U0756042

LITERATURE AND INTERCULTURALITY (3): FROM CULTURAL JUNCTIONS TO GLOBALIZATION

文学与跨文化研究（三）：从文化交汇到全球化

主　编：*Michael Steppat*
　　　　Steve J. Kulich（顾力行）

上海外语教育出版社
外教社 SHANGHAI FOREIGN LANGUAGE EDUCATION PRESS

图书在版编目(CIP)数据

文学与跨文化研究.三，从文化交汇到全球化：英文／（德）迈克尔·斯
代帕（Michael Steppat）主编；（美）顾力行（Steve J. Kulich）编. —
上海：上海外语教育出版社，2021
（跨文化研究）
ISBN 978 - 7 - 5446 - 6908 - 5

Ⅰ.①文… Ⅱ.①迈… ②顾… Ⅲ.①文学研究－世界－英文②文化交
流－研究－世界－英文 Ⅳ.①I106 ②G115

中国版本图书馆 CIP 数据核字(2021)第 160254 号

出版发行：上海外语教育出版社
（上海外国语大学内） 邮编：200083
电 话： 021-65425300（总机）
电子邮箱： bookinfo@sflep.com.cn
网 址： http://www.sflep.com
责任编辑： 许进兴

印 刷： 启东市人民印刷有限公司
开 本： 635×965 1/16 印张 29.25 字数 576千字
版 次： 2021 年 10 月第 1 版 2021 年 10 月第 1 次印刷

书 号： ISBN 978-7-5446-6908-5

定 价： 90.00 元

本版图书如有印装质量问题，可向本社调换
质量服务热线：4008-213-263 电子邮箱：editorial@sflep.com

魏　明（Cooper Wakefield　美国玛丽安大学）
徐欣吾（Danny Hsu　大连外国语大学）
颜静兰（华东理工大学）
严文华（华东师范大学）
张惠晶（美国奥尔巴尼大学）
张　睿（美国狄金森学院）
张雁冰（美国堪萨斯大学）
郑　萱（北京大学）
庄恩平（上海大学）
庄智象（上海外语教育出版社）

上外跨文化研究中心执行编委

张红玲（上外跨文化研究中心副主任）
王志强（上外跨文化研究中心副主任）
于朝晖（上外跨文化研究中心副主任）
周　怡（上外跨文化研究中心副研究员）
翁立平（上外跨文化研究中心副研究员）
迟若冰（上外跨文化研究中心副研究员）
张晓佳（上外跨文化研究中心副研究员）
英亚东（English，Alex　上外跨文化研究中心助理研究员）

The Editorial Board of
Intercultural Research

Contents

Section One

Exploring Cultural Junctions

Section Two
Interpreting Globalization

Appendix

Intercultural Research
Series Foreword

Michael H. PROSSER
Chair of the SII International Advisory Board
(prossermichael@gmail.com)

Ancient Athens served as an intercultural and intellectual crossroads for Asia and Europe. The Greek philosopher, Socrates' famous statement "I am neither a citizen of Athens, nor of Greece, but of the world" speaks eloquently of the impact of intercultural communication, comparative analysis, and the importance of identity clarification both in his and contemporary society. Greek philosophers Socrates, Plato, and Aristotle all looked outward from their own culture, identifying or debating major world value orientations such as goodness, justice, truth, and happiness. For East Asia, multiple schools of thought developed during the Spring and Autumn Period, shaping China's cross-state communication. Confucius' *Analects* articulated the role of *ren* (benevolence and kindness), *li* (propriety and right living through ritual), *de* (moral power), *dao* (internalized moral direction), and *mianzi* or *lian* (externalized social image and harmony). These Confucian orientations were integrated into what became the fabric of not only the Chinese state, but the educational and philosophical orientation of much of East and South-Eastern Asia.

All of these early cultural conceptualizations of identities and values strongly support the potentially positive intercultural, multicultural, and global world orientations that have enhanced a dialogue of civilizations and cultures, and stress factors that are unifying rather than divisive. The challenge continues to be substantial since intercultural, multicultural, and global communication might just as easily be highly negative with increasing war, poverty, crime, and pandemics. The goal of all those interested in promoting a better local and global society vastly prefers the former.

The location from which this series originates shows some of these dynamics and contradictions. Just as each nation and people must deal with highs and lows, China is grappling both with some of the positive dialogues of modernization and internationalization, and also the challenges of divergent cultural or global discourses. From the depths of the Wenchuan earthquake in Sichuan that rallied not only the nation's, but the world's sympathy, engagement and commitment to rebuild, to the heights of the spectacularly well-orchestrated and successful 2008 Beijing Olympics; from the ongoing challenges of natural disasters like floods or human tragedies and accidents or the global financial crisis, to the futuristic development of Shanghai and its visionary and record-breaking participation and cooperation at the 2010 Shanghai Expo, we see these human and intercultural dynamics at work.

I would suggest that intercultural communication as a field has emerged to embody and embrace both these challenges of human clashes and the dialogues across cultures and civilizations. The anthropologists Edward T. Hall and Ruth Benedict serve as the symbolic "grandparents" of intercultural communication in North America, though neither set out to begin a new field. Others in North America in the 1960s and 1970s and coming from various viewpoints (see Vol. 2 for the complete list of influencing scholars) and I sought early to develop an intercultural communication discipline or sub-discipline, which has now spread broadly through much of the academic world.

When the field of intercultural communication began to develop rapidly in China during the 1980s and 1990s, Chinese scholars each brought and sinicized many of these Western intercultural theories and practical implications for China. Concerned international scholars have also sought to indigenize social and cultural psychology and the humanities to strengthen Chinese scholarship on intercultural communication. Currently many Chinese scholars, either in China itself, in North America, or other regions around the world, have developed robust theories and models or have postulated newer ones, as documented in the premier volume of this series, *Intercultural Perspectives on Chinese Communication* (2007).

The SISU Intercultural Institute (SII) of Shanghai International Studies University (SISU), under Steve J. Kulich (Gu Lixing 顾力行), has accepted a mandate to undertake an *Intercultural Research* series of volumes which seeks to publish "cutting-edge and seminal articles on the state of the intercultural field" in a variety of areas.

As formulated in the establishment of the series, Kulich emphasized that "Each volume will focus on one primary domain and will include diverse theoretical and applied research from cultural, intercultural or cross-cultural approaches for that area, seeking to present and frame a 'state-of-the-art' or an extended development summary on the topic."

The SII is committed to close cooperation with both Chinese and international scholars, and that was reflected since the first, where domestic scholars of the CAFIC were joined by international scholars from various disciplinary or research perspectives to contribute IC research from their respective areas of focus. SII is also committed to highlight and bring some integration to the diverse disciplines that influence, contribute to or are informed by intercultural scholarship. This is illustrated particularly by efforts in that first and subsequent volumes to invite contributions from communication studies at both the interpersonal (*jiaoji*) as well as mass communication (*chuanbo*) levels and also to include the perspectives of cultural psychology, cultural anthropology and other related fields. The interdisciplinary nature of IC motivates the SII team to identify and integrate those aspects that contribute to shared foundations for the field, especially as these reflect intercultural, multicultural human development, or in short, to "develop a discipline to develop people."

This focus on cooperation continued first with disciplinary assessment and development seminars (in 2006, 2010, 2014, 2016, a continuing hallmark of the institute), the biennial thematic IC conferences held by Shanghai Normal University, dynamic cooperation among CAFIC Shanghai Branch institutions (which also includes regular cross-city scholar forums and the annual IC outstanding MA thesis conference) and international partners like the University of Bayreuth, Bavaria, Germany (from which the collaboration for this volume has emerged). Each volume has highlighted interdisciplinary and multi-perspective scholarship on *Identity and Intercultural Communication*, focusing on *I: Theoretical and Contextual Construction* (Vol. 2), and *II: Conceptual and Contextual Applications* (Vol. 3). Other volumes in the series take up the important topic of IC values — *Value Frameworks at the Theoretical Crossroads of Culture* (Vol. 4) and *Value Dimensions and Their Contextual Dynamics Across Cultures* (Vol. 5). Later volumes will focus on subsequent themes, like IC and acculturation (Vols. 6 and 7), IC and comparative literature, which now has nationally listed disciplinary status (Vols. 8 and 9), and other topics for IC disciplinary development.

Naturally, since Shanghai Foreign Language Education Press is publishing the series, Chinese academic contributions are especially encouraged, as well as those from the wider international academic community. In his foreword for the first volume, *Intercultural Perspectives on Chinese Communication* (2007), Guan Shijie noted that three features characterize the series: (1) It serves as an interdisciplinary platform for China's IC research; (2) It emphasizes the importance of scientific methodology in IC research; (3) It focuses on the localization of IC research. He concludes his remarks by saying that "The publication of this series is an occasion to celebrate for the entire Chinese community: My hope is that it develops into a series that is interdisciplinary, methodology-promoting, indigenized into the Chinese settings and blends well theories with practice (p. xvi)." As he also notes in that foreword, "In today's world, communication between various cultures have become an important task for human beings. Just as Lourdes Arizpe, chair of the Scientific Committee of the *World Culture Report* (2000), says, 'Cultural exchanges are in fact the axis of the new phenomena' as global cultures develop and change (p. ix)."

Since the initial books by Edward T. Hall, *The Silent Language*, *The Hidden Dimension*, *Beyond Culture*, and *The Dance of Life* began to shape the early study of intercultural communication theoretically and practically, so too, it is reasonable to assume that these volumes might provide new impetus for the academic study of various cultural contexts. The historical development, frameworks and research approaches presented both by well-established and emerging scholars in these volumes will surely move the academic understanding of key intercultural topic areas ahead. Each volume's contribution toward highlighting theoretical constructs, clarifying the "state-of-the-art" and presenting cutting-edge research and practical applications will hopefully contribute to a new apex in the field of intercultural communication. To the ongoing development of the intercultural communication discipline both in China and abroad this series is dedicated.

International Academy for Intercultural Research (IAIR)
2015 Lifetime Achievement Award Winner

Charlottesville, Virginia

Volume Preface

Sandra L. BERMANN

Cotsen Professor of the Humanities, Princeton University

The Preface to Volume 8 of this series as well as the Preface to the series as a whole are written by experts in the field of intercultural studies. So are (mainly) the important introductory chapters and appendices to Volumes 8–10, each offering information describing intercultural studies as a whole and the new program at SISU in Comparative Literature and Intercultural Studies. I write this brief Preface from a distinctly different angle, as a scholar of comparative literature, one intrigued by, though not directly involved with, what this new interdisciplinary connection promises for future studies of literature and its relation to the world.

As is well known, comparative literature is itself an unusually broad and complex field. Poly-linguistic in its reach, trans-cultural and trans-disciplinary in its research, it intersects regularly with other disciplines. Ideally dependent on what Gayatri Spivak has called "deep language learning" and an equally probing theoretical and cultural inquiry, it considers modes of literary expression as these appear in particular times and places, as well as their relation to changing modes of translation and transmission. So diverse is the field today that it might best be described as an active network — embracing literature's relation to various media, different disciplines, and a number of ethical, political, and aesthetic commitments. The rhetorical level of the text and the particular role of language, analyzed theoretically, culturally, and practically, often remain central to its thinking. This emphasis regularly extends to inquiries into translation, translation theory, and at times, experiential learning through community outreach. At its best, comparative literature produces conversations in which cultural traditions and creativity, theory and particular examples, literary history, experimental art, and an ongoing reach to public issues and the ethical questions they raise can within nation states leave their marks in most of the narratives studied.

Temporal mobility, though not as immediately evident, is at least as important. Not only might we say that the past is a foreign country (one well worth visiting through texts from earlier times); we can also note that themes of geo-linguistic migration inevitably shuttle between present and past. Histories, souvenirs, images of the past zigzag through the intricacies of memory as they unravel the forgotten repetitions of trauma and desire. Importantly, migration narratives also focus on encounters with foreign "others" — people, languages, lands, cultures, all with their own past stories — that will be embraced or resisted by specific characters. But these narratives look not only to the pasts of their protagonists and their "others"; they also often speak to the future, where fears of resistance and marginalization as well as hopes of economic betterment, freedom — or survival itself — come into play. Whether a hoped-for future is envisioned in terms of an actual geographic site, or in the vague outlines of fantasy, it will deeply affect the story's temporal dimensions.

Speaking of temporality, it is important to note that, though migration has been called the major human issue of the 21st century, both history and literature reveal that mobility has always characterized our humanity (see Bade and Livi-Bacci). Historians date our migrations back some two million years, and our earliest epics focus on characters in movement, on stories of nomadism and migration: the Bible, the Mahābhārata, Gilgamesh, the Iliad and Odyssey. Travel literatures, picaresque novels, the *bildungsroman*, many examples of poetry, drama, memoir, novels, non-fictional narratives — as well as films and digital expressions — serve as more current reminders of our longstanding fascination with migration. Not surprisingly, migration has had a major role in the field of comparative literature through the many literary texts claiming the field's attention. But it has also come to us through the lives of its best-known figures: Erich Auerbach, Leo Spitzer, René Wellek, Edward Said, Gayatri Spivak, and Homi Bhabha, to name but a few.

If translation and translation studies are by now central to comparative study, this is particularly the case when considering issues of migration. Whether translation focuses on the lives of men, women, and children as they learn and unlearn languages in the process of migration, or whether it concentrates on the literary and material encounters that create and transmit the palimpsest that we call a literary text, translation speaks powerfully to central issues of language(s), difference, opacity, "untranslatability," and relationality.

Once translated and transmitted, words spark conversations with new interlocutors in different contexts. They gain an ability to affect and transform. At times the translational migration of texts has had especially powerful results (see the vernacular translations of the Bible, the debates and translations of Buddhism in China, or the migrations and interpretations of Marxist texts around the world). Most often, the effects of translation are felt more subtly but pervasively through the rewritings that spur textual circulation, and the "intertextuality" that transforms the ways in which past, present, and future texts are written and read (see Kristeva).

Apt metaphors for our transformative times, literatures of migration with their mobile, polylogical, and often linguistically hybrid presentations are sometimes claimed as "a new world literature," as texts that might in some ways offer a salutary practice of "living together," to invoke Roland Barthes as well as Ottmar Ette. Through the encounters with otherness which they stage, stories of migration can both engage and query the reader, offering not only an image of otherness but an actual *practice* in understanding it. There are at least a couple of ways this can happen. The first entails literature's celebrated ability to create readerly identification and empathy, an "inside" view of a character or dilemma that might otherwise seem distant or "foreign." Through literary art's representational potential, and especially its enunciative strategies, narrative offers an "as if," which engages the reader in thinking *from the place of another*. But giving us this experience in living "other"*wise* is, it seems to me, only half the educational story.

For literary texts are, of course, not just representational, and are never transparent. As they invite the reader/interpreter into an imagined world of characters, situations, and encounters, they also refuse to grant full transparency. Aesthetic structures, figuration, and particular uses of language quite inevitably instill the text itself with something "strange," "other," something to challenge the reader's too easy imaginative progress. Gaps in meaning, metaphors, intertextualities and inter-lingual wordplay, changing narrative viewpoint and irony can ask us to stop and reflect — not only about what is "foreign," in the sense of outside national or cultural borders, but also about the foreignness within the rhetoric of the text itself, a rhetorical quality that can, of course, be enhanced, diminished, or otherwise transformed by the work of translation. These are important literary and educational effects, since between experiencing reader and multivalent text, moments of reflection and self-reflection can arise. Frames of reference and habitual modes of thinking can be questioned, internally debated. And here, the textual "foreign" can stand as a sort of "door" (evoking "foreign's" Latin root "fores") — a blocked passage causing a pause, but also inviting an opening, one dependent on the reader's insight and agency. In such textual involvement we find echoes of Bakhtin's "dialogism," Edouard Glissant's "relationality," Derrida's "différance," and Ette's sense of "trans." We can also find a compelling, if optional (we can, after all, always interpret otherwise) "education in living," an education that might indeed contribute to the public good.

Hopes and Encounters: Comparative Literature and Intercultural Studies

Given all of this, there seems little chance that literary texts focusing on migration — or other cross-cultural themes — would *not* make interesting additions to the work of Intercultural Communication Studies. Adding a new "key to perception," literature brings, as Steppat suggests, major questions of intercultural communication to the fore in compelling, "polylogical" ways: touching newly on questions of identity and cultural difference, on changing values and global mobility. Especially when such texts are approached with a keen awareness of language, narrative structure, and specific linguistic effects which comparative literature can offer, collaborative projects seem likely to enrich the research projects of intercultural communication.

Another question posed in these volumes is whether the more social-science dimensions of intercultural communication might offer new insights for the field of comparative literature. To my mind, the answer is yes, though with some minor qualifications. Many comparatists might, for instance, find it uninteresting to apply certain positivist methodologies to literary texts without a full engagement with their rhetorical or linguistic dimensions. But bracketing such attempts, gains could be substantial. For instance, as comparative literature increasingly speaks to pressing issues of our times such as migration, ecology, climate change, or inequality, knowledge from the social sciences will clearly be important.

Moreover, as comparatists know, the interpretive lenses of comparative literature (as well as the artistic texts they consider) are already deeply implicated in transcultural as well as translinguistic issues. Questions of language, but also questions of power and history engage the field at many levels. This inevitable juncture of language with other aspects of what we call "culture" invites further research and critical emphasis. The appendix by Steppat and Kulich on "The Challenge of an Intercultural Literature" in Volume 8 reminds us of this. Not only in the study of literature of migration, but also when approaching texts in colonial, postcolonial, and anticolonial contexts; or when considering those displaying multilingualism, dialogism, and polylogism; those questioning planetary inequality; or exploring issues of climate and sustainability — in each of these contemporary literary and cultural themes, transversal conversations among a variety of disciplines, including intercultural communication, can only expand our insights.

There are other reasons, emanating from the institutional status and Eurocentric "image" of comparative literature, to welcome the juncture of these fields and especially the newly instituted program of Comparative Literature and Intercultural Studies at SISU. The recent disciplinary developments described under its first rubric, "Studies in World Literature and Literary Concepts," will likely reinforce a number of underlying goals for translinguistic and transcultural study so important to comparative literature historically. Situating comparative literature in the context of "foreign literature/language" — as opposed to Chinese alone or for that matter, any other single language (including English) — also seems essential to the field as we see it today.

Developing a keener awareness of "Sino-Foreign Literary Relations," as described in rubric two, and particularly of the growing transnational significance of Chinese literature, will be a gain for all literary scholars. Similarly, emphases suggested in "Media-translatology" coincide in a number of ways with ongoing research in the U.S. and elsewhere in the field of translation studies. It would be intriguing to compare and expand upon these conceptions. Further studies in "Intercultural Communication and Its Theory" will likely be of special interest to literary scholars inquiring into cultural theory and its relations to literary study.

As these designated fields of the new program at SISU encounter the field of comparative literature in a strange parallel to migration narratives themselves, we might consider possible projects for the future. I mention a few of them here:

(1) Reflect on the intercultural importance of *language* and of *languages*, as well as their hybridizing potential. Continue to insist through teaching and research that the intercultural cannot be

studied monolingually, and certainly not in English — or Chinese — alone.

(2) Consider the role of translation, editing, and publishing in the transmission of texts and cultures. One might also pursue direct work on issues of translation with migrant and marginalized populations. What research topics might be envisioned here? What new knowledge — theoretical as well as practical — might emerge?

(3) Take up the study of stories — their roles, the questions they raise in different disciplinary as well as geo-linguistic and cultural domains: consider literary stories, anthropological, sociological, journalistic, political/governmental stories. What are their formal differences within and across languages and cultures? What or who is the object of these stories? Who acts as the story-teller and what is/ are the media outlet(s)?

Comparative literature as well as intercultural studies have much to offer and to gain in such transversal conversations.

References

Bade, Klaus J. *Migration in European History*. Translated by Allison Brown. Blackwell, 2003.

Bakhtin, Mikhail M. *The Dialogic Imagination: Four Essays*. Edited by Michael Holquist, translated by Caryl Emerson and Michael Holquist. U of Texas P, 1981.

Barthes, Roland. *How to Live Together: Novelistic Simulations of Some Everyday Spaces*. 2002. Translated by Kate Briggs. Columbia UP, 2013.

Britton, Celia M. "Globalization and Political Action in the Work of Edouard Glissant." *Small Axe*, vol. 13, no. 3 (30), 2009, pp. 1–11.

Derrida, Jacques. *Monolingualism of the Other; or, The Prosthesis of Origin*. 1996. Translated by Patrick Mensah. Stanford UP, 1998.

—. *Speech and Phenomena and Other Essays on Husserl's Theory of Signs*. 1967. Translated by David B. Allison. Northwestern UP, 1973.

Ette, Ottmar. *Writing-between-Worlds: Transarea Studies and the Literatures-Without-a-Fixed Abode*. Translated by Vera M. Kutzinski. De Gruyter, 2016.

Glissant, Edouard. *Poetics of Relation*. 1990. Translated by Betsy Wing. U of Michigan P, 1997.

Kristeva, Julia. *Desire in Language: A Semiotic Approach to Literature and Art*. Edited by Leon S. Roudiez, translated by Thomas Gora and Alice Jardine. Columbia UP, 1980. ("Word, Dialogue, and Novel" and "The Bounded Text.")

Livi-Bacci, Massimo. *A Short History of Migration*. 2010. Translated by Carl Ipsen. Polity Press, 2012.

Spivak, Gayatri Chakravorty. *Death of a Discipline*. Columbia UP, 2003.

Cultural Patterns of Communication-Values-Crossroads

Michael STEPPAT & Steve J. KULICH

Without a viable value discourse,
we are obliged to negotiate
a commotion of disorientational crises
amidst unadjudicated claims of validity
and diverse experiences of evaluation.
(John Fekete: *Life After Postmodernism*)

Our Interrelated Fields

Communication scholar John C. Condon has observed that "[1] iterature and film can enhance intercultural communication in two very important ways: one is by expressing the significance of certain relationships, values, communication styles, and so on that are representative of the culture being described; the other is by presenting intercultural issues themselves as the major theme of the film or literary work" (155). The complementary volumes we are presenting explore both of these ways. From a variety of perspectives, they affirm that devoting attention to the relationship between literature and interculturality not only represents a sizeable enterprise, but also has a key significance for understanding what Condon calls "cultural patterns of communication."

Therefore, after already having offered the first volume devoted to *Literature and Interculturality*, we are now pleased to be able to present further major focal areas, in two volumes. The present introduction is mostly valid for Volume 9 as well. Our companion Volume 8 inquires into concepts, applications, and interactions. The present book, like Volume 9, extends and complements that scope, this time exploring cultural junctions and globalization as well as lines of inquiry into values. The volumes are independent of each other, and each can be taken by itself without recourse to the other. As in Volumes 8 and 9, we are delighted that it has been possible to assemble a group of outstanding scholars from several continents who represent a broad range of connected interests. Each has activated a strong analytical capability to show us new pathways of thinking about our complex research object — an object that increasingly challenges our understanding while the world is becoming "a global village" (Triandis xix).

We hope this will enable us to contribute to fulfilling the expectations of China's Ministry of Education disciplinary register. In 2016, that ministry introduced a place for intercultural communication within the broader framework of foreign language and literature studies to form a converging field, Comparative Literature and Intercultural Studies. Accordingly, among the "hot topics" of research, Suo Gefei notes: "In the field of literature and comparative literature, scholars have made efforts integrating intercultural communication studies into comparative literature and comparative culture research" (106–07).

As these efforts move ahead, they will need nothing short of a "new intercontinent of conceptualization" (Jung 153). It is from our editorial vantage points in a Faculty of Literary Studies and Linguistics and an Intercultural Institute, on two continents as it happens, that we face this formidable task as well as we can. It is already some years ago that Jean-François Lyotard announced ways in which "the predominance of the performance criterion" would sound "the knell of the age of the Professor": such a capitalized grandee is "no more competent than interdisciplinary teams in imagining new moves or new games" in the production of knowledge (53). As an alternative, that may be overstated, but we should note the preference for imagination, as a "capacity to articulate what used to be separate" (Lyotard 52). Can we take some of the diagnosis as encouragement, to embark on such articulation?

We know that applications of intercultural communication research have tended to focus primarily on forms of knowledge suited to intercultural training to benefit education or international business, toward the cultivation of intercultural awareness, competence, and problem-solving in individuals or cultural groups for smoother exchanges or cooperation. Yet these foci have never been isolated among contributing disciplines. At the beginning of the very first volume in the present book series, the study of comparative literature (among others) is already placed in intercultural communication's interdisciplinary dimension (Kulich, "Introduction" 4). We do not want to forget that our cultural encounters happen in a context which includes a wide variety of "channels," involving how we respond to Others through the experience of reading a novel or watching a movie (Kulich and Weng 18). Recipients, after all, "may show effects of the story on their real-world beliefs" (Green and Brock 701; see also Appel and Richter 129).

If we want to ask how fictional art can contribute at all to knowledge, we might do well to consider a proposition by cultural critic Walter Benjamin. To overcome a lack of consistency in Immanuel Kant's guiding concept, Benjamin a century ago suggested relating knowledge to language. This would allow the creation of a concept of knowledge to which a concept of experience can correspond, thus preserving a multiplicity of knowledge which allows for the truth content of aesthetic representation (100 − 10). In this context, questions of identity already become important for Benjamin. In our time, comparative culture scholars are aware that reconsidering identity from contexted intercultural frames, as in literary works, "might facilitate more than our analysis — it might also help us talk to each other more meaningfully about our discoveries, processes, and reflections on who we are in all our complexity in this increasingly globalized world" (Kulich, "Constructing" 142–43).

For the methodological foundations of multiculturally oriented communication theory, indeed, it can make good sense to give attention and credibility to such genres as allegories, novels, and poems (see Miike 52). In various ways, our disciplinary fields partly converge to study and seek to attain meaning or signifying value. To the extent that they do, our efforts will go beyond any search that is not communicatively situated and oriented — between our institutional and discursive practices, our disciplinary boundaries. The meaning may well turn out to be meaningless without that communicative orientation.

Values/Multiplicities

As John Condon already argued, literature and film are especially capable of expressing the significance of cultural values. In devoting all have a role. Through its wide-ranging discussion, it highlights the mobile, multi-dimensional nature of literary (and related artistic) texts as it emphasizes their transforming and transformative effects.

Comparative literature's wide-ranging network of interests often intersects with topics raised by intercultural communication studies, a field growing from the work of North American anthropologists Edward T. Hall and Ruth Benedict. Though this field initially focused on a social-science-based training for individuals involved in international education or business, it soon developed research areas in identity formation and in value frameworks as these arise in different — and often distant — geo-historical cultures. Recently, literature and film have been invoked as important ways to expand the research of intercultural studies. As authors in these volumes suggest (Michael Steppat and Susan Arndt with special emphasis), the multi-perspectival insights into our social and individual lives offered by literature in fact create especially fruitful ground for this collaborative project. Central topics in literary and intercultural theory, such as alterity and difference, mestizaje, hybridity, creolization, and globalization represent ready areas of study, indeed already overlapping ones where much might be shared. The newly formed doctoral program in Comparative Literature and Intercultural Studies established by the Chinese government at SISU promises to join the two fields more closely and intentionally. Such trans-disciplinary research — to underscore the prefix "trans-" (see Ette 33–35) so appropriate to this work emphasizing mobility and intersection — is all the more likely to occur as the humanities engage increasingly with public issues that by their nature invite, even require, a thinking across disciplinary and cultural divides.

Migration Stories

One public theme appears prominently in these volumes, as in comparative and world literature more generally: migration. Indeed, migration can reveal the human face(s) of globalization. And themes of migration immediately gesture to the sense of mobility, encounter, and relationality (in Glissant's sense of not only harmonious but also contending interactions, interconnections, and rhizomatic connections) central to our time and to current projects in both the humanities and social sciences (see Glissant and Britton). Geographic movement, its trademark image, and border crossing of many kinds between and our attention to a range of valuation aspects, we are also guided by cultural studies scholar John Fekete's insight that "we live, breathe, and excrete values. No aspect of human life is unrelated to values, valuations, and validations" (i). Or: values *are* culture (Branco and Valsiner xiii). Yet if we accept the equation, we should be aware of the Nietzschean argument that "all value is *valuation*: value is necessarily always contingent and distributed rather than inherent" (McKay 59; see also Nietzsche 13–14). At the present time, indeed, there is a distinct process from values to valuation — in the sense of interdisciplinary dialogue (Brosch and Sander Ch. 19). Our book series has included two substantial volumes dedicated to the exploration of value frameworks and value dimensions across cultures, with a substantial chapter on reviews, definitions, and approaches to values studies. We thus have firm ground on which to build. For an overview, the present volume offers an Appendix on the research in this area, concerning both literature and intercultural communication. We can regard literary narration as "a process that creates values," as Paul Ricoeur in *Time and Narrative* agrees with Algirdas Greimas (*Du sens*, see Ricoeur 2: 50). This is possible because its topological syntax can be mapped onto the semiotic square. As functions of cultural norms, moreover, narratable actions "can be estimated or evaluated" and thereby receive "a relative value" (Ricoeur 1: 58).

As a consequence of such considerations, the study of values is "an interdisciplinary field of research, which is still one of the most controversial and, at the same time, most fruitful and fascinating areas in literary and cultural studies" (Baumbach et al. 12). It gains these qualities because literature "opens up a space where new possibilities of meaning- and value-making can be explored" (Neumann 136–37; see also Fisher, *Human* and "Narration" 8). Readers and audiences examine a narrative, as a communication scholar argues, in order to assess "the value of its values": do they make "a pragmatic difference in one's life and in one's community"? (Fisher, *Human* 88, 111; see also Mar and Oatley, "Function" 174–75 and "Exploring"). When mental systems and capacities become strongly focused on events occurring in a fictional narrative, social psychology regards this as a process which "can affect beliefs," and which can presumably occur when a story taps into important values but "even when a story is not immediately relevant to a reader's cherished values" (Green and Brock 714; see also Appel and Richter).

At "a moment when the legitimization of literary scholarship has become an urgent problem in many countries," investigating how narratives and films function as important tools for spreading values and their ensuing cognitive practices has considerable benefit for our societies (Nünning 53). From another research perspective, across cultures, we cannot but be aware that values are "an extremely important component in the meaningful study of cultural differences" (Kulich and Weng 1).

Values research has been operating with the concept of a "social-molecular bond" or "molecular model." We should look at this more closely for a moment. In the model values priorities, identity roles, beliefs, and behavioral preferences have "shared affinity bonds in a 'life orientation' mix" (Kulich, "Values" 37). If we look beyond social science, we will find a certain analogy to this in the admittedly intricate argumentation of Gilles Deleuze and Félix Guattari. They speak of a "molecular realm of beliefs and desires" (*Thousand* 219). It is a realm which appears in the shape of molecular lines of flight: "There is always something that flows or flees, that escapes the binary organizations, the resonance apparatus, and the overcoding machine: things that are attributed to a 'change in values'" (216).

This consideration of change counterpoints or at least complements research that tends to highlight a slow adjustment or even stability of values (see also Shearman 151–53; Hofstede 210). We should take note of the work of Pettersson and Esmer, who offer a differentiation between value change and cultural change: "values can change but cultures are much more resistant" (5).

So we can come back to Deleuze and Guattari: a molecular "quantum flow," they tell us, can be set off against but also interpenetrates "the molar segmented line" (*Thousand* 217). A molecular kind of line is rhizomatic, having "anomalous and nomadic multiplicities" which are transformational (505). Furthermore, quantum flows are "neither attributable to individuals nor overcodable by collective signifiers," so that in their realm this particular distinction loses its meaning (219). In "the molecular multiplicities that subordinate the structured crowd phenomena," any seemingly "lone particle" is not just a particle: it "has an associated wave as a flow that defines the coexisting space of *its* presences" (*Anti-Oedipus* 280). It may be no coincidence that Walter Benjamin, too, highlights a multiplicity of knowledge (108).

It's tempting to explore a connection here, to a certain extent, with Cao Shunqing's and Han Zhoukun's highlighting of a pluralistic orientation among literary cultures, of heterogeneous cultural traditions: literary works, after all, are "of all kinds" (in Lu Xie's classical assessment [261]).

As for the life-organization "mix" quoted above, it may be capable of opening toward Deleuze's "minute inclinations" with unstable molecular perception (*Fold* 99–100). In point of fact, one of the most frequent themes in *A Thousand Plateaus* is that "all semiotics are mixed" and that they "combine different regimes of signs" (for instance 119). We might also take heed that "[v]ery specific assemblages of power impose signifiance and subjectification as their determinate form of expression, [...] there is no signifiance without a despotic assemblage" (*Thousand* 180).

Yet also: with their inorganization, molecular elements are "pure positive multiplicities where everything is possible, without exclusiveness or negation, syntheses operating without a plan, where the connections are transverse, the disjunctions included, the conjunctions polyvocal" (*Anti-Oedipus* 309). The cultural affinity bonds we spoke of above are likely to harbor disjunctive multiplicities. And, if values are to be understood as converting drives into desirable goals, Deleuzian machines of desiring-production could prove suggestive in some regards. We might be able to track pathways of inquiry that can benefit from both social science and concepts such as these.

Values/Identity Struggles

When we turn back from philosophy to science and consider the pertinent research avenues, we will find or recall that such tools as Geert Hofstede's Values Survey Module and the Schwartz Values Survey have been extensively used and tested. We should not overlook the critical if somewhat sweeping view that values as extracted from questionnaires, rating scales, and interviews tend to appear as if they were "stable traits or characteristics," hardly as dynamic (Branco and Valsiner ix), and as being objective across all situations. These influential research directions, and those developing them further, tend to speak to organization and management culture, and hence need careful scrutiny before any attempt is made to apply them to the study of literature. Also, there are limits to direct articulation: values are "silent" in their operation, so that talking about them "breaks that silence, and no longer fully represents the values" (Branco and Valsiner xiii, 10).

We should bear in mind such bounds of research — and that

literary works mostly observe value emphases indirectly. Literature is able to represent and probe not only prevailing and socially sanctioned but also alternative, repressed, unsanctioned values and norms (Baumbach et al. 5), their internal competition or contradiction, their situational reordering. This latter aspect deserves attention. It's worth reflecting that an intention is always "embedded in its situation," as well as in human customs; an expectation, too, is embedded in "a situation, from which it arises" (Wittgenstein sections 337 and 581). In Aristotle's *Nicomachean Ethics*, prudence is concerned with knowledge of particulars, of single cases and circumstances (1104a4, 1141b7, 1142a5). In keeping with this, and notwithstanding Aristotle's *Poetics* 9, literary discourse in dealing with ethical concerns and values presents individual cases, the "experience of particular situations" all the way to "singular turns of tone, phrase, and figure" (Irwin xx; Nussbaum 37ff.; de Man 23; see also Grabes 48−49). This context is discussed further in the Appendix. Individual situations, at any rate, are closer to Deleuze's molecular flow than to large-scale molar aggregates.

Social science affirms that researchers can try to "identify culture" by studying a society's literature, chiefly seeking "underlying value emphases" (Schwartz 341). Indeed, literature as such has been studied from a values perspective (see for instance Baumbach et al.; Erll et al.; and partly Lopičić and Ilić). Yet that has rarely embraced a specifically inter- or transcultural orientation — which has become our task in this and the companion volumes.

Wherever possible, we seek to explore the common ground between valuation and identification issues, especially where they appear as processes rather than as products: the "orientation processes" of which Kulich and Weng speak (17; see also Hall 2). In our context, we are not concerned directly with the various aspects of Kenneth Burke's ideas of identification in *A Rhetoric of Motives*. Instead, we are strongly aware that "cultural values shape and are shaped by cultural identity struggles" (Buzzanell 18), and that these are not always easy to separate. In fact, cross-cultural studies of "cultural, ethnic, or national identity" are topics that were recommended for our book series from the beginning (Volume 1, p. 377).

No less important are dialogues. These occur between value and identity research foci, also between the two disciplinary fields of our volume title (and of China's new direction in Comparative Literature and Intercultural Studies), as well as the scholars contributing to our enterprise. At least equally important are dialogic processes between cultures, as "[b] eing dialogic and intercultural is to celebrate difference and plurality" (Xu 394). We welcome Cao Shunqing's advocacy of "cross-civilization dialogue" which should "not start unilaterally from a certain kind of cultural value system" (214). To enable such dialogue, concepts of variation and heterogeneity can become fruitful for literary circulation, to some degree, in our age of intercultural communication (as stressed by Cao and Han). What is more, we certainly have dialogue between our companion volumes. In their focus on intercultural dimensions, they show a research scope that is potentially valid for all literature: "traces of other cultures exist in every culture" (Kraidy 148); from another perspective, "we already live in the volatility of the pluricultural" so that "ours is a pluricultural vision" (Ihde 29, 66). Thus it is with literary cultures, their subtle trajectories of influence and transfer.

In pursuing these thematic clusters, like Condon we have welcomed attention to film as well as to literature in a traditional sense. The "discipline of film studies" has given the friendliest reception of any to "the textual paradigm" (Mowitt 141; see also Bellour). Zhang Yingjin has affirmed that academic border-crossing, as in the rise of culturally oriented film studies, has had effects "both profound and far-reaching" (8). As Mao Sihui reminds us in our previous volume, "[w]e all have films that we love for what they present to us: laughs, thrills, stunning audio-visual effects [...]". And what they present has at least as much effect on our (inter) cultural orientation as literary works in the classic sense.

Illustration: A Tragedy of Foreign Women

After the theorizing, let us consider a striking case. A volatility of cross-cultural valuations is explored in depth already in earliest Western culture: Athenian tragedy, Aeschylus' *The Suppliants* (c. 466 B.C.). Any reader who happens to be less interested in the specific literary illustrations may skip directly further along, to the "Building on Volume 8" paragraph.

Communication professor Walter R. Fisher has named Aeschylus' tragedies among works that foster values reaffirming the human spirit "as the transcendent ground of existence" ("Narration" 16). Austrian Nobel laureate Elfriede Jelinek has partly used *The Suppliants* for her own postdramatic work *Die Schutzbefohlenen* (2013 with updates in 2015), in which she creates a chorus to thematize fearful refugee voices and hold up a mirror to European policies:"Angst überall, Angst vor den Meinen, die ich verließ, daß ich wieder zurück muß, vor Ihnen aber noch mehr Angst [...]."

Aeschylus dramatizes the flight of the 50 daughters of Danaus with their father from Egypt, where Danaus' twin brother and rival Aegyptus is attempting to force the girls' marriage with his 50 Nilotic sons (see Vasunia 42). By means of a ship which Danaus builds, instructed by the goddess Athena, he and his daughters embark on a journey "with all speed over the waves of the sea" (Aeschylus line 14), becoming what we now might call "boat people." They finally end their journey on the shores of Argos (signifying Greece), home of a distant ancestor of Danaus (see also Brill). In a sanctuary there, the girls implore the gods, "the compassionate spirit of the land" (line 29), and especially Argos' king Pelasgus for shelter and protection. In chorus, they project a vivid sense of identity:"Behold me, your suppliant, a fugitive, running around like a heifer chased by wolves upon precipitous crags" (350). They present themselves as a "fugitive who has been impiously cast out and driven from afar" (420) — which is actually less than the truth. Their plea, at any rate, is accompanied by hardly veiled threats:"heavy is the wrath of Zeus, god of the suppliant" (347); "Beware pollution!" (375). They have a point when they invoke the Homeric Zeus Xenios or Hikesios.

Figure 1

Aeschylus, *The Suppliant Women*: Rogue Machine Theatre, The Getty Villa, LA Directed by Michael Arabian, translated by George Theodoridis, photo credit John P. Flynn

This is a liminal situation. In a remarkable part-analogy with ritual process conditions as analyzed by Victor Turner, it is attributed with religious properties, and regarded as "polluting" by those concerned with maintaining structure (*Ritual* 108–09). The drama itself serves as a form of ritual process: *Suppliants* is "a piece of ritual theater that combines the patterned emotional transformations of rite with a kinetic visual experience" (Lembke 207).

Yet the law of Aeschylus' Athens is not on the girls' side. We can assume that the audience would find it acceptable and binding. In keeping with the law, the Argive king disputes the girls' right to flee: "If the sons of Aegyptus have authority over you by the law of your country claiming that they are nearest of kin, who would wish to contest it?" (387). He fears his people's future judgment, "You honored aliens and brought ruin upon your own land" (400). At least equally fearing attack from the Egyptians, which would mean importing a foreign conflict into his own country, he refuses to accommodate the group. Conveniently, he treats them as mere strangers, since they are "clothed in foreign attire and luxuriating in closely-woven and barbaric robes": "you are more similar to the women of Libya and in no way similar to those native to our land," evidently from "a land neighboring the Aethiopians" (434 ff.). The Greek "Libya" designated most of the African continent. The girls' stage appearance and their speech are evidently designed to bear this out (see also Chad Turner); they are "a dark, sun-burned race" (Aeschylus 154–55). In fact, the Greeks in later times, too, tended to think of Danaus as a barbarian invader from Egypt (see Isocrates, *Helen* 10.68 and *Panathenaicus* 12.80).

The Danaids seem to have gotten on the wrong side of what will much later become Immanuel Kant's universalist assertion that the right to visit and associate "belongs to all men by virtue of their common ownership of the earth's surface" (Kant 16) — not, however, a claim to be a permanent visitor. This amounts to a decisive differentiation. To what extent, in any case, is the relationship to the foreigner regulated by law? The foreigner, and especially "a foreign woman," is not "the completely other who is relegated to an absolute outside, savage, barbaric, precultural, and prejuridical" (Derrida 73). Yet, awkwardly for the Danaid girls, the relevant law, supported by Athens, is that of the country from which they have fled, not that of Argos. Moreover, somewhat ominously, the Danaids hold "patently foreign and anti-democratic views" (Chou 44).

Barbarian Dealings?

The girls in a lengthy exchange not only seem to hint at an aversion to all marriage. They also clarify their threats by vowing to hang themselves from the statues of the Argive gods (465), hence morally tainting the country with innocent blood; later they envision a "plunge into the depths" (796), no doubt a similar taint. Indeed, the foreigner contests authority, "puts me in question" (Derrida 3) — a perplexing challenge built into any such encounter. Eventually the king reluctantly admits their claim, but insists that a majority of the Argive people would need to decide in their favor. At length the people do, so that the Danaids are allowed to stay. Yet before they can begin to enjoy the people's hospitality, their father sees a pursuing fleet from Egypt approaching, carrying the suitors with numerous "black limbs" (719): "Abominable is the lustful race of Aegyptus and insatiate of battle" (741), "of evil mind, and guileful of purpose" (750). Alarmed, the Danaid chorus dreads the impending "suffering wrought by violence [...] savagery beyond bearing" (830ff.).

The Egyptians' herald enters and, as they feared, begins to force the girls away from their sanctuary: "Wail and shout and call upon the gods — you will not escape the Egyptian ship" (874). Despairing, the girls now appeal to King Pelasgus:

Herald
If you will not resign yourself and get to the ship, rending will have no pity on the fabric of your garments.
Chorus
We are lost! O King, we are suffering impious violence! [...]
Listen! Chiefs and rulers of the city, I am threatened with violence!
[**Herald**]
I think I will have to seize you by the hair and drag you off since you are slow to heed my orders.
Enter the King with retainers
King
You there! What are you doing? What kind of arrogance has incited you to do such dishonor to this realm of Pelasgian men? Indeed, do you think you have come to a land of women? For a barbarian dealing with Hellenes, you act insolently. Many are the misses of your wits, and your hits are none.

Herald

And in this case where have I gone wrong and transgressed my right?

King

First of all, you do not know how to act as a stranger.

Herald

I not know? How so, when I simply find and take my own that I had lost?

King

To what patrons of your land was your notice given?

Herald

To Hermes, the Searcher, greatest of patrons.

King

For all your notice to the gods, you do them no reverence.

Herald

I revere the deities by the Nile.

King

While ours are nothing, as I understand you?

Herald

I shall carry off these maids unless someone tears them away.

King

If you so much as touch them, you will regret it, and right soon.

Herald

I hear you; and your speech is far from hospitable.

King

No, since I have no hospitality for despoilers of the gods.
(902ff.)

Pelasgus subtly shifts the clash from an uncomfortably legal level, and thus from the suitors' palpably justified claim, to the ethnic ("barbarian" versus "Hellenes"), hence to radically opposed value orientations. The audience will recall the Danaids' plaint about the aliens' black, lustful, and savage qualities. That the Egyptians' whole action belies the Danaids' tearful claim of being cast out is lost from sight. Eventually the king's resolute threat of war succeeds in forcing the Egyptian herald to retreat. Thereupon Hellenic kindness toward strangers, interwoven with democracy, shines brightly as he generously assures the fugitives: "A protector you have in me and in all the inhabitants, whose resolve this is that now takes effect" (964).

Relieved as they are, the girls are apprehensive about their future: "All the world is ready to cast reproach on those who speak a foreign tongue. But may all be for the best!" (974). For the exiles, the root- and lawless nomads, only their language is "their ultimate homeland" (Derrida 88) — their "best." Their final prayer has a somewhat ominously militant ring: may Zeus "award victory to the women!" (1069). It seems to strengthen the dark threat of line 347.

"The Perverseness of Values"

The militancy suggests that there is more to come. And indeed there is a decisive extension: *Suppliants* forms part of a tetralogy with further plays whose sequence cannot now be clearly determined. These are, regrettably, for the most part lost. From other sources, the actions of the subsequent plays, at least along general lines, have been largely reconstructed. As the audience might expect, war does break out with the Aegyptus. King Pelasgus is presumably killed: the inviting host, in Derrida's unsettling equation, has all along become "the hostage" as the guest becomes "the master of the host" (Derrida 125). Danaus is spared and allowed to rule Argos, on condition that he will no longer resist his daughters' marriage. Secretly, however, he conspires with them to put their Egyptian bridegrooms to the sword on the wedding night. (From Vasunia's analysis, one would hardly gather that Danaus has a hand in the affair.) Which is what they do, with one single exception: his daughter Hypermnestra refuses to kill her bridegroom (Lynceus), who is able to flee. Enraged, Danaus threatens Hypermnestra with a harsh sentence, presumably even death (as we hear in Ovid's *Heroides* 14:"aut illo iugulet, quem non bene tradidit ensem"), for disobeying. If we were to consider this within the network of the narrative program's axiological values, we would find that an insistence on "being able not to choose" (the enforced Egyptian marriage) either brings forth "not being able not to choose" (as abject obedience to father) or, more consistently, "being able to choose" (as free choice of marriage as well as of disobedience) (see Greimas 184, 190).

Along with the treatment of foreigners (women in particular) and the valorization of hospitality, a major issue in the sequence appears to be that of social roles in which values are enveloped. Actantial roles do not have to be stable; the values they carry can be variable and shifting. With moving eloquence, the Danaid girls plead for compassion when pursued by their oppressive cousins in another country. Yet will the Athenian audience recognize that they reveal themselves, with filial compliance, to be at least as much "of evil mind, and guileful of purpose" when occasion arises? Some vaunted cultural virtues on the Danaid side, which becomes Greek, can be no less savagely barbaric than the aliens'. It has been conjectured that it is none other than the Eastern/Egyptian Lynceus who will eventually become the protector of the Western/Hellenic people and values (see Chad Turner 46). What is more, in one specific cultural domain the girls act as a homogeneous group. Yet in another, one of them shows herself capable of a radically divergent, individual value orientation. They embody opposing answers to the need to preserve or even create a viable identity amid unfamiliar surroundings.

Julia Kristeva has reflected on how culture "forces everyone to take into account a value *and* its opposite, the same and the other, the identical *and* its alien," and how "the perverseness of values establishes the subtle norm of a culture conscious of its reversibilities [...]" (147). Also: as research on value dimensions since the significant work of Seligman (et al.) has shown, values (and not only attitudes and motivations) are dynamic, blended from various sources. They can thus be situationally determined, and hence reordered in response to situational manipulations. This is close to Aristotle's concern with knowledge of particulars and single cases (*Nicomachean Ethics* 1141b7, 1142a5). To discern, in any instance, whether and how far psychological and intercultural research is adaptable to the needs of literary analysis becomes the first operation suggested by transversal rationality, in the shape of "praxial critique" (see Steppat's Chapter 5 in Volume 8).

The literature of our time has explored further, no less painful ways to grapple with these issues.

Threshold People

We have a striking modern response to the situation of hapless migrants. Articulating social experience rather than myth, it is that of the "often forceful and visionary" poems (Gee 83) which anonymous Chinese men, who had faced hardship in their desire to leave their home behind, in the first half of the 20th century wrote and partly carved on the walls of Angel Island Immigration Station outside San Francisco. That is where they were detained to await jurisdiction on their appeals or on deportation. Their own language was largely Cantonese and Toisanese. Of course the situation, historical place, and poetical form are quite unlike those of the Greek drama, but "similarities in difference as well as differences within similarities" might surface (Chang 144). Somewhat like the Danaids, for all the contrasts, these are "liminal *personae* ('threshold people')" slipping through the positions of cultural space (Victor Turner, *Ritual* 95, see also Thomassen 19) — at the interstices of structure. Like them, they are not marginal: they do have "cultural assurance of a final stable resolution of their ambiguity," be it in admission or deportation (Turner, *Dramas* 233). Somewhat like the Danaid case, there are claims of citizenship by derivation if not by birth (*Island* 20). And not altogether unlike the Argive shore's sanctuary, the station is a liminal entity in a mutual definition with its alternative, the structured and differentiated society: "neither here nor there," hence "betwixt and between the positions assigned and arrayed by law, custom, convention, and ceremonial" (Turner, *Dramas* 233). The liminal condition, indeed, is characteristic of the intercultural (see Xie 6). Another study of liminal conditions is offered in Patrick Oloko's chapter in Volume 9. Nobody stands on both sides of the threshold between ownness and alienness, at least not at the same time — as we can learn from Bernhard Waldenfels (7). We also learn that the cultural alien can only be reached over a threshold; in a fuller sense, accordingly, not at all.

The poems speak of their writers' lingering hope, but also their anguish, frustration, and anger. Some vaunted American virtues can be those of "barbarians": "humanitarian" turns into "tyrannical," with no respect for "justice" (as in *Island* nos. 47 and 48, p. 100). We hear eloquent voices of lamentation: "When will they wrap your corpse for return? / You cannot close your eyes. [...] Before you could fulfill your ambition, you were buried beneath clay and earth" (no. 55, p. 106). From the records one can learn that there were suicides, both in the barracks and also on returning ships (*Island* 22, 48, 75, 114, 136; no. 66, p. 168: "I pray that the day you again enter the cycle of life / You'll not be a chap with a worthless life from a poor family"). There are pleas for pity, sometimes self-pity: "I am like pear blossoms which have already fallen; / Pity the bare branches during the late spring" (no. 27, p. 156). Occasionally there is a dark threat of revenge: "An advantageous position for revenge will surely come one day" (no. 42, p. 92); "If you have but one breath left, do not be discouraged from your purpose. [...] Only by wielding the lance can one avoid certain defeat" (no. 45, p. 94). Not quite like the ambivalence of cultural values in the Danaids' case, because responding from a position of acutely felt weakness to very real humiliation experiences, some of the poem writers imagine they will "sharpen their swords" or aim to "behead the barbarians and spare not a single blade of grass" (no. 35 [p. 84] and no. 45 [p. 94]). Could this be an allusion to Walt Whitman's *Leaves of Grass*?

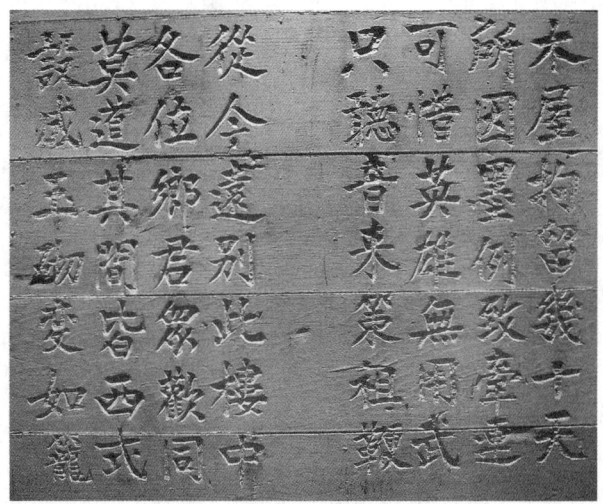

Figure 2
Angel Island Detention Center
Reproduced courtesy of Archive of Mobility,
Magdalene College, University of Cambridge

In some respects, these poetic voices form "a liminal phenomenon which fulfills the function of transition phase or, one can say, a 'transit carriage' between the reality ruled by force and distant cosmos elaborated by imagination" (Ratiani). They are a response to America's "boundary-producing rituals of representation" which suspected imaginary external threats to "fully made" White America as in the Chinese Exclusion Act since 1882, the context of the Angel Island station (Oliver Turner 78). Ritual processes here frame the counter-inscription embodied in the poems. Together, the latter form a dynamic of identity which, while being individually varied, belongs to the "transit carriage" situation: "I sigh because my compatriots are being forcibly detained" (*Island* no. 6, p. 38); "Over a hundred poems are on the walls. / Looking at them, they are all pining at the delayed progress. / What can one sad person say to another?" (no. 27, p. 62); "With a weak country, we must all join together in urgent effort" (no. 39, p. 88).

Can the poems be said to belong to "the vital literary legacy of

America" (Gee 83), if America in many cases refused their writers, strengthening "the foreignness of the Chinese" (Oliver Turner 78)? Surely it makes good sense to place the poems at the "intersection" of two literary traditions (Shan 394), hence betwixt and between: "the ideal reader is an Anglophone-Sinophone bilingual reader with some knowledge of Cantonese and pidgin English" (Shan 389).

Building on Volume 8

Liminal conditions, like marginal ones, are relevant to the inquiries that our volumes seek to encourage. Clearly there is a wider range of inter- and transcultural depictions, of cultural variance, context, and comparison to be studied. Our hope is that this book, like its companion volumes, will prompt those of us undertaking literary and intercultural research to think more seriously about the opportunities which the mutual disciplinary perspective will enable. Hence this volume seeks to build on the theoretical frameworks, cultural representations, and varied approaches found in Volume 8 with its eighteen chapters (Steppat and Kulich, 2018, *Literature and Interculturality (I): Concepts, Applications, Interactions*). That book's sections offer thoughtful new theoretical considerations and commentaries, moving from there to analytical studies of relevant works and their context. The first major thematic section in that volume is **Concepts and Orientations**: it presents conceptual reflections which aim to provide some orientation in relating to each other the various branches of literary study (including a comparative perspective) extending to film and of inter- as well as transcultural research. The section is not designed to be insulated against the further chapters, as the ideas presented do feed into the subsequent parts of the book in a number of ways. Moreover, to guide a focused research agenda, in Chapter 5 the section offers a sequence of analytical questions for the practice of literary analysis.

In Volume 8's following sections, the larger part of the chapters explore literature that deals with migrant situations and sociocultural minorities; partly overlapping with this focus, some studies contribute to comparative literary study and to the study of literary adaptation as well as forms of cultural transfer. The second major section is devoted to **Diasporic Discourses**, analyzing various literary representations of the experience of diasporic spaces and conditions: Chinese-Canadian fiction, then literature relating to diasporic situations between

Africa and North America, and situations between Africa, France, and the Caribbean. The third section (**Cross-Cultural Identities**), in which North America is again a prominent though not the only space, studies identity problems in cross-cultural situations. These extend the previous section's focus without foregrounding diasporic concepts to the same extent. The fourth and final section (**Variations of Cross-Cultural Transfer**) discusses cross-border transfers of cultural artifacts and practices, which include cases of literary and theater adaptation, comparative study, and translation. As the analyses show, when objects are transferred or transformed, ideas and values are usually transported with them. In addition, there are essays on "Intercultural Concepts of Identity" and "The Challenge of an Intercultural Literature"; the book also offers a study calling for "Reconsidering Intercultural Narratives: Prologue to Research on Rachel Davis DuBois and Early Textual Approaches to Interculturality."

The Scope and Contents of This Volume

Leading on from there, without trying to avoid intersecting the companion volumes' focal areas, we have recruited contributions highlighting the following specific themes: in Volume 9 (1) Comparative Analyses of Literary Value Constructions, (2) Perspectives on Migration, and now in this volume (1) Exploring Cultural Junctions, and (2) Interpreting Globalization. The volumes are independent of each other, and each can be taken without recourse to the other. In this volume, the actual sections are followed by an Appendix introducing readers to lines of inquiry on "Values and Valuations," in the context of literature and of intercultural communication. This enables a consideration of the potential usefulness of values research for literary study: it is argued that from interculturally-oriented values research, the analysis of literature should potentially receive impulses for tracing variable forms of cultural imprint.

The sections move from theoretical reflections to specific research studies, to show the range of possible applications. Our reading (or viewing) of "something other than what are, all things considered, the short and simple annals of one cultural parish at one historic moment" (Miner 3) activates a poetics that draws on intercultural evidence. We will keep this in mind, as we offer a brief introduction to the chapters and the research issues that are presented in the volume. This is what awaits you.

Section One: Exploring Cultural Junctions

This first section focuses especially on cultural crossroads and junctions. These do occur in other sections of our volumes as well, so that the chapters (reflecting the complex interconnections of our sociocultural reality) dovetail to some extent with approaches in other sections that trace different contexts. The section concentrates on re-thinking some conditions of comparative intercultural inquiry, on cultural interfaces of China (especially film, theater, drama, and ethnic minority literature), then on literary images of Russia and of West Africa. The section features an important thematic focus in terms of world minority literature, as opened in Chapter 2.

In Chapter 1 Ming Xie presents a reconsideration of key epistemological conditions of a research focus on comparative intercultural discourse. The conjunction of the intercultural and the comparative is an evocation of both what is given and what is not (yet). T. S. Eliot has likened efforts to read a remote literature to "trying to be on both sides of the mirror at once," and this suggests that in order to see a limit in Wittgenstein's sense one needs to see both sides of the limit. One would need, accordingly, to unveil the implicit structures of one's own thinking through the foreign. We are pleased to have secured permission to publish this update, to familiarize readers with Xie's rigorous analysis of the conceptual foundations and methodological challenges of intercultural inquiry. Comparative scholarship on cultural junctions can gain much from tracing Xie's concepts.

As Wen Peihong observes in Chapter 2, China's ethnic minority literatures have been undergoing notable changes in globalization in recent years. The mobility caused by migration and travel has promoted Chinese ethnic writers' cross-cultural writings and even twice-cross-cultural writings. They record a spiritual journey from the world of the ethnic mother tongue to that of Chinese, then to the English-speaking world in their artistic creations. Often, these "cultural triphibian" writers present a distinct ethnicity, localism, together with cosmopolitanism. The author offers a case study of the bilingual *Coyote Traces: Aku Wuwu's Poetic Sojourn in America*, which was translated from Chinese into English.

This is followed by an interview (Chapter 3) which Wen Peihong has conducted with Mark Bender, who is a pioneer in academic approaches to Sino-U. S. and world ethnic or minority literatures. Bender's life experience in Appalachia has greatly influenced his study of Chinese folk and ethnic literature. Bender speaks about his experience in and his views about translating Chinese folk literature and ethnic literature, and his views on the relationship between traditional culture and modern life.

Chapter 4 directs attention to film, as Mao Sihui observes the way films can be situated within a *glocalized* context, the dual process of *globalization* and *localization*. This chapter takes a semiotic approach to the study of an important Chinese film: Feng Xiaogang's *The Banquet* (2006), a transculturally creative adaptation of William Shakespeare's *Hamlet, Prince of Denmark*. Through a detailed analysis of some key features of the film (with a section comparing it with *Prince of the Himalayas*, 2006), Mao considers how cinematic meanings are constructed through verbal and visual codes/signs such as narrative structure, and how intertextuality can be fruitfully used to highlight the value of intercultural communication. He concludes that such Chinese film adaptations of *Hamlet* make Shakespeare not only *postcolonial* but also *glocal*.

In Chapter 5, Agota Revesz considers theater as a social act, with significant systemic divergences between China and Europe. She analyzes four specific case studies for an awareness of what is expected of a production concerning value orientations and how the concept of "theater" is used. The focus of analysis is a British, a German, and two Chinese performances: two different European *Hamlet*s and two Chinese versions of *The Orphan of Zhao*. Whereas in China, the performance gives occasion for an articulation of cultural identity, as iconic representation and reinforcement of the whole community, European theater tends to support the Adornian ideal of art as criticism disclosing social contradictions.

Liu Siyuan in Chapter 6 discusses Zaju drama (from the Yuan Dynasty) in connection with German dramatist Bertolt Brecht's *The Caucasian Chalk Circle*, which was composed in the USA. The play embodies a range of cultural interactions: these include Chinese, American, Japanese, and Russian influences. It suggests urgent questions about values concerned with ownership with which we are still confronted in today's world. Now that *The Caucasian Chalk Circle* has become one of Brecht's most frequently staged plays in the USA, as a part of American culture, we have more reason than ever to recall its Zaju origins as strongly contributing to this success.

In the 20th century, a mythical idea of Russia has been projected by British writers. Olga Sobolev and Angus Wrenn in Chapter 7 offer a critical appraisal of this process, making use of the socio-political theories of Edward Said and Pierre Bourdieu. The representation of the Other appears as a particular type of intertext — a dynamic product of cultural interference between "auto" and "hetero" images, shaped by a specific historical context with selective value judgments. This approach to interpreting the paradigm of Russian reception is rooted in imagology or representation studies. In thematizing perspectival image-making, the processes of creating perception contribute to the critical theory of national stereotyping and representation.

In Chapter 8, Charles Ngiewih Teke analyzes a case of cultural authenticity, enriched with traditional values, as communicated in an international space: Alobwed'Epie's novel *The Lady with a Beard* (Cameroon). It presents the prototype of an African community that conceptualizes itself primarily from within and not from without, with local cultural dynamics that resist incursions by external influences. While this appears to counter transcultural processes and junctions, a locally circumscribed cultural origin here receives an identification that goes beyond its own linguistic boundary to receive a transculturally communicative significance. The fiction thus brings forth a hybrid subject.

Section Two: Interpreting Globalization

This second section studies certain global aspects of cultural experience, with attention to China (China's "going abroad" discourses and the transcultural turn of memory studies focusing on the global south), the movement of cultural narrative from multiculturalism to a reconsidered cosmopolitanism, and also the Western phenomenological experience of space and movement as re-evaluated in two American narratives. Here, too, are fruitful overlaps with other sections in our volumes which help to integrate the range of focal research areas.

In a context of global Cultural Studies trajectories, in Chapter 9 Keyan G. Tomaselli and Du Yiwei examine how some trajectories of Cultural Studies research are responding to China's innovative "going abroad" initiative. Among the many topics that are being studied are television drama, travel writing, and also film translation. In this context it appears especially useful to consider Stuart Hall's appropriation of Jacques Derrida's concept of *différance* to formulate his theory of identity, which is extendable to international identity. This helps us understand how Cultural Studies and its *alter ego*, intercultural communication, are being applied as mechanisms enabling soft power to translate Chinese culture across the world.

The conjunction enables a global dialectical discussion which is likely to be of value to both China and the "West."

Based on the experience of 20th-century cultural politics, Zhou Min in Chapter 10 examines the assumptions of multiculturalism and explores the possibility of an alternative in terms of a community of common human fate. As multiculturalism has been contested, a concept proposed and practiced especially in Quebec is interculturalism, which believes in enabling minority groups to engage actively in the dominant culture. Yet the various concepts have drawbacks, so that we could gain a new and globally relevant cultural narrative from Ulrich Beck's proposal of a cosmopolitan realism, which has analogies with Confucian "Ren."

With the sweeping force of globalization, as Yuan Mingqing shows in Chapter 11, memory studies has encountered a "transcultural turn" and is accordingly freed from being conceptualized according to territorial, political, or national boundaries. A concept of "traveling memory" has been proposed, which aims to provide different perspectives for studying the interaction and cross-referencing of memories in the global era. Yet since memory answers the needs of cultural valuations, selections and modifications of memory may incubate dangers of partial subjective positioning. Making use of these concepts, Yuan examines the semi-autobiographical novel *Nairobi to Shenzhen* by Mark Okoth Obama Ndesandjo, half-brother of former U.S. president Barack Obama.

Geographical Information Systems (GIS) and satellite imagery, specifically Google Earth, are characteristic of the Western phenomenological experience of space and movement in an age of globalization and digitization. In Chapter 12, Inge van de Ven and Tom van Nuenen analyze two American novels and their global representations: William T. Vollmann's *The Atlas* and Mark Z. Danielewski's *Only Revolutions*. Vollmann and Danielewski do not attempt to cover up asymmetrical power relations between the U.S. and the rest of the world. Unlike Google's smooth zoom aesthetics, they do not sanitize their worlds of the messiness of our concrete global situation, and they invite the reader to rethink transnational relationality.

Conclusion

Many impulses from these chapters can help us in contributing toward a poetics that draws on intercultural research. This is a complex aim;

our volume has not yet met that goal, but the chapters not only remind us of the conditions for adequate inquiry but also provide some new insights to help us move ahead. Some contributions provide the cross-disciplinary field with fresh perspectives, others take us several steps forward. When we focus on cultural interplay as the study of "encounters" between literary cultures, extending to film, we are led to the fruitful insight that "intercultural understanding in the literary field is now more indispensable than ever before" (Gunilla Lindberg-Wada). It is all the more fruitful when, employing a range of mutually illuminating methods, we attempt to extend inter- and transcultural scrutiny toward a processual or interactive notion of culture as practice and meeting ground. The diversity and integration of literary culture, importantly including Chinese in its relation with other literatures and cultural experiences, is a major concern. For the significant challenges our societies face, locally and globally, in intercultural understanding and in our grasp of some key material problems in today's world, such diversity and integration are indispensable.

Thus our hope is that this book may supplement its Volume 8 companion in providing suitable resources toward designing new approaches, facilitating further steps on the path of understanding how inter- and transcultural inquiry can benefit and even change literary research. We believe that this undertaking is worth all our efforts as we work together. There is more complexity that needs to be disentangled, more context that needs to be accounted for in terms of a multi-methodological and multi-perspectival reality. We now have multifaceted, analytical, and reflective volumes, with historical orientations as well as current concerns, that bring together many of the methods and issues which are vital for a mutual disciplinary influence. As broadly sourced resource guides, they take us from locally situated analyses across all continents and into complex theoretical considerations as well as a range of contextual meanings. The contributions, like those in previous volumes, may well serve as a capstone for future research, pushing us forward to new areas. As numerous research pathways remain to be charted, this book with its preceding companion volumes offer stimuli that interested readers and future researchers are likely to find worthy of further investigation.

Words of Appreciation

As we conclude these introductory statements, we would like to express our thanks and appreciation to all those who have supported the endeavor and helped us bring about this volume. We are beholden to Prof. Feng Qinghua, the then Vice President of Shanghai International Studies University (SISU), for opening and addressing the international symposium "Literature, Comparative Studies, Interculturality" in 2015, which gave us important stimuli for our cooperative research. We wish to give our strong appreciation to Prof. Zha Mingjian, the then Dean of the Graduate School and Dean of the School of English Studies at SISU, now Vice President of SISU, for his personal initiative in furtherance of our work and in organizing that symposium, with untiring and valuable support from Prof. Wang Xin, School of English Studies at SISU. Prof. Mao Sihui, Executive Director of the International Association for Intercultural Communication Studies (IAICS), has not only strengthened the said symposium with his own prominent participation, but has given us essential impulses for our work. Prof. Zhang Hongling and the staff of the Office for International Cooperation and Exchange at SISU deserve thanks for decisive support in enabling the various stages of our cooperation. The Intercultural Institute staff at SISU has contributed very helpful service to our endeavor all along. What is more, the program organizers of the 22nd IAICS Conference in 2016 have enabled an especially fruitful environment for stimulating exchanges of ideas benefiting our work. Then, the organizers of the Sixth International Conference on English and American Literature at SISU in 2017, especially Prof. Li Weiping and Dr. Cheng Xin, have created an excellent platform for intellectual exchange and for expanding our research network in new directions. We are grateful also to Prof. Zheng Tiwu, Director of the SISU Institute of Literary Studies, for his intellectual support and his interest in the volume.

This publication project is part of a commitment to contribute to the internationalization and interdisciplinary cooperation of the Intercultural Institute and of SISU itself, by linking the cooperating and interculturally-oriented researchers on interdisciplinary research and writing projects, selecting and editing the best new work, and publishing continuing topical volumes in this monograph series of *Intercultural Research*. Our volumes seek to highlight benchmarks of international scholarship, in an effort to move the enterprise of our disciplinary cooperation forward. From the outset, this series has aimed to provide a set of monographs in which each volume is focused on one important topic area. Each chapter is meant to be a specially invited "state-of-the-art" analysis of a key topic in intercultural communication studies and its disciplinary partners. This volume, like its companions, attempts to fulfill the high goals we have for this series, having both international and Chinese scholars providing their best work as a reference or benchmark on which to further the research agenda. Researchers in several countries have helped us progressively clarify our ideas and approaches.

In Germany, the Bavarian Academic Center for China has granted a generous fund to enable the formative stage of our cooperative research cluster, with the additional backing of the Vice President and the International Office of the University of Bayreuth as SISU's partner institution. The University of Bayreuth's Faculty of Literary Studies and Linguistics has continuously supported the cooperation and cultural exchange which have made our partnership possible. A productive research environment has been provided by the Bayreuth Institute for American Studies for our cooperative work from the beginning. Doctoral and postdoctoral colloquium groups in Shanghai, Taipei, Moscow, London, Bayreuth, and at the John W. Kluge Center at the Library of Congress have contributed useful debates and ideas to our inquiry.

We owe great thanks, moreover, to Shanghai Foreign Language Education Press for its professional excellence in the printing of the volume.

We wish to take this opportunity to express our profound gratitude to each of the contributors to this volume, for having prepared excellent scholarly essays and engaging with us in fruitful discussion. Building on this experience, we feel strongly encouraged in looking forward to further explorations together. We will be grateful to all who will build on the chapters put forward here.

References

Aeschylus. With an English Translation by Herbert Weir Smyth. Loeb Classical Library. 2 vols. vol. 1. Heinemann / Putnam's, 1922.

Appel, Markus, and Tobias Richter. " Persuasive Effects of Fictional Narratives Increase over Time." *Media Psychology*, vol. 10, no. 1, 2007, pp. 113–34.

Aristotle. *Nicomachean Ethics*. Translated by Terence Irwin. 2nd ed. Hackett, 1999.

Barry, Brian. *Culture and Equality: An Egalitarian Critique of Multiculturalism*. Harvard UP, 2001.

Baumbach, Sibylle, Herbert Grabes, and Ansgar Nünning. " Values in Literature and the Value of Literature: Literature as a Medium for

Representing, Disseminating and Constructing Norms and Values." *Literature and Values: Literature as a Medium for Representing, Disseminating and Constructing Norms and Values*, edited by Sibylle Baumbach, Herbert Grabes and Ansgar Nünning, Giessen Contributions to the Study of Culture 2, Trier: WVT, 2009, pp. 1–15.

Bellour, Raymond. "The Unattainable Text." *Screen*, vol. 16, no. 3, 1975, pp. 19–28.

Benjamin, Walter. "On the Program of the Coming Philosophy." 1918. Translated by Mark Ritter. *Selected Writings*, Vol. 1 (1913–1926), edited by Marcus Bullock and Michael W. Jennings. Harvard UP, 1996, pp. 100–10.

Branco, Angela, and Jaan Valsiner. "Values as Culture in Self and Society." *Cultural Psychology of Human Values*, edited by Angela Uchoa Branco and Jaan Valsiner, *Information Age*, 2012, pp. vii–xviii.

Brill, Sara. "Violence and Vulnerability in Aeschylus's *Suppliants*." *Logos and Muthos: Philosophical Essays in Greek Literature*, edited by William Wians. State U of New York, 2009, pp. 161–80.

Brosch, Tobias, and David Sander, editors. *Handbook of Value: Perspectives from Economics, Neuroscience, Philosophy, Psychology, and Sociology*. Oxford UP, 2016.

Buzzanell, Patrice M. "Extending and Enriching the Scope and Boundaries of Intercultural Communication." Edited by Kulich and Dai, *Identity*, pp. 12–19.

Cao, Shunqing. *The Variation Theory of Comparative Literature*. Springer, 2013.

Cao, Shunqing, and Han Zhoukun. "The Theoretical Basis and Framework of Variation Theory." *CLCWeb: Comparative Literature and Culture*, vol. 19, no. 5, 2017, doi.org/10.7771/1481-4374.3108.

Chang, Hui-ching. "Touring the Field of Intercultural Communication: Finding Differences and Commonalities." *Identity and Intercultural Communication (I): Theoretical and Contextual Construction*, Intercultural Research Vol. 2, edited by Xiaodong Dai and Steve J. Kulich. Shanghai Foreign Language Education Press, 2010, pp. 125–49.

Chou, Mark. *Democracy Against Itself: Sustaining an Unsustainable Idea*. Edinburgh UP, 2014.

Condon, John. "Exploring Intercultural Communication Through Literature and Film." *World Englishes*, vol. 5, nos. 2–3, 1986, pp. 153–61.

Deleuze, Gilles. *The Fold: Leibniz and the Baroque*. Translated by Tom Conley. Continuum, 1993.

Deleuze, Gilles, and Félix Guattari. *Anti-Oedipus: Capitalism and Schizophrenia*. Translated by Robert Hurley et al. Preface by Michel Foucault. U of Minnesota P, 1983.

—. *A Thousand Plateaus: Capitalism and Schizophrenia*. Translated by Brian Massumi. U of Minnesota P, 1987.

De Man, Paul. *The Resistance to Theory*. Foreword by Wlad Godzich. *Theory and History of Literature 33*. U of Minnesota P, 1986.

Derrida, Jacques. *Of Hospitality: Anne Dufourmantelle Invites Jacques Derrida to Respond*. Translated by Rachel Bowlby. Stanford UP, 2000.

Erll, Astrid, Herbert Grabes and Ansgar Nünning, editors. *Ethics in Culture: The Dissemination of Values Through Literature and Other Media*. de Gruyter, 2008.

Fekete, John. "Introductory Notes for a Postmodern Value Agenda." *Life After Postmodernism: Essays on Value and Culture*, edited by John Fekete. Macmillan, 1988, pp. i–xix.

Fisher, Walter R. *Human Communication as Narration: Toward a Philosophy of Reason, Value, and Action*. U of South Carolina P, 1987.

—. "Narration as a Human Communication Paradigm: The Case of Public Moral Argument." *Communication Monographs*, vol. 51, 1984, pp. 1–22.

Gee, Emma. "Poems of Angel Island." *Amerasia*, vol. 9, no. 2, 1982, pp. 83–88.

Grabes, Herbert. "What Exactly Is the Case? Ethics, Aesthetics, and Aisthesis." Baumbach et al., *Literature*, pp. 43–53.

Green, Melanie C., and Timothy C. Brock. "The Role of Transportation in the Persuasiveness of Public Narratives." *Journal of Personality and Social Psychology*, vol. 79, no. 5, 2000, pp. 701–21.

Greimas, Algirdas Julien. *Maupassant: The Semiotics of Text. Practical Exercises*. Translated by Paul Perron. John Benjamins, 1988.

Hall, Stuart. "Introduction: Who Needs 'Identity'?" *Questions of Cultural Identity*, edited by Stuart Hall and Paul du Gay. Sage, 1996, pp. 1–17.

Hofstede, Geert. "Dimensionalizing Cultures: The Hofstede Model in Context." SISU, *Value Frameworks*, pp. 183–215.

Ihde, Don. *Postphenomenology: Essays in the Postmodern Context*. Northwestern UP, 1993.

Irwin, Terence, translator. Aristotle, *Nicomachean Ethics*. 2nd ed. Hackett, 1999.

Island: Poetry and History of Chinese Immigrants on Angel Island, 1910 – 1940. Edited by Him Mark Lai et al. San Francisco Study Center, 1980.

Isocrates. With an English Translation by George Norlin and Larue Van Hook. Loeb Classical Library. 3 vols. Harvard UP, 2014.

Jelinek, Elfriede. *Die Schutzbefohlenen*. Theaterverlag Friedrich Berlin, 2014.

Jung, Hwa Yol. "Transversality and Public Philosophy in the Age of Globalization." *Journal of Political Criticism*, vol. 12, 2013, pp. 139–88.

Kant, Immanuel. *To Perpetual Peace: A Philosophical Sketch*. Translated by Ted Humphrey. Hackett, 2003.

Kraidy, Marwan M. *Hybridity, or the Cultural Logic of Globalization*. Temple UP, 2005.

Kristeva, Julia. *Strangers to Ourselves*. Translated by Leon S. Rudiez. Columbia UP, 1991.

Kulich, Steve J. "Constructing Dynamic Theoretical Frames for Contextual Intercultural Identity Analysis." Kulich and Dai, *Identity*, pp. 105 – 54. *Identity and Intercultural Communication (II): Conceptual and Contextual Applications*. Intercultural Research Vol. 3, edited by Steve J. Kulich and Xiaodong Dai. Shanghai Foreign Language Education Press, 2012, pp. 105–54.

—. "Introduction: Linking Intercultural Communication with China Studies — Language and Relationship Perspectives." *Intercultural Perspectives on Chinese Communication*, Intercultural Research Vol. 1, edited by SISU Intercultural Institute (Steve J. Kulich, Michael H. Prosser). Shanghai Foreign Language Education Press, 2007, pp. 3–21.

—. "Values Studies: The Origins and Development of Core Cross-Cultural Comparisons." SISU, *Value Frameworks*, pp. 33–70.

Kulich, Steve J., and Weng Liping. "Introduction: Value Dimensions, Dynamic Contexts, and Beyond." Kulich et al., *Value Dimensions*, pp. 1–24.

Kulich, Steve J., Weng Liping and Michael H. Prosser, editors. *Value Dimensions and Their Contextual Dynamics Across Cultures*. Intercultural Research Vol. 5. Shanghai Foreign Language Education Press, 2014.

Kulich, Steve J., and Xiaodong Dai, editors. *Identity and Intercultural Communication (II): Conceptual and Contextual Applications*. Intercultural Research Vol. 3. Shanghai Foreign Language Education Press, 2012.

Lembke, Janet. Introduction to *Suppliants*. *The Complete Aeschylus*, vol. 2, edited by Peter Burian and Alan Shapiro, Oxford UP, 2009.

Lopičić, Vesna, and Biljana Mišić Ilić, editors. *Values Across Cultures and Times*. Cambridge Scholars, 2014.

Liu Hsieh [Lu Xie]. *The Literary Mind and the Carving of Dragons*. Translated by Vincent Yu-chung Shih. Columbia UP, 1959.

Lyotard, Jean-François. *The Postmodern Condition: A Report on Knowledge*. Translated by Geoff Bennington and Brian Massumi. Manchester UP, 1984.

McKay, Robert. "Invaluable Elephants, or the Against-Value of Critique (for Animals)." *Against Value in the Arts and Education*, edited by Sam Ladkin, Robert McKay and Emile Bojesen, Rowman & Littlefield, 2016, pp. 53–75.

Mao, Sihui. "Interfacing Literature, Culture, and (Intercultural) Communication Studies in the Digital Era." *Literature and Interculturality (I): Concepts, Applications, Interactions, Intercultural Research* Vol. 8, edited by Michael Steppat and Steve J. Kulich, Shanghai Foreign Language Education Press, 2018.

Mar, Raymond A., Keith Oatley and Jordan B. Peterson. "Exploring the Link Between Reading Fiction and Empathy: Ruling Out Individual Differences and Examining Outcomes." *Communications*, vol. 34, 2009, pp. 407–28.

Mar, Raymond A., and Keith Oatley. "The Function of Fiction Is the Abstraction and Simulation of Social Experience." *Perspectives on Psychological Science*, vol. 3, no. 3, 2008, pp. 173–92.

Miike, Yoshitaka. "Toward an Alternative Metatheory of Human Communication: An Asiacentric Vision." *Intercultural Communication Studies*, vol. 12, no. 4, 2003, pp. 39–63.

Mowitt, John. *Text: The Genealogy of an Antidisciplinary Object*. Duke UP, 1992.

Neumann, Birgit. "What Makes Literature Valuable: Fictions of Meta-Memory and the Ethics of Remembering." Erll et al., *Ethics*, pp. 131–52.

Nietzsche, Friedrich. *The Will to Power*. Translated by Walter Kaufmann and R. J. Hollingdale. Vintage, 1967.

Nünning, Vera. "The Ethics of (Fictional) Form: Persuasiveness and Perspective Taking from the Point of View of Cognitive Literary Studies." *Arcadia*, vol. 50, no. 1, 2015, pp. 37–56.

Nussbaum, Martha C. *Love's Knowledge: Essays on Philosophy and Literature*. Oxford UP, 1990.

Pettersson, Thorleif, and Yilmaz Esmer. Introduction. *Changing Values, Persisting Cultures: Case Studies in Value Change*, edited by Thorleif Pettersson and Yilmaz Esmer. Brill, 2008, pp. 3–6.

Ratiani, Irma. "Theory of Liminality." *Georgian Electronic Journal of Literature*, vol. 1, no. 1, 2007. www.litinfo.ge/issue-1/ratianiirma.htm.

Ricoeur, Paul. *Time and Narrative*. 3 vols. Translated by Kathleen Mclaughlin [Kathleen Blamey] and David Pellauer. U of Chicago P, 1984–1988.

Schwartz, Shalom H. "Mapping and Interpreting Cultural Differences Around the World." 2004. SISU, *Value Frameworks*, pp. 339–79.

Seligman, Clive, James M. Olson and Mark P. Zanna, editors. *The Psychology of Values: The Ontario Symposium*. Vol. 8. Lawrence Erlbaum Associates, 1996.

Shan, Te-hsing. "At the Threshold of the Gold Mountain: Reading Angel Island Poetry." *Sinophone Studies: A Critical Reader*, edited by Shu-Mei Shih, Chien-Hsin Tsai and Brian Bernards, Columbia UP, 2013, pp. 385–96.

Shearman, Sachiyo M. "Value Frameworks Across Cultures: Hofstede's, Ingelhart's [*sic*], and Schwartz's Approaches." SISU, *Value Frameworks*, pp. 137–80.

SISU Intercultural Institute (Steve J. Kulich, Michael H. Prosser, Weng Liping), editors. *Value Frameworks at the Theoretical Crossroads of Culture*. Intercultural Research Vol. 4. Shanghai Foreign Language Education Press, 2012.

Suo, Gefei. "An Examination of the Status and Future of Intercultural Communication Studies in China — A Pseudo-Delphi Grounded Theory Approach." *China Intercultural Communication Annual*, vol. 2, 2017, pp. 95–119.

Thomassen, Bjørn. "The Uses and Meanings of Liminality." *International Political Anthropology*, vol. 2, no. 1, 2009, pp. 5–27.

Triandis, Harry C. "Foreword to the Two Values Volumes." Kulich et al., *Value Dimensions*, pp. xix–xxxi.

Turner, Chad. "Perverted Supplication and Other Inversions in Aeschylus' Danaid Trilogy." *The Classical Journal*, vol. 97, no. 1, 2001, pp. 27–50.

Turner, Oliver. *American Images of China: Identity, Power, Policy*. Routledge, 2014.

Turner, Victor. *Dramas, Fields, and Metaphors: Symbolic Action in Human Society*. Cornell UP, 1974.

—. *The Ritual Process: Structure and Anti-Structure*. Foreword by Roger D. Abrahams. Aldine Transaction, 1969.

Vasunia, Phiroze. *The Gift of the Nile: Hellenizing Egypt from Aeschylus to Alexander*. U of California P, 2001.

Waldenfels, Bernhard. *The Question of the Other*. The Chinese U of Hong Kong P, 2007.

Wittgenstein, Ludwig. *Philosophical Investigations*. Translated by G. E. M. Anscombe. Blackwell, 1958.

Xie, Ming. *Conditions of Comparison: Reflections on Comparative Intercultural Inquiry*. Continuum, 2011.

Xu, Kaibin. "Theorizing Difference in Intercultural Communication: A Critical Dialogic Perspective." *Communication Monographs*, vol. 80, no. 3, 2013, pp. 379–97.

Zhang, Yingjin. "Engaging Chinese Comparative Literature and Cultural Studies." *China in a Polycentric World: Essays in Chinese Comparative Literature*, edited by Zhang Yingjin. Stanford UP, 1998, pp. 1–20.

Section One

Exploring Cultural Junctions

1

"Both Sides of the Mirror": Comparative Intercultural Inquiry[①]

Ming XIE
University of Toronto

Summary: This chapter presents a reconsideration of key epistemological conditions of a research focus on comparative intercultural discourse. The conjunction of the intercultural and the comparative is an evocation of both what is given and what is not (yet). T. S. Eliot has likened efforts to read a remote literature to "trying to be on both sides of the mirror at once," and this suggests that in order to see a limit in Wittgenstein's sense one needs to see both sides of the limit. One would need, accordingly, to unveil the implicit structures of one's own thinking through the foreign. This inquiry allows us to see the intercultural as a liminal condition, at intersections of cultures, with ceaseless transformation. As we are always translating within and between cultures and languages, we grow aware that the in-between is a space inscribed by values. As cultural interpretation requires a shared framework of evaluations, values are as objective as our attitudes toward truth-claims.

---

① An earlier version of this chapter was published in © Ming Xie, *Conditions of Comparison: Reflections on Comparative Intercultural Inquiry* (Continuum Publishing, 2011), where the chapter's contents form parts of the Introduction and the Epilogue. Permission to use the materials for the present version has been granted both by the author and by Bloomsbury Publishing Plc.

I

No interpretation can duplicate its conditions of possibility.

— Miguel Tamen

1.

In an introductory way, this chapter's concern is to explore, and seek to offer new ways of thinking about, the epistemological conditions of what I would like to call "comparative intercultural inquiry." It is a critical-comparative study of the epistemes, or presuppositional perspectives, of intercultural discourse. By focusing on how conceptual resources of cultures (such as underlying assumptions, implicit categories of thought and belief, and unconscious or semiconscious social imaginaries) may prefigure our perspectives and predetermine our habits of mind, I argue for the *cognitive*, *conceptual*, and *epistemological* nature of comparative intercultural inquiry, alongside with and apart from its historical, social, political, and ethical dimensions. Cultural exchange or dialogue may sometimes seem to be merely an ideal or even an illusion, but it is real in the impact of encounters between cultures. Comparative intercultural studies may often come across as an etiology of intercultural incomprehension or miscomprehension. But it is salutary to remember that trying to use such incomprehension (or non-comprehension) as an opportunity for a diagnostic self-understanding is probably more fruitful than being obsessed with its symptoms or causes.

Comparative intercultural studies is, of course, not a single or unified "field" or "area" of specialized academic study. It is hardly feasible to refer to the "facts" of intercultural encounter and communication, since it is the fluid nature of such facts or fields of study that *frames* the problematics of exchange, argument, and debate. The traditional sense of "comparative literature" or "comparative literary studies" has been greatly transformed in recent decades. Comparative literature now exists in a complex web of interrelations with world literature, translation studies, area studies, transnational studies, cross-cultural global studies, to name just a few related disciplinary orientations.② I shall use the term "comparative intercultural

---

② There are numerous recent publications in English that discuss comparative literary and cultural studies from a general and theoretical point (next page)

inquiry" to name the constellation of problems and concerns built on a new conception of "comparativity." "Comparative" names a mode of inquiry; it is in fact a mode of relating to different cultures. "Comparative" and "intercultural" may seem to overlap, but both are necessary terms in the current context and should not be collapsed into each other. If "the intercultural" denotes what seems to be already there, "comparative" points to what is not (yet) given, or pre-given, what is (yet to be) made and produced. But the intercultural can also be a particular mode of comparative inquiry. The conjunction of "comparative" and "intercultural" enables us to evoke both what is "given" and what is not, as well as what can be thought about them. "Inquiry" names a mode of ongoing and open-ended self-reflexivity. In short, comparative intercultural inquiry is concerned as much with what we need to know about a culture (our own or a foreign one), as with what we do not yet know about it.

One of the difficulties of comparative inquiry is that it may be impossible to distinguish the object of study from "its symbolic reverberation in the consciousness of the subject," to borrow Claude Lévi-Strauss' formulation, or from the imaginative and discursive organizing patterns on the part of the comparativist.[3] One of the first things we become aware of in thinking comparatively and interculturally is the cultural and perspectival embeddedness of our cultural theorizing. We can illustrate such embeddedness with the common trope of "mirror" or "refraction" in comparative discourse.[4] It

---

(continued) of view, with a variety of approaches and emphases. As important articles are too numerous to cite here, I will confine the following very selective list to the most important books published in recent years that are directly germane to the concerns of my approach. Books that discuss general and theoretical aspects of comparative literature, world literature, translation studies, and global intercultural studies include those by Apter, Bermann and Wood, Damrosch, Felski, Felski and Friedman, Fokkema and Ibsch, Gentzler, Li, Melas, Prendergast, Ramazani, Saussy, Spariosu, and Spivak. I would also like to mention the work of Graham Harman. I find the approach of his "object-oriented ontology" extremely interesting and helpful in thinking about comparative intercultural analysis. Important recent books that focus especially on Chinese comparative themes and East-West cultural relations but have broader critical implications include those by Billings and Bush, Bush, Cai, Chen, Chow, Davies, Eoyang, Hayot, Hayot and Saussy and Yao, Huang, Liu, Porter, Saussy, Shih, Tatlow, Yao, and Zhang.

[3] Claude Lévi-Strauss, quoted in Boon 54. I adopt the slightly less common name "comparativist," instead of the more usual "comparatist," to emphasize a distinction between conventional comparison and "comparativity."

[4] See, for example, Levin and Eoyang.

would not be an exaggeration to say that comparative intercultural studies may resemble a play of mirrors. In a letter to I. A. Richards, T. S. Eliot once compared reading in a remote literature to "trying to be on both sides of a mirror at once." Richards used the same metaphor for a later essay, "Mencius Through the Looking Glass":

> The odd title of this essay comes from T. S. Eliot. When I was working in Peking at *Mencius on the Mind* about 1930, he wrote to me (referring probably to his own early Sanskrit studies) that reading in a remote text is like trying to be on both sides of a mirror at once. A vivid and a suitably bewildering image. To ask how exact it may be would be to raise the prime question "What is understanding?" anew. (Richards, *So* 202)

Eliot might be wryly hinting at the impossibility of being on both sides of a mirror at once, the impossibility of being able both to hold onto the assumptions of one's own tradition and to entertain those of the foreign equally well to be in a position to compare and evaluate. The "mirror" image may nevertheless be quite pertinent to the central problematic of comparative intercultural inquiry. One way to take this mirror image is to say that the two sides of a mirror are like the two sides of a limit. As Wittgenstein alludes to the difficulty of drawing a limit of what is thinkable and what is not in the preface to his *Tractatus*, to see a limit, one needs to see both sides of the limit.⑤ Likewise, how can we define in advance, almost in an *a priori* way, a "problematic" when we don't know it yet, when we haven't encountered it before? The problematic can only come from the problems that the comparativist has encountered and experienced. In this sense, to be on the other side of the mirror is to be in a position to unveil the implicit categories and structures of one's own thinking through encountering something foreign. When we, as comparativists, are called into question by the very distance or discrepancy newly revealed between ourselves and the foreign culture, when we are reflected in the mirror of the strange or foreign, then we imagine and change ourselves through the mirror. It may often be the case that the mirror itself, different by virtue of different cultures,

⑤ "[T]he aim of the book is to draw a limit to thought, or rather — not to thought, but to the expression of thoughts: for in order to be able to draw a limit to thought, we should have to find both sides of the limit thinkable (i.e., we should have to be able to think what cannot be thought). It will therefore only be in language that the limit can be drawn, and what lies on the other side of the limit will simply be nonsense" (Wittgenstein 3–4).

merely reflects back to us the image of ourselves we are *expecting*. Yet it could also be a mirror in which our assumptions and preoccupations are reflected back to us as (new) *problems*. To be on both sides of a mirror at once is as much to see what is reflected in the mirror as to see what is literally behind the mirror, what makes the mirror function as a mirror. It is also to glimpse the other that is reflected in the mirror of one's own speculative instrument, to see *how* one sees, to see what enables one to see in a particular way. To be on the rear side of the mirror is also to see one's own "blind spot" or "ignorance" precisely as a condition of possibility for knowing the other and hence oneself.

This chapter can be seen as introducing a set of dialogically interrelated reflections on the meanings and implications of prefixes (such as "trans-" and "inter-") that address and connote forms of relation and process in the making and unmaking of cultural boundaries. Ours seems an age of prefixes (and also of suffixes). Take any substantive notion or concept and add various prefixes to it, what we get then is a new take on things, a new theory, a new model, or simply a new "turn." Examples abound: culture, nation, humanism, modernity, coloniality, discipline, for example. Each of these substantive concepts can be transmuted, with the help of some of these all-powerful prefixes, into a number of different things. Notable prefixes include the following: inter-, cross-, trans-, multi-, pluri-, post-, meta-, counter-, extra-, intra-, infra-, anti-, mono-, de-. Thus, to take "discipline": we get *inter*-disciplinary, *cross*-disciplinary, *trans*-disciplinary, *multi*-disciplinary, *post*-disciplinary, *meta*-disciplinary, *anti*-disciplinary, and so on. Such permutation may also seem to indicate a certain logic of progression from absence of disciplinary consciousness through transgression of disciplinary boundaries to the apparent transcending of disciplinarity itself, as if this is at all possible.

At the outset, I want to foreground "meta-" as the crucial trope, since there is hardly anything more reflexive than "meta-cultural." For example, the elision, enabled by the meta-relation between intra-cultural and inter-cultural as well as trans-cultural, can be demonstrated through a heuristic distinction between morality and ethics. If morality may be taken as *intra*-cultural, ethics can then be construed as *inter*-cultural, or even *trans*-cultural. The basic intellectual operation here is that of the *meta*-cultural, which may mean both *transcendence* (going beyond culture as currently understood or practiced) and *immanence* (still staying within culture and creating a new version of this same culture). In his *Notes*

Towards the Definition of Culture, published shortly after the Second World War, T. S. Eliot says, "We are [...] pressed to maintain the ideal of a world-culture, while admitting that it is something we cannot *imagine*. We can only conceive it, as the logical term of relations between cultures" (62). Eliot's last phrase is very suggestive but remains cryptic. I would argue that this "world-culture" is to be conceived not as a geographical or even geocultural entity, but as an ongoing work or process, as the very structuring logic of the intercultural. In other words, *the meta-cultural is the logic of the intercultural*. That is, it is not that there is first the cultural, then the intercultural, but the cultural is already intercultural. This is an ontological distinction, but also a meta-epistemological one and has methodological implications as well. Thus the intercultural has to do with both the nature and structure of the world and how we know cultural categorizations *as* epistemological frameworks that are historically transformable. Epistemology here is taken not in the sense that objects of knowledge are given naturally and are (more or less) accessible to our knowing, but in the sense of cultural categories of knowing. Critical intercultural inquiry as an epistemological approach thus highlights the reflexive *circularity* of intercultural knowing: we try to know by reflecting on the forms and categories of our knowing.

2.

Here, I would like to take the reader through some of the keywords formed with the main prefixes, terms commonly used to describe relations between cultures, by briefly discussing their definitions and connotations, the better to clarify why the term "intercultural" is the most precise for the purpose of this chapter. First, the term "cross-cultural" largely means crossing the boundaries between at least two cultures or cultural areas. Haun Saussy is quite right to point up in the term "cross-cultural" the hidden "idea of an encounter, a cross-roads, as well as that of a hybrid, or a crossing." Yet "cross-cultural" may just be a neutral, descriptive term, since "cross-cultural study is simply the recognition of a condition in which we all exist" (Saussy, "Teaching" 5–8). So "cross-cultural" is not quite the best term in the context of this chapter, as it may also seem to presuppose the fixity and self-evidence of the boundaries to be crossed and traversed.

"Trans-cultural" means extending across or going beyond particular cultures. "Trans-" is here both "going *across*" and "going *beyond*;" hence "trans-cultural" means both *passing through* particular cultures and *transcending* them at the same time, thus implying an idea of *supra*-cultural universality. A related term is "transculturation," which in fact means something different from "transcultural": a process of cultural transformation marked by the influx of new cultural elements and the loss or alteration of existing ones. "Transculturation" is a term first coined by Cuban historian Fernando Ortiz in his *Cuban Counterpoint: Tobacco and Sugar* to designate the process whereby "subordinated or marginal groups select and invent from materials transmitted to them by a dominant or metropolitan culture" (Pratt 6). But the term has come now to be used more generally and descriptively, beyond its originally colonial context, to refer to the process of both synchronic and diachronic movements of cultural forms, interacting with and generating each other. Elaborating Ortiz's favorite example of the adoption of tobacco for enjoyment by Europeans in the process of American colonization, Saussy further develops the apt metaphor of a "conceptual turbulence" in the wake of transculturation:

> In the end tobacco, like coffee and many other substances from the Americas, came to occupy a space midway between the categories of "food" and "medicine," and therefore altered the mental landscape of consumption among European peoples. If you were to map that landscape, the picture that came into effect after the introduction of tobacco would be qualitatively different from that before. [...] The new product actively reshapes the minds of the people who use it; the new habits and ways of thinking at time $t + 1$ cannot be reduced to the conditions of the previous understanding. ("Teaching")

For Saussy, the significance of such transculturation lies in how it actively alters the very *ground* of intercultural interaction and exchange. Finally, we should also note that "transcultural" may seem to imply a vertical or hierarchical dimension to cultures, whereas "intercultural" intimates a certain laterality, which is primarily horizontal and even "rhizomatic." What is important in the intercultural is a lateral sense of displacement, of emergence, of incompletion, and of continual creation.

"Multicultural," of course, means relating to or designed for several or many cultures. Multicultural, as a descriptive term, invokes diversity and implies multiple frames of reference. Multiculturality respects cultural entities as bounded and discrete. Multiculturalism tends to promote clear and fixed boundaries and barriers between diverse sections within the same state or society, which may lead to the (self-)ghettoization of suppressed or unfulfilled identities.⑥ The basic paradox of multiculturalism is that ethno-cultural minorities in a multicultural society are encouraged to be an active part of a liberal cosmopolitan culture of diversity, while at the same time their "authentic" and partly endangered identities are to be protected (or even excluded) from any cosmopolitan assimilation. However, this double bind makes it all the more difficult for a serious multicultural dialogue to take place. According to Werner Hamacher, any culture is always already "multiculture": "If the historical and structural *a priori* of every culture is its multiplication, then *one* multiculturalism cannot be enough, and there need to be *many* multiculturalisms" (298). The multicultural can also be distinguished from the pluricultural. If *multiculturality* refers to diversity *within* the "same" culture, then *pluriculturality* may be used to refer to diversity *across* cultures. What is crucial in pluriculturality is the impacting of cultures upon each other and the consequent bricolage of multiple visions, especially in relation to how the rise of technoscience goes hand in hand with the appearance of pluriculture. As Don Ihde observes, "For every contact the Euro-American technologized culture makes with the Other, there returns a countercurrent of the culture contacted. This is the phenomenon of what I shall call *postmodern pluriculture*" (28). This vision is thus both Western and post-Western, in that much of the matrix and framework of this technologized world culture remains largely Western in origin, but it is no longer Western in the sense that distinctly non-Western beliefs and value systems are now increasingly being placed side by side with those of the West.⑦ This postmodern pluriculture is not neutral, but is "acidic in its effect upon all deep monocultural traditions [...] pluriculture also changes culture, and that will be, in one way or the other, the result of the meeting of new technologies and old cultures" (Ihde 30 − 31). In this sense, the pluricultural has very subtly and effectively dislodged the so-called monocultures from their traditional certainties, because the pluricultural accentuates a certain

---

⑥ Multiculturalism is of course understood very differently and has very different histories in Australia, Canada, the United States, and European countries such as the Netherlands and Germany, to name just a few Western countries where multiculturalism has become a prominent issue.

⑦ I use terms such as "the West," "the Occident," "Western," or "non-Western" in a nominalist way, with full awareness of how such global notions are mostly distorting and misleading if used as substantive and essentialist concepts. The same is true of notions like the "Orient" and "Chinese."

genealogical *arbitrariness* of their historical developments and traditional values, which have so far simply been taken for granted. On the other hand, postmodern pluriculture has a strong tendency to become a global *monoculture*.

This is where the *intercultural* comes in: the place where culture or multiculture is ceaselessly created and recreated. "Intercultural" means existing between or relating to two or more cultures, as in intercultural contact or intercultural tension. But the intercultural is much more complicated than this simple definition allows. The intercultural can be construed in diverse ways. For example, the notion of *interculture*, as Anthony Pym has reminded us, can be used "to refer to beliefs and practices found in intersections or overlaps of cultures, where people combine something of two or more cultures at once" (*Method* 177). "Intersections" here should be considered hierarchically "secondary to a division of cultures" because "as soon as the line between cultures becomes non-operative, as soon as there is no functional barrier to overcome, interculturality loses its derivative status and becomes indistinguishable from general cultural practice" (Pym, *Negotiating* 5). The key point here is the real but unstable distinction between, on the one hand, interculture as derived from its two or more coterminous cultures and, on the other hand, simply culture or general culture. The shifting boundaries of such an interculture can also be evoked in terms of translation, as clarified by Gideon Toury:

> What is totally unthinkable is that a translation may hover in between cultures, so to speak: as long as an (hypothetical) interculture has not crystallized into an autonomous (target!) systematic entity, e.g., in processes analogous to pidginization and creolization, it is necessarily part of an existing (target!) system. (28)⑧

Interculture as such is certainly not an entity. We should rather say that the intercultural has to do with boundaries, since cultures themselves are not spatial wholes and their "territory" is in fact fluid in its boundaries. No culture can be abstracted from its boundaries, because boundaries are liminal and pertain to both the inside and the outside of a culture at once.

The intercultural can thus be taken as a liminal condition. The term "liminality," derived from the Latin *limen*, means "threshold."

---

⑧ Quoted also in Pym, *Method* 180.

The threshold is like a nodal point or pivot that is a point of ceaseless transformation. The liminal is necessarily ambiguous and indeterminate because of its in-betweenness. The in-between is not an entity, but a space without boundaries of its own. The intercultural is the modality of cultural de-realization and de-idealization. We may need to distinguish between the intercultural and the multicultural. Multiculturalism promotes the coexistence of, rather than movement among, cultures. Multiculturalism maintains as a principle the current status of the cultures involved, rather than expecting change from them. It addresses cultural traditions in more synchronic terms, whereas the intercultural would highlight these traditions in more diachronic terms, turning history into a determining force. The multicultural reinforces the *exteriority* of cultures, while the intercultural may create a (self-)conscious *interior* for them through the very process of exchange. The "inter-" in intercultural signifies not just the in-between, but particularly the active sense of interaction, confrontation, and even conflict. The intercultural in-between as the potential space of interplay can be further clarified with the help of D. W. Winnicott's notion in "The Location of Cultural Experience," though formulated in a different context from mine, of a potential psychic space that is neither inner nor outer. Winnicott describes an emergent property of the interaction between inner and outer in the context of subjectivity, yet what he highlights as "*the potential space between the subjective object and the object objectively perceived*" (100) is applicable to the intercultural as well. The intercultural is the emergent property of interaction between cultures. The intercultural is necessarily contingent and open-ended. It is at once the *actuality* and *virtuality* of cultures.

Thus the notion of the intercultural in fact presupposes a third realm, which is precisely the *intercultural* itself. Interculturality has a triadic structure: between any *two* cultures, there is the *intercultural*. Yet the intercultural does not enter into a world of already constituted and realized cultures, merely to intervene externally between the two cultures thus conceived. Rather, the intercultural itself already functions as the *middle* or *medium* of these cultures. The cultural is mediated and constituted by the intercultural, which is an intervention into the *intra*-cultural dynamics of contestation, bifurcation, and transmutation internal to a given culture. The basic opposition between *intra*-cultural and *extra*-cultural presupposes that the *intra*-cultural already embraces both internal consensus and dissensus. Analogously, the *extra*-cultural may be a way of seeing that is located both inside and outside a culture: it may be a way of seeing in the light of another culture, or a way of seeing that goes beyond cultures as such. In other words, the intercultural is paradoxically also the *outside* of the (mono)cultural *within* the (mono)cultural. I would argue that the intercultural is a paradoxical and dynamic space of both making and unmaking. The intercultural not only mediates between cultures, but also looks beyond the cultural *as such*.

II

When the truth is evident, it is impossible for parties and factions to arise.

— Voltaire

1.

Voltaire may be right, but the truth is not always evident, especially between cultures. As a way to move forward my argument about comparativity and intercultural critique, I turn to the idea of truth and the politics of truth, for in the context of intercultural cognition, it has proved to be a central concern in terms of the pragmatic or communicative dimension of cultural exchange. It is necessary to engage dialogically and comparatively with the various discourses on this topic. In particular, I want to show that, though I argue for an epistemological approach, my aim is not to set up epistemology and politics (or ideology) as binary oppositions but, rather, to accentuate the *epistemological* dimensions of intercultural politics as well as the *political* implications of intercultural epistemological inquiry. In short, intercultural politics is more than just political.

The question of truth evokes our sense of the real and how we come up with that sense. "What *counts* as the real world depends on our values," argues Hilary Putnam (137). Values such as purpose, interest, coherence, and relevance determine the kind of world we come to see and take as real. "Any choice of a conceptual scheme presupposes values [...] because no conceptual scheme is a mere 'copy' of the world. The notion of truth itself depends for its content on our standards of rational acceptability, and these in turn rest on and presuppose our values." Yet our values themselves ultimately depend on our assumptions about human nature, society, or the world. So our values can be revised and changed, "again and again as our knowledge has increased and our world-view has changed" (Putnam 215). In a fundamental sense, we are always already translating within and between cultures and languages. Even if we don't know how to locate the in-between, we know that it is a space inscribed by values — values such as economy, circulation, appropriation, and self-reflexivity. Translation is also necessarily motivated and underwritten by a sense of truth and truthfulness. This is an issue fundamental to intercultural discourses: we are constantly challenged by the need to recognize that there may be a common core shared by conflicting cultural traditions and values in their encounters precisely because such a core has been developed and expressed in different ways historically. For example, a strategy of comparative analysis may be historically informed while its essential problematics are not necessarily determined by such history. Bernard Williams has emphasized some of the ramifications of this dialectic of "central core and historical variation." This notion can prompt us to think further about intercultural value. A critical redefinition of value in the intercultural context would *seem* to rest on some notion of truth and truthfulness as having *trans*-historical and *trans*-cultural validity. This dimension of truth also pertains to the ethical implications of intercultural epistemology.

Bernard Williams calls the twin qualities of accuracy and sincerity the virtues of truth. The virtues of accuracy have to do with finding out the truth, as accurately as one can, and the virtues of sincerity have to do with those who communicate these truths to other people as honestly as they can. These two basic virtues of truth are derived from essential features of human communication, in what Williams calls the "state of nature" story. This "state" is a fictional construction in which Williams sets out the basic needs for such virtues of truth and truth communication in human society. This kind of pure *fictional* reflection on the needs of human communication in a schematic "state of nature" society is supplemented by Williams' genealogical reflection on *real* history. Such basic needs are constantly changed and transformed, differently embodied, and extended by historical experience. What interests us here is that the fundamental claim of Williams' *Truth and Truthfulness* concerns methodology: such needs and virtues can only be understood through a historical, genealogical knowledge of concepts. But to have a concern with truthfulness and its virtues of accuracy and sincerity is to presuppose the concept of truth (see Williams). Such genealogical inquiry into the origins of a custom or concept does not debunk or unmask it, nor leaves it hollow. Rather, such inquiry shows the contingency of all our concepts, and what the true potential for their realization can be.

An analysis of the relevance of Cornelius Castoriadis and Niklas Luhmann to critical comparativity could show that the concept of the praxis of truth points up its contingency, historicity, and relativity, but also, more important, its open-endedness and creativity. These dimensions of truth-praxis are especially important for intercultural critical comparativity. Truth as an intercultural concept is objective but not immutable, since it is a relational concept in the sense that truth may be just the *gap* between cultures, or the *contradiction* between cultures. If so, truth between cultures is not something trans-historical or trans-cultural that stands over and above cultures, but the very gap between them and how this gap can be brought into *explicit focus*. The chief value of comparative intercultural inquiry lies in the fact that it promotes a willingness to recognize contingency, hence the possibility of change and transformation in one's own cultural views, attitudes, and even values. Barbara Herrnstein Smith has forcefully argued that "all value is radically contingent, being neither a fixed attribute, an inherent quality, or an objective property of things but, rather, an effect of multiple, continuously changing, and continuously interacting variables" (30). We could balance this strong claim with a recognition of the relative validity of *socially and culturally validated values*, as we can see in the aporia of historicized relativity as opposed to the relatively synchronic coherence of our truth and value.

Contingency entails a notion of fallibilism. In this respect, comparative intercultural inquiry can further develop the arguments of contemporary philosophers with a pragmatist orientation. Donald Davidson, for example, maintains that

> what we will never know for certain is which of the things we believe are true. Since it is neither visible as a target, nor recognizable when achieved, there is no point in calling truth a goal. Truth is not a value, so the "pursuit of truth" is an empty enterprise unless it means only that it is often worthwhile to increase our confidence in our beliefs, by collecting further evidence or checking our calculations. ("Truth" 67)

On this view, truth is neither relative nor absolute. There are different degrees of perception of a truth. A truth can manifest itself *differently*. Hence the fallibilist notion of truth entails a notion of value pluralism, which would *seem* to be incompatible with a strong notion of the objectivity of value. But that impression would be reductive. Alison Assiter provides a stimulating perspective: "If values are objective, then there is a right set of values and a wrong set. Perhaps no one as yet has discovered this right set of values, and that explains the existing plurality of views about value" (72). This is certainly true, yet we may still want to question Assiter's implicitly framed irreconcilability between value objectivity and value pluralism, since pluralism in this case does not pertain to the *plurality* of values as such, but to the *inadequacy* of any commitment to one value or entity. My point is that, in intercultural terms, values can be objective in the ensemble of their complex interrelations or oppositions or even conflicts, but commitment to any one (or a very limited number) of them at the expense of all the others can make such commitment excessive and thus less objective. As Mencius puts it, "Why I dislike holding to one point is that it injures the *tao* (the way or principle). It takes up one point and disregards a hundred others" (Richards, *Mencius* 35). Moreover, values are as objective as our attitudes toward truth-claims, since cultural interpretation requires a shared framework of such attitudes and evaluations, which in turn constitutes a necessary condition for disagreement about values.⑨

2.

In thinking about intercultural truth, we need to remember that everything is underpinned by the *circuit* of communication. This is to say that communication is predicated on the indeterminacy and distortion of the meaning of what is and is not communicated. In this sense, comparative intercultural theory calls for a "constructivist" notion of knowledge and truth-claims, which do not pre-exist our construction of them. In spite of the ideal of transparent discursive communication, we have to confront the double bind of communication: we tend to miscommunicate in order to communicate at all. We tend to misunderstand in order to understand at all. This is no mere paradoxical way of speaking. Cultural misunderstandings or even conflicts are not (necessarily) due to defects or shortcomings of the cultures involved, but simply the inevitable *entropic* result of their very *interaction*. To try to understand another culture may perhaps

---

⑨ This is essentially Davidson's argument in "The Objectivity of Values" (*Problems* 39–59).

be necessarily to misunderstand or "misrecognize" it in important and consequential ways, and also, to a significant degree, to misrecognize one's own.

Here, I want to extend Pierre Bourdieu's concept of *méconnaissance* in comparative intercultural terms. Bourdieu uses it in the context of the economy of gift exchange, in which the required lapse of time between the gift and the counter-gift serves to mask the nature of the gift as an entirely gratuitous and unrequited act, but this lag is nevertheless needed to complete the gift-exchange and is guaranteed by *méconnaissance*, "this institutionally organized and guaranteed misrecognition" (171). *Méconnaissance* is defined as "deliberate oversight" whereby a group "conceals from itself its own truth" (6, 22). For Bourdieu, recognition or misrecognition presupposes forms of knowing or *failing* to know, yet these forms are in fact shared culturally and collectively. I think what needs to be brought out more explicitly in Bourdieu's concept is that misrecognition is not ignorance but *misconstrual* or, more precisely, a complicity with what is taken to be the invisible but natural order of things. Misrecognition lies behind misunderstandings. Thus, in a fundamental sense, misrecognition is really a kind of *un*-recognition, which means that misrecognition presupposes there is something that is *not* recognized. The importance of misrecognition as a concept in the intercultural context has to do with the implicit legitimation of what is "recognized" (but in fact "misrecognized") as the natural order of things, as the natural way or the only way to see or do things. The point is that often the fact of this misrecognition itself is not recognized. Knowledge is bound up with "misrecognition," a connection that is more directly evident in French: *connaissance* relates to *méconnaissance*. Thus misrecognition or misconstrual needs to be foregrounded as an important epistemological (and also political) fact in intercultural inquiry. It has profound implications not only for "misunderstanding", but also for "self-misunderstanding."

Moreover, we also need to recognize that there always seems to be something in a different culture, as well as one's own, that remains irreducible to our own (present) terms, something that is inassimilable and even inaccessible. In the encounter with what is unfamiliar, unexpected, and even unsettling is generated something that *exceeds* mere exchange and opposition. It would be more interesting to compare two cultures with a view to revealing the different assumptions that often turn into obstacles that affect communication between them, rather than simply to judge or evaluate them in terms of superiority or hierarchy. Communication puts into play what *fails* to communicate as well as what *cannot* be communicated. Communication is underwritten by what escapes (direct) communication.

To affirm the intercultural is thus not to affirm substantive identities of cultures, but to reflect on a fractal image of the very tension of sharing-in-common and inner conflict, which is reflected on every level of a culture's being, as well as between cultures. Incommensurability resides in principle within the same culture. Conflicts are contingent, in the sense that cultural objects and identities cannot be totally controlled through categorization. Contingency here relates to a reflexive relativism, which should in fact be a *self*-relativization — that is, a relativizing of one's own current assumptions and horizons. Commonality in this sense does not mean the possessing of something in common, but confronting ourselves *vis-à-vis* that which different cultures may help to bring forth into visibility, through communication (that is, disagreement). Commonality may be the very gap between reality and representation, not in terms of "correspondence," but in terms of acknowledging the reality of the real, as well as the reality of different cultures in their recalcitrant autonomy and interdependence simultaneously.

I would argue that comparative intercultural inquiry is fundamentally concerned with this intrinsic discrepancy between reality and representation, between objects and their interpretations and categorizations, between the world and the perspectives we can have on it. By arguing this thesis, I am trying to suggest the terms of a comparative intercultural inquiry that would enable us to rethink and reimagine the *actual* as *contingent* possibilities of the real. Such a comparative mode of thinking also provides the necessary distance as a vital precondition of opening existing cultures towards new and diverse modes and possibilities of being. Fundamentally, cultural confrontations are not just agonistic; they also compel and enable cultures (and individuals) to confront their own radical *freedom* and *creative capacity*. Comparative intercultural thinking enables us to see any actual or possible universal modes and values as no longer just ethno-cultural or particularistic in application (for example, as "Western" or "Chinese"), but as modes of being that enable us to become aware of the *actual* relations in which things have been contingently inserted and which could thus prompt us to rethink and re-actualize things differently, by putting them into new and different relations and contexts. Alternative relations, perspectives, or frameworks are always possible. Yet the arbitrariness of a perspective or framework is itself relative to something supposedly non-arbitrary. So there is a constant tension between what is taken to be arbitrary and what is not. Awareness of this tension entails a comparative approach that makes us appreciate our own contestability and hence also our freedom. This affirms the objectivity of our common world and our search for its many truths.

References

Apter, Emily. *The Translation Zone: A New Comparative Literature*. Princeton UP, 2006.

Assiter, Alison. "The Objectivity of Value." *Defending Objectivity: Essays in Honour of Andrew Collier*, edited by Margaret S. Archer and William Outhwaite. Routledge, 2004, pp. 63–74.

Bermann, Sandra and Michael Wood, editors. *Nation, Language, and the Ethics of Translation*. Princeton UP, 2005.

Billings, Timothy, and Christopher Bush, translators and editors. *Stèles by Victor Segalen: A Facsimile Critical Edition*. Wesleyan UP, 2007.

Boon, James A. *From Symbolism to Structuralism: Lévi Strauss in a Literary Tradition*. Blackwell, 1972.

Bourdieu, Pierre. *Outline of a Practice of Theory*. Translated by Richard Nice. Cambridge UP, 1977.

Bush, Christopher. *Ideographic Modernism: China, Writing, Media*. Oxford UP, 2009.

Cai, Zong-qi. *Configurations of Comparative Poetics: Three Perspectives on Western and Chinese Literary Criticism*. U of Hawai'i P, 2002.

Chen, Xiaomei. *Occidentalism: A Theory of Counter-Discourse in Post-Mao China*. Oxford UP, 1995; 2nd revised and expanded ed. Rowman & Littlefield, 2002.

Chow, Rey. *The Age of the World Target: Self-Referentiality in War, Theory, and Comparative Work*. Duke UP, 2006.

—. *Primitive Passions: Visuality, Sexuality, Ethnography, and Contemporary Chinese Cinema*. Columbia UP, 1995.

—. *The Protestant Ethnic and the Spirit of Capitalism*. Columbia UP, 2002.

Damrosch, David. *How to Read World Literature*. Wiley-Blackwell, 2009.

—. *What Is World Literature?* Princeton UP, 2003.

Davidson, Donald. *Problems of Rationality*. Oxford UP, 2004.

—. "Truth Rehabilitated." *Rorty and His Critics*, edited by Robert B. Brandom, Blackwell, 2000, pp. 65–74.

Eliot, T. S. *Notes Towards the Definition of Culture*. Faber & Faber, 1968.

Eoyang, Eugene Chen. *Two-Way Mirrors: Cross-Cultural Studies in Glocalization*. Lexington Books, 2007.

Felski, Rita. *Uses of Literature*. Blackwell, 2008.

Felski, Rita, and Susan Stanford Friedman, editors. "Special Issue on Comparison." *New Literary History*, vol. 40, no. 3, Summer 2009.

Fokkema, Douwe, and Elrud Ibsch. *Knowledge and Commitment: A Problem-Oriented Approach to Literary Studies*. John Benjamins, 2000.

Gentzler, Edwin. *Contemporary Translation Theories*. Revised 2nd ed. Multilingual Matters, 2001.

Hamacher, Werner. "One 2 Many Multiculturalisms." *Violence, Identity, and Self-Determination*, edited by Hent de Vries and Samuel Weber, Stanford UP, 1997, pp. 284–325.

Harman, Graham. *Prince of Network: Bruno Latour and Metaphysics*. re. press, 2009.

—. *Towards Speculative Realism: Essays and Lectures*. Zero Books, 2010.

Hayot, Eric. *Chinese Dreams: Pound, Brecht, Tel Quel*. U of Michigan P, 2004.

—. *The Hypothetical Mandarin: Sympathy, Modernity, and Chinese Pain*. Oxford UP, 2009.

Hayot, Eric, Haun Saussy, and Steven G. Yao, editors. *Sinographies: Writing China*. U of Minnesota P, 2008.

Huang, Yunte. *Transpacific Displacement: Ethnography, Translation, and Intertextual Travel in Twentieth-Century American Literature*. U of California P, 2002.

—. *Transpacific Imaginations: History, Literature, Counterpoetics*. Harvard UP, 2008.

Ihde, Don. *Postphenomenology: Essays in the Postmodern Context*. Northwestern UP, 1993.

Levin, Harry. *Refractions: Essays in Comparative Literature*. Oxford UP, 1966.

Li, Victor. *The Neo-Primitivist Turn: Critical Reflections on Alterity, Culture, and Modernity*. U of Toronto P, 2006.

Liu, Lydia H. *The Clash of Empires: The Invention of China in Modern World Making*. Harvard UP, 2004.

—, editor. *Tokens of Exchange: The Problem of Translation in Global Circulations*. Duke UP, 1999.

—. *Translingual Practice: Literature, National Culture, and Translated Modernity*. Stanford UP, 1995.

Melas, Natalie. *All the Difference in the World: Postcoloniality and the Ends of Comparison*. Stanford UP, 2007.

Porter, David. *The Chinese Taste in Eighteenth-Century England*. Cambridge UP, 2010.

—. *Ideographia: The Chinese Cipher in Early Modern Europe*. Stanford UP, 2001.

Pratt, Mary Louise. *Imperial Eyes: Travel Writing and Transculturation*. Routledge, 1992.

Prendergast, Christopher, editor. *Debating World Literature*. Verso, 2004.

Putnam, Hilary. *Reason, Truth and History*. Cambridge UP, 1981.

Pym, Anthony. *Method in Translation History*. St. Jerome, 1998.

—. *Negotiating the Frontier: Translations and Intercultures in Hispanic History*. St. Jerome, 2000.

Ramazani, Jahan. *A Transnational Poetics*. U of Chicago P, 2009.

Richards, I. A. *Mencius on the Mind: Experiments in Multiple Definition*. Kegan Paul, Trench, Trubner, 1932.

—. *So Much Nearer: Essays Toward a World English*. Harcourt, Brace &

World, 1968.

Saussy, Haun, editor. *Comparative Literature in an Age of Globalization*. Johns Hopkins UP, 2006.

—. *Great Walls of Discourse and Other Adventures in Cultural China*. Harvard University Asia Center, 2001.

—. *The Problem of a Chinese Aesthetic*. Stanford UP, 1993.

—. "Teaching Cross-Cultural Studies to Cross-Cultural People." *Ex/Change*, vol. 1, June 2001, pp. 5–8.

Shih, Shu-mei. *The Lure of the Modern: Writing Modernism in Semicolonial China, 1917–1937*. U of California P, 2001.

—. *Visuality and Identity: Sinophone Articulations Across the Pacific*. U of California P, 2007.

Smith, Barbara Herrnstein. *Contingencies of Value: Alternative Perspectives for Critical Theory*. Harvard UP, 1988.

Spariosu, Mihai I. *Global Intelligence and Human Development: Toward an Ecology of Global Learning*. MIT P, 2004.

—. *Remapping Knowledge: Intercultural Studies for a Global Age*. Berghahn Books, 2006. Spivak, Gayatri Chakravorty. *Death of a Discipline*. Columbia UP, 2003.

Tatlow, Antony. *Shakespeare, Brecht, and the Intercultural Sign*. Duke UP, 2001.

Toury, Gideon. *Descriptive Translation Studies and Beyond*. John Benjamins, 1995.

Williams, Bernard. *Truth and Truthfulness: An Essay on Genealogy*. Princeton UP, 2002.

Winnicott, D. W. *Playing and Reality*. Basic Books, 1971.

Wittgenstein, Ludwig. *Tractatus Logico-Philosophicus*. Translated by D. F. Pears and B. F. McGuinness. Routledge, 2001.

Yao, Steven G. *Translation and the Languages of Modernism: Gender, Politics, Language*. Palgrave Macmillan, 2002.

Zhang, Longxi. *Allegoresis: Reading Canonical Literature East and West*. Cornell UP, 2005.

—. *Mighty Opposites: From Dichotomies to Differences in the Comparative Study of China*. Stanford UP, 1998.

—. *The Tao and the Logos: Literary Hermeneutics, East and West*. Duke UP, 1992.

—. *Unexpected Affinities: Reading Across Cultures*. U of Toronto P, 2007.

2

Twice-Cross-Cultural Writing and "World Minority Literature"[①]

WEN Peihong

Southwest Minzu University, Chengdu

Summary: With constant physical migration from their indigenous

① I would like to thank all those team members of this intercultural translating, editing, and publishing project of *Coyote Traces*: the poet Aku Wuwu, co-translator and English poems reciter Mark Bender, the Chinese and American editors Shi Zhaohui, Mingru Li, and Hanning Chen, producers Galal Walker and Yin Jun, John N. Low, a Native American scholar, for his incisive comments, Sun Hong, the reciter of the original Chinese poems, and Jiaba A'san, the recordist. The present chapter might serve as a project report on this unique Sino-U.S. academic cooperation in minority literature translation and publication. Intellectually and spiritually, I owe thanks to scholars whom I have not personally known, but whose sparkling thoughts have inspired me, comforted me, and encouraged me greatly in the process of doing this self-study of the translating process: Lawrence Venuti, for "translator's invisibility;" Kenneth Rexroth, for the translator's "sympathy" with the poet, and his remarks on a translator's self-learning and mental growth in translation; and Jonathan Stalling, for calling attention to the lack of acknowledgment of translators in American academia. I owe much to Chadwick Allen, for his pioneering theory of "trans-indigenous literatures" which inspired me for the "world minority literature" concept in China. Special thanks go to Mark Bender, for his "constellations of competency in cosmographic translation," which I refer to as the main theoretical foundation for my own arguments in the chapter. I am thankful to China Scholarship Council for sponsoring me to be a visiting scholar (2017–2018), enabling me to do further research on the comparative study of indigenous literatures in China and the USA. Thus I owe thanks to Pacific University Library for providing great research resources and wonderful space for me to complete the current research.

    This essay was written with the support of the fund provided by China Scholarship Council. The project number is CSC [2017] 3059, No. 201708510070. The essay has also been supported by the Fundamental Research Funds for the Central Universities, Southwest Minzu University (Grant Number: 2020SYB18).

minority areas to mainstream urban centers, and then abroad, a few Chinese ethnic minority writers are becoming culturally "triphibian," shifting their concerns for ethnic minorities from local to global. This enables the forming of a concept of "world minority literature" from that of a comparative approach to "trans-indigenous literature." It should be understood as having an important focus on translation. For the work of translation, the author expands Sinologist Mark Bender's concept of "cosmographic translation" to refer to a larger process: the comprehensive cooperation between Chinese and non-Chinese translators, editors, and publishers in bilingual and intercultural book production, in more than one country. Such a communicative project takes its resources from what have been called "dialogic transactions" extending to dialogic institutional forms, as it is the practice of "various communities of investigators" that enable an understanding of configurations of meaning. Translation processes turn out to be twice-cross-cultural when the Chinese language functions not as a starting point, but as an intermediary between the native tongue and English, with intertextual networks to be traced. To illustrate, the chapter offers a case study of the making of Chinese ethnic Yi poet Aku Wuwu's bilingual poetry collection *Coyote Traces: Aku Wuwu's Poetic Sojourn in America* (2015), translated from Chinese into English by the author together with Mark Bender. On his journey to the West, Aku addresses some issues commonly faced by world minority peoples: endangered native languages, the threat of modernization for ethnic traditions, and the call for indigenous cultural survival and revival. Valuing "differential equality," Aku has launched cultural dialogues between indigenous peoples in China and the USA.

1. From Local to Global: Twice-Cross-Cultural Writing

Ethnic minority literatures in China have been undergoing notable changes as a result of globalization in recent years. The mobility caused by migration, immigration, and travels have promoted Chinese ethnic writers' cross-cultural writings and even twice-cross-cultural writings. These writers record their spiritual journey from the world of their ethnic mother tongue to that of Chinese and then to the English-speaking world in their artistic creations. In the process of their geographic shift as cultural expatriates, they experience preliminary cultural shock, then cultural epiphany, and eventual cultural hybridism. Very often, these "cultural triphibian" writers present their distinct ethnicity, localism, and cosmopolitanism at the same time. Their works convey their concerns about the survival of their native tongue, culture, environmental crises, and a strong sense of intercultural dialogues. They express their ideal of differential equality regarding ethnicity and cultural identities.

Native Americans in the Eyes of a Yi Poet

Aku Wuwu is such a plural triphibian poet, whose artistic creations are strongly affected by his multiple cross-cultural experiences. A poet of the Yi ethnic minority who writes in both Nuosu and Chinese, Aku Wuwu is a professor of Yi Studies at Southwest Minzu University, Chengdu, Sichuan Province (for Yi oral and written literary tradition, see Bender, "Poet" 504−05). He has published several volumes of poetry, literary criticism, and micro-blogs. His books *Winter River* (1994) and *Tiger Traces* (1998) are the first two collections of poetry written and published in modern Yi script.②

In the spring of 2005, Aku was invited to the USA by Mark Bender, a professor of Chinese and folklore studies at The Ohio State University, for his first academic visit and poetry reading. A few other such trips followed. While introducing his own indigenous culture to American communities, Aku also observed the diverse American society, especially in the Native American communities. With mobility and migration between different cultures, Aku, like other cultural expatriates or sojourners such as V. S. Naipaul, Ha Jin, or Bharati Mukherjee (see the chapter by Zhou Yi in the present volume), portrays his multi-cross-cultural experiences in his recent travel poems. These poems, written in Chinese, were composed during his various academic visits to the USA in the past decade. They were originally published in Chinese in 2008 under the title《密西西比河的倾诉》[*Mixixibi he de qingsu*] or *The Appeal of the Mississippi River*.

Coyote Traces: Aku Wuwu's Poetic Sojourn in America (2015) is a bilingual poetry collection. Most of the 80 poems in this collection first appeared in the 2008 Chinese version of *The Appeal of the Mississippi River*, and they were translated into English by the

---

② For more information about Aku Wuwu, please read the short introduction by Mark Bender: http://www. poetryinternationalweb. net/pi/site/poet/item/28064/0/Aku-Wuwu.

author of this chapter and Mark Bender. Most of the poems present Aku's unique perspectives on Native American culture and American multi-ethnic cultures as a whole. At the same time, he frequently recalls the hard survival and potential resilience of the indigenous language and the cultures threatened and endangered by industrialization and modernization in both countries. The ethnic identification of ethnocultural groups, as psychologists have found, chiefly involves cognitive orientation and values expressions (see Trimble et al. 254; also Phinney 920); literature is especially suitable for these. Accordingly, Aku desires to launch a cultural dialogue between two peoples and two cultures, both struggling to survive and revive in the dominant Han Chinese cultures and the mainstream Anglo-American cultures respectively. On his trips to the USA, Aku visited several reservations in the Midwest and Pacific coast areas in Washington and Oregon.

The Native American figures and tribal people he describes include Bannock ("Revival"), Wishram ("Salmon"), Chilkoot ("The Cannibal"), Paiute ("Poisonous Snake"), Umatilla ("Birdman"), Sioux ("Dancing Moon"), Sacajawea of Lemhi Shoshone ("A Mother"), and Chief Joseph of Nez Perce ("The Prayer of Chief Joseph"). He also sojourned along many major rivers in North America: the Mississippi River ("The Source of the Mississippi River"), the Columbia River ("On the First Sight of the Columbia River," "The Columbia River"), Willamette River ("The Future River"), Snake River ("Snake River"), Clearwater River ("The Moonlight at the Shore of the Clearwater River"), and such important historic sites as the Liberty Bell, the Lincoln Memorial, Independence Hall, and the Grand Canyon. In all of these poems, Aku reveals his view of American racial relations and especially the Native American cultural heritage and survival in the country from the perspective of a Chinese ethnic minority. Though social science research has stressed a similarity of cultural value orientations within nations, against a background of "cultural distance between nations" (Schwartz 357), clearly "there are quantitative and qualitative differences between Anglo-American majority values and American Indian minority values" (Lum 71). It is with a knowledge of this that Aku launches a dialogue between ethnic groups in two nations and their civilizations' two rivers, the Mississippi and the Yangtze. Through this dialogue, when translated into English, the poet and the translators hope to make American readers understand Chinese ethnic people's empathy for the Native Americans and the common challenges faced by the indigenous or minority people in the age of modernization. This carries the potential of a "world minority literature" concept, building on Chadwick Allen's comparative research (see also Adamson) by extending it to Asia; the present author aims to communicate the concept and focus it on the translation dimension.

The term "twice-cross-cultural writing" first appears as the title of an interview with Aku in the appendix to *Coyote Traces* (313). It refers to Aku and similar writers' multiple cross-cultural experiences, i.e., "from his native Yi culture to Han Chinese culture, then to American culture, the complexity of Aku's cultural backgrounds, and the 'cultural hybrid' nature of his poems." The multi-cultural migration in physical space enables Aku to think "globally," not only "locally." He insists on "mother-tongue" writing, but at the same time he also advocates "cultural hybridity," not "cultural purity" or "cultural isolation."

The basic and primary foundation for Aku to start this cultural dialogue between himself and the Native Americans across the Pacific is their common belief in spirits and Nature. In *Coyote Traces*, Aku resonates indigenous American belief with traditional beliefs in his own culture, as conveyed in the following poem:

> The shaman tells us that
> the sound of the Heavens is the Great Sound,
> and Nature is the Great Law.
> In explaining the truth of life,
> the world is not divided into strong or weak.
> Every species,
> every people,
> has their own subtle way of thinking
> and unconstrained expression
> for revealing the wisdom of Nature,
> and the truth of the soul.
> — "Shaman at the University" (*Coyote* 53)

Aku's imagination and creativity lie in his pantheism, i.e., nature worship and ancestor worship. Such poems as "Lissome Worship," "Serpent Mound," "The Sacred Indian Bear," and "Four Colors" illustrate similar beliefs in the "Great Spirit" of Nature. Though Aku knows little English, he can easily understand the core beliefs of the Native Americans on his various trips to the reservations or cultural exhibits in Native American museums. Qian Zhongshu（钱锺书）has appealed to a common "poetic heart;" accordingly, as Zha Mingjian（查明建）has maintained in our companion volume 8, it is surely possible to find "the commonality of literature in different cultural systems."

Aku laments the injustice and brutal treatment of Native Americans throughout American history. Native Americans had created great ancient civilizations. But the intrusion of the White Europeans brought about disasters and damages to their native land:

> The Indian people used animal bones
> to create large numbers of objects:
> arrows, drumsticks, powder horns,
> pearls, necklaces, and bracelets.
> Looking over the history of the Indians,
> I feel perhaps due to their harsh living conditions,
> in the process of making stone and bone tools,
> they spent too long a time
> and too much wisdom.
>
> When the ever triumphant iron weapons were threatening
> they were forced to wake up:
> In that place beyond imagination
> human cruelty
> far surpassed merciless Nature.
> — "Bones of Beasts" (*Coyote* 159–61)

Besides the great sympathy for the Native Americans' sufferings in American history, a few historical figures in Native American history, including Chief Joseph and Sacajawea, are also portrayed from Aku's own perspectives. Yet his view of Sacajawea, the Native American heroine who was of great help to the Lewis and Clark expedition in the early 19th century (see Howard), may not be what readers expect:

> I don't know whether her child was later
> killed by settlers or not,
> but I know it well that
> for being a mother,
> her deeds are due
> no simple moral judgment.
>
> By recording the story of Sacajawea,
> I mean to let such a woman
> live as a real mother
> in my verse.
> — "A Mother" (*Coyote* 143)

American historian Frederick Jackson Turner in his remarkable speech "The Significance of the Frontier in American History," presented at the World's Columbian Exposition in Chicago in 1893, analyzes how the concept of the American "frontier" has been shaped in the Westward Movement, and how "frontier" helps mold such American national characteristics as self-reliance, pioneering spirit, adventure, and independence. American people celebrate Thanksgiving to memorialize the Native people's contribution to this new nation and new country. And every November is "National Native American Heritage Month" to commemorate the historical injustice to which Native people have been subjected, and to highlight their unique cultural inheritance. Sacajawea's portrait appeared on the $1 coin in 2000 to highlight her special contribution to this nation.

However, the history of frontiersmen's settlement of the West, for the Native people, is nothing but a "Trail of Tears." The real history is cruel and bloody, not romantic. As James Fenimore Cooper in his novel *The Last of the Mohicans* implies, the "Last of the Mohicans" eventually paved the way for "the First of the Americans" (see also Zhuravleva). The land called "America" was once the land of the ancient peoples with great diversity in language, tradition, and custom. In this sense, the role of Sacajawea is paradoxical for the White settlers and for her Native people respectively.

Significantly, as the title of Aku's poem suggests, Sacajawea simply appears as a mother who (for whatever reasons or considerations) has to carry her baby on her back to help the Lewis and Clark expedition to the far West, her own Native land. The so-called "historical truth" no longer seems important for Aku. He refuses any moral judgement on Sacajawea — whether she is a "hero" of America, or a "betrayer" of her tribal people, for guiding the White pioneers to explore the West. Aku's portrayal of Sacajawea, a paradoxically historical figure in American history, leaves the reader much space to ponder American history and its historical figures.

Despite all the invasions, mistreatments, and injustices the Native Americans have suffered in history, Aku still firmly believes in the revival of Native languages and culture. His great sympathy and hope for the Native Americans' cultural survival echoes his expectations for his own native tongue and heritage, which are threatened by modernization and industrialization in contemporary China. In the following poem, Aku imagines that the legendary birdman *E-tsa-wis-no* will carry on the treasures of cultural heritage:

How wonderful it would be
if all the Indian tribes,

> before disappearing into
> forest, desert, and snowy mountain,
> had produced many birdmen like *E-tsa-wis-no*!
> For only birdmen
> can really understand
> the genuine character and personality of
> swans, the migrant birds.
> — "Birdman" (*Coyote* 129)

I will come back to the conceptual question of becoming-animal further below. In regard to intercultural relations, Aku believes in "equal though different." The whole collection expounds his ideals of humanity, equality, and diversity. He admits and respects differences within diversity. People with different linguistic, religious, and cultural backgrounds are equal in humanity. Here is one such example:

> In Columbus,
> in front of the African-American Cultural Center,
> there stands a sculpture
> with no facial expression,
> made by a Black artist.
>
> I know no deeper meaning of the sculpture,
> Yet, I do know,
> a blank facial expression means
> the refusal of narrow-mindedness and bias,
> and a refusal to be judged based on skin color.
>
> For humanity, the end purpose,
> the end point, will always be
> different but equal.
> — "The Sculpture with No Expression" (*Coyote* 177)

This ideal of "differential equality" is not new. We can find its counterparts in American literary history, as in Walt Whitman's *Leaves of Grass*: "I celebrate myself, and sing myself, / And what I assume you shall assume, / For every atom belonging to me as good belongs to you" (Whitman, "Song of Myself").

Heterogeneity, Localization, Return

As we study the cultural representation of Native Americans from the perspective of a Yi poet, Aku Wuwu's "Four Colors" (already mentioned above) illustrates how an awareness of the "Great Spirit" of Nature can become a gift across cultures without leading to a reductive homogenization:

> An American Indian friend
> gave me a special gift,
> "Four Colors," mysteriously woven
> with divine grass of
> red, yellow, black and white colors.
>
> They are especially sensitive to
> the colors of races,
> just as they were the first to
> determine the four directions of
> east, west, south and north.
>
> As long as human life is capable of abstraction,
> the cognition of who are one's enemies
> gives people much wisdom.
> — "Four Colors" (*Coyote* 65)

As we can learn from the National Museum of the American Indian in Washington D.C., especially the exhibit "Our Universes: Traditional Knowledge Shapes Our World," in some Native American mythologies the four divine colors are indeed associated with four directions and also with four seasons. Yet in different tribal mythologies, the four colors vary in their references: while for the Plains Indians Lakota (South Dakota), the colors are indeed "red, yellow, black, and white;" for the Pueblo of Santa Clara (New Mexico), the colors are referred to as "red, yellow, blue, and white" (see also Roediger 93). Aku's poem does not clarify the particular Native Americans of which it speaks, since most Chinese readers will not be aware of such distinctions. We can consider this to be a case of "heterogeneity" and of "literary domestication" (文学他国化), with assimilation into the target-language context, in Cao's concept of variation: a "literary domestic appropriation" process in which "the receiving country localizes the received literature by its own literary traditions, literary theories, and cultural rules," thus enabling the disseminated literature to "participate in the renewal and recreation of the receiving country's literature" (Cao 57). A mirror image can become relevant in this context:

> The interpretation of otherness is closely related to the understanding
> of oneself. No matter out of what kind of motive and desire and no
> matter having shaped what kind of foreign image, a writer of a

> country considers a foreign country as "otherness," which is a
> mirror to reflect the "self." Therefore, the analysis of "otherness" is
> actually a way to inspect, discover, construct, and complete
> oneself. (Cao 232)

While there is a considerable degree of homogeneity, which forms
the very foundation of intercultural dialogue among ethnicities around
the world, the Yi ethnic group does differ from the American-Indian
people in their specific beliefs and values, thus illustrating the partial
validity of Cao's emphasis on the core concept of heterogeneity (Cao
xxix ff.). By writing the American Indian "four colors," Aku is
reflecting on a Yi belief in the capacity for "abstraction" which
enables sensitivity.

Strengthening this capacity, there is a second case study of
variation or appropriation in *Coyote Traces*:

> The Willamette River in Salem City,
> I name it as "Future River." [...]

> I am attracted by its reputation,
> as if returning to my own village.
> Everyone here is so earnest and dear,
> all barriers disappear
> like haze on a hillside.
> Language is just a decoration,
> the river purifies my inner soul.

> Was it Coyote, the spirit,
> that let the "Future River" bear them
> such an optimistic outlook,
> or perhaps the immense sufferings they experienced
> let their generous spirit re-bloom in the depths of their life?

> At a heart-rending moment,
> the Willamette River
> has infused my veins
> with blood rushing towards the future.
> — "Future River" (*Coyote* 95–97)

How can the Willamette in Oregon get renamed as "Future River"?
The poem itself does not directly reveal an answer. It takes linguistic
awareness to recognize that the original name, which is actually that
of a Native American village, sounds like the Chinese 未来 (weilai in
pinyin), meaning "future." To "inspect, discover, construct" oneself

in a domestication process (Cao) is indicated in the key movement of "returning to my own village," which happens not in the Yizu community but in Oregon. Thus Aku's semantic play suggests the strong role of aesthetics in code switching and in the naming process, enabling him to extend the symbolic meaning through twice-cross-cultural writing and through translating sound to text. By cultural filtering, which enables creative "misreading" (Cao xxxiv) and adds signifying energy, Aku creates fresh meanings and new inspirations. The semantic play equally suggests the nature of literary traveling among different languages and cultures, the energy with which literature is in motion, as discussed by Susan Arndt in our companion volume: literary texts "weave themselves" into future text.

The river, as shown by the poetic speaker's "return" to an imagined home, is closely associated, like all rivers, with migration — and with the sacred serpent:

> [...] Beside the ancestors' tombs,
> they piled up earth in a snake shape.
> The ancient Natives used the power of the snake
> to prevent invaders from disturbing
> their forefathers' sacred space.
> As snakes are also symbols of rivers
> Native civilizations
> were inseparable from
> the ancient rivers of North America.
>
> Serpent Mound — a cipher of their
> migration routes,
> Serpent Mound — marking recognition of
> the directions,
> Serpent Mound — perhaps —
> a shrine to worship heaven and earth.
>
> The ancient Natives,
> took the land of North America as a canvas
> with their feet.
> Among their many cryptic portraits,
> the richest in wisdom of the East
> is the Serpent Mound in Ohio.
> — "Serpent Mound" (*Coyote* 37–39)

The lyrical speaker marks his reading of the shaped landscape with "perhaps" and "cryptic," employing an etic perspective — one that does not impose itself on the object — to demarcate possible interpretive horizons. The external viewpoint enables cautious domestication which carries a signifying function for the receiving culture. For non-indigenous American readers of the translated version, this function may become no less relevant. Chadwick Allen focuses attention on a storied performance in which the indigenous representation becomes trans-indigenous:

> As in the recognition of the importance of rivers, […] the speaker emphasizes Indigenous movement — performance — and he links this intentional, purposeful performance on and across the land — the "ancient Natives" do not *find*, but rather take the land "as a canvas" — to Indigenous expression, self-representation, and wisdom. Although his speaker does not hear voice or song emanating from the mound, nonetheless, similar to Hedge Coke, Howe, and Mojica, the Yi poet perceives the effigy's "snake shape" as embodied story; he imagines the Serpent Mound not as emblem of death or loss, but as enduring evidence of embodied Indigenous performance. (Allen, "Performing" 411)

Here too, the enduring evidence points toward a future (with "blood rushing") which is given lyrical shape. The symbolic expression is perhaps that of "ancient Natives" but at least as much that of the poetic persona; archeology, ethnology, anthropology, and literature come together in the "trans-" movement, that of "migration routes" which create a bond between the Ohio landscape art and the Yi poet. As on the hillside of "Future River," on the bluff of Serpent Mound "all barriers disappear."

Aku Wuwu and Awareness of Minority Literatures

Coyote Traces is an example of cross-cultural writing and, as we have seen, an attempt to communicate between two indigenous cultures. Aku's travels in the USA are brief, and his English is not good. Mostly he relies on translators to communicate with English speakers. Partially due to this, his observations of this country and the people are different from those who can speak English. His observations and thoughts are strongly affected by his own Yi culture. He does not have to know the English language in order to feel sympathy for the Natives, for there are many similarities in culture and beliefs, especially worship of nature, worship of ancestors, and pantheism.

In the Introduction to his recent book *The Borderlands of Asia: Culture, Place, Poetry* (2017), Mark Bender sums up the common themes of "borderlands" poems:

What is comparable about these poems is a mix of themes and perspectives which involve local environments and traditional cultures. There is concern over the fate of local languages in the face of overwhelming mainstream "languages of interaction." There are parallels in attitudes towards self, group, and community. There is indexing of oral and written histories that speak of migration, invasion, evasion, rebellion, accommodation, and accomplishment. (2)

Bender points out that the poems he collected in the "borderlands" are highly diverse in their geographical, historical, linguistic, and cultural contexts. Despite this, as the above passage reveals, they share common features in many ways, and thus it is valid for him to compile them in the same collection. The indigenous people of East Asia share common concerns about the environment, traditional cultural survival, and self-identity in the age of modernization and industrialization. Indigenous peoples in East Asia and North America are facing the same challenges: the survival of the native languages and cultures and the adaptation to new environments, or what Bender calls "place competency" (*Borderlands* 15). As many instances show, literary articulation is especially able to represent and probe not only prevailing and socially sanctioned but also alternative, repressed, unsanctioned values and norms (Baumbach et al. 5). As in earlier minor American writing, it has been "possible to clarify one's dissent from existing values and offer alternative values as *exempla* to others" (Partridge 2). Thus the common concerns of indigenous people in China and the USA make it possible for them to engage in dialogue, to respond strongly to each other's call.

Aku Wuwu's increasing international influence and reputation can be attributed to the closer attention given to worldwide ethnic minority literatures in this age of globalization and multiculturalism since the Civil Rights Movement in the USA in the 1960s, and China's "Reform and Opening-Up" policy since the late 1970s. Compared with many other ethnic minority Chinese poets, Aku is unique in the following ways:

- Firstly, Aku is bilingual (in his native tongue and Chinese). Many other ethnic minority Chinese writers write only in Chinese, not their native tongues. Aku is widely known for his advocacy of mother-tongue writing, which for him is not only a choice of language, but more importantly a major issue of preserving his own cultural identity as "a buttress against acculturalization" (Bender, "Poet" 502).
- Secondly, Aku is not only a poet, but also a professor and a

literary critic in Chinese ethnic minority literatures. He is familiar with his own native Yi language, poetics, and folklores as well as Han Chinese literary theories, and additionally Western literary theories through translation. Aku coined the terms "second mother tongue," "second Chinese," and "culture hybrid" to analyze poets like himself who occasionally experience the dilemma of being cultural in-betweens. But he is always proud of his native tongue, and determined to carry his two identities reflecting two cultures as "cultural hybrid."

- Thirdly, and most noticeably, Aku is a performer of poetry recitation (not only a poet). His astoundingly powerful oral performance of his best-known poem "Calling Back the Soul of Zhyge Alu" (the legendary spiritual hero of the Yi people) ③ in the Nuosu language has become a classic which is very much liked by audiences nationally and internationally. His mother tongue is unknown to many of his audiences, yet the emotion is universal and transferable. On many such occasions, they echo with his calling "*O la*" "*O la*" ("Come back") to call back the ancestor's soul and spirit, which has been lost among many modern people in the processes of modernization and globalization. This poem was translated from the Nuosu language into English by Mark Bender, and appears in the trilingual poetry collection *Tiger Traces* (Aku and Bender). Its contexts are detailed by Bender ("Poet" 500ff.).

Yet the growing attention attracted by Aku's mother-tongue language and poems did not happen in a day. Twenty-five years ago, in the 1990s, the young poet Aku Wuwu had two collections of poetry and prose in the Nuosu language published by a local publishing house. Though some of his poems were collected in primary school students' textbooks, he was still largely unknown to the outside world. And twenty-five years ago, in the mid-1990s when doctoral candidate Mark Bender intended to choose Yi folklore as his dissertation topic, he was discouraged from choosing such a remote, marginal topic.

But changes took place 15 years ago. At an international conference on *Ashima* (《阿诗玛》), the Chinese Yi poet and the American scholar got to know each other. They were introduced to each other by well-known Yi scholars, the Bamo sisters. Since then, Bender has cooperated with Aku to translate Aku's Nuosu language. In 2006, Aku and Bender published the ground-breaking trilingual *Tiger Traces* (2006), the first poetry collection of the Nuosu language ever presented to the English-

---

③ For Aku Wuwu's reciting of his Nuosu Yi poem "Calling Back the Soul of Zhyge Alu," please see https://www.youtube.com/watch?v = PXGHXZ0ZX_M.

speaking world. Through their collaboration and the efforts of many other scholars and translators, Aku's poems have been translated and studied by more and more scholars around the world. His works are now included in prestigious literary anthologies such as the *Norton Anthology* and *The Oxford Handbook of Modern Chinese Literatures*.

Not only have Aku and Bender cooperated in translating Yi epic and Aku's Nuosu poems into English, in 2010 they also launched an annual cultural exchange program between students from Southwest Minzu University and The Ohio State University. Every year Aku and Bender, along with related friends and faculty members, work hard on the schedule and the launch of the one-month cultural activity. This annual communication process among young people from China and the USA is of great significance. The Yi college students at Southwest Minzu University and the American students from The Ohio State University attend the same lectures by both Chinese and American experts, take cultural field trips to Yi minority areas, and teach English to Yi primary school students in villages.

This is an interculturally oriented communication opportunity for all those participating. Every year, ethnic minorities are also represented in the group of American students; they gain first-hand fresh cultural experience of ethnic areas in Southwest China. My own lectures to this unique group of college students from China and the USA on the translation of Aku's poems, including "A Mother," "Serpent Mound," "Mother Tongue over the Phone," in which Aku addresses Native American culture and history or his deep concern for the marginalized and endangered ancient languages in modern times, inspire them to think more deeply about their own national history and cultural survival.

This is an ideal way for everyone participating in this annual series of cultural events to acquire a deeper understanding of "different but equal," with better appreciation of each other's language and culture. If *Coyote Traces* is a literary attempt to build a bridge between indigenous people in China and the USA, then the actual personal exchanges launched by Aku and Bender among young people from both countries creates stronger ties for future generations. Such intercultural communication is of literature, but it is also beyond literature.

2. "World Minority Literature" in China's Academia

In 2012, two papers (Jin and Liu; Bender "*Ogimawkwe*") on the comparative study of Aku's poems with ethnic American literatures were published in American academic journals. Chinese-American critic Wen Jin from Columbia University, Chinese critic Liu Daxian from the Institute of Ethnic Literature, Chinese Academy of Social Sciences, and Mark Bender made the first attempts to approach Aku's poems under the category of Sino-U.S. comparative ethnic literatures, from which we can develop the concept of "world minority literature." Advancing this concept, and focusing it on translation, is one of the present chapter's main objectives.

Jin and Liu's paper "Double Writing" offers a historical review of the history of cultural exchanges between Sino-U.S. ethnic writers and scholars starting in the 1980s. According to this essay, the Chinese Ewenki writer Wurertu took part in the Writers' Workshop at The University of Iowa in 1986. A trip to the nearby Native American reservations changed his later life after he returned from the USA. The paper narrates the decades of academic cooperation between anthropologist Stevan Harrell, a professor of Yi studies at University of Washington, and the Yi sister scholars Bamo Ayi and Bamo Qubumo from the Chinese Academy of Social Sciences. It chronicles their visits to reservations in Washington State and the visit of two Makah Indian scholars to the Chinese Academy of Social Sciences. Besides the historical review, the paper presents a comparative study of Aku's *The Appeal of the Mississippi River* with Chinese-American writer Alex Kuo's novel *Panda Diaries* (2006). Aku's great sympathy for the forced assimilation of Native Americans into mainstream Anglo-American society is presented alongside Kuo's concerns over the forced agrarian turn of the Chinese ethnic Oroqen people in modern China (see also Shan) and the forced migration of Plains Indians in the 19th century. The paper also expounds such terms as "indigenous" and "ethnicity" in different historical, cultural, and academic contexts in China and the USA.

Mark Bender's essay "*Ogimawkwe Mitigwaki* and 'Axlu yyr kut'" is based on his translating of Aku's Nuosu poems into English, years of research on Chinese folklore and recent East Asian ecological poems, and his own background of living in the Great Lakes area where the Potawatomi legends and folktales originated and spread. Bender's essay starts by citing the Indian folklorist Soumen Sen's remark on the relationship between oral and written literatures based on his Khasi people. *Ogimawkwe Mitigwaki* or *Queen of the Woods* (1899) is an autobiographical work by the Pokagon Potawatomi chief Simon Pokagon. It is the second book ever written in English by a Native American writer. Simon Pokagon narrates the peaceful and romantic life before the European settlers' intrusion and the tragic fate of his people with the threat brought by the Whites, such as drugs and alcohol, which started with their first encounter with Europeans several centuries earlier and lasted until the late 19th century. Along with the main narration in the English language, Simon Pokagon intentionally keeps many Potawatomi words in his book as a cultural "monument" for future generations of his people.

Similar to Simon Pokagon's masterpiece, "Axlu yyr kut" ("Calling Back the Soul of Zhyge Alu") is Aku's best-known Nuosu poem, already introduced above. Aku uses Yi legends and folktales. In his English translation, Bender purposefully keeps the sounds and spellings of many Yi words, such as *Abbo* (father), *Amo* (mother), and *O la* (come back). He adds many notes to these poems to illustrate the rich material culture of the Nuosu people. The title of Bender's essay explains his critical approach: the two indigenous writers in China and the USA, though quite different in time and space, share a common concern for the native-language survival in cultural transition. For Pokagon, the transition problems are as just explained; for Aku, it is the dilemma of many members of his people in the process of migration from mountain villages to big cities in industrialization and modernization processes.

The above two essays can be regarded as milestones of "Sino-U.S. Comparative Minority Literature," a research program which I intend to propose here.

Aku Wuwu is one of the few Chinese ethnic minority poets whose works have been relatively fully translated and researched in English-language academia. This is particularly due to the increasing interest in multiculturalism in an age of globalization, with the worldwide development of ethnic literatures as background. It is thus part of the continuing interest in multicultural, marginal, and under-represented peoples and cultures since the 1960s. In recent years, the important literature awards around the world, such as the Nobel Prize in Literature, Pulitzer Prize, and Booker Prize, have been given to marginalized writers. In this age of multiculturalism and critique of orientalism, Aku's nationally and internationally growing reputation is understandable.

In the USA, journals such as *MELUS* (*Multi-Ethnic Literature of the USA*, Oxford University Press), *NAISA* (*Native American and Indigenous Studies Association*), and *Journal of Transnational*

American Studies (University of California, Santa Barbara) publish criticism on the country's non-White, minority literatures. They hold annual conferences and publish essays on U.S. ethnic literatures. In China, there is such a leading prestigious journal on Chinese ethnic literatures as *Studies of Ethnic Literature* (Institute of Ethnic Literature, Chinese Academy of Social Sciences).

Yet ethnic literatures in China and the USA lack opportunity to directly converse with each other. For a long time, Aku planned to hold a conference at Southwest Minzu University in Chengdu to lead Chinese minority literatures into the world's academia and the world's minority literatures into China. He and Bender, as well as a few leading scholars in China, acted as the main organizers of such a conference and worked for years to make it possible. On 29−30 October 2016, the "First Symposium on World Ethnic Minority Literature" was held at Southwest Minzu University, thus finally realizing Aku's long-cherished dream. The host university, where students from all of China's 56 ethnic groups, with linguistic, cultural, and religious diversity, study at the campus, was an ideal place to hold such an international symposium. Domestic scholars and foreign scholars from the USA, Japan, and Vietnam attended the symposium.

One important outcome of the symposium has been the launching of "Equality, Justice, and Love: The Manifesto for World Ethnic Minority Literature." Aku, leading scholars and writers in China's minority literatures, and foreign scholars had heated discussions to work out the final draft of this innovative manifesto, with its highlighting of key values embodied in such literature, in Chinese and in English.

This symposium and the manifesto are of great significance for Chinese academia. It is an innovative effort of Aku and related Chinese scholars to link Chinese minority literatures to the rest of the world. For the first time, Chinese ethnic writers and ethnic writers of marginal place in other parts of the world started to address each other on the same issues: endangered ethnic native languages, threats to indigenous traditions in modernization, dilemmas between ethnic cultures and mainstream cultures, difficulties of assimilation into the mainstream, and environment changes resulting from industrialization. At the symposium, scholars had discussions over the most accurate English terms, i.e., world ethnic minority, indigenous people, minority, and the like. After all, ethnic identity has major dimensions which interact in complex ways: "cultural socialization, experience in society, the way one is perceived by others, and one's own construction of these experiences" (Phinney 925). The principles in the "Equality, Justice, and Love" manifesto combine the margin and the center, the majority and the minority, the oral and the written, the general common language and the ethnic native tongues.

Aku made great efforts to highlight worldwide "minority literatures": not only in Chinese mainland, but also the Asian-American, Native American, African-American, or Aboriginal literatures in Chinese Taiwan, Japan, or Australia. This shows the scope of trans-indigenous research as it moves beyond what was proposed by Chadwick Allen. Though scholars at the 2016 symposium argued and debated with each other about the appropriate terms in Chinese and their English translations — 少数民族,少数族裔,民族文学,土著文学, or ethnic minority, Native, aboriginal, and indigenous — this symposium has for the first time globally highlighted the importance and the contributions of some ever-marginal, less prestigious, under-presented, ever-ignored literatures in China communicating with other parts of the world.

Aku and his Chinese fellow researchers' efforts to link Chinese and world minority literatures, together with the manifesto, are a milestone in comparative literature study in China and the world. This manifesto, one of whose main drafters is Aku, reflects his primary academic pursuit: to build a bridge between China and the rest of the world by highlighting ethnic literatures around the world. It is a continuation of Aku's sense of combining the local and the global, China and the rest of the world in the concept of ethnic minority literatures:

> "Minority" and "majority," "margin" and "center," "tributary" and "mainstream" coexist relatively, and their relationships keep shifting. The existence of ethnic minority literature not only means the existence of a specific nationality, or a specific ethnic literature, but also the existence of the mutual relevance and reliance among literatures in the world. Ethnic minority peoples desire liberty, equality, and justice. We are in pursuit of coexistence, conversation, and common prosperity. We are the most ancient and the most strong-willed seeds ever sowed by any Deity. Ethnic minority literatures coexist with Heaven and Earth, dialog with the Sun and the Moon. (qtd. in Bender, "Brief Report")[4]

---

[4]   For more details of this ground-breaking conference, and the complete manifesto, see Mark Bender's "Brief Report on the International Symposium on World Minority Literature and Manifesto of World Minority Literature," https://u. osu.edu/mclc/2016/12/13/world-minority-literature-conference-report/.

The concept thus links the concepts of ethnic minority and comparative study, as well as a strong desire to draw strength from natural energies. In the USA, there are already several transnational cultural and literary studies, with the important initiatives of Chadwick Allen in comparative studies, and scholars such as Wen Jin and Mark Bender ("Ogimawkwe") have already started such pioneering academic approaches to Sino-U.S. and world ethnic or minority literatures. However, in China, for a long time, ethnic Chinese literature has been classified under the subject of "Chinese literature," while "ethnic American literature" has been classified under the subject of "American literature"; between these there appears to be little space for communication and dialogue. Yet we should not simply conclude that they are just too different from each other. In this sense, the launching of the manifesto functions as a milestone for the concept of "world minority literature" to be introduced in Chinese academia. Chinese ethnic writers and critics intend to build this platform to communicate with the rest of the world. We might be able to adapt the idea, suggested by Deleuze and Guattari, that the minoritarian is "a potential, creative and created, becoming": we can think of minorities as "seeds, crystals of becoming whose value is to trigger uncontrollable movements and deterritorializations of the mean or majority" — in the sense of a "continuous variation" which doesn't leave the majority's norms and standards unaffected but brings about modification by means of overstepping the majority's standards (*Thousand* 106).

The 2016 symposium is just a beginning — a beginning of intercultural dialogue between ethnic minority Chinese writers and ethnic minority American writers, allowing a dialogue between scholars in these two seemingly very different areas. We can expect more such conferences and dialogues among indigenous literatures in the world to be carried out in the future.

3. "Constellations of Competency" and *Coyote Traces*

Cosmographic Translation and Cooperation

The term "cosmographic translation" first appeared in several public speeches given in China by Mark Bender. Bender gave a keynote speech on "Constellations of Competency in Cosmographic Translation" at the 9th National Symposium on the Translation of Chinese Classics held at Jiangnan University, Wuxi, Jiangsu Province on 13 Nov.

2015. He recalled his personal experiences of visiting and doing research among the local people in Southwest China since the 1980s and more recently in Northeast India. He summed up the various competencies needed in translating ethnic literatures or folk literatures. In that speech, Bender concluded from his own decades of cooperating with various Chinese ethnic poets and folklorists that a workable, cooperative translating mechanism is needed.

Bender's views are that folk/minority literature translation is totally different from translating classic poems from Chinese into English. It is much more complex and demanding. The translator of folk or ethnic literatures cannot just retreat into the study or library to complete the translation. He or she needs to be outgoing, to visit remote settlements and villages to talk with local people, the folklorists, story-tellers, medicine men, meditators, recorders, and the poets themselves. It requires a considerable time exploring, learning, and establishing relationships with the local communities. An experienced translator can complete the translation of Tu Fu or Li Bai in his or her study in the USA without bothering to travel to China for cultural contacts in order to translate ancient poems. Translators of ancient classic texts can complete a relatively acceptable translated version in their studies in the West.

However, translating contemporary Chinese ethnic or folk literatures is different. The translator must travel to meet community members in their home villages, to see the material cultures, to feel what the local people feel. That is what Bender has been doing for his Chinese folklore and ethnic literature studies. Bender's recent book *The Borderlands of Asia* (2017), an ambitious anthology of poems from Asian countries, east of the Himalaya, contains 48 poets' works from India (Northeast India), Myanmar, China (Southwest China, Qinghai, Gansu, Inner Mongolia), and Mongolia. Bender visited all these regions himself, meeting in person most of the poets whose works would be collected in the book. Based on his academic experience of translation and research, Bender sums up the various constellations of "cosmographic translation":

> One of the things I keep wondering about is what does "I translated" mean? Or what does the word "cooperation" entail? Looking back to my first experiences in the early 1980s, I realize that in many or most cases the "I translated" is not very accurate. In most cases I must admit that it is a "we translated", though the "we" can be many things. I am certain that many of us have been in a similar situation, in which we draw on the help of others to translate a work

of literature, or in some cases collaborate as pairs or even teams.
("Constellations" 5)

This explanation is analogous to "mutual interaction and synthesis" between cultures; for cross-cultural integration, "a person moves back and forth between the dominant culture and the minority culture. In the process, a person sees relationships between distinctive similarities and differences" of the cultures in question (Lum 61). At the same time, we need to be aware that "our bubble of centrism may sometimes be seen to travel with us, to convey, when we leave our home environment and penetrate the Other's safe space" (Starosta 58).

In recent years, influenced by ecocriticism, Bender tends to use "cosmographic" rather than "ethnographic" (see "Landscapes"). He explains that the former is more inclusive, while the latter is human-centered, excluding non-human beings (*Borderlands* 13). Bender's "cosmographic translation" is a sum of his decades of translation and study of ethnic minority folktales in East Asia. A successful translation of ethnographic or cosmographic poetry (*Borderlands* 15, "Cambria") is often based on a cooperation between Sino-U. S. translators and editors with different academic backgrounds. We can thus understand it as a mode of "comprehensive" translation. It has this comprehensive aspect in common with the otherwise rather different *Cosmographie*, a chorography of the world composed by Peter Heylin in 1652.

As Bender explains, "competency" is a concept that he borrowed from Dell Hymes and Richard Bauman, the leading scholars of the "performance school" of folklore studies in the 1970s and 1980s in the USA. His main arguments on the translator's competency are as follows:

> Translators, like performers, must demonstrate competence in producing translated works that will be utilized and evaluated by their target audiences. ("Constellations" 8)
> In terms of translation, I argue that translators need deep knowledge of situated culture and the local environments to really understand the folk material being translated. ("Constellations" 7)
> Ideal teams for translating cosmographic epics would be comprised of two groups of competent specialists who can work together; 1) basic constellation [...] and 2) extended cohort. ("Constellations" 13–14)

Since translating "ethnographic" or "cosmographic" texts is complex, demanding the cooperation of various specialists, a single translator alone cannot do it. It needs the cooperation of specialists in different fields (see also Chapter 5 in our companion volume 8). A translator is not a bilingual machine who can "switch" freely and automatically between two languages. Moreover, in ethnic literature translation usually a third or even fourth language and culture are involved. This adds great difficulties for the translator. In this case, the translator is not just a language code switcher, he or she needs to learn the third or fourth ethnic minority language and culture. To explain comparative intercultural inquiry, Ming Xie adapts T. S. Eliot's metaphor of being "on both sides of a mirror at once": to see "what makes the mirror function as a mirror [...] to see *how* one sees [...] to see one's own 'blind spot' or 'ignorance' precisely as a condition of possibility for knowing the other and hence oneself" (3). This is an experience which, as I wish to argue, is also characteristic of a cosmographic translator, so that an important purpose I am pursuing in this chapter is to extend the latter concept by doing justice to what the cosmographic approach does with the translator.

In his 2017 book of eco-poems from East Asia, Bender raises another "competency" concerning indigenous people's survival in a changing environment and landscape:

> One theme that I raise in the Introduction is that of "place-competency" — the deep familiarity with local environments and how to live in a place — knowledge threatened by new styles of living that require new competencies for survival. Many of the poets in this volume have written poems that reflect their own adjustments to changing circumstances, and often speak for their local communities. ("Cambria")

After decades of doing research on Chinese folk and ethnic literatures, Bender deeply understands the complexity of translating orally-related poetry and rich material cultures. He thus illuminates the following main principles in translating indigenous people's ethnographic or cosmographic poetry:

1. It is vital for the translator to acquire various competencies in knowledge of folklore, legends, material culture, and research methodology, which can only be obtained through extensive fieldwork in the areas where the poems originate. Language competency alone is less than enough.
2. A close and comprehensive cooperation between foreign translator and local experts and professionals is crucial for any such translation project.

In the following parts, I intend to adapt Bender's theory of "constellations of competency" to present arguments for co-translating Aku Wuwu's *Coyote Traces* in a research partnership. While Bender uses "cosmographic translation" to refer specifically to cosmographic poetry translation, I expand the term to refer to the cosmographic translation process: to a sustained and comprehensive cooperation between (in this case) Sino-U.S. translators, editors, and publishers in the process of bilingual and intercultural book production.

"Empathy-Competency" and *Coyote Traces*

After 8 years of translating Aku's ethnographic poems from Chinese into English, I have gained a deeper understanding of the various competencies needed in translating such multi-cross-cultural texts. "Twice-cross-cultural writing" and "Twice-cross-cultural translation" are the terms I use to sum up this complex, multi-level, cross-cultural activity. Due to the diverse sources of the cultural images, myths, and folktales, in poem composing, the translation of such texts is all the more demanding for a translator, who must gain various competencies to be qualified for such tasks.

Here I would like to base my arguments on Bender's "cosmographic translation" in analyzing the complex intercultural tradition of Aku's poems in *Coyote Traces*. The term sums up the whole process of collecting, recording, compiling, translating, publishing, and of acceptance. It refers to the formation, the qualification, and the teamwork or cooperative spirit needed in translating oral or folk literatures.

Besides the "constellation of competency in cosmographical translation" and "place-competency," I would add the requirement of "empathy-competency." By this I mean not only a strong interest in and curiosity about the original text, but also a strong urge to learn and know more of the contextual, less familiar myths and folklores, which underpins the desire to disseminate the original text into the target cultures in another language.

The translating of Aku Wuwu's *Coyote Traces* is such a case. Though the poetry is originally written in Chinese, the contents, the images, and the material culture it deals with are not about Han Chinese. And though the target language is English, the poems are not about Anglo-American mainstream society and culture. Instead, as we have already seen in Part I, they are about Native American myths and legends, while occasionally the poet recalls his own ethnic Nuosu language and culture. As translators from China and the USA, we are neither Yi nor Native American, and we are linguistically and culturally "outsiders" of the poet's culture and language. We will thus not be in danger of "becoming blinded by the overly familiar;" as a social science discipline tells us, one needs to "render 'strange' for ethnographic practice what is perceived to be 'normal' to the insider" (Ybema and Kamsteeg 103). Here lies a problem and challenge. As geographical and biological "outsiders," the translators must become intellectual and linguistic "insiders" of the folk people and their culture as Aku portrays them in his Chinese poetry. This requires a process of many years of learning and exploration. There is a fruitful tension in "the play between both the strangeness and the familiarity of the foreign or the past or the remote" (Xie 62)— because to become "insiders" opens a space of intercultural interpretation and translation, one "where the interpreted and the interpreter condition and transform each other" (Xie 34).

Besides being linguistically competent, beyond Chinese and English, the translator-interpreter must be culturally competent, which involves a quality of being folklore-competent: one must have adequate knowledge in both Yi and Native American folklores, myths, and worldviews. Besides the above competencies, "empathy competency" (or Roscommon's "sympathy" competency) is crucial: empathy with both the poet and the target audience. This qualification needs to do justice to the fact that a Mandarin version does not render Han Chinese experience, which is familiar to a Chinese translator, but that it is already a cultural translation from indigenous experience — while such a version needs to be converted into the English which inevitably speaks of Anglo-American cultural experience, not that of Native Americans. We know that the terms we employ in formulating what belongs to Foucault's "order of things", "themselves determine whatever order there is to be found"; accordingly, translation "is precisely what brings the untranslatable into being" (Xie 27, 28). The many practical issues of mutual understanding, funding, editing, and publishing function as a mirror to this insight, which is an important reason for the cross-cultural cooperation from different academic backgrounds that we need.

Why: A Translator's Motivation

If one looks at the textbooks for "foreign literature" courses in a Chinese Language Department, one may notice that very often the translated versions do not include the translators' names. Students thus read Shakespeare's major plays in Chinese translations as if they

were reading the original 16th-century English versions. But what
they are in fact reading is likely to be the beautiful 20th-century
translations by Zhu Shenghao（朱生豪）, one of the most talented
translators of Shakespeare. Similarly, when English readers read Lu
Xun's（鲁迅）*The True Story of Ah Q in* English translation, they
seldom realize that what they are reading is not Lu Xun's 1921–1922
original but Yang Xianyi's（杨宪益）and Gladys Yang's 1960 English
translation. In both China and the USA, a certain neglect of the role
of translators is not rare in academia: "Only a translation purged of
the translator's presence allows consumers to indulge the fiction of
equivalence. The illusion of equivalence demands the elision of the
translator as a subject in the text"; an enunciating subject besides the
lyrical persona or the narrator is no longer discernible (Hermans,
Conference 27). Yet Italian-American translation theorist Lawrence
Venuti has rightly warned that "such a translation simultaneously
reinforces the major language and its many other linguistic and
cultural exclusions" (*Scandals* 12). As against such reinforcement,
translation can be seen as "a complex transaction taking place in a
communicative, socio-cultural context," which requires bringing the
translator "as a social being fully into the picture" (Hermans,
"Norms" 26).

Venuti in *The Translator's Invisibility*, too, analyzes this condition.
What is more, Jonathan Stalling (endorsed by Nicky Harman)
comments on the fact that a reviewer of the translated version of
Chinese Nobel Prize winner Mo Yan's book fails to give credit to the
English translator Howard Goldblatt:

> So while Xiao quotes liberally from the English text (sans
> citations), she never mentions even once that the book under
> review is not《檀香刑》, which was published well over a decade
> ago, but is instead its English translation. Of course, any review of
> translated literature will necessarily focus on the merits of the
> original, but at the very least professionalism requires a reviewer to
> acknowledge the work of the translator in some form.

If the translator becomes "visible" only for bad translation or
interpretation, a skeptic might ask: "why translate?" Stalling offers
an answer:

> Translators work for many of the same mysterious reasons writers
> do — not because it pays well (though I hope this can be remedied
> soon), but to contribute to the cultural work of our time, to
> participate in the global conversation of literature itself. If our work

as translators is not discussed in reviews of our work (or even simply acknowledged), when, pray tell, will it be?

A further answer is offered by Tie Ning, chair of the Chinese Writers' Association, at the 3rd Conference on Sinologists' Translation of Chinese Literatures, in speaking of the relationship between author and translator:

> Author and translator, enjoy the most magic relationship in the world. Like you found the twin brother or sister, whom you have lost long ago. He/She and you live totally different lives, and you speak different languages. Yet gradually you realize that we are so dear to each other, we hear the empathy between us. That is the joy brought by writing and translation. (My translation)⑤

The well-known American poet and translator Kenneth Rexroth, in his famous 1959 speech "The Poet as Translator" at the University of Texas, commends the Earl of Roscommon's 1685 concept of the translator's "sympathetic bond" for the poet he or she is translating:

> [...] the translation of poetry into poetry is an act of sympathy — the identification of another person with oneself, the transference of his utterance to one's own utterance. The ideal translator, as we all know well, is not engaged in matching the words of a text with the words of his own language. He is hardly even a proxy, but rather an all-out advocate. His job is one of the most extreme examples of special pleading. So the prime criterion of successful poetic translation is assimilability. (Rexroth 171)

Along with Stalling's explanation of the translator's desire to "participate in the global conversation of literature itself," I endorse Roscommon's/Rexroth's "sympathy" theory, coupled with "learning a great deal about yourself": he or she is expecting to grow mentally in the process. Comparativity is "to see *oneself* while seeing oneself as other," with an emphasis both on receptivity and construction (Xie 38): "Thus the otherness of the other suspends our usually hidden prejudices and assumptions and makes them *visible to ourselves*" (Xie 64). This experience should be available no less to the recipient of a translated text, through awareness of the mediation

---

⑤ "作者和译者,是这个世界上一种奇妙美好的关系,就好像你找到了失散已久的孪生兄弟或姐妹,他或她过着另一种生活,说着另一种语言。但渐渐地,我们发现,原来我们是这样的亲和近,我们听到了生命深处的共鸣。这是写作和翻译带来的欢悦。"——铁凝:"第三次汉学家文学翻译国际研讨会上的讲话"(http://www.chinawriter.com.cn/2014/2014-08-26/215915.html).

process. As Sandra L. Bermann explains in our companion volume 8 (Chapter 2), translation has "the potential to open a relation with the Other, to transform our selfhood."

In earlier years, Aku's Chinese poetry collection *The Appeal of the Mississippi River* (2008) failed to arouse much critical attention among critics and readers after publication. Yet someone like myself, from the vantage point of having taught Native American literatures in China for years, could not fail to realize immediately these poems' value in Sino-U.S. cultural exchanges. I had read some Native American folk stories before reading Aku's poetry, focusing on features such as coyote trickster, birdman, Sacajawea, and the works by Cherokee Indian woman writer Diane Glancy, who led Aku to visit the source of the Mississippi River. I wondered how a Chinese ethnic minority poet with little English language competence, after several poetry reading and academic trips to the USA, would view this country and its people.

When I eventually finished this translation project, there was a feeling of having been pregnant and, like so many predecessors of far superior competency, giving birth to a form of new life. That new life was not only the completed textual work. I had indeed learned much about myself through knowing the other, and realized that my chief motivation had been my own benefit: "To understand this country, which is both familiar and unfamiliar to me, from the perspective of translating Aku's poems is an important motivation for me to do this work" (Aku, *Coyote* 371). As an American literature specialist in China, I had read works by some well-known African-American, Native American, and Asian-American writers, yet my knowledge about the target country came from my readings and mass media. Aku's poetry provided me with a pair of "eyes" to see the country not only from my own Chinese cultural perspective but from the vantage point of an ethnic minority Chinese poet, being (as it were) on both sides of a mirror and thus seeing *how* one sees, "what makes the mirror function as a mirror" (Xie 3). As Kenneth Rexroth puts it: "[...] translation saves you from your contemporaries. You can never really model yourself on Tu Fu or Leopardi or Paulus the Silentiary, but if you try you can learn a great deal about yourself" (190).

Who: Sino-U.S. Translators

A Chinese translator who wishes to start a process of translating ethnographic poetry from Chinese (and other minority languages and cultures) into English should know that it will be a long process of research. Translating ethnic literature from Chinese into English is not our primary strength; since English is not our native tongue, a version by a single Chinese translator can hardly be accepted by native speakers, though there may possibly be a small number of exceptions in history.

Since the translation of ethnic minority poetry involves much additional knowledge, the work should be done by mutual cooperation between Chinese and American scholars. The Chinese can understand the original text better, while the native-speaking scholar or poet is more capable of expression in the target language. Exploring cultural translation, Mao Sihui urges scholars to engage with colleagues in other countries in discussions and reflections (281); as in social constructionism, people "jointly construct" their understanding of social life, thus developing meanings "in coordination with others" (Leeds-Hurwitz 2: 891). We can understand a communicative project as one that takes its resources from "dialogic transactions and institutional forms," the practices of "various communities of investigators and interpreters" who attempt to understand configurations of meaning (Schrag 57). The American professional editor knows more about American markets, reading habits, and expectations than their Chinese counterparts, so that the close and effective cooperation of different languages and academic backgrounds is the key to the success of such bilingual and intercultural books. While an accurate understanding of the original text, down to its minute implications, is the strength of the Chinese side, accurate poetic expression in the target language is that of the American side:

> I think the magic thing is that different people in this world are interested in the same thing. We found each other, and cooperate with each other. Some people like to finish a project all by themselves, but I like to work with the others, I like cross-national, cross-ethnic work. It is challenging, but meaningful. (Bender and Wen 45, my translation)⑥

My own field is ethnic minority literatures in the USA, while Bender's is ethnic and folk literatures in China. Experience confirms that his research and translations of orally-based folk literatures and

---

⑥ "我认为最奇妙的事情就是：世界上不同的人对同样的事情感兴趣，我们找到了彼此，然后一起合作。有些人喜欢独自一人完成项目，而我喜欢和他人一起工作，喜欢跨国、跨民族的合作。这很有挑战性，也非常有意义。" See also the interview with Mark Bender in the present volume.

Chinese ethnic literatures thus qualify him as an ideal cooperator in this unique intercultural literary translation project.

How: Two Translating Processes

(1) Yi → Chinese → English

In the twice-cross-cultural poetry collection *Coyote Traces*, Aku addresses many Native American folktales and myths. At the same time, he occasionally recalls his own Nuosu legends. He makes use of many Nuosu legendary figures, traditions, and worldviews between the verse lines. As Zha Mingjian explains in our companion volume, an adequately broad understanding of intertextuality refers to the relationship between any individual text and the knowledge, codes, and signifying practices that in total form the text's meaning — as a signifying process, oral or written, passes between sign systems (see also Graham Allen). The intertextual concept also calls attention especially to the content's forming process in a text, which is the chief issue I am anatomizing in the present chapter. Because of the need for con- and intertextual reference, anyone outside the cultures involved will feel puzzled without consulting experts or doing further research.

Here are some examples：

快渡过密西西比河吧
快祈求河神保佑你们
快去吧，朝着加拿大的方向
你们的敌人就要追来

在古印第安人
从猎人变成猎物
被残酷追猎的历史深处
密西西比河畔
一棵光秃秃的树上
出现过世界上第一群
吉祥的乌鸦

几千年以来
彝族人用一部神奇的经书
破译着乌鸦的语言
乌鸦传递噩耗
乌鸦是灾难的使者

我站在密西西比河岸

关切印第安人
苦难的命运时
那群吉祥的乌鸦
一定飞往金沙江边
曾被玷污太久的杉树林
继续鸣唱
——《吉祥的乌鸦》(74-76)

Be quick, cross over the Mississippi River, and
ask the River God to bless you.
Hurry, towards Canada,
for your enemy is chasing after you.

In the depths of history,
when ancient Natives were no longer hunters,
but were cruelly hunted,
there along the Mississippi,
appearing on a bare tree
was the first group of
crows with good omens.

For thousands of years,
Nuosu people in accordance with *Hxati tepyy*,
a magic book,
have decoded the language of crows,
informing the world confidently that
crows transfer bad news, and
crows are messengers of disaster.

Standing on the banks of
the Mississippi River
I contemplated the bad fortune of the Indians.
That group of crows with good omens
are certainly flying toward the
Golden Sands River.
The fir woods besmirched for so long
go on singing.
— "Propitious Crows" (75-77)

"曾被玷污太久的杉树林" literally means "The fir woods besmirched
for so long," which was puzzling. When I encountered this poem, I
had access neither to Nuosu folklores nor to the different cultural
meanings of "crow" for Native Americans and the Yi people. In

Aku's original Chinese collection *The Appeal of the Mississippi River* (2008), there are no explanatory notes. A few notes are added to *Coyote Traces* to explain the implied meanings of certain local and cultural images. The original pronunciations of the Nuosu words are also provided. Such notes are added to allow the target-language reader to know more of the cultures and original vocabularies.

If a translator chooses an easy way, the notes would be of no use. As a switcher of language, he or she will not have to bother much to make such cultural encodings clear for the target readers. Though Bender and I could translate literal meaning, which would amount to remaining on the text surface without giving much attention to the intertextual network, we decided to make it clearer by adding notes to explain the cultural implications. The procedure includes consulting with the poet, searching for documents, listening to lectures, and watching movies. The whole process is one of exploring, discovering, discussing, and of epiphany, employing various methods. Sometimes one can get the answer to a puzzlement directly from the poet, but the answer may not explain everything, and it may not always be forthcoming. The need to be mobile and travel, with the need to seek multiple procedures, recalls Deleuze's preference for transformational and nomadic multiplicities which combine different regimes of signs forming mixed semiotics — as frequently thematized especially in *A Thousand Plateaus*. Here are the notes we added to the original after consulting the poet and related research documents:

Note 1. *Hxati tepyy*, the scripture of interpreting the language of crows, is a book of divination. Nuosu people believe that crows always herald something evil or unfortunate.

Note 2. The Golden Sands River is a tributary of the Yangtze River, the longest river in China.

Note 3. In Nuosu idiom, if a crow breathes the smoke of a cremation, it will pollute nine (many) forest areas. (*Coyote* 77)

I sum up the process of this type of language transfer as follows:

Step 1.   Yi folktales in Yi language,
Step 2.   Yi folktales translated from Nuosu into Chinese, and presented in Aku's composition of the poems in《凯欧蒂神迹》,
Step 3.   Yi folktales being translated from Chinese into English in *Coyote Traces*.

In this process, Step 1 is completed by a Yi folklorist in the native language; Step 2 is completed by Aku in his Chinese language poems; Step 3 needs to be completed by the translators. As cultural outsiders, the translators need to figure out these Yi folktales and add notes to the original poems for the target English-speaking readers. This twice-cross-cultural translating process becomes more difficult at Step 3.

The following poem "Avenging Deer" is another example of this type of language transfer:

> At dawn, on the meadows along the highway,
> the deer draw pictures
> with their frozen bodies
> that even God above cannot see.
>
> My memory flashes back to the Yi lands,
> To those who regain dignity by
> paying the price with their life
> hurting their enemy by hurting themselves;
> those daring avengers face death unflinchingly,
> akin to those innocent suicidal deer.
> My heart knows those deer too
> are groups of avengers.
> — "Avenging Deer" (*Coyote* 33)

As with the previous example, Bender and I added a note to the title "Avenging Deer":

> Note: In Yi culture, the concept of "*sy jjy bbyx*" (i.e., resistance through death) is concretely demonstrated by committing suicide. The belief is that one's suicide is caused by one's enemy, and suicide is a form of resistance in situations where a person's dignity is harmed. "*Sy jjy bbyx*" is unique to Yi people, for whom dignity is preferable to life. This belief conveys aspects of the Yi world view and shows that the weak sometimes adopt extreme measures to maintain dignity. (*Coyote* 35)

In this case, we keep the pronunciation of the Nuosu language "*sy jjy bbyx*" (and even now, I remember how eagerly Aku tried to teach me to say the Nuosu words). The poet and the translator met many times in order to solve all the similarly puzzling cultural implications in translation. The poet cherishes his own mother tongue, and wishes that the words, the sound of his native tongue, could be caught by me as translator, and then be exactly transferred into English in my version. So, by keeping the original sounds of Nuosu words, we intend to show respect to this ancient language, which now, in mainstream modern life, is more and more marginalized and endangered.

As Dean of the Institute of Yi Studies at Southwest Minzu University, Aku has been making great efforts to promote Yi language teaching not only at universities, but also in primary schools and middle schools among his native people in Liangshan, Southwest Sichuan Province. Aku's persistence in promoting his endangered and marginalized mother-tongue writing is also an important factor which Western scholars like Mark Bender appreciate.

As Kenneth Rexroth claims, the translator is anything but a mechanical and soulless machine. For many years, I had assumed Yi culture to be very remote from my life, even though these people were living on the borderlands of my own country. I only began learning about the culture for an academic purpose. But once this translation project began, the culture became less and less remote. The "Avenging Deer" can become highly meaningful for a translator, a woman, a mother, a female intellectual. It has in fact provided me with new insight into my own life. Can "*sy jjy bbyx*" enable an English-speaking audience to pause for a moment to think about the fate of this remote group of ethnic people, who, when faced with oppression, injustice, and humiliation (for such minority experiences, see also Phinney 919), would choose the path of self-sacrifice of life to regain dignity? Across genres, the poem can remind the translator of Lu Xun, who exposes similarly negative developments in his period, as in the memorable *Ah Q* in his novella.

I confess that the Yi concept of "*sy jjy bbyx*" aroused my own thinking. I started to sympathize with helpless victims as evoked here, especially women, not only Aku's Yi people, and to wonder how they could survive such experiences. Moved by Aku's bittersweet humor, I came to agree with what the poet declares in an interview:

> A translated poem can trigger the reader's inner emotion, and arouse empathy towards the beauty of the language. Of course, a poet should firstly trigger the emotion, wisdom and imagination of the translator, through whom the target-language reader is affected. The expansion and intensification of the reader's emotion originate in my poetry. (*Coyote* 345)

The poetic experience links me, an outsider of Yi culture, to the insider. Perhaps it is adequate to think of what Deleuze and Guattari call the affect (*What* 164, 173): the poem "is independent of the creator through the self-positing of the created, which is preserved in itself. What is preserved — the thing or the work of art — is *a bloc of sensations*, *that is to say*, *a compound of percepts and affects*." It is a zone where more than one thing and person "endlessly reach that point that immediately precedes their natural differentiation." We can also consider that, as explained briefly above, "cosmographic translation" is capable of not only being human-centered. In the "deer" image, as in "Birdman" (discussed further above), we are close to what Deleuze repeatedly characterizes as Becoming-Animal:

> Becomings-animal are neither dreams nor phantasies. They are perfectly real. [...] What is real is the becoming itself, the block of becoming, not the supposedly fixed terms through which that which becomes passes. Becoming can and should be qualified as becoming-animal even in the absence of a term that would be the animal-become. (*Thousand* 238)

A "politics" of becoming-animal is elaborated in assemblages that "express minoritarian groups, or groups that are oppressed, prohibited, in revolt, or always on the fringe of recognized institutions" (*Thousand* 247). In seeking to grasp the "deer," the translator may come close to losing herself, but will actually become herself. At every step of twice-cross-cultural translation, there is a possibility of transference: "Poetry is not what is lost in translation; it is rather what we gain through translation and translators" (Bassnett and Lefevere 74). For the target audience, the translators' work serves as a pluralized offer of interpretations, of standpoints, and of views on culture and politics.

(2) English → Chinese → Back into English

The so-called "twice-cross-cultural translation" takes another form in the case of *Coyote Traces*:

Step 1. There are folktales about "coyote" (a trickster in many Native American legends) in English.

Step 2. When composing a few poems in *Coyote Traces*, Aku possibly read the Chinese version of Jarold Ramsey's *Coyote Was Going There*《俄勒冈印第安神话故事》translated by Li and Shi, and presented a few coyote folktales in his Chinese poems in *Coyote Traces*. A form of obscurity (for the translators) occurred in the adaptation of the original myth in the Chinese version of the poems.

Step 3. Wen and Bender translated these "coyote" folktales back into English in *Coyote Traces*.

In this process, Step 1 is done by American folklorists such as Ramsey; Step 2 by Aku in a few of his poems; Step 3 by the translators. In some cases, the poet's presenting of the "coyote" folktales may appear obscure due to its poetic expression. Thus, the translators need to work with the original English version.

Ethnographic translation demands that the translator cannot rely only on the poet. The poet usually does not tell enough to convey the connotation of material cultures in another language, enabling a transfer from Nuosu to Chinese and then to English, or from English to Chinese ... and then back into English. This process of twice-cross-cultural translation (or back-translation) can be complex.

Translating the poem "Stealing Fire" is such an example. In both processes above, for the translators (who, as explained above, are non-Yi people, non-Native American, i.e., not "insiders") the most important task is to figure out adequate English expressions to fit either the original Yi or Native American folk images and material cultures. To cope with this task, the translators should not only familiarize themselves with Yi language and culture, but also Native American cultures and history.

A typical example of twice-cross-cultural translation follows. Some Native American folktales of "coyote," the trickster, are imagined and re-created in Aku Wuwu's《凯欧蒂神迹》*Coyote Traces*. Bender recommended Jarold Ramsey's *Coyote Was Going There: Indian Literature of the Oregon Country* to Li Wusheng (李务生) and Shi Kun (史昆) to be translated into Chinese. It was published in China in 1983. Then, Bender introduced the Chinese version《俄勒冈印第安神话故事》to Aku. Aku was inspired by the Native American folktales in this book, and composed a few "coyote" poems in his《凯欧蒂神迹》*Coyote Traces*.

Now, at Step 3, the translators of Aku's book《凯欧蒂神迹》needed to find the origin of the folktales, which was not always easy. But we did not at first realize that it was partially under the inspiration of Li and Shi's translated version of Ramsey that Aku composed some of the coyote poems. There are, however, two Mandarin characters 彭恩 in Li and Shi's version. In Aku's collection of Chinese poems《密西西比河的倾诉》*The Appeal of the Mississippi River*, the second stanza of the poem 盗火 ("Stealing Fire") goes like this:

> 为了让更多的人／能够拥有火种／在众鸟和乌龟的协助下／成功地盗走过／沙塔人的火种／从此火种传遍了／所有的印第安山林／结束了彭恩一家／独占火种的历史(阿库乌雾 *Appeal* 69)

In the final Chinese version, we changed 彭恩 into 沙塔人(Shasta), and the English version then goes like this:

> Only the magic Coyote, / to help more people own fire, and /

assisted by birds and turtles, / succeeded / in stealing fire from the Shasta people. / Since then, / fire spread to all Indian villages, / ending the history of fire / being possessed only by the Shasta.
— "StealingFire" (*Coyote* 119)

This is the story of an intertextual traveling of the magic word, the trickster Coyote "Pain," in three different languages with different spellings, forms, and characters. This shift of the same object, with different names in twice-cross-cultural migration for the translators, remained a mystery until we eventually found the clue to the origin. The journey of the "coyote" went from the English word "Pain" (Ramsey's original word in *Coyote Was Going There*) to the Mandarin characters "彭恩" (Peng'en in *pinyin*, Li and Shi's version), then to Aku's poem composed by using "彭恩," and on to my original back-translation into "Penn" (rightly disapproved by Bender, since it did not sound like an Indian name). We almost deleted the whole poem due to the uncertainty of this detail. It was only some months later, after the manuscript had been presented to the publishing houses, that we came across the source of Aku's story. Yet it was too late to change the manuscript, so we left the English version appearing like a legendary "Shasta" story, without mentioning either "Pain" in English or "彭恩" in Mandarin.⑦

---

⑦ To document how "twice-cross-cultural translation" (or back-translation) proceeds in an actual translating process, I will quote from the exchange of e-mails between the two translators of *Coyote Traces* from China and the USA. In the following, "Wen" stands for Wen Peihong, "Bender" for Mark Bender.

Wen: Hi, Mark, I happened to read Li Wusheng and Shi Kun's Chinese translation of the book *Coyote Was Going There: Indian Literature of the Oregon Country* by Jarold Ramsey today. The translators acknowledged your suggestion of translating this book and the precious help provided by you in the process. It is an old book, published in 1983. I remember you mentioned Shi Kun in the interview! I was so excited to get it unexpectedly. When I read the story "The Theft of Fire" from this book, I got the Chinese characters "彭恩" (Peng-en in *pinyin*) who is a Shasta Indian trickster. I suddenly realized the origin of Aku's poem "Stealing Fire." It is this very story in this book that had inspired Aku to write this poem! (Perhaps it was you who gave this book to Aku?) Aku used the characters "彭恩" in his poem, and I translated back into the English word "Penn." Yet this translation "Penn" was questioned and disapproved by you. You told me that "Penn" doesn't sound like an Indian name. After some futile researches, I still could not find its origin in last May, so we gave up and just deleted the name in the translated version. Do you still remember this? Now, I finally find the source of Aku's poem. But still I cannot figure out the original English word for "彭恩." So, if you have this book by Jarold Ramsey, would you please check it for me? Thanks. Perhaps you still remember how hard we've tried to find (next page)

What: Interview Questions and Names

Two interviews appeared at the back of *Coyote Traces*, along with the poet's "Postscript" and co-translator Mark Bender's "Foreword." These serve as important background information for readers, especially the poet's thematic concerns over the compositions and his theoretical views on "mother-tongue writing," "second mother tongue," "second Chinese," and "cultural hybrid."

The first interview which I conducted with Aku, "Persistence in Vanishing" (in Chinese), was originally published in *China's Ethnic News* (1 June 2007). I was once told by Aku's Yi people that the very first question I raised, about Aku's various names, appeared unexpected and astounding. It goes like this:

> *Wen:* Thanks so much for accepting my interview. I'll read this statement from your poem: "The chain of my names, from 'Apkup Vytvy' to 'Aku Wuwu,' then to 'Luo Qingchun' is very rusty." [Translator's note: The name Aku Wuwu is how the Yi name Apkup Vytvy ("ap kup vyt vy") is pronounced in Standard Chinese, which does not have the "v" sound. The "p" and "t" in the Yi name mark linguistic tones and should not be pronounced for phonetic value. For the names, see also Bender, "Poet" 499.] Subconsciously, who do you think you are? Do you often ask yourself: "Who am I?" Which name would you prefer others to call you? For me, I am somewhat

---

(continued) the English word and almost have deleted the whole poem completely from the book because of this obscure name.

    Bender: Hi Helen — yes, I remember — yes, I did work on that project and was the silent translator. I will try to find it — yes, I think I introduced the book to Aku, if I recall. Thanks for your footwork on this... Mark.

    Bender: Hi Helen — I found the name! It is on p. 216 of Ramsey's *Coyote Was Going There* — I will send you a PDF later. It is really funny — I think Shi Kun and Li and I translated it wrong back in 1981. It looks like the word Pain (*tong*) was translated for its sound — not its meaning. So the word/name is actually Pain (meaning it hurts — i.e., the fire will make you hurt if you get too close).

    Wen: Hi, Mark, it's so funny to figure out all this... So, I am looking forward to reading the original English story to find out what has bothered me so much in my translation of Aku's poem! Thanks. — It sounds weird for me that "Pain" (*tong*) is an Indian family name in Ramsey's story. It doesn't sound like a name, does it? Anyway, I am glad that you stopped me using "Penn" in time. Otherwise...

    Bender: It is not an Indian family name. "Pain" is a feeling ("ouch") — but it is personified (to use our modern term). It is talking about the origin of why fire makes us hurt when we touch it. Isn't that interesting? That would be a good example to use in a translation class.

puzzled. Would you please tell me how I should address you — Professor Luo, or Aku Wuwu? (*Coyote* 271)

In fact, this question about Aku's name changing in twice-cross-cultural experiences did not arise out of nothing. It stemmed from my own cross-cultural experience. Some years earlier, I had traveled to Melbourne, Australia, for a teachers' training event. It was the first time for me to go abroad, and I had no such intercultural experiences previously. I was asked by my Australian teachers what my name was, and my response was Wen Peihong. However, it turned out to be somewhat hard for them to pronounce my name. And many times I was asked about the meanings of my name. In some of the Australian teachers' mouths my name sounded weird, so I decided to announce that my English name is Helen. During that whole month in Australia, I was "Helen," which was natural enough for Australians to pronounce. It seemed to be easier too for me to achieve cultural communication when using "Helen." Yet I suddenly lost my own identity, and became "foreign." Clearly, there are "meaning making processes involved in marking 'passage points' in one's biography by changing one's name" (Watzlawik et al. 17). The practice of Asians' choosing a Western name may "either be a sign of 'protecting' one's given name(s) and thus be a sign of identification" or it may be "an indicator of a weakened identification" (Watzlawik et al. 16). There is as yet no convincing empirical evidence to support either hypothesis. When I was addressed as "Helen," I could certainly react and respond, yet I occasionally asked myself who I actually was. "Helen" is a mask, while in my perception "培红" (in Chinese characters, not in *pinyin* Peihong) carries the soul. In that linguistic and cultural environment, my own name "文培红" in characters no longer mattered.

Gradually, from my readings of ethnic minority American literatures, and everyday encounter with students and colleagues with their diverse ethnic and linguistic backgrounds at Southwest Minzu University, I realized that my puzzlement in Melbourne was not unique at all. Anyone having a cross-cultural experience will be renamed (either in sound or spelling form) and will adapt to the new name and identity carried by the new name. I gradually realized the relationship between one's name and identity in this cross-cultural experience.

While in Melbourne, I visited the Immigration Museum. One of the display boards caught my attention. In plain words, it tells an important truth about immigration: the change of one's name and forced adaptation to the new name and the cultural identity implied in the name. It runs like this:

> What we are called:
>
> Our names can be a blessing or a burden. Love or hate them, keep or change them or constantly have to explain them.
>
> The name we are given is our first step towards a separate identity. Names can also signal a connection to our family or a particular religion, language or community.
>
> There are times when our names set us apart. People ask: "How do you pronounce that?" "That's an interesting name. Where does it come from?" or "How do you spell that?"
>
> The impulse to change our name can be compelling. Getting married? Need to disappear? Feeling pressure to assimilate or fit in?
>
> Ali becomes Alan.
>
> Xiao Yun becomes Claudia.

Such ethnic American authors as Amy Tan, Maxine Hong Kingston, Alex Haley, Sandra Cisneros, and N. Scott Momaday have written about names and identities. The Pulitzer-Prize-winning Native American novelist Momaday's memoir *The Names* includes discussions about the relationship between one's name and identity. For Aku Wuwu as a "cultural triphibian," naturally the issue of his various names is quite significant. This similarity between Aku and indigenous people in the USA was the academic foundation for me to raise that first question about names in my interview. It went like this:

> *Wen:* As your life is advancing in the direction of "Luo Qingchun," does it mean that you are farther and farther from "ap kup vyt vy"?
>
> *Aku:* It would be like that for an ordinary person. But as a writer, I have the strong desire for and the capability of self-reflection on my own life experience. I was trained to write in the manner of spiritual retrospection and contemplation of the past via poetry. On the one hand my writing is a review of the past, but on the other it is a step forward. I not only identify with "Luo Qingchun" self-consciously, but also persist in being "ap kup vyt vy," striving to absorb Yi and Chinese wisdom, to whole-heartedly experience the unique bilingual life.
>
> *Wen:* "Both... and..." not "either... or...?"
>
> *Aku:* Now, I cannot be "either... or..." You can clearly see the journey of my heart, and that of my life. The only fortunate thing for me is that though having lived in the world of "Luo Qingchun," I have never forgotten "ap kup vyt vy." And this is the eternal theme and motivation of my writing. Subconsciously, I constantly return to "ap kup vyt vy." In the meantime, I have a strong sense of

responsibility and an inner calling to pursue a mission in life as Luo Qingchun. It is between these two roles, two names, that I get inexhaustible passion for artistic creation. (*Coyote* 275)

As for the origin of this concept of "both... and..." or "either... or..." I received the former from Linell Davis, an American sociologist and my former teacher at Sichuan University. Linell Davis wrote *Doing Culture: Cross-cultural Communication in Action* (2001), based on her years of teaching and living in China. By tracing the origin of this concept, I reflected on how the interview with Aku, in fact, greatly reflects the interviewer or translator's own mentality and her teacher's. Even before the translation was finished, this bilingual book was destined to be a product of the cross-cultural experiences of many people, not only explicitly Aku's, but also the implied translators' own spirit and character.

I summed up this book's various themes in a "Translator's Note":

Firstly, there is his interest in beliefs concerning the spirit world, which for Aku resonates with traditional beliefs in his own culture. He also comments on some negative aspects of Native American history. In regard to inter-culture relations, he believes in "equal though different." The whole collection is replete with feelings of humanity, diversity and care for the others. (*Coyote* 365)

In Alice Walker's short story "Everyday Use" (1973), a black college student named Dee changes her name to "Wangero Leewanika Kemanjo," an African name which she chooses in order to suggest African roots at the peak of the Civil Rights Movement in the early 1970s. She totally ignores how the name "Dee" can actually be traced back to many generations of her female ancestors in the new world, who could be a source of identification. But she declares that "Dee" stems from oppressors (implying the slave owner who forced the black slaves to give up their African names and adopt the slave owner's). The individual, we can gather, is thus "knowable externally," but "can also interpret him- or herself as 'other'" (Watzlawik et al. 2): Dee is discovering not so much a self but rather othering and losing herself. As Alice Walker shapes the narrative, the "privilege of seeing what was unclear" becomes the mother's, not Dee's (Sadeq and Al-Badawi 159). From this narrative, we have a way of understanding the relationship between one's name, identity, and cultural heritage preservation in ethnic cultures (see also Smith for semiotic concepts of naming). For this purpose we should compare other ethnic American writers' works, such as Amy Tan's novel *The*

Joy Luck Club and N. Scott Momaday's memoir *The Names*.

We should realize, at any rate, that there is one major difference between naming practices in the USA and China: for black slaves, the assimilation and change of name were enforced in slavery. In contemporary China, the change of names of minority people, as Aku's case, is motivated by the self-choice of migration from remote villages to major cities for a better life in a modernization process. When Aku Wuwu launches a poetic dialogue between Yi culture and indigenous culture in the USA, the translators and the interviewer started an academic dialogue between Chinese and American ethnic literatures. Together, the twice-cross-cultural writing and twice-cross-cultural translation comprise a significant part of "world minority literature."

4. Multiple Intercultural Dialogues in Twice-Cross-Cultural Writing

The bilingual poetry collection *Coyote Traces* is co-translated by two translators, then co-edited and and co-published by academic publishing houses in Beijing and Columbus, Ohio. This mode of comprehensively intercultural cooperation in ethnic minority literature book production is unusual. It is the first poetry book by a Chinese ethnic bilingual writer (in his native tongue and Chinese) about ethnic groups in the USA. By producing such a work, the whole team attempts to strengthen the cultural communication between minority communities in China and the USA. These communities share worldviews and beliefs, and are faced with common challenges as marginalized minority ethnic groups in their respective countries.

The book's bilingual publication could enlarge the potential audiences who are interested in ethnic Chinese and American literatures. From very beginning the poet, translators, editors, and publishers needed to have a clear idea about the target readers of the book: Native American people (scholars, poets, college students, readers) and other ethnic minority American readers; sinologists and students majoring in Chinese language and literature, or who are interested in translation between English and Chinese; American readers who are interested in multi-ethnic Chinese culture; and Chinese readers who are interested in American history and its multi-ethnic cultures.

With this in mind, the book's contents and format have to appeal to the needs of the target readers. The first major question is thus: how should we arrange the original Chinese poems and English translations? Shall we put the Chinese ones in the first half, and the English ones in the latter half? If we had designed the format in this way, the editing and type-setting would have been much easier and saved the editors much time and energy. But finally, after careful discussion, we decided to put the English translations along with the Chinese poems side by side. This would definitely make editors' type-setting more complex, for it is often hard to match the two in length. But we assumed that many of the book's potential readers will be either Chinese majors in the USA or English majors in China who would know both the source language and the target language. Putting the translated versions side by side with the originals would make it more convenient for such readers to learn the language and to study translations. Even for readers who speak only one language, this arrangement will not cause any trouble. The editors from both countries finally agreed upon this arrangement.

We provide online poem recitation on the website of the American publishing house. One expert in Chinese poetry performance was invited to recite all 80 of the Chinese poems, and folklorist Mark Bender read the English ones. In this way, we offer the readers more alternatives for appreciating the poems and opportunities to learn language and culture. For a poet like Aku, the sounds of words are as significant as the written words. We predict that the online option will provide another means of appreciating Aku's poems.[8]

This project has required years of cooperation between Sino-U.S. scholars and publishers at various levels. The editorial process itself is a constant cultural dialogue. The design, format, and pictures of native American culture and Yi ethnic culture — images of material cultures of the Nez Perce National Historic Park in Idaho, and the exhibits of Nuosu Yi material cultures in Liangshan, Sichuan Province, where many Yi people reside — are presented in their specific geographical and cultural spaces. The intercultural dialogues take place in different ways: between the poet and the translators, between the translators, between translators and editors, between Chinese and American editors, also between oral and written literary articulations and between the signifying elements of intertext. They take place between the oral recitations, and between recitations and

---

[8] For a bilingual recitation of all the 80 poems in *Coyote Traces*, see "East Asian Audio Books": http://u.osu.edu/eaab/aku-wuwus-coyote-traces/coyote-traces-page-1/.

visual images. We are fully aware that using several semiotic forms enables "interrelationships between co-present modes" for complementary or even dissonant meanings, and thus "intersemiotic" relationships (Lyons 279); they are composed of "multimodal microevents in which all the signs present combine to determine their communicative intent," in our case oriented toward communication between cultures (Van Leeuwen 8). As for the book's title, there were alternative choices: *The Appeal of the Mississippi River*, *Drifting in America*, *Native American Dream*, or *Turtle Island*. Eventually we chose *Coyote Traces* as title, aiming to echo the previous collection published ten years earlier in the USA, *Tiger Traces* (2006), which Bender translated with Aku. Thus these two English translations of poetry collections form a dialogue with each other, a spiritual echo.

This whole process of Sino-U.S. cooperation in producing the bilingual poetry collection illustrates Bender's concept of "cosmographical translation." Apart from referring to the poetic inclusiveness of human as well as non-human beings, the concept refers to comprehensive cooperation and to the adaptation of multimodal means of presentation, to encourage cultural communication between the peoples involved.

As the above analyses show, the bilingual *Coyote Traces* is an example of intercultural writing as an attempt to communicate between two civilizations. The book's author and the translators desire to establish a cultural dialogue between Chinese and American ethnic writers and readers. This chapter offers a self-analysis not only of a translated product (a text with extensions), but rather of the translating process (the context). I have tried to answer the following questions: What happens in twice-cross-cultural writing and twice-cross-cultural translation, from a Chinese version to a bilingual text? What factors are involved in language transfer, and how do they affect the book's final version? Since this is an exercise in comparative intercultural thinking, in which second-order observation is inherent (Xie 46), what is the relation between emotion and cognition in the translator's self-observation?

Ethnic literary translation is not as simple as "in other words" — to use the title of Mona Baker's popular coursebook. Indeed, it is the translator's re-creation of a spiritual echo between translator and poet. As a form of writing culture, an ethnographic twice-cross-cultural poem is often the carrier of material as well as intangible ethnic culture. Ethnographic poetry combines rich information on material culture and intangible cultural images. Translating objects of material culture from ethnic languages into English often involves complex and multiple steps of language transfer. In Mark Bender's "cosmographic translation" concept, successful operations tend to require cooperation between translators and editors from different cultural and academic backgrounds, to enable a development of meanings "in coordination with others" (Leeds-Hurwitz 2: 891). The concept should be combined, as I have argued, with comparative intercultural inquiry. Accordingly, it is to be hoped that "world minority literature" will receive a significant place in our collective academic thinking.

References

Adamson, Joni. "Whale as Cosmos: Multi-Species Ethnography and Contemporary Indigenous Cosmopolitics." *Revista Canaria de Estudios Ingleses*, vol. 64, 2012, pp. 29–45.

阿库乌雾 (Aku Wuwu).《密西西比河的倾诉》(*The Appeal of the Mississippi River*). China's Writers' Press, 2008.

Aku Wuwu. *Coyote Traces: Aku Wuwu's Poetic Sojourn in America*. Translated by Wen Peihong and Mark Bender. Ethnic Publishing House & Foreign Language Publications, 2015.

Aku, Wuwu, and Mark Bender. *Tiger Traces: Selected Nuosu and Chinese Poetry by Aku Wuwu*. Foreign Language Publications, 2006.

Allen, Chadwick. "Performing Serpent Mound: A Trans-Indigenous Meditation." *Theatre Journal*, vol. 67, no. 3, 2015, pp. 391–411.

—. *Trans-Indigenous: Methodologies for Global Native Literary Studies*. U of Minnesota P, 2012.

Allen, Graham. *Intertextuality: The New Critical Idiom*, Routledge, 2000.

Bassnett, Susan, and André Lefevere. "Translating the Seed: Poetry and Translation." *Constructing Cultures: Essays on Literary Translation*, Shanghai Foreign Language Education Press, 2004.

Baumbach, Sibylle, Herbert Grabes and Ansgar Nünning. "Values in Literature and the Value of Literature: Literature as a Medium for Representing, Disseminating and Constructing Norms and Values." *Literature and Values: Literature as a Medium for Representing, Disseminating and Constructing Norms and Values*, edited by Sibylle Baumbach, Herbert Grabes and Ansgar Nünning, Giessen Contributions to the Study of Culture 2, Trier: WVT, 2009, pp. 1–15.

Bender, Mark. *The Borderlands of Asia: Culture, Place, Poetry*. Cambria Press, 2017.

—. "Brief Report on the International Symposium on World Minority Literature and Manifesto of World Minority Literature." *MCLC Resource Center*, 13 Dec. 2016. http://u.osu.edu/mclc/2016/12/13/world-minority-literature-conference-report/.

—. "Cambria Press Author Mark Bender (AAS 2017 Speech)." *Cambria Press*, 30 Mar. 2017. http://cambriapressacademicpublisher.wordpress.com/2017/03/30/cambria-press-author-mark-bender-aas-2017-speech/.

—. "Constellations of Competency in Cosmographic Translation." *Studies on Translation of Chinese Classics* (The Eighth Collection),《典籍翻译研究》(第八辑)edited by Wang Hongyin（王宏印）. Foreign Language Teaching and Research Press, 2017, pp. 4–15.

—. "Landscapes and Life-Forms in Cosmographic Epics from Southwest China." *Chinese Literature Today*, vol. 5, no. 2, 2016, pp. 88–97.

—. "*Ogimawkwe Mitigwaki* and 'Axlu yyr kut': Native Tongues in Literatures of Cultural Transition." *Sino-Platonic Papers*, vol. 220, 2012, pp. 1–28.

—. "Poet of the Late Summer Corn: Aku Wuwu and Contemporary Yi Poetry." *The Oxford Handbook of Modern Chinese Literatures*, edited by Carlos Rojas and Andrea Bachner, Oxford UP, 2016, pp. 498–520.

Bender, Mark, and Wen Peihong. 从阿巴拉契亚到喜马拉雅：美国学者马克·本德尔访谈录. ("From the Appalachia to the Himalayas: A Talk with the American Scholar Mark Bender").《文化遗产研究》(*Cultural Heritage Studies*), Sichuan UP, 2015, pp. 39–49.

Cao, Shunqing. *The Variation Theory of Comparative Literature*. Springer, 2013.

Davis, Linell. *Doing Culture: Cross-cultural Communication in Action*. Foreign Language Teaching and Research Press, 2001.

Deleuze, Gilles, and Félix Guattari. *A Thousand Plateaus: Capitalism and Schizophrenia*. Translated by Brian Massumi, U of Minnesota P, 1987.

—. *What Is Philosophy?* Translated by Hugh Tomlinson and Graham Burchell, Columbia UP, 1994.

Harman, Nicky. "Reviewing Translations: Jonathan Stalling, Chinese Literature Today." *Paper Republic: Chinese Literature in Translation*, 8 Jan. 2014. paper-republic.org/nickyharman/reviewing-translations-jonathan-stalling-chinese-literature-today/.

Hermans, Theo. *The Conference of the Tongues*. Routledge, 2007.

—. "Norms and the Determination of Translation: A Theoretical Framework." *Translation, Power, Subversion*, edited by Román Álvarez and M. Carmen África Vidal, Multilingual Matters, 1996, pp. 25–51.

Howard, Harold P. *Sacajawea*. Foreword by Joseph Bruchac. U of Oklahoma P, 1971.

Jin, Wen. *Pluralist Universalism: An Asian Americanist Critique of U.S. and Chinese Multiculturalisms*. The Ohio State UP, 2012.

Jin, Wen, and Liu Daxian. "Double Writing: Aku Wuwu and the Epistemology of Chinese Writing in the Americas." *Amerasia Journal*, 2012, pp. 45–63.

Leeds-Hurwitz, Wendy. "Social Construction of Reality." *Encyclopedia of Communication Theory*, edited by Stephen W. Littlejohn and Karen A. Voss, Vol. 2, Sage, 2009, pp. 891–95.

李务生, 史昆译(Li, Wusheng, and Shi, Kun, translators).《俄勒冈印第安神话故事》(*Coyote Was Going There: Indian Literature of the Oregon Country*). Jarold Ramsey, China Folk Arts Publishing House, 1983.

Lum, Doman. "Cultural Values and Minority People of Color." *The Journal of Sociology & Social Welfare*, vol. 22, no. 1, 1995, pp. 59–74.

Lyons, Agnieszka. "Multimodality." *Research Methods in Intercultural Communication: A Practical Guide*, edited by Zhu Hua. John Wiley, 2016, pp. 268–80.

Mao, Sihui. "Translating the Other: Discursive Contradictions and New Orientalism in Contemporary Advertising in China." *The Translator:*

Studies in Intercultural Communication (Manchester), vol. 15, no. 2, 2009, pp. 261–82.

Partridge, Colin. *Minor American Fiction, 1920 – 1940: A Survey and an Introduction*. Rodopi, 1984.

Phinney, Jean S. "When We Talk About American Ethnic Groups, What Do We Mean?" *American Psychologist*, vol. 51, no. 9, 1996, pp. 918–27.

Ramsey, Jarold, editor. *Coyote Was Going There: Indian Literature of the Oregon Country*. U of Washington P, 1977.

Rexroth, Kenneth. "The Poet as Translator." *World Outside the Window: The Selected Essays of Kenneth Rexroth*, edited by Bradford Morrow, New Directions, 1987, pp. 171–90.

Roediger, Virginia More. *Ceremonial Costumes of the Pueblo Indians: Their Evolution, Fabrication, and Significance in the Prayer Drama*. U of California P, 1991.

Sadeq, Ala Seddin, and Mohammed Al-Badawi. "Epiphanic Awakenings in Raymond Carver's *Cathedral* and Alice Walker's *Everyday Use*." *Advances in Language and Literary Studies*, vol. 7, no. 3, 2016, pp. 157–60.

Schrag, Calvin O. *The Resources of Rationality: A Response to the Postmodern Challenge*. *Studies in Continental Thought*. Indiana UP, 1992.

Schwartz, Shalom H. "Mapping and Interpreting Cultural Differences Around the World." *Value Frameworks at the Theoretical Crossroads of Culture*, Intercultural Research, Vol. 4, edited by Steve J. Kulich, Michael H. Prosser and Weng Liping. Shanghai Foreign Language Education Press, 2012, pp. 339–79.

Shan, Patrick Fuliang. "Ethnicity, Nationalism and Race Relations: The Chinese Treatment of the Solon Tribes in Heilongjiang Frontier Society, 1900–1931." *Asian Ethnicity*, vol. 7, no. 2, 2006, pp. 183–93.

Smith, Grant W. "Theoretical Foundations of Literary Onomastics." *The Oxford Handbook of Names and Naming*, edited by Carole Hough, Oxford UP, 2016, pp. 295–309.

Stalling, Jonathan. Letter, Chinese Literature Today. *Paper Republic: Chinese Literature in Translation*, 8 Jan. 2014. http://paper-republic.org/nickyharman/reviewing-translations-jonathan-stalling-chinese-literature-today/.

Starosta, William J. "Expanding the Circumference of Centrisms: On the Reframing of Identity." *Identity and Intercultural Communication (I): Theoretical and Contextual Construction*, Intercultural Research Vol. 2, edited by Xiaodong Dai and Steve J. Kulich, Shanghai Foreign Language Education Press, 2010, pp. 53–68.

Tie Ning(铁凝). "Speech at the 3rd Conference on Sinologists' Translation of Chinese Literatures." 2014. www.chinawriter.com.cn/2014/2014 – 08 – 26/215915.html.

Trimble, Joseph E., Janet E. Helms and Maria P. P. Root. "Social and Psychological Perspectives on Ethnic and Racial Identity." *Handbook of Racial and Ethnic Minority Psychology*, edited by Guillermo Bernal et al., Sage, 2003, pp. 239–75.

Turner, Frederick Jackson. "The Significance of the Frontier in American History." 1893. *The Frontier in American History*, Henry Holt, 1920, pp. 1–38.

Van Leeuwen, Theo. "Ten Reasons Why Linguists Should Pay Attention to Visual Communication." *Discourse and Technology: Multimodal Discourse*

Analysis, edited by Philip Levine and Ron Scollon. Georgetown UP, 2004, pp. 7–19.

Venuti, Lawrence. *The Scandals of Translation: Towards an Ethics of Difference*. Routledge, 1998.

—. *The Translator's Invisibility: A History of Translation*. 2nd ed. Routledge, 2008.

Watzlawik, Meike, Danilo Silva Guimarães, Min Han and Ae Ja Jung. "First Names as Signs of Personal Identity: An Intercultural Comparison." *Psychology & Society*, vol. 8, no. 1, 2016, pp. 1–21.

Whitman, Walt. *Leaves of Grass*. Edited by Sculley Bradley and Harold W. Blodgett. Norton, 1973.

Xie, Ming. *Conditions of Comparison: Reflections on Comparative Intercultural Inquiry*. Continuum, 2011.

Ybema, Sierk, and Frans H. Kamsteeg. "Making the Familiar Strange: A Case for Disengaged Organizational Ethnography." *Organizational Ethnography: Studying the Complexity of Everyday Life*, edited by Sierk Ybema, Dvora Yanow, Harry Wels, and Frans H. Kamsteeg. Sage, 2009, pp. 101–19.

Zhuravleva, A. P. "The Image of the American Adam in James Fenimore Cooper's Novels." *Writing Identity: The Construction of National Identity in American Literature*, edited by Michael Steppat and Natalia Morzhenkova. MGOU, 2016, pp. 77–83.

3

From Appalachia to the Himalayas: An Interview with Mark Bender

Interviewee: Mark Bender
(*The Ohio State University*)
Interviewer: Wen Peihong
(*Southwest Minzu University*)

Summary: At folklore symposia on material culture, Prof. Mark Bender has been speaking about the material culture in parts of the Appalachian areas of Ohio, where he spent much of his childhood. As an American folklorist and expert on Chinese ethnic literature, Bender has talked about the mutual influences between American Indians and the white settlers in the frontier history of the area and about local cultural traditions and historical revivals that are observable today. In my interview with Bender, he looks back on his own ever-expanding academic career: from the study of Suzhou chantefable to Chinese ethnic minority literature and folklore, and to contemporary eco-literature and "ethnographic poetry" in Eastern Asia. The two common threads linking these interests are traditional culture and nature. In the interview, Bender speaks about his experience in and his views about translating Chinese folk literature and ethnic literature. He narrates his encounters over the last three decades with a number of Chinese and American scholars, such as Zha Ruqiang (查汝强), Zhong Jingwen(钟敬文), Sun Jingyao(孙景尧), Gary Snyder, and John Miles Foley. He also speaks about the activities of Sino-U.S. college students' cultural exchanges, and his views on the relationship between traditional culture and modern life.

Wen: Thanks a lot for your acceptance of my interview, Mark. I'd like to start with the lectures you gave at East China Normal University in 2014. In the past three decades, you've been doing research and giving lectures on Chinese folklore and Chinese ethnic minority literature. But you have also talked about the material culture in the Appalachian Mountains. It was the first time for you to talk about your own cultural background in public. Did you feel differently when talking about Appalachian culture as an insider, compared with talking about Chinese ethnic minority culture as an outsider? How has your early life experience in Appalachia influenced your study of Chinese folk literature?

Bender: When I was invited to participate in that folklore symposium, they wanted me to focus on material culture in America, for they needed some new perspectives. So I decided to talk about the Appalachian areas of Ohio, and other parts of Appalachia, which I am familiar with. In the past 30 years, I always talk to some Chinese people about other Chinese people. Now I want to talk about my own background. But my part of America is kind of unique because few American people understand things there. Besides, I felt the topic "material culture" was very good. I've done most of my research on oral tradition, but I've also found a lot of connections between oral tradition and material culture. And one of the things that have attracted me to the oral performance, the minority cultures or local cultures in China, is its material culture.

Giving these lectures provided me with an opportunity to retrospect and rediscover my own cultural background. When I was giving the lectures, I seemed to see what I'd never seen about myself before. I was sort of discovering something inside me. I noticed the strong response of the audience when I showed the pictures of the pottery and cupboard made by my father, the quilts and gardens made by my mother, the iron tools made by my son, the muzzle-loading rifles made by me, etc. And when I was showing the picture of me and my father beside the grave, I could tell some people responded to that emotionally. You may see my feelings toward the local material culture as an insider. However, even when I was talking about my own family, I distanced myself. I took a certain kind of objective position as an outsider. Besides, when talking about the Amish in Holmes County, I am an outsider, not an insider. I am not Amish.

From a very young age, I was interested in the history and material culture of the places where I lived in the Appalachian area. I used to do lots of things, like going to the forest, hunting, fishing, trapping, etc. All of those things involve material objects. Every year, my family would go camping for one month. We would live in tents and we traveled around places. Also, later, I took some training in blacksmithing and learned how to make muzzle-loading rifles. I learned some of these skills from some local people, one of whom was the town barber. And also, remember that old Appalachian hunter I mentioned in my lecture, Skip Yeager? I stayed with his family the whole summer when I was 11. He influenced me a lot as well. So I learned lots about that kind of lifestyle. And that's part of the attraction that I actually have especially for the material culture of Yi people or Hmong people. When I go to these places, I understand what they are doing. I've done something similar before, though it is in a different cultural context.

Wen: It seems that your early life experience in Appalachia has greatly influenced your study of Chinese folk and ethnic literature, for the Yi poet Aku Wuwu(阿库乌雾)once told me that both you and he believed in animism. What do you think of this statement?

Bender: It's an interesting statement. I don't know what Aku believes, but I do think that we are both on the same wave length. Like radio, you have to be on the same wave length to communicate. We had similar life experiences of living in mountains. We are sensitive to similar things. I think the ways we connect with the natural world are quite similar. Some people try to reject their rural backgrounds, but people like Aku and myself don't do that. To some extent we combine our habits and customs into a modern urban life style.

Wen: In the past few decades, you traveled a lot in East Asia to do research work. I assume this spirit of sojourner has something to do with your own family history. Is that right? What influences have you got from your parents?

Bender: My parents are very nice and kind. All my family members regard my parents as living Buddhas, or "Saints." My father participated in the Civil Rights Movement in the 1960s. A young pastor at that time, he marched with Black leaders in our community. And I was only 6 or 7 years old then. My mother once worked as a nurse for 6 or 7 years, and then she worked in a library. So all of my brothers and sisters have jobs associated with books or libraries. My mother told us stories every night. She read stories to us each night. Many of the stories were about the East. I was fascinated by dinosaurs when I was 4 or 5 years old. My mother told stories about how Chinese and Mongolians went to seek for dinosaur eggs with the explorer Roy Chapman Andrews. I went to Hohhot to see the dinosaur eggs in the local museum in 1982.

My parents also took us (my siblings and me) to the retirement home to visit those old missionaries who had been in China for over 30 years. I was very curious about their experiences. They were so old. They talked about nothing else but China; they told me what kind of place China was.

Wen: I noticed that your academic research fields are quite diverse, from Suzhou *Pingtan*, to Southwest Chinese ethnic minority literature, to the comparative study of it with Northeast Indian literature, to eco-poetry in East Asia. Would you please say something about your ever-expanding academic development?

Bender: In terms of my academic development, I had a sort of unofficial training with Sun Jingyao at Guangxi University, and earlier from my undergraduate teachers at Ohio State. I took some comparative literature courses and anthropology. But back then I cared very little about grades, for I had to work while studying at university. Despite this, I never dropped a class. I went to class every day. I also spent quite a lot of time reading Ezra Pound.

I never met any Chinese people until I was 18 or 19 when I went to college. I met teachers and students who were from Chinese Taiwan. These relationships were very meaningful to me in many ways. I generally got along with the Chinese people I met. And the more I learned the culture, the better I began to understand some things. Then things got even more interesting when I went on a study abroad trip to Taiwan around 1977, and even more so when I went to the Chinese mainland in August 1980 for what became a long-term stay.

When I went to graduate school, I studied folklore theory and traditional Chinese literature, especially Ming/Qing literature. Patrick B. Mullen is the teacher who taught me folk literature theory after I returned to the USA. I had just come back from China, and attended his class. He introduced folklore performance theory. Wow! My mind was opened. I could now express myself since I had attended quite a lot of folk activities in China.

I originally wanted to write my dissertation on Yi traditional literature. For some practical reasons, however, my advisor Timothy Wang thought that topic was too far away from the norm. He felt that if I did it, I would never find a job. He said the project should be in *Hanyu*（汉语）-related literature. So I said OK. I chose to do some local type of literature. It's a local（Han）type of thing, with a very strong local cultural identity. A lot of problems I encountered in translating local literature are the same as translating minority literature. *Suzhouhua* is a local dialect that most Chinese can't understand. And there is still a very strong material culture dimension in this performance culture. I found it's arguably the most complex oral performance style in China. I wanted to study it for that reason. It is so rich with tradition, and so rich in narrative style. Because I had been starting to be influenced by the oral performance school of folkloristics, I had the theory to deal with it. Not very many people were using that kind of theory to study Chinese literature at that time. Only Susan Blader was experimenting with it. I think I expanded the use of it in the study of Chinese oral performance. There is a kind of gap between people who study Chinese performance theory and folklore theory. But now my students know all about the performance approach, and all the background.

Then, I've always been interested in translating Chinese ethnic minority literature over the years. When I was studying Yi language, I was told that there were people whose spoken language was related to Yi and some other languages in Northeast India. Then I had a chance to attend a conference in Northeast India, and I found there are many ethnic minority people there, with cultures quite similar to those in Southwest China. A lot of them speak Tibeto-Burman languages. They have legends of migrating from China, across the borders disputed between India and China. So I thought it was a very unusual place. In both places, the poets talk about nature, close relationships with the environment, and how the tradition is threatened to disappear. Then, a few years ago, I went to Mongolia for the first time. I met some local poets and was aware of the similar situation there. And I visited Myanmar, hoping to find some poets there. The study of the ethnographical poetry about the environment in East Asia is a new phase in my academic life, but there is always a tie — the interest in folk culture, and traditional images. These are something in common among the poets. [Note: These and other trips resulted in the book *The Borderlands of Asia: Culture, Place, Poetry*, published by Cambria Press in 2017.]

Wen: You've expanded the oral performance theory to the study of Chinese folk literature. I think this is your unique and special contribution. What do you think is your most important contribution as a sinologist and folklorist?

Bender: If I've made any contribution, I think that is I've drawn some people's attention to local ethnic literature and oral literature in China. I mean I wrote that book on Suzhou *Pingtan*, and translated versions of the Miao epic *Butterfly Mother*. I think those are some of my accomplishments to date. I think I was one of the first to start using the contextual/performance approach in Chinese folklore study.

We should view oral performances as a dynamic and multi-dimensional process in different social situations. And I think that helps us understand the cultural meaning of certain performances in particular situations, which is not easily got in many cases. It concerns not only the ways of looking at the performance, but also its meanings to the audience. There are certain sorts of dynamic interaction between the audience and performer. The performer should meet the needs of the audience. It means in some cases some sorts of performances are specially designed to guide the audience to react in certain ways. But when audiences freely attend the performance, they have a choice about whether they want to stay or to leave, or they want to encourage the performer or deride the performer. Especially in the context of traditional epics, the audiences may already have lots of knowledge about the stories. Therefore, they can judge the performer's abilities, and also directly or indirectly they may influence how the story is told. We have such examples from many traditional performances.

Another question is: How do performances work? I noticed there is a set of similar effective performance techniques across various East Asian traditional performances, such as China's Sichuan *Pingshu* and Suzhou *Pingtan*, Japanese *Rakugo*, and Korean *P'ansori*. We see a lot of effective techniques in story-telling—stylized and patterned movements and facial expressions, such as hand gestures, and the use of simple story-telling tools, such as percussive devices or fans, in all these traditions. I think there are some basic story-telling techniques transmitted over centuries. The reason why they could survive over centuries is because they work. They work in an interaction dynamic with the audience, gaining and keeping attention. I think performance theory allows us to understand the cultural meaning of performance. This is one of my present projects, to look at the story-telling techniques across East Asia. I'll compare some of the means of performance across cultures, across parts of Asia.

Wen: I am really amazed by your language competence! Just imagine a 100% American is greeting the audience, many of whom are Yi, including those who can no longer speak their native tongue! This contrast is really astonishing for me. I think you are a soul-caller like Aku Wuwu at that moment. How did you learn the Yi language and Hmong language?

Bender: I don't really know Yi or Hmong/Miao, I just work with them. I do know something about the Hmong grammar. I can tell what has been changed when it is made into a text; I know some vocabulary, but I can't speak it. I just never had enough time to do the field work there, as I have been working on other projects. As for Yi language, I'm still learning it. I practice at home, but I don't have anybody to practice with. And I try to give a speech in Yi language every time I go to Southwest University for Nationalities (which is now Southwest Minzu University). I know some of the vocabulary, but my conversation in Yi is still very basic. I wish I could do better.

Translating poems helped me know the structure of the language. It is a kind of decoding. When working with native speakers, you will have much better understanding of that language. So usually, I work with native speakers.

Wen: You once mentioned the idea of "Chinese filter" coined by Victor Mair. When did he propose this term for the first time? And how do you solve this problem of the "Chinese filter" in your own translation of Chinese ethnic minority literature?

Bender: Victor has been talking about that for at least 20 years. I don't know the first place he used that, but he is a very creative guy. You know most of the ethnic minority literature in China is written in Chinese (*hanyu*). Victor feels that in the process of textualization and translation, some things in the original version get changed and filtered. In fact, "filter" always happens in the translation between any two languages. But if a third language is in between, there will be even more changes. In collecting and translating folk literature, editors may combine several versions together, and make a super version out of them. The *Miao Epics* collected and edited by Ma Xueliang (马学良) and Jin Dan (今旦), and the Yi epic *Hnewo teyy* edited and translated by Feng Yuanwei (冯元蔚) are of this category. In fact, a lot of folk literature in the world goes through a somewhat similar process when editors smooth out the language or otherwise tinker with texts. In the USA, they used to take out all the references to sex in North American Indian stories. So China is not the only situation to let that happen.

Chinese folklorists have also addressed these issues. A number of them have written articles (since the late 1970s) about translation practices in the 1950s or 1960s. The editors at the time had to follow strict editorial guidelines concerning content. Anyway, that is the idea of "Chinese filter." In that book which Victor and I published, we did use some texts that were originally in another language, then translated into Standard Chinese. In some cases I had only the Chinese version, and could not get the original version. So sometimes, you have to go with that. There is no other way.

Wen: What do you think of the processed or filtered master texts, such as *Butterfly Mother*?

Bender: *Butterfly Mother* is a composite text, firstly collected by Jin Dan and other people under the guidance of Ma Xueliang. The version I first translated was an edited one in Chinese. It is somewhat like the *Kalevala* from Finland. In *Kalevala* there is more than one voice speaking, as the editor put many songs together as one text. If you say *Butterfly Mother* is not valid, you have to say that *Kalevala* is not valid either. Despite this, if you look at it from certain scholarly perspectives, it definitely has some defects. These items are not first-hand oral literature. They've been edited, or processed. Some scholars look askew at such texts. But if the purpose is creating a master text, I think the only way you can do so is to put different versions together, and then the whole story is there. It's OK as long as you just put all versions together and don't make things up. It's not the same sort of text as what we're trying to do with *Hnewo teyy*. But it's still valid for some audiences, and has a different intent. A rich master text may be useful in carrying on the tradition in some fashion for later generations, especially in situations where the oral performance dimension is endangered or appears to have died out. In fact, the latest version of the *Butterfly Mother* text, which is titled *Hmong Oral Epics* in English, is a tri-lingual text with lengthy introductions that was designed by Jin Dan and Wu Yiwen (吴一文) as a monument to the epic tradition.

Wen: So the translation of *Hnewo teyy* is somewhat different from the versions of *Butterfly Mother/Hmong Oral Epics* you worked on. Is that right?

Bender: Yes, it is. In regards to the textualization and translation of oral folk literature, there is another view: it is better to translate directly from the original language to the target language, without the interference of Chinese language. So in this way we have just one filter in this project.

Bamo Qubumo (巴莫曲布嫫) of the Institute of Ethnic Literature of the Chinese Academy of Social Sciences has studied different versions of *Hnewo teyy*. What Aku and I have been working on is just one version. We decided to rely on this version only, not anything else. Of course, this hand-written version of *Hnewo teyy* that we are working on is also de-contextualized, for I am not certain about how it is used in everyday life. I don't even know whether it has ever been used. We see only parts of the songs were sung in funerals. The text was supplied to us by a local tradition-bearer named Jjivo Zoqu (吉伍作曲), who does perform parts of it in his own unique style.

Wen: What kinds of problems do you meet when you translate *Hnewo teyy*? How do you solve them?

Bender: Aku Wuwu and I speak Chinese most of the time because his English is not so fluent. But I usually have him recite the poem passages in Yi language when we translate. We spend a lot of time on the Yi texts. We decode the text by first writing it out in Yi Romanization, which is easier for me than the Yi graphs, then assigning Chinese equivalents to each Yi word. And each line is discussed over and over until I can formulate the poem in colloquial English.

The hardest thing for Aku is to find out the meaning line by line. He ran into lots of these problems because the text is written in ancient Yi language. There are some places we kept going over and over again because it was just too obscure. I can't proceed until Aku makes sure of everything line by line.

Also, we never had enough time to work on it. Usually our time is broken. We both have duties toward our students. And he is extremely busy! We work on it, then stop, work on it, then stop. And we both have many other projects.

In addition, I have to know much about Yi culture. I wish I could go and stay there for one or two years. I wish I could have started doing that 10 years ago, because things are changing so fast. Some old people are dying off with time going on. There is a kind of new Yi culture emerging.

I guess that's why our work is meaningful. Because if the future generations want to understand what has happened before, they'll have to look to people like us to figure it out. Otherwise it will be lost forever. History is whatever somebody else says it is unless you've experienced it yourself. So Aku and I work on this project to leave the future people something to read. We mean to leave behind the precious cultural heritage to future generations, and to wider audiences. I think this is the significance of our work.

Wen: What are the audiences for your translations of Chinese folk stories and epics? Will the factor of audience affect your translation strategies?

Bender: That's a good question. Supposedly the audiences determine everything even as we pretend that we are writing for ourselves. I try to present things that are accessible to people who are interested. They don't know Chinese or Yi/Miao language and thus cannot read the original text. My potential audience is anyone who is interested in looking at the world from diverse perspectives.

I write notes and introductions in my books. Some people don't like to have any notes, they don't want to have any introductions. They just want the text in front of them. If they want to have that, it's fine — but again, it's up to the reader. I am writing for the audiences with that kind of expectation. I am not talking to millions of people around the world, only a few dozens, or maybe a few hundreds.

Wen: What motivated you to do the translations of Chinese folk stories, epics, or contemporary poems in native tongues? Is it just out of interest, or a sense of mission, or any other considerations?

Bender: I believe I do have some sort of mission. It's not very formulated, though. From the very beginning, I've kept getting feedback from the people in China. They want to work with me, which is a signal to me that my work is meaningful. If I don't think it is meaningful, I won't keep on doing it any more. I think the greatest thing is that I really enjoy working with Chinese people. I like this international and transnational cooperation, and got a lot out of that. It is like: different spirits who are interested in the same things find each other on the planet, and then cooperate to do something together. They are larger than themselves. I will just continue to do it as long as the green light is on.

Some people just want to do everything by themselves. But I like to work with other people who are interesting and intelligent. Sometimes, you get more done that way. That is something I noticed about Chinese folklore study: many people are involved in the projects. So I think the Chinese approach is quite good in that regard.

Wen: And what are your suggestions for translating and exporting Chinese ethnic minority literature to the English-speaking world?

Bender: People who commit to do this work must learn the local culture in China as much as they can, and go to spend as much time as possible there. You must try to understand what is going on there. You have to train yourself to translate properly, you must do accurate translation.

Wen: In your essay "Hunting Nets and Butterflies: Ethnic Minority Songs from Southwest China" (2001) published in *Manoa*, you recalled your translation and field trip experience in the 1980s with some Chinese scholars, such as Sun Jingyao, Jin Dan, and others. How important was the experience of working with these Chinese scholars in your early years for your later career?

Bender: I think my relationship with the Chinese scholars has defined my work. If I hadn't met the people I have met, I don't know whether I would ever have had a career. I would be nothing.

When I came to China for the first time in 1980, the first Chinese scholar whom I came in contact with was the late Zha Ruqiang from the Chinese Academy of Social Sciences. I met him at Huazhong

University of Science and Technology, Wuhan, where he was on a short-term English program. He wanted to have a speaking partner to improve his English. Every night, he and another fellow, we walked around in the courtyard. He introduced me to the situation of China and encouraged me to stay in China. He said that China was going to develop and was to stand up within 30 years. These experiences with him still exert a great influence on me today.

He helped me contact the New World Press in Beijing for my translation of *Seventh Sister and the Serpent*. He also introduced Zhong Jingwen to me, and led me to visit his home. Zhong Jingwen told me: "You need to go to the South if you want to study the ethnic minority literature." Zha Ruqiang knew Hou Depeng (侯德彭), the vice president of Guangxi University. I stayed in Wuhan for one year, and in Guangxi for 6 years. There I got to know the late Sun Jingyao in the first week. He had just moved in. We stayed in the campus guest house that first week, we got to know each other there. He was not very good at English, and I was not good at Chinese at that time, but we still created a certain kind of communication.

One day, we chatted and got the idea of compiling a journal of comparative literature called *COWRIE* (《文 贝 》). During the Cultural Revolution, Sun was dispatched from Fudan University to Guizhou, then afterwards got to Guangxi University, and then to Suzhou University a few years later, and finally to Shanghai Normal University. You can say those years of working with Sun Jingyao at Guangxi University are when I got my first M.A. Not an officially acknowledged M.A., but substantially an M.A. He and I started to compile the journal. We started to translate Suzhou *Pingtan*, for Sun is from Jiading, Shanghai, and he knew all things about *Pingtan*. He introduced me to *Pingtan*, which I got interested in. There was a movie of two sisters playing *Pingtan* in the 1980s. I went to watch the movie, which interested me a lot. Sun said that story took place in his hometown. Later I had further cooperation with him. He also introduced me to some scholars of Chinese literature; I attended their meetings. I got to know quite a lot of people, including Jia Zhifang (贾植芳) from Fudan University and, indirectly through letters, Qian Zhongshu (钱锺书). So I got to be influenced by the perspective of Chinese comparative literature, I got to know the angle of Chinese scholars.

So, the 1980s were a very precious period for me. As I said, I came to China in 1980. It was a very special period in Chinese history, it was the beginning of reform and opening-up. You could try some new things in this age. Hou Depeng was bold enough to grant us money to compile the journal. We translated each article; it was very hard work. Several of Sun's graduate students and I translated them. Sun did not translate himself; He led us to discuss what should be translated. I came to China with a B.A. As I said, my "first M. A." was earned while working with Prof. Sun. Then I returned to the USA in 1987 and got my real M.A. in 1989, and Ph. D. in 1995.

We had a particular issue of *COWRIE* that included works of ethnic minority literature. I got to know Li Zixian (李子贤) from Kunming; he edited *Mountain Flower*, a journal of ethnic minority literature. Later, Li Zixian introduced me to some older local scholars in Chuxiong, Yunnan Province. I also got to know Ma Xueliang through correspondence (though I never met him in person). I translated one essay by Ma (on translating ethnic minority oral literature) in *COWRIE*.

Later, at a local Xinhua Bookstore, I happened to find a book of Miao epics. I found it was valuable and I should translate it into English. Later, I got to know Jin Dan through Ma Xueliang, for Ma Xueliang and Jin Dan once cooperated in collecting and translating the Hmong/Miao epics in the 1950s and 1960s. Jin Dan is a Hmong/Miao. In 1985, my fiancé and I went to Guizhou and found Jin Dan. Jin Dan led us to southeast Guizhou, I saw quite a lot of the folk customs and material culture. When I started to translate the *Hmong Oral Epics*, I found that I did not know many of the things referred to in the text. I had hundreds of questions waiting to be answered, and I had no way to deal with them. So, in the process of translation, you must go to those places, and must have some connection with them. At least, you must find the local tradition-bearers and get to know them, for the knowledge is local. It's hard to explain it otherwise. I asked some teachers at Guangxi University or the folklorists about these questions, even they could not understand them. They did not necessarily know these customs. I found this is a long learning process. I started to cooperate with Jin Dan from 1985. I went there again several years later; we kept in contact in all these years. The English version of the Miao epic *Butterfly Mother* was published in America in 2006. When I went there again in 2004, Jin's children had already grown up. They are also interested in the Miao epics. They helped their father recollect the materials and revise them. They invited me to participate, since they needed a tri-lingual version. This book *Hmong Oral Epics* in Miao, Chinese, and English was published in China in 2012.

As for the Yi areas, I went there four times in the 1980s before I came back to the USA for further education. But some people I knew there passed away in the years after I left. Then, around the year 2000, I got to know Bamo Qubumo at a conference. Prof. Zhong Jingwen had already showed her my translation of *Seventh Sister and the Serpent*. She already knew who I was. She and her elder sister introduced me to Aku Wuwu. At a national conference held in Shilin, Yunnan Province, I got to know Huang Jianming (黄建明) from Minzu University of China in Beijing. We had some cooperation in translating Yi epics. I started to translate Aku's poems after I got to know him. And recently, I cooperated with him to translate some traditional Yi literature. Also, we had some academic cultural exchange activities, exchange of students. So, really, I can never set myself apart from these Chinese partners.

Wen: You stated in the essay "Hunting Nets and Butterflies": "Though several of my guides and teachers have passed away, their encouragement, patience, and generosity are not forgotten." For me, you are a person who is always grateful to those who have helped you. Even though you are now an internationally well-known scholar in your field, you never forget where you are from. You never forget your roots. We respect you not only for your academic achievements, but also for your character of modesty and gratitude.

Bender: That is because I never feel far from those experiences. I am still a small potato. My academic roots are mostly in China. Some overseas Chinese lived in the USA; I attended their Chinese lessons at The Ohio State University. Most of those old men were from the Chinese mainland, they went to the USA via Chinese Taiwan. They also exerted great influence on me. They were skilled in calligraphy, painting, the art of tea, etc.; they had kept those traditional customs. They were the first Chinese I met in the USA.

The USA and China didn't establish a diplomatic relationship until 1979. When I came to China in 1980, I was one of those Americans who came to China very early, though I was not the earliest. And I stayed for a long time. It is not unusual for a foreigner to stay in China for seven years now. But back in the early 1980s, it was not that easy, especially in such places as Guangxi. But for me it was fine — no problem. I felt comfortable to go to and stay in places like Guizhou, Yunnan, and Sichuan.

Wen: You've talked about your relationship with some Chinese scholars and its significance. I assume that, as an American sinologist, you must also have been influenced by some American scholars. Would you please talk about it a little?

Bender: You may call me a "Chinese school" scholar. But I have also been influenced by European and American literature and scholarship. Most likely the American scholar who has influenced me most is the late John Miles Foley, for he helped me a lot in several aspects. Foley helped anyone with potential and talent if he really appreciated the person. He helped me and gave me confidence. He helped me participate in some academic activities. Foley had just completed a book entitled *Singer of Tales as Performance* when I was writing my Ph.D. dissertation. One of my teachers, Amy Shuman, whose focus is narrative study, told me Foley was writing that book, and to see whether he could let me read the manuscript. So I sent him an email. He said "OK"! And he let me read his book, which had not been published. I cited him in my dissertation, then I attended a conference at his university. I went to his home; I gave him the last muzzle-loading gun I made, just for him. It was really touching! He got cancer a few years ago. I was invited to attend the 25th-year anniversary of the Oral Tradition Center at his university, he invited me to give a special speech. He was in very bad health at that time. He said he had prepared a surprise for me. He opened the computer: it was a picture of that gun I gave him. I had asked my cousin Dan to make a silver inlay to put on the gun, it was the kind of harp played by Homer, which was meaningful. So you see, the growth of a scholar cannot be independent of the encouragement and support of the older generation of scholars. So now, when I meet any promising young persons, I'll encourage them. I'll try my best to help them as long as they are talented and enthusiastic about their work.

Besides, Gary Snyder also influenced me a lot. It happened after I came to China. We were pen pals for some years. Although I attended a poetry reading he gave at The Ohio State University in about 1977, I never really met him. But years later we corresponded by letters. He helped me publish my translations of Yi literature in Japanese and American journals.

Wen: I read that essay you wrote in the 1980s about how Gary Snyder has been influenced by Chinese culture. You mentioned in that essay that Snyder taught his son arrow-shooting to pass on a cultural heritage. Similarly, in a lecture you have talked about how you taught your son the skills of a blacksmith. So I assume that to some extent, you are similar to Gary Snyder in temperament and goals in life?

Bender: Snyder and I shared something in common. Both of us were from the countryside, different from those who came from big cities. I felt that he had something that was unique. I once wrote to Snyder telling him about my activity with my son. He wrote back, saying that was a very good way to cultivate a child, that I was "raising him right."

Wen: You and Aku Wuwu have cooperated for quite a few years in translating Yi epics and poems, and your achievement in introducing Yi literature and culture to the English-speaking world is really admirable. Now, you have been expanding this cooperation from an individual level to university level. What is your comment on the cultural exchanges between The Ohio State University and Southwest University for Nationalities (now Southwest Minzu University)? Do you have any plans to promote the cooperation further?

Bender: Bringing these students from America to China is part of the "China Gateway Program." We have done the program already for seven years. This has been a wonderful thing for these American students. Some of them are from small towns in Ohio, some are from Appalachia. Some are minorities, like the Yi students who participate. I think the Americans develop good relationships, for whatever reasons, with the Yi students. Sometimes there are some similarities in their backgrounds. Yi students are very kind and sincere people, and Americans respond to them very well. I think the Yi students appreciate their friendship with American students very much. A lot of the Yi students never have a chance to deal with foreigners in that way. But now they have that experience, hopefully it motivates them. And a lot of American students have developed an appreciation for the Yi culture.

Wen: In the process of modernization, urbanization, and economic development, the material culture and oral tradition are greatly threatened to survive. What do you think about this situation?

Bender: The whole world is changing rapidly. If life is too difficult, or some custom doesn't function properly anymore, you may change it. But it doesn't necessarily mean something has to be forgotten or dropped. Should we just throw away all of that, or keep some kind of record, so in some way we can experience it, even if it is just on some special occasions, such as putting on *Minzu Fuzhuang* ("native dress") during festivals? That is a way of keeping in touch with the treasures and knowledge of the past. I think this is an important way for people to feel proud of their tradition. These cultures have been created for hundreds or thousands of years, they can still have a place in modern society.

That's also the American story. Usually the children, the grandchildren of the immigrants no longer speak the language their ancestors once spoke. A lot of American people don't even know where their relatives came from. They've been there for many generations; nobody kept any records. Some people don't even know what parts of Europe or Africa their ancestors came from, but to some extent, they may keep certain parts of that identity. America is an interesting case. China is quite a little different; they had to build a new China — they had to build a new world. Things changed so fast! That is the thing about the poets that interests me, because through them I realize it is not an easy change for everybody. But on the other hand, it also presents other possibilities for people. Aku has taken advantage of this, publishing, printing, being a professor, all this stuff. It would never have been possible before. So, you know, there have always been different sides to these situations.

Wen: Finally, I wonder in what ways have years of translating and researching Chinese folklore and ethnic minority literature affected your own life? How are the two related, literary study and life itself?

Bender: Firstly, I have met a lot of interesting people in this process. I like working with these people; I like to see their enthusiasm for their own culture; I like seeing their creative activity; I like hanging out with them; I like to get to know them. It has changed my habits in life in terms of thinking. And secondly, I have gotten new ways of experiencing life from other perspectives. I realize what some of the people in other areas are like around the world. And I like the interaction when I do the translations, in this kind of cooperation between them and me. Our goal is to bring more attention to their literature, or themselves as poets. I find it satisfying and it makes me happy. I think I'm uniquely positioned to do this. Since I have this academic position and background, I think I should do more, to make more contributions. That is what Zha Ruqiang told me: "I think you can make some contributions." I have always remembered it: everybody can make contributions to the world, large or small. So some of the ideas of the Chinese I work with have definitely cultivated me, because America is still a very fresh and new society, while China has a much longer tradition. There is a lot I can learn in dealing with the people of China, regardless of their background. So I think it has definitely changed me a lot in different ways.

The funny thing is that I never expected to make a career out of it! I was interested in Appalachian culture or American Indian cultures — all of the things I'd been familiar with when growing up. I've always been interested in reading things about other cultures. I became interested in East Asia when I was quite young. I never planned to be a professor; it just kind of happened step by step.

There was a professor named Larry Tyler from the USA who visited Guangxi for half a year. He looked at what I was doing. He said I'd better go back to America to go to graduate school. I'd never really thought about that before. I had been sort of unknowingly preparing for that after years in Guangxi. I actually took his advice and went back to The Ohio State University. I started out thinking of just getting a master's degree. Then they kept giving me money, and I got a Ph.D. And later, they hired me to work there, and now I am the department chair. I don't know how it happened; it just happened.

Very early, I realized life presents opportunities to everyone. But you need to prepare to take advantage of them! When opportunity comes, you should take it. Davy Crockett, the American frontiersman, always said "Stop and think. If you know you are right, just go ahead" — and then see what happens. That is what I have believed in over the past 30 years: you just do it. You just have to keep working hard; otherwise you cannot get it done. Just like making a tool, making a muzzle-loading gun. Gary Snyder talked a lot of such things.

Wen: Many thanks indeed, Mark, for this interview!

Earlier versions of Mark Bender's interview responses have appeared as 从阿巴拉契亚到喜马拉雅：美国学者马克·本德尔访谈录.《文化遗产研究》 (*Cultural Heritage Studies*). Sichuan UP, 2015, pp. 39-49.

4

Film Semiotics, Shakespeare, and *Hamlet*'s Chinese Cousin: Decoding the Narrative of Feng Xiaogang's *The Banquet*

MAO Sihui

College of Liberal Arts, Shantou University

Summary: In cinematic terms, films as series of images create a narrative in their own language. They can be situated within a *glocalized* context, the dual process of *globalization* and *localization*. After a brief review of the development of film semiotics and screen adaptations of the Shakespeare canon in world cinema, this chapter takes a semiotic approach to the study of an important Chinese film: Feng Xiaogang's *The Banquet* (2006), a transculturally creative adaptation of Shakespeare's *Hamlet, Prince of Denmark*. To decode a cinematic text is to uncover the various systems of assumptions, beliefs, ideologies, and values embedded in images and discourses, to demonstrate how such structures generate myths, connotations, points of view, modes of address, and their significance. Through a detailed analysis of some features of the film (with a section comparing it with *Prince of the Himalayas*, 2006), this chapter considers how meanings are constructed through cinematic verbal and visual codes/ signs such as narrative structure, and how intertextuality can be fruitfully used to highlight the value of intercultural communication. It concludes that such Chinese film adaptations of *Hamlet* make Shakespeare not only *postcolonial* but also *glocal*.

Snapshots: Film Semiotics

Films are cultural artifacts which are made up of a series of individual images called frames. In cinematic terms, these series of images create a narrative in their own language. As the story of film-making leads us back to the first public screening of projected short motion pictures in 1895 by the French Lumière brothers, film semiotics (the study of cinematic codes and signs) takes us back to the Swiss linguist Ferdinand de Saussure. In his seminal *Course in General Linguistics*, Saussure (1916) proposes a science that studies the life of signs within society. Going against Greek philosophers such as Plato or the Scholastics who believed that there must be some connection between a signifier and the object it signifies, Saussure insists on the arbitrary nature of the sign: no word is inherently meaningful. He divides a sign into its two constituent elements — the physical form (as perceived by our senses) which he calls "the signifier" and the mental concept of what the physical form refers to, which he calls "the signified." A word is only a "signifier," which is the representation of something, and must be combined in the brain with the "signified." He stresses that a sign can properly be understood only in relation to other signs in the same code or system.

This linguistic line of thought was taken up by the French cultural critic Roland Barthes, who helped popularize and extend semiotics as a science for both linguistic and film studies in the 1960s. In his most influential book *Mythologies*, Barthes applied semiotic readings not only to his analysis of novels, plays, and photographs, but also to "popular" texts, activities, and everyday objects such as films, striptease, wrestling, cooking, cars, plastic, steaks and chips, wine and milk, soap-powders, and detergents. In the essay "The Romans in Films" (Barthes 26–28), he decodes the fringes, hair-styles, and faces of the Romans in Mankiewicz's film *Julius Caesar* in order to demystify the signs, signals and symbols of the language of mass culture.

In the 1960s, Christian Metz greatly advanced film semiotics with the publication of his book *Film Language: A Semiotics of the Cinema* (1968), in which he used semiotics as a method in analyzing cinema by constructing a model to explain how a film embodies meanings. He sees "shot" as the basic filmic unit, which is neither symbolic nor arbitrary but iconic and laden with specific meanings, suggesting that film is a language in which each shot used in a sequence works like a unit in a linguistic discourse. In his theoretical model *grande syntagmatique*, Metz argues that individual cinematic texts, rather than sharing a unified grammar, construct their own meaning systems. In Metz's terms, what is being seen or consumed, in fact, is the cinematic apparatus — the instrumental, the technological, the ideological, and the symbolic. As we come to concepts such as *the basic apparatus*, *the cinema-machine*, or *the institution of cinema*, we are not simply referring to the cinema industry but the "interior machine" of the psychology of the spectator, the social regulation of spectatorial metapsychology, or what Metz ("Imaginary" 19) calls the "mental machinery" of cinema, cinema as "technique of the imaginary." Focusing on the psychoanalytic constitution of the cinematic apparatus, Metz explores what relations the cinematic apparatus has with the mirror phase, the infinite movement of desire, the position of voyeurism, the primal scene, the twists and turns of disavowal.① When examined in structuralist and psychoanalytic terms and seen as local manifestations of a more widespread linguistic turn, film semiotics becomes the theory of film-as-a-systems-of-signs. It is crucial that film semiotics should focus on discovering the various symbolic codes that give film its importance as a work of art. Therefore, films are read as "texts" and interpreted with the implication that such a method of reading, understanding, and consuming films does not only activate similar processes of semiotic decoding but also has "enormous consequences for the way film studies as a discipline has tended to frame questions about visual meaning and communication" (Prince 99).

From the mid-1970s to the early 1980s, Metz's theories were largely replaced in film studies debates by an interest in Lacanian psychoanalysis. Greater attention was given to the role of the "reader" (audience) in producing meanings out of textual resources. In Lacanian terms, cinema was viewed as discourse, thus assuming a symbolic relationship with ideology and becoming an effective vehicle for the transmission of "political" messages and cultural value systems. In *Questions of Cinema*, Stephen Heath challenges Metz that all cinema is concerned with representation and that representation itself is a

① See Metz's essay "The Imaginary Signifier." For a detailed critical introduction to Metz's semiology of the cinema, see Part III of Andrew's *The Major Film Theories*, pp. 212–41.

form of language equivalent to Saussure's linguistic model of "langue." The relationship between cinematic texts and the world becomes a matter of representational convention. Heath argues that "the match of film and world is a matter of representation, and representation is in turn a matter of discourse. [...] [I]n this sense at least, film is a series of languages, a history of codes" (26). Drawing on Lacanian psychoanalysis, Heath sees film as a signifying practice and the cinema as a social institution of meanings.

It was also during this period that film semiotics was forced to extend its enquiry into gender issues, especially the different representations of men and women in narrative cinema. Laura Mulvey, in this regard, made a considerable contribution to the development of semiotics and gender politics with the 1975 publication of a very influential essay "Visual Pleasure and Narrative Cinema." Her basic argument is that women in narrative cinema are framed in their traditional role and are "simultaneously looked at and displayed, with their appearance coded for strong visual and erotic impact so that they can be said to connote to-be-looked-at-ness," whereas a male movie star's glamorous characteristics are "those of the more perfect, more complete, more powerful ideal ego."②

To decode a cinematic text is to uncover the various structures — systems of assumptions, beliefs, ideologies, and values embedded in images and discourses — to demonstrate how such structures generate myths, connotations, point of view, mode of address, and their significance for the work. An image of the master drawing a Japanese sword in Quentin Tarantino's film *Kill Bill*, for example, is a signifier that would offer (or provoke in) the spectator a fairly wide range of socio-psychological as well as aesthetic and cultural meanings: as a unique weapon related to the history and myth of the samurai, as sacred Japanese art, as a symbol of Japanese masculinity and violence, as a master-pupil ritual, as a representation of reverence for Japanese swordsmanship, as Tarantino's homage to and commercialization of "Oriental" martial arts, and others still.

Starting from the mid-1980s, poststructuralist theory began to adopt some new approaches to the semiotic studies of cinema together with new discoveries in sociology, philosophy, and history of intellectual thought. Building on his observations of the systems of

---

② See Mulvey's "Visual." For diverse applications of Mulvey's theory by other film and visual culture critics, see among others Silverman's *Subject*, Hansen, Easthope, Bergstrom and Doane, Cohan, and Mao.

punishment in Western European history, Michel Foucault in *Discipline and Punish* formulates a theory of what he calls "the political technology of the body" which presupposes that the body is mapped on a political terrain, that power relations "invest it, mark it, train it, torture it, force it to carry tasks, to perform ceremonies, to emit signs," that this politically invested body is bound up with its "economic use" in accordance with a network of power relations which "go right down into the depths of society" because of the forces of domination and resistance (*Discipline* 25–26). Constructing a history of Western European sexuality within a philosophical framework of rethinking the meaning of the self as a desiring subject, Michel Foucault published his most important and influential work *The History of Sexuality* (in three volumes), giving the subject philosophical legitimacy by delineating the technologies of production, of sign systems, of power, and of the self. According to Foucault, subjectivity, gender, and sexuality are fundamentally shaped by discourse and representation. In *The Use of Pleasure*, Foucault sees the body as a signifying site for deployment of various discourses such as those of madness, medicine, punishment, and sexuality. He says that the history of desiring man is a story about "an ethics for men: an ethics thought, written, and taught by men, and addressed to men [...] [a] male ethics, consequently, in which women figured only as objects" (*Use* 22). This line of thought was to shape the way we look at power relations in the arts, humanities, and social sciences in general and not only in visual (especially cinematic) representations of male and female bodies in particular. Although its main function was still to specify how meaning is socially created, subject to power relations like other kinds of social production, film semiotics enjoyed a major cross-fertilization with Marxism, new historicism, feminism, postcolonialism, and various other sociological approaches throughout the 1980s to early 1990s.[3] Film semiotics started to develop in a more political and sociological manner: the foregrounding of cinema's social function and political position of film directors and producers and their impact on particular groups of viewers, the importance of historical contexts within which different interpretations emerge, the function of cinema with its socio-psychological impact as a form

---

[3] During this period, there was an unprecedented number of interdisciplinary works on these subjects such as Bhabha's "The Other Question," Kuhn's *The Power of the Image*, Seidler's *Recreating Sexual Politics*, and Bad Object-Choices' *How Do I Look?*. Also see Sedgwick's *Between*, Spivak, Mulvey's *Visual*, Sedgwick's *Epistemology*, Stam et al., Silverman's *Male*, and Merck.

of mass entertainment.

From the early 1990s to the first decade of the 21st century, there has been a rise and popularity of gender and ethnic *identity politics* which focuses on defining the shared qualities that characterize a particular group or community or nation-state in relation to national/ transnational cinema, history, culture, and capitalism. Because of the huge impact of postcolonial theories, feminist and "Subaltern Studies" on arts, humanities, and social sciences, film studies has displaced earlier concerns with cinematic aesthetics and technologies, going beyond grand theories of history, linguistics, and psychoanalysis.④ Film semiotics has started to take a more (multi)culturally sensitive perspective, thus enabling us to think about cinema in relation to specific social reality, ideological framework, ethnicity, gender and cultural identity. This is why film critics today tend to stress issues of social, cultural, ethnic, and sexual stereotypes in cinematic representations, calling for "positive images" and searching for "alternative" forms of narrative that are more in line with shared values of a community, an ethnic group, or a nation. Such a search has brought forth not only a flowering of an enriched semiotic approach to the study of world cinema, but also some major developments in critical practices in relation to the re-writing of film history as well as re-situated perspectives from the "Native," the "Subaltern," the "Local," the "Non-Western," the "Ethnic," the "Marginalized," and the "Queer."⑤ Taking into account the social, historical, cultural, economic, ideological, and sexual issues as well as formal, linguistic, and aesthetic factors, semiotic film studies has become more and more interdisciplinary in its approach.

Shakespeare's Cinematic Renaissance: Enter Chinese *Hamlet*

As the most internationally acclaimed playwright and possibly the biggest "job provider" in the literary, theatrical, and visual world,

---

④ See, for example, Bhabha's *Nation*, Hall's "Cultural," Hooks, Said's *Culture*, Bhabha's *Location*, Shohat and Stam, Murray on gay and lesbian film and video, Young, Williams, and finally Gledhill and Williams on film as mass culture, return of history, genre and aesthetics, and cinema in the age of global media.

⑤ See, among others, Shohat and Stam on representations of colonialism, national identity and multiculturalism, Browne et al., Ehrlich and Desser, Austin, Lu, McQuillan and Byrne, Mao, Moore,Landy, Hu, Kaplan and Wang.

William Shakespeare as the Bard has been a permanent source of inspiration, wielding incomparable semiotic impact and cultural influence over literature and culture for the last four centuries. In the last hundred years, Shakespeare's plays have been extensively appropriated, recycled, and adapted for the screen, big or small, by directors of different ethnic, political, and cultural backgrounds from Scotland to Africa, from Hollywood to Beijing.⑥ After a tidal wave of adaptations of Shakespeare's plays for the screen by cinematic giants such as Laurence Olivier (*Henry V* in 1944, *Hamlet* in 1948, *Richard III* in 1955), Orson Welles (*Macbeth* in 1948, *Othello* in 1952, *King Lear* in 1953, *The Chimes at Midnight* which was based on *Richard II*, *Henry IV*, *Henry V* and *The Merry Wives of Windsor* in 1965), and Akira Kurosawa (*Throne of Blood* which was based on *Macbeth* in 1957), there came a relatively quiet period in the 1960s and 1970s, although there were hugely successful adaptations such as *West Side Story* (a musical based on *Romeo and Juliet*) by Robert Wise and Jerome Robbins in 1961 and *Macbeth* by Roman Polanski in 1971.

A major breakthrough in screen adaptation of Shakespeare plays came with Akira Kurosawa's *Ran* (based on *King Lear*, 1985) which took the whole world by storm. Kurosawa's masterful re-construction of the original drama, his artful cinematography with a powerful and painterly use of color became the major pillars of his semiotic empire. In the late 1980s, we saw the "Age of Kenneth Branagh," who almost single-handedly started and continued to lead a revolution in adapting Shakespeare for the big screen with his *Henry V* (1989), *Much Ado About Nothing* (1993), *Hamlet* (1996), and *Love's Labour's Lost* (2000). Indeed, this revolution ushered in a cinematic renaissance of Shakespeare in the late 20th century that reached a new height with John Madden's *Shakespeare in Love* (1998), which won seven Academy Awards at the 1999 Oscars.

Since the turn of the 21st century, the literary and cinematic

---

⑥ For a complete filmography of works based on Shakespeare's plays up to 1998, see Hong. See also the ShakespeareFlix List of Shakespeare Movies on DVD. For a not wholly authoritative survey of Shakespeare screen adaptations, see "List of William Shakespeare screen adaptations." According to this web site, more than 410 feature-length film versions of William Shakespeare's plays have been produced. As of July 2018, the Internet Movie Database lists Shakespeare as having writing credit on 1,371 films. This means that Shakespeare has been the most filmed author ever in any language. For a detailed chronicle of Shakespeare filmography, see Rothwell et al.

world has witnessed not only a revival of Shakespearean stories (especially the Hamlet story) adapted for contemporary novels such as John Updike's *Gertrude and Claudius* (2000), Matt Haig's *The Dead Fathers Club* (2006), and Lin Enger's *Undiscovered Country* (2008), but also a new series of movies (nearly 30 titles in all) that are based on the Shakespearean canon from the English-speaking countries as well as other countries such as Brazil, India, Italy, and China. Representative film adaptations include Michael Hoffman's *A Midsummer Night's Dream* (1999), Gil Junger's *Ten Things I Hate About You* (based on *Taming of the Shrew*, 1999), Julie Taymor's *Titus* (2000), Michael Almereyda's *Hamlet* (2000), Andrzej Bartkowiak's *Romeo Must Die* (2000), Klaus Knoesel's *Rave Macbeth* (2001), Billy Morrissette's *Scotland, PA* (based on *Macbeth*, 2001), Tim Blake Nelson's *O* (based on *Othello*, 2001), John Farrell's *Richard the Second* (2001), Kristian Levring's *The King Is Alive* (with *King Lear* as play within film, 2002), Trevor Nunn's *Merchant of Venice* (2003), Michael Radford's *Merchant of Venice* (2004), Bruno Barreto's *Romeo and Juliet Got Married* (2005, Brazil), the BBC's *Shakespeare Re-Told* series (2005), Andy Flickman's *She's the Man* (based on *Twelfth Night*, 2006), Kenneth Branagh's *As You Like It* (2006), Geoffrey Wright's *Macbeth* (2006), Vishal Bharadwaj's *Omkara* (based on *Othello*, 2006, India), Mike Cahill's *King of California* (based on *The Tempest*, 2007), Oscar Redding's *The Tragedy of Hamlet Prince of Denmark* (2007), Lim Won-kook's *Frivolous Wife* (based on *Taming of the Shrew*, 2008, South Korea), Volfango De Biasi's *Iago* (based on *Othello*, 2009, Italy), Bruce Ramsay's *Hamlet* (2011, Canada), V. K. Prakash's *Karmayogi* (based on *Hamlet*, 2012, Malaysia), Vishal Bhardwaj's *Haider* (partly based on *Hamlet*, 2014, India), Justin Kurzel's *Macbeth* (2015, UK and France), Aparna Sen's *Arshinagar* (a Bengali musical romance drama film based on *Romeo and Juliet*, 2015, India), Gabriel Manwaring's *M4M: Measure for Measure* (all-male cast, 2015, USA), Jayaraj's *Veeram* (English: *Valour*, based on *Macbeth*, 2016, India), and Casey Wilder Mott's *A Midsummer Night's Dream* (2017). And the list goes on ... but let us turn to China.

As most of us are aware, the growing interconnection between China and the rest of the world has made it necessary for the Chinese working in the film industry to balance domestic social, economic, and cultural priorities and international challenges, risks, and opportunities by a more *glocal* way of thinking: think globally and act locally. In Chinese cinema, various conscious efforts have been made to bridge the global and the local while critically reflecting on the concurrent dual process of *globalization* (dominated by the West and the various conflicting discourses thus generated) and *localization* (characterized by active resistance but also adaptation to that Western domination). In the following sections, I shall, within this general context of *glocalization*, take a comparative semiotic approach to the study of an important Chinese film — Feng Xiaogang's *The Banquet*, a transculturally creative adaptation of William Shakespeare's *Hamlet, Prince of Denmark*. Through a detailed analysis of some selected scenes/shots from both works, we shall see how meanings are constructed through cinematic verbal and visual codes and signs, such as narrative structure, and how intertextuality can be fruitfully used to highlight the value of intercultural communication.

Narrating Hamlet with Chinese Characteristics

For the last four hundred years since its "birth" at the turn of the 17th century, William Shakespeare's *Hamlet* has remained one of the most powerful and influential tragedies written in the English language. The play offers a perfect plot capable of endless retelling and adaptation by artists of diverse cultural and ethnic origins for different media such as paintings, novels, operas, and films. Being one of Shakespeare's most popular plays, *Hamlet* has been "the world's most filmed story after Cinderella" (Thompson and Taylor 17). Although film audiences and critics all over the world have seen great adaptations of *Hamlet* on the screen by directors from different countries such as Britain (e.g., Laurence Olivier in 1948, Kenneth Branagh in 1996), Japan (e.g., Akira Kurosawa in 1960), France (e.g., Claude Chabrol in 1962), Russia (e. g., Grigori Kozintsev in 1964), Italy (e. g., Franco Zeffirelli in 1990), and the United States (e.g., Michael Almereyda in 2000), the Hamlet story did not get rewritten on the Chinese/ Tibetan screen until 2006 when Feng Xiaogang and Sherwood Hu presented the world with their own narrative films *The Banquet* and *Prince of the Himalayas*. Since the very beginning of cinema, telling stories has been a major concern for filmmakers, and weaving an intriguing narrative has always been a key component in how we watch, think about, and reflect on the cinema. In these two films, the story of the "Permanent Prince" has been re-told in the Chinese and Tibetan historical contexts. For lack of space, I will focus on the former while referencing the latter when it is needed.

Using a familiar tale of passionate love, conspiracy, betrayal, and revenge based on the narrative template of Shakespeare's *Hamlet* with some *Macbeth* undertones, Feng Xiaogang succeeds in translating the story into an intriguing drama within the extravagantly adorned palace of ancient China. The time is 907 A.D. The once mighty empire of the Tang Dynasty (618–907) has fallen into ruins. Rebellion has spread across the land with its insurgents proclaiming their own kingdoms. This is the period known as the "Five Dynasties and Ten Kingdoms" (907–79). It is a chaotic era plagued by widespread turmoil, treachery amongst government officials, and a bitter struggle for power within the imperial family. Against this backdrop the Chinese Hamlet story begins. A tender affection has blossomed between the maiden Little Wan (Zhang Ziyi) and young Prince Wuluan (Daniel Wu), but his father, the Emperor, marries Little Wan himself. Desperate and heartbroken, Prince Wuluan disappears into the southern heartlands, seeking solace in the art of song and dance. Three years later, Prince Wuluan's uncle (Ge You) murders his brother, the Emperor, and usurps the throne. Empress Wan secretly sends her messengers to warn Prince Wuluan, urging his return. But she is unaware that the new Emperor, Emperor Li, has already dispatched assassins to prevent Prince Wuluan's return. Now, the Emperor, the Empress, the Crown Prince, Minister Yin Taichang (Ma Jingwu), and his son General Yin Sun (Huang Xiaoming) all have their own enemies they would like to finish off at the grand midnight banquet. As the desire for power, incestuous lust, jealousy, hate, and betrayal darken almost every character, tragedy becomes inevitable, and so is the destruction of the innocent Qing Nu — Minister Yin's daughter (the Chinese Ophelia) — who is in love with Prince Wuluan.

While retaining a similar narrative template or formula as Shakespeare's original story, a tragic tale of murder and revenge in the royal halls of medieval Denmark, with ingredients such as a ghost, poison, love, madness, and death, *The Banquet* focuses more on the intricate relationships between the five major characters — the Prince (Hamlet Wuluan), the King (Claudius Emperor Li), the Queen (Gertrude Empress Wan), the Minister (Polonius Minister Yin Taichang), and his daughter (Ophelia-Qing Nu). There are many commendable aspects in the film that we can highlight and talk about, such as the first-class performances by the leading actors/actresses, the stunning cinematography by Zhang Li, the great original music by Tan Dun (with traditional Chinese and modern

Western musical instruments, as he composed for Ang Lee's *Crouching Tiger, Hidden Dragon* and Zhang Yimou's *Hero*), the gorgeous costumes, fine props, effective use of masks, and creative editing, which all combine to move the narrative forward. But here let us focus on some major changes in the narrative of the Chinese *Hamlet*, re-created in the Chinese cultural and media contexts (Zhang Ziyi and Ge You as two of the most popular film stars from "the Orient"), an intensive epic drama that bridges and fuses different genres of love story, history, and action cinema.

First of all, there is a conspicuous shift of centrality and importance in the narrative structure of *The Banquet* from the Prince to the Queen. In other words, the narrative focus in the film is no longer on the Crown Prince (Wuluan) but on the Queen (Empress Wan). Empress Wan (formerly "Little Wan" and four years younger) is Prince Wuluan's former lover, who becomes his stepmother when the King takes her from the Prince and later when his uncle kills the King and also marries her. With this undercurrent of double incest running throughout the film (going far beyond the normal dose of "Oedipus complex" in Hamlet), Empress Wan becomes the pivotal point connecting all the other major characters as well as the controlling force that dominates the fate of all except her own. If we simply look at the conversational "exchange structure"⑦ and compare the number of turn-taking utterances in the original play *Hamlet* with that in *The Banquet*, we can clearly see this shift of focus (Figure 1) which reflects the change of power relations among the characters:

Figure 1: Number and percentage of turn-taking utterances in *Hamlet* and *The Banquet*

Character \ Play/Film	Prince Hamlet vs. Prince Wuluan	Ophelia vs. Qing Nu	King Claudius vs. Emperor Li	Queen Gertrude vs. Empress Wan	Total
Hamlet	358 (61.2%)	58 (9.9%)	102 (17.4%)	67 (11.5%)	**585** (100%)
The Banquet	67 (21.9%)	48 (15.7%)	91 (29.7%)	100 (32.7%)	**306** (100%)

⑦ According to Vimala Herman, "In the analysis of the dramatic discourse [...] many linguistic devices emerge as significant in unraveling the relation of power and levels of ideology. The exchange structure, for instance, emerges as a powerful device for not only the analysis of the discourse structure of drama, but also for studying the power relations among the characters of the play" (182).

In Shakespeare's original play *Hamlet*, the "Permanent Prince" registers over 60% of the total turn-taking utterances (358 out of 585) while Prince Wuluan makes slightly over 20% (67 out of 306) in *The Banquet*. The sharp drop of utterances for Prince Wuluan is made even more conspicuous by the equally sharp increase in turn-taking utterances by Empress Wan, from 11.5% to over 30%. Another significant shift is between King Claudius (17.4%) and Emperor Li (29.7%). In other words, the absolutely dominant position of the Prince in *Hamlet* is fundamentally weakened in *The Banquet* while the position of both Empress Wan and Emperor Li (the murderer and usurper) is considerably strengthened, as their complex relationship takes "center stage."

This "re-distribution" of power and dominance can be seen in the entire narrative structure of the film with long takes and big sequences that are conceived for and move around Empress Wan. After a short prologue on the historical context and Prince Wuluan's "self-exile" at the Song and Dance Theater of the Yue Heartland, the film dedicates a long sequence to Empress Wan with a two-minute tracking shot of her back while she walks down the lushly decorated and glittering yet somewhat gothic hallways of the imperial palace to the bedchamber of Prince Wuluan's uncle, who has usurped the throne. This revision of the play, centering around Empress Wan as a Lady-Macbeth-like woman of beauty and ambition, creates a large amount of dramatic tension and cinematic effect compared to the *Hamlet* storyline, making it more complicated and unpredictable. Yet the opening sequence already foretells her tragic fate as both a victim (an object in male traffic from the Prince to the Emperor to the Usurper) and victimizer who uses all means including "sacrifices" ("I have sacrificed more than enough for you and your father"), "vile exchanges," and direct or indirect killing/murdering to survive and conquer in the feudal patriarchal machinery — from a free-spirited Little Wan, to the Empress of the Late Emperor, then the Empress of the Usurper (Emperor Li), and finally Empress Her Majesty (short-lived as she is immediately back-stabbed by a dagger from an unknown source — maybe from her servant Ling but perhaps symbolically from the invisible hand of the omnipresent, feudal patriarchal system). The film depicts the process of her inevitable downfall.

Indeed, rather than "revenge," as in Shakespeare's original *Hamlet* and Olivier's film adaptation, "desire for power" becomes the dominant driving force in *The Banquet*'s narrative. In this intriguing Chinese tale of treachery, betrayal, and corruptive power, we see a "family" of plotters, conspirators and usurpers. Empress Wan's stunning seductive beauty is not only matched by her desire for power and dominance, but also balanced by the various unmitigated ambitions of the characters and their dark flaws as well as the purity and innocence of Qing Nu (literally meaning "green girl"), Minister Yin's daughter and General Yin's sister. Feng's film is ultimately about Empress Wan. It is the dark political world that triumphs, not the affective world Qing Nu dearly cherishes.

Secondly, we see a very different Ophelia in *The Banquet*. On the surface, Qing Nu in *The Banquet* is presented as a victim (of "unrequited love" and Hamlet's "madness") like Ophelia. Yet in true Shakespearean tradition, the Chinese film succeeds in re-creating Qing Nu as the tragic moral center to counterbalance both the destructive force of desire in Empress Wan and her inevitable downfall in the imperial court. Unlike Ophelia in *Hamlet*, Qing Nu is sunny and pure but never naïve. She is innocent and insistent, believing in love. At the royal banquet, just when Emperor Li is about to drink the poisoned wine prepared by Empress Wan in the name of honoring the Emperor, Qing Nu unexpectedly bursts into the palace hall, asking the Emperor to allow her and the palace dancers to perform "The Song from Yue." When asked why, Qing Nu replies, "It was the Crown Prince's favorite song. I want him to know that even if the whole world abandons him, I shall never do so, and my love for him will never die."

Earlier in the film, when Emperor Li "appoints" Prince Wuluan as "Ambassador to Khitan" (but in private instructs his Imperial Guards to kill the Prince near the border), Qing Nu begs the Emperor and Empress to allow her to accompany the Prince. Defying all obstacles and challenges (partly due to the amazing performance by Zhou Xun, one of the most talented and accomplished actresses in Asia), Qing Nu remains the moving spirit to the end when she dies of the poisoned wine, crushed by the multiple clashing sides (including her father, the Minister, and her brother, the General, in the name of "love and care") in a brutal and tragic struggle for the throne. In other words, the presentation of the character Qing Nu goes beyond "the Personal" to "the Socio-Political." In many ways, Qing Nu is a much more developed character in *The Banquet* than Ophelia in *Hamlet*.

Thirdly, compared with *Hamlet* and Olivier's film adaptation, *The Banquet* makes significant changes in terms of other important characters. For example, while *The Banquet* does not include characters like Horatio, Rosencrantz, Guildenstern, or Fortinbras, we see a significant change of two relatively important characters — Polonius (the King's Chief Counsellor) and his son Laertes (Ophelia's brother) into Minister Yin Taichang and his son General Yin Sun. This "localization" shows Feng Xiaogang's great insight and narrative skills in film-making, as it undoubtedly adds great narrative complexity to the power struggle and conspiracy in the Imperial Palace. They both genuinely care about Qing Nu, but they care more about their status and life in the palace. They are survivors but could not survive the power struggle there.

Let's hear the conversation between the father and son analyzing the critical situation and making their plan:

> **Father:** [...] Rather than wait to be discarded, she [Empress Wan] will take the risk and strike first.
> **Son:** She want to rule herself?
> **Father:** Exactly! Once she has succeeded in the assassination, she intends to denounce the Emperor as murderer and usurper. She will say that she is carrying out justice on behalf of the late Emperor. She wants us to rally and support her claim to the throne. This woman! Ah, this woman ...
> **Son:** Father, whose side should we take?
> **Father:** We have no choice. She has planned everything perfectly. When she took your sister in her hands, then asked you to save the Prince, it was not for personal reasons alone. It was to turn us into her accomplices so that we have nowhere to stand except by her side. She knows that we have no option now. If this woman succeeds, we must denounce her straightaway as a traitor and an assassin. The person who deserves to ascend the throne is not she but you.
> **Son:** (*Taken aback*) Father!
> **Father:** Are you afraid?
> **Son:** (*Firmly*) No! If heaven bestows this gift upon me, to refuse would be to disobey the gods.
> (*Father and son clinch their hands tightly together.*)

As the narrative develops, we see that their plan fails. Minister Yin, who has served three previous emperors with "honor and loyalty," is banished by Empress Wan in the end to a remote place with no chance of return, and General Yin, the son, in an attempt to kill Empress Wan after seeing his sister Qing Nu's death, is stabbed to death in the neck by the Empress. As a matter of fact, the change for these two characters in the film has great historical relevance.

Such characters (usurpers, traitors, rebels, murderers, and assassins, especially in the Chinese Imperial Court of so many dynasties) are not alien to the Chinese audiences (or readers) because they are found in almost every chapter of the long Chinese history, as recorded in many Chinese history books such as "Ranked Biographies" of *Records of the Grand Historian* by Sima Qian, which covers a 2500-year period from the age of the legendary Yellow Emperor (2717 B.C.–2599 B.C.) to the reign of Emperor Wu of Han (156 B.C.–87 B.C.) in Sima Qian's own time. In the last two decades, these "dark characters" increasingly find their way to the big screen in China, such as Jing Ke, the assassin in Chen Kaige's *The Emperor and the Assassin* (1998); traitorous Duke Wuhuan in his *The Promise* (2005); murderous General Tu'an Gu in his *Sacrifice* (2010); the three assassins Long Sky, Flying Snow, and Broken Sword in Zhang Yimou's *Hero* (2002), Leo and other rebel members in his *House of Flying Daggers* (2004), and assassins and "yin-yang" characters in his *Shadow* (2018).

Fourthly, another significant change to the original *Hamlet* or Olivier's *Hamlet* is the spectacular addition of Chinese *Kung Fu* or *Wuxia* (martial arts) as a prominent and integral part of the narrative, not as "an icing on the cake." In Greater China, when one mentions *Wuxia / Kung Fu Dianying* (martial arts films), some of the first few names that come to mind would be Bruce Lee, Jackie Chan and Jet Li. Yet when we talk about designer/choreographer for Wuxia / Kung Fu films, the very first name would be Yuen Woo-ping. Apart from being an accomplished film director, Yuen has also been the action choreographer / fight advisor for numerous Chinese / HK Cantonese film classics and some Hollywood action movies such as *The Bloody Fists* (1972), *Born Invincible* (1978), *Drunken Master* (1978), *Fist of Legend* (1994), *Lethal Weapon 4* (1998), *The Matrix* series (1999, 2003), *Crouching Tiger, Hidden Dragon* (2000), *Kill Bill I & II* (2003, 2004), *Kung Fu Hustle* (2004), *Fearless* (2006), *The Forbidden Kingdom* (2008), *The Grandmaster* (2013), *Once Upon a Time in Shanghai* (2013), *Man of Tai Chi* (2013), and *Ip Man 3* (2015), to name but a few.

Altogether there are six long sequences of *Kung Fu* fights or combats in *The Banquet*, which are all designed by Yuen Woo-ping, being both producer and action choreographer for the film. These sequences are designed not only to create visual splendor and excitement for the audience, but also to push forward the narrative and further intensify the multipolar conflicts among the characters in this epic drama: from the bloody slaughter at the Prince's Art

Theater by black riders (the assassins) sent by his uncle (Emperor Li), to the ambush by the emperor's men to kill the Prince at the snowy border with the Khitans' kingdom in the north, from the symbolic love combat dance between Empress Wan and Prince Wuluan in the imperial chamber to the dancing, fighting, killing, and deaths in the catastrophic finale. If we say that Shakespeare's Prince has been interpreted and presented in a thousand and one ways in different cultures over the centuries, it is the first time that we've had a *Kung Fu Hamlet* with distinctive Chinese characteristics.

Visual Power and Contributions of *The Banquet*

Compared with Shakespeare's original *Hamlet* and Laurence Olivier's film adaptation, *The Banquet* can be further examined in terms of its visual power and special contributions to both film language itself and the visualization of Shakespeare's dramatic language through its masterful production. As is well known, Feng Xiaogang used the same production team behind Ang Lee's internationally acclaimed *Crouching Tiger, Hidden Dragon* (2000). *The Banquet*'s spectacular visual power lies in the ingenious script based on Shakespeare's play with quasi-historical characters from ancient China, the outstanding cinematography by Zhang Li et al., the specially built extravagant palace and the exquisite Art Theater among the swaying lush bamboo forest by the Oscar-winning art director and designer Timmy Yip Kam-tim with meticulous attention to every detail, the innovative *mise-en-scène* (lighting, color, composition, camera/character movement etc.), the original music score by Tan Dun including the superior performance of singing by three top Chinese singers — Teng Ge'er, Zhang Liangying, and Zhou Xun, who also plays Qing Nu in the film, the rich and detailed costume designs including the use of so many kinds of masks (as homage to Greek-style tragedies), Yuen Woo-ping's amazing choreography including the numerous *kung fu* stunts, the masterful editing work by Liu Miaomiao, as well as the overall high quality of first-class performances of the leading and supporting actors/actresses. All these elements combine to create a mesmerizing and dream-like beauty in this quasi-historical epic drama. In many ways, *The Banquet* has successfully updated Shakespeare's *Hamlet* in terms of narrative structure, characterization, and language. Feng has rightly been called "the embodiment of a 'cultural broker'— a major player in the transnational circulation of cultural and commercial capital" (Ko 2, citing Yomi Braester).

In *The Banquet*, Prince Wuluan does not suffer from Hamlet's prolonged indecision or "madness," real or pretended, although melancholia is still one of his traits. If we look more closely, the Chinese adaptation has made the Prince both artistically and physically strong (er). No longer troubled by the philosophical question "To be or not to be," he becomes a man of action with few words, fully capable of not only performing, singing, dancing, and martial arts (busy ducking swords and spears), but also planning and executing his revenge on his uncle, the usurper. Unlike Hamlet in the original play and Olivier's film, Prince Wuluan even succeeds in consummating his sexual desire by making aggressive and violent advances upon Qing Nu, who genuinely loves the Prince.

It is also interesting to see that in Olivier's film adaptation of *Hamlet*, most of the dialogue that explains the reasons for Hamlet's excessive indecision and melancholia is cut out. But his acting advice to the players is almost entirely kept. Let's briefly look at "The Mousetrap" (the play's centerpiece) as an example. This is the key scene where Hamlet discovers that Claudius is guilty of murdering the old king (the confirmation of the murder story told by his father's ghost). The Prince announces:

> [...] I'll have these players
> Play something like the murther of my father
> Before mine uncle. I'll observe his looks,
> I'll tent him to the quick. If 'a do blench,
> I know my course. The spirit that I have seen
> May be a dev'l, and the dev'l hath power
> T' assume a pleasing shape, yea, and perhaps,
> Out of my weakness and my melancholy,
> As he is very potent with such spirits,
> Abuses me to damn me. I'll have grounds
> More relative than this — the play's the thing
> Wherein I'll catch the conscience of the King. (2.2. 594–605)

This soliloquy carries critical information as it is a crucial moment for both Hamlet and the development of the plot. But in Olivier's film, all this is gone except the last couplet. In *The Banquet*, the plan is fully visualized through several sequences, and the murder story (play-within-play) is effectively re-created as a Chinese mime show. The performance comes as a shock to the entire court as well as Empress Wan, and Emperor Li, who tries to conceal his outrage and guilt. He could have ordered his Imperial Guards to kill the

Prince, but instead he starts to clap his hands to "congratulate" the Prince and then issues an imperial order:

> **Emperor Li:** My dear nephew, I have been expecting you. Won't you take off your mask and let me look at your face?
> (*Wuluan reluctantly but calmly takes off his mask* .)
> **Emperor Li:** You're covered with sweat!
> **Prince Wuluan:** They're tears.
> **Emperor Li:** Come. Let me wipe them away for you.
> **Prince Wuluan:** (*Shouting*) No! Your sleeves are soaked with erysipelas. They reek of black scorpions.
> **Empress Wan:** (*With great concern*) Wuluan, you are not acting in a play now.
> **Emperor Li:** What a talented artist! How much you have grown in the last three years. It's time to take some serious responsibilities now.
> (*To Lord Chamberlain*)
> The Crown Prince is henceforth appointed Ambassador to Khitan. He will be escorted by the Imperial Guards and will depart promptly today. By command of the Emperor.
> **Empress Wan:** (*Controlling her sadness and helplessness*) His Majesty is doing this for your own good.

Indeed, one of the important innovations in *The Banquet* is the profound characterization of the major characters, especially Emperor Li, the usurper. He is not created as a typical Shakespearean or Greek archvillain but a character richly layered with many levels, who defies being generalized as a simple or flat character. At an intimate moment in the royal bedchamber, we hear the following conversation between him and Empress Wan:

> (*Emperor Li wearing the armor and helmet of the late Emperor*)
> **Empress Wan:** This helmet does not sit well on you.
> **Emperor Li:** To call Your Emperor "you" is not appropriate. The correct address is "Your Majesty."
> **Empress Wan:** It is hard for me to adapt so quickly, Brother-in-law.
> **Emperor Li:** Indeed this is not a good fit. I shall have a new one made. The kingdom shall not wait. Seal the door, Sister-in-law.
> **Empress Wan:** The correct address is "Empress." Your brother should not have trusted you.
> **Emperor Li:** The death of the late Emperor had nothing to do with me.
> **Empress Wan:** Is the Crown Prince still alive?

> **Emperor Li:** Sister-in-law seems very concerned.
>
> **Empress Wan:** I am his step-mother after all.
>
> **Emperor Li:** He is four years older than you are.
>
> **Empress Wan:** Brother-in-law knows how I remove my make-up?
>
> **Emperor Li:** Not just your make-up but also the way you enter your bath.
>
> **Empress Wan:** Will brother-in-law let the Prince go free?
>
> (*Li puts his hand down Wan's breast and Wan tries to stop it.*)
>
> **Emperor Li:** Will you let my hand go free?

In this sequence, Emperor Li is presented not simply as someone cold-hearted who can commit murder (of his brother) for the throne and prevent the Crown Prince from the throne by "appointing" him "Ambassador to Khitan" (to have him killed at the Khitan border), but also someone who is capable of expressing his loving feelings (while giving the Empress a thorough Chinese-style massage with effective camera work under soft lighting) for the woman he has always adored and perhaps even loved, although he is well aware that "a beautiful woman is great danger to his kingdom."

A most revealing moment comes at the grand finale when Emperor Li realizes that it is Empress Wan who has planned to kill him by poisoning his wine and also when Prince Wuluan declares that he wants to finish the business between them with his sword. Holding the poisoned wine cup in his hand, Emperor Li delivers a speech (mainly a series of rhetorical questions), addressing the Crown Prince as the rest of the whole imperial court is in the grip of horror:

> Was it the desire for revenge that hauled you out of the valley of death?
>
> Or was it your melancholy that touched the hearts of women so that their tenderness wove a web of protection around you?
>
> Or perhaps, a million calculations cannot compare with one pure heart?
>
> (*Looking up*)
>
> Or maybe it is you, brother, who has been protecting your son all along, so that he can spill my blood and restore your honor?
>
> If this is what you want, brother, then let me appease you tonight.
>
> (*Going up to Empress Wan with the poisoned wine*)
>
> You offered me a toast.
>
> How can I refuse?
>
> (*He drinks the wine and dies in Empress Wan's lap.*)
>
> **Lord Chamberlain:** (*declares*) The Emperor has passed away!

Taking his own life by drinking the poisoned wine, Emperor Li seems to have partially regained some dignity and even honor. Perhaps the director wants to convey to the audience that no matter how evil or treacherous Emperor Li might be, there is still some human decency, in a Shakespearean sense, that is buried or lies dormant in a deep corner of the human heart, although the film repeats a few times that the most poisonous thing in the world is the human heart. This philosophical paradox is found in several characters in the film, especially in the Emperor and the Empress. This genuine humanistic concern is one of the factors that seem to distinguish Feng Xiaogang from many other contemporary Chinese film directors.

An Extra Scene for the Chinese-Tibetan Prince

As an intertextual cross-reference for Feng Xiaogang's adaptation of Shakespeare's *Hamlet*, it may be helpful to add a brief comparison between *The Banquet* and another adaptation of the same play in the Chinese-Tibetan context: Sherwood Hu's film *Prince of the Himalayas*, also produced in 2006 and set in ancient Tibet under the shadow of the Himalayas. The young prince Lhamoklodan (Hamlet) learns of his father's mysterious death and returns to the Kingdom of Jiaobo. Troubled by the sudden remarriage of his mother Nanm (Gertrude) to his uncle Kulo-ngam (Claudius), he swears he will find out the truth of his father's death. His obsession of revenge overwhelms his spirit and overshadows his love for Odsaluyang (Ophelia). When he points his sword at the new king, Queen Nanm finally tells her son the true identity of his uncle — her true love and the prince's biological father. In the struggle to face his destiny and fight his demons, a new king is born.

Compared with the original *Hamlet* and *The Banquet*, we can see four major changes / shifts in the Tibetan narrative:

(1) The focus is on Prince Lhamoklodan and his relationship with the Queen, his Uncle, and the love between the Prince and Odsaluyang (Ophelia).

(2) Old King is the intruder (evil ghost) while the Uncle is the Queen's real lover.

(3) Odsaluyang gives birth to a new king in Fairy Lake (Buddhist Reincarnation).

(4) The Wolf Lady is added as witness, mediator, narrator, and philosopher.

Figure 2: Number and percentage of turn-taking utterances in Hamlet, The Banquet, and Prince of the Himalayas

Play/Film \ Character	Prince Hamlet vs. Prince Wuluan vs. Lhamoklodan	Ophelia vs. Qing Nu vs. Odsaluyang	King Claudius vs. Emperor Li vs. Prince's Uncle	Queen vs. Empress Wan vs. Queen Nanm	Total
Hamlet	358 (61.2%)	58 (9.9%)	102 (17.4%)	67 (11.5%)	585 (100%)
The Banquet	67 (21.9%)	48 (15.7%)	91 (29.7%)	100 (32.7%)	306 (100%)
Prince of the Himalayas	113 (44.7%)	27 (10.7%)	54 (21.3%)	59 (23.3%)	253 (100%)

In *Hamlet*:
Hamlet (61.2%) → King Claudius (17.4%) → Queen (11.5%) → Ophelia (9.9%)

In *The Banquet*:
Empress Wan (32.7%) → Emperor Li (29.7%) → Prince Wuluan (21.9%) → Qing Nu (15.7%)

In *Prince of the Himalayas*:
Prince Lhamoklodan (44.7%) → Queen Nanm (23.3%) → Prince's Uncle (21.3%) → Odsaluyang (10.7%).

Umberto Eco points out that, in a cinematic text, there are so many transformations involved from the object to the representation of the object that the image itself has none of the properties of the object represented, but that, at most, the iconic sign reproduces some of the conditions of perception. Indeed, like literary narration, a narrative film provides a set of representational, organizational, and discursive cues that deliver the story information to the audience. It can be analyzed in relation to history, language, culture, and society as well as modes of production, style, and aesthetics.

In many ways, *Prince of the Himalayas* can be seen as another good example of reproducing Shakespeare's *Hamlet* as a *glocalized* Chinese-Tibetan text. As the story unfolds amidst the mythical beauty of the landscape of Tibet, home for China's Tibetan Buddhism, the *mise-en-scène* of film offers the audience a very different viewing experience from what they have in *Hamlet* or *The Banquet*. *Mise-en-scène* in our context refers to how the director, the script writers, set and costume designers, cameramen, music composers, and other film artists work together to create the spatial elements which form a coherent filmic world which the fictional characters inhabit and where they stage their new *Hamlet* drama: we have the towering Himalaya Mountains, the

Tibetan Royal Court, the Tibetan costumes and objects/props, the Evil King on horseback, the knowledgeable, wise, and kind Wolf Lady appearing and disappearing without warning, the uncle as a kind, patient, thoughtful lover/husband and also a loving father. We also have the Tibetan Ophelia, who dies of childbirth on Fairy Lake and has a spectacular Buddhist water burial, as well as the Tibetan Hamlet, who suffers from indecision and melancholia but rides naked on horseback and later becomes a father. All these Tibetan (Buddhist) elements, through effective composition and the articulation of space, carry a different kind of narrative power and construct different meanings, just as the characters' dialogues in the Tibetan language do.

Conclusion: Shakespeare *Postcolonial* and *Glocal*

The success of *The Banquet* in China, as one of the best examples of films that can strike a good balance between commercial and art cinema, shows Feng Xiaogang's great confidence in his command of visual codes and story-telling skills, making one rethink whether the domination of Hollywood over the rest of the world by its visual hegemony defeats the logic of its own intellectual egalitarianism. Although Hollywood continues to be deeply rooted in American values and politically and artistically conservative, it is no longer just "American" or "Western" but "culturally cosmopolitan." Sincere homage to Western literary classics such as Shakespeare's *Hamlet*, combined with profound awareness of the wealth and gravity of Chinese history, the forces of the market (known as "Socialist Market Economy with Chinese Characteristics"), the power of Hollywood, and the value of Kung Fu tradition, seems to speak a new style of Chinese visual hybridity in the postmodern age of *glocalization*. This hybridity, as can also be seen in Sherwood Hu's *Prince of the Himalayas*, fashions the "East" as an alternative visual space to appropriate and articulate the great value of both the Chinese literary and cultural legacy and the Shakespearean heritage as intercultural communication for a new generation of audiences.

The American-Chinese scholar Gu Mingdong observes that under the heavy pressures of digital revolution and STEM (science, technology, engineering, mathematics), literature departments around the globe are facing a bleak reality: the dwindling of a reading public and shrinking numbers of literature majors in colleges. Gu points out that many scholars in the West, "in response to Derrida's prophecy about the death of literature, have contemplated the awkward situation of refined literature and raised two practical questions":

(1) In colleges today where STEM courses predominate, how can literary teaching re-energize itself?

(2) In the world dominated by new media and telecommunications, how can we revive the public's interest in reading classic literary works?

Gu briefly examines C. P. Snow's idea of "Two Cultures" and the public's strong interest in science fiction, but carefully explores the close connections between digital games and James Joyce's fiction and investigates the possible functions of science fiction and digital games in resuscitating the public interest in literature. Reflecting on "the way out" for traditional literature pressurized by telecommunications, Gu proposes the concept of "greater literature" in preparation for the coming of a post-literary era. This would, undoubtedly, call for a new way of thinking about our shared literary heritages (Chinese and Western) and also our changing social reality in inter-/intra-/trans-cultural terms.

Films such as *The Banquet* and *Prince of the Himalayas* in China seem to have begun to break our cultural singularity and the insularity of ethnocentrism as well as the prominent ideology that represents, imagines, and translates the incomprehensible " Other " through creative visual codes and cinematic conventions. In this historically, linguistically, and culturally transformative process of film adaptation from literary texts to media products, Shakespeare in general and *Hamlet* in particular have become both *postcolonial* and *glocal* in the post-literary era. If we understand cinema as a Promethean apparatus that visualizes, in one way or another, the concerns, issues, fears, and hopes of our contemporary world, we would then agree that this would not be the "shimmer of a single dream," as the theme song of *The Banquet* says, but a burning bush for cinema's social and aesthetic future as well as for enlarging/extending the great role of literary texts (ancient and modern classics from both the East and the West) for effective intercultural communication among us all.

References

Andrew, J. Dudley. *The Major Film Theories: An Introduction*. Oxford UP, 1976.

Austin, Guy. *Contemporary French Cinema: An Introduction*. Manchester UP, 1996.

Bad Object-Choices. *How Do I Look? Queer Film and Video*. Bay Press, 1991.

Barthes, Roland. *Mythologies*. Editions du Seuil, 1957. Translated by Annette Lavers. Vintage, 1972, 2000.

Bergstrom, Janet, and Mary Ann Doane, editors. "The Spectatrix." Special issue of *Camera Obscura 20−21* (1989).

Bhabha, Homi. *Location of Culture*. Routledge, 1994.

—, ed. *Nation and Narration*. Routledge, 1990.

—. "The Other Question — The Stereotype and Colonial Discourse." *Screen*, vol. 24, no. 6, 1983, pp. 18−36.

Blackmore, Susan. *The Meme Machine*. Oxford UP, 1999.

Browne, Nick, Paul G. Pickowicz, Vivian Sobchack, and Esther Yau, editors. *New Chinese Cinemas: Forms, Identities, Politics*. Cambridge UP, 1994.

Buckman, Lorne M. *Still in Movement: Shakespeare on Screen*. Oxford UP, 1991.

Cohan, Steven. "Masquerading as the American Male in the Fifties." *Male Trouble*, edited by Constance Penley and Sharon Willis. U of Minnesota P, 1993, pp. 203−32.

Easthope, Anthony. *What a Man's Gotta Do: The Masculine Myth in Popular Culture*. Paladin Grafton, 1986.

Eco, Umberto. "Articulations of the Cinematic Code." *Cinematics*, vol. 1, no. 1, 1970, pp. 590−605.

Ehrlich, Linda C., and David Desser, editors. *Cinematic Landscapes: Observations on the Visual Arts and Cinema of China and Japan*. U of Texas P, 1994.

Foucault, Michel. *Discipline and Punish: The Birth of the Prison*. Translated by Alan Sheridan. Allen Lane, 1977.

—. *The Use of Pleasure*. *The History of Sexuality* Vol. 2. Translated by Robert Hurley. Pantheon, 1985.

Ghosh, Ranjan, and J. Hillis Miller. *Thinking Literature Across Continents*. Duke UP, 2016.

Gledhill, Christine, and Linda Williams, editors. *Reinventing Film Studies*. Arnold & Oxford UP, 2000.

Gu, Mingdong. "On the Way Out for Traditional Literature in the Post-Literary Era: Science Fiction, Digital Games, and Joycean Novels." *Foreign Literature Studies*, vol. 3, 2018, pp. 77−87.

Hall, Stuart. "Cultural Identity and Diaspora." *Identity, Community, Culture, Difference*, edited by Jonathan Rutherford. Lawrence & Wishart, 1990, pp. 222−37.

Hand, Molly. "Review of *Ye Yan/The Banquet* (directed by Feng Xiaogang)." *Shakespeare*, vol. 4, no. 4, 2008, pp. 429−33.

Hansen, Miriam. "Pleasure, Ambivalence, Identification: Valentino and Female Spectatorship." *Cinema Journal*, vol. 25, no. 4, 1986, pp. 6−32.

Heath, Stephen. *Questions of Cinema*. Indiana UP, 1981.

Herman, Vimala. *Dramatic Discourse: Dialogue as Interaction in Plays*. Routledge, 1995.

Hong, Hong. "Shakespeare Filmography." *Film Appreciation Journal*, no. 91, 1998, pp. 52−56.

hooks, bell. "Representing Whiteness in the Black Imagination." *Cultural*

Studies, edited by Lawrence Grossberg, Cary Nelson and Paula A. Treichler, Routledge, 1992, pp. 338–46.

Hu, Jubin. *Projecting a Nation: Chinese National Cinema Before 1949*. Hong Kong UP, 2003.

Internet Movie Database (IMDb). William Shakespeare. www.imdb.com/name/nm0000636/?ref_ = fn_al_nm_1. Accessed 17 Aug. 2018.

Kaplan, E. Ann, and Ban Wang, editors. *Trauma and Cinema: Cross-Cultural Explorations*. Hong Kong UP, 2008.

Ko, Yu Jin. "Martial Arts and Masculine Identity in Feng Xiaogang's *The Banquet*." *Asian Shakespeares on Screen: Two Films in Perspective*, Special issue, edited by Alexa Huang, *Borrowers and Lenders: The Journal of Shakespeare and Appropriation*, vol. 4, no. 2, 2009. www.borrowers.uga.edu/.

Kuhn, Annette. *The Power of the Image: Essays on Representation and Sexuality*. Routledge, 1985.

Landy, Marcia, editor. *The Historical Film: History and Memory in Media*. Rutgers UP, 2001.

"List of William Shakespeare screen adaptations." Edited 13 Aug. 2018. Wikipedia. Accessed 17 Aug. 2018.

Lu, Sheldon Hsiao-peng. *Transnational Chinese Cinemas: Identity, Nationhood, Gender*. U of Hawaii P, 1997.

McQuillan, Martin, and Eleanor Byrne. *Deconstructing Disney*. Pluto Press, 1999.

Mao, Sihui. *Technologising the Male Body: British Cinema 1957 – 1987*. Foreign Language Teaching and Research Press, 1999.

Merck, Mandy, editor. *The Sexual Subject: A Screen Reader in Sexuality*. Routledge, 1992.

Metz, Christian. *Film Language: A Semiotics of the Cinema*. Translated by Michael Taylor. Oxford UP, 1974. (*Essais sur la signification au cinéma*, 2 vols., 1968, 1973.)

—. "The Imaginary Signifier." *Screen*, vol. 16, no. 2, 1975, pp. 14–76.

Moore, Rachel O. *Savage Theory: Cinema as Modern Magic*. Duke UP, 2000.

Mulvey, Laura. *Visual and Other Pleasures*. Macmillan, 1989.

—. "Visual Pleasure and Narrative Cinema." *Screen*, vol. 16, no. 3, 1975, pp. 6–18.

Murray, Raymond. *Image in the Dark: An Encyclopedia of Gay and Lesbian Film and Video*. TLA Publications, 1994.

Nienhauser, William. "Sima Qian and the Shiji." *The Oxford History of Historical Writing, Volume 1: Beginnings to AD 600*, edited by Andrew Feldherr and Grant Hardy, Oxford UP, 2011, pp. 463–84.

Prince, Stephen. "The Discourse of Pictures: Iconicity and Film Studies." *Film Quarterly*, vol. 47, no. 1, 1993, pp. 16 – 28. (*Film Theory and Criticism*. Edited by Leo Braudy and Marshall Cohen. Oxford UP, 1999.)

Rothwell, Kenneth S. et al. "Shakespeare on Screen: An International Filmography and Videography." internetshakespeare.uvic.ca/Theater/spotlight/2005–10/filmintro1/. Accessed 17 Aug. 2018.

Said, Edward. *Culture and Imperialism*. Chatto & Windus, 1993.

—. *Orientalism*. Pantheon, 1978.

Saussure, Ferdinand de. *Course in General Linguistics*. 1916. Translated by Wade Baskin, edited by Perry Meisel and Haun Saussy. Columbia UP, 1959.

Sedgwick, Eve Kosofsky. *Between Men: English Literature and Male Homosocial*

Desire. Columbia UP, 1985.

—. *Epistemology of the Closet*. U of California P, 1990.

Seidler, Victor J. *Recreating Sexual Politics: Men, Feminism, and Politics*. Routledge, 1991.

Shakespeare, William. *The Riverside Shakespeare*. Edited by G. Blakemore Evans. Houghton Mifflin, 1974.

The ShakespeareFlix List of Shakespeare Movies on DVD. www.shakespeareflix. net/2011/06/shakespeareflix-list-of-shakespeare.html. Accessed 17 Aug. 2018.

Shohat, Ella, and Robert Stam. *Unthinking Eurocentrism: Multiculturalism and the Media*. Routledge, 1994.

Silverman, Kaja. *Male Subjectivity at the Margins*. Routledge, 1992.

—. *The Subject of Semiotics*. Oxford UP, 1983.

Sima Qian. *Records of the Grand Historian*. Translated by Burton Watson. Chinese Univ. of Hong Kong, 1993.

Spivak, Gayatri Chakravorty. *In Other Worlds: Essays in Cultural Politics*. Routledge, 1987.

Stam, Robert et al. *New Vocabularies in Film Semiotics*. Routledge, 1992.

Thompson, Ann, and Neil Taylor, editors. *Hamlet*. The Arden Shakespeare. 3rd Series. Thomson Learning, 2006.

Tsai, Hsiu-chih. "Consolation to the Lovelorn? The Return of the Unforgotten in *2046*." *Chinese Semiotic Studies*, vol. 1, 2009, pp. 279–94.

Williams, Linda. "Film Bodies: Gender, Genre, and Excess." *Film Theory and Criticism*, edited by Leo Braudy and Marshall Cohen, Oxford UP, 1999, pp. 701–15.

Wollen, Peter. *Signs and Meaning in Cinema*. 3rd ed. Secker & Warburg, 1972.

Young, Robert. *Colonial Desire: Hybridity in Theory, Culture and Race*. Routledge, 1995.

5

They Do But Jest? — Theater in Different Cultural Ecosystems

Agota REVESZ
Free University Berlin

Summary: This chapter considers theater as a social act, with significant systemic divergences between China and Europe. It offers four specific case studies for an awareness of what is expected of a production concerning value orientations and how the concept of "theater" is used. The focus of analysis is a British, a German, and two Chinese performances: two different European *Hamlet*s and two Chinese versions of *The Orphan of Zhao*. What is analyzed is not the performances, but discourse analysis of what has appeared about them in the online mainstream media. It turns out that, in China, the public performance of a narrative gives occasion for an articulation of cultural identity, serving as the iconic representation and consequently the reinforcement of the whole community. By contrast, European theater tends to consider the work of art as one artist's communication with the community: the Adornian ideal of art as criticism disclosing social contradictions and bringing about emancipatory social change is at the heart of contemporary European theater production.

Introduction

The present study has grown out of my work in China in the area of cultural diplomacy and my more recent research on current developments in traditional Chinese theater. While I was busy facilitating cultural exchange projects, it struck me that Europe and China have widely diverging understandings of the concept of theater. By "theater" I mean here neither the actor's work, nor the physical appearance of a production — I am talking about the very basics of why people gather together at a particular place to watch a narrative acted out by live performers. In this study I look at theater as a social act, "representing and establishing relationships which fulfill social functions" (Fischer-Lichte and Riley 26, similarly Alter 15–16), and will try to point at differences in theater's social mission. Initially I was trying hard to avoid the standard comparative aspect based on an East-West binary, but as I reached deeper into the topic, certain very conspicuous elements stood out, and it became increasingly difficult not to see significant systemic divergences.

The reader will be guided through four specific case studies to an awareness of what is expected of a production and how the concept of "theater" is used. The focus of my analysis will be a British, a German and two Chinese performances: two different European *Hamlet*s and two Chinese versions of *The Orphan of Zhao*. I decided to choose contemporary performances of such established literary works in order to see the approach to what is considered an iconic cultural treasure.

This will *not* be an analysis of the performances, but discourse analysis of what has appeared about them in the online mainstream media. Those are the outlets that reflect and shape public opinion the most, and I have tried to select and introduce a wide variety of these texts. I have chosen to focus on the reviews, as they tend to be "the most influentially constitutive of memory and value," since the critic's "presence at the performance acts as a surrogate for our own" (Prescott 4, 5) — although Prescott writes about Shakespearean performances, this statement seems generally applicable to the process and afterlife of theater criticism. For Europe I have concentrated on what has appeared in the English and German languages, for China I have selected Chinese texts only, as my focus was on the domestic reception of these productions. All translations in the current article are mine.

I. Two Hamlets

Hamlet 2008

(Schaubühne Berlin, director: Thomas Ostermeier, Hamlet: Lars Eidinger)

The performance that from now on I will call *Hamlet2008* was jointly produced with Festival Athens and Festival Avignon, and first performed at Athens Epidaurus Festival in July 2008. Since then it has toured 28 major cities worldwide, and has become a brand name for German theater. From among the ample supply of criticism, I will pick out those chains of thought that seem to be the common denominator in the reviews.

Most critics, especially in the English-language media, stress the production's being "live" theater (see Gardner, Kellaway, and Orr). While on the one hand "live" apparently stands for a concept of theater as non-text-based and essentially independent from the literary sources, this designation also seems to convey deeper expectations. It stands out as very apparent that critics hail Ostermeier's playing against the rules, and consider this directorial stance as the starting point for the performance's superiority.

> This is a ripping-up of the rule book — if there were ever any rules to staging Shakespeare. More than anything, this mind-blowing, spit-hurling, earth-moving evening [...] is about what theatre can do. (Kellaway)
>
> [...] *live* theatrical experience, where neither actor nor audience can escape the clutches of the direction. Directors take note: *this* is the theatre we need. [...] The conventions of theatre are stripped away, and [...] there is much mockery of theatre as an art, as a device and with it the audience itself. (Orr, italics in the original)
>
> But that is precisely the piece's thrill: to watch Ostermeier sink his teeth into the text and shake the carcass for his own ends. That is, perhaps, the only way to get to its heart today. (Trueman)
>
> Director Thomas Ostermeier seems intent on proving a thesis that others might have pondered but dared not posit. (Fisher)

The critical discourse constructs a set of dichotomies: conventional–unconventional, cowardly–daring, and hence dead–live. These dichotomies are strongly interdependent, and convey an understanding that a director (whose figure necessarily defines the borders within any kind of "director's theater") wishing to create "live" theater needs to go against whatever is codified as "tradition." One must admit, though, that there has never been an actual "rule book" — as Kellaway herself posits this question — but a steady sequence of epochal/generational performance characteristics, in which each new generation is expected to redefine itself in opposition to their predecessors. The one thing that seems to be the constant of this establishment is an expectation of deconstruction and disorder — a strongly anti-traditionalist approach. It does not and cannot mean completely doing away with the perceived traditions at any given time, as the very essence of each new work of art is an active and deconstructionist dialogue with these same traditions. The claim that Ostermeier's theater is "not for purists" (Kellaway, similarly Trueman) signals a new declaration of identity and simultaneously the creation of a new tradition.

Reading through the English-language criticism of *Hamlet2008*, we can discern sharp disapproval of what the critics deem as the current British practice.

> If theatre is a live product then Thomas Ostermeier's *Hamlet* is a wake-up call to British directors who continually present the undead of theatre [...] It is a *Hamlet* that reaches out and demands that you take notice, but there's also a distinction between those directors who dare to question our classics, and those who merely reproduce dead pieces. In this instance, I'd take Ostermeier's live *Hamlet* than any other attempted version. This is what an audience needs — a living, breathing piece of theatre. (Orr)

When they [i.e., Ivo van Hove or Ostermeier] stage Shakespeare, they do so with an urgent vividness that persuades us that he could indeed be our greatest living playwright. (Gardner, "British")

> In Britain, we tend to take our Shakespeare as it comes. Directors that dare draw out — or worse, impose — particular concepts are best advised to round off the edges and tie up the loose ends. The warning message: please don't feed the purists. (Trueman)

There is thus a further aspect (and further items) to add to the above list of dichotomies: that of "us—them," with "us" standing for general British theater practice, while "them" are the innovators from outside (van Hove is Belgian, Ostermeier German) offering a higher-standard approach. The authors — no doubt unknowingly — apply a national cultural essentialism in their effort to reproach their "own" theater makers for not living up to present-day expectations and reproducing only "the undead of theatre." It seems there is an understanding that innate directors cannot live up to the greatness and originality of their "own" bard, either because they do not dare to act as iconoclasts, or because their view is restricted. Cultural distance is interpreted as an important aspect of innovative artistic creation: the further you are from the cultural icon, the more freedom of expression you apparently enjoy — a badly needed freedom, if you are expected to "tear open classic plays, mash together their innards and reassemble them" (Bowie-Sell).

The fact that the protagonist in *Hamlet 2008* is depicted as literally mad is also deemed unanimously positive among British critics. The authors do not straightforwardly apply the idea of divine madness, but Hamlet's (and the production's) unconventionality connects to the perception that insanity represents a deeper understanding than sanity. Through this "real" madman we gain something that would otherwise not be discernible:

> [M]ad, manic and almost deafeningly raucous, [...] the whole two hours and 45 minutes of the finest acting is bonkers. (Fearon)

> Yet this is still a Hamlet which feels supremely truthful. As Eidinger splutters and cavorts his way through his role you can see a raw embodiment of the visceral internal struggle of Shakespeare's words.
>
> There's an irreverent brutality to Ostermeier's direction. He is intent on making each moment of insanity and rage onstage remind us of our own frustrations: "It's all theatre" Hamlet smirks at one point, "and yet also reality." (Bowie-Sell)

> Hamlet's madness becomes, not a plot device, but the plot itself. "Is Hamlet really mad, or just acting?" is the key question students ask of the play. (A more contemporary question is to ask if Hamlet is clinically depressive).
>
> The most famous moment in the play is not one of action, but of morbid self-reflection: "To be or not to be." This is what, in the 20th century, would be called "existential angst" (or self-obsession). [...] Shakespeare anticipated, or invented, the modern condition. (Murphy)

In their fascination with insanity, the reviewers employ the ideas of 18th century Romanticism: as "in [Goethe's] *Tasso* the poet enters for the first time upon the historical stage as if to dramatize the madness that produces literature itself" (Thiher 135), here madness — both the protagonist's and the production's — produces theater itself. Especially for the representation of the "modern condition," for the realization of "our own frustrations," for a raw and straightforward "In-Yer-Face Theatre" (Fisher) we seem to need "mutilation and excess" (Fisher).

In close connection with the idea of insanity, the performance also evokes the Bakhtinian grotesque and the carnivalesque (see

Bakhtin 328). Hamlet's body in the fat-suit is increasingly distorted, protrudes into the outer world; the stage, covered in mud and gradually in garbage, sinks into physical chaos. As Fisher notices: "actors [...] do the strangest and most unsettling things and even invade the audience." This evokes a generally positive response among critics, giving them the opportunity to applaud it with a combination of adjectives that knead what is considered to be the basest (e.g., bodily fluids) into one dough with emotional or rational depth: "mind-blowing, spit-hurling, earth-moving" (Kellaway); "dirty, blood-spurting and heart-pounding" (Orr); "brash and noisy, sometimes infuriating, frequently illuminating, occasionally heart-stopping" (Gardner, "Hamlet"). It is rare to find a critic like Nice to see it as "Ostermeier's oddly dated theatre of repulsion."

The very same criteria apply to the acting of Lars Eidinger, who is hailed for his identification with the role. As Nestruck writes: "It was the first time I wondered not only whether Hamlet was going crazy, but whether the actor playing Hamlet was as well." Eidinger does his best to reinforce his image of achieving such a level of stage presence that it is reaching into the "real." In an interview with *Zeit Online* he said "There have been performances of Hamlet, when I thought I would fall dead"①(Kalle). His ecstasy gets associated with divine madness, where the self's boundaries are blurred and the agent opens an insight into other realms: "Eidinger's Hamlet is not a pretty sight, and you can't take your eyes off of him. Mad, certainly; magnificent and doomed, too" (Gardner, "Hamlet").

The play on balancing between artefact and life brings us back to the question of "live" theater. Critics are also unanimously enthusiastic about Eidinger's constant improvisations with the audience. In Orr's opinion, confronting the audience turns the play "into more than just a presentation, but an engagement." Crawley finds that "freedom [...] makes it one of the most arresting interpretations of the play," and cites Ostermeier saying "sometimes I have to swallow my anger because he [Eidinger] doesn't always hit the points he should — but it's part of the freedom he got." Eidinger in a different interview confirms the above statement: "This is what theater is about. You know, it's just there for the moment. This is also why I am trying to improvise — be more electric" (Renz-Hotz).

"Freedom" and "life/energy" seem to have their foundation in

---

① "Es gab schon Vorstellungen von Hamlet, da dachte ich, dass ich gleich tot umfalle."

the ephemerality of theater, and the concept that theater reaches its peaks when it crosses the border and becomes not so much a work of art, but rather a work of life. Contemporary English-language theater criticism seems to owe a lot to the Stanislavski method, even if on the surface we might sense a departure from it. Ephemerality also involves instability and unpredictability, and the co-creative presence of the audience: sharing the same time and space is a challenge not only for the actor, but also for the audience as well. "Liveness" (Fischer-Lichte) is the personal encounter between performer and spectator at every passing moment, and also the basically tragic experience of the passage of time.

At this point, it is worth a thought that none of the critics mention the lack of Fortinbras. The need for a correction of the time "out of joint"[2] is completely missing, not only from the performance, but also from the reviewers' expectations. The existence of a corrective power is neither possible nor desirable: this is a revenge tragedy where the reestablishment of justice is not even discussed.

Ostermeier has said in an interview: "[I]t's also important to say I don't at any moment think of this as a definitive version of the play. It's just one way of looking at it" (Crawley). Yet, even though European "director's theater" prides itself in the endless creation of new readings, the necessary coexistence of multiple mirrors, it is *this* particular *Hamlet* production that has become *the* emblematic version of *Hamlet* and also *the* representative piece of German (and in the wider international context: European) theater of the past decade: "110 percent fitting for tours and festivals"[3](Brug).

At this point I have already moved over to the world of German theater critics, who seem to share an opinion different from their British counterparts. Although they do write about the production's being "unconventional" and "radical," and while there is praise that it attracts a lot of young people who find it "better than a movie"[4] (Bylow, Diekmann, and Sokolowski), the overall tone of the reviews is one of disappointment.

When they talk about the figure of Hamlet, the stress is not so much upon his depiction as crazy or Eidinger's talent in sculpting a convincing image of a madman — they seem instead to miss psychological precision throughout the play:

---

[2] William Shakespeare, *Hamlet* Act 1, Scene 5.
[3] "zu 110 Prozent tournee- und festivaltauglich."
[4] "besser als Kino; kinder-/jugendfreundlich."

It is atmosphere and action that define this production from the very beginning rather than psychology or subtle character development. [...] [Eidinger] throws himself with much, far too much energy into the role. This is quite rough; it seems emotional under- and overtones are less in the focus than going through the role.⑤(Krug)
A lot of fluids, a lot of earth, a lot of artificial blood, the necessary intermediality. To the physical [bodily] limits and beyond them. A sensational Hamlet from Lars Eidinger, who this evening, however, as an actor imitates the personality of Hamlet far too much.⑥(Führer)
Hamlet stays without development, a clinical symptom repeated to the point of exhaustion, the analysis of a condition.⑦(Marcus)

Critics appear to take the stance that they "see through" the tricks, do not let themselves be deceived by the innovations in the performance, and wish to disclose the shortcomings of the actor's work. They have the authoritative voice of a strict professional jury that clearly distances itself both from the "general" audience and from the production's creators. Most of them are far from enthusiastic about the translation of Marius von Mayenburg: the new text prepared for this particular performance is "colorless"⑧(Krug) and has become "flatter, lost a dimension of hidden meaning"⑨(Mustroph). When summarizing the overall experience of the performance, the negative elements dominate again:

Thomas Ostermeier was unable to find a uniform style for the play, he just uses all currently popular effects. [...] The production sways to and fro between body-centered action theater and the conventional "spoken theater" of German municipal stages. [...]⑩(Krug)

---

⑤ "Von Beginn an bestimmen Atmosphäre und Action diese Inszenierung mehr als Psychologie oder subtile Figurenentwicklung. [...] [Eidinger] wirft sich von Beginn an mit viel, mit allzu viel Kraft in die Rolle. Das wirkt vor allem grob, emotionale Unter- und Nebentöne scheinen weniger gefragt als das Ausstellen einer Rolle."

⑥ "Viele Flüssigkeiten, viel Erde, viel Kunstblut, obligatorische Intermedialität. Bis zu den körperlichen Grenzen und darüber hinaus. Ein sensationeller Hamlet von Lars Eidinger, der an diesem Abend allerdings als Schauspieler den Charakter seiner Figur allzu sehr nachahmt."

⑦ "Denn Hamlet bleibt ohne Entwicklung, ein bis zur Ermüdung erzähltes Krankheitssymptom, die Analyse eines Zustands."

⑧ "Neu an dieser Übertragung ist leider nur ihre Farblosigkeit."

⑨ "flacher, hat eine Dimension an versteckter Bedeutung verloren."

⑩ "Thomas Ostermeier sucht und findet keinen einheitlichen Stil für das Stück, sondern benutzt alle aktuell gängigen Effekte. [...] Es ist eine Inszenierung, die zwischen körperbetontem Actiontheater und herkömmlichem 'Sprechtheater' des deutschen Stadttheaters mächtig hin und her schwankt. [...]"

The too many different stylistic elements can be amusing, but the heterogeneity can also rob a production of its deeper reasons.⑪ (Mustroph)

Even if there were some reason behind the one-dimensionality: after two and a half hours it is tiring.⑫(Wahl)

What began as stylistic device, soon becomes a burden. [...] [After the interplay between theater and reality] the play cannot regain its rhythm. The out-of-play elements are too distractive as detours — and they are too incoherent as general stylistic devices. What mostly remains is confusion.⑬(Führer)

Thomas Ostermeier sifts skilfully through his catalogue, and satisfies all expectations accordingly. [...] An evening of rehearsed poses:"More matter, with less art" — the queen justifiably once calls out.⑭(Brug)

For the critics cited, it goes without saying that theater can and actually should detach itself from the script — this is no longer a question. The emancipation of theater that started with an experiment at the Meiningen Court Theater in the late 19th century (see Osborne), and ripened into an almost complete split between theater and literary studies also on the academic level, lies at the very basis of the evaluation. Reviewers take it for granted that the performance is not to be judged in comparison with the Shakespearean script, but rather in the context of other present-time productions and the director's own oeuvre. The requirement is more than individual style: the authors seem rather weary of the familiar elements of Ostermeier's theatre, and tend to dismiss it as a "suitcase of directorial clichés"⑮(Brug). What they miss the most about the production is a strong individual narrative with cohesion.

Hamlet 2015

(Barbican Theatre London, director: Lyndsey Turner, Hamlet:

---

⑪ "Zu viele unterschiedliche Stilelemente mögen für Kurzweil sorgen, die Heterogenität kann aber auch eine Inszenierung ihres tieferen Grunds berauben."

⑫ "Selbst wenn diese Eindimensionalität Methode haben sollte: Ermüdend ist sie über zweieinhalb Stunden schon."

⑬ "Was als Stilmittel begann, wird schnell zur Last. [...] [N]ach dem Bruch [zwischen Theater und Realität] findet das Stück keinen Rhythmus mehr. Die Irritationen sind als Exkurs zu ablenkend. Als allgemeines Stilmittel sind sie wiederum zusammenhangslos. So bleibt vor allem: Verwirrung."

⑭ "Thomas Ostermeier spult gekonnt seinen Katalog durch, befriedigt auch jede Erwartungshaltung. [...] Ein Abend einstudierter Posen:'Mehr Inhalt, mit weniger Rhetorik', ruft zu Recht einmal die Königin."

⑮ "Regiemusterkoffer."

Benedict Cumberbatch)

Similar is the case of the recent Barbican production of *Hamlet*, which received extreme publicity due to Benedict Cumberbatch's starring in the lead role. Authors invariably start their reviews weighing the anticipations against the final outcome, frequently in a tone somewhat ridiculing both the actor and his fans, and thus signaling their objective distance:

> Does small-screen beau Benedict bring home the Dane's bacon? (Letts)
>
> [T]he most hotly anticipated Hamlet in living memory has been unveiled. One of the burning questions of the age — does Benedict Cumberbatch deliver the goods? (Cavendish)
>
> [A] respected stage actor now in the unfortunate position of being the most famous thesp on the planet. (Lukowski)
>
> Irony quite often becomes pronounced in the rhetoric, as reviewers apparently sense an urge to counterbalance the production's perceived importance, while also trying to add a personal touch to their texts:
>
> If you spent £125 for a ticket to see Benedict Cumberbatch hold a mirror up to nature, you're now getting a clearer vision than those who paid the same price in week one. (Maltby, "Hamlet")
>
> They're a constant focus [...] at the dark heart of the production. That darkness is occasionally literal — as lit by Jane Cox, the action is frequently played in crepuscular shade. (Shenton)
>
> The most knowing wink comes in the first big ensemble scene where Hamlet sits sulking during a ceremonial banquet, positioned like Christ in da Vinci's *The Last Supper*. [...] [S]ome film or stage producer should consider casting him as Jesus next. (Felperin)

The authors operate with strong contrasts: £125 — the very essence of Shakespeare ("mirror up to nature"); dark heart — stage lighting considered insufficient; Cumberbatch uniting the figures of Jesus and a sulking Hamlet. What we hear is a variety of highly individual voices: critics are apparently looking for details that have not been noticed by anyone else, and then go to great lengths to crack a joke that will probably stick in the readers' minds — they are using the production as an occasion to display their sharp tongue and quick wit, and thus acquire authority.

Reading through several reviews, one discerns a consensus, though, that the overall level of the production does not match the accomplishment of Cumberbatch:

Yet this Hamlet seldom seems to relate to anyone else onstage. [...] This production would benefit greatly, though, if it allowed him to play well with others, too. (Brantley)

This is a fine Hamlet in a patchy, occasionally puerile production. (Letts)

Cumberbatch, in short, suggests Hamlet's essential decency. But he might have given us infinitely more, if he were not imprisoned by a dismal production that elevates visual effects above narrative coherence and exploration of character. (Billington)

[D]irector Turner has aimed to make an accessible, digestible Hamlet that won't much frighten the horses. There are an infinite number of ways to open up, color and carve the play, making it a pliant vehicle to explore madness, sexuality, gender, what have you. But there's almost no palpable subtext here [...] (Felperin)

It just strikes me that Turner and team spent so much energy thinking about the extraordinary look and feel of this production that they got sidetracked from the business of textual interrogation. (Lukowski)

There is a general feeling of dissatisfaction, as authors all seem to point to the same problem: the lack of a strong and coherent directorial vision. Benedict Cumberbatch is not depicted as the star of the day, but rather as the victim of a deficient production. It is also apparent from the texts that it is not visuality that makes a production valuable and unique, but an individual (directorial) perspective that digs into the Shakespearean play and brings to light a new aspect, while subjecting all other stage elements (including the star actor) to it. Exploratory content and contextuality are considered not an obstacle but an assistance for the actor to live up to his full professional capacity. Concern with visual elements is regarded with a certain contempt as a kind of escape from facing the real task, and this time it is no excuse that the production has become popular among youngsters. The first review by Kate Maltby in *The Times* bears the title: "What a waste! It's Shakespeare for the kids." *Hamlet* is neither a star show, nor a picture book — *Hamlet* is here considered an intellectual challenge. But within that category, it is what you make of it.

Interpretation is a requirement, and at this point I wish to emphasize briefly an important aspect of it before turning my camera toward China. It is the dynamic between tradition (represented by earlier dramatic work) and theater maker in *Regietheater*, and also the very similar dynamic of theater production and its reviewer. The two seem to repeat the same pattern, and by doing so reinforce an underlying approach. The act of interpretation goes beyond the need to reflect on the work; it means entering the work (i.e., drama or production) from the outside with force, and by doing so decentralizing and disempowering it. Contemporary European theater overwrites tradition and gains power over it, just as the public (represented by the figure of the reviewer) gains an upper hand over the production and its celebrity. It is this gesture of dislocating the center that is at the very heart of production and critique in Europe. In this process it is not so much the result that matters, but the drive behind creativity: the constant shift in the focus, the movement from periphery to center, the desire "to unlearn what we have learnt."⑯ In contemporary European theater production and criticism, this transformative act is a universal credo, applicable on the global scale. But is it? In the following, let us a take a brief look at the dynamic between tradition and current theater production in China.

II. Two Orphans of Zhao

To take a look at critical reflections on theater productions in China, I have chosen two performances of *The Orphan of Zhao*. Due to the specific nature of Chinese media, in some cases I selected reviews that introduce the existing productions preceding a certain guest performance. It is also due to the same reason that there are instances where the original online source is no longer available, so I have refer to a secondary source that republished the text. It is a very common practice in China for texts to reappear unchanged in several online news outlets. In these cases I indicate the original source in the References together with the URL of the secondary source.

The first textual version of the "Zhao Orphan" narrative is a *zaju* from the Yuan Dynasty, attributed to Ji Junxiang. Its classification as a revenge tragedy and its outstanding status within Chinese dramatic literature and theater history make it readily comparable to *Hamlet*. Both performances belong to traditional Chinese theater, also called Chinese opera or sometimes by its Chinese name: *xiqu*. As China had no prose theater until the beginning of the 20th century, *xiqu*, i.e., a story narrated through song and dance, was theater itself. This is why in the following I will use the term "traditional

---

⑯ Homi K. Bhabha at the symposium "Haben wir die richtige künstlerische Bildung?", Rolex Arts Weekend, Deutsches Theater Berlin, 4 Feb. 2018.

Chinese theater." I will refer, however, to the two particular genres as "Beijing opera" and "Henan opera" simply because these are the generic terms used in a huge bulk of Western academic literature, and the English-language reader might find them easier than the Chinese names *jingju* and *yuju*.

Zhao 2011

(*The Orphan of Zhao*, Shanghai Beijing Opera Theatre Company, director: Ma Qian, Cheng Ying: Wang Peiyu)

This performance — to which in the following I'll refer as *Zhao2011* — is a Beijing opera version jointly produced by Shanghai Beijing Opera Theatre Company and Shanghai Grand Theatre. The lead role of Cheng Ying, belonging to the "old man" role type, is played by a young actress, Wang Peiyu.

All critics hail her artistic achievement, and credit the creative work to her rather than the director — in fact, director Ma Qian is not necessarily mentioned in the reports. The texts attribute the production's innovative quality to two aspects. The first one is a unique combination of two distinct schools of Beijing opera: "the joint beauty of Ma and Yu." The performance goes back to the 1960 version of the renowned actor Ma Lianliang, but Wang Peiyu, who received her training along the lines developed by Yu Shuyan, combines the singing technique of the Yu school and the acting technique of the Ma school in this role. The expression "the joint beauty of Ma and Yu"[17] appears in several texts (Hei, Mei, and Pan) as a kind of epithet of the performance — always in quotation marks but without indication of the source. Its four-syllabic structure functioning as assistance for quick memorization reminds the reader of traditional proverbs as well. This usage seems to imply that it is common knowledge, as the consensual opinion of a community of connoisseurs, and as such offers a reliable basis also for those who are less erudite in opera matters.

The second aspect is expressed with an even more frequently employed set phrase "ink painting version," used without exception in all reviews of the performance, most often already in the title. It refers to the stage design that uses ink paintings in the traditional ("national") Chinese style as backdrop images. It is also a four-syllable expression, which most probably originates from the creative

---

⑰　马余兼美。

team itself, and has been used to identify this particular production ever since, evoking a strong visual image even for those readers who are unfamiliar with the performance. The reasons for and the results of producing an "ink painting version" are also given ample space in the reports:

> The combination of national essence Beijing opera with national painting and calligraphy, the introduction of the distant artistic concept of ink painting [...] created a unique aesthetic effect.[18] (Hei)
>
> [The stage] transmits the unadorned and concise beauty of suggestive painting. The so-called ink painting version Beijing opera is an ingenious introduction of landscape painting into stage design: an innovative crossover and combination of the two national essences: "national painting" and "Beijing opera" — a big artistic highlight of the present *The Orphan of Zhao*.[19] (Pan)
>
> Instead of the commonly seen real props there are only landscape paintings highlighting the suggestive beauty of Beijing opera. As Wang Peiyu said herself: "The substance of Beijing opera cannot be changed, only its packaging can be innovative."[20] (Mei)
>
> [What] we can see on the stage is a crossover fusion of two oriental [sic] art forms: "Beijing opera" and "national painting."[21] (Zhang, Huang, and Liang)

I translate the Chinese term *xieyi* as "suggestive", because all other, frequently used terms ("abstract", "symbolic," or "essentialist" — the latter used by Chi 2017) are loaded with connotations that might derail the reasoning. *Xieyi* had been in circulation for fine arts aesthetics, but its widespread use for theater began as late as the early 20th century with Yu Shangyuan, and continued later in Huang Zuolin's work. *Xieyi* is one half of a binary (*xieyi-xieshi*), and as such carries in itself the idea of cultural contrast: Chinese art being non-representative, hence "suggestive" of spiritual qualities, while Western art represents physical reality and is consequently "concrete" and "realistic." Thus the very application of *xieyi* places the discourse in a

---

[18] 将国粹京剧与国画、书法相结合,引入水墨丹青的悠远意境,[⋯⋯] 打造出独特审美效果。

[19] [舞台] 传递出古朴简约的写意之美。所谓墨本丹青版京剧,是指将山水丹青画卷巧妙融合进舞美设计之中,"国画"与"京剧"两种国粹开创性的跨界混搭,也是此次《赵氏孤儿》的一大艺术亮点。

[20] 只用山水丹青画卷代替了常见的实景道具,凸显京剧写意之美。对此,王珮瑜这样解读,"京剧的本体不能动摇,但在包装方式上可以有创新。"

[21] 在舞台上实现"京剧"与"国画"两种东方艺术的跨界融合。

culturally comparative context.

The same pertains to the widespread use of the term "national essence" (*guocui*), which also goes back to the early 20th century and has its roots in China's patriotic intellectual movements. The very idea of "nation" was new to China at the time of the Opium Wars, when the country was forced to enter into international treaties and define itself as one among several nations within the Westphalian system (see Feng 3). As the gradual creation of nationhood brought forth the need for "national culture," certain elements that were commonly perceived as outstanding cultural achievements — kung fu, traditional Chinese medicine, Beijing opera, and calligraphy (together with ink painting characterized by the freehand style) — were defined as national essence. The above critics apparently deem the "combination of the two national essences" highly innovative: as a means to achieve an even more distilled and condensed expression of what one may call "Chinese culture."

I have managed to locate only one blogger who found this reasoning insufficient:

> After all, what is this ink painting version? Is it just an empty construction, where the form is bigger than the content, or is it tightly connected to the main topic? After watching the whole performance it is still not clear to me. This so-called ink painting version seems to be nothing more than some application appearing on the level of stage design.[22] (Zhang Jing)

At the other end of the palette, one review stands out that discusses the production solely in the context of cultural identity. In order to introduce the author's train of thought I cite several parts of the article:

> *The Orphan of Zhao* advocates and expresses the strong sacrificial spirit and noble moral power in Chinese culture. [...] It might well be, that the true portrayal of the ordinary person as hero starts from *The Orphan of Zhao*. [...]
>
> Talking about foreigners, they can look up to a God with respect and have a hope for transcendental care. The Chinese people had no native religion, so they had to rely completely on the sense of justice and loyalty flowing in their veins — could they bear the heavy load of strong virtue and spirituality? [...] [T]heir strong

---

[22] 究竟墨本丹青是什么？是形式大于内容的虚设，还是与主题紧紧相贴？看完后我仍不明白。所谓墨本丹青，仅仅就是在舞美呈现上的一些运用。

hope and trust in the ethics of social equality, justice and political sobriety have become the spiritual pillars they would even die for. [...]

During the Cultural Revolution we slid into one extremism, smashed the cultural psychological composition that the Chinese people had constructed throughout several millenia, and destroyed the moral pillars of the Chinese people. We discarded the most precious kernel of our national spirit, and this resulted not only in the malignant overgrowth of the individual psyche, the crazy quest for development in the economy, and the superficial and short-sighted pursuit of material wealth, but even our national art, which should rely on the national spirit, has run into a cul-de-sac. [...]

The stage [of the ink painting version of *The Orphan of Zhao*] becomes a meeting point [crossover] of two oriental [*sic*] arts: "national painting" and "Beijing opera." Although the desire is to assert innovation and exploration in performing arts and stage design, the production's objective significance is unmistakably clear: the ultimate goal is the theatrical portrayal of the national cultural spirit.㉓(Cai)

What the author says about virtue and spirituality as depicted in the play is not only the most commonly used argument for its exceptional values, but also often considered to be the quality that took this Yuan *zaju* — and with it the appreciation of Chinese culture — to Europe in the 18th century (see Zhang Guogang 107). In an earlier part on his article, Cai refers to Voltaire as someone who "acknowledged *The Orphan of Zhao*, acknowledged Chinese culture," and "received inspiration"㉔ from Ji Junxiang's work. *The Orphan of Zhao* seems to be a play that on the one hand served to educate the domestic society on Confucian morals, while on the other hand became one of the earliest cultural export pieces. Voltaire's fascination with the story is

---

㉓ 《赵氏孤儿》倡导与表达的就是中国文化里强烈的牺牲精神与高尚的道德力量。[……]真正描摹了平民英雄的可能要从《赵氏孤儿》起算。[……]
　　一个人完全依靠血液里流淌的正义、忠勇,能够支撑那么沉重的道德和精神的负荷吗?[……]而是他们对社会公平、政治清明、善恶有报的基本道德正义的强烈希望和信任,这是他们毅然赴死的精神支柱[。][……]
　　"文革"几乎砸碎了几千年形成的文化心理结构,摧毁了很多人的精神支柱。我们自己丢弃了最珍贵的民族精神内核,其结果不仅仅造成人个体的恶性心理膨胀、片面追求物质利益的短视行为,就连依靠民族精神支撑的民族艺术也同样会走向死胡同。[……]
　　"在舞台上实现'国画'与'京剧'两种东方艺术的跨界。"尽管他们主张的更多的是在表演艺术和舞台艺术的革新与探索,但作品的客观意义却明白无误地昭示:民族文化精神的戏剧化塑造才是他们的终极追求。
㉔ 伏尔泰肯定《赵氏孤儿》,肯定中国文化[……]他从《赵氏孤儿》里受到的启发。

often cited by Chinese authors as a proof that *The Orphan of Zhao* is a successful medium for the international communication of the Chinese psyche. In the domestic arena, an urge for social justice and stability even at a price of huge personal sacrifices has thus come into the foreground, while the international reception paraphrases these in the context of "national spirit," thus allocating them to a particular social space defined as the "nation."

Cai seems to be concerned with national cultural boundaries, relying heavily on a comparative aspect in defining what is "Chinese" and what is not. He hails the production for its endeavor to create an ultimate performative representation of what he considers a national cultural identity. From this aspect, it is interesting to see that "national" seems to be interchangeable with "oriental"[25] for several authors (Cai; Wang Jia; Zhang, Huang, and Liang), indicating an uncertainty about what exactly constitutes "nation": whether it is an ethnic term or denotes a broader cultural identification with Confucian civilization. This uncertainty is a symptom of the fact that the discourse is a continuation of the late-19th- and early-20th-century landslide-like shift in Chinese perceptions about the structure of the world. Cai actually writes about a need to return to a world of Confucian morals, and paints a strongly idealized image of this now distant past.

In this context, the preservation of tradition gains special emphasis, and reviewers find the safest guarantee for this in the person of the performer. First and foremost, Wang Peiyu's professional superiority is emphasized — the recurrent phrase is "Boss Yu" (*Yu Laoban*). The articles invariably list that she is a "national first-grade actress," winner of the prestigious Plum Blossom Prize, and the epithet "Today's Meng Xiaodong"[26] — referring to a former famous Shanghainese Beijing opera actress — also appears regularly (Hei; Mei; Wang Jia; Zhao; Zhang, Huang, and Liang). This information is generally placed at the beginning of the text, anchoring the topic to social recognition and setting a "no nonsense" tone.

It is also often mentioned that she is a fourth-generation disciple of the Yu school (see Hei, Pan, and Zhao), which places her in a historical context and implies that she has responsibility for the perpetuation of her predecessors' work. The difficulty of transmission is a recurrent topic in contemporary Chinese theater discourse. Several authors emphasize that her forte is a combination of traditional

---

㉕　东方。
㉖　当代孟小冬。

technique and an onstage-offstage presence that appeals to younger audiences:

> "All I have to do is decorate the traditional halls with a touch of individual Wang Peiyu color" — she says. Revision through "redoing the old into the old" might recall the classics for many an old opera fan, while at the same time might introduce a more colorful Beijing opera world to the young people who have just become initiated into Beijing opera.[27](Hei)
>
> Onstage she is a dignified and composed female "old man," offstage she is a fashionable, short-haired girl in jeans and sneakers. [...] She communicates with young fans through the newest forms of media: interacts with followers through her blog, and listens to their suggestions on the transmission and innovation of Beijing opera.[28](Zhao)
>
> Onstage she impersonates a multitude of men with a female body, offstage she still retains the graceful beauty of South-of-Yangtze girls. [...] Her abundant experience grants her composure and tranquility that set her apart from her peers. [...] This female "old man," who dresses relaxed offstage, and plays men with a tragic fate onstage, has a lot of softness in her heart.[29](Mei)

Critics are more concerned with the very distance between the performer's self and the role(s) she plays than the specifics of her acting. In fact, very little has been written on this particular Cheng Ying, the emphasis is always on the oscillation between the real (young and cool) person and the impersonated (old and troubled) character. Reviewers are fascinated to witness how the performer moves between two extremes, but rarely tackle the actual process of character formation. Interestingly enough, not even the journalist who prepared an in-depth interview with Wang Peiyu asks about the challenges she faces when entering an "old male" role (see Meng). She does not need to identify with the role — on the contrary: her very conspicuous distance from the character is a huge asset. In this

---

[27] "我所要做的只是在传统厅堂上点缀一抹属于王珮瑜个人的色彩。"她说,这次 "修旧如旧"的改编,希望唤回老戏迷记忆中的经典,也让刚接触京剧不久的年 轻人通过王珮瑜看到一个更加丰富多彩的京剧世界。

[28] 台上是正襟危坐、端庄儒雅的女老生,台下是帅气板寸、着牛仔裤板鞋的时尚 潮人,[……] 她以各种创新方式与年轻戏迷进行沟通,在网络上通过博客等 方式与粉丝们互动,听取他们对京剧传承和创新的建议。

[29] 舞台上,她以女儿身演绎男子百态;舞台下,她还原一个江南女子的娟秀文雅。 [……]丰富的经历让她比同龄人多了些淡然、平和。[……]这个台下打扮中 性、台上演着人生沧桑的女老生,心中也颇多柔软处。

sense, Chinese critics hit an almost Diderotian tone about detachment as the prerequisite for the actor's professionalism.

It is only Zhang Jing who is critical about the way the character is sculpted:

> Even when facing death or separation Cheng Ying is still surprisingly calm, as if it were none of his concern, letting people feel his being self-possessed and righteous. [...] When his own son gets killed and people disperse, he stays with the small body but does not express any emotion at all; we see him as cold-blooded. Is it a directorial problem? Or perhaps the actress' performance falls short? Or what? [...] But Wang Peiyu is still young, she still has a long road ahead of her: if she walks it right, she will be worthy of the fame — if she walks it wrong, she won't.[30] (Zhang Jing)

Although the blogger expresses dissatisfaction with emotional expressivity, she also dissolves the problem in the wider context of artistic career: a performer's achievement can only be judged after she has accumulated an oeuvre. She will also work longer on the role of Cheng Ying: it is a common practice for Beijing opera performers to polish their most important roles for decades.

This gradual and meticulous career construction process as well as the star cult developing around the performer are both viewed as necessary for the survival of Beijing opera. Tradition gains new meaning through the performer's bringing in a tiny individual touch: the "Wang Peiyu color," which might attract spectators "who are not opera fans, but want to see Wang Peiyu"[31] (Wang Peiyu about herself as cited in Hei). She needs to balance it out, however, to create "a performance based on tradition and breaking through tradition"[32] (Hei), because after all her biggest task is to preserve Beijing opera while attracting young audiences. She has "learned bone-old pieces, mastered all the ancient techniques," and "sings living up to [...] her [legendary] Beijing opera predecessors"[33] (Hei).

---

[30] 面对生死,面对骨肉分离,程婴竟然出奇地平静,好像事不关己一样,让人深觉此人的"淡定"与"大义"。[……]程婴亲子被狠狠地摔在地上,众人离开后,面对亲子那弱小的身体,程婴仅仅是一个刹那的极不到位的表情,让人深觉此人是这样冷血。或许是导演的问题? 也或许是演员自身的表现不足? 还或许是……[……]好在,王珮瑜还年轻,艺术的路子还很漫长,走正了,名副其实;走歪了,名不副实。

[31] 如果不是戏迷,可以来看王珮瑜。

[32] 演出立足传统而又尝试突破传统。

[33] 潜心学习骨子老戏,唱念做表皆深具古风,[……]演唱[……]深得[……]前辈京剧名家赏识。

The particular performer is viewed as one link between all other former and future performers, and as such he/she functions in the context of a long linear time scale.

It is part of the artist's task to reconnect both in space and in time: "The performance coincides with the 120th anniversary of the birth of school founder Yu Shuyan, so fourth-generation disciple Wang Peiyu works with all her heart in the hope to 'give new life to the old traditions' and thus pay respect to her predecessors"[34] (Pan). She needs to reconnect also with her own roots: "Wang Peiyu will show the elders in her hometown a few successful attempts at the creation and dissemination of Beijing opera" — writes Mei preceding a Suzhou performance. The performer's artistic and social embeddedness constitutes a fundamental context for her work.

At this point, it is worth mentioning that the frequent repetitions in the different articles indicate that on the one hand reviewers rely heavily on press release and on formerly published material, while on the other hand they consider most of the information a kind of "community consensus" — a common understanding to which they need to give voice, but cannot/should not alter in any significant way. They rely on consensual opinion and the reiteration of facts rather than taking a critical stance. Although Wang Peiyu's being exceptional is emphasized throughout the reviews, what exactly constitutes this individuality in theatrical terms never seems to come into the focus.

Zhao 2002

(*Cheng Ying Rescues the Orphan*, Second Troupe of Henan Yu Opera House, chief director: Huang Zaimin, director: Zhang Ping, Cheng Ying: Li Shujian)

This Henan opera version of *The Orphan of Zhao* was given the title *Cheng Ying Rescues the Orphan*, but in my own text I'll refer to it as *Zhao2002* in order to emphasize its retaining the same narrative.

Although the articles that have appeared about the production tend to center around a different set of topics, the routine of positioning the production on a scale of professional recognition at the very beginning of the review stands out as a basic requirement. The performer in the main role, Li Shujian is invariably introduced

---

[34] 又适逢余派创始人余叔岩先生诞辰 120 周年,作为余派第四代传人的王珮瑜,也希望以这部"为老传统注入新生命"的心血之作向先贤致敬。

as "Vice President of the Chinese Theatre Association," "Director of Henan Yu Opera House," and "winner of a second Plum Blossom Prize." His exceptionally high professional status functions as guarantee for unquestionable quality and also as support for the authors, who regularly use direct citations from him.

The narrative created around him is completely different, though, from that for Wang Peiyu. He is not seen as a "cool" figure of innovation, but is more often referred to as someone having weathered many hardships — and as such standing close to the character of Cheng Ying. He belongs to the generation who grew up during the Cultural Revolution, and "he says his expertise at depicting tragic characters goes back to his own experience: many things he has lived through in his life find their way into his art on the stage"[35] (Wang Jianhong). It seems as if there were an almost Stanislavskian expectation here in a reliance on personal emotional memory — as opposed to the lack of such memory, consequently the lack of such expectations, in the case of Wang Peiyu.

He is quoted as saying that "the real stage for the actor is in the hearts of the people"[36] (Wang Jianhong) and "playing to the people should be like playing to your own mother and father"[37] (Zhou). An imaginary but highly intimate audience is created consisting of the older generation: the "people" who probably share a similar life story and a similar understanding of the world. Li Shujian's social role is to give voice to these people, elevating them to the tragic fate and heroism of Cheng Ying, who in turn receives more attention in these reviews than in those about *Zhao2011*:

> From Cheng Ying radiates the glory of humanity, he embodies the national spirit of tenacity and perseverance. [...] Li Shujian once said, "Chinese traditional opera always aspires to give the audience a sense of 'good ending.'"[38] As we witness how Cheng Ying saves the orphan from death out of loyalty, we feel the heart-rending artistic effect of this traditional play.[39] (Liu Huan)

---

[35] 他说自己擅长演绎悲剧人物与他的经历有关,生活中的不少经历都被他用到了舞台上。

[36] "一个演员的真正舞台,是在老百姓的心坎上。"

[37] "给老百姓演戏要像给爹娘演戏。"

[38] I am trying to avoid translating this expression as "happy ending," as that would be gravely misleading.

[39] 程婴身上闪耀着人性的光辉,折射出坚忍、顽强的民族精神。[……]李树建曾说:"我国传统戏曲为迎合观众的'善终'心理,总以程婴福禄双收大团圆结束,我们则将程婴的结局安排成忠心救孤终被杀害,赋予这部传统剧目震撼人心的艺术效果。"

Li Shujian's Cheng Ying is mature and flawless, his singing is rich and colorful; he can transport the traditional virtues of China — loyalty and honesty — from a distance of millennia to the audience of the present, and evoke their strong response. A classical old piece can have contemporary educational value.[40] (Liu Ping)

Some people say in *Cheng Ying Rescues the Orphan* Li Shujian acts out "the trembling heart of a tragic character." Actually, the relentless pursuit for art also shows his own fierce inner struggle.[41] (Liu Yuqin)

Cheng Ying Rescues the Orphan [...] demonstrates even more strongly the "loyalty" and sacrificial spirit of Cheng Ying in the face of crisis, while at the same time bestows upon this traditional "loyalty" a new meaning.[42] (Jia)

"Loyalty," a basic Confucian value, is stressed (see also Higgins), as well as the character's inner conflict. While the concept of tragedy rarely appears in the texts about *Zhao2011*, here the critics seem to deem it necessary to place the narrative in the context of extreme personal inner struggle — also relating it to the personal experience of the particular performer (Li Shujian) and his generation. The Confucian idea of sacrificing personal happiness for the sake of order and justice in society — i.e., an ultimately "good ending" — definitely resonates within the performer's generation. At the same time, this is also a message to the younger generations, warning them to preserve the same values.

The concept of tragedy in connection with *Zhao2002* has acquired an even more complex meaning after the production started touring abroad. Interestingly enough, after the 2002 launch of the production,

Henan Opera House repeatedly invited famous opera masters to assess, comment on and improve the performance. It was not until 2007, after several great opera masters had concluded that the production was mature enough and reached its perfection, that the Opera House took it out to the world.[43] (Li Shujian as cited in Wang Shengxi)

---

[40] 李树建出演程婴,其人物火候把握恰到好处,唱腔运用丰富多变,把中华传统美德——忠诚信义,穿越千年历史时空再次传递给现代观众,引起强烈共鸣,经典老戏仍具有现代教育意义。

[41] 有人说,《程婴救孤》中,李树建演出了"一个悲剧人物的心灵颤抖"。其实对艺术执着不舍地追求也描摹出李树建艰辛奋斗的心路历程。

[42] 《程婴救孤》[⋯⋯]强化了程婴在危急时刻表现出来的"忠义"和牺牲精神,同时又赋予这种传统的"忠义"以新的内涵。

[43] "河南豫剧院[⋯⋯]多次邀请戏曲名家反复进行指点、推敲、修改。到2007年,很多戏曲大家都认为该剧已经成熟、臻于完美的时候,才呈现给世界。"

In the reports about the performances abroad, especially those in the United States, the authors tend to emphasize that the play is "a great tragedy"[44] (Jia and Liu Ping), that it displays "the beauty of a tragedy"[45] (Wang Shengxi), or narrates "a story of tragic twists and turns"[46] (Zhang Chaoqun). Reviewers writing about *Zhao2011* sometimes do mention the fact that the original *zaju* script can be classified as tragedy, but rarely identify the production in this way.

Although the present chapter's scope does not allow me to dwell on the question of genre definition in more detail, I want to at least mention briefly that the concept of "tragedy" is itself a loaded one. The Aristotelian concept from *Poetics* came as an import to Chinese literary studies in the late 19th century, and although it has become widely adopted (see the volumes edited by Wang Jisi: *Ten Chinese Classical Tragedies* and *Ten Chinese Classical Comedies*), there is a scholarly debate on whether the application of the Western terms is a healthy process in Chinese academic disciplines (see the 2003 essay by Hua on the dangers of "Westernization as part of 'modernization'").

It is conspicuous how often critics write on the actual reception of *Zhao2002* — compared to the reviews of *Zhao2011*. The critics of *Zhao2002* tend to comment on its being suitable for international audiences, and sometimes also add illustrative details about audience reaction:

> The story of *Cheng Ying Rescues the Orphan* is one of loyalty and honesty, of suffering in silence. It evoked a sympathetic response in the West, received the acknowledgement of American white-collar people.[47] (Wang Shengxi)
>
> During the climax of the performance in the ninth scene many spectators were watching the stage overwhelmed while wiping away their tears with their hands.[48] (Zhang Chaoqun on a Los Angeles performance)
>
> During the two-hour performance, the audience seemed to "enter the play", tears were flashing in their eyes. At every point of brilliance there was a burst of applause indicating the spectators' emotions. [...] The Henan opera *Cheng Ying Rescues the Orphan* is

---

[44] "一部伟大的悲剧。"
[45] 悲剧的美。
[46] 悲壮曲折的故事。
[47] 《程婴救孤》所讲述的忠义诚信、忍辱负重的故事,与西方文化产生了共鸣,得到了美国白领阶层的认可。
[48] 演出到第九场高潮部分时,不少观众一边聚精会神地看戏,一边用手轻轻擦拭脸上的泪水。

the first [Chinese opera] performance since the foundation of the new China [...]; the American theater world calls Henan opera "the Chinese opera."⁴⁹ (Jia on a Beijing performance)

[The performance] has also been on Broadway, has told the Chinese story, spread the Chinese voice, [...] and conquered the international audience with oriental [sic] aesthetics and virtues! [...] The curtain fell, and an enthusiastic applause burst out from the spectators, who were full of tears. They celebrated not only the actors, but also the loyal hero and the loyal spirit that came forward from the distant past, and that deeply touched China and the whole world.⁵⁰ (Liu Ping on a Hebei performance)

It appears that the emphasis on audience reactions and on the international appreciation of the production provides the discourse with a new context. It is not merely a performance on the stage any longer, but the whole of China: getting the world's long-overdue recognition after an extended period of distress. Cheng Ying stands out as an allegory: his sixteen years of silent suffering equal the injustice and tragic fate China had to endure. This also explains the accentuation of tragedy in the reviews. The narrative on the stage becomes the body of China evoking the Bakhtinian image of the classical body: noble, smooth, and finished. (I need to remind the reader here of the long polishing process before *Zhao2002* was brought to foreign audience.) The audience's strong emotional response is an inherent part of the performance, as it brings the relief of a "good end" that has finally been arrived at on the world stage.

There is direct or indirect reference to Confucian values — Liu Ping uses the ambiguous expression "oriental aesthetics and virtues" to denote a sphere of cultural influence which is not limited by national boundaries. These virtues also appear among the "core socialist values" propagated by the Xi administration, where they constitute the basis of the China Dream. "Telling the Chinese Story" and "Spreading the Chinese Voice" are tasks that have been considered as

⑭ 两个多小时的演出过程中,观众仿佛全都"入了戏",眼角闪着泪花。每到精彩之处,一阵阵热烈的掌声诉说着观众的心声。[……]豫剧《程婴救孤》是中华人民共和国成立后第一个登上美国百老汇剧院的剧目,[……]豫剧被美国戏剧界称为"中国歌剧"。

⑮ [豫剧《程婴救孤》]还曾登上美国百老汇的舞台,讲述中国故事,传递中国声音[……],以东方审美和道德情怀征服了世界观众! [……]幕布落下,满含热泪的观众把最热烈的掌声送给舞台上的演员们,也送给那些从中国历史深处走来,感动着中国也感动着世界的忠义之士、忠义之魂。

imperatives for the media ever since President Xi Jinping announced them at a Publicity Seminar in 2013 (Ni). Henan opera apparently brings a local identity into the focus, as Henan province prides itself in representing the whole of China — "the Chinese opera" in the eyes of the American theater world (Jia) — on the international stage.

Conclusion

So "what do we talk about when we talk about theater?" In China, the public performance of a narrative — especially an ancient one with a wide circulation and an inherited (operatic) form — gives occasion for an articulation of cultural identity. It serves as the iconic representation and consequently the reinforcement of the whole community. Theater does not open a space for public debate — on the contrary: the basic function of theater is the ritual re-enactment of community values. All participants — audience members as much as reviewers — are given specific roles in this performative event of celebration. This is the reason why reviewers find it extremely difficult to position themselves as distinct from the creative team: they are actually co-creators of the meta-narrative.

As a major public event, theater has been viewed as having huge responsibility for spreading Confucian values, and thus improving social stability. In the present-day context art needs to be more supportive than ever, as Cai says in his review: "the excellent Chinese tradition is the spiritual lifeline of the Chinese nation, [...] the solid foundation of our firm footing in the global cultural turmoil."⑤ This also explains why Xiong, analyzing a spoken drama version of *The Orphan of Zhao* in which the youngster hesitates about revenge, titles his essay "The Cultural Identity and the *Betrayal* [my italics] of Chinese Tragedy."

Contemporary traditional Chinese theater production views itself as one of the last bastions of the preservation of cultural values, and as such it does not consider its task to address urgent social issues. It contextualizes itself in the paradigm of national identity, and finds its mission in the construction of a unified national community — as opposed to other national communities, meaning that it feeds on the perpetuation of an East-West binary. Historically, it reaches back to

---

⑤ 中华优秀传统文化是中华民族的精神命脉，是培养社会主义核心价值观的重要源泉，也是我们在世界文化激荡中站稳脚跟的坚实根基。

late-19th- and early-20th-century patriotism, and continues to concern itself with national cultural identity and fears for national cultural survival. Against the background of an emotionally highly charged environment — as feelings of superiority, inferiority and vulnerability are all there in the package — traditional theater forms find their social space in being a pledge for stability. This theater (including its critics) is constantly recreated in order to celebrate ritually an idealized image of how society operates — and how the individual cooperates.

As much as traditional Chinese theater may appear to be obsessed with the theme of social order, the European theater world, with subtle differences between critical cultures, seems to idolatrize individual values, priding itself in its mission of being society's "critical conscience." In a two-step separation process it is a theater that, as a first step, needs to stand apart, to dissect whatever it gets into its hands, transform it, uglify it, squeeze some new meaning out of it, and finally push the image in society's face. It is a grotesque act of penetrating the body of society with the disfigured body of an art object. The second step is that of critical reception: autonomous figures weigh whether this disfigured body has added enough new perspective to the ongoing social discourse. They expect a highly individual vision of the world: the discovery of an idea (of an intended or, in most cases, originally unintended subtext) in the traditional work of art, thus revealing some truth for the present. It is one single artist's communication with the community, based on analytical precision and the artist's social responsibility to be critical of the same community. The Adornian ideal of art as criticism disclosing social contradictions and bringing about emancipatory social change is very much at the heart of contemporary European theater production: artworks as the "social antithesis" of society embody a "difference from a bewitched reality," and "[t]heir enchantment is disenchantment" (Adorno 8, 227).

It appears, then, that Shalom Schwartz's theory of cultural value orientations is highly applicable to this difference in the public performances of traditional narratives: whereas theater in Europe fulfills requirements for autonomy, especially intellectual autonomy, the traditional theater forms of China accentuate embeddedness. The European demand for acute observation and sharp critique is based on the needs of civil society, which is viewed as a composition of autonomous beings. It becomes the task of theater, the major art form addressing larger groups, to engage these people in public debate in contemporary Europe. We would need to go back at least to the 18th-century beginnings of European modernity to see the decisive historical and political reasons behind this development, an analysis which is far beyond the scope of the present study. Yet autonomy and egalitarianism seem to define the social space for European theater, which in turn further strengthens these value orientations.

Both understandings of theater are firmly rooted and are considered as matter-of-fact in both cultures, which makes it all the more difficult to operate not only with the concept of "theater," but also with other, related concepts. Underlying differences rarely get articulated; touring with theater productions of the traditional dramatic corpus is generally considered safe, apolitical territory, where dialogue is made easy. A lack of contextual understanding, however, can pose a major problem for all levels of cultural exchange: audiences, media, and the artists themselves.

References

Adorno, Theodor W. *Aesthetic Theory*. Edited by Gretel Adorno and Rolf Tiedemann, translated by Robert Hullot-Kentor. Athlone Press, 1997.

Alter, Jean. *A Sociosemiotic Theory of Theatre*. U of Pennsylvania P, 1990.

Bakhtin, Mikhail. *Rabelais and His World* [1941]. Translated by Hélène Iswolsky. Indiana UP, 1984.

Billington, Michael. "Hamlet Review — Benedict Cumberbatch Imprisoned in a Dismal Production." *The Guardian*, 26 Aug. 2015, www.theguardian.com/stage/2015/aug/25/hamlet-barbican-review-benedict-cumberbatch-imprisoned-prince.

Bowie-Sell, Daisy. "Hamlet, Schaubühne Berlin, Barbican, Review." *The Telegraph*, 2 Dec. 2011, www.telegraph.co.uk/culture/theatre/theatre-reviews/8931119/Hamlet-Schaubuhne-Berlin-Barbican-Review.html.

Brantley, Ben. "Review: Benedict Cumberbatch in 'Hamlet'." *The New York Times*, 25 Aug. 2015. www.nytimes.com/2015/08/26/theater/review-benedict-cumberbatch-in-hamlet-cocooned-in-an-aura-on-a-london-stage.html.

Brug, Manuel. "Narziss mit Prollmund." ["Narcissus with a prole-mouth."] *Die Welt*, 9 July 2018, www.welt.de/welt_print/article2193168/Narziss-mit-Prollmund.html.

Bylow, Christina. "Es ist wahnsinnig erotisch, Schauspieler zu sein." ["Being an Actor Is Incredibly Erotic."] *Berliner Zeitung*, 12 Dec. 2014, www.berliner-zeitung.de/lars-eidinger-es-ist-wahnsinnig-erotisch---schauspieler-zu-sein--2679876.

Cai, Xiaojiang. "剧评 | 从墨本丹青版《赵氏孤儿》想到的" ["Critique — Thoughts on the Ink Painting Version of *The Orphan of Zhao*"]. *Radio Tianjin*, 19 Sept. 2016, chuansong.me/n/863784652454.

Cavendish, Dominic. "Hamlet, Barbican, Review: 'Justifies the Hysteria'." *The Telegraph*, 25 Aug. 2015, www.telegraph.co.uk/theatre/what-to-see/benedict-cumberbatch-as-hamlet-barbican-review/.

Chi, Yumei. "The Attempt of *Xieyi*（Essentialist）Theatre 寫意話劇 in the History of the Chinese Spoken Theatre." *Intercultural Communication with China: Beyond（Reverse）Essentialism and Culturalism?*, edited by Fred Dervin and Regis Machart. Springer, 2017, pp. 79–90.

Crawley, Peter. "Ostermeier's 'Hamlet': What Did You Expect?" *The Irish Times*, 23 Aug. 2014, www.irishtimes.com/culture/stage/ostermeier-s-hamlet-what-did-you-expect-1.1901339.

Diekmann, Patrick. "'Sein oder Nichtsein?' Das ist keine Frage mehr! Die Erfolgsgeschichte des 'Hamlet' an der Berliner Schaubühne mit Lars Eidinger." ["'To be or not to be?' This Is Not a Question Any More! The Success Story of 'Hamlet' at Schaubühne Berlin with Lars Eidinger."] *BerlinOnline*, 2014, www.berlinonline.de/magazin/abgefeiert/3715341-3564159-sein-oder-nichtsein-das-ist-keine-frage-.html. Accessed 17 Nov. 2017.

Fearon, Alana. "Thomas Ostermeier's Hamlet Review: A Shakespearean Play — But Not as You Know It." *Irish Mirror*, 28 Sept. 2014, www.irishmirror.ie/whats-on/arts-culture-news/thomas-ostermeiers-hamlet-review-shakespearean-4338600.

Felperin, Leslie. "'Hamlet': Theater Review." *The Hollywood Reporter*, 25 Aug. 2015, www.hollywoodreporter.com/review/benedict-cumberbatch-hamlet-theater-review-816761?utm_source=twitter.

Feng Tianyu. 2012. "'中国''中华民族'语义的历史生成" ["The Historical Development of the Meaning of 'China' and 'Chinese Nation'"]. *Journal of Henan University*, vols. 1–6, no. 11, 2012, retrieved from www.wanfangdata.com.cn. Accessed 7 July 2017.

Fischer-Lichte, Erika. "Quo Vadis?: Theatre Studies at the Crossroads." *Modern Drama*, vol. 44, no. 1, Spring 2001, pp. 52–71, doi.org/10.1353/mdr.2001.0004.

Fischer-Lichte, Erika, and Jo Riley. *The Show and the Gaze of Theatre: A European Perspective*. U of Iowa P, 1997.

Fisher, Philip. "Hamlet." *British Theatre Guide*, 2011, www.britishtheatreguide.info/reviews/hamletbarbican-rev. Accessed 17 Nov. 2017.

Führer, Till. "Livekritik zu Hamlet." ["*Livekritik* on Hamlet."] *livekritik.de*, 17 Mar. 2014, www.livekritik.de/livekritiken/livekritik-von-till-fuehrer-zu-hamlet/.

Gardner, Lyn. "British Shakespeare Productions Need More than Scene-Stealing Stars." *The Guardian*, 30 Jan. 2014, www.theguardian.com/stage/theatreblog/2014/jan/30/shakespeare-help-hindrance-british-theatre.

—. "Hamlet-review." *The Guardian*, 2 Dec. 2011, www.theguardian.com/stage/2011/dec/02/theatre-shakespeare.

Hei, Mei. "如果不是戏迷,可以来看王珮瑜" ["If You Are Not an Opera Fan, You Might Want to See Wang Peiyu"]. *Zhongguo Wenhua Bao*, 22 Mar. 2012, ent.ifeng.com/zz/detail_2012_03/22/13357443_0.shtml.

Higgins, Kathleen M. "Loyalty from a Confucian Perspective." *Nomos*, vol. 54, 2013, pp. 22–38.

Hua, Ming. "悲剧的话语与话语的悲剧" ["The Discourse of Tragedy and the Tragedy of Discourse"]. *Comparative Literature in China*, no. 2, 2003, pp. 62–76, retrieved from www.wanfangdata.com.cn. Accessed 18 July 2017.

Jia，Yutao. "《程婴救孤》" [*Cheng Ying Rescues the Orphan*]. *Zhongguo Wenming Wang*，29 June 2016，www.wenming.cn/specials/goodstoryofchina/artistory/cyq/gsldzp/201606/t20160629_3479420.shtml.

Kalle，Matthias. "Lars Eidinger. Der kleine Prinz." ["Lars Eidinger. The Little Prince."] *Zeit Online*，10 June 2010，www.zeit.de/2010/24/Schauspieler-Lars-Eidinger/komplettansicht.

Kellaway，Kate. "Hamlet：Schaubühne Berlin — Review." *The Guardian*，4 Dec. 2011，www.theguardian.com/culture/2011/dec/04/schaubuhne-berlin-hamlet-shakespeare-review.

Krug，Hartmut. "Lautsein oder Nichtsein." ["To Be Loud or Not to Be."] *nachtkritik.de*，7 July 2008，www.nachtkritik.de/index.php?option = com_content&view = article&id = 1583.

Letts，Quentin. "Hamlet. By William Shakespeare，London's Barbican." *The Daily Mail*，26 Aug. 2015，www.dailymail.co.uk/tvshowbiz/article-3210853/Alas-poor-Benedict-fine-Hamlet-s-let-second-rate-stars-hype-incomparable-critic-s-night-verdict.html.

Liu，Huan，editor. "豫剧《程婴救孤》老戏新唱 李树建简约程式化表演" ["The Henan Opera *Cheng Ying Rescues the Orphan*：An Old Play Sung New — Li Shujian's Compact and Stylized Performance"]. *Dahe Wang*，11 Dec. 2015，www.chinanews.com/cul/2015/12–11/7666583.shtml.

Liu，Ping. "豫剧历史大戏《程婴救孤》诠释忠诚信义" ["A Tale of Loyalty and Honor — the Historical Henan Opera 'Cheng Ying Rescues the Orphan'"]. *Hebei Daily*，4 Oct. 2016，he.xinhuanet.com/jujiao/20161004/3471134_c.html.

Liu，Yuqin. "看遍人生各种风景——李树建：高亢悲凉唱'程婴'" ["Seeing All Facets of Life — Li Shujian：The Resonant and Tragic Voice of Cheng Ying"]. *People's Daily*，27 Sept. 2007，www.360doc.com/content/14/0802/15/4250371_398830077.shtml.

Lukowski，Andrej. "Hamlet. Theatre，Shakespeare." *Time Out*，25 Aug. 2015，www.timeout.com/london/theatre/hamlet-43.

Maltby，Kate. "Hamlet at the Barbican，EC2." *The Times*，26 Aug. 2015，www.thetimes.co.uk/article/hamlet-at-the-barbican-ec2-cckt3msvzbw.

—. "What a Waste! It's Shakespeare for the Kids." *The Times*，6 Aug. 2015，www.thetimes.co.uk/article/what-a-waste-its-shakespeare-for-the-kids-t938xl92qgp.

Marcus，Dorothea. "Ostermeiers 'Hamlet' in Avignon. Terrorist aus der Familienzelle." ["Ostermeier's 'Hamlet' in Avignon. Terrorist from the Family Cell."] *taz.de*，18 July 2008，www.taz.de/!5178788/.

Mei，Lei. "王珮瑜：让更多年轻人爱京剧" ["Wang Peiyu：Let More Young People Love Beijing Opera"]. *Suzhou Daily*，16 Feb. 2012，www.dongdongqiang.com/liyuanzouma/2012–02–16/32216.html.

Meng，Weihong. "'当代孟小冬'王珮瑜：用最现代的方式推广京剧" ["'Today's Meng Xiaodong' — Wang Peiyu：Using the Most Modern Methods to Promote Beijing Opera"]. *Chengdu Daily*，15 June 2011，scopera.newssc.org/system/2011/06/15/013201546_01.shtml.

Murphy，Colm. "Theatre：'Hamlet' … as You've Never Seen It Before." *Independent.ie*，20 July 2014，www.independent.ie/entertainment/theatre-arts/theatre-hamlet-as-youve-never-seen-it-before-30442060.html.

Mustroph，Tom. "Eindrücke vom Athener 'Hamlet'-Spektakel mit der Berliner Schaubühne." ["Impressions of the Athens 'Hamlet' Spectacle with Schaubühne Berlin."〕 *Frankfurter Rundschau*, 9 July 2008, www.fr. de/importe/fr-online/home/hamlet-in-athen-tschuldigung-a-1175331.

Nestruck, J. Kelly. "Why Anarchic German Actor Lars Eidinger Loves to Break the Fourth Wall." *The Globe and Mail*, 23 May 2015, www.theglobeandmail. com/arts/theatre-and-performance/why-anarchic-german-actor-lars-eidinger-loves-to-break-the-fourth-wall/article24581220/.

Ni, Guanghui. "习近平：胸怀大局把握大势着眼大事　努力把宣传思想工作做得更好"〔"Xi Jinping: Let's Grasp the Situation, Focus on the Major Issues — Let's Improve Propaganda and Ideological Work"〕. *People's Daily*, 21 Aug. 2013, cpc.people.com.cn/n/2013/0821/c64094-22636876.html.

Nice, David. "Hamlet, Schaubühne Berlin, Barbican Theatre." *theartsdesk. com*, 2 Dec. 2011, www.theartsdesk.com/theatre/hamlet-schaub%C3%BChne-berlin-barbican-theatre.

Orr, Jake. "Review: Hamlet." *A Younger Theatre*, 4 Dec. 2011, www. ayoungertheatre.com/review-hamlet-thomas-ostermeier-schaubune-barbican-centre/.

Osborne, John. *The Meiningen Court Theatre 1866–1890*. Cambridge UP, 1988.

Pan, Yu. "墨本丹青版《赵氏孤儿》下周加演"〔"The Ink Painting Version of *The Orphan of Zhao* Is Again on Stage Next Week"〕. *Oriental Morning Post*, 4 Mar. 2011, www.dongdongqiang.com/liyuanzouma/2011-03-04/19648.html.

Prescott, Paul. *Reviewing Shakespeare: Journalism and Performance from the Eighteenth Century to the Present*. Cambridge UP, 2013.

Renz-Hotz, Ashlee. "Is America Ready for the Real 'Hamlet'?" *Pyragraph*, 13 Aug. 2015, www.pyragraph.com/2015/08/is-america-ready-for-the-real-hamlet/.

Schwartz, Shalom H. "Mapping and Interpreting Cultural Differences around the World." 2004. *Value Frameworks at the Theoretical Crossroads of Culture*, Intercultural Research Vol. 4, edited by SISU Intercultural Institute (Steve J. Kulich, Michael H. Prosser, Weng Liping), Shanghai Foreign Language Education Press, 2012, pp. 339–79.

Shenton, Mark. "Hamlet." *The Stage*, 26 Aug. 2015, www.thestage.co.uk/reviews/2015/hamlet-cumberbatch-barbican/.

Sokolowski, Andre. "Lars Eidinger im Februar." 〔"Lars Eidinger in February."〕 *KULTURAextra*, 15 Feb. 2015, www.kultura-extra.de/theater/spezial/rosinenpicken331_hamlet_schaubuehneberlin.php.

Thiher, Allen. *Revels in Madness: Insanity in Medicine and Literature*. U of Michigan P, 2004.

Trueman, Matt. "Review: Hamlet, Barbican Centre." *Matt Trueman*, 4 Dec. 2011, matttrueman.co.uk/2011/12/review-hamlet-barbican-centre.html.

Wahl, Christine. "Der kleine Horrorladen." 〔"Little Shop of Horrors."〕 *Der Tagesspiegel*, 19 Sept. 2008, www.tagesspiegel.de/kultur/berliner-schaubuehne-der-kleine-horrorladen/1328296.html.

Wang, Jia. "王珮瑜墨本丹青版《赵氏孤儿》昨夜满座满堂彩"〔"Wang Peiyu's Ink Painting Version of *The Orphan of Zhao* Receives Full House and Standing Ovation Last Night"〕. *Chengdu Daily*, 15 Apr. 2012, news.163. com/12/0416/05/7V6I4L4N00014AED.html.

Wang Jianhong. "苦难都是他的财富——著名豫剧演员李树建专访"〔"Suffering Is His Wealth — Interview with Famous Opera Actor Li Shujian"〕. *Xinmin*

Evening News，30 Apr. 2017，kknews. cc/zh-my/entertainment/oylxyym. html.

Wang Jisi. 中国十大古典悲剧集［*Ten Chinese Classical Tragedies*］. Shanghai Literature & Art Publishing House，1982.

—. 中国十大古典喜剧集［*Ten Chinese Classical Comedies*］. Shanghai Literature & Art Publishing House，1982.

Wang Shengxi.“河南豫剧院《程婴救孤》：向海外观众展现忠义之美”［“Henan Opera *Cheng Ying Rescues the Orphan* Shows the Beauty of Loyalty to Overseas Audiences”］. *Guangming Daily*，11 Nov. 2016，culture.people. com.cn/n1/2016/1111/c22219-28853133.html.

Xiong，Yuanyi.“中国悲剧的文化认同与背叛”［“The Cultural Identity and the Betrayal of Chinese Tragedy”］. *Journal of Hubei University of Economics*，vols. 1–2，no. 3，2004，retrieved from www.wanfangdata.com.cn. Accessed 16 Mar. 2017.

Zhang，Chaoqun.“古装豫剧《程婴救孤》在洛杉矶上演感动观众”［“The Los Angeles Performance of Henan Costume Opera *Cheng Ying Saves the Orphan* Moves the Audience”］. *Xinhua News Agency*，20 Oct. 2016，ent. news.cn/2016-10/20/c_1119752394.htm.

Zhang，Guogang.“《赵氏孤儿》为什么会风靡欧洲?”［“Why Did *The Orphan of Zhao* Become Popular in Europe?”］. *Nanfeng Chuang* no. 8，2015，pp. 106–07，retrieved from www.cnki.net. Accessed 17 Oct. 2017.

Zhang，Huiling，Huang Teng and Liang Man.“墨本丹青《赵氏孤儿》”［“The Ink Painting Version of *The Orphan of Zhao*”］. *Tianjin Ribao*，22 Sept. 2016，news.xinhuanet.com/local/2016-09/22/c_129293344.htm.

Zhang，Jing.“京剧《赵氏孤儿》”［“The Beijing Opera *The Orphan of Zhao*”］. *Guose Tianxiang Xiqu Sheying Gongzuoshi de Boke*，30 May 2011，blog.sina. com.cn/s/blog_5fc76fac01017ghk.html.

Zhao，Weijun.“听‘京剧界李宇春’唱《赵氏孤儿》”［“Listening to the ‘Li Yuchun of Beijing Opera’ Sing *The Orphan of Zhao*”］. *Shanghai Beijing Opera Theatre Company*，6 Apr. 2012，www.pekingopera.sh.cn/Eight-cont. aspx?id = 11709.

Zhou，Guoliang.“‘瞧这角儿’——‘霸气’李树建：豫剧《程婴救孤》登上百老汇”［“‘Look at This Star’ — A Domineering Li Shujian Performs Henan Opera *Cheng Ying Rescues the Orphan* on Broadway”］. *Hebei Xinwen News Network*，29 Sept. 2016，hebei.hebnews.cn/2016-09/29/content_5923584. htm.

6

Zaju and *The Caucasian Chalk Circle*

Liu Siyuan
Shanghai International Studies University

Summary: During his sojourn in the United States between 1941 and 1947, German dramatist Bertolt Brecht wrote *The Caucasian Chalk Circle*, commissioned by a contract for Broadway production. It is the only Brechtian play which is based on a genuine Chinese drama, specifically a Zaju work from the Yuan Dynasty. For some time, however, the original Chinese elements in Brecht's play did not receive much critical attention in the USA. This chapter seeks a better understanding of how Chinese elements in the dramaturgy, the narrative, and the characters' stylized performance construct a dialectical theatrical space for inquiring into the nature of an ideal social order, and how these elements remain politically expressive in a modern context. Brecht's play embodies a range of cultural interactions: these include Chinese, American, Japanese, and Russian influences. It suggests urgent questions about values concerned with ownership with which we are still confronted in today's world. Now that *The Caucasian Chalk Circle* has become one of Brecht's most frequently staged plays in the USA, as a part of American culture, we have more reason than ever to recall its Zaju origins as strongly contributing to this success.

Introduction

The Caucasian Chalk Circle was the only play which German dramatist Bertolt Brecht (1898–1956) wrote during his sojourn in the United States from 1941 to 1947. Unfortunately, the playwright did not have the chance to see it staged before he left America in 1947. It was a play commissioned by a contract for Broadway production, and the only play that Brecht wrote with "the viewing habits of the Broadway theater public in mind" (Weber, "Is" 233). The mid- and late 1950s with the popularity of the Theater of the Absurd witnessed a growing interest in Brechtian drama in the U.S. (see Weisstein 374), when the English versions of *The Caucasian Chalk Circle* were republished and commercial theaters realized it was a piece worth being staged. Peter Brook once said that Brecht's "ideas have decisively influenced American theater and film-making" (see Lyon, *Bertolt* xi). Among the American dramatists whom Brecht influenced are Tony Kushner, Robert Schenkkan, George C. Wolfe, Anna Deavere Smith, and others (see Weber, "Brecht" 353).

For some time after its premiere in 1948 in Northfield (Minnesota), in an unauthorized English version, a characteristic concern of Anglo-American critics of *The Caucasian Chalk Circle* was to study the political implications of the *Prologue* and of its relation to the play-within-the-play.① In contrast, the Chinese elements in the play, including the so-called arrogating narrator (to be explained below) and the stylized performance of characters, for some time received far less critical attention. This could be the result of a misreading shaped by an antagonizing ideology when the play was first published and staged in the late 1940s, the beginning of the Cold War. When Brecht's work was introduced into the U.S. in the early 1930s, he was labeled a communist playwright and poet. Even after the Pearl Harbor Attack in 1941, when the U.S. became allied with the Soviet Union, this situation did not change much. Ideological concern was one of the major problems that baffled the publication and the staging of Brecht's plays in the 1940s and early 1950s.

---

① This forms a contrast with Chinese scholarship on the play, which can be divided by two major concerns: its reference to *The History of the Chalk Circle*, a Zaju written in the Yuan Dynasty, and the effect of estrangement in the play, a Brechtian theatrical theory and practice which took shape after Brecht's watching Mei Lanfang's Beijng opera performance.

On the one hand, it steered Anglo-American academia from the play itself to its legitimacy on the American stage. In the summer of 1966, Eric Bentley in "An Un-American Chalk Circle?" adopted careful wording in his defense of Brecht, arguing that the resolution of the play's conflict about ownership was based not on communism but on reason in general, and that Brecht like his American audience cherished a "democratic hope." On the other hand, wishing to defend Brecht by arguing that the playwright worked continuously for a better social order as a universal truth through dramatic imagination, Bentley drew a conclusion that both the Soviet Georgia setting in the *Prologue* and the Chinese plots of the chalk circle should be taken as equally "exotic externals" (68). Such an interpretation ran the risk of overlooking the significance of Chinese elements, which are able to construct a dialectical theatrical space for inquiring into the nature of an ideal social order which could bring about justice. This was an urgent question in Brecht's time, and remains so in ours.

One might surmise that interpretations of Brecht's borrowing of Asian theater dramaturgy were preconditioned by a collective unconscious of Orientalism, which has had much influence in Anglo-American theater circles if not in the academia. This resulted in considering why and how Brecht borrowed from exotic performing arts, but less what the borrowed dramaturgy in the original Chinese performance was intended to express — and even less what the dialectic relation between its original Chinese dramatic expression and that of its Brechtian adaptation can reveal. It was not always fully realized that *The Caucasian Chalk Circle* is the only Brechtian play which is not a make-up *chinoiserie* piece but one based on a genuine Chinese drama. This chapter explores how the Chinese elements in the dramaturgy, the narrative, and the characters' stylized performance construct "a more dialectical, synthesizing perspective" of a new social order (Silberman et al. 101), and how these elements remain politically expressive in a modern context.

The Caucasian Chalk Circle and Li Qianfu

The Caucasian Chalk Circle is an adaptation of a Zaju written by Li Qianfu (courtesy name Li Xingdao)② in the Yuan Dynasty (1271–1368) titled 灰闌記 or *Hui Lan Ji* (*The History of the Chalk Circle*,

---

② Also transliterated as Li Hsing-tao.

which can be expanded as *Used by Pao the Governor as a Skillful Stratagem for Discovering the Truth*). The original play is a Gong'an play, a law-case drama which ends with virtue rewarded, evil punished, and justice enforced (see also Yu and Lovrich as well as Idema). Gong'an works that often express a call for justice were popular during the Yuan Dynasty, when the Han nation suffered severe discrimination and oppression under the rule of Mongolian invaders. Zaju is a dramatic one-prologue-and-four-scene genre,③ which became a mature performing art in the period. The prologue is often a prose narrative by a character, while the scenes consist of singing, each scene adopting a different Chinese key signature. *The History of the Chalk Circle* is a story about Zhang Haitang, a girl who is forced to become a "woman of pleasure" so as to support her mother. Haitang marries a wealthy merchant Ma Junqin as his second wife, and bears him a son. Mrs. Ma, his jealous first wife, poisons her husband, claiming that Haitang is the murderer and that she herself is the boy's mother. The drunken judge of Zhengzhou court, bribed by Mrs. Ma, makes Haitang admit her "guilt" after she is beaten, and sends her to Kaifeng court where she is to await her sentence. Mrs. Ma has a sexual relationship with Zhao, an officer serving at Zhengzhou court, whereupon he bribes the two men traveling with Haitang and orders them to kill her in the quiet woods before they arrive in Kaifeng. Luckily, the three encounter Haitang's brother Zhang Lin. Despite a dispute and misunderstanding he has had with his sister, Zhang Lin saves her.

At the court of Kaifeng, Baozheng,④ the most just judge and governor in Chinese history (see also the chapter by Sun Yan in our companion volume), has the boy placed in a chalk circle between Haitang and Mrs. Ma, and orders them to pull him from opposite ends as a means to distinguish the true mother from the false one. Being afraid of hurting her son, Haitang refuses to pull at him. Baozheng then decides she is the true mother, giving her the child as well as the deceased Mr. Ma's property. He also pronounces a death sentence for Mrs. Ma as murderer as well as for her relationship with Zhao, and punishes all the others that were engaged in evil conduct.

The History of the Chalk Circle is the only complete play by Li

---

③   The literary translation of Zaju form is one-*Xiezi*-and-four-*Zhe*. *Xiezi* is similar to prologue, which I will explain below. *Zhe* means scene rather than act, for it is more about change of scene than development of plot as action in the Aristotelian concept of drama.

④   Baozheng was translated as Pao in Stanislas Julien's French version.

Xingdao which has been preserved. It was one of the first Chinese plays translated into a European language. It was first rendered into French by Stanislas Julien, published in London in 1832. Julien supplied his version with notes that explain the meaning of words without equivalents in European languages (see Berg-Pan, *Bertolt* 194). Several later versions including Frances Hume's 1954 English translation were based on Julien's (ibid. 194–95). Brecht saw Alfred Henschke's play adaptation *Der Kreidekreis*, written under the pen-name of Klabund, in 1925 in Berlin. Though Klabund made changes in the original plot and characters according to his will, he maintained the "intermingling of lyrical verse with prose and dramatic dialogues," which may be the feature that attracted Brecht when he saw Klabund's play (Berg-Pan, *Bertolt* 196). It is believed that Brecht read the English translation of the Chinese play during his exile in Scandinavia (Berg-Pan, "Mixing" 219). Obviously it had lingered in his mind (see Berg-Pan, *Bertolt* 197). He "used the chalk circle imagery in 'The Elephant Calf', a ludicrous interlude in his 1925 version of *Man Is Man*" (Mumford 101). He then attempted to write a play adaptation titled *Odenser Kreidekreis*, but gave up after jotting down a few pages of notes. In 1940 he wrote *Der Augsburger Kreidekreis* as a short story in Denmark (see Mumford 101), Augsburg being a city in southern Germany and Brecht's hometown (see Brecht, *Collected* 328). Except for a change of setting during the Thirty Years War in the seventeenth century and a comparatively minor role for the judge, the short story presents exactly the same plot as the inset play of *The Caucasian Chalk Circle*; the maid-servant who decides to save the baby is of few words, like her theatrical equivalent Grusha. The dramaturgy Brecht adds to his play consists of the prologue, the singer, and the chorus.

New Adaptation

The success of Klabund's play on the American stage in the late 1930s and early 1940s, as well as a contract for a Broadway production secured for Brecht by Luise Rainer, the Academy Award winner and established German-American actress (Liu Xiaoqing 147 wrongly asserts that she was Australian), who starred as female protagonist in Klabund's play, encouraged Brecht to try out a new adaptation of the Chinese play for the American audience. Of course Brecht did not write the play for merely commercial interests; it was also intended to construct a theatrical space as social institute for negotiating an ideal social order with the help of the ancient Chinese play's dramaturgy. The Chinese elements of *The Caucasian Chalk Circle* do not exist on the play's locutionary level such as the setting, names of characters, and costumes, but rather on the illocutionary level, the narrative and the stylized performance of characters in the play's historical context — for a theatrical discourse which then became fruitful in an interculturally oriented social and political context. Brecht's use of the medieval Chinese play has been discussed as metonymic translation (see Liu Xiaoqing).

It is possible that Brecht gained the inspiration for the *Prologue* from a dramaturgy of the Japanese Noh play in the 1920s, at a time when German society was fascinated by Japanese culture and arts (see Berg-Pan, *Bertolt* 138–45). However, if one takes into consideration that Brecht had close relations with Russian theater avant-gardists in the 1910s (see Bai 402 – 13) who had borrowed theatrical forms heavily from Chinese theatre, and that Brecht used every means to learn from Chinese culture and followed the process of its communist revolution, which he believed promised a utopian future, one can assume that China, whose arts enjoyed incomparable prestige, served as a symbol for Brecht firing both his theatrical and his political imagination. Clearly, the influences on the work represent a range of cultural interactions. There is little doubt that it is the traditional Chinese plays and performing arts that shaped Brecht's conception of *Verfremdungseffekt*, a dramaturgy to which he devoted considerable energy to awaken a carefree middle-class audience from the enchantment of Aristotelian, empathetic theater productions so as to make them observe and judge through a critical and detached view (see also Bai, Tian). Certainly the conception is traceable to Russian formalism, as in Viktor Shklovsky's "priem ostranenniya" (the device of making strange), but it has earlier roots.

The prologue or prelude of a play was called *Xiezi* in Zaju theater in the Yuan Dynasty. *Xiezi* means wedge, chock, or cleat in Chinese. In Zaju it is a short section in which one of the play's characters introduces the time, the place, the relationship between characters, and the events before the play starts. *Xiezi* is usually found at the beginning of a play but may sometimes be placed between scenes, as an efficient dramaturgy to enable the audience's basic understanding of the plot or to inform the audience of events between scenes that could not be conveyed by performers within a short time. It is a dramaturgy to strengthen the relation between the scenes and maintain the pace of the play within a psychologically endurable time span (see Xu 72, 76). The Yuan Dynasty's Zaju features a one-prologue-and-four-scene structure that could be staged within two to three hours, which proves to be manageable by the performers and acceptable for the audience (see Xu 89). The narrator of the *Xiezi* in Zaju does not necessarily have to be the protagonist. It may also be another character in the play, as is often the case (see Xu 73), so that the character "steps out of the fictional narrative level of the play and talks directly to the audience, offering an explanation of the plot as well as describing the scene, which pushes forward the plot" (Gong 105).

Xiezi Narrative Levels

In *The History of the Chalk Circle*, Haitang's mother introduces the family's financial standing, the reason why Haitang became a "woman of pleasure," the relationship between her daughter and wealthy merchant Ma Junqin, and the dispute between Haitang and her brother Zhang Lin. This prepares the audience for the first scene, in which Mrs. Ma maltreats Haitang and accuses her of murdering Mrs. Ma's husband and feigning to be the boy's mother. Such "character-arrogating narrative" reveals that Zaju maintains the narrative features of performing arts from before the Yuan Dynasty. Though plays that could stage a complete story had been available before the Yuan Dynasty, most performing arts had been much like the Italian *commedia dell'arte* as being less-text-based funny performances of sketches, whereas fictional stories were performed by dramatic narrators as storytelling rather than staging of characterization. This can also be proven by the original work's extended title, which takes the form of a title for a narrative with chapters. There are two narrative levels: one level on which characters convey the story and another level on which the playwright narrates through a character in the *Xiezi* (see Gong 106). In addition to their function in pushing forward the plot, Brecht found that the double narrative levels constructed in *Xiezi* could also shape a philosophically critical interpretation of a play from a non-empathetic perception (see also Du 316–17; Tatlow 291ff.). This ancient dramatic form, similarly to modern meta-drama, unexpectedly foregrounds the playwright's intention and attitude toward the play (ibid. 106).

The singer in the play is another device to construct such a narrative. The *Prologue* was first published with the play at the request of Brecht's primary English translator Eric Bentley in *Tulane Drama Review* in 1959, three years after the playwright's death, though another six years passed before it was staged by Minnesota Theatre Company at Guthrie Theater in 1965 (see Bentley, Introduction 11; Connelly 96). In the *Prologue* of *The Caucasian Chalk Circle*, the singer introduces the play ready to be staged for both the peasant audience on stage and the real audience off stage. His introduction contains several pieces of information: *The Caucasian Chalk Circle* is "from the Chinese," the play's title and origin, then a wish that "the voice of the old poet also sounds well in the shadow of Soviet tractors," how the play is to influence "reality" on the stage, as "old and new wisdom mix admirably," and how the play is to change reality off the stage. When Brecht advised Bentley not to publish or stage the *Prologue* of the play in the late 1940s (Bentley, Introduction 11), he was in fact deleting the *Prologue*'s direct reference to the political and military tension between the two sides in the Cold War over their respective geographical extension. This is the reality of which his American audience and readers at the end of the World War were tired and which they would be inclined to neglect. This is also a reality that may have alerted the U.S. authorities to Brecht's political standing, and doomed the production of his plays.

The singer, the only character who appears both in the *Prologue* and in the play-within-the-play, addresses the character in the inset play, the audience on the stage as a character in the framing *Prologue*, and the audience off the stage. The singer's role is different from either the classical drama's chorus, who often plays the role of a second character or of the audience on stage, or the playwright on the framing narrative level, who mostly addresses the audience off the stage by making comments on the play. His ability to step out of his role as a character from time to time when necessary was the ideal manner of performance for which Brecht had long been searching. Brecht wished to find a dramaturgy to prevent the actors' identification with the characters, so as to prevent the audience from empathizing with the character on the stage and to maintain the ability for a detached and sound judgement of the play as a key value.

The Zaju Singer as Narrator

It was when he met the famous Beijing opera actor Mei Lanfang in

Moscow in 1935 and saw some of his performances that Brecht declared he had found what he had been looking for. Brecht admired the Chinese actor of the Beijing opera, who was the character and the performer at the same time. Mei, Brecht observed, used some gestures which had a designated meaning shared by both the performers and the audience. It was this manner of performance that he wished his actors could adopt to achieve *Verfremdungseffekt*, a dramaturgy that helps the audience construct a critical distance for perception (see also Bai). Nevertheless, the gestures of the Beijing opera took a long time to develop, form, and become accepted by both the performers and the audience. Brecht may have realized that he should replace the gestures of Beijing opera performers with a theatrical "gesture" or *gestus* that would work in the same way to build a distance between the audience and the performers (see also Brooker 219ff.). A narrator who could "arrogate" a layer of meaning constructed by a specific narrative level proved to be Brecht's supplementary method.

However, what Brecht did not realize was that the singer's role as an arrogating narrator was similar to the role of Baozheng, the judge and governor of Kaifeng court, in the handling of suspense. The singer's ability to move between two narrative levels and address three audience groups constructs a manner in the play's storytelling which is in accordance with the narrative tradition of Gong'an plays. In *The History of the Chalk Circle*, when Baozheng first appears on stage in Scene Four, he introduces himself and recalls how he has been appointed as judge and governor by the emperor with a golden card, which grants him the right of a final judgment of all cases before reporting them to the emperor.⑤ He then expresses his hatred of corruption, and declares his determination to rid the court of it. Baozheng's self-introduction is a narrative in the fictional "reality," while the expression of his hatred of corruption is closer to a narrative addressed to the audience's reality. It sounds more like the playwright's declaration of the theme of the play and the values it represents through Baozheng's voice. Thus the first item of information is addressed to the audience off the stage, while the following three items could be addressed to both the audience off the stage and the characters on the stage, especially to Haitang. All four items are articulated in one paragraph.

---

⑤ Self-introduction is a performance convention in Zaju, a time-efficient measure to stage a new character. Brecht evidently noticed the narrative feature in self-introduction, but did not relate it to his dramaturgy.

This efficient dramaturgy both informs the off-stage audience that Haitang will be proven innocent, from the playwright's narrative point of view, and constructs another perception of the case through Baozheng's character. Baozheng is both a character on the narrative level of fictional reality (Haitang's case) and a critic of social ills on the level of reality of the off-stage audience. Then, after he decides who is the true mother, Baozheng adds an explanation about how he solved the case with the chalk circle. This could seem surprisingly strange for European audiences in Brecht's time, who were used to suspense that pushes forward the plot. Such an "arrogating" narrator does invite the off-stage audience to judge what happened on stage, so as to encourage referentiality in their judgement of good and evil in their social life. This relates his apparently individual identity to that of the audience.

Baozheng's handling of suspense also results from Yuan viewing habits. Gong'an works were very popular in the Yuan Dynasty, for the Mongolian administration featured many practices of injustice. They divided men and women into racial rankings. The Han nation ranked the third, while the Mongolian and the Semu ranked the first and the second. People from these privileged nations faced few legal responsibilities, while Han and Nanren, ranking third and fourth, could be punished by death for minor legal transgressions. The royal families and nobles of the Mongolians frequently took farmers' lands by force to turn them into hunting fields. The national examination for selection of officials was suspended, leaving young scholars no means to support themselves. Zaju was the performing art of the Han nation. Law-case plays that end with evil punished and justice restored expressed Han people's desire to restore proper social order with equality and justice. As the audience members mostly lived with the social ills depicted in the plays, the cultural values inscribed in dramatic art allow insight into their being more concerned with how Baozheng judged the case rather than whether Baozheng would judge the case with wisdom and restore justice.

Thus plays that develop a double narrative level in which certain characters arrogate levels in their storytelling steer the audience's attention from suspense in the plot toward the denouement of the conflict. Such a narrative form is shaped by these plays' content, which in turn is shaped by the historical context of Gong'an plays, steering audience attention from what happens toward how justice is restored. This is also Brecht's concern in writing *The Caucasian Chalk Circle*.

The Brechtian Singer

The singer's function in *The Caucasian Chalk Circle* as a narrator who arrogates two narrative levels and talks to the audience amid three layers of reality can be understood as the same device to steer the audience's attention from *what* the judgement is to *how* the case is judged. In addition to describing the scene, he foretells what will happen by revealing the characters' inner minds and giving instructions to characters in the inset play. The latter begins with the scene in which he sits together with the chorus as "listeners" with a "well-thumbed notebook in his hand" (Brecht, *Caucasian* 27). His recitation "makes it clear that he has told his story over and over again" (ibid. 27). His skillfulness suggests not only his familiarity with the story, but also his authority in shaping its interpretation and his confidence in helping the audience both on- and off-stage discover the answer to their respective questions about ownership. When two soldiers walk in with the governor in chains, his songs foretell the governor's death:

> You won't be moving into a new palace
> But into a little hole in the ground.
> Look about you once more, blind man!
> Does all you had please you?
> Between the Easter Mass and the Easter meal
> You are walking to a place whence no one returns. (*Caucasian* 35)

The singer's songs inform both the audience on and off the stage what will happen next. When ironshirts are chasing Grusha, he gives her instructions on where to flee. When she reaches a farm, he tells her to sit and eat. These instructive songs ensure both the audience on and off the stage that Grusha can escape with the child from the town. They relieve the audience members both on and off the stage of anxiety about what will happen next, and also of possible empathy with Grusha's experiences. Instead they will probably be more concerned with how Grusha can keep her child.

Compared to the chorus, who only expresses the characters' feelings in singing, the singer's role is capable of changing. In the first three acts, the singer's songs mostly take the standpoint of a playwright overseeing the staging of his play, but in Act Four when Grusha and Simon meet after the war, his songs jump from a third-person narrative point of view to a first-person point of view as he enters the mind of Simon and Grusha:

> I trod on the first, left the second behind, the third was run through
> by the captain.
> One of my brothers died by steel, the other by smoke,
> My neck caught fire, my hands froze in my gloves, my toes in
> my socks.
> I fed on aspen buds; I drank maple juice; I slept on stone, in
> water. (*Caucasian* 82)

And for the first time, his song enters Grusha's mind.

> I found a helpless infant
> I had not the heart to destroy him
> I had to care for a creature that was lost
> I had to stoop for breadcrumbs on the floor
> I had to break myself for that which was not mine
> That which was other people's
> Someone must help! (*Caucasian* 83)

The singer's changing roles from the playwright of the inset play at its beginning in the fictional "reality" to the role of audience both on and off the stage, and then to the playwright's role again at the play's end, commenting on the logic behind the judgement of this case of ownership and motherhood, serves as the theatrical "gesture" or *gestus* that makes him both a character and a performer, and therefore always keeps the audience members at a critical distance to work out their own judgement of the play.

Stylization, *Verfremdung*, Muteness

Like other plays by Brecht, *The Caucasian Calk Circle* is a dramaturgy-based play: it is a play whose meaning relies on dramaturgy rather than on the characters or a particular performance. This is the reason why his play did not initially find a market in the U.S., where theater tends to be a business of making stars and stars making plays. At first sight, Brecht's idea of characters seems to be in conflict with traditional Chinese theater, which relies strongly on the actors' performing skills. However, traditional Chinese theater is made up of the stylized performance of characters, and actors need to learn one character's stylized performance before they take roles in a play. In traditional Chinese theater, there was a division between performance gestures according to differently stylized characters. One stylized character would adopt one style of face mask, one style of body movement, one style of singing, and one style of diction in narrative.

Dan originally means the female performers who are capable of singing and dancing. Before the Southern Song Dynasty (1127–1279) only *Jing*, the "painted face," and *Mo*, the middle-aged or elderly man, took their forms. These were characters who made impromptu comic performances with quips and jokes. When Zaju emerged in late Southern Song as a text-based dramatic genre different from impromptu comic performance (see also Brandon 27ff.), singing and narrative replaced quips and jokes as the major performing forms of plays, and *Dan* therefore became a most important stylized character in plays (see Liu Xiaoming 273). In each Zaju play, there is only one singer, and the rest of the characters will perform in narrating. Almost half of the Zaju works in the Yuan Dynasty have *Dan* as the single singer, so that one would speak of the *Dan*-book.

This development gives the female characters more space to express themselves, and thus to articulate and strengthen their sense of identity. It dramatically contrasts with women's life in social reality, where they are more confined within a domestic space and can seldom make their voice heard. *The History of the Chalk Circle* is one such work that gives scope to the *Dan* performance. The *Dan* who plays Haitang sings at the beginning of each scene and sometimes in the middle of a scene. Her singing is mostly a lyrical expression of her emotions and sentiments. In addition, as one of the origins of stylization is the character's social status, for stylized character types there are formal requirements governing performance by which performers should abide and which they should never break, no matter in what situation the character finds herself. Therefore, sometimes the character's mental conflict is presented by a tension between the performance format which restricts expression of emotions and the performer's attempts to find expression within the format. In *The History of the Chalk Circle*, no matter how much Haitang suffers from false accusation, the character will never resort to physical action but will articulate her misfortune in narrative and singing. When her case is to be heard at the court of Kaifeng, instead of telling Baozheng what happened, she becomes mute. Her muteness is a stylized externalization of her desperation, for she has exhausted all means to prove her innocence.

It is the stylized performance of characters that helps to shape

Brecht's dramaturgy in *The Caucasian Chalk Circle*. He strictly divides the performance between characters and the assignment of formated performance to stylized character to achieve the desired *Verfremdungseffekt*. Brecht allots the narrative to the singer and the action to Grusha. Grusha is a woman of action. She sees the baby, takes it, flees with it, abandons it, brings it back, feeds it, and takes care of it. Differently from its Chinese origin, only the singer and the chorus in the play sing. Their songs do more for the narrative than serving as lyrical expressions of Grusha's emotions. This arrangement denies Grusha the chance to express herself.

Brecht has been criticized for his over-confidence as playwright and director in shaping his characters in dramatic texts and the actors' performance on the stage. The technique of muteness as stylized externalization in performance, in any case, is adopted as an effective theatrical measure to express more than words could. That is why when Simon returns, Grusha stands mute on the other side of the river. If stylized performance was a practical measure to pass on performing skills from generation to generation in ancient China, Brecht deliberately implements a strict division between characters' performance and stylized characters' formated performance, to prevent the actors from sensationalized performance that might arouse empathy in the audience. Azdak the judge is another stylized character, closer to *Jing* in Zaju. He reverses right and wrong, and accidentally does justice with a mistake as a joker.

With Azdak's stylized performance, Brecht guides his audience from relief and joy at Grusha's winning of her case and her reunion with Simon to questioning the legitimacy of ownership and the origin of justice: Who has the right to claim ownership? Who has the authority to decide what is justice? These were urgent value questions concerning an ideal social order when Brecht wrote his play toward the end of World War II in 1944, and they remain urgent questions with which we are confronted in today's world. In suggesting them in his time, Brecht in *The Caucasian Chalk Circle* adopts a number of American artistic elements to enable its dramatic effect (see Lyon, "Elements"). And now that *The Caucasian Chalk Circle* has become one of Brecht's most frequently staged plays in the U.S., as a part of the American culture which was Brecht's "target system" (see Liu Xiaoqing 153–54), we have more reason than ever to recall its Zaju origins as strongly contributing to this success.

References

Bai, Ronnie. "Dances with Mei Lanfang: Brecht and the Alienation Effect." *Comparative Drama*, vol. 32, no. 3, 1998, pp. 389–433.

Bentley, Eric. Introduction. *The Caucasian Chalk Circle* by Bertolt Brecht (Revised English Version). Grove Press, 1967.

Bentley, Eric. "An Un-American Chalk Circle?" *The Tulane Drama Review*, vol. 10, no. 4, 1966, pp. 64–77.

Berg-Pan, Renata. *Bertolt Brecht and China*. Bonn: Bouvier, 1979.

—. "Mixing Old and New Wisdom: The 'Chinese' Sources of Brecht's *Kaukasischer Kreidekreis* and Other Works." *The German Quarterly*, vol. 48, no. 2, 1975, pp. 204–28.

Brandon, James R., editor. *The Cambridge Guide to Asian Theatre*. Cambridge UP, 1993.

Brecht, Bertolt. *The Caucasian Chalk Circle*. Translated by Eric Bentley, Revised English Version. Grove Press, 1967.

—. *The Collected Short Stories of Bertolt Brecht*. Edited by John Willett and Ralph Manheim. Bloomsbury, 2015.

Brooker, Peter. "Key Words in Brecht's Theory and Practice of Theatre." *The Cambridge Companion to Brecht*, edited by Peter Thomson and Glendyr Sacks, 2nd ed., Cambridge UP, 2006, pp. 209–24.

Connelly, Stacey. "Brecht's Out-of-Town Tryout: The World Premiere of *The Caucasian Chalk Circle*." *Theatre History Studies*, vol. 17, 1997, pp. 93–119.

Du, Wenwei. "The Chalk Circle Comes Full Circle: From Yuan Drama Through the Western Stage to Beijing Opera." *Asian Theatre Journal*, vol. 12, 1995, pp. 307–25.

Gong Dequan. "An Explanation of the Legitimacy of Arrogating Narrative in Yuan-*zaju*." *Drama: Journal of the Central Academy of Drama*, vol. 145, no. 3, 2012.

Idema, Wilt L. *Judge Bao and the Rule of Law: Eight Ballad-Stories from the Period 1250–1450*. World Scientific Publishing, 2010.

Li, Xingdao. *The Story of the Circle of Chalk: A Drama from the Old Chinese*. Translated by Frances Hume. Rodale, 1954.

Liu, Xiaoming. *A History of the Formation of Zaju*. Zhonghua, 2007.

Liu, Xiaoqing. "A Metonymic Translation: Bertolt Brecht's *The Caucasian Chalk Circle*." *Translation: A Transdisciplinary Journal*, 2013, pp. 133–58.

Lyon, James K. *Bertolt Brecht in America*. Princeton UP, 1980.

—. "Elements of American Theatre and Film in Brecht's *The Caucasian Chalk Circle*." *Modern Drama*, vol. 42, 1999, pp. 238–46.

Mumford, Meg. *Bertolt Brecht*. Routledge, 2009.

Silberman, Marc, Steve Giles and Tom Kuhn. *Brecht on Theatre: Bertolt Brecht*. 3rd ed., Bloomsbury, 2015.

Tatlow, Antony. *The Mask of Evil: Brecht's Response to the Poetry, Theatre and Thought of China and Japan*. Peter Lang, 1977.

Tian, Min. "'Alienation-Effect' for Whom? Brecht's (Mis)interpretation of the Classical Chinese Theatre." *Asian Theatre Journal*, vol. 14, no. 2,

1997, pp. 200–22.

Weber, Carl. "Brecht and the American Theatre." *A Bertolt Brecht Reference Companion*, edited by Siegfried Mews, Greenwood, 1997, pp. 339–55.

—. "Is There a Use Value? Brecht on the American Stage at the Turn of the Century." *Bertolt Brecht: Centenary Essays*, edited by Steve Giles and Rodney Livingstone, Rodopi, 1998, pp. 227–39.

Weisstein, Ulrich. "Brecht in America: A Preliminary Survey." *Modern Language Notes*, vol. 78, no. 4, 1963, pp. 373–96.

Xu Fuming. *The Art of Zaju of Yuan Dynasty*. Shanghai Guji Publishing, 2014.

Yu Zhang and Nicholas Lovrich. "Portrait of Justice: The Spirit of Chinese Law as Depicted in Historical and Contemporary Drama." *Global Media and China*, vol. 1, issue 4, 2016, pp. 372–89.

7

The Myth of Russia as an
Intertext in British Culture

Olga Sobolev
Angus Wrenn
London School of Economics and Political Science

Summary: The aim of this chapter is a critical appraisal of the idea of Russia or the Russian myth projected by the British, examined through the structural framework of the socio-political theories of Edward Said and Pierre Bourdieu. The approach is rooted in imagology, or representation studies, concerning the structural analysis of discursive articulation with regard to ethnotyping. The representation of "the other" is thus a particular type of intertext — a dynamic product of cultural interference between an "auto" and "hetero" image, shaped by the hallmarks of a specific historical context with selective value judgments. To examine this, the authors discuss a range of literary sources from the early modern period until the early twenty-first century. The processes through which one culture's perceptions of another are (re)created are highly relevant to intercultural communication. In thematizing the literary legacy of perspectival image-making, the processes contribute to the critical theory of national stereotyping and representation.

Introduction

This chapter offers an interdisciplinary approach to the critical appraisal of the idea of Russia or the Russian myth projected by the

British, examined through the structural framework of the socio-political theories of Edward Said and Pierre Bourdieu. We will argue that, right through to the early twentieth century, the representation of Russia in Britain largely falls within the framework of Said's concept of Orientalism (see also Neboit-Mombet 457–58). Following Said's thesis on the significance of artistic discourse in the formation of the Orientalistic viewpoint, we shall look more closely at the post-1910 years to establish whether the unprecedented interest in the Russian theme among the British cultural elite had a crucial impact on and led to a radical change in the signifying function of the icon, viewed rather as a new emblem of the British intellectual prestige or a fashionable contribution to cultural capital, understood in Pierre Bourdieu's sense of the term.

Our approach to interpreting the paradigm of Russian reception is rooted in imagology, or representation studies, concerning the structural analysis of discursive articulation of national stereotyping (see Beller and Leerssen; also Cao Chapter 4.3). Recent advances in this area are focused on the constructivist perspective, considering any image of national character as culturally constructed within the framework of the given socio-historical context (see also Soboleva and Wrenn, Introduction). The representation of "the other" should, therefore, be effectively treated as a particular type of "intertext" — a dynamic product of cultural interference between the "auto" and "hetero" image, shaped by the hallmarks of a specific historical context. In another context, Robert van Gulik's constructions of China have been analyzed from imagological perspectives (see Wang and Mo 517–18, and Sun Yan's chapter in this volume). In this light, especially since the impact of the context can never be discarded, the very notion of the discursive image turns out to be intrinsically linked to the semantics of a myth — hence, the use of this term in the course of our discussion, which essentially concerns the projection of the myth of Russia constructed by the British.

When examining the characteristics of the projection, we try to go deeper than the simple binaries of the literary and artistic impact, and focus on the conceptual avenues through which the idea of "the exotic other" was appropriated and internalized in the artistic world of the British authors. We go beyond the limits of the mere reproduction or representation of the material and cultural condition of its genesis, and into such areas of fictional and poetic creation that may generate other perspectives on reality, alternative registers of the complex "other" than those afforded by the political realities of its time or the boundaries of the established perception of the "self."

We believe that the importance of such an approach transcends the field of a simple literary investigation, and that the findings are of interest to a wider circle of human and social sciences scholars. As Elizabeth Goering explains, with recourse to symbolic interactionism, "[a]n intriguing but understudied aspect of intercultural communication is the communication processes through which one culture's perceptions of another culture are created and recreated." The methods and concerns brought together here are on the one hand defined by the specificity of comparative literary imagology, and — on the other — by a dialogue with the more general field of scholarship concerned with the issues of national representation and identity constructs. The ultimate framework, however, will remain within the sociohistorical and literary study of image making: the representation and construction of Russian cultural stereotypes — not the theory of national identity and the mechanisms of its cultural formation.

We aim to show that the image of Russia in British literature, when viewed over its entire chronological extent, has developed according to a broadly dialectical pattern, alternating between extremes of demonization, for the majority of the time, interspersed with shorter, but highly significant periods in which Russian culture has been equally fetishized within literature in Britain, as a synecdoche of sophistication (for a more detailed analysis of this subject, see Soboleva and Wrenn). Our context is "the field of social theories of cultural reception, aimed at analysing the paradigms of intercultural representation and their re-contextualising and re-shaping in the process of cultural reproduction and transmission" (Soboleva and Wrenn 18). As such, the history of Russia's image within British literature serves as a critique of, as well as an exemplification of certain key notions within imagology (hetero- and auto-image), Bourdieu's concept of cultural capital, and Geert Hofstede's typology of cultural dimensions.

Ethnotypes and Intertexts

The standard work in the field of the study of national archetypes in comparative literature is surely *Imagology* by Beller and Leerssen, which is in many ways an ambitious survey, covering entries on some fifty different countries. It makes a vital preliminary point that imagology concerns not the societies of individual countries but the mental images which are formed of those countries and their inhabitants: "Our images of foreign countries, peoples and cultures mainly derive from selective value judgements (which are in turn derived from selective observation)" as in literary representations (Beller 5). As regards the purpose of this research, the authors say:

> It is the aim of imagology to describe the origin, process and function of national prejudices and stereotypes, to bring them to the surface, analyse them and make people rationally aware of them. But it would be illusory to think that we can remove the affective reasons for our prejudices, like the Hydra's heads, they grow back again continually. (Beller 11–12)

The "default value of humans' contact with different cultures" tends to be ethnocentric: what deviates from accustomed domestic patterns "is 'Othered' as an oddity, an anomaly, a singularity" (Leerssen, "Imagology: History" 17). Almost as if in response, Russian identity with its understanding of cultural values has been analyzed as "the only one of its kind," as uniquely "*contra* any and all (potentially adversarial) frameworks" (Sinekopova 435–37). Imagology, then, aims to understand "a discursive logic and representational set of cultural and poetic conventions," examining ethnotypes whose empirical truth value is undecidable: "Instead of an ethnotype's truth value, the research focus is on its persuasive poetical and rhetorical power, and that in turn depends on its recognition value and on the effectiveness of its discursive presentation" (Leerssen, "Imagology: On" 19).

In the domain of intercultural communication, "everybody tends to form their views within a certain mind-set of preconceptions, and an attempt to break the stereotypes essentially means replacing them by the new ones" (Soboleva and Wrenn 140). Beller and Leerssen include a focus on Europe, which appears somewhat incomplete. They devote most of their volume, after the Survey articles, to a long series of entries for some fifty population groups (not necessarily nation states), covering countries or continents from Australia, North and South America, also comprising some twelve subheadings for groups or nations from Asia, and they give some 60 detailed entries or definitions under the heading "Relevant Concepts, Related Disciplines." Yet at no point in their work do they spell out exactly what geographical area, or grouping of countries, constitutes Europe. There are, for example, entries on Poland and Finland, but not on the Baltic States, Estonia, Latvia, and Lithuania, and none on Belarus or Ukraine. Admittedly, some of these countries had achieved independence from the Soviet Union only a decade before the end point of Beller and Leerssen's five-hundred-year survey. But what is germane for the discussion undertaken in the present chapter is that nowhere is Europe's eastern border made clear. It is not self-evident whether Russia, which merits an entry of some four pages, is classified overall as a European or non-European nation.

By contrast, the question of whether Russia is to be considered a European or an Asiatic nation gets very much to the heart of the present chapter. For, during the period of nearly five hundred years which (like Naarden and Leerssen 226−30) we cover, Russia went from being a more or less completely isolated, only newly autonomous Grand Duchy of Moscow — following the end of the kingdom of Rus' and the emergence of western Russia from the centuries of domination by the Mongol Horde — to becoming, by the beginning of the seventeenth century, a growing power under Peter the Great, looking westward to assert itself in territorial wars with Sweden and Poland. The turn westward was more profound than a mere concern with the acquisition of territory, and by the early years of the eighteenth century Peter the Great was visiting the Netherlands and Britain, with an important trip to Greenwich, which bore fruit with the founding of the port city of St. Petersburg, destined to displace Moscow as the imperial Russian capital.

The most westerly of Russian cities, St. Petersburg was modeled on Amsterdam and, perhaps still more so, on French and Italian cities, with architects Jean-Baptiste Alexandre Le Blond and Bartolomeo Francesco Rastrelli employed. By the days of Peter's successor but two, Catherine the Great, it could boast a highly-reputed university. The Empress was able to attract the French *philosophes* Voltaire and Diderot, just as Frederick the Great had earlier invited the older thinker to his court at Sanssouci in Potsdam. The majority of Russia's population remained tied to the land in a rural economy, and the institution of serfdom was actually growing in the eighteenth century, representing some 37% of the nation's population. Yet the owners of the serfs, the nobles, were freed in 1751, under Elizabeth of Russia, from the traditional obligation placed upon them to render military service to the Tsar. That legislation facilitated the rise of the phenomenon of the émigré Russian aristocrats who undertook the Grand Tour of Europe (see Tosi 266) and spent extended periods at Baden-Baden, Nice, or in Florence or Rome.

In the nineteenth and early twentieth centuries, Russia made significant contributions to science as it developed within a European and later also American context. Russia produced Dmitri Mendeleev, whose periodic table of the elements became rapidly and firmly adopted throughout science on a global basis, while Ivan Pavlov undertook pioneering work, scarcely less widely influential, in the fields of physiology and conditioning; from the eighteenth century onwards Russia abounded in major contributors to mathematical science. In the same period ballet, originally French in its conception and imported for the exclusive, elite culture of the Tsar's court, became available to commoners, and by the last years of the nineteenth century Russia was established as a world leader in this art form. Ivan Clustine moved from the Bolshoi to France from 1903 and was recruited, in preference to French candidates, as head of the ballet at the Paris Opera in 1909. Our study examines the ways in which these modernizing developments were reflected (or, no less significantly, at certain points failed to be reflected) in the prevailing image of Russia in British literature.

Our choice of a lengthy timespan for this survey of the development of the image of Russia in literature in Britain may seem, at first glance, hard to justify. It must, however, be borne in mind that the field of study here is primarily the cultivation of the Russian stereotype in British literature and the emergence of an "intertext." Although our study does indeed stretch back to the first commercial and diplomatic visits to Russia by English diplomats and traders in the mid-sixteenth century, and although references to Russia and Russians began to appear in English literature almost immediately thereafter, the process cannot be considered to be in any significant degree reciprocal at this early stage.

For Russian literature developed at a remarkably late date, compared to literature in Western Europe. The first major Russian literary figure to establish any reputation abroad, active not only in poetry and drama, but also in prose, was Alexander Pushkin. Though he was dead by 1837 and enjoyed fame elsewhere abroad somewhat more rapidly (Dupont's French translation of *Eugene Onegin* appeared in 1849), Pushkin's most celebrated work did not appear in English translation until 1881. With prose and drama it was likewise. Until 1885 Tolstoy's name was barely known to the British readership, familiar mainly with the early translations of the writings of Turgenev, to the extent that *The Contemporary Review* ("Contemporary" 1885) could refer freely to Dmitrii Tolstoy, the Russian Minister of Home

Affairs, simply as Count Tolstoy, without any fear that his identity might be mistaken. At the end of the 1870s there appeared a couple of publications that tried to attract attention to Tolstoy's writings, but they were very sparse; see for instance Henley (1878), Ralston (1879), and Turner (1882). Henry James' notable essay on Turgenev's literary legacy as well as his 1884 "The Art of Fiction" make no mention of Tolstoy's writings. Many of Turgenev's novels were still being translated into English for the first time in the 1890s by Constance Garnett, and Dostoevsky's novels had to wait longer still.

Thus the Tolstoy craze, apart from an admittedly influential élite of British and American authors who were fluent enough in French to read *War and Peace* (from 1879) and *Anna Karenina* (from 1885) in that language, and apart from the 1884 Clara Bell translation (itself from the French translation rather than from the original Russian), did not reach a mass English-language readership until the English translations by Constance Garnett (1894) and Aylmer and Louise Maude (1922–1923).

A similar position applied to Dostoevsky. According to Rachel May (27), the Russian author was generally greeted as unreadable. Henry James was said to be "unable to finish it." A signal exception was Robert Louis Stevenson, who declared *Crime and Punishment* "easily the greatest book I have read in the last ten years" (May 28). May points out, moreover, that both the American and the Scotch novelist were reading Dostoevsky in French translation. Though Dostoevsky's works had been available to German readers for sixty years, and to French readers since 1890, according to May (following Maurice Baring), it was not until the second decade of the twentieth century that Constance Garnett's translations began to establish him as arguably the preeminent novelist of a Russia "craze." This was facilitated by sympathy among British radical intellectuals for the failed revolution of 1905, and by the general atmosphere of the Triple Entente, which grouped Russia with France against the Kaiser's unified Germany and its already outmoded and conservative neighbor, Austria-Hungary, combined with Italy as a considerably less enthusiastic ally.

"The Only Topic of the Hour"

The remarkable volte-face in terms of the stereotype of Russians in literature in Britain in this period is seen most forcefully in the transition away from the norms which informed Rudyard Kipling's

Kim, at the very beginning of the century. In Chapter 12, an Indian Hurree Babu says of Russians:

> By Jove, they are not black people. I can do all sorts of things with black people. They are Russians, and highly unscrupulous people. I — I do not want to consort with them without a witness. (Kipling 272)

Here are all the hallmark, negative character traits of Russians as found in earlier centuries, among which moral duplicity and untrustworthiness predominate. In Kipling's novel Russians are deemed even less amenable to civilization than the colonized races. By contrast, little more than a decade later, Virginia Woolf in her early Bloomsbury novel *The Voyage Out* (1915) presents a more multi-faceted view of Russians. They can still be regarded as "other" — bracketed with outright Orientals such as the Chinese by the character Evelyn Murgatroyd — and yet the same character in the novel also yearns ardently to align herself with the revolutionary movement in Russia:

> I've just had a letter from a friend of mine whose brother is in business in Moscow. They want me to stay with them, as they're in the thick of all the conspiracies and anarchists; I've a good mind to stop on my way home. It sounds too thrilling. (Woolf, *Voyage* 342)

In this context one should take into consideration the extensive imports of Russian culture that marked the early-twentieth-century period. These years are most often associated with the Sergei Diaghilev seasons (1911–1914). Leonard Woolf recalls in his autobiography that the British audience was completely enthralled by the performance: "Night after night we flocked to Covent Garden," he maintains, "entranced by a new art, a revelation to us benighted British, the Russian Ballet in the greater days of Diaghilev and Nijinsky" (37). The newspapers and fashionable magazines were full of superlatives and praising comments; and the fact that Diaghilev's premiere in London was scheduled during George V's coronation festivities speaks for itself. The big stores (Heal's and Harvey Nichols) changed their shop window styles in imitation of Bakst's designs for Diaghilev seasons. Fashionable middle-class ladies acquired fur-trimmed outfit and learned to glide like Russian peasants; the wife of the British ambassador sent dresses from St. Petersburg, for the dignitaries to shine at the opulent Slavic theme parties that were spawning all over London (Green and Swan 65; Garafola 303).

In 1912 the second Post-Impressionist Exhibition, "British, French and Russian Painters" (curated by Roger Fry and Clive Bell), featured two highly successful contemporary artists, Mikhail Larionov and Natalia Goncharova (see Reed 290–96; also Soboleva and Wrenn 43ff.). The latter was to make an unforgettable impression on an even wider audience with her designs for *Le Coq d'or* — Rimsky-Korsakov's opera performed by Diaghilev's company in 1914 (Theatre Royal, Drury Lane). These magnificent productions of Russian opera during the 1913–1914 seasons, which appeared as a real celebration of performance art, captured the imagination of the most refined viewers. According to Sir Osbert Sitwell, they raised the standard of music drama to an unprecedented level:

> The Russian operas never before performed in London until these years relieved one suddenly from the Viking world of bearded warriors drinking blood out of skulls, that had been for so long imposed by Germany. They pleased the eye at last, as well as the ear. (Sitwell 263)

In the words of Rosa Newmarch, these spectacles "rescued" the city's social life in the days just before the assassination of the Archduke:

> Russian opera, perhaps, is the only topic of the hour on which educated people can meet on a common ground of admiration. Ulster, the suffrage, Lloyd-Georgian finance, Mr Winston Churchill, are all dangerous subjects which divide house against house and estrange life-long friends. ("The Russian Invasion")

In 1916 Macmillan published a very handsome book with an impressive list of British and Russian contributors, titled *The Soul of Russia*. The "Soul" was presented with a wide range of subjects from early icons, peasant crafts, and popular folk-songs to the music of Igor Stravinsky and the paintings of Natalia Goncharova. There were poems by Valery Bryusov and Konstantin Balmont, and some prose pieces by Fyodor Sologub, Anton Chekhov, and Alexander Kuprin — all in an attempt, according to the editor Winifred Stephens, to embrace Russia's "noble but sometimes unfathomable soul" (Stephens vi).

This vogue for all things Russian represented an instance of cultural capital on which British figures could trade in sophisticated London cultural circles. It extended to the Woolfs starting their extended series of Russian language lessons with Samuel Koteliansky, the Russian-speaking émigré and close friend of D. H. Lawrence and H. G. Wells, who had come to Britain before World War I (see Diment 132). It constitutes a major shift away from the dominant dismissal of Russia as emblematic of the barbarian, unsophisticated and uncivilized, which had dominated since the sixteenth-century voyages by Turberville, Chancellor, and Hakluyt. At that initial point the stereotype of the Russian bear entered English literature, and is already to be found in Shakespeare's work of the 1590s.

By the 1920s, Woolf was writing with the utmost enthusiasm about Dostoevsky, Chekhov, and Tolstoy in "The Russian Point of View," where she says of the first writer:

> The novels of Dostoevsky are seething whirlpools, gyrating sandstorms, waterspouts which hiss and boil and suck us in. They are composed purely and wholly of the stuff of the soul. Against our wills we are drawn in, whirled round, blinded, suffocated, and at the same time filled with a giddy rapture. Out of Shakespeare there is no more exciting reading. ("Russian" 226)

Woolf uses this impression to express dissatisfaction with the formal concerns of English fiction (see also Soboleva and Wrenn 254). When the Russia "craze" or "Russophilia" gripped Western Europe in the last years of the nineteenth century and the first three decades of the twentieth (see also Rybakov for Germany), Russia was by no means a new topic of discussion or virgin territory. In fact, Virginia Woolf's 1929 novel *Orlando*, which has an outrageously non-realistic and non-naturalistic timeframe, proves apt in terms of the Russian components of its plot. The eponymous courtier-hero, still at this stage prior to a change of sex which takes place later in the seventeenth century, has a romance with a visiting Russian princess in the first years of the reign of James I (1608). At that date, real-life contacts between England and the Grand Duchy of Muscovy had been taking place for half a century, since Willoughby's first, ill-fated expedition — he and all his men died in an ice-locked ship. Later visitors such as Chancellor, Willoughby, and Turberville had enjoyed more success, reached Moscow, and found Ivan IV eager to establish trade deals (for this context, see Stout). Indeed, the Russian monarch was at one point considered as a possible spouse for the English Virgin Queen Elizabeth. The discourse initiated with those first sorties into Muscovy is characterized by hyperbole and superlatives. These may express approval or admiration, or they may give voice to disdain and even phobia.

Before the Twentieth Century

Bears and Caviary

The earliest written reports by English visitors set the tone which was to predominate for generations and indeed centuries thereafter. In the wake of Richard Hakluyt, Giles Fletcher, Sir Jerome Horsey, and George Turberville all routinely employ a vocabulary which abounds in generalization and hyperbole when describing what they witnessed first-hand. They were, of course, struck by the sheer scale of Russia's geography which, given the primitive state of roads, must have dominated their experience. They speak of the Russians themselves, in terms of their physique, as being enormous, with bellies which "overhang the waist" and the men uniformly and extravagantly bearded, a considerable contrast with the elegant and refined goatee beard which had come into vogue at the court of Elizabeth I and was to be sported by her successor James I .

Russian social practices are depicted as anachronistic and less civilized, by contrast with England, where the towns had been in the ascendant and the disappearance of serfdom had begun as early as the Peasants' Revolt of 1381, with the very last vestiges of serfdom abolished by Elizabeth just a few years after the first voyages to Russia, in 1574. England was a country where Parliament was a major force within society, destined to challenge a monarch espousing a Divine Right of Kings within two generations from the time of writing. In diametric contrast, Russia is seen as coming under the absolute autocracy of the early Romanov czars, and slavery or at any rate serfdom is the dominant system throughout the majority of what was to remain until the nineteenth century a rural, agrarian, and feudal economy.

In matters of religion, we must note that the English eyes viewing Russia in the sixteenth century witnessed a country very much dominated by Orthodox monasteries with their hierarchy and power structures, in marked contrast to the situation in England, where Thomas Cromwell had spearheaded the wholesale dissolution of the monasteries in the 1530s. In Russia, no challenge to the monasteries' economic dominance within the agrarian system was mounted before the time of Catherine the Great. And in terms of religious practice, much is made by English travel writers of the veneration accorded to icons, both in religious services and in everyday life and the domestic sphere. This is dismissed pejoratively as "idolatry" by writers from Protestant England, a country which had witnessed the iconoclasm which ensued upon the unsuccessful Pilgrimage of Grace in the 1530s, and which was to embark upon a sustained anti-Catholic culture in the wake of the Spanish Armada of 1588. As Galina Sinekopova has analyzed, it is "as if Russia's value has constantly been questioned" (428).

In the drama of this period, the stereotype of the Russian bear is introduced famously by way of Shakespeare's *Macbeth*, where the tragic (anti-)hero responds to the ghost of Banquo:

> What man dare, I dare.
> Approach thou like the rugged Russian bear,
> The arm'd rhinoceros, or th' Hyrcan tiger,
> Take any shape but that [...] (3.4.98–101)

This is not Shakespeare's only memorable bear. In *The Merry Wives of Windsor*, young Abraham Slender prides himself in having taken the bear Sackerson "by the chain" (1.1.296); in *Henry V*, the French compare the English troops to mastiffs "that run winking into the mouth of a Russian bear" (3.7.143–44); in *The Winter's Tale* we have the well-known stage direction "*Exit pursued by a bear*" (3.3.58). The bears were most likely imports from Russia (see also Stříbrný 155), a practice which commenced following the voyages undertaken by Hakluyt and others. The native wild bear in the British Isles had been exterminated thanks to over-hunting, as far back as 1000 A.D. It is ironic indeed that the rugged bear stands for the wildness of Russia while the baiting of Russian bears was routinely carried out for public entertainment, virtually on the doorstep of the Globe Theatre in Southwark (see Velten 99–100). An analytical overview shows that in Shakespeare's dramatic work "the sympathy is on the side of the bear, whose defiance of the horror of his position is admired" (Stříbrný 155).

However, even in this early period, Russia simultaneously became a byword for certain aspects of luxury. Besides the wealth of minerals and metalwork for which the country was famed, by 1603 caviar could already be used metaphorically in front of a London stage audience. Hamlet praises an earlier speech by the First Player:

> [...] for the play, I remember, pleas'd not the million, 'twas caviary to the general, but it was — as I receiv'd it, and others, whose judgments in such matters cried in the top of mine — an excellent play, well digested in the scenes, set down with as much modesty as cunning. (2.2.435–40)

Given that the first instance of the word "caviar" cited in the *Oxford English Dictionary* is Giles Fletcher's *Of the Russe Common Wealth* (1591), this suggests that the term became rapidly synonymous with high chic in London, indicating that Russia was from the earliest days capable of becoming associated with extremes of luxury to counterbalance notions of crudeness and barbarian wildness. Harold Jenkins comments on Hamlet's caviar as "a novel delicacy," adducing early-seventeenth-century sources which take it to be a black soap. The *Oxford Dictionary of Phrase and Fable* "translates" Hamlet's reference to caviar as "[a] good thing unappreciated by the ignorant." Nevertheless, it must be conceded that more commonly both Fletcher and Turberville, a diplomat who had served as Elizabeth I's envoy to Russia for some years, associate Russians with negative character traits, such as habitual drunkenness and a tendency both to be disbelieving of others and to be themselves habitual perpetrators of lies.

Daryl Palmer has argued persuasively that Shakespeare, whose work is invariably drawn from other literary or documentary sources, in *The Winter's Tale* was reflecting current relations between the Jacobean court and Muscovy. This was a continuation of a trend starting in the 1580s for things Russian in English society, which extended to other major writers of the period such as Sir Philip Sidney (whose *Astrophel and Stella* was published in 1591):

> Now even that footstep of lost liberty
> Is gone, and now like slave-born Muscovite
> I call it praise to suffer tyranny. (*Astrophel and Stella* 254)

Already deemed by Sidney before 1586 to be sufficiently strongly embedded in his readers' minds to be used with confidence as a simile, as it is here, the Russia obsession was also referred to by John Donne in his "Epistle to Mr E. G." Having made mention of bear-baiting, which persisted while plague had closed the theatres, Donne uses a heavily laden trading ship from Russia as a simile for the self: "As plenteously / As Russian Marchants, thy selfes whole vessel load" (52 – 53). The equation speaks of an abundance of desirable Russian goods, as a model for the self.

Then, in the late seventeenth century, English voyages to Siberia may have been the documentary source which inspired one of the founders of the novel in English, Daniel Defoe, to include this most remote region of Russia in the sequel he published to capitalize on the success of *Robinson Crusoe* (1718). *The Farther Adventures of Robinson Crusoe* (1719) concludes a truly global sequence of travels which take Robinson, gripped by wanderlust and dissatisfaction with life in England, to South America, Madagascar, the Bay of Bengal, and then Indochina and China. While for Dr. Samuel Johnson in *The Vanity of Human Wishes* (1749) the eastern extreme of the global purview may have been China —

> Let Observation with extensive View,
> Survey Mankind from *China* to *Peru* (Johnson 12) —

Defoe's sequel, by contrast, ends not in China but in Siberia ("wild uncultivated country" but also "pleasant, fruitful, and agreeable") with its capital Tobolsk. This arguably reflects the period's political and demographic shifts. Following the decline of the Golden Horde, by the fifteenth century European Russia (Muscovy) had become increasingly expansionist in an easterly direction. The beginning of the eighteenth century saw nearly a quarter of a million European Russian settlers established in Siberia. Against this backdrop, Defoe's choice of Siberia for the conclusion of Crusoe's adventures is consistent with Russia's expansionist status at the time (see Bridges).

The Irish novelist Laurence Sterne's most substantial work *The Life and Opinions of Tristram Shandy* (1759) was to prove a pivotal inspiration for the French *philosophe*, encyclopaedist, and novelist Denis Diderot, who journeyed to St. Petersburg and became an intimate of Catherine the Great. However, in *Tristram Shandy* Sterne is disparaging and dismissive of Russia (see Stewart 127): the novel's hero declares that in Russia "to perceive some small glimmerings of wit" you must "hold your hand over your eyes and look very attentively" (Sterne 52).

"Peter's Polish'd Boors"

In the early years of the nineteenth century, Lord Byron, surely the English poet who enjoyed the most widespread reputation across Europe during his age, takes the eponymous hero of his satirical epic *Don Juan*, by way of Ottoman Turkey, to the Russia of Catherine the Great. Depicted as "a well-known modern Amazon" (Solovyova 355), the Empress is a caricature of sexual licence, with a retinue of Russian lovers whose physique conforms to a stereotype established since the sixteenth century: "mostly nervous six-foot fellows, / All fit to make a Patagonian jealous" (Byron 318), in contrast with the "slight and slim, / Blushing and beardless" Don Juan. He nonetheless attracts the voracious Empress' attentions:

> Our hero (and, I trust, kind reader, yours)
> Was left upon his way to the chief city
> Of the immortal Peter's polish'd boors,
> Who still have shown themselves more brave than witty.
> I know its mighty empire now allures
> Much flattery — even Voltaire's, and that's a pity.

> For me, I deem an absolute autocrat
> *Not* a barbarian, but much worse than that. (Byron 253)

Byron's purpose is to "mock this uncertain Russian identity," as the country is "confused about its new role and identity" (Vallucci 330). In these court scenes, love is "a play, associated with the institute of favoritism" (Solovyova 352). A "Russophobia" on Byron's part, shared by Whig politicians, is spurred on by the Napoleonic campaign (Vallucci 328). Ironically, if not surprisingly from the author of the *Ode to Napoleon*, Byron suggests that Russian soldiers are more controlled as invaders, less barbarous than the French under Napoleon:

> In one thing ne'ertheless 't is fit to praise
> The Russian army upon this occasion [...]
> Much did they slay, more plunder, and no less
> Might here and there occur some violation
> In the other line; — but not to such excess
> As when the French, that dissipated nation,
> Take towns by storm [...] (Byron 245)

This is "a fake eulogium" as Byron's target of mockery is not actually Russia but the Marquis of Castelnau's *Histoire de la Nouvelle Russie* (Vallucci 330). Byron's depiction of Russia focuses more on the Empress Catherine the Great than on the land and people themselves. Indeed, writing in the aftermath of the Napoleonic Wars, Byron even suggests that the Russian army shows greater restraint in terms of acts of rape associated with battle. Nevertheless, Byron ironically characterizes the Russian monarch as not being barbarous — "much worse than that."

In William Wordsworth's "The Russian Fugitive" (1829) we are told that "[t]he Czar full oft in words and deeds / Is stormy and self-willed [...]," though pacified by Lady Catherine, and the fugitive heroine envisages his "lawless will" (8: 161, 162). At the same time, Wordsworth gives the poem a happy ending which modifies the Czar's status as an epitome of autocratic caprice.

The mid-Victorian novelist and playwright Edward Bulwer-Lytton characterizes Russia, in the ferment of the Crimean War, as a nation "that threatens all that is dear to civilisation and freedom," and justifies the waging of the war, in contrast to "doves" like Lord John Russell, as an enterprise "to preserve Europe from the outlet of barbarian tribes" (Mitchell 202). As for literary genres, Neboit-Mombet, studying the image of Russia in French fiction during the period, discusses the category of "roman populaire" as being suited to this inquiry (10–11), highlighting adventure fiction (e.g., 28); there is an especially large number of works featuring the Russian empire in France (12).

In the same period Alfred Lord Tennyson, appointed Poet Laureate and the monarch's favorite poet, author of "The Charge of the Light Brigade," which was printed in *The Times* during the conduct of the war, in a similar vein views Russia as a benighted, barbarous society governed by cruelty and exercising repression over subordinate nations within its sphere. *Maud: A Monodrama* is first and foremost a personal, psychological drama of romantic love against family opposition, but its conclusion, after the eponymous heroine's death and her lover's recovery from madness, shows him enlisting for the Crimean War. This occasions the following justification of the war from Tennyson, in Part 1: "Shall I weep if a Poland fall? Shall I shriek if a Hungary fail? / Or an infant civilisation be ruled with rod or with knout?" (217). *The Spectator* comments:

> Raving madness follows this chronic excitement of the brain, from which an appearance of Maud in a dream begins the cure; and the final restoration to a healthy activity is caused by the war with Russia, and the consequent hopes for the world and the elevation of the tone of the English nation. ("Tennyson's Maud" 813)

The poem was, of course, written at the height of Britain's engagement in the Crimean War, the enemy being its sometime ally in the Napoleonic Wars, Tsarist Russia. As Isobel Armstrong observes (125), the forbidding father at the personal level of the poem's "domestic" plot is paralleled with the Tsar as father of his people, yet one who rules by violence and the threat of violence.

The last years of the nineteenth century and the very earliest years of the twentieth saw Britain's political relations with Russia strained — from the time of the Great Eastern Crisis in the 1880s (see also Soboleva and Wrenn 37 – 38). Despite the reverses it suffered in the Crimean War, which led to the serfs' emancipation, and the need to sell off Alaska to the USA, Tsarist Russia was still viewed by Western European nations as a country with expansionist, imperialist ambitions. This might apply in the Baltic States and Poland, which it had annexed since the late eighteenth century; the Balkans (where Russia was perceived as having ambitions to fill the vacuum created by the Ottoman Empire, which was in long-term decline, and having the objective of establishing a naval presence beyond the Black Sea, in the Mediterranean itself); or equally on the northwest borders of British India. In this regard, Kipling's most famous novel *Kim* (1901) is a pivotal text. The backdrop to this work, which combines elements of the picaresque, the *bildungsroman*, and the road novel genres, ends with the orphan hero, on reaching maturity, becoming a player in the so-called Great Game, the espionage campaign conducted by Britain and Tsarist Russia as they vied for competitive advantage in the region of North-West India (modern-day Pakistan and Afghanistan). In this context, Russia appears as an uncivilized, non-European, absolutist political system which is in rivalry with and threatening to subvert British imperial interests. These, by contrast, are presented as missionary and civilizing, as well as being territorially expansionist.

The beginnings of a pro-Russian interest, or at least a responsiveness to aspects of Russian culture in Britain, are most likely to be found in the 1880s when Nikolai Gogol's, Mikhail Lermontov's, and Pushkin's works were making an impact for the first time. Mikhail Glinka's and Mily Balakirev's music made limited inroads into British culture, and posthumously the work of Modest Mussorgsky. From 1880, by comparison, French-Russian relations "vont devenir de plus en plus chaleureuses, surtout dans la conscience populaire" (Neboit-Mombet 16).

That Russia could be viewed as a wild, impulsive "other" by contrast with Western Europe, and suspiciously tinged with oriental features, may be partially attributed to problems in some quarters in the later nineteenth century regarding Russia's "auto-image." This is seen clearly in the attitudes adopted by some of those at the radical end of the political spectrum. The putting down first of the Decembrists and later of the 1863 rebellion against Russian rule in Poland (partitioned between Russia, Austria, and Prussia since the late eighteenth century) prompted a flight into exile of numerous radicals, some communists, some anarchists, and some more mainstream, moderate socialists. Nikolai Morozov, one of the more prominent, as an exile in London in the 1870s, came into contact with Karl Marx, who had been in refuge in London since 1848. Marx's theory of class struggle and history, articulated for instance in *Das Kapital*, dictated that Russia must first become a predominantly industrialized and urban nation, giving rise to a proletariat. Only then, as a proletariat, rather than latter-day feudal peasants could the majority of the population mount an effective revolution against their oppressors. Marx spells this out in a letter to Nikolai Danielson which is really directed at Nikolai Mikhailovsky, a leader of the Narodniki movement:

> If Russia tries to become a capitalist nation, in imitation of the
> nations of western Europe, and in recent years she has taken a
> great deal of pains in this respect, she will not succeed without first
> having transformed a good part of her peasants into proletarians;
> and after that, once brought into the lap of the capitalist regime,
> she will be subject to its inexorable laws, like other profane nations.
> (Letter 111)

The Twentieth Century and Thereafter

Thriller Fiction

After Marx's death, in the latter stages of the nineteenth century
and first two decades of the twentieth, a dispute was conducted
between Vladimir Ilyich Lenin and Georgi Plekhanov, both in exile
in the West and divided, after the failed revolution of 1905, between
the Bolshevik and Menshevik factions. Since the 1890s, Plekhanov
had been arguing that historically Muscovy, hence western and
nominally European Russia, was in its social character essentially
Oriental and despotic: "Old Muscovite Russia was distinguished by its
completely Asiatic character. In social life, its administration, the
psychology of its people — everything in it was alien to Europe and
very closely related to China, Persia, and ancient Egypt" (quoted in
Baron 28). In his work *The History of Russian Social Thought*,
published before and during World War I, Plekhanov went further:
"Peculiarities [...] very noticeably set it apart from the historical
process of the European West and recall the developmental process
of the great Oriental despotisms" (quoted in Baron 36). According to
Samuel Baron, Plekhanov was not arguing that Russia had been
directly molded by the Mongol Horde, but that Old Russia had
developed more or less independently in a manner that produced an
institutional order strikingly like those of China, Persia, and ancient
Egypt. The most prominent feature was an omnipotent state
authority (the despot and his governing apparatus) which, through
its control of the means of production, reduced all classes of the
population to utter dependence (see Baron 36).

The ideas Plekhanov expressed and debated with Lenin run
parallel to the pronouncements of Marx himself in the middle of the
nineteenth century: "England has to fulfil a double mission in India:
one destructive, the other regenerating the annihilation of old
Asiatic society, and the laying the material foundations of Western

society in Asia" ("Future"). These words are quoted by Edward Said in *Orientalism* (154), when he asserts that both Marx and John Stuart Mill conform to conventional European "orientalist" thinking in regard to India. Said earlier says that Mill

> made it clear in *On Liberty* and *Representative Government* that his views there could not be applied to India (he was an India Office functionary for a good deal of his life, after all) because the Indians were civilizationally, if not racially, inferior. The same kind of prejudice is to be found in Marx. (Said 14)

It was not too difficult, apparently, to infer from India in some regards to Russia. Whether it was in his exile in the West that Plekhanov developed his idea that Russia is too oriental in its civilization to make the country a candidate for imminent proletarian revolution (on the grounds that as such it lacks the requisite Western-style proletariat, since Sergei Witte's industrialization is regarded as very much in its infancy), or whether the idea had already come to him while in Russia, remains unclear. Nevertheless, it is of great significance that the notion of Russia as oriental and non-European was not a concept confined to foreign observers but was espoused by those within Russian society, albeit those who sought revolution, and can be considered an element of the Russian "auto-image."

If the quotation from Virginia Woolf's early novel above shows how rapidly the Russian stereotypes in Kipling's *Kim* began to undergo transformation, it is also worth observing that one of the genres to which it belongs, the espionage novel (admittedly something remote from the emerging sensibilities of Bloomsbury), was also experiencing transmogrification in British culture. This process can be illustrated by reference to the career of William Le Queux (1864–1927), whose *The Great War in England in 1897* (1894) involves an invasion of Britain by allied French and Russian forces, which is successfully repulsed and leads to Britain victoriously invading French Algeria and central Asian areas of the Russian Empire bordering on the Raj. In 1900, the same year as Kipling's *Kim*, John Buchan wrote *The Half-Hearted*, in which the hero Haystoun defends British India against invading Russian Cossacks. By 1906, with Britain now in alliance with France as part of the *Entente Cordiale*, Britain is invaded by the Kaiser's militaristic Germany in Le Queux's *The Invasion of 1910* (1906). Although Conrad's classic *The Secret Agent* casts absolutist Tsarist Russia as the enemy of liberal Britain with its constitutional monarchy, we should remember that Conrad, born Josef Korzeniowksi, as an exile from the Tsarist partitioning of Poland was hardly a straightforward Briton. Moreover, the drafting of the novel was begun before the *Entente Cordiale* was extended to include Russia in 1907.

A focus upon Germany as Britain's habitual enemy (which had first emerged in 1871 in George Chesney's improbably named *Battle of Dorking*, reflecting Prussia's defeat of France the year before) had also been foreshadowed by Erskine Childers' *The Riddle of the Sands* (1903) and was then developed further by William Le Queux in *The Invasion of 1910*, Gerald Du Maurier's *An Englishman's Home* (1909), Saki's *When William Came: A Story of London under the Hohenzollerns* (1913) and, most memorably of all, drafted in the months before the outbreak of World War I by John Buchan in *The Thirty-Nine Steps* (1915). In the same author's *Greenmantle* in the following year, the earlier novel's hero is rescued from the German threat by Russian Cossacks (see Bydder 2). The post-First-World-War period saw the rise of the idea of a Russian threat, but this arguably surfaced more in the fictions created by real-life intelligence services than in spy fiction.

The period immediately following the end of World War I saw a rise in thriller fiction of spy novels concerning a Bolshevik threat to Britain. To give but a few examples, Cyril McNeile's *Bulldog Drummond* (1920) involves the unmasking of a plot by the villain Peterson to instigate a Bolshevik uprising. By 1935 John Buchan, formerly praising Russians and casting them as his character Sir Richard Hannay's saviors at the turn of the century, in *The House of the Four Winds* was issuing warnings articulated by a prince about a threat posed to the Balkans:

> The present Government must go, and at once, for it is too gross a scandal. If we delay, there will be a blind revolution of the people themselves. You will say — let Juventus restore Prince John. Juventus will do nothing of the kind, since Prince John is not its own candidate. If we restore him, Juventus will become anti-Monarchist. What then will it do? I reply that it does not yet know, but there is a danger that it may set up one of its own people as dictator. That would be tragic, for in the first place Evallonia does not need or desire a dictator, being Monarchist by nature, and in the second place Juventus does not want a dictatorship either. It is Nationalist, but not Fascist. Yet the calamity may happen. (Buchan 28)

Michael Annesley (who also wrote as Michael Webster) significantly cast the British hero's wife in *Spies Abounding* (1945) as half-

Russian (writing at the height of the Grand Alliance following the USSR's entry into the war after the 1941 invasion of Russia by Hitler). Yet he made the same character, retaining the first name, half-Polish in *Spy Corner* in 1948 (see Bydder 3). This maps fairly closely the shift from wartime alliance with "Uncle Joe Stalin" to his emergence as the perceived oppressor of Eastern Europe. Setting up his series of communist buffer states, after his death to be formalized as the Warsaw Pact, Stalin became a Machiavellian figure behind opposition to the reunification of Germany and the man who imposed the Berlin Airlift in an attempt to cow the country's former capital into submission.

Harry Edmonds in the genre thriller *Red Invader* (1933) imagines a future invasion of Britain by Soviet and Nazi German forces acting in concert, surely at this date a purely chance anticipation of the 1939 Molotov-Ribbentrop Non-Aggression Pact. The same author had cast the USSR and USA as still more unlikely allies in *The Riddle of the Straits* (1931) against scarcely more plausible fellows in arms, Britain and Japan.

Eric Ambler, who had at one point entertained sympathies for Soviet communism as the most effective bulwark against fascism during the era of Appeasement, included a positive view of two Russian KGB agents, Andreas and Tamara Zaleshoff, who save the British hero Kenton (a flawed figure with a gambling habit) in *Uncommon Danger* (1937); there is still a positive portrayal of a Russian heroine in Webster's *East of Kashgar* (1940). However, Ambler became disillusioned by the implications of the Molotov-Ribbentrop Pact, and after 1940 did not publish in the espionage genre again until the 1950s. In *Judgment on Deltchev* (1952), Ambler now depicted the Soviet Russians as a malign influence, by means of Stalin-inspired purges and show trials, exerted over smaller nations in the Balkans.

In *From Russia with Love* (1957), perhaps the Ian Fleming novel most concerned with Russian Cold War stereotypes, the hero James Bond embarks on a flight from Britain to Istanbul reading Ambler's thriller *The Mask of Dimitrios* (see Fleming 144). This is an intertextual hint, as that novel was much admired by Fleming and also has a setting in Istanbul. However, as Jake Kerridge observes, it is significant that Bond does not actually proceed far with reading the Ambler novel, and Kerridge makes the point that Bond is a much less ambiguous and multi-faceted conception on the part of his author than were Ambler's heroes, who also inspired more high-brow writers such as Graham Greene and, after World War II, John Le Carré.

From Fleming to Burgess

From Russia with Love was written in 1957, in the middle of the so-called Krushchev Thaw, from 1953 and Stalin's death through Krushchev's overthrow by Brezhnev in 1964. This period saw modifications in the image associated with Soviet Russia. Millions were released from the Gulag prison camps in Siberia, and censorship was relaxed to the extent that Solzhenitzyn's 1960 exposé of the Stalin-era Gulag, *One Day in the Life of Ivan Denisovich*, could be published (albeit briefly) in the Soviet Union itself when it first appeared. There were increasing gestures toward the West, in so far as Krushchev made a 1955 official trip to the USA, although in terms of foreign policy the new leader could be every bit as aggressive as Stalin. The Thaw coincided with the Soviet military crackdown on the 1956 anti-Soviet insurrection in Hungary, as well as unrest in Poland. In 1961 Krushchev oversaw the building of the Berlin Wall, while the following year saw the Cuban Missile Crisis, arguably the most perilous episode of the Cold War with nuclear stand-off between the USSR and USA. In the 1950s the USSR, a nuclear power since the beginning of the decade, made impressive advances in terms of Sputnik satellite technology and entered the space race with the USA, being the first nation to put a man into orbit in 1961. Bernard Baruch commented:

> While we devote our industrial and technological power to producing new model automobiles and more gadgets, the Soviet Union is conquering space [...] It is Russia, not the United States, who has had the imagination to hitch its wagon to the stars and the skill to reach for the moon and all but grasp it. America is worried. It should be. (Crompton 4)

At the date of the publication of *From Russia with Love*, there was a widespread Western perception that the USSR was overtaking the USA and the West in general. Although the Berlin Airlift had successfully challenged Stalinist aggression, the USSR still maintained a presence over the eastern half of Europe, which it was to keep until the end of the 1980s. Significantly, the genesis of the plot of this Bond novel is owed to the liminal figure of Red Grant, half Irish and half German, an orphan psychopath, who has done his compulsory military service in the British Signals Corps and defected to the East while serving in Berlin, because he was disgraced as a cheat at boxing. He is attracted to the USSR on the strength of its reputation for brutality: "He liked all he had heard about the Russians, their brutality, their carelessness of human life, and their guile, and he decided to go over to them" (Fleming 22). He has acquired fluent Russian. His cover name as a Soviet double agent posing as a Briton is Nash, which in Russian means "ours." He is eventually outwitted by Bond's resourceful ingenuity in evading certain death from shooting.

The female Russian agent Tatiana Romanova — a surname as absurdly redolent of Tsarism as Huxley's (28) Lenina Crowne in the *Brave New World* (1932) is evocative of Bolshevism — has a less clear motivation. She too is a double agent, but she seems to become genuinely attracted to Bond, despite being manipulated by the KGB. At the end of the novel, it is unclear whether she will ever come round fully from sedation. For that matter, although Rosa Klebb (Romanov's controller and Bond's ultimate adversary) is captured, she appears to poison the British hero fatally before the novel's end. Bond responds to the offer by Mathis, his British controller, to obtain for Bond "The best dinner in Paris. And I will find the loveliest girl to go with it" by saying "I shan't need a girl René" (Fleming 136). It is unclear whether he means he is about to die or he has already found the love of his life in Romanova, though the track record of Bond's philandering in other Fleming novels does not suggest monogamy. Of course, one might cynically assume that Fleming is manipulatively keeping his readers on tenterhooks. Fleming's biographer Andrew Lycett says the ending "reflects Fleming's uncertainty whether to continue his hero's exploits in the future" (293).

The novel's ending is of significance, given the Thaw context with the Soviet Union seemingly in the ascendant. In the 1950s, the West had been undermined by espionage trials involving the Rosenbergs, the Krogers, the 1951 defection of the Cambridge spies Burgess and Maclean. The USSR gave every appearance of becoming something of a success, with a now widely literate populace, able to challenge the USA for supremacy in the Space Race and to thwart U.S. hegemony in the proxy war being fought in Vietnam. In that context the ambiguous, apparently doomed ending of *From Russia with Love*, so much at odds with the uncomplicated unswerving belief in Western capitalist supremacy which is found more or less everywhere else in the Bond novels, seems almost to be a response showing a recognition of real achievement made by Russia by this date. In a larger sense, James Bond films in the period 1962—2012 mostly evoke existing stereotypes about Russia and frames Russians as "others" with negative labeling (see Lawless).

Fleming's novel was turned into a box-office bestseller film in 1963. Both the novel and the film make an instructive comparison with another British book which was published in the same year, Anthony Burgess' *Honey for the Bears*. Drafted in 1962, presumably at much the same time as the tension which culminated in the Cuban Missile Crisis, following a trip which Burgess and his first wife had made to Leningrad in the summer of 1961, the novel involves a black-market-driven scheme by a Sussex antiques dealer, Paul Hussey, to sell nylon dresses in Leningrad, illegally imported there, albeit with the more altruistic motive of helping an impecunious friend. Early on Hussey describes Krushchev's Soviet Union as "that country bloated with cosmonauts, starved of consumer goods" (Burgess, *Honey* 19), a theme which is developed throughout the novel. The fictional British character's trip to Leningrad coincides with Yuri Gagarin's triumphant appearance, as the first man in space, in Britain. The black-market scheme backfires, and the Briton ends up helping a Russian who appears to be a recently institutionalized psychopath to defect to the West.

This contrasts markedly with *From Russia with Love*, where it is the Western-born psychopath Red Grant who regards Russia favorably on account of its reputation for brutality and who defects to the East. The "Bears" of Burgess' title are consistent with the characterization of the Russians whom Hussey encounters as much given to black marketeering, cynical about the ideology of communism, and brutally violent, homophobic, and dipsomaniac. These are all hallmarks of the traditional and pejorative aspects of the Russian stereotype, recurrent since the first voyages by Britons in the sixteenth century. Burgess is by no means unaware of this tradition, and indeed he brings in a British academic expert on Hakluyt in the scenes toward the novel's end, as well as earlier making literary allusions to Dostoevsky — aptly, a St. Petersburg rather than Moscow novelist.

The experienced expatriate in Russia, Madox, gives a positive summing-up of the nation at the novel's outset, when Hussey and his wife are on board the Russian liner in the Baltic bound for Leningrad, contending that the Cambridge spies may in fact have defected for non-political reasons "'like those diplomats that went over that time. For all anybody knows they might have gone over because of their stomachs. In Russia,' he told Paul, 'nobody gets indigestion. Everything is cooked in the best butter. A worker's country,'" he explains (Burgess, *Honey* 8); though on the same page the "patrician parrot," an "ancient creature" also traveling over from Britain, dismisses music in the officially approved Soviet style as "precisely circus music. You will *never* civilize these people" (*Honey* 8). Yet the contingent of musicians on board the boat is met by "an outward-bound goodwill mission called The Little Sputniks" (*Honey* 8), Soviet students who take issue when the "ancient creature," who dismisses this music and claims to have known Russia before the Revolution, compares Russians to benighted Orientals: "They are only Orientals. They have their sulks and their losing face. Believe me, I have known them since before their Lenin and Trotsky were ever heard of. They even count with bead-frames" (*Honey* 9).

The reference to "bead-frames" is a supremely ironic indicator of entrenched Western attitudes toward Russia, which is projected here by this character as a country still as numerically backward as it had been illiterate until the twentieth-century mass education drive. The stereotype willfully overlooks the fact that Leonhard Euler spent most of his career in St. Petersburg, and Nikolai Lobachevsky and Pafnuty Chebyshev and Dmitri Egorov were but a few among dozens of leading Russians who made pioneering contributions to mathematics.

The oriental references in Burgess' work are valuable to compare with the stereotypes found in Fleming's. In the Bond novel it is a deviant Briton, Red Grant, who can pass for a Russian-speaking native of the Baltic states, which are regarded as Russian or Soviet "provinces": "Grant spoke Russian excellently but with a thick accent. He could have passed for a national of any of the Soviet Baltic provinces. The voice was high and flat as if it was reciting something dull from a book" (Fleming 14).

Fleming's oriental characters are not Russian but German-Chinese (*Dr. No*, 1958) or Korean (Oddjob in *Goldfinger*, 1959). Fleming significantly makes Goldfinger a Latvian rather than a Russian, and he does not, despite the typically Jewish name, appear to be regarded as Russian-Jewish. In Fleming's work there are important elements of both the Russian and the oriental, but the two are generally distinct. In *The Man with the Golden Gun* (1965), for example, British intelligence forces have to persuade the Japanese to divulge secret codes captured from the Russians; Bond becomes at one point amnesiac and lives as a Japanese fisherman, and Bond is brainwashed by Russian intelligence forces in Russia while suffering memory loss. If the term "oriental" is interpreted to signify "middle eastern" as well as far eastern — a central contention of Said's key work on this phenomenon — then Fleming can be seen as a practitioner. Bond's local, Istanbul-based henchman on behalf of British intelligence in *From Russia with Love* is called Darko Kerim. The highly politically incorrect first name (which was removed even as early as the 1963 film version) speaks of an earlier, imperial age, consonant with Kipling's patronizing attitudes toward Indians, be they Moslem or Hindu, in *Kim*.

We should bear in mind that *From Russia with Love* appeared prior to Harold Macmillan's "Wind of Change" speech, which effectively sounded the death knell for the British Empire. Clement Attlee's Labour Government had overseen the independence of India, the Empire's largest constituent colony, and saw this as the prelude to further decolonization. That process was halted by Sir Winston Churchill's return to power in 1951, but subsequently (post-Suez 1956) a later Conservative Prime Minister acknowledged imminent change. During the 1960s, 27 British colonies in Africa, Asia, and the Caribbean won independence. Born in 1908, Fleming espoused attitudes from the era of the British Empire, and his death in 1964 came in the same period as the death of that empire.

Burgess' "Jeu D'Esprit"

As Burgess presents it, the reality which Hussey discovers in Leningrad is a world where no-one takes the Soviet system entirely seriously, and where Christianity appears to persist in various forms:

> He was far too short to be a good advertisement for Soviet Russia. As for the system, he seemed not really to understand it. He had shown Dyadya Pavel a photograph of his family round a Christmas crib; he had once performed, in the dining saloon, an obscene mime of Krushchev, whom he called Bolshoi Zhivot or "Big Belly"; he thought sputniks and vostoks a waste of public money; the most valuable achievements of the West he considered to be Gordon's Gin, Princess Margaret, drip-dry shirts, stock-car racing, Mr Harold Macmillan. (*Honey* 22–23)

This represents a revival of the age-old stereotype from the sixteenth-century travelers' reports, of Russian giants whose stomachs hang down below their waists, while additionally framing Soviet Russians as a populace in thrall to the more frivolous, consumerist, and sensational aspects of life in the West.

Honey for the Bears is conceived as a satirical comedy, which means exaggeration must be expected. Nevertheless, it also provides some more penetrating reflections on twentieth-century history. The central character Paul Hussey has a knowledge of the Russian language, thanks to Britain's wartime Grand Alliance with Stalin's Soviet Union. He was sent on a Russian language course rather than being asked to fly with the RAF. Much is made of the Russian language, and in Burgess' previous novel, the far better-known *A Clockwork Orange*, set in a Britain of the near future, the teenage gangs speak a slang language called "Nadsat." This is drawn from Russian vocabulary, combined with the principles of indigenous British Cockney rhyming slang. Burgess himself affected disdain for *A Clockwork Orange* as "a *jeu d'esprit* knocked off for money in three weeks" (Burgess, *Flame* 267). However, he is surely selling his own achievement short, and certainly something of the violence found in the previous year's dystopian novel seems to have spilled over into the treatment which Hussey receives during his time in Leningrad, whether at the hands of Soviet Secret police or disaffected Leningrad youth. He is repeatedly beaten up, has his teeth knocked out, and is left lying unconscious in the street overnight.

Besides the Russian language, *Honey for the Bears* includes a number of references to Russian literature which allow it to be considered to some extent an exercise in intertextuality. Paul Hussey recalls Pushkin from his World-War-II study of Russian: "Here in the Baltic summer there was no real dark. Pushkin had written beautifully about the white nights of northern Russia; Paul had tried to read Pushkin on that course" (*Honey* 18); he despairs of the approved Soviet taste in Western literature: "on his knee was one of the few readable books in English that the ship's library possessed. Oh God, those Londons and Cronins" (*Honey* 16). Meanwhile, approved Russian Social-Realist literature is parodied and disparaged:

> The book was an immense Soviet novel by T. S. Pugachev, all the characters (the hero a jig-maker) Soviet Man or Woman and hence not characters at all. Soviet literature would kill itself because of its inherent contradictions. [...] (*Honey* 17)

Contemporary Russian literature is brought in by way of Boris Pasternak's *Doctor Zhivago* (1957). The novel had been banned in the USSR for exposing the excesses of the Bolshevik Revolution and the setting up of the Soviet Union, and also caused controversy when published in the West. (The Italian communist party expelled the publisher Feltrinelli from its ranks for publishing an indictment of

Soviet communism.) Pasternak was awarded the Nobel Prize *in absentia*, and had died by 1960, but the novel became a bestseller in the period in which Burgess was writing and, just afterwards, one of the box-office successes of the cinema in the 1960s, when filmed by David Lean (1965). Yet in *Honey for the Bears* the novel is associated with the cynicism of a Western character. Hussey deliberately brings a copy with him into the USSR in order to distract attention away from the suitcases full of smuggled "chemical dresses bought wholesale at thirty shillings each" (*Honey* 19). These he intends to sell for financial gain on the Russian black market. As if to make a point which recurs as the novel develops, the immigration and customs officials prove unconcerned:

> "It's this book I'm really worried about," said Paul, presenting *Dr Zhivago*. "Can I bring this into the Soviet Union?"
> The customs-man examined it with little interest, flicked through the pages as if looking for old tram-tickets, then handed it back. "*Mozhna*," he said. "Can." (*Honey* 40)

Later, stranded in Leningrad while his American wife is taken ill, Hussey grows closer to some of the younger generation, who for him evoke Russian literature: "The faces of the young Leningraders grew names — Vladimir, Sergei, Boris, Feodor, a Pavel like himself; it was the cast-list of a Russian novel coming alive" (*Honey* 94); Sergei declaims Pushkin to Hussey's wife, "a luscious growling poem of infinite lyric sadness" (*Honey* 94). However, Dostoevsky's *Crime and Punishment* is disparaged by one of the young Leningraders with whom Hussey comes into contact. According to Andrew Biswell, Burgess' biographer, Burgess had been told in a conversation with a Leningrad waiter regarding Dostoèvsky's novel "that it was a crime to write it and a punishment to read it," and gave that line to a character in his novel (Biswell 237). The same cynicism which had been shown by the Westerner Hussey, in bringing in *Doctor Zhivago*, is thus displayed by a native Russian.

While there are important allusions in *Honey for the Bears* to Russian classic literature, such as to *Anna Karenina*, ultimately the novel's dominant intertextual relationship is arguably with another novelist altogether, in origin at least culturally much closer to Burgess, sharing the latter's upbringing as a "cradle catholic." In *A Clockwork Orange*, the multilingual "Nadsat" wordplay which is constantly at work, involving puns simultaneously in high and lowbrow English and Russian, surely takes its inspiration from Burgess' lifelong literary hero James Joyce, and especially the Joyce of his late period and *Finnegans Wake*. This emerges when Hussey is trying to communicate with his sickly wife:

> He shook her quite violently and heard strange words, words from the underworld: "Gart ... fairgrow ... lubu ..."
>
> How strange! She knew no Russian, and yet here was an approximation to the Russian word for "love" bubbling up from the depths, as though James Joyce had really been the inventor of everybody's unconscious. Earwicker was Everybody. Robert had been, for a time, quite keen on that. Robert had taught him quite a bit he supposed. (*Honey* 47)

Burgess was later to publish *Here Comes Everybody: An Introduction to James Joyce for the Ordinary Reader* (1969). Here, the fictional collectivism of Soviet Man and Soviet Woman ("hence not characters at all") in the work of "T. S. Pugachev," bemoaned as the death of Soviet literature, is given a rather different, approving expression by reference to the high modernist James Joyce, who at least until the Thaw, if not in considerable measure beyond, was in fact regarded as anathema by Soviet cultural authorities (see Wicht 71).

Bradbury's Diderot Project

Leningrad, freshly renamed St. Petersburg in the recent aftermath of the Soviet Union's collapse in 1991, is the setting for Malcolm Bradbury's final novel *To the Hermitage* (2000). Like Burgess' novel of 37 years before, this is a comedy — although, as an example of the "university novel" genre to which Bradbury together with David Lodge is one of the most prominent and acclaimed contributors, it is distinctly highbrow by contrast with the works of Kipling, Buchan, and Ambler which we have mentioned earlier in this chapter. It wears its intertextuality as a badge of postmodern pride, and its plot is highly artificial and contrived. This is justified by reference both to the postmodern, present-day context and to high theory, most notably deconstruction à la Jacques Derrida, and also the eighteenth century. An unnamed British academic's trip to St. Petersburg is brought about by his inclusion in the sketchily defined, distinctly Utopian "Diderot Project," a pan-European and indeed global academic research venture whose leading lights are Swedes. The novel involves following the footsteps of Denis Diderot toward St. Petersburg in the eighteenth century, when he was recruited by Catherine the Great as an advisor, much as she had earlier recruited Voltaire.

The self-conscious style of intrusive narration, with the author/ narrator in dialogue with his readers and characters, and the episodes in the eighteenth-century sections of the novel presented as unadorned dialogue which could as easily be the script of a play, is a tribute to the style of Diderot's *Jacques Le Fataliste* (1796). Perhaps the novel is also a tribute to a rather more recent contribution to the ranks of "European" fiction from elsewhere in Eastern Europe: Milan Kundera's *The Unbearable Lightness of Being* (1982), itself profoundly indebted to Diderot. The journey made by an assortment of Western academics and performing and applied artists to St. Petersburg coincides with the *putsch* which led to Boris Yeltsin's facing down Soviet hardliners determined to reverse Mikhail Gorbachev's reforms in the perestroika era. The epithets which had been assigned to Russians' own bodies in the accounts of earlier Western visitors to Russia are now transposed to the material trappings of the fast-disappearing Soviet Union:

> The wide seaway we're sailing is busy with big-bellied Russian factory ships, their funnels tricolored in pre- or post-Marxist livery. All of them seem to be running westward toward the world's richer economies. Meanwhile we're beating eastward, to political turmoil, economic crisis, maybe a new civil war. (Bradbury 211)

The novel juxtaposes chapters set in the present of 1991 with chapters covering the meetings between Denis Diderot and Catherine the Great in the eighteenth century. In one of the chapters set in that century, the question of Russian racial identity is raised in the context of the decline of Muscovy: "Moscow rots with disease and disorder; its buildings constantly burn or collapse. But Sankt Petersburg is a new city, a new idea. Its people claim to be from everywhere, and see the world afresh" (Bradbury 211). Observing as a Western foreigner, Diderot then goes on to wonder:

> Yet who are the true natives, the Russian people, the ones who are not émigré, Huguenot, Swiss, Prussian? Some claim they all descend from the noble Vikings, others say the Slavs. Yet half are Tartar, Cossack, oriental, speak a strange repertory of languages, write, when they are able to, an alphabet that has wandered up from a Mediterranean monastery, and which he's already begun to replan and improve. (Bradbury 327)

And having introduced the Oriental stereotype made familiar by earlier visitors to Russia, Bradbury's Diderot then questions Russian culture's claim to be considered European:

> If some are freemen of Europe, hunting an opportunity, many are the slaves off the steppes, brought here by imperial fiat or obligation, herded in off the Siberian wastes. Even nobles and gentlefolk are often brute souls, brought off distant estates by draconian laws to serve at court or in the army, before disappearing into war, drunkenness, exile, servitude. (Bradbury 327)

To Diderot, the Russian Orthodox clergy "are bearded fanatics — more like Musselman mullahs than the abbés and prelates he's known all his life [...] nearer a frank band of brigands. Not people you'd care to entrust a prayer to on a dark night" (Bradbury 330). Bradbury makes his Diderot conform with and reinforce the Western stereotype of Russians as non-European and, in this instance, non-Christian.

In the present-day (late-twentieth-century) episodes, Bradbury's British narrator repeats the stereotype of Russians as "drab," "resentful," and "sullen," with a tendency toward xenophobia: "Lively stewards have turned into drab resentful hotel waiters, spry stewardesses into invisible chambermaids, as if the very fact of being in Russia has reminded them that a sullen hostility is the proper way of life" (Bradbury 142). Yet in the same chapter we are also told that post-Soviet Russia is rapidly becoming, in the spirit of glasnost, open to individuals and less of a police state: "gone, apparently, is the dark age when much of Russia was red-mapped and foreigner-hostile country, and where a journey off-course would inevitably lead to arrest. Personal touring is being encouraged" (Bradbury 344).

Surely the most moving character, standing out from both the postmodern academics, epitomized by Jack-Paul Verso (an American "funky professor" with a Deconstruction baseball cap), and the various glib Scandinavians is the ageing Russian tour guide Galina. In Bradbury's otherwise rather uncommitted fiction (given that its twentieth-century action coincides with a moment of seismic political change, with Rutskoy's hardliner challenge to the reformist Yeltsin), Galina stands out from the various Russian stereotypes which have been presented. She has kept culture alive through the Soviet era, and now looks with doubt upon forthcoming change. Bradbury tells us: "Then slowly she admits to the life I can't see: a husband, a painter, who was arrested in the 1950s in the time of Stalin and disappeared in the Siberian camps" (Bradbury 410). And Bradbury goes on to reveal that this is not simply an episode confined to the Stalin era, but has continuing human consequences: "There are two children who grew up and went to Moscow. They were turned against her, and don't come back any more" (Bradbury 410). Galina then articulates an important variant on the sullen resignation which is either identified by Bradbury's Diderot in the nineteenth century or attributed to the Russian serving staff in the 1990s:

> Hopeful? Please, I am Russian. I live in a land of mad hopes, long queues, lies and humiliations. They say about Russia we never had a happy present, only a cruel past and a quite amazing future. Of course we worship another crazy leader, another false tzar. We are used to being repressed. We are the people who invented the equality of misery. All we like here is one strong man who tells us what to do. Yeltsin, well, think, he survives because everyone else is so much worse. But maybe you understand why I prefer to spend my days with Voltaire and Didro. (Bradbury, 347)

The Galina character, whose death is reported with great regret before the end of the narrative, stands out as a representation of the Russian character in a novel whose genre is not normally associated with this degree of emotion. However, perhaps equally important if this novel is to be taken as an index of Russian society in recent decades is a character who goes by the name of Chichikov, whom the group meets during Galina's guided tour of St. Petersburg. The name is an allusion to the character in Gogol's *Dead Souls* (1842) who stands for the embodiment of the Russian concept of "poshlost," which is strictly untranslatable but includes the notions of corruption and philistinism.

It is fitting that his name should be borrowed intertextually from a character in fiction since he appears as a confidence trickster on Bradbury's fictional action level, in keeping with which the character's identity in Bradbury's novel is bogus. As the author-narrator feels that the name sounds vaguely familiar, Galina reminds him of the source in Gogol's novel. Being a generation and more younger, he stands as what might be called a "New Russian" looking Westward: his clothes have "an Englishy sort of cut" (Bradbury 355); he produces numerous, doubtlessly forged documents purporting to come from an array of officials. He stands for the Western capitalist concept of market value based upon reputation rather than strict material use value, as espoused by the fast-disappearing Soviet system. Accordingly, he announces: "In Russia right now everything is for sale. Don't go yet, listen to me, wait. There has to be something you want. Icons? Old cameras?" (Bradbury 359).

In many ways, it is the *soi-disant* Chichikov who points forward most to the future at this novel's end. The author-narrator seems to be somewhat unconvinced by a multicultural future, and the real-life Bradbury, like his character Galina, did not live far enough into the Yeltsin era to see the Russian oligarchs' rise to prominence. The author who might be said to have taken up this theme of the Russian confidence trickster most obviously at our time of writing, although a Slav in origin, is a writer whose debut novel is written in her adoptive language: English. Vesna Goldsworthy's 2015 novel *Gorsky* is every bit as intertextual as Bradbury's *To the Hermitage*. It is modeled closely on Scott Fitzgerald's American classic of the Jazz Age, *The Great Gatsby* (1922; see also Nefedova). Yet it transposes its action to London, and more specifically to Chelsea, alternatively known as Chelsky or Londongrad in recognition of its status in the early twenty-first century, as one of the favored expatriate playgrounds of Russian oligarchs who enriched themselves during the Yeltsin and Putin years. Goldsworthy herself has explained: "A Serbian song I like speaks about loving 'the Russian way', Russian being synonymous with measureless, yet doomed, passion. The Russians have written some of the greatest love stories: Eugene Onegin, Anna Karenina, Doctor Zhivago"; she avers that her novel's "mix of tragedy and comedy owes more to my reading of Chekhov than it does to my shakier knowledge of Fitzgerald" ("I Started").

That its intertextuality involves an American who spent most of his successful novelist's life as an expatriate in Europe is significant. It would appear that, while Bradbury's Chichikov might seek to gain credibility by dressing in British clothes, American rather than British literature has so far provided the best literary lens for examination of Russians, as they are perceived outside Russia itself, in the early twenty-first century.

A Postmodern Culture

Overall, our examination has sought to show that literature in Britain has tended to maintain a stereotype of the Russian character which has remained identifiable throughout these periods. For most of the time, the idea of Russians as barbarous, crude, and insensitive, and frequently displaying non-European features (or at least characteristics deemed thus in Britain and elsewhere in the West) has been to the fore. Having said that, there have also been periods where Russian culture has either been encouraged because of political alliances (especially during wartime) or spontaneously — thanks above all to influences like Diaghilev's Ballets Russes, the English translation of Chekhov's dramas, and the prose of Dostoevsky, Turgenev, and Tolstoy. In such periods, it can be said that Russian culture has genuinely acted as a source of "cultural capital" *à la* Bourdieu.

On the one hand, such a mode of "imagological" alterations can be regarded as a simple example of a supererogatory motion. The pendulum swung to the opposing side of the spectrum: one extremity was replaced by another; and the array of pejorative epithets associated with all things Russian was eclipsed by another set of superlatives with a markedly positive slant. This did not mean that the old descriptors were immediately abrogated and forgotten, but rather that they were "relieved" *pro tem* from their operational function. They remained subliminally present in the vocabulary range connected to the Russia discourse, to be reactivated should the situation or opportunity arise. This, in fact, was the case in the Cold War era, when the image of Russia as a dangerously hostile power coincided with the generally accepted political message of the day.

At the same time, Bourdieu's concept of "cultural capital" always implies the idea of progression, a spiral rather than cyclical motion. In this sense, a parallel with "linguistic capital" comes to mind. It is enhanced by the fact that imagology is intrinsically rooted in both literature and language studies, and that these two elements play a major role in the process of identity construction and projection. Language use, after all, symbolically represents fundamental dimensions of social behavior and interaction. The notion is simple, but the ways in which language reflects behavior can often be complex and subtle. Furthermore, the relationship between language and society affects a wide range of encounters — from narrowly based interpersonal contacts to broadly international relations.

It is part of the cultural history of English speakers that they have always adopted loanwords from the languages of whatever cultures with which they have come in contact. There have been few periods when borrowing became unfashionable, and there has never been a national academy in the English-speaking countries to attempt to restrict new loanwords, as there has been in many continental European countries. As a result, English has a much larger vocabulary than either the Germanic languages or the members of the Romance language family to which French belongs (see also the Oxford Living Dictionaries web site). Borrowing is a consequence of cultural contact between two language communities. Borrowing of words can go in both directions between the two languages in contact, but often there is an asymmetry, such that more words go from one side to the other. In this case the source language community has some advantage of power, prestige, and/or wealth that makes the objects and ideas which it brings desirable and useful to the borrowing language community. For instance, after the Norman Conquest in 1066 English as a Germanic language was significantly influenced by Norman French. Anglo-Norman became the language of the ruling class, their "linguistic capital," for a considerable period of time (see also Ingham). The end of the era of this fashionable Latinization toward the end of the fifteenth century, however, did not mean that the accumulated vocabulary was obliterated and elapsed; it resulted in a more nuanced and linguistically complex level of communication affecting a wide range of social interactions. Viktor Živov has examined transformations of linguistic capital in Russian in the twentieth century.

Largely in the same vein, the return to the cliché-image of a barbaric Russian in the Cold War era's spy thrillers did not mean going back to the initial level of *tabula rasa*. Acting in the same way as the pressure of cultural heritage and tradition, the former vogue of Russian culture added a certain level of complexity to the contextually required re-configuration of the image, suggesting, to use the terms of Claude Lévi-Strauss (26), a bricolage rather than an ontological manifestation of the national myth. In this context, it is significant to mention, however, that the works of Russian culture which have had the greatest impact upon literature in Britain have hardly ever been contemporary. With the exception of Stravinsky's scores and the ballets into which Diaghilev as impresario turned them, the Russian work which has been most influential in Britain has always been much older. The Bloomsbury Group showed little interest either in Russian futurist art or the then contemporary and revolutionary Russian poetry of Vladimir Mayakovsky. Goldsworthy's 2015 novel undertakes the reworking of a classic now almost 100 years old (and for that matter from the USA) in order to highlight Russia, or at least Russians as they behave abroad, in the early twenty-first century; Bradbury's *To the Hermitage*, for all the postmodernity and deconstruction of its university novel plot, depends upon a Russian novel of the early nineteenth century. At the same time, we have seen that the doxa of old Russian stereotypes continues well into twenty-first-century Britain. They are perpetuated and are given a new boost of life even in the post-Soviet years, though within a framework of the postmodern platform's situational irony.

198 SECTION ONE EXPLORING CULTURAL JUNCTIONS

Analyzing Western film representations of Russia, Alexander Fedorov finds that "on the whole Western cinematographic 'Rossika' fully inherited the traditions of the Western attitude to Russia: in the majority of fiction films of 1946–2013 the image of Russia is treated as an image of something 'alien,' 'different,' often hostile to Western civilization" (1064). Yet in literature, where they are used half-heartedly, these cultural clichés are used half-seriously. Meant to be recognized as distinct cultural markers, they nonetheless invoke and perpetuate the connotation of any readily available stock image — they avoid being taken in a serious way.

Considering the reconfiguration of the Russian image, one can say that in the second half of the twentieth century it has undergone a definitively "ironic turn." With the rise of postmodernist thought with its anti-essentialism and its strong emphasis on the constructed nature of identity categories, it is used as a prevalent aesthetic and narrative device characteristic of the movement's major proclivities. Identity negotiation concepts likewise emphasize construction according "to the dictates of a social scene" as well as to choices among position possibilities in narrative (Cooks 366). It is no coincidence that Volume 3 in the present book series is devoted to "theoretical and contextual constructions" of identity: "Identity is always under construction, definition, enactment." As for the reconfiguration:

- Firstly, in the period of globalization, cultural diversity, and blurring the barriers of national borders, the very use of national characterization often thematizes the clash between the limited knowledge of fictional characters and the inherently more complex real-life matters which they only partially apprehend. Often employed as a means of ironic deconstruction, the use of stereotypical characterization contributes to the notion of virtual reality (as an essential characteristic of the postmodern), which gives characters a false sense of cognitive control.

- Secondly, in the novels with a multicultural perspective such as Anthony Burgess' *Honey for the Bears* or Michael Bradbury's *To the Hermitage*, this becomes part of stylistic playfulness: national stereotypes are not used seriously (as they would have been a century before) but metafictionally or conceptually — as a postmodern game of conventions or as a light-hearted dialogue between the author and the reader. As Galina Sinekopova has stressed, building on an argumentation by Mikhail Epstein, "Russia can be conceptualized as a postmodern culture *par excellence*"; meanings are unstable and signs lack exteriority (437).

Conclusion: How We See

In sum, a European perspective on seemingly "distant" nations and societies like Russia has always been Eurocentrically foreshortened. It has always been designed to reduce real-world complexities into simplified clichés even more radically than in the case of the intra-European process of cross-cultural stereotyping. It would certainly be far too ambitious an endeavor to "undo" the effects and consequences of this time-honored tradition, but the very process of thematizing the existing literary legacy of perspectival image-making offers some insights into the notion of a constructed Russian paradigm. In turn, when viewed in light of the constructivist perspective of modern imagological studies, the process makes a certain contribution to the critical theory of national stereotyping and representation. Comparative intercultural studies has been said to resemble a play of mirrors, "trying to be on both sides of a mirror at once," as Ming Xie gathers from T. S. Eliot; accordingly there is a potential advantage in seeing "what makes the mirror function as a mirror"— hence "to see *how* one sees" (Xie 2–3). The importance of such a multifaceted perspective, then, lies in its transcending the boundaries of a unidimensional literary investigation: while casting new light on questions of the reception of Russia in Britain, such an approach places the perspective in line with the pan-European debate on the concept of imagological simplification, and with the ways in which literary interaction with the myth of Russia has shaped and deepened these cultural views.

References

Armstrong, Isobel. "Tennyson in the 1850s: From Geology to Pathology — *In Memoriam* (1850) to *Maud* (1855)." *Tennyson: Seven Essays*, edited by Philip Collins, Macmillan, 1992, pp. 102–40.

Baron, Samuel H. *Plekhanov in Russian History and Historiography*. U of Pittsburgh P, 1995.

Beller, Manfred. "Perception, Image, Imagology." Beller and Leerssen, *Imagology*, pp. 3–16.

Beller, Manfred, and Joseph Leerssen, editors. *Imagology: The Cultural Construction and Literary Representation of National Characters*. Rodopi, 2007.

Biswell, Andrew. *The Real Life of Anthony Burgess*. Pan Macmillan, 2006.

Bourdieu, Pierre. *Distinction: A Social Critique of the Judgement of Taste*.

Routledge, 1984.

Bradbury, Malcolm. *To the Hermitage*. Picador, 2000.

Bridges, Richard M. "A Possible Source for Daniel Defoe's *The Farther Adventures of Robinson Crusoe*." *Journal for Eighteenth-Century Studies*, vol. 2, 1979, pp. 231–36.

Buchan, John. *The House of the Four Winds*. Kelly Bray: House of Stratus, 2008.

Burgess, Anthony. *Flame into Being: The Life and Work of D. H. Lawrence*. Arbor House, 1985.

—. *Honey for the Bears*. Heinemann, 1963.

Bydder, Jillene. "Red Snow on Their Boots: Russian Characters in Spy Thriller Fiction Published during the Two World Wars, 2017." *Peer-Reviewed Proceedings of the 8th Annual Conference Popular Culture Association of Australia and New Zealand (PopCAANZ)*, 10–11 July 2017, edited by Paul Mountfort, Wellington: *PopCAANZ, 2017, pp. 1–10*.

Byron, George Gordon. *Don Juan*. J. B. Smith, 1859.

Cao, Shunqing. *The Variation Theory of Comparative Literature*. Springer, 2013.

"Contemporary Life and Thought in Russia." *The Contemporary Review*, vol. 47, 1885, pp. 727–36.

Cooks, Leda M. "Identity Negotiation." *Encyclopedia of Identity*, edited by Ronald L. Jackson II and Michael A. Hogg, vol. 1, Sage, 2010, pp. 365–67.

Crompton, Samuel. *Sputnik/Explorer I: The Race to Conquer Space*. Chelsea House, 2007.

Diment, Galya. *A Russian Jew of Bloomsbury: The Life and Times of Samuel Koteliansky*. McGill-Queen's UP, 2011.

Donne, John. *The Poems of John Donne*. Vol. 1. Routledge, 2014.

Fedorov, Alexander. "The Image of Russia on the Western Screen: The Present Stage (1992–2013)." *European Researcher*, vol. 47, no. 4–3, 2013, pp. 1051–64.

Fleming, Ian. *From Russia with Love*. Penguin, 2006.

Garafola, Lynn. *Diaghilev, Ballets Russes*. Oxford UP, 1989.

Goering, Elizabeth M. "(Re) Presenting Russia: A Content Analysis of Images of Russians in Popular American Films." Symposium of the Russian Communication Association, 2004, Paper. www. russcomm. ru/eng/rca _ biblio/g/goering_eng.shtml.

Goldsworthy, Vesna. *Gorsky: A Novel*. Overlook Press, 2015.

—. "I Started from Gatsby as a Greek Dramatist Starts from Antigone." *The Guardian*, 22 March 2016. www. theguardian. com/books/2016/mar/22/vesna-goldsworthy-paperback-writer-novel-gorsky-great-gatsby.

Green, Martin, and John Swan. *The Triumph of Pierrot: The Commedia dell'Arte and the Modern Imagination*. Penn State UP, 1993.

Henley, W. E. "New Novels." *The Academy*, vol. 329, 1878, pp. 186–87.

Hofstede, Geert. *Cultures and Organizations: Software of the Mind*. 3rd ed. McGraw-Hill, 2010.

Huxley, Aldous. *Brave New World*. Vintage, 2004.

Ingham, Richard. *The Anglo-Norman Language and Its Contexts*. York Medieval Press, 2010.

James, Henry. "The Art of Fiction." *Longman's Magazine*, vol. 4, 1884, pp. 502–21.

—. "Ivan Turgénieff." *Atlantic Monthly*, vol. 53, 1884, pp. 42–55.

Jenkins, Harold, editor. *Hamlet*. The Arden Shakespeare. Methuen, 1982.

Johnson, Samuel. *The Major Works*. Oxford UP, 2008.

Kerridge, Jake. "Eric Ambler's heroes." *The Daily Telegraph*, 18 June 2009. www. telegraph. co. uk/culture/books/bookreviews/5568185/Eric-Amblers-heroes.html.

Kipling, Rudyard. *Kim*. 1901. Penguin, 1987.

Lawless, Katarina. "Constructing the 'Other': Construction of Russian Identity in the Discourse of James Bond Films." *Journal of Multicultural Discourses*, vol. 9, no. 2, 2014, pp. 79–97.

Leerssen, Joep. "Imagology: History and Method." Beller and Leerssen, *Imagology*, pp. 17–32.

—. "Imagology: On Using Ethnicity to Make Sense of the World." *Revue d'études ibériques et ibéro-américaines*, vol. 10, 2016, pp. 13–31.

Lévi-Strauss, Claude. *La pensée sauvage*. Librairie Plon, 1962.

Lycett, Andrew. *Ian Fleming*. Turner, 1996.

Marx, Karl. "The Future Results of British Rule in India." *New-York Daily Tribune*, 8 Aug. 1853.

—. Letter to Nikolai Danielson, 15 Aug. 1877. *Karl Marx and Friedrich Engels: Selected Correspondence, 1846 – 1895*, edited by Dona Torr and Vladimir V. Adoratsky, Martin Lawrence, 1934.

May, Rachel. *The Translator in the Text: On Reading Russian Literature in English*. Northwestern UP, 1994.

Mitchell, Leslie. *Bulwer Lytton: The Rise and Fall of a Victorian Man of Letters*. Bloomsbury, 2003.

Naarden, Bruno, and Joseph Leerssen. "Russians." Beller and Leerssen, *Imagology*, pp. 226–30.

Neboit-Mombet, Janine. *L'image de la Russie dans le roman français (1859–1900)*. Presses universitaires Blaise Pascal, 2005.

Nefedova, Olga I. "F. Scott Fitzgerald's *The Great Gatsby* and the Making of American National Character: Jay Gatsby as an American Errant Knight." *Writing Identity: The Construction of National Identity in American Literature*, edited by Michael Steppat and Natalia Morzhenkova. Moscow Region UP, 2016, pp. 51–56.

Oxford Dictionary of Phrase and Fable. Edited by Elizabeth Knowles. Oxford UP, 2006.

Oxford English Dictionary. 2nd ed. Edited by John Simpson and Edmund Wiener. 20 vols. Oxford UP, 1989. (Also *OED Online*.)

Palmer, Daryl W. "Jacobean Muscovites: Winter, Tyranny, and Knowledge in *The Winter's Tale*." *Shakespeare Quarterly*, vol. 46, no. 3, 1995, pp. 323–39.

Ralston, W. R. S. "Novels of Count Leo Tolstoy." *Nineteenth Century*, vol. 5, 1879, pp. 650–69.

Reed, Christopher, editor. *A Roger Fry Reader*. U of Chicago P, 1996.

Rybakov, Alexei. "Deutsche Russophilie zu Beginn des 20. Jahrhunderts: Rußland in den Werken von Rainer Maria Rilke und Thomas Mann." *Deutsche Rußlandbilder im 20. und 21. Jahrhundert*, edited by Nikolaus Lobkowicz et al., Forum für osteuropäische Ideen- und Zeitgeschichte, vol. 12, no. 1, 2008, pp. 13–28.

Said, Edward. *Orientalism*. Pantheon Books, 1978.

Shakespeare, William. *The Riverside Shakespeare*. Textual editor G. Blakemore

Evans. Houghton Mifflin, 1974.

Sidney, Sir Philip. *The Last Part of the Countesse of Pembrokes Arcadia: Astrophel & Stella and Other Poems*. *The Complete Works*, Vol. 2, edited by Albert Feuillerat. Cambridge UP, 1922.

Sinekopova, Galina V. "Sacredness of the Ordinary: Changing Russian Values." *Value Dimensions and Their Contextual Dynamics Across Cultures*, edited by Steve J. Kulich, Weng Liping, and Michael H. Prosser, Intercultural Research Vol. 5. Shanghai Foreign Language Education Press, 2014, pp. 427–40.

Sitwell, Osbert. *Great Morning*. Little and Brown, 1947.

Soboleva, Olga, and Angus Wrenn. *From Orientalism to Cultural Capital: The Myth of Russia in British Literature of the 1920s*. Peter Lang, 2017.

Solovyova, Natalya. "*Don Juan* and Russia." *Aspects of Byron's* Don Juan, edited by Peter Cochran, Cambridge Scholars Publishing, 2013, pp. 347–56.

Stephens, Winifred. Preface. *The Soul of Russia*, edited by Winifred Stephens, Macmillan, 1916, pp. v–viii.

Sterne, Laurence. *The Life and Opinions of Tristram Shandy, Gentleman*. 1759–1767. Ingram, Cooke, 1853.

Stewart, Neil. "From Imperial Court to Peasant's Cot: Sterne in Russia." *The Reception of Laurence Sterne in Europe*, edited by Peter de Voogd and John Neubauer, Continuum, 2008, pp. 127–53.

Stout, Felicity. *Exploring Russia in the Elizabethan Commonwealth*. Manchester UP, 2015.

Stříbrný, Zdeněk. *The Whirligig of Time: Essays on Shakespeare and Czechoslovakia*. Edited by Lois Potter. U of Delaware P, 2007.

Tennyson, Alfred Lord. *Selected Poetry*. Edited by Erik Gray. Broadview Press, 2014.

"Tennyson's Maud and Other Poems." *The Spectator*, 4 Aug. 1855, pp. 813–14.

"The Russian Invasion." Review of Rosa Newmarch's *The Russian Opera*. *The Spectator*, 27 June 1914, p. 1089.

Tosi, Alessandra. *Waiting for Pushkin: Russian Fiction in the Reign of Alexander I (1801–1825)*. Rodopi, 2006.

Turner, C. E. *Studies in Russian Literature*. Kessinger, 1882.

Vallucci, Valeria. "Byron's *Don Juan* and Russia: A Double Perspective." *Aspects of Byron's* Don Juan, edited by Peter Cochran, Cambridge Scholars Publishing, 2013, pp. 326–35.

Velten, Hannah. *Beastly London: A History of Animals in the City*. Reaktion Books, 2013.

Wang, Jin, and Mo Wan-yi. "A Historical Review of Robert van Gulik and His *Judge Dee Mysteries* in Chinese World (1996 – 2016)." *Journal of Literature and Art Studies*, vol. 7, no. 5, 2017, pp. 513–20.

Wicht, Wolfgang. "The Disintegration of Stalinist Cultural Dogmatism: James Joyce in East Germany." *The Reception of James Joyce in Europe*, edited by Geert Lernout and Wim van Mierlo, Continuum, 2004, pp. 70–88.

Woolf, Leonard. *Beginning Again: An Autobiography of the Years 1911 to 1918*. Hogarth Press, 1964.

Woolf, Virginia. "The Russian Point of View." *The Common Reader*, Hogarth Press, 1925, pp. 219–31.

—. *The Voyage Out*. Random House, 2012.

Wordsworth, William. *The Complete Poetical Works*. 10 vols. 1904. Cosimo

Classics, 2008.
Xie, Ming. *Conditions of Comparison: Reflections on Comparative Intercultural Inquiry*. Continuum, 2011.
Živov, Viktor. "Il capitale linguistico e la sue trasformazioni nella storia linguistica del secolo scorso." *Studi Slavistici*, vol. 9, 2012, pp. 71–84.

8

Intrinsic and Extrinsic Cultural Mutations: Alobwed'Epie's *The Lady with a Beard*

Charles Ngiewih TEKE
University of Yaounde I

Summary: Using Alobwed'Epie's novel *The Lady with a Beard* (2005) as an example, this chapter underscores the open-ended nature of cultural valuations and identity within and without the confines of a specific cultural location. The novel, through which the author engages various facets of the Bakossi culture of Cameroon's South West Region, illustrates both the intrinsic and extrinsic nature of cultural dynamics, in accordance with Stuart Hall's articulations of cultural identity. Identification is always "in process" of becoming, never fully grasped as a finite discursive category so that identification is conditional, lodged in contingency. Enriched with traditional values, while there is already the presence of Western Christianity as signaling an unavoidable transcultural reality, the novel highlights cultural authenticity as communicated in an international space. In this fictional encoding, using a language which is not that of the Bakossi, a locally circumscribed cultural origin receives an identification that goes beyond its own linguistic boundary to receive a transculturally communicative significance. The fiction thus brings forth a hybrid subject, for "a whole range of new and distinctive enterprises" (Bill Ashcroft).

Introduction

Culture, however semantically pluralistic the term, is very important when an individual or community articulates and represents identity as well as a sense of belonging. In *Post-Colonial Transformation*, Bill Ashcroft explicitly articulates culture in the direction which concurs with the conceptual framework and discourse in this chapter. He asserts that

> [c]ulture describes the myriad ways in which a group of people makes sense of, represents and inhabits its world, and as such can never be destroyed, whatever happens to its various forms of expression. Culture is practiced, culture is used, culture is made [...] All cultures move in a constant state of transformation. The attempt to understand how post-colonial cultures resisted the power of colonial domination in ways so subtle that they transformed both colonizer and colonized lies at the heart of post-colonial studies. (2–3)

This chapter underscores the intersectionality between postcolonial literature and inter/cultural studies in Alobwed'Epie's seminal novel *The Lady with a Beard* (2005). The chapter demonstrates how artistic creativity is rooted in cultural conditioning, identity, representation, and transformation. In essence, it underscores the open-ended nature of cultural valuations and identity within and without the confines of a specific cultural location. It emphasizes the richness of discourses in postcolonial intercultural encounters and experiences.

Why cultural mutation, in the spectrum of what I call the dynamics of intra-cultural/internal and extra-cultural alterations, internally or externally motivating change factors? My conception of the intrinsic and extrinsic nature of cultural dynamics was shaped by Stuart Hall's articulations of cultural identity and the diaspora (1996, 1990). Hall is undoubtedly a seminal cultural critic whose articulations on questions of culture and representation shape the theoretical trajectory of this chapter. Conscious of his transnational and transcultural identity, Hall has contributed immensely to the understanding of global processes concerning culture, cultural change, and intercultural intelligence. Alobwed'Epie's *The Lady with a Beard* aptly showcases cultural mutations born of encounters within and without a cultural location. Culture as dynamic experiencing goes beyond questions of diaspora orchestrated by displacement and repositioning; changes are made or experienced within the same locations of culture as well.

In "Cultural Identity and Diaspora" Stuart Hall's contention about cultural transmutation can be well contextualized in the present discourse:

> Cultural identities come from somewhere, have histories. But, like everything which is historical, they undergo constant transformation. Far from being eternally fixed in some essentialised past, they are subject to the continuous "play" of history, culture and power. Far from being grounded in mere "recovery" of the past, which is waiting to be found, and which when found, will secure our sense of ourselves into eternity, identities are names we give to the different ways we are positioned by, and position ourselves within, the narratives of the past. (225)

This excerpt inspires two pertinent views. The first is that it is a pointer to the misconstrued oppositionalities, positionalities, and representations of cultural identity particularly with regard to postcolonial resistance and resilience to Western cultural dominance. Paradoxically, the grandeur of the colonized is inscribed in its "resistance" to acceptance of influence and not in its resignation or capitulation to cultural assimilation, effacement, or annihilation as designed in the colonialist agenda to produce both the colonial and postcolonial subject.

The second view wrestles with what I call intra-cultural dynamics. The premise is that culture undergoes changes without necessarily being subject to external influences. Cultural evolution and representation can occur with regard to the dire need to alter or modify certain values, practices, or thoughts which are deemed inevitably necessary by a people in the making of their cultural history. This change, in other words, does not result from intercultural dialogue or synergy. Adherence to cultural values, codes, norms, and symbols does not mean that culture is static. The complexity of culture and its myriad transformative contexts of operation explain why interculturality is a permanently unending phenomenon.

In his articulation of the postmodernist identity, Hall has deconstructed what he calls the essentialist cultural identity which is stable, unchanging and serving as "continuous [frame] of reference and meaning" that reflects the general, shared cultural codes and common historical experiences of a people (223). Hall convincingly argues that displacement and the diaspora have led to the crisis and plurality or heterogeneity of identity.

In the Introduction to *Questions of Cultural Identity*, Hall reiterates his convictions about the heterogeneity of identity. The notion of integral, originary, and unified identity has been demolished. The postmodernist turn with its dominantly deconstructive criticism has dismantled any essentialist notion of identity and self-authentification. Identity and identification are always "in process" of becoming, never completed or fully grasped as a finite discursive category so that identification is conditional, lodged in contingency. Hall rearticulates his conviction that

> [w]e need to situate the debates about identity within all those historically specific developments and practices which have disturbed the relatively "settled" character of many populations and cultures, above all in relation to the processes of globalization, which I would argue are coterminous with modernity [...] and the processes of forced and "free" migration which have become a global phenomenon of the so-called post-colonial world. (4)

It is evident that Hall's central position on cultural identity is based on inter-culturality or cross-culturality. He is not concerned with how change processes may occur within the same location of culture, identity, and representation. In the matrix of this chapter, even if a culture regards itself as essentialist, that does not presuppose that the culture is static or unfaltering. Nor is identity dismantling reduced only to questions of hybrid/pluralistic identities, but we can regard the positioning of a specific culture as enshrined in the poetics of becoming rather than the illusionary permanence of being. The conditionality or "becoming" nature of culture is construed in the context of intrinsic and extrinsic factors as exemplified in *The Lady with a Beard*.

Alobwed'Epie: African (Bakossi) Community and Transformation

Alobwed'Epie is an icon in Cameroon's literary landscape. That he uses English as medium of artistic expression instead of a Cameroonian language is a significant sign of cultural concession and intercultural competence, since the language is considered a part of Western cultural capital. From a postcolonial perspective, English is undoubtedly a global language which is subject to as well as capable of various forms of interculturality. *The Lady with a Beard* is a novel through which the author engages various facets of Bakossi culture of the South West Region of Cameroon. The cultural dimension of orality, particularly the proverbial richness of Bakossiland, gives the work its deserving aesthetic and thematic potential. Reconstructing gender, perpetuating culture, cultural (r)evolution, and ontological rootedness are major issues discussed in this critical inquiry.

Ali Mazrui in *The Africans* argues that the West has always tried to make Africans perceive themselves from a Western, particularly Eurocentric spectrum. The West invented Africa by unmaking the continent to look like a distorted portrait, and narrating her not only as a single story, but also a grossly falsified and flawed single story. The attempt has always been to efface any epistemological and ontological substance which would authenticate the intrinsic values of the continent's multivariate cultures. Alobwed'Epie's work is an attempt to deconstruct this invention by presenting what one may call a prototype of an African community that conceptualizes itself primarily from within and not from without, while it inevitably connects without and exhibits signs of transformation. Bakossiland, even though implicated in processes of modern transformations, holds strongly to its mostly unblemished though not ossifying cultural heritage. Unlike Kenjo Jumbam's novel *The White Man of God* (1980), where Christianity and Western cultural epistemology have a strong and active presence, albeit subtly disrupted and subverted, *The Lady with a Beard* is predominantly about local cultural dynamics amid a passive or subdued Western Christian presence, though not without its own perceptible impact.

The Lady with a Beard is an enthralling story evolving around Emade, a woman of great cultural taste and mastery. She is not educated in a Western way, but is richly conscious of her cultural construction, conditioning, identity, and representation. Emade is a widow who, after the death of her husband, challenges traditional norms by refusing to relocate to a position in her village where she can have appropriate protection, and by influencing the village council to move the sacred grove where *Muankum* is incarnated from her husband's house to the chief's compound. She goes through a series of complex experiences which affect her cultural reasoning, and which alter certain long-held traditional beliefs and practices among her Bakossi folk. Believed to be ill-fated and "glued with the wax of misfortune," she is strong and determined to fight against all odds and give meaning to her existence, by relying on her cultural values. Not only has she lost her husband, her daughter has fallen and broken her most treasured utensils. Socio-cultural interpretations of these occurrences and Emade's reaction earn her unpopularity. She is ostracized by the women folk and obliged to leave her native Atieg to take residence temporarily with her sister Ahone at Ekenzu. Her stay in Muabag, where she partakes of the burial of her sister, does not ease life for Emade, who seems to defy a number of roles culturally assigned to men like beating of drums and digging of graves. Having returned to Atieg and becoming reconciled with her women folk, calamity still befalls Emade as her daughter's confession to have fallen into a sacred brook raises more cultural concerns. Besides, she kicks her ill-omened foot and must search the mystery behind this. The novel ends with Emade's search for satisfying answers to her existentialist trauma and self-performed ritual to purge and free herself from overwhelming burdens.

As a text that is enriched in traditional values even though there is already the presence of Western Christianity, signaling an unavoidable transcultural reality, the novel highlights cultural authenticity in a postcolonial and international space. The text showcases an emancipatory and dynamic vision of culture. Culture is manifested in all its diverse aspects of spiritual and transcendental consciousness: the burial of the dead with its rites, the world of ancestors, marriage, child birth and naming, song and dance, etc. My analysis attempts, though not exhaustively, to assess certain key aspects of the representation of Bakossi culture. When Alobwed'Epie writes in English, he articulates inevitable and externally influenced changes in Bakossiland, while he especially wrestles with intrinsic cultural change which perpetuates the Bakossi people's adherence to their identity.

The Cultural Way of Learning: Proverbial Grandeur

This chapter's discourse underscores cultural identity and representation from the perspective of oral literature as epistemological pedagogy. An important peculiarity of *The Lady with a Beard* is the extensive use of proverbs drawn from Bakossi oral literature. Orality is infused into the written text to drive home the identity of a people and the fertility of the spoken word. The novel's proverbial density represents a subset of the vast cultural identities of Africa. All proverbs are culturally bound. As a cultural vector, Alobwed'Epie brilliantly succeeds in transliterating Bakossi oral literature into written English. While rendering the oral text into English rather than *Akóóse* (the language of the Bakossi people) may be a marker of cultural concession, the depth of knowledge is basically Bakossi. In *Standpoints on African Orature*, Nol Alembong asserts that "proverbs are the most widespread, popular and widely collected of what has been described as 'shorter' or even 'minor' forms of Orature" (129). He provides a number of definitions drawn from research on oral literature. That of Wolfgang Mieder suits the context analysis of Bakossi proverbs: "A proverb is a short, generally known sentence of the folk which contains wisdom, truth, morals, and traditional views in a metaphorical, fixed and memorizable form and which is handed down from generation to generation" (3). Bakossi proverbs are therefore highly pedagogic in nature. They undoubtedly demonstrate depths of knowledge in which social and cultural life is grounded.

The characters who use proverbs in Alobwed'Epie's novel possess maturity and depth in understanding oral social and cultural data. Age and cultural immersion are important factors. Mastery of proverbial expressions is therefore a marker of cultural education and intelligence. It evinces a deeply rooted civilized epistemology. Emade, Ahone, and Sango Mesumbe are examples of culturally educated people, bearers of Bakossi core values and identity. Their level of wisdom and sense of discernment are showcased through proverbs.

Emade's reaction to the group of women who come to sympathize with her following her daughter's fall and the losses incurred in the incident is that of accusing them of propagating her demise:

> For one thing, she who organises a hunting expedition, and she who actually kills, are equally responsible for the death of the animal. If what happens was the work of wizards, then all of you who are magnifying it are witches. (*Lady* 16–17)

Emade is angry because village women are taking the incident out of proportion, and in so doing, they are worsening her situation. The women of Atieg take her reaction as a sign of impudence, however, and are resolved to deal with her. Yet one of the women called Munge cautiously warns, "She who wants to fight a tiger must have claws and fangs" (17). Eduke, Emade's arch-enemy, is bent on influencing the women to take action against Emade. The proverb is therefore used to give knowledge of the character and mettle of Emade as an exceptionally strong woman in her socio-cultural milieu.

Mboke is one of the Atieg women who show sympathy for Emade. She relates Eduke's conspiracy to Emade, who intelligently answers, "A quarrel across the valley does not bleed." With regard to

Eduke she says, "an empty hand is of no good to the mouth" (19), meaning that sooner or later Eduke's followers would realize that she is a loud-sounding nothing. The inevitable outcome is that Emade is ostracized.

Ntube, Emade's daughter, is strongly affected by the banning of her mother from all women activities. Yet Emade's intelligence is seen again as she drills Ntube with proverbial wisdom: "When the back is cudgelled the mouth yelps. People can't hate a dog and love its muzzle" (25). Ntube should understand that hatred toward her mother can also be directed toward her as daughter. Regarding Ahone's arrival in connection with Emade's problems, Emade axiomatically resolves to give Atieg women the same problem dose they are giving her: "As the file wears out the cutlass so does the cutlass wear out the file" (26).

Strong and determined as she is, Emade's resolve to shoulder and face her problems is again expressed through a powerful proverb: "The plantain stem begets the bunch but it is the bunch that dictates where the stem will incline. If the stem and the bunch agree where to incline they would withstand not only storms but gales" (27). Two meanings can be deciphered from this saying. The first is that, as a member of her cultural setup, Emade would be defiant in determining her direction and destiny. The second implication is that she and her daughter would, together, brave any storm that comes their way, and they would certainly incline in a direction which would enable them to resist any adversity. This latter attitude would be a clear sign that Emade is engaged in cultural change regarding norms in her community. She is signaling transformation not in terms of debunking Bakossi female identity and representation, but of altering long held-views which are essentially the fabric of her culture.

An important part of Emade's mothering and nurturing responsibility is the cultural education of her daughter. Several occasions substantiate this. From the novel's outset, Emade educates Ntube on why she calls her *mother* and also on domestic science regarding cooking. It is important to note that in most African cultures names are significant. Emade calls Ntube *mother*, because Ntube is a representation of Emade's mother. She therefore possesses the qualities of her grandmother, and should be brought up with this cultural knowledge. Allowing her to go through the process of strong-heartedness gives Emade confidence in culturally bringing up Ntube. "The quality of good pepper can be judged from the way the pepper plant grows" (30) is a proverb which expresses pride in seeing her daughter endure the sight of

Mechane's illness (Emade's sister) and stench from her faeces. Emade also expects her daughter to have fortitude of character; like mother, like daughter.

The burial of Mechane generates more problems for Emade as she announces the death through expert drumbeating like a man, digs the grave in a strategic part of Mechane's compound, and argues for the appropriateness of the grave's positioning. Kolle, who is a member of the Christian choir, suggests that they should incarnate the spirit *Muankum* to deal with Emade for transgressing or defying tradition. Contrary to Kolle's suggestion, however, Sango Mesumbe, the oldest man in Muabag village, uses wisdom to judge the situation with a rationality that would not pass for male chauvinism or patriarchal dominance over women. His explanations no doubt indicate that Emade should not be treated in such a way as to empower her as a man, but nonetheless her inevitable influence earns her due respect as a woman. Sango Mesumbe takes recourse to proverbs drawn from his cultural repertoire rather than Christian theology: "A spear launched in anger misses its target [...] you see, some problems are like porcupines. No matter how right you are, you don't grip them with bare hands [...] It is difficult to handle mudfish out of the net" (50, 51). These proverbs indicate that Emade is quite a complex person to deal with, particularly as she comes from a different Bakossi village, Atieg, with a nuanced cultural outlook not identical with that of Muabag. The paradox is that those who are bent on seeing Emade punished by incarnating *Muankum* are members of the Christian choir who are incontestably rooted in Bakossi culture. For them Christianity is an extrinsic factor; it has come to transform the lives of the Bakossi people in several ways. But the internal alterations which Emade is orchestrating are not influenced by the Christian presence. Atieg and Muabag are microcosms of the greater ensemble of Bakossiland. The tension is not from outside Bakossiland; it is from within, a cultural clash amid a people who are not truly Europeanized because of Christianity.

Ahone advises Emade to be prudent and avoid any further trouble in Atieg after the purification rite on Ntube: "The legs that have no shoes should be careful with the way they move on a stony road" (103). Emade does not only acknowledge her sister's cautionary note on being extremely careful in her fragile position, but is intelligent and farsighted enough to be pre-emptive in her environment:

> I shall bear no person a grudge. But let me tell mother-of-the-sugarcane grove, if a rat mole returns from an expedition and meets

a new clearing at the entrance to its burrow and does not move house immediately, it becomes the broth of the next day meal. (103–04)

Ntube's fall into the Brook-of-the-Serpent is culturally interpreted as a symptom of danger for Emade's daughter, who on Ahone's advice needs to be protected despite the rite which has been performed: "It is when the inside throws out that the outside picks ... If the first thrown spears misses its target, the second does not" (103). Emade resolves to take Ntube to the Mission, where she thinks conditions will be safe for her. Her cautious move is expressed as such: "A cockroach is a cockroach, and even one with a mane should take refuge under a cardboard if it expects to see the next day" (104). To be forewarned is to be forearmed: that is the circumstance of Emade's preventive action.

Though some of these proverbs can indeed have a transcultural and transnational connotation, they are drawn from Bakossi culture. Cultural and situational determinants of proverbs lend credence to the idea that cultural specificity matters in epistemological and ontological processes of human existence. These proverbs constitute the core substance of Bakossi philosophical ordering, justifying an uncontested age-old civilization which Western or other external incursions cannot eclipse. Thus Alobwed'Epie obviously transliterates proverbial texts and is aware of their connotation beyond the individual culture, but it should be re-emphasized that the epistemological and ontological substance of the texts is Bakossi. At the same time, in this fictional encoding the locally circumscribed cultural origin has more than a local identity. It receives a written identification that goes beyond its own linguistic boundary to receive a transculturally communicative significance: texture, sound, or rhythm may be "carried over from the mother tongue to the adopted literary form," just as "the appropriated english is adapted to a new situation" and English is thus "readily available for appropriation and liberation by a whole range of new and distinctive enterprises" (Ashcroft et al., 51–52). Ambanasom has perceptively suggested in another context that the superimposition of a European language (and culture) upon the African experience can create a "hybrid subject," with a text appropriately celebrating "diversity, difference and hybridity" (144).

Contestations of Space: Bakossi Spiritual Roots and Christian Epistemology

Two kinds of contestation of space are construed in *The Lady with a*

Beard regarding the interpreting of cultural transformation. The first wrestles with Christian incursions of Bakossiland and the extent to which these establish themselves and alter cultural identification. The second and most important contestation centers on the dynamics of cultural change from within. This is very important in postcolonial studies because African cultures are far from being archaic or obsolete. As mentioned earlier, cultural alteration must not be orchestrated only by external forces, that is, by contact with and influence of an/other culture(s). All cultures are evolutionary, as evinced in Emade's contestations of gender politics. When Mechane dies, Emade assumes the responsibility to pass on the information through drumming. This act has essentially been considered a male prerogative. Her defiance in assuming a male role is not without a carefully thought explanation that is pregnant with cultural implications:

> Women who guard village entrances must not only understand but must also know how to play the drum, not only the drum announcing death but also the drum announcing war. All the people of this village have gone to the bush. How do we get them if we rely only on the men playing the drum? [...] how many men are in this village? When you get to a village where men shriek to call each other, you call such husks men? Were we not drenched with dew this morning when we got to this village's section of the road? If there were men here won't they have cleared their section of the road? Anyway, blowing the nose once only, does not heal a catarrh attack. A woman playing the drum once cannot destroy the intrepidity of the Muabag men. (*Lady* 35–36)

This excerpt requires cautious cultural analysis. One may think that Emade is exhibiting resistance to male dominance, but this would be a misconception of her cultural context. Her defiance in this context speaks of cultural intelligence and not disrespect for cultural norms, but an attempt at reactivating dormant men who seem not to be inclined to embody the norms. In terms of a hierarchy of power, she has carved out a recognized space for herself within her macro-cultural matrix. Though it is not in Atieg but in Muabag, where she is named "the lady with a beard," her actions are more geared toward the preservation of Bakossi cultural values than a determined fight to assert herself as woman against male dominance. The expressions "blowing the nose once only, does not heal a catarrh attack" and "A woman playing the drum once cannot destroy the intrepidity of the Muabag men" show Emade subtly advocating a cultural alteration that could allow women to assume certain responsibilities in the face of the absence of men or the presence of those who are culturally feeble. Her challenge could even be read as an attempt at overcoming men's docility.

Emade's decision to dig Mechane's grave in the middle of her compound instead of near her deceased husband's behind the house is a challenge to existing cultural order. She is a woman and is considered to be doing the wrong thing. Yet no amount of dissuasion would stop her from doing what she has resolved to do. Existing cultural conditioning and practice allows young boys to dig the grave and be duly entertained. Any person other than a man or boy digging the grave would pose a stiff challenge to Muabag manhood. These factors do not weaken Emade's determination. Her grave-digging act is not motivated by her coming from Atieg to disorientate conceptions of maleness in Muabag. Her refusal to relocate from the entrance of Atieg into the village after the death of her husband is already proof of defiance and expression of fortitude of mind and spirit. These localities are all Bakossi villages, but they are ones which cannot hold on to a static, non-evolutionary, and essentialist notion of culture. Emade's reasons are very plausible and go a long way to ascertaining positive cultural alteration. She is a vector of internal cultural change:

> *Ahieg* and *ngandu* are temporary celebrations and people interested in the celebrations will bear the little inconvenience the grave will cause. Secondly, a grave is not frightening in a crowd. A grave is a permanent thing. This is Wobe. She is married in Nigeria. She may never come here again. What will keep watch over this compound? What will keep away grabbers of land? If we bury Mechane behind the compound, in less than five years, one of those opposing burial in the courtyard will come and build in this strategic compound and own it by creating new genealogies and new folktales. If for anything sake the going gets rough with Wobe and she decides to come back, will she be able to dislodge the new owner of the compound? Nobody will like to build on a non-relative's grave. So the grave in the middle of the courtyard is the sure guard of the compound. If there is war people flee the cities and seek refuge in the villages. So, Wobe, as you look ahead, you should look behind also. (47–48)

Through the force of persuasive argument, Emade is infusing an innovative cultural outlook which would alter previous ways of positioning certain graves in Bakossiland. Caused by the dynamics of internal modifications, this is a vital aspect of cultural change which is often overlooked in postcolonial criticism. This perspective broadens the critical implications of an "Emade syndrome" (94) in the paradigm of cultural mutations not triggered by extrinsic forces, but by reformation from within the fabric of a culture in flux. The flux is strengthened by the cultural distance of marriage in another country, Nigeria, which enables a new discursive perspective on the received Bakossi practices. Without acting as a direct result of external influence, then, Emade relies on her intuition to do what she believes is culturally profitable.

Though we find a foreign presence (Christianity), the story is more about the richness of people who are proud to have a civilization that is neither Western nor Eurocentric. Christianity is present but somewhat eclipsed by the dominant cultural patterns of Bakossi life. Alobwed'Epie appears to either snub the church or be indifferent to its expected spiritual role in the cultural life of Bakossiland, because the church's presence in this case does not signal genuine intercultural dialogue. The school and hospital are certainly welcome institutions which are involved in changing lives, but innate aspects of culture are unshaken. Apart from the choir, which sometimes appears to be more inclined to aspects of Bakossi tradition rather than Catholic orthodoxy, the burial rites of Mechane follow a purely traditional model, the customs of the land. No church authority is present to perform a Christianizing ritual at the funeral ceremony. Christian prominence is thus lacking, contrary to the representation in Kenjo Jumbam's *The White Man of God*.

Christianity is evidently present in Bakossi cultural space, though it does not have a hold on the people of the Atieg and Muabag villages. It plays a passive role, is not resisted, not rejected; it is simply incorporated into the social life style of the people while it is strongly overshadowed by their cultural practices. The burial rites of Mechane at Muabag attest to the passivity of the Catholic faith, which does not really impact the lives of Bakossi people. It is Emade who is at the center stage of the rite; she addresses the corpse:

> Daughter-of-the-deities-of-Kupe-Muanenguba-mountains, Wife-of-the-water-source, Twine-of-the-spreading-pumpkin-plant [...] return to your forebears in peace. When you arrive identify yourself with this cloth (*abad d'esake*) which the deities themselves left with us as sign of solidarity and oneness with the underworld. Let it be the bridge between us. Let each of us who touched it be considered as one of them. And when you share what you are taking along, share in equity so that the "down" may live in harmony and bounty and the "up" also. (54–55)

This is ritualistic performance in essence, finely enshrined in an incantatory mood. The strong belief in a bond between the dead, the living, and even the unborn is evident. Ancestral veneration is typical in this context. The return to the forebears presupposes that Mechane was sent by the ancestors with whom she would be reunited through the passage of death, which is a transition to a more fulfilling life. In *Standpoints in African Orature*, cultural critic Nol Alembong has stressed that

> an incantation is a verse form, the words of which are believed to have a magical effect when spoken or chanted during the performance of rituals or any other occasion that calls for the intervention of the supernatural in human affairs. This verse form manifests itself in such categories as blessings, curses, invocations, prayers and spells. (71–72)

Alembong goes on to talk about the levels of ritualization and rites performed. The ritualization level here is family, and the rite performed is death. The transcendental link between the ancestors and the living culminates in a realm of existence which is propelled by a transitoriness of physical death; reincarnation justifies the cyclical nature of existence in the Bakossi mind-set. Sone Enongene echoes Alembong's definition, stressing that "the incantation is the most significant form of Bakossi religious poetry" and that incantations "constitute a 'vital force' for survival in Bakossi society" (309). Emade's message falls within this cultural logic, irrespective of her gender. Her mastery of oral content and performance context showcase her as a cultural authentifier.

With the already established reputation that Emade has in Muabag, her leading role in this burial ceremony should not be conceived as female agency against patriarchy or male dominance, even if her cultural matrix apparently lends credence to this view. She may have challenged the men of Muabag by digging a grave and dexterously playing drums during and after the burial, but her primary ambition is nonetheless to safeguard time-honored cultural practices. What is important is that vital dictates of Bakossi tradition are adhered to. No Bakossiman or Bakossiwoman in Atieg and Muabag is left indifferent to Emade's cultural dynamism, especially regarding Mechane's death and its aftermath. Nsango Mesumbe, Muabag village patriarch, heartily praises her for the role she plays during the gift ceremony, and is thrilled by Emade's mastery in drumming. This move is a strong marker of cultural flux, and is proof of the non-exclusionary power relations in Bakossi culture. Emade is making that change possible.

Drumming is very important in most African societies, because it signals different layers of significance. In Bakossiland it is used as a means of information and of entertainment involving rhythmical and soulful bonding. Emade fully understands the effect and significance of drumming: "The drum must talk. It must penetrate the nerves. It must possess the mind. It must unite not only the body and soul, but also the living and the dead. And from that fusion, dance comes" (*Lady* 63). The significance that the Bakossi attach to drumming certainly has more than auditory and bodily manifestation; its spiritual dimension creates a synergistic moment in which harmony overflows. This is exactly what Emade does when she is persuaded by Muabag men to drum and ignite an expected totality of effect. When she handles the lead drum, the vibration of the compound heightens with the music producing a bewitching effect:

> She made the lead drum speak. It spoke to the living and the dead in a compelling tone. Inexplicable sounds of whirling storms, interlaced with voodoo shuddering of shoulders and mysterious shrieks of joy took possession of all and sundry. And as the music exploded in them, they danced as they had never danced before. (68)

Failure of Universalist Discourse

On the question of the church's (that is, Rev. Father's) dismissal of the power of *Muankum* as a spirit, claiming it is just a disguised human being in the context of belief in witchcraft, Ebude retorts, "Is the Rev. Father a Bakossi Man? Does he know our tradition?" (94). The question implies that the Father does not master the depth of the people's ontology, and so cannot pass condemnatory judgement on what is sacred to them. The Father's preaching on Sunday shows his consternation at the Atieg people's continuous rootedness in their traditional beliefs: "I am flabbergasted with the shaky grounds the church still has among you." The question is whether it is possible for Christianity to build its fortress, as it were, or superimpose itself on a culturally grounded Bakossi people. The church has done so much for twenty-seven years to eradicate any specter of traditional belief and witchcraft, but in vain: "Yet, faith is still on very timid grounds here" (98 – 99). Even if the Bakossi were to adhere to certain

Christian principles, it would not presuppose the effacement of their cultural identity.

Like his counterpart in *The White Man of God*, Big Father, Reverend Father has failed to understand Bakossi culture simply because it is not compatible with what he takes to be the supremacy of Christianity. He cites Harvestcam, another Father, who had burned Bakossi idols without anything happening, neither did the gods avenge themselves nor did anybody die. The word "idols" as used in this context conveys a sense of denigrating or altogether dismissing Bakossi traditional symbols or emblems. The Reverend introduces a fresh complication by telling the congregation that children come and confess that they fell in the Brook-of-the-Serpent, so God should forgive them. The reaction of the Bakossi people sidelines his church and its supremacist values. Their eventual performative act of condemning the Reverend lends credence to Homi Bhabha's articulation of sly mimicry, as in "Of Mimicry and Man," as a strategy of subverting the dominant cultural discourse by pretending to act it out to the pleasure of the cultural master. Bhabha argues that mimicry connotes camouflage and pretense; it repeats rather than represents. The Bakossi Christians pretend to act as a site on which Christianity, and by extension the Western grand narratives, are successfully inscribed. Their refusal to adhere to Christianity's condemnation of their cultural beliefs points to the fact that they simply appear to be Christians in church. In reality, they are strongly attached to their cultural values. Going to church is therefore a sly mimicry; a performative act of mockery on Christianity.

The Reverend's biased position against the cultural and philosophical mindset of the Bakossi people is that of a particular theologico-philosophical Western representative. His preaching is totalizing and problematically universalist; it is unacceptable in postcolonial discourse. He preaches a brand of Catholicism which refuses dialogue or conversation with local beliefs, and fails unfortunately to inscribe itself on the people. D. A. Masolo has argued fervently for African apprehension of the spiritual and transcendental with regard to the Reverend's accusations against the Bakossi. Writing contemptuously against the misconstrued Western thinking that African religions are animist, Masolo asserts in *African Philosophy in Search of Identity*:

> Witchcraft and magic in African religion, or the significance of the attributes of God to natural objects and phenomena are based on the simple criterion of analogical symbolism. Thus God is called the sun because He, like a celestial body, is powerful despite the great

distance between Him and human beings on earth. In this way, believes Mbiti, Africans try to explain the nature of the invisible spiritual world by means of ordinary language and with reference to objects and phenomena of ordinary experience. (67)

This excerpt testifies to an epistemological and ontological consciousness that is characteristic of Africans. The concluding part of Rev. Father's preaching has far-reaching implications in its opposition to Masolo's assertion:

... belief in God is the marriage between the human soul and the spirit of God. Once God has taken possession of our hearts, there is no room for belief in witchcraft. So, let those who profess in the brook of the serpent know that God sowed his seed in them, they allowed the devil to interplant it with bad weeds. The devil has no power over those who believe in God. (*Lady* 99)

This is a religiously turned imperialist notion aimed at cultural erasure. While witchcraft and (d)evil are phenomena that have been common to all humanity, the Reverend's mission appears to be to tag these traits on Africans as an excuse for bringing them out of the abyss of demonism and ungodliness through a "civilizing mission."

Ntube's confession on the question of the Brook-of-the-Serpent and the resulting severe cultural tensions can only be solved by reverting to the customs of the land. The reaction of the church members and the opinion of the elders with regard to falling into the Brook-of-the-Serpent are unequivocal:

The church hummed in surprise. Who might have gone to confess that he fell in the Brook-of-the-Serpent? "If a person falls in the brook, is that a sin against God or the serpent? Our people have always maintained the tradition that if a person falls in the Brook-of-the-Serpent, whether seen or not seen, he should appease the serpent by offering a goat — church or no church. That is what our forefathers did and that we do and shall do, church or not church," the elders of the congregation whispered among themselves. (98)

This instance lends credence to the question of analogical symbolism. The Brook is a kind of heterotopic cultural space into which the Christian church is not supposed to enter and meddle. It is a sacred place which is reserved for initiated people. The reaction of the entire congregation and most significantly elders inside the church is symbolic of the vulnerability of the Western institution and ideology which this structure here embodies. Apart from the Brook-of-the-Serpent, there are other traditional signposts which mark the cultural and religious inclinations of the Bakossi.

As discussed earlier, Big Father does the same thing in Jumbam's *The Whiteman of God*, the complex climax of which is the kicking and unmasking of the ritual figure of Kibarankoh (143). Both Big Father and Pa Matiu (Matthew) condemn Nso beliefs and practices as heathen and pagan. It is the mother of the boy Tansa who, despite her strong Catholic Christian faith, asks Tansa, "Are you more of a Christian than Big Fadda?" (Jumbam 145). The implication in this context of cultural difference is that there is a superiority of Big Father's Christianity over that of the villagers who are still in the process of becoming closer to his religious status. The question is, how does this fit into the agenda of the Biblical narrative of God's children as one and the same? Mama is still naturally tied to tradition, expressing organic hybridity in Bhabha's terms. Both Papa and Mama express fears of what can befall Tansa on claiming that he saw the person who was in the Kibarankoh mask. According to the traditions of the Nso people, it is an abomination to acknowledge having seen a spirit-possessed entity. The gods must be appeased with animals for cleansing and purity. In Alobwed'Epie's novel, the Brook is a sacred space to the Bakossi, and the new church can do nothing to alter their cultural mind-set regarding this long-held belief. The appropriateness of the question, quoted above, as to whether the Reverend Father is a Bakossi man capable of being audacious to condemn their transcendental belief, positions the Bakossi people as conscious of their space and identity. Theirs is the first space, the actual site and location of their culture, which must not be uprooted by an incoming and foreign one which they are nonetheless trying to accommodate in terms of intercultural dialogue.

Global Forces and Belonging

The Bakossi people have neither refused nor rejected the church. They are syncretic, open to intercultural dialogue, but they strongly adhere to the ways of their ancestors, justifying a civilization that had existed long before the intersection of Christian theology. Even though Ntube, daughter-of-the-upstream-python, stays at the Mission where the Christian God would protect her, Emade is resolved to bring her home after the cleansing ceremony. She would thus also rely on traditional protection, which has been part of Bakossi civilization: "I shall take all precautions. I shall fortify myself, and fortify the daughter-of-the-upstream-python. Nyango Madiba will fortify us in her shrine. I know she is the toughest traditional medicine woman in all the land" (*Lady* 105). The shrine is a sacred space for divinatory and incantatory pronouncements of individual and collective wishes. It is a site of transcendental communication with ancestors and the Supreme Being in Bakossiland.

Most of the world's societies are culturally and philosophically inclined to asking questions about the mysteries of existence and humanity's rational limitations in dealing with such mysteries. Obi Maduakor has stressed the importance of the cosmological vision of African societies as regards spirituality:

> The cosmos, in the African imagination, is a looming reality, still threatening in its intensity. In this environment, man maintains a close contact with nature, but his life is a life of fear: fear of ferocious beasts, fear of anger of the gods, fear of an unwitting infraction of the laws of nature, the taboos, and the social mores that bind society. The goal of life is that harmony can only be generated through constant communication with the gods. (274)

One can thus discern that humanity's metaphysical and transcendental roots are inextricably linked to supernatural phenomena and supernatural humans, animals, or other symbolic entities. Alobwed'Epie's cultural representation in *The Lady with a Beard* conveys such tendencies. Belief in totems and looming spirits, names like "Daughter-of-the-upstream-python" (Ntube), "Widow-of-the-upstream-python" (Emade), "Daughter-of-deities" (Emade), "Wife-of-the-incarnator-of-Muankum" (Emade), "Spoon-that-stirs-steaming-broth" (Emade), "The daughter-of-the-deity-of-Kupe-and-Muanenguba" (Emade, Ahone, and Mechane), "Daughter-of-the-roaring-lion" (Mboke), "Daughter-of-the-deities-of-Kupe-Muanenguba-mountains" (Mechane), "Wife-of-the-water-source" (Mechane): all resonate with Maduakor's description.

As cultural vectors/actors, Emade and Ahone are progressive, steadfast, culturally conscious, and rooted. As in many African communities, child-naming is a culturally valued ceremony among the Bakossi. Though the cultural critic Ekanjume-Ilongo has argued that intercultural interference is weakening the deeper undercurrents that constitute naming among the Bakossi, Alobwed'Epie concentrates on a typical traditional ceremony devoid of external influence.

Ahone is keen on seeing her granddaughter's naming ceremony done in the culturally prescribed manner, and is accompanied by Emade and Ntube to Kodmin village for the occasion. Nyango Diele, chief celebrant of Etame's and Etane's child-naming, is undoubtedly a custodian of Bakossi culture, given the expertise with which she handles the rite. The church has no impact on the process, though many Bakossi attend different church services. After mixing the child's ground umbilical cord with red oil in a clay pot, Nyango Diele in typical oral tradition first rubs the child's chest and speaks of psychosomatic bonding, the mother's sacrifice, and subsequent responsibilities toward the mother when age tolls on her. The second phase of the ritual concerns the mother, whose left breast is rubbed with the mixture, and she is lauded for her endurance amid the inconveniences of pregnancy among other difficulties. The highlight of the rite is the incantatory pronouncement of metaphysical bonds, after which the celebrant empties the remaining mixture against the plantain sucker where the child's placenta is buried:

> Umbilical solution, I pour you here to reinforce the mystical bond between the living and the dead. I pour you here to reinforce the link between the buried placenta, the nursing and the child. Let the bond act like magnet to pull mother and child to where the placenta is buried. [...] Your placenta is buried behind the hut to show that you belong to this family, village, clan and tribe. Let no force on earth ever pull you out of this tribe. (*Lady* 78)

This transliterated text embodies the physical and transcendental link between the living and the living, and most especially between the living and beyond. However global the child may turn out to be, her cultural rootedness cannot be effaced from her location of birth and her initial cultural epistemology. Likewise, the family and tribe are capable of becoming a "force on earth" of global proportions, empowering a sense of belonging that reaches across cultures. If we take recourse to Alembong's classification, Nyango Diele's context obviously fits the realm of the family as the level of ritualization, and the rite performed is one of cultural birth. The ceremony, graced with eight birth songs, is backed with ancestral blessings, and serves as a cultural lesson for Ntube, whose mother has strategically involved her in all the phases. After the ceremony Ntube brilliantly answers her mother's questions. This is a clear and satisfactory signal that Emade is appropriately implementing what was previously her own cultural experience and learning (80). Cultural knowledge is effectively transmitted, its survival and continuity firmly ascertained.

It is important to note that Emade has knowledge of healing as she provides a therapy for Mbole's traumatizing breast problem, and re-establishes the distorted psychosomatic bond between Mbole and her supposedly possessed or bewitched son whose love instincts have been reversed. Before Emade prepares herbs to cure the troubled child and treat the mother's breast, she performs a ritual aimed at psychologically redressing the child and reactivating the umbilical link manifested by the physicality of sucking. Emade's treatment is so successful that both Mbole and her husband promise to name their next son after Emade's father, "Akwe-Kome, the deity-of-Kupe-and-Muanenguba mountains" (87). She succeeds in doing what only Sango Kape is reputed to have expertise in, and thus once more demonstrates her loyal attachment to Bakossi culture and its preservation. Mbole's treatment also solves Emade's perplexity over a strange dream and state of unease that urged her to go to church. The church as a Christian space does not by itself alleviate Emade's burdened mind. Yet her going to church connects her with Christina Nange, who takes her to Mbole's house. The church thus serves as a contact point toward the resolution of a culturally grounded problem.

Bakossiland and the Power of Divination

Clairvoyance, prediction, or foresight is a common phenomenon in most of the world's cultures. The different male and female diviners otherwise known as soothsayers in *The Lady with a Beard* also have a substantial role in the cultural lives of Bakossiland. As telepathists and agents dealing with esoteric realms of existence, they act as intercession between humans and the spirit world, unraveling mysteries and forewarning of danger. Emade's search for unfolding the mystery of an ill-omened stubbing of her toe on her way to the Mission where she takes Ntube reveals a significant aspect of how she understands her cultural identity. After twenty-one nights of Ntube's stay at the Mission, Emade resolves to take her back so as to cast away any suspicion that she is afraid of further cultural reprisals on Ntube.

The foot stubbing incident ignites worrying questions: "What did stubbing the foot signify? Was it a premonitory sign that Ntube's stay at the Mission would be ill-fated, or that her return to Atieg would be ill-fated? What, what was the meaning of the sign? Who will unravel the mystery?" (105). Answering these puzzling questions requires culturally imbued resources such as diviners/spiritualists. A Westerner who is not knowledgeable in Bakossi practices might consider Emade's reflection as mere superstition, in a strategy of demeaning African cultural reality.

Yet in Bakossi culture, as evinced in Alobwed'Epie's representation, divinatory science is carefully categorized. Foot or toe stubbing requires a specialized breed of seers who cannot claim mastery in every other aspect of clairvoyance. For the period of two years and nine months, Emade visits about nine different diviners in diverse Bakossi villages to disambiguate the mystery. She needs a female diviner to decipher her enigma. Yet on the suggestion to meet a female soothsayer from Banso at the Kumbo quarters, Emade retorts, "I heard about that woman. The problem is, she is a non-native. I don't see her being capable of plying into the secrets of our ancestors. But since the legs that searched don't get tired, I shall try her too" (109). Emade is right because she is eventually asked by this non-native prophetess, who acknowledges her limitations, to see a native male diviner to interpret her problem (110). This specificity in cultural difference is not only a gender matter, it also indicates that divinatory power has its culturally localized limitations. At the same time, it testifies to the potential capacity of "non-native" diviners in carefully circumscribed problem areas.

Emade's encounter with a palm wine tapper, her psychosomatic experience of belching and airing her mind, and her resolve to adhere to the tapper's advice to fix matters with her people, shed light on her problem. She is overwhelmed to learn that the palm wine tapper has solved it. Her return to Atieg and her eventual, self-performed ritual of purgation illuminate the Bakossi conception of the human being. Mirabeau Sone Enongene states:

> It is believed among the Bakossi that a human being is both physical and spiritual. He is thought to be endowed with both physical and metaphysical powers that he can use for both good and evil. However, only a select few can exercise influence at the spiritual level, and these are referred to as people with a double nature. (313)

There is no doubt that Emade has a strong sense of the spiritual dimension of her abilities after having met numerous diviners. What she does on the foot-stubbing spot and the attendant physical and psychic relief is proof of her innate spiritual strength.

Could Emade be considered as a feminized African (mother Africa) voice that defies the grand narratives of the West? Aware that it is possible to look at her character from a feminist perspective, as a writer/critic like Anne Tanyi-Tang might do (for instance "Theatre for Change"), one could argue that the forces Emade opposes in a bid to ascertain a distinctive stance are an external and infringing Self, as a Western and dominant male presence — as against a passive, raped, and subjugated female African Other, one that has come to self-consciousness to reassert its overshadowed existence and voice, even if amid stiff challenges.

Could Emade's fate be described as a variant of cultural determinism? Are the circumstances surrounding her life to be interpreted as paying the price for transgressing cultural values which are not ascribed to her jurisdiction? Is her ritual performance not truly within the cultural epistemology of the Bakossi dynamism? And has her power been weakened in the course of time? It may be hasty to make any conclusion. Her travails appear fairly normal after all; perhaps she is just entering another phase of life. The question of her place in Bakossi culture is not entirely judged in *The Lady with a Beard*, a title which designates her. The sequel to this novel, *The Lady with the Sting*, inspires other critical trajectories of cultural ordering and representation.

What is the significance of the end of the novel in terms of my argument on cultural lines, the interplay between Christianity and the local tradition and the relation between Emade and her cultural environment? The story is about cultural representations in intrinsically mutating circumstances. It is about the immense impact of cultural re-orientation as orchestrated by a woman whose chief goal is that of fostering her community.

Conclusion

I refer once more to Stuart Hall to articulate my considerations of intraculturalism and interculturalism. Underscoring cultural flux and representation, Hall states:

> Though they seem to invoke an origin in a historical past with which they continue to correspond, actually identities are about questions of using the resources of history, language and culture in the process of becoming rather than being: not "who we are" or "where we came from", so much as what we might become, how we have been represented and how that bears on how we might represent ourselves. Identities are therefore constituted within, not outside representation. (*Questions* 4)

Alobwed'Epie's *The Lady with a Beard* aptly demonstrates the "becoming" of cultural identity predominantly from the perspective of change processes which occur within the same cultural matrix. In the domain of African cultural studies and intercultural dialogue from an international perspective, it is imperative to redress biases and stereotypes which blur both cultural identity and flux. With the English articulation of the fictionalized Bakossi culture, carrying the native cultural expression into the appropriated ex-colonial language, the becoming of identity is inscribed in a manner celebrating its intrinsic hybridity.

References

Alembong, Nol. *Standpoints on African Orature*. U of Yaounde P, 2011.

Alobwed'Epie. *The Lady with a Beard*. Editions CLÉ, 2005.

Ambanasom, Shadrach A. *The Cameroonian Novel of English Expression: An Introduction*. Langaa Research and Publishing, 2009.

Ashcroft, Bill. *Post-Colonial Transformation*. Routledge, 2001.

Ashcroft, Bill, Gareth Griffiths, and Helen Tiffin. *The Empire Writes Back: Theory and Practice in Post-Colonial Literatures*. 2nd ed. Routledge, 2002.

Bhabha, Homi. "Of Mimicry and Man: The Ambivalence of Colonial Discourse." *October*, vol. 28, 1984, pp. 125–33.

Ekanjume-Ilongo, B. "The Naming Practice in Akoose: Deviation from Cultural Stereotypes." *International Journal of English and Translation Studies*, vol. 2, no. 2, 2014, pp. 228–35.

Hall, Stuart. "Cultural Identity and Diaspora." *Identity: Community, Culture, Difference*, edited by Jonathan Rutherford, Lawrence and Wishart, 1990, pp. 222–37.

—. "Cultural Studies and Its Theoretical Legacies." *Stuart Hall: Critical Dialogues in Cultural Studies*, edited by David Morley and Kuan-Hsing Chen, Routledge, 1996, pp. 261–74.

—. "The Question of Cultural Identity." *Modernity: An Introduction to Modern Societies*, edited by Stuart Hall, David Held, Don Hubert, and Kenneth Thompson, Wiley-Blackwell, 1996, pp. 595–632.

Hall, Stuart, and Paul du Gay, editors. *Questions of Cultural Identity*. Sage, 1996. Jumbam, Kenjo. *The White Man of God*. Heinemann, 1980.

Maduakor. Obi. *Wole Soyinka: An Introduction to His Writing*. Garland, 1986.

Masolo, D. A. *African Philosophy in Search of Identity*. Indiana UP, 1994.

Mazrui, Ali A. *The Africans: A Triple Heritage*. BBC / Little, Brown, 1986.

Mieder, Wolfgang. *Proverbs: A Handbook*. Greenwood Press, 2004.

Sone Enongene, Mirabeau. "Religious Poetry as Vehicle for Social Control in Africa: The Case of Bakossi Incantatory Poetry." *Folklore*, vol. 122, no. 3, 2011, pp. 308–26.

Section Two

Interpreting Globalization

9

Identity, *Différance*, and Global Cultural Studies: China Going Abroad

Keyan G. Tomaselli
University of Johannesburg
Du Yiwei
Shaoxing University

Summary: Based on close observation of the priorities evident in recent influential congresses in China, in this chapter we examine how some trajectories of Cultural Studies research are responding to the innovative China "going abroad" initiative. Among the many topics that are being studied are television drama, travel writing, and also film translation. In this context it appears especially useful to consider Stuart Hall's appropriation of Jacques Derrida's concept of *différance* to formulate his theory of identity, extendable to international identity. This helps us understand how Cultural Studies and its *alter ego*, intercultural communication, are being applied as mechanisms enabling soft power to translate Chinese culture across the world. Yet at the same time we can observe a diminishing of originary British Cultural Studies as a historically informed agent of fundamental social change into a discipline of textual analysis offering descriptive, uncontextualized, ahistorical readings of texts which are not clearly identified as located within the political economy. Giving more attention to the inherently self-reflective, self-critical, and historicized character of Cultural Studies would regain the field's full cognitive potential. In this situation, Raymond

Williams' dynamic concept of "structures of feeling," which has been called a "happy marriage of the aesthetic and the socio-historical or the socio-political," can offer new impulses. Making use of "difference as/is dialogue," China certainly can communicate within the rapidly changing global semiosis.

Introduction

This chapter tries to understand how some trajectories of scholarship on Cultural Studies (CS) are responding to the China "Going Abroad Initiative," which was inaugurated in 1978 when the then-Chinese leader Deng Xiaoping initiated the reform of China's economy. Our focus relates more particularly to developments since the turn of the millennium, when the work of the Birmingham School was translated into Chinese (see Huang, "Entering," as well as Luo). Some contemporary processes rupturing what one might consider to be "Western" Enlightenment values have meanwhile appeared to herald a post-truth, even a post-American age (see Zakaria).

Where post-modernism critically examined the grand narratives that went before, the post-truth age deliberately discards what went before, replacing it with fictions that deny history or, at least, those histories that don't fit with dominant discursive hegemonies. Lies and lying, as Umberto Eco has revealed, are "the *proprium* of semiosis" (59), now becoming a socially legitimate (dis-)communication practice which spurns anything that does not fit preferred discourses. A "politics of violence" belongs in a similar category (see Bhatt).

The nature of China's reform project that now promotes economic growth occurred at precisely the moment that the aftermath of the centuries-long Enlightenment had come under stress in the "West." This occurred co-terminously with the rise of right-wing populism in the USA and Britain, and to a lesser extent in the Netherlands and France.

These impressions underpin our observations on the Sino-U.S. relationship through the prism of CS. When President Trump was elected, and when he assumed office in January 2017, geopolitics and multiculturalism are no longer the same as they were; the European political and economic project came under siege everywhere; and globalization is being spatially re-bordered and walled off, with migration now managed in extraordinary detail though refugee numbers are burgeoning in many regions.

Though it is a borderless field, CS assumes particular contours during different conjunctures at different places. We will map how and to where, with what articulation, CS has traveled, and identify the kinds of utilitarian forms it has adopted in totally different contexts and periods.

Once known in the "West" for its activist and humanist intellectualism, the field has been everywhere re-articulated into doing different kinds of work: translation, literary studies, cultural economy, marketing and advertising, audience and reception studies, policy analysis, discourse analysis, and studies of identity. As we argue below, the field and its *alter ego* of intercultural communication (which according to Hua has positivist, interpretive, critical, constructivist, and realist paradigms) are being applied as mechanisms enabling soft power to translate Chinese culture across the world in the context of the "Belt and Road" and the "21st-Century Maritime Silk Road" initiatives. Among the effects of the initiatives could be stimulating the translation and dissemination of major literary works from the cultures of the countries concerned. Or, inspired by this and instances such as Amitav Ghosh's ethnographic semi-fiction or the imaginative historiography of Timothy Brook, literature may emerge that can give new impulses to understanding the global implications.

Where Tomaselli ("Seeing") addressed one particular Chinese appropriation of CS compared to early British, Australian, South American, U.S. American, and South African experiences, this chapter develops a further specifically Chinese dimension, with special reference to the concept of identity and its derivation from Jacques Derrida as read by the seminal British scholar Stuart Hall, and appropriated in China by scholars like Jin Huimin and Zhao Bing. The discourse analyses of "Cultural China" (Shi) in understanding a globalized market economy following the end of the Cold War can be comparatively examined in relation to other CS trajectories that relate to intercultural negotiation, international diplomacy, and digitization, though we cannot trace all aspects of the relationship in the present chapter. We will discuss the implications for global CS in terms of the ideological metaphor of the color "red" (as in revolutions [cultural, political, guerilla] and so on). We will explain this further below.

1. Histories of Cultural Studies

For a historical context, we need to give a very brief and simplified overview of major developments in CS. With its strong interest in power relations (see for instance Guillem), CS emerged during the 1970s in different ways in different places, in response to similar post-Cold-War political and economic impulses. British CS was critical of Soviet structuralism but also of "Western" neo-liberalism, which spread across the Anglo-Saxon world from the early 1970s.

Below is a schematic overview of global CS trajectories, in order to place Chinese CS in a historical perspective.

• **Early British** scholars constituted themselves as organic intellectuals (to use a term introduced by Antonio Gramsci) whose analyses of power relations, circuits of culture, and text–context relationships attempted to counter the rise of Thatcherism in the context of the Cold War when capitalism had failed to generate humanistic values. British CS dismissed the conservative morality of "social deviancy," recasting such practices as legitimate forms of collective resistance to dominant hegemonies exhibited by ordinary people who expressed themselves through subcultures of style (see Hebdidge).

Apart from intercultural studies, CS's other *alter ego* that directly engaged it was anti-theory Thompsonian culturalism (see Thompson), which eschewed structuralist Marxist class analysis in favor of a concept of class-as-consciousness. This workerist emphasis was opposed alike to capitalism, as it was argued to operate as anti-humanist structures that reduced humans to unfeeling wage slaves.

• **South American CS**, like that of the 1980s South African trajectory (see Tomaselli, "Alter-Egos"), took its cue from Marxist scholarship and activism, engaging in revolutionary actions against neo-fascist military states. Middle-class academics in these contexts did not necessarily think of themselves as organic intellectuals, but as facilitators (often liberation theologians) working alongside labor and social movements in identifying and enabling organic intellectuals from the working classes and *lumpenproletariat* to resist and overthrow state repression (see Martín-Barbero).

• **Australian CS** was less riven by intractable class struggles during the 1990s. Scholars like Tony Bennett developed an affirmative trajectory that adopted and adapted Michel Foucault's concept of governmentality into a strategy that was applied to the generation of organizational practices, enabling civic management in the creation of cultural and creative industries policy (see Sterne). Simultaneously, it critically examined issues of representation and identity, and the historical conjunctures out of which these arose. Where British CS was decidedly oppositional, Australian cultural policy research was critically collaborative, affirmative, and tactical, enabling civic developments within a much more benign and socially inclusive political and public sphere. Australian academics operated more like technical intellectuals working in conjunction with municipal and state agencies in embedding popular access and a critical citizenry within government structures and democratic processes.

• **U.S. American CS**, initially indebted to the British derivation, lost much of its activist and political-economic dimension after the crossing of the seas, becoming a text-bound close reading activity. Such an approach confirms oppressive regimes but tends to eschew an affirmative dimension, an essential ingredient in the work of any social movement.

For a much fuller overview of cultural studies globally in a historical context, see Connell and Hilton as well as Gilroy et al.

We should see the growth of CS in China against the backdrop of these orientations as well as of China's own rapid development. In response to neo-liberal market economics, China's economy was transformed within 20 years "from a closed backwater to an open centre of dynamism with sustained growth rates unparalleled in human history" (Harvey 1). This extraordinary shift was accompanied by intense intellectual ferment — known as "culture fever" (*wenhua re*) — in the search for "an alternative intellectual framework" to replace "official ideology" (Gu 389; see also Wang Jing and Tsou). The key tactical terms are marketization (see also Tao et al. 4), foreignization, and translation. Marketization refers to translating Chinese enterprises as "created in China," an indication of consumerist post-modernity. Foreignization refers to translating Chinese culture abroad, as can be done by promoting Chinese films globally, the establishment of Chinese studies and/or Confucius Institutes at universities across the world, and by means of educating foreigners at the country's "Foreign Studies" institutions. Finally, translation means basically how to enable intercultural communication between China and the world at large.

The Global North/West region (for which see Nayak and Selbin 2) during the post-1970s conjuncture, coinciding with the decade of the Chinese "reform era" (Wang Jing), vigorously imposed inflation-curbing monetary policy. Neo-liberal policies to manage economies and nations targeted trade union power, while stagnation was tackled through deregulation, liberalization, and privatization. The co-incident rise of the Asian Tigers in the east influenced China to substitute market socialism for central planning (see Harvey 1 and Huang, "Entering" 237).

The era of China's "going abroad" (see Sun) or "encountering the world" (Dai 170) followed from the excesses of the Cultural Revolution. National image-building is indicated by China's hosting of the 2008 Olympic Games, the 2010 World Expo, and the global publicity around the "Belt and Road Initiative" from 2015 onwards. Simultaneously, Chinese universities developed intercultural communication strategies to enable strategic parity with the USA and Asia. This "going abroad" discourse was the gist of a keynote delivered by Zha Mingjian at the 2016 International Association for Intercultural Communication Studies conference, strongly supported by students in their cross-cultural case studies between China and the USA, often signifying their own attempts as positioning of self in different and unfamiliar cultural contexts as they shifted between them.

By the turn of the millennium, the global economy was remade largely in the name of neo-liberalism. Neo-liberalism can be understood as a set of political and economic practices which claim that the quality of life is most efficiently secured by liberating individual entrepreneurial freedoms and skills. These are to be managed within a state framework characterized by private property rights, free markets, rule of law, and free trade. This was the economic world into which China was entering. As Wang Xiaoming expresses this condition in his "Manifesto":

> Appeals for "modernization" swept the nation in the mid-1980s — anyone over thirty today will remember the slogans of that time: "separate politics and business", "stop price-fixing", "destroy the common pot", "smash the iron rice bowl", and the posters declaring "efficiency is money". Scholars were especially keen on the maxims "change systems of ownership", "the market economy is the height of efficiency", and "the market economy is modernization". The model of modernity, naturally, was Western Europe and America. (278)

An ensuing, but less chaotic "Western" theoretical emphasis has underpinned much subsequent discussion among Chinese scholars in art, media, and language realms, as they have examined translation and related topics pertaining to China-communicating-with-the-world. In discourse analysis studies and elsewhere, this is termed "Branding China" (see for instance Loo and Davies; Wang Jing, *Brand* 134ff.). A special issue of *Critical Arts: South-North Cultural and Media Studies* on this topic (see Cao and Wu) examines how China was propelled to global prominence through its economic growth rather than by political-military-technological means. As "a developing country," China is at pains to manage its own transformations while trying to carve out an international identity amidst its growing global roles. Studies published in this special issue examine how the formation of China's international image is fused with the creation of new identities within the country. More crucially, under examination is how China's self-portrayals are communicated to the world and how they interact with the current, prevalent and "Western"-defined modernity-dominated ideologies. The special issue examines how China's political, cultural, and business elites see China's past, present, its positions in the world, and its future directions, and it considers the consequences of the "new voice" from China in a fast-changing world.

2. Descriptive Readings or Critical Approaches

With these contexts, for an understanding of how CS is conceptualized in Chinese academic sites in relation to its historical manifestations elsewhere, we want to show how some Chinese scholars have tended to take CS and/or discourse analysis and its methods for granted, offering theorized and often descriptive, uncontextualized ahistorical readings of texts without locating them within the political economy which had generated them. What appeared to be a "culture fever" in the 1979–1989 period, as already noted, "engaged with great eagerness in searching for an alternative intellectual framework, derived from modern 'Western' theories in social sciences and humanities, to replace the official ideology" (Gu 389). These kinds of critical approaches characterized the debates of meetings organized by the International Association for Intercultural Communication Studies (IAICS) as well as by China's Academy of Social Sciences (CASS), to which we will come back further below. We can also remind ourselves of how CS, upon being introduced into the Chinese context, became integrated with existing practices of cultural history and comparative literature studies to enable a closing of the gap between elite and popular culture (see Wang Ning, "Cultural").

To study the major contributions to CS for our purpose, we have examined over 1,200 conference abstracts linked to intercultural, business communication, and CS conferences between 2015 and 2017. We participated in many sessions, and studied full papers where these were available. The 2015 International Association of Intercultural Studies (IAICS) conference held in Chinese Hong Kong, for example, included studies of Gangnam style (Piyawan), streets (Radwanska-Williams), TV drama (Tu), travel writing (Zhang), and also film translation (dubbing, subtitling, fansubbing, etc.). We can learn, for instance, that popular TV drama series in both China and the USA "place women in a position where they still have to be rescued by men," and that TV series present "role models that audiences emulate" (Tu). We could also compare the dramatized TV reconstructions of courtroom proceedings in China and other countries, as studied earlier in the present book series (see Goering et al.). At the same time we can observe that, even if "compared with American and British TV series, Chinese productions still need to improve artistry and imagination," the Chinese series "Princess Agents" from Hunan Satellite TV, for instance, has become "one of the hottest Chinese TV productions shown in Western countries" (Wei Xu). In the IAICS context, most studies involving translation drew on discourse analysis, examining branding, marketing, and translation, and the ways in which institutions (academic, retail, or media) present and represent themselves.

3. International Association for Intercultural Communication Studies 2015, 2016, and 2017

So does China, in terms of its preferred CS orientations, hold a shared identity with what is known as the "West"? We begin our exploration of the question with a consideration of the recent IAICS conferences. At the 2015 conference one innovative student presenter, Feng Lei, engaged with Stuart Hall's "Two Paradigms" article (1980) and the incompatibilities between CS (including Edward P. Thompson's culturalism) on the one hand and conventional, mainly positivist, cross-cultural theory on the other. In this reading, CS meshes structuralism (or objectivity) with anti-theory culturalism (or subjectivity) into a third, combined pathway that analyzes human agency (that of ordinary people) in its relation to overarching structures of class power, regulated through an economy's relations and modes of production. Cross- and inter-cultural communication studies, in contrast, is presented as being located largely within structural functionalism, which examines how institutions and social practices work as cybernetic systems. Where the former is thus intensely historicized in terms of Marxist class analysis and political economy, the latter is seen as offering frameworks for building theory and examining societies as complex organic systems whose interacting parts cohere to promote solidarity, stability, and predictability.

Feng Lei, who studied in Australia where he first encountered CS, observes of the descriptive-instrumentalist trend:

> My own impression of what makes cultural studies distinct from other disciplines is that it creates complexity but not conformity. The significance of cultural studies lies not in its utility, but in the reflexive and critical mode in which researchers deal with theories and politics. Therefore, unlike cross-cultural communication which has its root in American pragmatism, cultural studies should never work to serve existing political institutions and business interests. This position also leads to my ambivalence towards the case of the "affirmative" type of cultural studies which is expected to solve "real life problems", as I find it very hard to integrate the act of knowing with that of living in research.

The above quote encapsulates much of the schizophrenia that characterizes the field of CS globally. It is never quite clear what it is, what it does, or what it can deliver. This is both a strength and a weakness, as Raymond Williams has observed.

3.1　Textualization: A Make-No-Difference Methodology

Many 2015 IAICS delegates were groping for a handle on a methodologically fuzzy but theoretically very precise field that one of the founding fathers, Raymond Williams, early on described as "a vague and baggy monster" (*Politics* 158), one that treats empirical inquiry "with suspicion" (Pickering 1). We should note that, in the shape of cultural materialism, Williams' concepts for analyzing cultural phenomena in their social and historical context have received considerable attention in China (see the discussion by Yin). Universality, ubiquity, and utility are among CS's strengths, but are also the field's weakness. In contrast, inter- and cross-cultural approaches can address clearly identified, usually contemporary research questions, in familiar scientific paradigms that offer implementable, replicable, and useful guidelines to inter-cultural and cross-cultural interaction.

With the exceptions of some IAICS plenaries at the 2015, 2016 and 2017 IAICS conferences (see also House), most of the theories and methods were generally Western or Anglo-American (see also Gu 389). These were unproblematically applied as highly elaborated and idealized schemata awaiting application and critical interrogation (see Wei as well as Chen, "Beyond"), whether of the intercultural, or less so of the CS kind. As useful as these are, Chinese philosophies did often filter through, often in a carefully considered manner (e.g., Chen, "The *yin*," "On Identity"). Overall, however, the discussions of Chinese theory were offered in ahistorical and idealist forms, short on discussion of gender relations, class analysis, and forms of governance and resistance. Confucianism with its harmonization imperative proposes functionalism in contemporary China as an outcome of multiple forces, including the market economy and state governmentality. As Feng Lei observes:

> Challenges may come from, [...] a kind of Confucian governmentality that reinforces a functionalist attitude in favor of national development. In Confucianism, self-development, family regulation, and national administration belong to one and the same trajectory. The state is considered as an intimate senior family member. The obligation of traditional intellectuals (literati) is to devote themselves to the ruling power and therefore to restore social harmony. This might explain, in a historical dimension, why functionalist theories like cross-cultural communication tend to travel more quickly and easily among Chinese scholars. (Personal e-mail, 21 July 2016)

In the USA, positivist and structural functionalism became known as "administrative research," where academics tended to vacate their critical selves and undertake studies useful to prevailing hegemonies, whether in the public sphere or in business. Analogously, there was little evidence in the IAICS abstracts and meetings in which we participated of the cultural strategies adopted by critical intellectuals in the 1980s who simultaneously concealed and articulated "their antiofficial stance through the seemingly nonideological means of cultural expression" (Dai 170).

To recall: CS started as a critique of high culture. It then critiqued Thatcherist supply-side economics that privatized state assets and restricted money supply, resulting in the soulless commoditization of social value and the alienation of the individual from the collective. In short, some trajectories of CS have been institutionally tamed and thereby conceptually traumatized. As Wang

Xiaoming explains with regard to an affirmative and "baggy" CS in China, CS must track the new ideology

> without undue respect for disciplinary restrictions or specialized fields. Above all, cultural studies must not, in the name of becoming modern, let itself be trapped by the compartmentalization of life and regulation of knowledge operative in increasingly detailed academic-administrative systems that are themselves one of the conditions of nurturing the new ideology. (290)

The diminishing of originary British CS as a historically informed agent of fundamental social change into a discipline of textual analysis, regulated via academies that have been criticized as neoliberal, could be conceived of as "red panty" approaches. We here, of course, invoke "red panty" ironically. As *parole* (or accent), "red" signifies fertility and celebration (see Yu Hui-chih 59), hence in our context the sexy sub-textual regimes of signification that often mask *langue*, the structural determinants and marketing discourses which order the capitalist political economy and consumption patterns within it. Our point is that much contemporary CS in this sense is analytically frivolous rather than engaging in active social praxis. Let us hasten to add that we are not questioning frivolity: more often than not such work is innovative and analytically prescient. Rather, such analysis needs to be aware that consumption itself acts a form of hegemony, and that hegemony arises out of the structuration of historical contexts (see for instance the work of Douglas Holt, who in "Distinction" offers a poetics based on Bourdieu and analyzes taste as "effective exclusionary resource," with high cultural capital resource informants showing "more interest in the qualities of the writing and acting, and less concern about the relevance of the content that is being represented"). In the intellectual context of CS, it can be argued that literary studies can "give a convincing interpretation to mass culture in an era of consumption" (Tao et al. 33).

The use of red also counterpoints the Chinese experience after the founding of the People's Republic of China. During the later Mao era, a contextual and communitarian Cultural Revolution drew on connotations of "red" as pro-collectivist, anti-individualistic, and anti-consumption-for-consumption's-sake. Politically-inclined individuals during the 1980s who were considered more "expert" than "red" were excluded from revolutionary currents, such as Jin Guantao, who became the author of the novel *Open Love Letter*. During the Cold War period, in the so-called West "red" evoked a double connotation, what was typified as the "red" political and military menace and also sexuality (individualistic, as the sexually secretive come-hither). Picking up some suggestions from Jing Wang (*High*), we could use the color metaphor of "yellow" to describe accumulation via sexual activity, "black" for the criminal subterranean economy, and "red" for the political, as in the Cultural Revolution's so-called five red categories, or later as they apply to the "new rich" (see Dickson). In the classic novel *Dream of the Red Chamber* (or *The Story of the Stone*), red signifies "good fortune or prosperity" as well as youth and spring (Hawkes 1: 45). In associating a new red with the new rich, one can re-articulate its prior meaning, contesting the narrower myths represented in the Cultural Revolution period, and suggest that consumption has become the political policing device. The new class formation soon adopts conspicuous consumption, allowing "red" as a ("Western") signifier of virility and enticement to come into play within new social classes across the global economy.

From the viewpoint of "Western" scholarship, a red panty trajectory will diligently search texts (anything that signifies, including film as Bellour's "unattainable text") for hidden meanings, society's grubby underwear, discursive patterns that actually speak of oppression, class and gender subjugation. It attempts to identify and explain (away) the hegemonic relationship between consent and coercion. As context, hedonistic consumerism is often driven by hi-octane, hyper-sexualized advertising and music video regimes. Consumer desires for certain commodities, in everyday interactions, may clash with the ways consumers can "elaborate nice discourses" about desiring to be guided in life by completely different values (Branco and Valsiner ix).

3.2 Textualization and Activism

For the effects of the diminishing of CS, our point of reference is again Feng Lei. He agrees that CS nowadays is often reduced to a sort of red panty "textual analysis":

> Despite the fact that deconstructionist reading may produce in-depth and complex knowledge, the knowledge is largely confined in its own immediate/subjective context and may therefore lose its validity on a social level. The focus on cultural texts — even in the form of discourse and ideological analysis that usually serves the politics of social equality — does not take readers too far, for texts are often the outcome but not the cause of social consciousness. Rather, it is the structures or relationships which lie within social

consciousness that dictate the shared and constraining nature of culture. I particularly enjoy Williams' (1977) notion of "structures of feeling" as "a particular quality of social experience ... that is being lived" (p. 131). This notion not only connects individuals with society, but also strikes a balance between both the enabling and disabling sides of human experience, between knowledge and power. For me, this exemplifies one of the best moments of cultural studies' way of thinking.

Yin Qiping confirms the importance of the "dynamic vital structures of feeling which in turn suggest a superb example of aesthetic judgement," with a "happy marriage of the aesthetic and the socio-historical or the socio-political" in cultural materialism (179). Textualization is certainly one useful approach. While original CS has always been self-reflective, self-critical, and historicized, textual approaches offer close readings that do not themselves critique methods, theories, or researcher positions.

Much contemporary CS has harnessed itself to a circularity of constructing deconstruction. This constructs little but a reverse semiosis, which, as Du Yiwei argues, is parasitic and of limited value in understanding Chinese modernity. When concepts like "deconstruction" and "post-modern" gained favor in academia, the results did not have much to do with "making a difference" (see Tomaselli and Durden, also Zhao). Still, emphasis on discourse analysis and translation offers comparative insights between China and the U.S. especially, involving differing representations of sexuality in *Cosmopolitan* (see Wu and Chung), modern women professionals (Wu and Chung), and involving politics (see Wu). While such studies discuss activism, they are not themselves activist. Critical research, Feng Lei argues, as everywhere else, has a long way to go. For example, Feng explains how he learned during his undergraduate days that the purpose of research is to improve social welfare and contribute to the "harmonious society." This objective is certainly to be lauded, but self-reflectivity and dialectics (see for instance Guillem) are what underpin any critical analysis that aims at fostering an involved critical citizenry, as is the Australian cultural policy imperative. In this regard, the annual competition for the national research grant, with its aim at winning what scholars sometimes call the "lottery," would appear to be ideologically weighted.

So skepticism occurs when reminders of CS as activism, one that takes sides, one that demands social justice or human rights are offered. This CS originary, grounded in critical theory, appears disorientating and discomforting to institutions. Its "critical cut" (Chambers) has a political objective — in a broad sense — to change the world. Activist CS does not do research just for research's sake, or deconstruction for deconstruction's sake, or discourse analysis for its own sake. It is much more than mere content or discourse analysis (see Connell and Hilton); CS does matter (see also Grossberg as well as Dai). It must make a difference, never more so than in a world experiencing recurring massive intercontinental refugee crises, genocide, human trafficking, huge and growing disparities in wealth, and new forms of neo-colonialism via the globalization of the relations of production, internationalization of poverty, and often inhumane living and working conditions for the masses that feed excessive consumption of the few. CS projects are capable of illuminating many of these. Add to these crises the human factor in rapid climate change and the emergence of pandemics like HIV, Ebola, and Zika, and the loss of potency of antibiotics. Governments thus have started planning for potential environmental and public health catastrophes that arise from war, drug immunity, and post-Cold-War "marketization" and allied interests represented in the so-called "clash of civilizations" (see, for instance, Xia).

3.3 Cultural China

The Cultural China approach centers on intercultural and business communication and tends toward translation studies and discourse analysis, especially applied to advertising, business linguistics, branding, and understanding the idea of markets, as the economy shifted after 2002 from *danwei*'s pre-marketization era characterized by the "work unit," relating to state or collectively-owned factories, and by high accumulation for the nation and low consumption of the mass (see Feng Jie-yun 61). Overlaid on these structural and culturally oriented economy imperatives (read through linguistic, discursive, and business frames) are attempts to make sense of the Other — especially "Western" culture, economy, industry, and consumerist ways of doing things that interpellate citizens as individualistic and hedonistic. For the neo-Confucian conceptualization of Cultural China with its three symbolic universes ("The Periphery as the Center"), see Tu Weiming's discussions; also Yeh's comments on cultural hegemony.

Our impression is that Cultural China scholars have been attempting to address a number of simultaneous questions (see Wu) as the society has been shifting from state-owned means of production to a market economy in a globalizing world that has been extracting the country from its previous isolation, interfacing it with other "dominant cultures" globally (Shi, "Towards" 244). From a reading of this corpus of work, we conclude that the approach is seeking to understand

- marketization, global regulation, financial integrations, and associated practices of consumerism and market economies through a study of "Western" theories and examples of branding①
- how the study of advertising explains shifts in the contemporary Chinese political economy as it globalizes
- how Chinese scholars interact with European, British, and American analytical discourses trying to make sense of a different imaginary
- to what degree cultural defensiveness has been evident when discussing these questions in China (See Shi, "Why"), and
- what critical frameworks have been systematically imported into the Cultural China discussion to mobilize dialectical thinking better (e.g., Wang, *High*; Dai; Gu).

These questions are flagged as driving an emergent CS strand as articulated at the 2015, 2016, and 2017 IAICS conferences, and also from the broader literature now emerging from Chinese cultural scholarship, particularly in the areas of business and advertising studies, identity, and globalization. From an analysis of conference abstracts of Chinese students studying at U.S. universities and in China, we can gather that CS has been leveraged to:

a) enable the students to reposition themselves from unspeaking national subjects to speaking global subjects, even if through "Western" frames of analysis, in order to address ... commonly human problems beyond the binary limitations of either Oriental or Occidental, and also proposing a multiculturalist in-betweenness research position (see Shi, "Towards" 248);

b) draw on local intellectual legacies when engaging and taming what have been called "the rampant generalization of Euro-centric concepts and values" ("Towards");

---

① As China has entered the market economy and is increasingly influenced by the culture ideology of consumerism, studies have revealed distinctive changes in Chinese advertisements: from promoting values such as family and tradition to promoting modern "Western" values such as hedonism and self-fulfillment. The different value systems can overlap and be used in mutually complementary ways. See for instance Zhang and Shavitt, also Shen. While *danwei* advertising referred to the descriptive promotion of work units, after 2002 advertising took on more familiar "Western" visual contours hailing affective responses (see Feng Jie-yun).

c) link the historical Cultural China with the economic in a period of change;

d) help reposition China … to creative industries in a regulated world; and

e) engage in cultural transformation that rearticulates the terrain of global relations from that of cultural imperialism — the domination of one geographically bound national culture by another — to the amorphousness characteristic of supranational imagined communities where the market is regulated by international agreements.

The "Cultural China" (usually thus capitalized) imagination of culture equality is different from the above-mentioned national derivations in that it has been geared, from the outset, toward understanding how to make meaning of and harness global, market-driven economies. It does this through the study of branding and of TV characters as cultural indicators of a "deterritorialized" and "de-ideologized" China which admits difference but talks of values of a single, homogeneous, and harmonious collectivist society, with a form of "Daoist libertarianism". Capitalism, under these circumstances, cannot "improve anything other than living standards" (Kelen 297). To this extent Cultural China remains an affirmative discursive mechanism examined through a CS-framed structural functionalism.

If the Cultural China approach is affirmative, it is also defensive and culturally re-assuring, a trajectory superficially similar to the Australian re-articulation of governmentality as a way of moving CS beyond critique and into usefulness. It does not stand alone in this regard. Similarly, in South Africa during the 1990s, an affirmative CS drawing on the Australian cultural policy impetus contributed to the forging of national policy (see Tomaselli and Mpofu). This is not only a form of intercultural communication, but more crucially of inter-cultural, inter-generational, and inter-periodized negotiation (see Coetzee and van der Waal). During the decades prior to 1990, American and British CS had come under siege from higher or central authority and its potential remained unrealized in opposition, though British CS remained defiantly activist. In contrast, in South Africa, CS underpinned much early cultural and media policy adopted by the new liberation government (see Tomaselli, "Alter-Egos").

In this context, in China the state has aimed to reduce its presence from the market and quotidian social spheres, that is to move from *danwei*, toward enabling the growth of civil society institutions, a neo-liberal society, and permitting advertising, which had been banned during the Cultural Revolution as being associated with corrupt capitalism (see Feng Jie-yun 20–21). The methods applied to analyzing advertising genres as representative of transitional political and economic arrangements, however, are not those common in "Western" CS and certainly not in business studies. "Cultural discourse" analysis has been proposed as a means to overcome a "Western"-style prioritizing of the speaker's discourse and her/his meaning, in favor of the value of taking the hearer as participating in the relationship; research should then consider what the hearer can make of the speaker's utterance, and how a society or culture should react (see Shi, "Why"). The approach incorporates a dimension of power, while it remains confined to the "textual space" (Feng Jie-yun 19).

4. CASS 2016 — The Epistemological Issues

A cognate trajectory to the Cultural China discourse was assumed at the 2016 CASS conference, which has a key significance in offering impulses for future development. Here, 38 papers offered over two days dealt with difference, structuralism, east-west dialogue, identity, geopolitical power, and the translation of "Western" scholars into Chinese academic dialogues. The names of Adorno, Benjamin, Foucault, Habermas, Hall, Heidegger, Locke, Macherey, Saussure, and Spivak, among others, recurred often. Hegel seems to have influenced the current debate quite significantly. Indeed, dialectical reasoning is the basis of modern thought. Dialectics is here understood mainly as the grasping of opposites, whether logical concepts or definitions of consciousness and its objects, in their unity, or of the positive in the negative (Hegel, for instance *The Science of Logic*, Part 1 in the 1832 revised edition). Hegel's parallel observation that when a nation loses its metaphysics it loses its inner purpose (see also Magee) is key. Cultural life, we may infer, must include metaphysics — which we can identify as experience. But metaphysics in a certain sense has sometimes been thought of as anti-dialectical. Do we need both modes of thought? If dialectics is analytical, metaphysics is best understood as cultural/spiritual/ontological, while experience is the real author of *growth* and *advance* in philosophy (Hegel, *Encyclopaedia of the Philosophical Sciences*, Part 1). If the analytical method is suited to negotiation and interaction (and probably AIDS planning), the metaphysical triad just suggested is where meaning resides.

Knowing, for Hegel in *Phenomenology of Spirit*, is something one does; it is an act (see Lauer, for instance p. 193). It is also presence of mind ("Gegenwart und Wachen des Geistes"; Hegel's speech 29 Sept. 1809). The "Belt and Road Initiative" is about acting in this sense, reshaping global consciousness together with spatial and economic relations. It is about long-term planning and the use of transport networks to create new markets and new opportunities. But as Kelen cautions, development in this model is not necessarily accompanied by a "Western" form of democracy, by openness, or intra-national debate. To return to Hegel, he seems to hold out the vision, even the experience, of thinking as self-presence or self-presentation of spirit ("Gegenwärtigung"; see for instance Sallis). Certainly, China is now self-present in the world. The "One Belt, One Road" evidences a huge undertaking with many participants. The envisaged investment is $1 trillion spread through 60% of the world's population and one-third of GDP involving 68 countries, which export to China the raw materials and energy it needs (see Pethiyagoda).

As expansive as is the scale of the "One Belt, One Road" infrastructure initiative, as wide is the academic Belt that has emerged to support the project intellectually. What was striking at this CASS meeting was the critical engagement with "Western" philosophy, in what appear to be attempts to engage in inter-cultural geopolitical dialogue, as Chinese institutions "go abroad" into the wider world. This focus enables a global dialectical discussion which must surely be of value to both China and the "West" in the era of globalization, when markets and relations of production, financial systems, and educational facilities become ever more interlinked and interdependent.

4.1 China's Identity: From Saussure to Derrida and to Hall

Philosophy is a relevant concern for Stuart Hall, though it may not be a key feature of his published work. The paper by Zhao Bing provides a prehistory of how Hall appropriates Derrida's concept of *différance* to formulate his theory of identity. Hall accepts Derrida's critique on Ferdinand de Saussure's dyadic semiology, which examined formal differences within linguistic structures as contributing to the creation of meaning through grammatical structure. Derrida questions the inherent sign stability assumed by Saussure. He criticizes Saussure's distinction between "signified" and "signifier," because such a distinction can easily lead to the misunderstanding that the former precedes the latter. The instability of a sign occurs when denotation is superseded by associated connotative meanings that have nothing to do with the item signified. The form of semiosis occurs when one sign gives rise to another sign, destabilizing the meanings that the sign attracts to itself. According to Hall, meaning occurs when semiosis is terminated. In other words, meaning occurs when there is an arbitrary closure, or when the shift pauses for the time being. Meaning, that is, can only be obtained when there is a "full stop" in the seemingly endless signification process or semiosis ("Minimal" 45). The position of the stop, as in the case of Caribbean cultural identities, is related to several cultural "presences" (as Hall in "Cultural Identity" adapts Aimé Césaire's and Léopold Sédar Senghor's metaphor). These in turn are rooted in what Charles Sanders Peirce (*Collected Papers* 8) calls the "final interpretant" or "the way in which every mind would act," when actual agreement on interpretation is reached by a community of scholars. Nonetheless, regarding the full stop or period mark, according to Jacques Derrida (following Søren Kierkegaard), "the instant of a decision is a madness," a "finite moment of urgency and precipitation" (*Acts* 255), one that is also surely a full embodiment of presence — a metaphysical rather than dialectical expression. Thus Hall's theory of identity as the articulation of difference arises from his reading of Saussure from Derrida's perspective.

Hall's seminal "encoding" and "decoding" model thus jettisons the dyadic Saussurian semiology, which is replaced with a Peirceian semiotics. This includes the interpreter and thus the triangular relationship in which meaning is made by individuals and interpreter communities (see Tomaselli, "Encoding"). The full stop is a temporary one, which Hall metaphorically explains as moorings and loosening of the moorings.

The construction of identity by different groups, societies, and nations occurs in the discursive matrices of Derrida's *différance*, that is a "sameness which is not identical," a spatial and temporal differing, an endless deferral of meaning as it shifts from fixed origins toward dynamic destinations. Identity (as analyzed from various angles in Volumes 2 and 3 of the Intercultural Research series) is often popularly understood as being rooted in tradition, in the past and that which is familiar. This static construction of identity obviously exists in an uneasy relationship with the concept of *différance*. The former is moored, forced to be unchanging, safe, and reassuring. The latter recognizes instability and unpredictability, and is future-oriented.

Extrapolating this framework from the individual to the nation, we conclude that China has hitched its identity to dynamic change, that is the "routes" metaphor (Hall, "Introduction", "Random") as signified by the "One Belt, One Road" discourse. China is thus graduating from the fixed, static, rooted understanding of national identity that was prevalent prior to the Deng period; China has rearticulated and re-discovered the value of *différance*. In contrast, for that matter, South Africans appear ill-prepared for the routes enabled by globalization, competitive markets, employment opportunities, and worker/manager mobility required by transnational business and commerce. Attacking and making it difficult for the Other (whether foreigner or non-black South African) to work is easier than positioning ourselves for international competitiveness.

Différance introduces an array of heterogeneous features that enable wider experiences of the world that were not previously permitted or feasible. The "West," and specifically America, is being engaged by China in terms, one could say, of the principle of *différance*. The meanings of these relations as they are negotiated in the current era have become destabilized and rearticulated, being in a constant state of flux.

Hall agrees with Louis Althusser regarding the omnipresence of ideology. For Althusser, ideology is inscribed in social practices and is class-based. But Hall is doubtful about Althusser's idea that ideology is "always already inscribed." Instead, he thinks that ideology only provides temporary ways of connecting signifier and signified, and such connections are only a part of the permanent shift. In a word, Hall has been mindful of extremes of slipping into an endless emptiness when using Derrida's approach to meaning and regarding ideology as a finished work in an Althusserian manner. Destabilized signs always stabilize in new contexts — until changes and shifts occur. As we have argued above, Chinese international diplomacy is well aware of shifting meanings, of how its interaction with the "West" is changing perceptions in China. Accordingly, the concepts of identity, the conditions of construction of identity, and mobilizing through identity to negotiate with other (national) identities were the basis of the CASS discussions.

When the concepts of identity and *différance* dominated CASS discussions, they enabled a new emphasis which is indicative of China's new global role and foreign policy where the country needs to negotiate and manage intercultural differences with other nations. This would appear to offer Chinese foreign policy a strategy to engage with different (and deferred) ways of making sense, to argue the merit of difference but also of dialogue, as a way of keeping the peace. The approach thus applies an affirmative dimension to the ways that CS is studied in China (and also Australia) but not anywhere else, where CS remains in opposition to prevailing national hegemonies.

In relation to indigenous Chinese approaches, what one could call received "Western" theory is developing reframed concepts and debates of relevance to the current conjuncture. As Jin Huimin observes in this regard,

> [w]ith the philosophically loaded concept of globality, which we would foreground as *global dialogism*, we will re-observe the phenomena of cultural flows referred by the dispute of cultural imperialism. Culture has never stopped flowing. Culture is always clashing, dividing, merging and looking for new heterogeneities to merge. No national culture today is born independent, and no nation has one single origin. (38)

We might recall Marx's and Engels' diagnosis "All that is set and stolid [solid] turns to vapour [melts into air]" (46); also Zygmunt Bauman's assumption regarding "patterns of dependency and interaction whose turn to be liquefied has now come" (8). Modernity thus mutates into postmodernity ... and then globality.

"Western" social theory emphases underpin most IAICS presentations, as we showed above, while the keynote speakers have tended to work within these emphases and CS as they examined translation and other related topics pertaining to China-communicating-with-the-world. As for CASS, the key concepts that we discerned from the 2016 conference as underpinning the discussions are: 1) Hegel's notion of dialectical reasoning, to some extent a precursor to the concept of *différance*; 2) Jacques Derrida's notion of *différance*; and 3) Stuart Hall's related notion of identity linked to dialectical reasoning and *différance*. It is also linked to Spivak, interpreted as speaking for non-Western states in general rather than sub-groups like street people, politically oppressed groups, and those denied access to local and national communication grids. These epistemological tasks have taken the CASS-affiliated scholars, all positive to the concept, to Hegel and to Heidegger, but also to Habermas and others (routed via Hall and Derrida), into issues generated by postmodernity and the associated contradictions that emerge.

The general notion of subaltern nations (as opposed to individuals or small groups) was then applied to questions of China's growing influence and role in the world.

4.2 Facing the Other

As the CASS discourses have explored, the idea of Cultural China (as a speaking subject) in the age of globalization and in the context of China's rise to global power enables the balancing of global power both militarily and discursively (also thematized in the studies by Shi as well as Wu). Difference is considered to be positive; it can be theorized and linked to articulations of national foreign policy via an intensive study of "Western" ways of making sense in relation to Chinese concerns.

Accordingly, Chinese foreign policy objectives can be achieved through the application of "soft power" (e.g., 2008 Olympic Games, 2010 Expo etc.). The so-called West certainly has the power to speak, but as China becomes more powerful a rebalancing of power relations generates the need to speak "with" (rather than "at") each other, in a "mutual-looking relationship" based on dialogue: "He-to-you. We-together, I and you" (Gao). It's easier to talk when the balance of power is more even — as indicated by equalized military strength and geopolitical power. The idea of "otherness" is seen critically as it objectifies the other, suggesting that a shift from monological "otherness" or third personness to "you-ness" or second personness should be adopted, to enable more engagement and fair play.

China should thus develop its own solutions, drawing on French and German theorists, especially on the concept of difference and how to overlap differences. Where Gottfried Wilhelm Leibniz believed in exposing oneself to conflicting concepts to obtain knowledge (as shown in extensive research by Marcelo Dascal), and Gilles Deleuze holds difference in tension, the acknowledgement of difference enables intercultural dialogue. Difference cannot always be resolved, nor does it always need to be resolved. This point is foregrounded by Jin Huimin, the CASS conference organizer, who gives prominence to the shift of the idea of *différance* — from one that distinguished China at the center (referred to as "Xia," the first dynasty) from the tribes and aboriginal peoples at the periphery to one that distinguishes China from the "West" in the present age. Jin examines "difference" through the development of "Western" philosophy, identifying four different areas of theorization of difference and concluding that difference is presupposed by dialogue: "difference is dialogue." The four areas identified by Jin are French poststructuralism,

British and American post-colonialism which has been influenced by poststructuralism, the German inter-subjectivity discourse which tries to eliminate difference and otherness, and the discourse of globalism since the 1990s.

4.3 Understanding the Other (The "West")

Maintaining the peace, as is argued in the CASS discourses, entails studying the Other's philosophical concepts and developing intercultural strategies via which negotiation can take place. Such strategies entail more than just language competence; they include contextual understanding, cultural sensitivity, acceptance of difference, capacity to be empathetic, and also acknowledgement of ontological diversity. In the following, we will track some of the major contributions leading on from there. We do not claim to give an adequate, let alone authorized summary of each of these contributions, since we merely pick out what seem to us to be the most salient ideas emerging from each.

Ding Zijiang, in examining the concepts of "intercultural," "cross-cultural," and "trans-cultural," describes the USA as individualistic, pluralistic, and particularistic, while China and continental Europe appear holistic, singularistic, and universalistic. Attempts to eliminate misunderstanding may easily produce more misunderstanding, and a comparison of Eastern and "Western" philosophies may fail, necessitating a dialogue between the philosophy of democracy, liberty, and non-normativity and one that dwells on authority, conservativeness, and normativity.

Su Gu argues that dialogue can best come into being when all parties agree to talk on the basis of a universal reason that transcends all ethics. This is the precondition for any dialogue, to prevent monological rationality. It includes "people having the right to question policy," so that "the policy makers should give reasonable explanation," and "there should be no double standard." Thus one should abandon the concept of relativity in ethics to enter the global dialogue.

Luo Ruchun alters this perspective in contending that the concept of dialogue cannot include everything, and that over-centralization of dialogics leads to a form of despotism. Instead, different forms of difference are the issue — how to identify them, mobilize a Hegelian process, resolve the contradictions, and then how to continue identifying the ensuing new contradictions, in a never-ending dialectical process. At times when the USA, for instance, seems to desire to maintain national differences China wants to discuss rather than erase them. CS in China, in whichever trajectory, seems to serve such national priorities, in what appears to be both a discursive and a policy moment.

Liu Yuedi distinguishes three areas of intercultural studies: one that compares cultures to look for differences and similarities, one that tries to bridge gaps, and one that aims at integration. He extends the concept of "inter-subjectivity" into "inter-culturality," to suggest that this could be used as a strategy for Chinese academia to participate in global academic dialogue. That this strategy is possible is indicated by the active participation of non-Western scholars of Greek, Russian, Indian, and Chinese intellectual cultures in the 23rd World Congress of Philosophy. While "Western" philosophy tends to focus on "reason," the congress' aim to consider "Philosophy as Inquiry and Way of Life" is indicative of opportunities for Chinese scholars, as "way of life" in Ludwig Wittgenstein's concept of "Lebensform" ("die Tatsache, daß wir so und so handeln"; see Nida-Rümelin 17– 18) is more in line with the Chinese philosophical tradition.

Huang Zhuo-yue ("Distinction"), reviewing the development of "Western" social theories, claims that unlike earlier periods when concepts of universality were pursued, the post-modernist age embraces an individualism which entails the resurrection of nationalism. Huang argues that such a theoretical divide is over-simplified; dualism is merely an abstract form of philosophizing, while reality features more of the fuzzy and intermediate. Discussions in the field of social science and philosophy tend to distinguish between China and the "West," a dichotomy that should be re-considered (see also Zhang Longxi's chapter "The Tao and the Logos Revisited" in Volume 8 of this series, and Chang Hui-ching's in Volume 2).

Gao Liping focuses on Gayatri Spivak's resistance against central structures of mainstream "Western" thought, as she suggests doing fieldwork among ordinary people. A number of Chinese researchers actually do such fieldwork, but since they are not located in the academic Global North/West their work may get less global exposure; also they may not write in the CS code which is the prime academic currency needed for citation in the North/West. If subalterns are to speak, moreover, they must be able to read and understand what academics write about, and become joint authors. Yet such forms of shared authorship would tend to be rejected by most peer reviewers and university managers. Scholars aiming for the center of attention will be inclined to use hegemonic English academic codes to ensure their own insertion within academic networks. Yet as they do so, they ironically erase the voice of the poor by the way that they speak/write. As Andrew Pendakis (in a focus on Globalization and Culture) has observed, for quotidian studies the subaltern include street scavengers with their overloaded carts. They see the world from their particular street point of view, as composed of bits and pieces, picking up bricolage as they find and load other people's junk during their daily collection of found items: "To see the present from the perspective of the scavenger is to see every whole as a tentative ecosystem of moveable parts and pieces" (Pendakis 39). Perhaps the act of scavenging is the future of productive labor? In the "West," these are the sites of CS research which analyze ordinary people and how they cope in the world. Ethnography is needed to keep academics grounded in the empirical world. Hence we need to know about how all social groups perceive and cope with the world, from presidents to 收破烂的人.

In summary, as we can gather from the CASS discourses in these and also in further contributions, there are two levels of understanding the Other. The one is an aim to understand "Western" theories and concepts, based on realities in China. This would enable an understanding of China itself, through a process of conceptualization as China has opened itself, whether passively in 1840 or actively in 1978. In this sense, as China moves forward it is no different from other parts of the world, as theories based on different realities in different times and places become appropriated.

At the other level of understanding, China is separate from the so-called "West" or the rest of the world. As it faces the world, it is trying to understand the Other as an object, something not having much to do with itself, and needing a reaction from its separated position. In this dialogic sense, China is not a member, holding a shared identity with others. However, we might remember that "difference as/is dialogue": China is different, *and* it can communicate within the larger semiosis. With its growing connections across the world, it is a matter of course that China needs to identify itself thus. Most significantly, in 2016 the Chinese Ministry of Education made two additions to the list of categories under "Foreign Language and Literature Studies." This had been composed of ten categories of literary studies of different countries and areas, and one category named "Foreign Linguistics and Applied Linguistics." Out of these, the newly added "Translation Studies" and "Comparative Literature and Intercultural Studies" were formed and thus upgraded. Whereas the field had been about reading and analyzing the productions of

Others, now an identity of China is emerging. Important aspects of CS as described by Wang Ning ("Cultural") may well find a home in the newly integrated intercultural studies field. In other regional contexts, studies of intellectual formations linking the arts with social sciences to strengthen awareness of the material and nonmaterial value of CS regarding such matters as oral and written textualities, or poetics in relation to politics, have gained ground (see *Eastern African Literary and Cultural Studies*, with its founding Editorial in 2014).

The IAICS approaches would need to examine not only Chinese histories, but also those of "Western" branding, which itself has become a fetishized, ideologized, totemized set of beguiling discourses that massively over-emphasize the ecstasies promised by hyper-individuated over-consumption at the expense of the broader collective. A discussion of Middle East CS has generated studies that offered what a guest editor called "a third voice" which speaks in a "third space," one that brings diversity of experience and history into a dialogue (Jayyusi 2). CS in China certainly has a positive role to play, while China is inching forward with a growing economy. For a context of CS in global comparison, see the discussion in Tomaselli (2016).

5. In Conclusion: How Vague, How Baggy?

Articulations of CS in different contexts and historical conjunctures, for different purposes, can be oppositional, critical, and also an aid in governmentality. This is the utility of the field, its flexibility, in that it evades being fixed into a single position. The trajectory with which we have been concerned is the narrower cultural framework and its associated methodologies as applied to an understanding of marketization, branding, and globalization, while retaining indigenous philosophical emphases. At IAICS conferences and their journal, *Intercultural Communication Studies*, what is labeled as CS is, in other contexts, named communication studies of somewhat positivist kinds. At root, CS's strength is its dialectical and historical engagement with the world. To lose this interaction would be to lose its value.

Editor's Note

An earlier version of a part of this chapter was published as "'Seeing

Red': Cultural Studies in Global Comparison." *Journal of Multicultural Discourses*, vol. 11, no. 4, 2016, pp. 375–88. We are pleased to have Keyan Tomaselli's permission to publish this updated and extended chapter here.

References

Althusser, Louis. *For Marx*. Translated by Ben Brewster. Verso, 1969.

Bauman, Zygmunt. *Liquid Modernity*. Polity, 2000.

Bellour, Raymond. "The Unattainable Text." *Screen*, vol. 16, no. 3, 1975, pp. 19–28.

Bennett, Tony. "Intellectuals, Culture, Policy: The Technical, the Practical, and the Critical." *Cultural Analysis*, vol. 5, 2006, pp. 81–106.

Bhatt, Chetan. "The Politics of Violence and Arts of Terror: The Salafi-Jihadi Political Universe." *Theory, Culture and Society*, vol. 31, no. 1, 2014, pp. 25–48.

Branco, Angela, and Jaan Valsiner. "Values as Culture in Self and Society." *Cultural Psychology of Human Values*, edited by Angela Uchoa Branco and Jaan Valsiner, Information Age, 2012, pp. vii–xviii.

Cao, Qing, and Doreen Wu, editors. *Brand China: A New Voice to the World? A Special Issue of* Critical Arts: South-North Cultural and Media Studies, 2017.

Chambers, Iain. "Cultural Studies under Mediterranean Skies." *Critical Arts: South-North Cultural and Media Studies*, vol. 28, no. 5, 2014, pp. 871–74.

Chang, Hui-ching. "Touring the Field of Intercultural Communication: Finding Differences and Commonalities." *Identity and Intercultural Communication (I): Theoretical and Contextual Construction*, Intercultural Research Vol. 2, edited by Xiaodong Dai and Steve J. Kulich, Shanghai Foreign Language Education Press, 2010, pp. 125–49.

Chen, Guo-ming. "Beyond the Dichotomy of Communication Studies." *Journal of Asian Communication*, vol. 19, no. 4, 2009, pp. 398–411.

—. "On Identity: An Alternative View." *Identity and Intercultural Communication (I): Theoretical and Contextual Construction*. Intercultural Research Vol. 2, edited by Xiaodong Dai and Steve J. Kulich, Shanghai Foreign Language Education Press, 2010, pp. 23–51.

—. "The *Yin* and *Yang* of Conflict Management and Resolution: A Chinese Perspective." *Conflict Management and Intercultural Communication: The Art of Intercultural Harmony*, edited by Xiaodong Dai and Guo-Ming Chen, Routledge, 2017, pp. 144–54.

Coetzee, Ingrid, and Gerhard-Mark Van der Waal, editors. *The Conservation of Culture: Changing Contexts and Challenges*. Pretoria: SACCC, 1988.

Connell, Kieran, and Matthew Hilton, editors. *Cultural Studies 50 Years On: History, Practice and Politics*. Rowman and Littlefield, 2016.

Dai, Jinhua. "Behind Global Spectacle and National Image Making." *Positions: East Asia Cultures Critique*, vol. 9, no. 1, 2001, pp. 161–86.

Derrida, Jacques. *Acts of Religion*, edited by Gil Anidjar. Routledge, 2002.

—. "Differance." Translated by David B. Allison, *Speech and Phenomena and*

Other Essays on Husserl's Theory of Signs, Northwestern UP, 1973, pp. 129–60.

Ding, Zijiang. "The Multi-dimensional Dialogue Between the East and the West." International Symposium on "Difference and Dialogue in the Context of Globalisation" and the 5th Forum on East-West Studies, July 2016, Chinese Academy of Social Science, Beijing. Paper.

Du, Yiwei. "From Tradition to Modernity and Post-Modernity — Revisiting Derrida's 'Relevant Translation.'" IAICS/CAFIC Conference, 15–18 July 2015, Hong Kong Polytechnic U. Paper.

Eco, Umberto. *A Theory of Semiotics*. Indiana UP, 1976.

Feng, Jie-yun. *Advertising Discourses and Social Changes in China*. U of International Business and Economics P, 2014.

Feng, Lei. "Rethinking New International Communication Research: A Case Study of Cultural Representation in Global Trade." IAICS/CAFIC Conference, 15–18 July 2015, Hong Kong Polytechnic U. Paper.

Gao, Liping. "Global Dialogism and Post-colonial Theories." *Comparative Literature in China*, vol. 4, 2016, pp. 20–35.

Gerbner, George, et al. "Growing Up with Television: Cultivation Processes." *Media Effects: Advances in Theory and Research*, 2nd ed., edited by Jennings Bryant and Dolf Zillmann, Lawrence Erlbaum, 2002, pp. 43–68.

Gilroy, Paul, Lawrence Grossberg and Angela McRobbie, editors. *Without Guarantees: In Honour of Stuart Hall*. Verso, 2000.

Goering, Elizabeth, Andrea J. Krause, and Liu Yifei. "The 'Collective Programming of the Mind': A Thematic Analysis of Values Re-constructed in Reality Courtroom Television Programs in the United States, Germany, and China." *Value Dimensions and Their Contextual Dynamics Across Cultures*, Intercultural Research Vol. 5, edited by Steve J. Kulich, Weng Liping and Michael H. Prosser, Shanghai Foreign Language Education Press, 2014, pp. 337–64.

Gramsci, Antonio. *Selections from the Prison Notebooks*. Translated by Quintin Hoare and Geoffrey Nowell Smith. Lawrence & Wishart, 1971.

Grossberg, Lawrence. 2010. *Cultural Studies in the Future Tense*. Duke UP, 2010.

Guillem, Susana Martínez. "Rethinking Power Relations in Critical/Cultural Studies: A Dialectical (Re)Proposal." *The Review of Communication*, vol. 13, no. 3, 2013, pp. 184–204.

Hall, Stuart. "Cultural Identity and Diaspora." *Identity: Community, Culture, Difference*, edited by Jonathan Rutherford, Lawrence and Wishart, 1990, pp. 222–37.

—. "Cultural Studies: Two Paradigms." *Media, Culture and Society*, vol. 2, 1980, pp. 57–72.

—. "Encoding/decoding." *Culture, Media, Language*, edited by Stuart Hall, Dorothy Hobson, Andrew Lowe, and Paul Willis, Hutchinson, 1980, pp. 128–38.

—. "Introduction: Who Needs 'Identity'?" *Questions of Cultural Identity*, edited by Stuart Hall and Paul Du Gay, Sage, 1996, pp. 1–17.

—. "Minimal Selves." *Identity: The Real Me*, Institute of Contemporary Arts Documents, no. 6, 1987, pp. 44–46.

—. "Random Thoughts Provided by the Conference 'Identities, Democracy, Culture and Communication in Southern Africa'." *Critical Arts: South-North Cultural and Media Studies*, vol. 11, nos. 1–2, 1997, pp. 1–16.

Harvey, David. *A Brief History of Neoliberalism*. Oxford UP, 2005.
Hawkes, David, translator. *The Story of the Stone*, by Cao Xueqin, Vol. 1. Penguin, 1973.
Hebdige, Dick. *Subculture and the Meaning of Style*. Methuen, 1979.
Holt, Douglas B. "Distinction in America? Recovering Bourdieu's Theory of Tastes from Its Critics." *Poetics*, vol. 25, 1997, pp. 93–120.
—. "How Consumers Consume: A Typology of Consumption Practices." *Journal of Consumer Research*, vol. 22, June 1995, pp. 1–16.
House, Juliane. *Translation as Communication Across Languages and Cultures*. Routledge, 2016.
Huang, Zhuo-yue. "Entering into the Expressway of Cultural Studies: Practices in China." *Cultural Studies 50 Years On: History, Practice and Politics*, edited by Kieran Connell and Matthew Hilton, Rowman and Littlefield, 2016, pp. 233–43.
—. "The Distinction of Universality." International Symposium on "Difference and Dialogue in the Context of Globalisation" and the 5th Forum on East-West Studies, July 2016, Chinese Academy of Social Science, Beijing. Paper.
Jayyusi, Lena. "Introduction: Speaking in a Third Voice." *Critical Arts: South-North Cultural and Media Studies*, vol. 21, no. 1, 2007, pp. 1–5.
Jin, Huimin. "Existing Approaches of Cultural Studies and Global Dialogism: A Study Beginning with the Debate Around ' Cultural Imperialism.'" *Critical Arts: South-North Cultural and Media Studies*, vol. 31, no. 1, 2017, pp. 34–48.
Kelen, Christopher. "Crossing the Road in Macao." *Critical Arts: South-North Cultural and Media Studies*, vol. 23, no. 3, 2009, pp. 283–320.
Khiabany, Gholam. "Is There an Islamic Communication? The Persistence of ' Tradition ' and the Lure of Modernity." *Critical Arts: South-North Cultural and Media Studies*, vol. 21, no. 1, 2007, pp. 106–24.
Kronenberg, Clive. "Contesting the Mechanisms of Disinformation: Part II. Castro, Cuba and the Empire: 'You Are Not a Liberator.'" *Critical Arts: South-North Cultural and Media Studies*, vol. 23, no. 3, 2009, pp. 253–82.
Lauer, Quentin. *A Reading of Hegel's* Phenomenology of Spirit. 2nd ed. Fordham UP, 1993.
Liu, Yuedi. "Uniqueness of Humanities in China: How Softness Overcomes Hardness by Interculturality." *Theoretical Studies in Literature and Art*, vol. 35, no. 1, 2015, pp. 56–61.
Loo, Theresa, and Gary Davies. "Branding China: The Ultimate Challenge in Reputation Management?" *Corporate Reputation Review*, vol. 9, no. 3, 2006, pp. 198–210.
Luo, Gang, and Liu Xiang-yu, editors. *Cultural Studies: A Reader*. China Social Sciences Press, 2000.
Luo, Ruchun. "A Post-Differentialist Cultural Dialogue." International Symposium on "Difference and Dialogue in the Context of Globalisation" and the 5th Forum on East-West Studies, July 2016, Chinese Academy of Social Science, Beijing. Paper.
Magee, Glenn Alexander. "Hegel as Metaphysician." *Hegel and Metaphysics: On Logic and Ontology in the System*, edited by Allegra de Laurentiis, De Gruyter, 2016, pp. 43–58.
Martín-Barbero, Jesús. *Communication, Culture and Hegemony: From the*

Media to Mediations. Translated by Elizabeth Fox and Robert A. White, Sage, 1993.

Marx, Karl, and Friedrich Engels. *The Communist Manifesto*, edited and translated by L. M. Findlay, Peterborough, Ontario: Broadview Press, 2004.

Nayak, Meghana, and Eric Selbin. *Decentering International Relations*. Zed, 2010.

Nida-Rümelin, Julian. "Philosophie und Lebensform." *Philosophie und Lebensform*, edited by Wolfram Hogrebe, Bonn UP, 2010, pp. 13–50.

Ouyang, H. *Remaking of Face and Community of Practices: An Ethnography of Local and Expatriate English Teachers' Reform Stories in Today's China*. Peking UP, 2004. (Dissertation, City Univ. of Hong Kong, 2000.)

Peirce, Charles Sanders. *Collected Papers*, vols. 7, 8, edited by Arthur Burks, Harvard UP, 1958.

Pendakis, Andrew. "收破烂的人 (*Shou Polan de Ren*): On the Historical Materialism of Scavenging." *Plastic Blue Marble*, edited by Ted Hiebert, Victoria & Seattle: Noxious Sector Press, 2016, pp. 27–40.

Pickering, Michael, editor. *Research Methods for Cultural Studies*. Edinburgh UP, 2008.

Piyawan, Charoensap. "Dissecting Gangnam Style Through the Lens of Cultural Studies." IAICS/CAFIC Conference, 15–18 July 2015, Hong Kong Polytechnic U. Paper.

Radwanska-Williams, Joanna. "Reading the City: The Linguistic and Semiotic Landscape of Macao's San Ma Lo (新馬路)." IAICS/CAFIC Conference, 15–18 July 2015, Hong Kong Polytechnic U. Paper.

Sallis, John. "Imagination and Presentation in Hegel's Philosophy of Spirit." *Hegel's Philosophy of Spirit*, edited by Peter G. Stillman, State U of New York P, 1987, pp. 66–88.

Shen, Feng. "Appeals and Cultural Values in Chinese Television Commercials." *International Business Research*, vol. 6, no. 4, 2013, pp. 25–31.

Shi, Xu. *Discourse and Culture*. Shanghai Foreign Language Education Press, 2013.

—. "Towards a Chinese-Discourse-Studies Approach to Cultural China: An Epilogue." *Discourses of Cultural China in the Globalizing Age*, edited by Doreen D. Wu, Hong Kong UP, 2008, pp. 243–50.

—. "Why Do Cultural Discourse Studies? Towards a Culturally Conscious and Critical Approach to Human Discourses." *Critical Arts: South-North Cultural and Media Studies*, vol. 26, no. 4, 2012, pp. 484–503.

Sterne, Jonathan. "Cultural Policy Studies and the Problem of Political Representation." *The Communication Review*, vol. 5, 2002, pp. 59–89.

Su, Gu. "Political Dialogue and Legitimacy in a Plural Society." International Symposium on "Difference and Dialogue in the Context of Globalisation" and the 5th Forum on East-West Studies, July 2016, Chinese Academy of Social Science, Beijing. Paper.

Sun, Youzhong. "Intercultural Teaching Principles and Methods: An Evaluation of *Think English* Textbook Series." IAICS Conference, 1–3 July 2016, Shanghai International Studies U. Keynote paper.

Taguba, Emmanuel Boon II. "Guerrilla Social Media: Decoding 'Ang Bayan,' the Official YouTube Platform of the Communist Party of the Philippines." IAICS Conference, 1–3 July 2016, Shanghai International

Studies U. Paper.

Tao, Dongfeng, Lei He and Yugao He. *Cultural Studies in Modern China*. Springer Nature, 2017.

Thompson, Edward P. *The Making of the English Working Class*. Victor Gollancz, 1963.

Tomaselli, Keyan G. "Alter-Egos: Cultural and Media Studies." *Critical Arts: South-North Cultural and Media Studies*, vol. 26, no. 1, 2012, pp. 14–38.

—. "Encoding/Decoding, the Transmission Model and a Court of Law." *International Journal of Cultural Studies*, vol. 19, no. 1, 2016, pp. 59–70.

—. "'Seeing Red': Cultural Studies in Global Comparison." *Journal of Multicultural Discourses*, vol. 11, no. 4, 2016, pp. 375–88.

Tomaselli, Keyan G., and Alum Mpofu. "The Re-Articulation of Meaning of National Monuments: Beyond Apartheid." *Culture and Policy*, vol. 8, no. 3, 1997, pp. 57–86.

Tomaselli, Keyan G., and Emma Durden. "Theory Meets Theatre Practice: Making a Difference to Public Health Programmes in Southern Africa." *Curriculum Inquiry*, vol. 42, no. 1, 2012, pp. 80–102.

Tomaselli, Keyan G., Nyasha Mboti and Helge Rønning. "South-North Perspectives: The Development of Cultural and Media Studies in Southern Africa." *Media, Culture & Society*, vol. 35, no. 1, 2013, pp. 36–43.

Tu, Haijing. "From *The Good Wife* to *Hot Mom!* An Ideological Analysis of American and Chinese Motherhood on TV." *Intercultural Communication Studies*, vol. 25, no. 2, 2016, pp. 99–110. (IAICS/CAFIC Conference, 15–18 July 2015, Hong Kong Polytechnic U. Paper.)

Tu, Weiming. "Cultural China: The Periphery as the Center." *Daedalus*, vol. 120, no. 2, 1991, pp. 1–32.

—, editor. *The Living Tree: The Changing Meaning of Being Chinese Today*. Stanford UP, 1994.

Wang, Jing. *Brand New China: Advertising, Media, and Commercial Culture*. Harvard UP, 2008.

Wang, Ning. "Cultural Studies in China: Towards Closing the Gap Between Elite Culture and Popular Culture." *European Review*, vol. 11, no. 2, 2003, pp. 183–91.

Wang, Xiaoming. "A Manifesto for Cultural Studies." *One China, Many Paths*, edited by Wang Chaohua, Verso, 2003, pp. 274–91.

Wei, Xu. "Chinese TV Dramas Appealing to an International Audience." *Shanghai Daily*, 26 Aug. 2017, p. A7. www.shine.cn/archive/feature/Chinese-TV-dramas-appealing-to-an-international-audience/shdaily.shtml.

Wei, Yong-kang. "Rhetorical Traditions in Comparison: High Context vs. Low Context." IAICS/CAFIC Conference, 15–18 July 2015, Hong Kong Polytechnic U. Paper.

Willems, Wendy. "Provincializing Hegemonic Histories of Media and Communication Studies: Toward a Genealogy of Epistemic Resistance in Africa." *Communication Theory*, vol. 24, no. 4, 2014, pp. 415–34.

Williams, Raymond. *Marxism and Literature*. Oxford UP, 1977.

—. *Politics of Modernism: Against the New Conformists*. Verso, 1989.

Wu, Doreen D. "Globalization and the Discourses of Cultural China: An Introduction." *Discourses of Cultural China in the Globalizing Age*, edited by Doreen D. Wu, Hong Kong UP, 2008, pp. 1–10.

Wu, Doreen D., and Agatha Man-kwan Chung. "Glocalising Voice and Style of *Cosmopolitan* in China." *Translation and Cross-Cultural Communication Studies in the Asia Pacific*, edited by Leong Ko and Ping Chen, Brill, 2015, pp. 407–20.

Wu, Doreen D., and Sihui Mao, Guest eds. "Media Discourses and Cultural Globalisation: A Chinese Perspective." *Critical Arts: South-North Cultural and Media Studies*, vol. 25, no. 1, 2011, pp. 1–6. Special issue.

Xia, Guang. "When China Globalizes Its Presence: Revisiting the 'Civilizational Clash.'" IAICS/CAFIC Conference, 15–18 July 2015, Hong Kong Polytechnic U. Paper.

Yang, Kenneth C. C., and Yowei Kang. "Social Media, Political Mobilization, and Citizen Engagement: A Case Study of the March 18, 2014, Sunflower Student Movement in Taiwan." *Handbook of Research on Citizen Engagement and Public Participation in the Era of New Media*, edited by Marco Adria and Yuping Mao, Hershey, PA: IGI Global, 2017, pp. 360–88.

Yeh, Michelle. "International Theory and the Transnational Critic: China in the Age of Multiculturalism." *Boundary 2*, vol. 25, no. 3, 1998, pp. 193–222.

Yin, Qiping. "Space, Cultural Materialism and Structure of Feeling: Reflections on the Chinese Reception of Raymond Williams." *The Cambridge Quarterly*, vol. 41, no. 1, 2012, pp. 163–79.

Yu, Hui-chih. "A Cross-Cultural Analysis of Symbolic Meanings of Color." *Chang Gung Journal of Humanities and Social Sciences*, vol. 7, no. 1, 2014, pp. 49–74.

Zakaria, Fareed. *The Post-American World and the Rise of the Rest*. Norton, 2008.

Zha, Mingjian. "Cross-Cultural Exchange Between China and the Rest of the World: From the Perspective of Comparative Literature." IAICS Conference, 1–3 July 2016, Shanghai International Studies U. Keynote paper.

Zhang, Jing, and Sharon Shavitt. "Cultural Values in Advertisements to the Chinese X-Generation: Promoting Modernity and Individualism." *Journal of Advertising*, vol. 32, no. 1, 2003, pp. 23–33.

Zhang, Wen-Yu. "Images of Xinjiang in Modern European Travel Writings under the Perspective of Cultural Studies." IAICS/CAFIC Conference, 15–18 July 2015, Hong Kong Polytechnic U. Paper.

Zhao, Bing. "From Difference to 'Unities-in-Difference': Hall's Appropriation of Derrida and Althusser." International Symposium on "Difference and Dialogue in the Context of Globalisation" and the 5th Forum on East-West Studies, July 2016, Chinese Academy of Social Science, Beijing. Paper.

Zhu, Hua. "Identifying Research Paradigms." *Research Methods in Intercultural Communication: A Practical Guide*, edited by Zhu Hua, Wiley Blackwell, 2016, pp. 3–22.

10

From Multiculturalism to Social Cosmopolitanism: Toward a New Narrative Mode*

ZHOU Min
Shanghai International Studies University

Summary: Based on the experience of 20th-century cultural politics, this chapter examines the historical symptom of multiculturalism and explores the possibility of a community of common fate for humankind. Multiculturalism became a contested topic after World War II; it is a normative, a descriptive, as well as a policy-oriented concept with great influence on economics, politics, culture, and education, but especially cultural practices. Yet it has been frequently questioned, if not attacked, in countries that have practiced it, not least in Canada. An alternative concept proposed and practiced especially in Quebec is interculturalism, which believes in opening up the minority groups' cultural space, so that they can engage more actively in the dominant culture. This, too, has revealed some drawbacks. We could gain a new cultural narrative from Ulrich Beck's proposal of a cosmopolitan realism; it has analogies with Confucian "Ren," a dynamic interconnection between Self and Other. When one enters imaginatively into value orientations that appear remote, a communication process allows the development toward a "full" human identity.

---

* The writing of this paper was supported by National Higher Education's Basic Research Grant.

I. Introduction

In May 2017, *Write Magazine* of The Writers' Union of Canada published the then-editor Hal Niedaviecki's opinion piece titled "Winning the Appropriation Prize" in an issue devoted to Indigenous writing:"In my opinion, anyone, anywhere, should be encouraged to imagine other peoples, other cultures, other identities. I'd go so far as to say that there should even be an award for doing so — the Appropriation Prize for best book by an author who writes about people who aren't even remotely like her or him" (Lederman and Medley). The publication of this paper immediately sparked great outrage, and the dispute between the First Nations People and the "mainstream" Canadian culture was fiercely set on fire again. The Writers' Union of Canada had to issue an apology, and the editor resigned from his position. Reflecting on the causes of this "literary event," in spite of the fact that there had long existed issues between the aboriginal and the dominant culture, we find that a return to the "meta" problem embedded in culturalism became inevitable. Isn't Canada a society of multiculturalism? How come the conflicts between different ethnic groups are still so intense? Surprisingly, multiculturalism no longer seems to be a ready weapon stored in the text corpus of "political correctness." On the contrary, the "death knell" of multiculturalism is now being echoed across the world. What has happened to multiculturalism? How can individuals live with each other in the increasingly interconnected (but perhaps also separated) reality of the world? Based on the cultural politics of the 20th century, this chapter will try to look into the historical symptom of multiculturalism and explore the possibility of a community of common fate for humankind.

II.

"Multiculturalism" as a concept became a hot word around the 1970s, into the 1980s. A similar term, "cultural pluralism," came into being at the beginning of the 20th century as a reaction against the notion of "Americanization." Horace M. Kallen first used the value-laden concept of "cultural pluralism" when he was teaching at Harvard around 1906 or 1907 (see Ratner 185). For Kallen, cultural pluralism can promote equality between different cultural groups, exactly what is needed in a democratic society (see Kallen 10). In 1922, an American travel writer first used the term "mosaic" to describe the notion of co-existence of multiple cultures in Canada (see Hayward 187). After World War II, with the movement of decolonization and the U.S. civil rights movement, as well as the deepening of the conflicts between French ethnic groups and English ethnic groups inside Canadian society, the issue of multiculturalism became a much contested topic. But first of all, what is multiculturalism? For C. W. Watson, multiculturalism, as a notion of culture, a notion of history, and a notion of education, is also a form of public policy (see Watson 1). Multicultural discussions refer to many situations — integration policies and welfare-state regimes, the legal and political accommodation of cultural diversity, the management of immigration and national borders, the recognition and respect of cultural/religious difference, living with "difference" in daily contexts, the ideological representation of identities, cultures and "the good society," to name but a few. They involve different disciplines — philosophy, sociology, anthropology, social psychology, political science, pedagogy, and cultural and post-colonial studies (see Colombo 801). Indeed, the term "multiculturalism" has an array of meanings in contexts as different as sociology and political philosophy, and in every-day use. Sociologically, it refers to a society that comprises different ethnic groups. Politically, it involves ideologies and policies that advocate equal respect for different cultures in a society, as well as cultural diversity: it "implies multiple frames of reference" and "respects cultural entities as bounded and discrete" (Xie 5). Many debates around multiculturalism have been carried on around ways to deal with the issues of diversity and integration. It has been used both as a descriptive and a normative term, as well as a term for particular types of government policies. As a *normative* term, multiculturalism affirms cultural diversity and provides normative grounds for accommodating this diversity. As a *policy-oriented* term, multiculturalism refers to a variety of government policies that aim to accommodate people's cultural differences — most notably, different types of culturally differentiated rights (see Vitikainen). The main focus of the debates on multiculturalism within political philosophy has been on normative multiculturalism, the broader normative questions relating to appropriate grounds for responding to people's cultural differences. Multiculturalism has exerted great influence on economics, politics, culture, and education, but especially cultural practices. A. Robert Lee sees the task of studying multicultural American literature as mapping and comparing "the arising literary fictions of Afro-America, Native America, Latino/a America and Asian America" (2). For Canada, Smaro Karoumbeli's anthology *Making a Difference: Canadian Multicultural Literature* has included First Nations writers while excluding "Anglo-Celtic" authors. It has been proposed to analyze the multicultural character of Canadian literature in terms of the narrative strategy of "literary code-switching, i.e., parts of texts written in more than one language," a strategy whose function is "constructing a discourse on multilingualism and multicultural identities in Canada" (Casagranda 78, 79). On the whole, there seems to be no exact definition of "multiculturalism"; it seems to take on different meanings in different times and situations. The term's ambiguity brings with it a constant reinterpretation — a discursive practice, as the "Godfather of multiculturalism" (Butler), Stuart Hall, put it.

From the perspective of the history of ideas, "multiculturalism" could be understood as a consequence of postmodernism, which advocates respect for and recognition of the values of "difference" and "otherness." Postmodernism dismantles a unified rationality and, as a result, elements that were marginal, non-mainstream, and heterogeneous were endowed with equal positions to the central, mainstream, and homogeneous. Multiculturalism emphasizes the significance of the recognition of difference from perspectives of both philosophy and politics. With philosophy, what matters is individual identification, self-realization, and social participation. With politics, what matters is to give voices to previously marginalized groups so as to overcome unfairness and exploitation. Meanwhile, it is not enough just to recognize the rights of individuals, because that is based on illogical assumptions that the individual is separated from society, rather than belonging to social relations. Only through dialogues with others can an individual feel that she or he belongs to a certain community, and establishes her or his independent identification. The objective of multiculturalism is to empower the once underprivileged, to fight for the once unrepresented, and to challenge once fixed standards so as to change their institution and discourse.

From the perspective of social reality, "multiculturalism" could be viewed as the consequence of globalization, which is believed to be the "transnational practices of immigrant communities, the flow of cultural notions, and global processes come together to create 'a new kind of citizen, the diasporic citizen, and to imagine some of the ramifications and consequences of this modus vivendi for the citizen-subject'" (Chierici 44). The cultural encounters that come with the phenomenon of globalization seem to rebut the very meaning of multiculturalism, hitherto understood banally "as the availability of different 'ethnic' foods, music, art and literature in the one society" (Milner and Browitt 142). Together with the movement of capital went the process of colonialization and the decolonization that followed it, which made multiculturalism a necessary policy in reality. As a political policy, it was a national strategy that Canada, Australia, the Netherlands and other countries had adopted since the 1970s and 1980s to address the problems caused by large flows of immigration, with an intention to ease the conflicts between the settlers and new immigrants. Canada was the first country to implement multiculturalism in 1971. In 1988, The Canadian Multiculturalism Act was passed, showing that multiculturalism had become the mainstream ideology in Canada. After his visit to Canada in 1973, the Immigration Minister in Australia introduced multiculturalism into his country. In 1975, after Canada and Australia, Sweden declared multiculturalism its national policy. In the 1980s, with the increase of immigrants in Western Europe, how to deal with the relationship between the natives and the immigrants had become common concerns for these countries. Therefore, countries like the UK, France, Belgium, and Denmark all to some degree began to practice multiculturalism. In these countries, immigrants were protected to maintain their own culture because of the policy of multiculturalism. Van de Vijver has studied the nomological network of the multiculturalism concept, regarded psychologically as "the acceptance of and support for the plural composition of a society," mainly in Europe (167). In America, "multiculturalism" was raised as a way to fight against a reality in which the minority, the subculture, and the underprivileged were not given equal treatment. It is the voice of the other, emphasizing the existence of multiple cultures in the society. Consequently, "recognition" and "equality" are basic tenets of multiculturalism because multiculturalism involves the coexistence of one community and other social communities with different social experience (Bolaffi et al. 183).

III.

As a "politics of recognition" (Glazer 35), multiculturalism is closely related to politics of identity and politics of difference, which all believe that, to re-evaluate the identity of the discriminated and to change the mainstream way of representation and communication that caused the marginalization of certain groups, it is vital to acknowledge the multiplicity of cultures. However, the difference among communities emphasized by multiculturalism might be totally different from the recognition that is demanded by such communities. This might be the reason why multiculturalism's intention to solve such problems backlashed. In spite of its good intentions, multiculturalism has been questioned, if not attacked. In the foreword to *Multiculturalism and Interculturalism*, Charles Taylor wrote that "in one short period in recent years, first Merkel, then Cameron, then Sarkozy informed us that multiculturalism had 'failed' in their respective societies, where it would have been much more accurate to say that it had never been tried" (viii). A fair society should recognize the importance of minority cultures and allow its members to protect their culture against majority practices and rules. Nevertheless, not all claims of cultural protection can be accepted on a basis of liberal assumptions (see Colombo 805). Conservatives accuse multiculturalism of supporting the identity and culture of the minority group at the cost of the native culture. For them, cultural conflicts are a zero-sum war that only favors the narrow-minded, the anti-modernist and anti-democratic minority communities: the majority communities are often condemned as ethno-centric or racist. Blind respect for and unquestioned acceptance of the minority group's customs, habits, values, and language are weakening people's identification with Western social systems and beliefs. For such critics, multiculturalism provides the fiery minority group with more support but ignores the special and unique historical value of the free and democratic Western culture, which may lead to its disappearance (see Colombo 809).

For Slavoj Žižek, multiculturalism is the best ideological form of global capitalism, which surpasses the relationship between the colonizer and the colonized in the framework of nation-states:

> This relationship is best designated as "auto-colonization": with the direct multinational functioning of Capital, we are no longer dealing with the standard opposition between metropolis and colonized countries; a global company as it were cut its umbilical cord with its mother-nation and treats its country of origins as simply another territory to be colonized. (Žižek 43)

Global capitalism treats each local culture the way the colonizer treats the colonized. At the same time, there are only the colonized with no colonizers in a strict sense, as the colonizing powers are no longer nation-states, but corporate companies (Žižek 44). Multiculturalism is not grounded in any specific culture when it advocates the Eurocentrists' respect for local cultures. This respect is in one sense a form of alienation — it is the respect that I give to you to make you an Other. It treats each local culture the way the colonizer treats colonized people: as "natives" whose mores should be carefully studied and respected. Therefore, multiculturalism is the best form of ideology for global capitalism: it is "a disavowed, inverted, self-referential form of racism, a 'racism with a distance' — it 'respects' the Other's identity, conceiving the Other as a self-enclosed 'authentic' community toward which he, the multiculturalist, maintains distance rendered possible by his privileged universal position" (Žižek 44). Multiculturalists are not neutral, as they proclaim to be; they are racists who empty their own position of positive content. The reason why multiculturalists respect the Other's specificity is as a way of asserting their own superiority. Their line of reasoning is right, Žižek argues, but for the wrong reason. Multiculturalists' respect for the Other culture does not mean that they are against the universalism that is advocated by the dominant culture. It is in essence a false, neutral position that steals the Other's culture with capital so as to tame that Other.

In countries that practice multiculturalism, many have expressed criticism of it. In *The Menace of Multiculturalism: Trojan Horse in America*, Schmidt has argued that the claims of cultural equality made by multiculturalists would not stand empirical scrutiny because they contradict people's daily life experiences. When multiculturalists believe in an equal values of all cultures, they are in contempt of culture. No-one could then reject any culture, for example, Sati (the burning of live widows in India), Melanesians' witchcraft worship, Kukuku culture, Padaung culture, Female clitoridectomy in African countries, and further cultural practices. These practices are not just different, but morally wrong and inhumane. Moreover, if all cultures are equal, it will not be necessary to introduce values, beliefs, and practices to enrich or reform American culture, as "there is no gain in exchanging one dollar bill for another dollar bill." If America were to fully accept the multiculturalist doctrine of cultural equality, it would harm its national and cultural pride (Schmidt 33 – 40). If America completely accepted the notion of cultural equality advocated by multiculturalists, it would mean the disappearance of almost 300 years of American culture and its influence, even the end of America. For Schmidt, therefore, multiculturalism has brought great damage to America. People's freedom of thought and speech have been severely hurt by so-called political correctness. In order to protect the soul of American culture, an attack should be launched against multiculturalism (see Schmidt 176).

Voices against multiculturalism are likewise strong in the Canadian academic world. Canada is the first country in the world to have enacted multiculturalism into law, as mentioned above. The efficacy of the policy, however, falls short of ensuring that all receive equal treatment under the law. Many therefore believe that multiculturalism is but a strategy which the Federal government uses to ease people's resistance against the bilingual policy in order to win votes from the minority group. Also, the "instrumental value of multiculturalism is seen in better serving external markets and improving the country's sales image" (Moodley 328). Li and Bolaria believe multiculturalism is a failed illusion rather than a policy. To try to deal with the problem of racial inequality and prejudice, whose causes are political and economical, by cultural policies can only be an illusion (Li and Bolaria 1). In *Selling Illusions: The Cult of Multiculturalism in Canada*, Neil Bissoondath has described the perception that, while in pre-immigration times Canada was mainly made up of White people and of Christians, multiculturalism has seriously damaged the formation of Canada's identity; Canadians no longer know who they are, as immigrants have been approved of and given too many rights — yet are still asking for more. What is left for the mainstream society is only confusion and shame (see Bissoondath 147).

Obviously, in spite of its good intentions, multiculturalism has encountered challenges from different perspectives.

IV.

Having first implemented multiculturalism as a national policy, Canada is facing the challenge of replacing it with interculturalism. This is especially so in Quebec, because multiculturalism is believed to have homogenized the difference among ethnicities in the context of a Federal discourse which failed to distinguish between ethnic minorities and national communities (see Gagnon 15). "Ethnic minorities" here refers to people who came to Canada through immigration, "national communities" to French-speaking Quebec people and the First Nations. National communities are not only defined by language and culture, but also by the character of their own political institutions, these being "nationality-based political units," so as to distinguish themselves from other immigrant communities. Nationalists in Quebec and First Nations people tend to believe that the policy of multiculturalism is a strategy adopted by the federal government whose real motivation is to negate the fact of the existence of the two kinds of community. Yet for them, the difference between the two communities is vitally significant. On the one hand, multiculturalism makes their long-term effort of striving for a unique society futile; on the other hand, multiculturalism is weakening Canada's fundamental characteristics as a federal state: for nationalists in Quebec, the Federal Government of Canada is a dual-nation federalism made up of two founding nationalities, English and French; for First Nations, that government is a treaty federalism as the First Nations are among those who signed the treaty, without which there would be no federal government. In Quebec criticism of multiculturalism has been particularly strong, and all elected governments of Quebec have categorically rejected federal multiculturalism, which is believed to be designed to slow down and even defeat integration. It is understood to consist in encouraging immigrants to retreat into their communities of origin, thus encouraging ghettoization because too much positive recognition of cultural differences will accelerate a retreat into ghettos, with a refusal to accept the political ethics of liberal democracy itself (see Taylor, "Interculturalism" 414). People in Quebec therefore tend not to believe that multiculturalism is in line with their values, and tend to think of it as imposed on them by the English-speaking Canadians. The narrative of Canadian multiculturalism has revolved around the "dethroning" of the Anglo-normative understanding: "People of non-British origin were not quite on the same footing" (Taylor, "Interculturalism" 416). In Quebec, more than 70% of the population are descendants from the original Francophone settlers, and their French language has been under threat of assimilation. Multiculturalism, then, could never take in Quebec because it just does not suit (Taylor "Interculturalism" 417).

In place of multiculturalism, what is proposed by Quebec and practiced there is interculturalism. Differing from the cultural mosaic under federal multiculturalism, interculturalism believes that what is most important is to open up the cultural space of the minority groups, so that they can engage more actively in the dominant culture. Taking into consideration the history of Quebec, interculturalism does not ask the immigrant groups to give up their native culture, but urges them to take French as the common language in the public sphere. In the official discourse, interculturalism exists in the form of a moral contract between the immigrant groups and Quebec society. In 1991, the Quebec government outlined the meaning of interculturalism, which contended that

> the incorporation of immigrants or minority cultures into the larger political community is a reciprocal endeavor — defined by a "moral contract" between the host society and particular ethno-cultural groups, which is the aim of establishing a forum for the empowerment of all citizens — a "common public culture". Through such a framework, the objective was to foster an evolving and plural "common public culture" that was conceptually distinct from past attempts to privilege a majority culture as a reference for integration and as a dominant pole of cultural convergence. (Meer et al. 115)

The purpose of this common public culture is to establish a Francophone, democratic, and multicultural society, which recognizes and appreciates the traditional culture of the society, which in Quebec means French culture. For Quebec, although interculturalism is important for giving necessary equality to the minority groups, it is also important for granting some privilege to the foundational culture, because to refuse this would mean to refuse the foundational cultural identity. At the same time, the unity and solidity of any society is important; unity and solidarity can only be realized by encouraging intercommunication and connection among different communities so as to achieve a common goal. The emphasis is thus on what they have in common rather than what is different. Nonetheless, a common history "with the francophone relatives of 'Mère France'" is not culturally dominant as recent Quebec feature films "increase the distance from their European and French roots"; their protagonists reflect "constant interaction between more or less European (Québécois) and US models and ideas of values and norms" (Müller 282). Quebec cinema "plays a discernable part in negotiating the Québécois community's linguistic and cultural foundations" (Müller 279).

The Achilles heel of the "inter" discourse, as Taylor has said, is the fear it can arouse that "they" may change "us." The notion that "they" can be equal collaborators in remaking the common culture rings alarm bells in all who share this anxiety (Taylor, "Interculturalism"

420). Rather than focusing on collaborative differences that may change "us," interculturalism encourages different communities to develop common cultural memories, as well as loyalties to common values and institutions. The essence of Quebec's interculturalism, accordingly, has been defined by Gagnon and Iacovino as follows:

> Interculturalism attempts to strike a balance between individual rights and cultural relativism by emphasizing a "fusion of horizons" through dialogue and consensual agreement. Through the participation and discourse of all groups in the public sphere, the goal of this approach is to achieve the largest possible consensus regarding the limits and possibilities of the expression of collective differences based on identity, weighed against the requirements of social cohesion and individual rights in a common public context. The recognition of cultural differences is assumed in such a view — the sources of meaning accrued from cultural identity are acknowledged as an explicit feature of citizen empowerment — yet an obligation is placed on all parties to contribute to the basic tenets of a common public culture. (101–02)

Quebec interculturalism, therefore, in comparison with Canadian multiculturalism, places more emphasis on togetherness, cultural convergence, liberalism, and an ongoing identity negotiation. They operate in two essentially different modes. With multiculturalism, there is a multiple mode in which individuals and communities share equal positions; interculturalism is a two-dimensional mode whose multiplicity or duality is built on the relationship between the minority immigrant groups and the society's foundational majority groups. Emphasizing the community's difference and uniqueness might lead to social segregation, while interculturalism aims to break the segregation and separate states between different communities by offering them a common identity (that of French-speaking Quebec) as well as respect for each cultural identity.

V.

There have appeared many discussions and disputes around the narratives of multiculturalism and interculturalism. Between them there exist many overlapping ideas as well as different understandings. As for alternatives to multiculturalism, apart from the discourse of interculturalism as just described, there is also the notion of cosmopolitanism. Cosmopolitanism, as we know, originated in ancient

Greece and was rediscovered in the Renaissance. Ulrich Beck has proposed a novel way to understand the world's diversity. Faced with an increasingly diversified world, our thoughts are often restricted to the confines of methodological nationalism and methodological cosmopolitanism, which, he believes, should be questioned and challenged. What Beck has proposed is a type of cosmopolitan realism, of cosmopolitanization rather than the old notion of Euro-centric cosmopolitanism. It counters methodological nationalism, which, as Beck explains, assumes that the nation, state and society are the "natural" social and political forms of the modern world. Multiculturalism, as one of many concepts and modes of dealing with cultural differences, actually means monoculturalism: by referring to collective categories of difference, it has a tendency to essentialize them by the nation-state social fabric of cultural differences. Multiculturalism, that is, perceives cultural differences as "little nations" in one nation. There is, accordingly, a strong correspondence of multiculturalism with the conventional mode of the nation-state, since a similar sense of either-or identity is presumed to characterize a people and multiple cultures. Beck thinks that the language of multiculturalism is a severe obstacle to describing and understanding the changing landscapes of cultural diversity. The national and the multicultural both revolve about identity, and identity as such excludes. For every "We" there is a "Them," the people who are not like "us."

Cosmopolitanism signifies what is excluded by both positions: the acknowledgement of the dignity of difference and equality at the same time. The cosmopolitanism proposed by Beck is not philosophical cosmopolitanism but rather an "impure cosmopolitanization" from below, a social cosmopolitanism. Whereas the philosophical version is normative, the social is descriptive and analytical. The notion of cosmopolitanization refers to the objective conditions and processes on a macro as well as a micro level. Regardless of ethnic background and political beliefs, we live in an age of cosmopolitization: the erosion of clear borders separating markets, states, civilizations, religions, cultures, life-worlds of common people — which implies the involuntary inclusion of the global Other (Beck 52–58).

The notion of cosmopolitization, differing from the notions of multiculturalism and interculturalism, aims more strongly at a global perspective, referring to a world or cosmos of interconnectedness. In *Economic and Philosophic Manuscripts of 1844*, Karl Marx wrote that

> Man is a species-being, not only because in practice and in theory
> he adopts the species (his own as well as those of other things) as

his object, but — and this is only another way of expressing it — also because he treats himself as the actual, living species; because he treats himself as a *universal* and therefore a free being. (31)

As "species-beings," as Marx also maintains, humans need a social fabric, a community to survive and develop. In this increasingly interconnected and fragmented world, whether we like it or not, in this age of the so-called Anthropocene with hazards of climate change, we share a common fate, belonging to a community of common fate. It does not matter what theories we believe in, be they multiculturalism, interculturalism, or cosmopolitanization: what is of real significance is that we forget the fragmentational view of the world and return to a holistic view. We still need a story, a story that tells about our belongings and aspirations. This story can be the story of the community of common fate for humankind. With this story, we can find commonness in difference. Angela McRobbie has an important point: "[...] if we all recognise the particularity of our cultural values then that requires us to find a wider context beyond these particulars so that others might make their demands" (McRobbie 30). Yes, we are in need of a new type of universality: this is not the "rationality" advocated by the Enlightenment, nor is it Immanuel Kant's "transcendentalism," nor Hegel's "absolute spirit," nor Mike Featherstone's "global knowledge," nor the neoliberal's "end of history." Rather, to use Confucius' word, it is "Ren" or 仁, a dynamic interconnection between the Self and the Other (see *Analects* 6: 30). This is a new type of universalism, of "whole culture." In *The Crooked Timber of Humanity*, Sir Isaiah Berlin has argued:

> Members of one culture can, by the force of imaginative insight, understand (what Vico called *entrare*) the values, the ideals, the forms of life of another culture or society, even those remote in time or space. [...] if they open their minds sufficiently they can grasp how one might be a full human being, with whom one could communicate, and at the same time live in the light of values widely different from one's own, but which nevertheless one can see to be values, ends of life, by the realisation of which men could be fulfilled. (10)

By thus entering imaginatively into value orientations that appear remote, a communication process allows the development toward a "full" human identity, with a global perspective. The "imaginative insight" is one which can be significantly strengthened by a perceptive response to fictional literature. Returning to the dispute about "cultural appropriation" spoken of at the beginning, we may say that, in essence, it comes out of a fragmented view of culture (without any intention to ignore the suffering of the First Nations in history), behind which lies a problematic relationship mode between the universal and the particular, the Self and the Other. If we choose to believe the future is a shared one, we will need to look for a new narrative mode to preserve and represent our history, to rethink the cultural tradition that has made us, and to rethink the place of our own cultural tradition in the global cultural network. Tradition is of course there, just as difference is there. Can we try to look at the reality of our history from a point of view of non-determined and variable futures: can we identify a re-reading of tradition with what is to come, locating difference within commonality (and vice versa)? For better or for worse, we belong to a community of common fate. With this perspective, we may find a novel mode of discourse to surpass the paradoxes in those of multiculturalism, interculturalism, and cosmopolitanism.

References

Beck, Ulrich. "Multiculturalism or Cosmopolitanism: How Can We Describe and Understand the Diversity of the World?" *Social Sciences in China*, vol. 32, no. 4, Nov. 2011, pp. 52–58.

Berlin, Isaiah. *The Crooked Timber of Humanity: Chapters in the History of Ideas*. 1990. Edited by Henry Hardy. Pimlico, 2003.

Bissoondath, Neil. *Selling Illusions: The Cult of Multiculturalism in Canada*. Penguin, 1994. (Revised ed. 2002.)

Bolaffi, Guido, Raffaele Bracalenti, Peter Braham and Sandro Gindro. *Dictionary of Race, Ethnicity and Culture*. Sage, 2003.

Butler, Patrick. "'Godfather of Multiculturalism' Stuart Hall Dies Aged 82." *The Guardian* 10 Feb. 2014. www.theguardian.com/education/2014/feb/10/godfather-multiculturalism-stuart-hall-dies.

Casagranda, Mirko. "Switching Identity in Multicultural Canadian Literature: Codes-witching as a Discursive Strategy and a Marker of Identity Construction." *Central European Journal of Canadian Studies*, vol. 6, no. 1, 2008, pp. 77–87.

Chierici, R. M. "Caribbean Migration in the Age of Globalization: Transnationalism, Race, and Ethnic Identity." *Reviews in Anthropology*, vol. 33, 2004, pp. 43–59.

Colombo, Enzo. "Multiculturalisms: An Overview of Multicultural Debates in Western Societies." *Current Sociology Review*, vol. 63, no. 6, 2015, pp. 800–24.

Fourny, Jean-François. "In Defense of the State: On Neil Bissoondath's *Selling Illusions*, Michael Lind's *The Next American Nation*, and Tzvetan and Todorov's *Morals of History*." *Research in African Literatures*, vol. 28, no. 4; Multiculturalism, 1997, pp. 142–53.

Gagnon, Alain-G. "Canada; Unity and Diversity." *Democracy and Cultural Diversity*, edited by Michael O'Neill and Dennis Austin, Oxford UP, 2000, pp. 12–26.

Gagnon, Alain-G., and Raffaele Iacovino. *Federalism, Citizenship, and Quebec: Debating Multiculturalism*. U of Toronto P, 2006.

Glazer, Nathan. *We Are All Multiculturalists Now*. Harvard UP, 1997.

Hall, Stuart. "The Multicultural Question." Milton Keynes; Open University Pavis Papers in Social and Cultural Research 4, 2001.

Hayward, Victoria. *Romantic Canada*. Macmillan, 1922.

Kallen, Horace M[eyer]. *Culture and Democracy in the United States*. Boni & Liveright, 1924; Transaction, 1998.

Karoumbeli, Smaro, editor. *Making a Difference: Canadian Multicultural Literature*. Oxford UP, 1996.

Lederman, Marsha and Mark Medley. "Writers' Union of Canada Editorial Sparks Outrage, Resignations." *The Globe and Mail*, 10 May 2017. www.theglobeandmail.com/arts/books-and-media/writers-union-of-canada-editorial-on-cultural-appropriation-sparks-outrage-resignations/article34952918/.

Lee, A. Robert. *Multicultural American Literature: Comparative Black, Native, Latino/a and Asian American Fictions*. UP of Mississippi, 2003.

Li, Peter S. and B. Singh Bolaria. *Racial Minorities in Multicultural Canada*. Garamond Press, 1983.

McRobbie, Angela. *The Uses of Cultural Studies: A Textbook*. Sage, 2005.

Marx, Karl. *Economic and Philosophic Manuscripts of 1844*. Translated by Martin Milligan. Progress Publishers, 1932.

Meer, Nasar, Tariq Modood and Ricard Zapata-Barrero, editors. *Multiculturalism and Interculturalism: Debating the Dividing Lines*. Edinburgh UP, 2016.

Milner, Andrew and Jeff Browitt. *Contemporary Cultural Theory*. 3rd ed. Allen & Unwin, 2002.

Moodley, Kogila. *Canadian Multiculturalism as Ideology: Ethnic and Racial Studies*. Routledge, 1983.

Müller, Jürgen E. "In Search of Otherness or Sameness; Traces of Americanism in *Cinéma Québécois*." *Americanisms: Discourses of Exception, Exclusion, Exchange*, edited by Michael Steppat, Universitätsverlag Winter, 2009, pp. 271–83.

Ratner, Sidney. "Horace M. Kallen and Culturalism." *Modern Judaism*, vol. 4, No. 2, May 1984, pp. 185–200.

Schmidt, Alvin J. *The Menace of Multiculturalism: Trojan Horse in America*. Praeger, 1997.

Taylor, Charles. "Foreword." *Multiculturalism and Interculturalism: Debating the Dividing Lines*. Edited by Nasar Meer, Tariq Modood and Ricard Zapata-Barrero, Edinburgh UP, 2016, pp. vii–ix.

—. "Interculturalism or Multiculturalism?" *Philosophy and Social Criticism*, vol. 38, nos. 4–5, 2012, pp. 413–23.

Van de Vijver, Fons J. R. "Multiculturalism; Definition and Value." *Value Dimensions and Their Contextual Dynamics Across Cultures*, edited by Steve J. Kulich, Weng Liping and Michael H. Prosser, Intercultural Research Vol. 5, Shanghai Foreign Language Education Press, 2014, pp. 165–90.

Vitikainen, Annamari. "Multiculturalism and Political Philosophy." *Oxford*

Research Encyclopedias. May 2017. politics.oxfordre.com/view/10.1093/ acrefore/9780190228637.001.0001/acrefore-9780190228637-e-252.

Watson, C[onrad] W[illiam]. *Concepts in the Social Sciences: Multiculturalism*. Open UP, 2000.

Xie, Ming. *Conditions of Comparison: Reflections on Comparative Intercultural Inquiry*. Continuum, 2011.

Žižek, Slavoj. "Multicultualism, or, the Cultural Logic of Multinational Capitalism." *New Left Review*, vol. 1/225, Sept.–Oct. 1997, pp. 28–52.

11

Memory for Transcultural Understanding? Reading *Nairobi to Shenzhen*

Yuan Mingqing
University of Bayreuth

Summary: With the sweeping force of globalization, memory studies has encountered a "transcultural turn" and is accordingly freed from being conceptualized according to territorial, political, or national boundaries. "Traveling" or "transcultural memory" is a concept (Astrid Erll) which aims to provide different angles for studying the interaction and cross-referencing of memories in the global era. Yet since memory represents and answers the needs of cultural valuations, selections and modifications of memory may incubate dangers of partial subjective positioning. The semi-autobiographical novel *Nairobi to Shenzhen* (2009) by Mark Okoth Obama Ndesandjo, half-brother of former U.S. president Barack Obama, features an unreliable narrator who faces challenges to his single perspectivization on the past as well as his interpretive framework of the present, creating a newly signifying and valorizing bridge across the global south.

Introduction

Even though connections between China and Africa can be dated back to ancient times (Li 10–16), the presence of Africans in China or interactions between Chinese and Africans on a local level are rarely studied (see Li 22; Thornber 697). With the rising Chinese economic power and the growing interactions between China and African regions, more and more Africans come to China in pursuit of financial benefits, cultural exchange, or their own "Chinese dream." Since there are no official statistics of the exact number of Africans in China, it is estimated that around 20,000 Africans are living at least in the southern city of Guangzhou (see Lan 298). The African community in the city of Guangzhou, which prospers as a consequence of the blossoming relationship and cooperation between China and much of Africa, is named "Chocolate city" or "Little Africa" (Lan 298). In addition to attracting more business contacts, the Chinese government is also providing scholarships to African students to encourage them to come and study in China. It is estimated that "more than 35,000 Africans are now pursuing degrees at Chinese universities" (Thornber 699).

Connections and interactions on the personal, local level between Chinese and the African diaspora are becoming more intricate, more complex, and more intertwined. However, in contrast to the increasing research on economic, military, medical, and political interactions between China and Africa, few studies are undertaken from perspectives outside these fields: "Both the impacts of economic and political ties on actual human lives, and the informal interactions and personal relationships between Africans and Chinese" are seldom discussed (Thornber 697). A more nuanced and deeper insight into the interactions and connections on a micro-level between China and Africa is required.

Literature provides a unique perspective to look into the issue. The novel *Nairobi to Shenzhen: A Novel of Love in the East*, which was published in 2009 as a semi-autobiography, is a reflection and description of this increasing trend of south-south migration. The novel was written by Mark Okoth Obama Ndesandjo, who is the half-brother of former U.S. president Barack Obama and also the author of the memoir *An Obama's Journey: My Odyssey of Self-Discovery Across Three Cultures*. He has set up the Obama Ndesandjo Centre at Beijing Normal University for Art Education and Research, and is an adjunct professor at Beijing Normal University. The novel narrates the experience of the protagonist David in China, with constant reminiscences of the past. David was born and brought up in Kenya, went to the U.S. to receive higher education, and then worked there for around thirty years after graduation. After the 9/11 events in 2001, he lost his job and decided to move to China for a new life or in search of his "Chinese dream." Shenzhen is close to Guangzhou and Hong Kong, a relatively new city constructed just after China's economic reform and opening-up in the 1980s. David's encounter with China is narrated in parallel with his attempts at cultural recall through photos, emails and narrators across temporal, spatial and cultural borders.

Even though the novel is often said to be semi-autobiographical,① on the first page of the book the author claims that all "characters and events portrayed and the names herein are fictitious" (Ndesandjo Foreword). "It's a work of fiction, but there's a lot going on in there that parallels my life," Ndesandjo explains in an interview (Richburg). He asks "Where does an author end and a character begin?" and answers "You want to give authenticity to your character. And the character you best know is yourself" (Richburg). These explanations reveal autobiography's paradoxical aspect, having a reference to memory of reality as well as being fictionalized. As Saunders puts it, "The distinction between autobiography and other forms such as biography or fiction is thus always already blurred" (321). In this sense, life writing such as semi-autobiography is a medium which records, rewrites, and represents individual memory as well as constructs, produces, and circulates cultural memory, which echoes with the notion of "universalized individualism" that "it was only in the individual mind that the universal had its existence" (Saunders 325). Individual experiences may differ greatly from each other, but they always have a dimension in and connection to a larger context. *Nairobi to Shenzhen* is not only a narrative of subjective, unique, individual experience but also an account of a current state and of historical events around the globe.

Since "[v]ersions of the past change with every recall, in accordance with the changed present situation" (Erll, *Memory* 8), and "memory is closely aligned with memory" (Rothberg 4), (re)-construction of the past has an undeniable link with what is happening in the present and an indispensable connection with the anxiety of identity. This chapter examines how the past is recalled, rediscovered, and reconstructed in response to the present with the help of the conceptualization of transcultural memory, to see what roles ideologies and values play in understanding the past and the present and how transcultural memory helps to mediate and construct

---

① See for instance http://www.foxnews.com/world/2011/08/18/obamas-brother-in-shanghai-to-promote-bio-novel.html.

a joint vision for the future.

Transcultural Memory

In 1999, German philosopher Wolfgang Welsch proposed the concept of "transculturality," which opposes "the old homogenizing and separatist idea of cultures" while it focuses on "the inner differentiation and complexity of modern cultures" (Welsch 197). Since then, the concept and perspective of transculturality, which emphasizes the fluid, hybrid, "multi-meshed and inclusive" (Welsch 200) aspect of culture, has been settling into different disciplines with a sweeping force. Under this influence, memory studies encountered the "transcultural turn" (Bond and Rapson 9), a shift of focus from national and collective memory to "cosmopolitan memory" (Levy and Sznaider 88), "multidirectional memory" (Rothberg 3), and "traveling memory" (Erll, "Traveling" 12). Levy and Sznaider focus on how Holocaust memories transform into cosmopolitan memory and form "a common European cultural memory" through representations in the global media in the era of globalization (87).

Meanwhile, Rothberg emphasizes the "ongoing negotiation, cross-referencing, and borrowing" aspect of memory in different historical contexts (3). As we will see, the negotiation aspect enables cross-fertilization with the concept of intercultural identity negotiation. He proposes taking the public sphere not as a "pregiven, limited space" of zero-sum game among memories of different groups, but as "a malleable discursive space in which groups do not simply articulate established positions but actually come into being through their dialogical interactions with others" (5). Both concepts acknowledge the continued influence, the mixings and collages of memories of different groups, and the exposed multilayered, intertwined, interactive aspects of memory across space and time. No memories are pure or belong only to a certain group, and the public sphere is not a space for competition among different memories.

In contrast to simply exposing and exploring the nature of memory as being cosmopolitan or multidirectional, Erll's concept of "traveling memory" and understanding of "transcultural memory" accentuates memory's traveling process. "The incessant wandering of carriers, media, contents, forms, and practices of memory, their continual 'travels' and ongoing transformations through time and space, across social, linguistic and political borders" are in the limelight of transcultural memory (Erll, "Traveling" 11). For Erll, "*all* cultural memory *must* travel, be kept in motion, in order to 'stay alive', to have an impact both on individual minds and social formations" ("Traveling" 17). This conceptualization expands the scope of transcultural memory to include not only mnemonic traveling within, across, and beyond cultures, but also memories shared among friends, families, and different cultural groups. Remembrance is no longer a static and unanimous entity owned by groups or nations, but rather a fluid and dynamic force moving back and forth, through and across the constantly changing, fuzzy distinctions or differences between cultures. Memories are by their nature mixed, shared, and always on the move through transcultural encounters. The "becoming" and "traveling" instead of the "being" aspect of memory reveals a dynamic and dialogic process of remembering and forgetting as well as the collages, negotiations, hybridizations, and creations of memory.

However, as Erll points out herself, "memory studies should develop an interest in mnemonic itineraries, follow the non-isomorphic trajectories of media, contents and carriers, the paths, and path-dependencies, of remembering and forgetting" ("Traveling" 14). The dialectics of remembering and forgetting, and the workings of the past in response to the present in the process of memory traveling as well as the localizations of traveling memory, need further discussion and development. On the one hand, what is remembered, commemorated, and narrated is always under the influence of the dominant discourse. Or more precisely, "the public articulation of memory is informed by the discourses and institutions of the public sphere that mediate and authorise such recollection" (Crownshaw 2). On the other hand, since "memory is the past made present" (Rothberg 3), recalls and reworkings of the past always represent and answer the need of the present. In Radstone's words, "even when (and if) memory travels, it is only ever instantiated locally, in a specific place and at a particular time" (114). In this sense, even though the concept of transcultural memory dissolves the boundaries of nations, regions, communities, or any restricting categories, it still has a spatial dimension as the "locatedness of instances of transmission" (Radstone 114) and a temporal dimension as "the living, or the life of 'the past' in the present" (Radstone 113). In this sense, the novel *Nairobi to Shenzhen* offers an example of how transcultural memory travels across time and space while still being attached to locatedness.

A Co-Present Time

The novel *Nairobi to Shenzhen* is narrated from the third-person omniscient point of view, with occasional retrospections of the protagonist David as well as citations from emails from his mother and his diaries of the past. Upon arriving in China in the wake of 9/11 and the onset of a war, the protagonist is forced to confront his early experiences in Kenya and the U.S. as a result of his growing love for a beautiful Chinese woman and a young orphan. Parallels between his own upbringing and the potential family that lies before him lead to questions about his true identity, the complexities of his multi-racial family, and the relationship he had known with his father. As the author declares, "Many Americans, and more and more people around the world are going through this globalization of race, culture and religion. And we're discovering that we don't represent just one culture, but two or three" (Williams). David's reminiscence of the past and his nostalgia for Kenya are always awakened by events in the present, and are attributed meanings and significance according to the present point of view. Yet this also generates a sense of disorientation and "apprehensions of spatial dislocation and disjuncture" (Radstone 114). When David walks into an electronics market in Shenzhen not long after his arrival there, he feels that "[o]utside on the street the human waves of Chinese pedestrians and hawkers resemble a Wall Street rush hour compressed into minutes" (Ndesandjo 19). Inside the electronics market, he feels himself actually in "the Nairobi open air supermarket at Westlands, where spinach, mangoes, lettuce, potatoes, tilapia fish, slabs of beef, oranges, and other produce and viands were sold in unregulated abandon, the ground filthy with mud and squashed and rotting vegetables" (19–20).

Flashbacks of the past occur at an unexpected moment, and the sense of disorientation calls for meaning-making for the new life in the present. The resemblance between Kenya and China not only arouses his nostalgia for the past, but also reveals his being out of place in the new location. Recalls of the past in this situation help to mitigate his anxiety and the new environment's unfamiliarity. The comparisons of electronic components with food not only depict a chaotic, crowded, and prosperous picture of markets, but also establish a comparison between China and Kenya in economic development.

Though many differences exist on the levels of technology, variety of products, and trading volumes, both China and Kenya are emerging markets that are prospering and progressing at the novel's publishing time.

In addition to the occasional retrospection, at the beginning of each chapter there is always a short paragraph cited mainly from David's father's journal as a foreword of the following chapter, even though the whole journal and his father's whole life story appear at the end of the novel as an epilogue. This means that the cited paragraphs are open to be interpreted out of the context and to be associated with the coming chapter, regarding what has been happening and what will happen in the present. An exception is one foreword, which is about an excerpt from a local newspaper about the establishment of the special economic zones in Shenzhen, while the others are all journal entries following a chronological order. The first chapter's foreword is about David's father's memory of the day his grandmother leaves his father, while the chapter "The Beginning" cites the whole email from David to his mother, which is sent after his arrival in China. If leaving his mother marks a beginning of David's father's new life of sadness and suffering, David's arrival in China and his email to his mother enquiring for more information about his father is a new start of his journey into himself and into family memory.

Due to different social and political contexts and different upbringings, the emails from David's mother and the appearance of his father's journal at the end are in fact the route of how transcultural memory travels as well as a revelation of how memories intermingle and intersect with each other. On the one hand, David's childhood memory of domestic violence is confirmed by his mother. The violence is attributed to family upbringing:

> Regarding your father, he was often beaten as a child. Men in those days were often autocratic and dictatorial. His life growing up with a very hard father was difficult. His mother was often abused and eventually ran away and left him. Maybe your father didn't know any other way. (83)

As the author explains about himself, "Because of the issue of domestic violence, I instinctively gravitated towards my mother and bonded with her, her values and her culture, Western culture" (Williams). Having experienced these events, David attempts to forget and move away from the memories, while they haunt him from time to time. On the other hand, even though David's father admits his addiction to alcohol and his unreasonable blaming of his wife, his journal reveals a bigger context: the author "finds his own closure by inventing his father's diary, which gives the book's protagonist insight into his father's philandering, outbursts and a self-destructive decline that paralleled Kenya's descent into corruption and tribal conflict" (Jacobs). Ndesandjo accounts for his motivation:

> [...] I imagined what would my father have said about his life if he had written a diary that detailed the most significant moments of his life. I started to write this diary because I wanted to imagine the good parts as well as explore where the bad parts had actually come from. But at that point it was no longer an autobiography. ("Brotherly")

It is the father's journal that decides the work's genre and makes it a novel.

His father "was a police guard, an askari, for the British magistrate assigned to Alego and its district" (Ndesandjo 326), while "he is too smart to have been an askari" (336). The constant humiliation, discrimination, and even violence of serving in the colonial period make his father become withdrawn, bitter, and constantly enraged, which leads to his ventilation of these feelings onto his wife and children. Growing up in this way, David's father had experienced segregation as well as violence since childhood (see for instance Brendon 350ff.; Anderson, Brown and Louis Chapters 11, 23).

After independence, he dreams of mastering knowledge so that he "would not have to kowtow to the whites. They would kowtow to me" (Ndesandjo 330). However, this dream withers after his witnessing of the death of trade unionist and politician Tom Mboya and his realization of corruption within the government as well as the rising tribalism in the new nation (340−41). Even though the incomplete and fragmented journal cannot offer the whole story of David's father's life, a broken, wretched man living in the shadow of colonialism, the composition still makes David feel "no bitterness" and "help[s] him understand himself a little more" (342): Ndesandjo, too, affirms that David "tries to understand himself through understanding his father," composing his text ("Brotherly").

By his realization of the burden of history from his father's generation, by facing the pain of the past, and by retrieving and negotiating long-forgotten memories with his own memory, David feels both relieved and empowered. It is difficult to imagine futures without anchors in the past, without memories which constitute and form the self. David's rediscovery of his father's journal and his mother's account of the past entitle the claim of his right to his dreams and futures. Transcultural and transgenerational understanding is formed through the textual traveling of memories through emails and a journal; as the text forms travel through each other, they enable the author's "own closure." Transcultural memory thus serves as a medium to rekindle David's dreams and to form his identity.

When he leaves the U.S. after losing his job due to "a corporate downsizing," David feels that after 9/11, "[t]he USA, once a place of hope and eternal optimism, had become a place of systematic and growing suspicion" (Ndesandjo 3). While being in China,

> [a]t times he was seized with the thrill of this land. A shiver would travel up his legs and through his arms, and give him a jolt of energy. How wonderful to live in a place that was all about expectations and promise. At these times, the storyline wasn't about China or its advance in the world. It was about personal possibilities. It was about the future and the desire to live a better life than one's parents. (29)

The fast development and the seemingly enormous possibilities in China bring him hopes for the future. The totally different cultural context, language, histories, and people, the revitalizing and rejuvenating spirits of working and living, serve as an alternative route different from his old paradigm. This to some degree situates the connections between China and Africa on the global stage, in which China is sometimes seen as an alternative opportunity or mode of development for Africa, since China maintains what it considers a "valueless" foreign policy in contrast to the West's interventions in Africa.

To some extent, the past and the present co-exist in David's life, or more precisely, are "operating with co-present time perspectives: The multi-temporal levels of the past and the present intermingle in manifold and complex ways" (Neumann 336). Retrospections and citations of emails and journals are constantly disrupting the chronological narration of the present, while at the same time David's retrospection, his mother's account of the past, and citations from his father's journal all follow a parallel chronicle order in a different time and space, which draw the three timelines to a comparison and converging point. In this case, for the three braids of narrations of the past, the present becomes the "reference frame in which each event is related to others in both a forward and backward direction: Each event is both marked by all preceding events and evokes expectations about events to come" (Neumann 336).

A Shared Sense of Exile

In addition to transcultural memory across time, transcultural memory across space enhances the narrative's complexity. Stories and recalls of the past from David's friends trigger his recalls of the past and form a new group identity. On the one hand, memories traveling between memory carriers serve as a bridge to construct transcultural understanding and emotional bonding as well as to form "complex constellations of intersecting group allegiances" (Erll, "Traveling" 14). On the other hand, the narration of the third-person point of view renders the memories unreliable; they already appear hybridized and localized.

In the novel, music is an indispensable part of the plot. David gets the chance to learn more about Chinese culture, including the story of butterfly lovers (Ndesandjo 103); important in this process are his Chinese friend and later girlfriend Spring and his student Zhen Rui during piano lessons at the orphanage. Zhen Rui is an orphan who loves music but suffers severely from a heart disease. David localizes and hybridizes the story of Beethoven into the Chinese context to cheer him up and strengthen his desire to stay alive. In the adapted story, the people whom Beethoven fights and despises are not the nobility class but Chinese businessmen and their use of his music to earn money (197 – 99). He is despised by a Hongkonger in Shenzhen for his sloppy appearance in a restaurant (199), only being recognized and taken as a celebrity in the street by "a fat pink woman (probably an English teacher hired by a local school) with a huge black afro and darkened eyebrows" (201). David compares his own experience in China to "a fugue of Bach's," being "like snakes between one's fingers, sometimes dissonant, other times consonant, but with direction, perpetual motion, and, occasionally, a superb grace" (29). Music serves as a bond that connects David and his friends. The changing of the context as well as the plots of Beethoven reveals how capital works and functions to promote globalization and commoditization; yet with the help of capital, a boundary-crossing solidarity between cultural forms is constructed over the distinctions of nation-states.

In addition to David's encounter with Zhen Rui, he meets Spring in a tea house, and is immediately attracted by her. After she reveals herself to be a Manchu in majority-Han China, David is reminded of his experience in Kenya of being distrusted as a Luo, isolated, and called "chotara, half caste" at school (52). There is a "shared sense of exile and solitude that attracted them to each other" (54), even though Spring confides in him with pride about her family being special, and being "once kings and queens" (53). When David and Spring visit an orphanage in Shenzhen, Spring is silent, because "as she held the child, she remembered her own childhood, her mother and father" (69). Then certain sufferings during the "Cultural Revolution", her father's compulsory sterilization due to the one-child policy, and a love story connected to the Tangshan earthquake all flood back to Spring's consciousness (72–75). However, her distance and silence at the orphanage are explained by her being embarrassed at "[l]etting foreigners see shameful parts of China" and her clinging to a Chinese concept of family with distinctions between one's own children and adopted children, since the "Chinese had lived among their own for so long, they could *smell* otherness" (75, 76). Together with the presumptuous reasoning of Spring's silence, such homogenization of the Chinese unveils the narrator's essentialist attitude and unreliability.

"A Citizen of the World"

As Neumann observes, "the interplay between individual memory and identity is staged through the tension — constitutive for homodiegetic narration — between the experiencing or remembered and narrating or remembering I" (336). In this sense, tensions and conflicts will occur when "the remembering I is not able to adjust his memories to his current needs in a meaning-creating manner" (Neumann 337). Identity will then be open to questions, doubts, and challenges, so that it will encounter further changes and become more fluid and less stable. We have a negotiation process in the struggle for identity, a "dynamic process of verbal and nonverbal message transaction and meaning attribution coordination between the two (or more) communicators in maintaining, threatening, or uplifting the various sociocultural group-based, role-based, or unique personal-based identity images of the other" (Ting-Toomey and Dorjee 54, as explained also similarly in the companion Volume 8's appendix on "Intercultural Concepts of Identity"). Linking cultural values and self-conception, the process involves the experience of identity dissonance coupled with interactional "unpredictability," while this disequilibrium can eventually lead to personal growth and resourcefulness (Ting-Toomey and Dorjee 18, 104). As we can learn from Ndesandjo's work, the process operates through memory trajectories, while it also becomes effective there through the textual dialogue between David's narrative and his father's journal as a fictional device. The opportunity for a similar textual dialogue is also discussed by Shen Weiwei in Volume 9. In *Nairobi to Shenzhen*, David undergoes a series of events in China which manifest a perspectivation and interpretation of the past from different vantage points.

Even though David claims to be "determined to avoid these national flaws," and "Kenya, America, white, black, Luo, Judaism, even Lithuanian ancestry were all parts of him" (Ndesandjo 90), he still categorizes cultures according to nations and tries to classify a superiority or inferiority of cultures. He "was proud to be American," because "the quintessence of being American" is absorption through which he "sought to identify the deficiencies and strengths of different cultures" (88) — even though his grandmother had a nervous breakdown when she learned that her daughter intended to marry a black man.

The ambiguity and self-contradictions in David's account reveal his own dilemma and confusion about his identity, and they incur conflicts and difficulties for his transcultural understanding of China. About himself, Ndesandjo explains "I've been able to take some of the good things from each of the cultures and tried to mold them into one. The process takes years, but you eventually develop a unique identity that has Chinese, Kenyan and American aspects" (Williams). In the narrative, the reader can see the difficulties David experiences with such attempts.

His "American" attitude fuses into his comparison of Chinese history with Wagner's music, which the narrator does not understand:

> it stretched for ages upon boring ages, only punctuated by brief moments of unforgettable brilliance and genius. Thus, to him, ever since Master Kong, known to the West as Confucius, with his students created, implemented, and destroyed all other thought structures after him, there had been nothing at all remarkable about those five thousand years. (Ndesandjo 120)

— with a few exceptions. This comparison indicates a linear thinking of time and history instead of the more commonly held belief that

Chinese history is circular. In addition, the discussion of historical "brilliance and genius" is no less problematic. What can be classified as historical brilliance, understood as powerful personages capable of making far-reaching decisions, is not a simple issue of individual preference but within contesting realms of power constellation. Confucius, as a "floating signifier" (cf. Nylan and Wilson 97), becomes a representation of Chinese history, stripped of complex historical and cultural context. Such a simplification of history ignores the complexity and multilayering of transcultural interactions. Even though David has articulated his pain in being categorized, and his identification as being "a citizen of the world" (Ndesandjo 343), he still assumes the role of being a judge in classifying cultures according to national boundaries, assessing civilizations, adhering to categories, and constructing a hierarchical order accordingly. This echoes with his claims of being American when asked (97), enjoying mobility and accessibility, entertaining the sense of representing freedom, independence, and being a human rights advocator, and adopting a somewhat patronizing and belittling attitude toward indigenous knowledge and traditions. Through the learning of Chinese, he simply

> wanted to understand China, but he did not want to be Chinese. In particular he did not want to be one of the crowd. / The crowd was rapacious. / The crowd was unfeeling. / The crowd was unthinking. / The crowd was vulgar and beneath him. (121)

This sense of superiority might also be one of the reasons for his hitting his student in the face in class when he is ignored (168–69), because a neglect and "rejection" from the crowd whom he despises generate a stronger sense of "failure, inadequacy, uselessness" (168). There may possibly be an echo of a competitive value system which, for Kenya as well as the U.S., tends to highlight "the winner takes all" (Hofstede's country comparison tool). As Ketter and Arfsten show, however, there are certain nuances between ethnic communities, so that David does not simply function as embodying an abstract Kenyan culture. David's attempt at understanding, at any rate, is built on maintenance of his own pride and superiority, of otherness as against "the crowd," and of taking cross-national contacts as sufficient transculturality.

This further explains David's rage in a conversation with a taxi driver in Shenzhen. When the taxi driver asks whether he is from India, he answers that he is from America. When the taxi driver expresses a hatred toward Americans, who "are always fighting.

Iraq, many places. Americans suck" (Ndesandjo 97), David retorts by asserting that "China has a history of more than 4000 years of war" (97). The taxi driver and David may both be speaking from their memory of certain kinds of information that they receive from the media, which is one of the main ways that memory travels and becomes localized, serving ideologically for a political agenda, linking the local dominant discourse and politics in the international arena. A monoculturally unified America and China are imagined, and histories are interpreted with isolation from other histories.

Ndesandjo himself has explained that the experience of his father's propensity to domestic violence made him gravitate toward his mother: he "bonded with her, her values and her culture, Western culture. [...] I love Western culture in many, many ways" (Williams). The conflict between David and the taxi driver shows different interpretations of the past, representing "the related pluralization of the remembered worlds" (Neumann 338), and reinforces the narrator's unreliability. It could thus be read as emphasizing the importance and success of transcultural understanding, which depends on the dissolution of one's own bias and deconstructing essentializing concepts of nationality or ethnicity. As for Ndesandjo, he has confessed "I've experienced the warmth and the graciousness of the Chinese people [...] If we can continue seeing the mutual positive points in these two great cultures, I think it'll be good for the world in general" (Ling Woo Liu).

At the end of the novel, David is dismissed from the school where he is teaching, his favorite student Zhen Rui dies from disease, while Spring refuses to answer his call or meet him again. It is then that the rediscovery of his father's journal offers him an opportunity to rethink and reassess himself. There is the germ of dialogic interaction: the journal "enters the speech that frames it not in a mechanical bond but in a chemical union (on the semantic and emotionally expressive level); the degree of dialogized influence, one on the other, can be enormous" (Bakhtin 340). A double voice thus emerges, for readers who are aware that it is the author who is composing the father's discourse.

Just like the adapted rendering from a Tang poem written by Li Shangyin at the novel's end ("I leave tonight / My life has spun its course / Like silk from dead worms / [...] / The hundreds of flowers / The east wind blows / Into my soul"), transformation and changes in identifications occur through the narrator's discovery of different versions of the past, with different voices, and transcultural understanding through transcultural memory.

Conclusion

As an unreliable narrator, David exposes the ambiguities, contradictions, and discrepancies of his memories and interpretations of the past. He relies on his subjective beliefs and values, and his application of these in a different context, creating tension between the past and the present as well as conflicts between himself and other people. The appearance of his father's journal and his own experience in China and encounters with the Chinese challenge his single perspectivization on the past as well as his interpretation framework of the present, creating a newly signifying and valorizing bridge across the global south. It is these that induce changes and transformations of his approach to identification.

The realization of the challenge and a determination to change at the novel's end signal a degree of hope for transcultural understanding. In what Ndesandjo has called "this globalization of race, culture and religion," traveling memories across time and space serve as initiators and media to enable the forming of transcultural and transnational alliances, while they point to gaps and unfruitful competitions as well as to negotiations and intersections of memories.

References

Anderson, David. *Histories of the Hanged: Britain's Dirty War in Kenya and the End of Empire*. Phoenix/Orion, 2005.

Bakhtin, M. M. *The Dialogic Imagination: Four Essays*. Edited by Michael Holquist, translated by Caryl Emerson and Michael Holquist. U of Texas P, 1981.

Bond, Lucy, and Jessica Rapson. "Introduction." *The Transcultural Turn: Integrating Memory Between and Beyond Borders*, edited by Lucy Bond and Jessica Rapson, Walter de Gruyter, 2014, pp. 1–28.

Brendon, Piers. *The Decline and Fall of the British Empire 1781 – 1997*. Jonathan Cape, 2007.

"Brotherly Love: Obama's Half Brother Searches for Identity." *The Washington Post*, 12 Nov. 2009. Online.

Brown, Judith M., and Wm. Roger Louis, editors. *The Oxford History of the British Empire*, Vol. 4. Oxford UP, 1999.

Crownshaw, Rick. "Introduction: Transcultural Memory." *Transcultural Memory*, edited by Rick Crownshaw, Routledge, 2014.

Erll, Astrid. *Memory in Culture*. Translated by Sara B. Young. Palgrave

Macmillan, 2011.

—. "Traveling Memory." *Parallax*, vol. 17, no. 4, 2011, pp. 4–18.

Hofstede, Geert. *Hofstede Insights*. www.hofstede-insights.com/. Accessed Nov. 2017.

International Institute for Asian Studies, "China's Policy Toward Africa: A Chinese Perspective." *The Newsletter*, 60, Summer 2012 (The Focus: Africa and the Chinese Way), iias.asia/sites/default/files/IIAS_NL60_2627.pdf. Accessed Nov. 2017.

Jacobs, Andrew. "An Obama Relative Living in China Tells of His Own Journey of Self-Discovery." *The New York Times*, 4 Nov. 2009, p. A10.

Ketter, Christopher K., and Michael C. Arfsten. "Cultural Value Dimensions and Ethnicity Within Kenya." *International Business Research*, vol. 8, no. 12, 2015, pp. 69–79.

Lan, Shanshan. "The Shifting Meanings of Race in China: A Case Study of the African Diaspora Communities in Guangzhou." *City & Society*, vol. 28, no. 3, 2016, pp. 298–318.

Levy, Daniel, and Natan Sznaider. "Memory Unbound: The Holocaust and the Formation of Cosmopolitan Memory." *European Journal of Social Theory*, vol. 5, no. 1, 2002, pp. 87–106.

Li, Anshan. "African Diaspora in China: Reality, Research and Reflection." *The Journal of Pan African Studies*, vol. 7, no. 10, May 2015, pp. 10–43.

Ling Woo Liu. "Obama's Half Brother Makes a Name for Himself in China." *Time.com*, 17 Nov. 2009.

Ndesandjo, Mark Obama. *Nairobi to Shenzhen: A Novel of Love in the East*. Aventine, 2009. 2nd ed. 2010.

Neumann, Birgit. "The Literary Representation of Memory." *A Companion to Cultural Memory Studies*, edited by Astrid Erll and Ansgar Nünning, Walter de Gruyter, 2010, pp. 333–44.

Nylan, Michael, and Thomas Wilson. *Lives of Confucius: Civilization's Greatest Sage Through the Ages*. Doubleday, 2010.

Radstone, Susannah. "What Place Is This? Transcultural Memory and the Locations of Memory Studies." *Parallax*, vol. 17, no. 4, 2011, pp. 109–23.

Richburg, Keith B. "Obama's Half Brother Goes Public with New Book." *The Washington Post*, 5 Nov. 2009. Online.

Rothberg, Michael. *Multidirectional Memory: Remembering the Holocaust in the Age of Decolonization*. Stanford UP, 2009.

Saunders, Max. "Life-Writing, Cultural Memory, and Literary Studies." *A Companion to Cultural Memory Studies*, edited by Astrid Erll and Ansgar Nünning, Walter de Gruyter, 2010, pp. 321–32.

"Strategic Dialogue on South Asia Conference Report." International conference organized jointly by CERI-Sciences Po (Paris) and the Brookings Institution (Washington, DC), Paris, 29–30 June 2006, www.brookings.edu/wp-content/uploads/2012/04/20060629.pdf. Accessed Nov. 2017.

Thornber, Karen L. "Breaking Disciplines, Integrating Literature: Africa-China Relationships Reconsidered." *Comparative Literature Studies*, vol. 53, no. 4, 2016, pp. 694–721.

Ting-Toomey, Stella. *Communicating Across Cultures*. Guilford Press, 1999; Shanghai Foreign Language Education Press, 2007.

Ting-Toomey, Stella, and Tenzin Dorjee. *Communicating Across Cultures*.

2nd ed. Guilford Press, 2019.

Welsch, Wolfgang. "Transculturality: The Puzzling Form of Cultures Today."
Spaces of Culture: City, Nation, World, edited by Mike Featherstone and
Scott Lash, Sage, 1999, pp. 194–213.

Williams, Kam. Interview with Mark Obama Ndesandjo. *Pittsburgh Urban
Media*, www.pittsburghurbanmedia.com/PUM-One-on-One-Mark-Obama-
Ndesandjo-The-An-Obamas-Journey-Interview-/. Accessed Nov. 2017.

12

Revaluing the Earth Through the Book-Bound Novel

Inge van de Ven
Tilburg School of Humanities, The Netherlands
Tom van Nuenen
Department of Digital Humanities, King's College London

Summary: The book-bound novel is proving to be a fitting receptacle for imaginative reflections both on the vast un-representability of the globe *and* on the intersections of the U.S. and the rest of the world. We analyze two American novels and their global representations: William T. Vollmann's *The Atla* (1996) and Mark Z. Danielewski's *Only Revolutions* (2006), in the context of Geographic Information System (GIS) and satellite imagery, specifically Google Earth. This service is characteristic of the Western phenomenological experience of space and movement in an age of globalization and digitization. In representing the globe, tensions between objective and subjective perspectives, partiality and totality, bounds and boundlessness, are striking. As cultural phenomena revolve around negotiations and exchanges, the narratives draw attention to relational, perceptual, and experiential factors in assigning cultural values. Vollmann and Danielewski do not attempt to cover up asymmetrical power relations between the U.S. and the rest of the world. Unlike Google's smooth zoom aesthetics, they do not sanitize their worlds of the messiness of our concrete global situation. In reimagining the world as book, they invite the reader to rethink transnational relationality.

Under the influence of conjoined processes of digitalization and globalization, our world seems to be at once smaller and larger than ever. On the one hand, it exceeds every possible representation in its vastness, as one of the most important instances of Kant's mathematical sublime: "That [...] which even to be able to think of demonstrates a faculty of the mind that surpasses every measure of the senses" (§§ 25, 34). Trying to comprehend or imagine its size intuitively, we always become aware of an idea of its totality, which we demand of ourselves but which we can never resolve without resorting to reason. Conversely, there is no outside position from which we can form a satisfactory total representation of the world, because we take part in it; we are *of* this world, even when we observe it from space.

The same world, however, seems to have condensed. Until recently, the idea of traversing its surface implied entering uncharted territory. Now, travel takes place in a world that is comprehensively known and mapped. To the expanding middle classes of the Global North, globalization and mobility have gone hand in hand. The vast decrease of airline travel costs, as well as the increase of car ownership and leisure time, have made post-World-War-II travel increasingly affordable and comfortable. From the 1980s onward, the development and popularization of the Internet have made it possible not only to travel globally, but also to globally spread and receive information. Online-distributed knowledge of the traveled world is continuously being produced by governments, individuals, and of course the tech giants of the 21st century. Accurate, high-resolution digital images of locations, from cities to streets to individual buildings, can be accessed at the touch of a button or screen. In this informational context, the global distribution of American cultural imagery and ideology, existing since the early 1900s under the broad banner of "Americanization," attains new relevance.

The book-bound novel is proving to be a fitting receptacle for imaginative reflections on both the vast un-representability of the globe *and* the intersections of the U.S. and the rest of the world. Thematically, these issues figure prominently in the works of Karen Tei Yamashita, Jonathan Franzen, Roberto Bolaño, and David Mitchell. In rare cases, the material book *itself* becomes a meaningful site for working through such negotiations. In this chapter we analyze two American novels and their global representations: William T. Vollmann's *The Atlas* (1996) and Mark Z. Danielewski's *Only Revolutions* (2006). Both strive to make sense of spatial experiences and scale discrepancies. They do so by incorporating their material properties as book-bound novels in their narratives. They make us experience the book as a space that is self-enclosed and simultaneously exceeds all representations. Shape and texture of book, page, and print all play into this dynamic. In doing so, these authors reinvent the book-bound narrative as a "navigable space" (Manovich, *Language*), bringing narrative or diegesis back to its original Greek meaning of both "guiding" and "transgressing" (De Certeau 129). Both *The Atlas* and *Only Revolutions* spatialize the reading experience.

We are going to analyze these novels in the context of current-day Geographic Information System (GIS) and satellite imagery, specifically Google Earth. This service is characteristic of the Western phenomenological experience of space and movement in an age of globalization and digitization. It fosters for its users an instrumental and frictionless global imagination. Yet, as we will argue, in representing the globe, tensions between objective and subjective perspectives, partiality and totality, bounds and boundlessness, remain striking. We argue that book-bound literature offers a productive lens through which to engage with these frictions, when it exemplifies them formally, thematically, and materially.

Reading Vollmann together with Danielewski will make manifest the novel's potential to comment on global situations in a meaningful way, refuting the conflation between representation and reality that characterizes today's data-informed media culture. Literature can imaginatively construe alternative relations between book and world that allow for critical reflection on our global situation in the digital age. This will give us insight in how analog, book-bound novels are able to comment on and maintain a critical distance from globalization, without denying that they are themselves implied in these processes, and are in fact products of the global imbalances they seek to address.

Google's Earth

As a contrastive framework, we discuss recent visual representations of the globe by a well-known Geographic Information System (GIS). Since 2005, the "Googlization of everything" (Vaidhyanathan) has yielded Google Earth, a "planet-modeling" service that allows users to explore a simulacrum of the Earth, captured by increasingly accurate satellite images, from an elevated viewpoint. We focus on

Google Earth because it allows us to critically assess contemporary practices of representations of the globe — specifically those that harbor implicit promises of total visibility of and mastery over the globe. Systems like Google Earth instantiate a politics of space that, in Michel de Certeau's words, "makes possible a panoptic practice proceeding from a place whence the eye can transform foreign forces into objects that can be observed and measured, and thus control and 'include' them within its scope of vision" (36). These phantasms of panoptic control are part of a broader logic of Western imperialism, here accommodated by the U. S.-based information empire of Google, and they offer a prism through which we can view the themes of Americanization and nationality expressed by Vollmann and Danielewski. As we noted, these literary works exploit their material instantiation to make sense of experiences of being-in-the-world under late globalization — experiences of a radically immanent world.

We ought to start by stating the obvious: phantasms of a "total worldly overview" are inherently unstable. As Fredric Jameson has pointed out, "totality is not available for representation, any more than it is accessible in the form of some ultimate truth (or Absolute Spirit)" (*Political* 39; see also Lyotard, *Postmodern* 25-26). Jameson expresses, in line with Kant, our cognitive failure when confronted with an excessive order of magnitude, the moment that comprehension turns into apprehension: "It is [...] as if the imagination included a sound barrier," he writes in *The Geopolitical Aesthetic*, "undetectable save in those moments in which the representational task or program suddenly collapses" (4). In these moments of collapse, we find that the world is un-representable as a totality: we can only list its parts in a seemingly infinite, yet always incomplete enumeration.

Pointing out the mental incapacity of a total overview may seem trivial, but is quite necessary in the context of the positivist epistemology we find in systems like Google Earth. Even if postmodern theory in cartography established decades ago that maps are always partly subjective and necessarily contain blind spots (MacEachren 10; Wood and Fels 60), new possibilities of mapping the earth through digital media have led to a new ideology of approximating the "real" territory. As Google Earth zooms in on the planet from a supposed distance, the "disembodied master subject" as theorized by Donna Haraway "see[s] everything from nowhere" (189). These representations are thought to be *objective*; they are meant to "simply" be immediate images of reality and, as such, they are taken to reside outside the realm of cultural interpretation. As Mei-po Kwan writes, the problem with GIS as software that gathers empirical data and presents it as factual is that such "scientific objectivity" typically privileges those in power. Enthusiasts of digital implementations of GIS make it seem as follows: firstly, we could measure the world on a scale that somehow lies *outside* that world; secondly, we humans as creators of these representations are not ourselves a part of that which we seek to map; and thirdly, the very measurements and mapping practices do not affect their objects.

Mapping the Unmappable

We ought to note that the acts of collection and ownership of geographical data demand reconsiderations of the parameters of American imperialism — or at least the relations between the U.S. and the rest. Google has started to seem "too big to fail" due to the magnitude of its datasets, and will surely play a role in the representation and navigation of space for millions in the years to come. If we are to agree that these knowledge frameworks are inherently ideological, we need to take note of the ways in which GIS make representational choices. For instance, Google Earth's startup screen virtualizes the analog image of a floating ball in space. This first image of the medium, the view of the Earth floating in space, is discursively connected to the aesthetics of the Apollo 14 photographs and to religious modernism, which is foundational to an imperialist geographical imagination. Google Earth's ancestry is colonial cartography, and its tools of aerial and satellite imagery are grounded in militaristic uses (Farman 882). While earlier iconic representations of this analog image, such as the "Whole-Earth" photographs of the Apollo space missions, were rhetorically employed to remind people of their finitude and dependence upon a fragile ball in space, Google's representations of the earth provide their (mostly Western) users with a sense of power (Farman). They can "fly" over the surface of the earth, and smoothly zoom in and out from the planetary to their own homes, or those of others.

The question, of course, is what kind of knowledge we are talking about here. We can turn here to the concept of "scale variance," a relatively recent field of scholarly attention, which holds that our observations and the operation of systems are subject to different scales. Scale is *beyond measure*. It is not an absolute unit, but a comparative relation: you need two scales to talk about scale at all (Woods 134).① The deceptively friction-less aesthetics of scale with which Google Earth's users are endowed, effectuated by the smooth zoom effect, opposes scale variance. By allowing users to effortlessly move between first- and third-person perspectives, between the world as interface on eye level and as a ball in space, Google Earth smooths and glosses over the incongruences between scales. There is only an apparent homogeneity to the earth in this representation: it is a world overlaid with all kinds of information sourced from other divisions of Google's data-infrastructure, from viewing star systems to real-time traffic monitoring. Media studies scholar Wendy Chun reminds us that interfaces, as mediators between the visible and the invisible and as means of navigation, invest in forming "informed" subjects who can overcome the chaos of global capitalism by mapping their relation to the totality of the global-capitalist system. As she notes, "The dream is: the resurgence of the *seemingly* sovereign individual, the subject driven to know, driven to map, to zoom in and out, to manipulate, and to act" (8).

The nature of such a transformability is explained further in De Certeau's *The Practice of Everyday Life*. The ground-level experience of being immersed in a city and seeing its image from a distance, to De Certeau, are a matter of control versus participation:

> To be lifted to the summit of the World Trade Center is to be lifted out of the city's grasp. One's body is no longer clasped by the streets that turn and return it according to an anonymous law; nor is it possessed, whether as player or played, by the rumble of so many differences and by the nervousness of New York traffic. When one goes up there, he leaves behind the mass that carries off and mixes up in itself any identity of authors or spectators. [...] His elevation transfigures him into a voyeur. It puts him at a distance. It transforms the bewitching world by which one was "possessed" into a text that lies before one's eyes. It allows one to read it, to be a

---

① Scale variance begins to satisfy recent calls by critics such as Dipesh Chakrabarty, Timothy Clark, Ursula Heise, Mark McGurl, Rob Nixon, and others, to think scale in cultural theory. In their texts, scale critique emerges as a means of reflective and analytic response to scale difference and its mediation. In texts concerned with problems of scale, the presence or absence of scale variance makes a crucial difference in the analysis. In "Scale Critique for the Anthropocene," Derek Woods argues that scale variance should therefore be a central concept when it comes to "reworking categories such as history, society, aesthetics, and technology in light of the geo-historical conditions" (133).

solar Eye, looking down like a god. (92)

Viewed from a distance, the city becomes a map that can be read and captured, in its totality. Perceiving the world in this way, the viewer is in a position of power, since she does not risk absorption. Moving at street level, however, the walker is at the city's mercy. Herself part of the creation of this space, she is only able to perceive parts. What retreats beyond the horizon of "Google Earth's earth" is precisely this sense of being-in-the-world that De Certeau describes, including the frictions, the messiness of social life, and the ethics of global relations and transnational concerns. Thus the un-representable, as something that goes beyond the limits of human senses and reason, is brought back to the scales of human perception and cognition, in a movement of what Manovich in 2002 has called the "anti-sublime."

It is worth noting that this panoptic empowerment is not just spatial but also temporal. Since version 5.0 of the software, Google Earth includes Historical Imagery, allowing users to travel back in time and study earlier stages of any place by clicking on the "clock" icon in the toolbar. This opens a time slider, permitting the observation of an area's changes over time. The slider is another frictionless mechanic, a "floating point" system with which the user commands changes in the representation. As Google accumulates more longitudinal data about the world, users will be increasingly able to warp through time as they do through space.

Smooth and effortless as these immaculately designed operations may be, we should take note of their ideological effects. The frictionless relation to time that Google Earth operationalizes produces a form of historical amnesia in its users, for whom the past is reconstructed in suspended animation, completely still and decontextualized. The changes in the urban landscapes that the user sees are completely devoid of history, of any motives or consequences that surround these landscape changes. They are effects without human, social, and cultural causes. The nostalgia incited in the user turning back the hands of time is founded on the proto-American values of renewal, autonomy, and restlessness. The American Dream, Google reminds us, is a rootless one; it needs to eliminate history so that the wayward adventure on the road may begin. Understood as such, Google Earth reads much like an American road novel. It asks us to pioneer, to move beyond all frontiers of both space and time — but it does so without producing the obstructions inherent in both. We can roam endlessly and romantically, untouched by culture, "forever young."

Consequently, Google Earth constitutes something of an anti-chronotope. Mikhail Bakhtin's famous concept, we recall, refers to the intrinsic connectedness of temporal and spatial relationships. Bakhtin notes that space and time can only be explained or measured by referring to each other — we only notice time, after all, because it influences the spatial world, and moving through space, conversely, means moving through time. The chronotope is "a place where the knots of the narrative are tied and untied" (250): specific organizations of space-time determine particular identities or genres that take place in it. Sliding and zooming, the user cuts the knots between space and time as Bakhtin envisioned them, resulting in a landscape without history and culture, and a history devoid of people.

Google Earth's image of the world, in short, "shares with Spaceship Earth something of the quality of a fetish, a shimmering image meant to be consumed, perhaps as an icon of nostalgia for an Earth we may be about to lose" (Helmreich 1219). It offers the viewer the right angles to aesthetically appreciate an otherwise unimaginable object, presenting the world we inhabit as a "distant planet that seems strangely suspended from the chaos of sociality and life" (Munster 46). In short, Google Earth maps the "unmappable" (King), transforming the earth from something of which we are a part to something readable and playable. As such, it also attains the status of a videogame — something that is underscored by specific features of the program. Version 4.2, for instance, introduced the "hidden feature" (currently openly visible) of Flight Simulation mode, which could be accessed by entering the "cheat code" Ctrl, Alt, and A. It allowed users to command one of several aircraft from a cockpit perspective with the keyboard, mouse, or a plugged-in joystick.

These gamified elements are further enhanced in the recently introduced VR version of the software, in which users are immersed in the 3D rendition of Earth, while using controllers to manipulate both the planet and their virtual bodies. They can rotate the globe, turn day into night, fly over the landscape, and so on. Google's earth takes the appearance of a frozen totality when experienced in VR, as its surface is strangely suspended from the chaos of sociality and human lives — a playground to be explored at will and without social or physical restrictions. Yet users who "fly" to their homes may immediately note that their house, street, city, or country looks similar but, uncannily, not the same. This is an effect of Google Earth VR's algorithmic modeling of the terrain: the software not only works with photos and satellite information but also "renders" the world through approximating the 3D models from these images, which can be accessed by zooming in to the point of standing on the earth's surface. This rendering is marked by imperfections: if the user moves too close to the earth, the landscape is transmuted into a patchwork of smudgy textures and frozen polygonal objects; a product of the programmatic attempt to transform satellite images into 3D renditions (the effect can be seen in the actual VR). Even within the partial, ground-level experience on offer, the un-representability of the global landscape becomes immediately evident. The first-hand, phenomenological experiences that users have of the world "fight back" against its algorithmic approximation.

Google's representational project is one in which the main criterion is always accuracy, as bigger and bigger data is injected into each new version of the immersive software. But despite the apprehensive effects that it may produce, it ultimately proves to generate, in its users, Kant's mathematical sublime: where imagination and representation fall short, we take refuge in representation as *calculus*, in engaging with earth through our faculty of reason. Google measures the earth non-intuitively and quantitatively, by means of strictly numerical concepts. It constantly makes demands on the idea of totality — and in Kant's words, we may *apprehend* the world in this way, but it remains beyond the intuitive norm by design, and we can never *comprehend* it.

The Book and the World

The reason why we elaborate on these systems is that both Vollmann's and Danielewski's novels foreground precisely these limits of our experiences of worldliness under the influence of globalization. They do so by using the unique possibilities that the codex offers, precisely because of its delimited form. Both novels can be described as "hybrid": rather than being "merely" illustrative, materiality and visual design are here fully integrated as a structural dimension of the narrative. In novels like these, word and image "breed to produce a new creature" (Sadokierski 3). As Johanna Drucker argues,

> The structural boundedness of the book and the discreteness of the delimited page make the expansions produced by intercutting, insertion, or other means, into significant gestures, inserting tension in the necessarily finite form of the codex; the theoretically infinite extension of an electronic document can't register such

> elements as a meaningful transgression of limits. The space within a
> book can be understood as both literal and conceptual. (99)

Vollmann and Danielewski exploit this capacity of the book to bind
and encapsulate narrative spaces. Their hybrid works employ these
characteristics in a meaningful integration. The shape and texture of
book, page, and print all play into this dynamic.

In a sense, we have chosen atypical works by both these authors
as a focus for this chapter. Both Vollmann and Danielewski are best
known for their centrifugal, excessive works. Danielewski obtained
his status as a cult author with *House of Leaves* (2000), a novel that
attempts to "incorporate all different kinds of discourses, sign
systems, and information into itself, engorging itself in a frenzy of
graphomania" (Hayles 16). In addition, the first, 880-page volume
of his projected 27-part series of novels, *The Familiar*, has just been
published. In these works, the reader's attention span is pushed to
(and perhaps beyond) its limits by writing that fills and overfills the
pages. Vollmann, as one of the most notoriously prolific literary
writers of our time, tops Danielewski's output. Since the publication
of his debut novel in 1987, he has written no less than twenty-four
books (ranging from fiction to journalistic reportage), half of which
are over 600 pages, and the grand total of his output surpasses 10,
000 pages. His editors have repeatedly tried to persuade him to
shorten his work, but the verbose Vollmann will not hear of it:
"They want me to cut, and I argue, so they cut my royalties, and I
agree never to write a long book again" (McGrath). For Vollmann,
refraining from catering to the shortening of attention spans and
readers' entertainment needs is a matter of artistic autonomy.

The book-world trope that Vollmann and Danielewski explore,
it should be made clear, is by no means a postmodern invention. In
fact the ambition to capture the world between the covers of the
book in general, or the novel in particular, has been persistent
throughout the history of literature. The idea of the book-as-world
has known many forms: from Bakhtin's conceptualization of the
novel as containing, like the societal world, numerous voices or
"heteroglossia" (1981) to Blanchot's *Le livre à venir* (1959); from
Mallarmé's famous insistence that "everything in the world exists to
end up in a book" (qtd. in Arnar 312) to Joyce's *Ulysses* as "book as
world" (French) and the attempts of Goethe scholars to create the
"Book of Everything" (Piper); and from Vargas Llosa's *novela
totalizadora* (Brody) to Elizabeth Eisenstein's historical account of
early print technology and the vision of the book usurping all media,

Hans Blumenberg's *Die Lesbarkeit der Welt* and of course Borges, for instance in his "Library of Babel" (1941). And the idea can be traced further back to St. Augustine and to Shakespeare's "all the world's a stage" from *As You Like It*. The age-old dream of "fitting the whole world inside the single text" (Portelli 100) is pervasive.

Yet, our objects of research for this chapter constitute special cases of the book-as-world trope, as they use the material form of the book to express it. Exploiting the bound nature of the book-object and the spatial delineation of the page, in *The Atlas* and *Only Revolutions* the authors do something else besides "building the novel to scale" (Pressman, "Big Novels"). They exploit the medium-specific features of the codex such as boundedness, finitude, linearity, and three-dimensionality, in order to transmit a sense of enclosure which we experience as the world becomes global. In *The Atlas* and *Only Revolutions*, the book object formally enacts an experience from which the protagonists suffer, and which we denote as a lack of a "beyond" or an "outside." As we will demonstrate, the main characters are curiously aware of being contained in the material form of the book. Conceptually, this being-enclosed relates to the constraints the characters face in trying to attain a totalizing perspective of the world. Michael Hardt and Antonio Negri have diagnosed this situation in terms of a collapse of the (spatial and conceptual) division of the world into an "inside" and an "outside" domain: "In the passage from modern to postmodern and from imperialism to Empire there is progressively less distinction between inside and outside" (187). We argue that both novels use the enclosed space of the book to situate characters in, and thus reflect on, this late-global predicament.②

They compose their narratives according to an approach we might call "scale variance," an awareness that the realities they represent change according to the distance or proximity of the observer. As a narrative strategy, scale variance centers on the idea that the realities these novels represent change according to the distance or proximity they take in relation to these realities. There is a continuous mutual impingement at work in these novels between the local and the global. While gesturing toward the global in their

---

② The phase of late globalization that we are generally thought to inhabit was inaugurated with the fall of the Berlin Wall in 1989. Late (or: "hypernetworked" or "strong" globalization), according to Christian Moraru, is characterized by a "geographical structure of co-presence" and an emphasis on worldly being-in-relation (34).

scope, both novels overtly implicate themselves in American traditions of literature and myth making of which they are critical, but which they do not pretend to transcend. Especially in Vollmann's case, we will see that this also has problematic dimensions of reiterating long-standing American archetypes like the lone cowboy who "collects" women in the towns he visits, but always leaves behind. Both create literary worlds that maintain a referential relation to the horizons of our concrete world, yet do not attempt to cover up asymmetrical power relations between the U.S. and the rest of the world.

Trapped Inside the Atlas: Vollmann's Journey to the Covers of the Earth

Born in 1959, Vollmann is an artist of the 1980s and 1990s, who witnessed the emergence of a radically globalized world. His way of moving in the world is quite literally errant or digressive. He traverses the globe for his journalistic work and out of personal interests, chasing a promise of alterity that always recedes. These quests of the author-witness are doomed from the beginning. In a world without a "beyond" or outside position, the interminable project of traveling and collecting leads to a search that cannot be completed. Despite perpetuating problematic Romantic notions like these, his novel *The Atlas* offers new insights into the relevance of world-making in a global, digitized world. This novel is informative precisely where it fails. Vollmann's narrator cannot shake off his male, American perspective on what he encounters, and thus fails to register anything objectively. His oeuvre is a meditation on the impossibility of objectively "recording" a global situation, and, as such, it points to the illusory nature of "mastery," even or rather especially for the white American male.

    The Atlas is a blueprint of almost all the themes and motives (flight, travel, escapism, moral digression, transgression, sex, violence) of his other, longer novels, as well as their aesthetic structures and preoccupation with the visual-material aspects of the book. The novel engages with these themes in the relatively compressed space of 455 pages, which makes it a short-read by Vollmann's standards. At the same time, it is the most explicitly "global" in scope of all his works. *The Atlas* is a collection of numerous fragments that record an American traveler's experiences all over the world — Bosnia-Herzegovina, Mexico, the U.S., Thailand,

Australia, Cambodia, etc. Like pages in a real atlas, the novel includes a Gazetteer (*Atlas* xvii–xxii) which gives us the exact coordinates of these places on the earth's surface, such as "Resolute Bay, Cornwallis Island, Northwest Territories, Canada 74.40 N, 95.00 W" and "Paris, Département Paris, Région Parisienne, France 48.52 N, 2.20 E."

The global scope of *The Atlas* is inscribed within the limited material space of the book-bound novel and, thereby, manifests itself in the form of the fragment. As Stefano Ercolino argues, the form of the fragment "is the only textual system possible for a literature of global aspirations; the only textual system possible for a novel that dares to challenge the complexity of the world" (56). In a "Compiler's Note" (*Atlas* xv–xi), Vollmann reveals that his specific use of fragments in the novel was inspired by the "palm-of-the-hand stories" of the Japanese writer Yasunari Kawabata, whose novel *Snow Country* (1935–1947) likewise consists of a collection of extremely compressed miniature vignettes. In *The Atlas*, as in most of Vollmann's works, the structure of the text is an indispensable element of the meaning of the work. Therefore, it is necessary to first examine its unique composition.

An Atlas of Cultural Values

After a section titled "Opening the Book" follow twenty-six numbered chapters. At the center of the novel is a novella called "The Atlas" and, after this, another twenty-six chapters follow. This time, the chapters are numbered backwards from 26 to 1. The novel's structure is symmetrical, revolving around the spine's rotational axis, an axis of convergence for both the narrative structure and the materiality of the book. Thematically and structurally, the collection of stories is arranged like a palindrome: "the motif in the first story is taken up again in the last; the second story finds its echo in the second to last, and so on" (*Atlas* xvi). Vollmann emphasizes the presentation of his travels as an inherently regressive way of traversing the globe, as suggested by the Greek root of "palindrome," meaning *recurring* or "running back again." In the palindromic structure of *The Atlas*, the absence of beginning or end determines the form of the novel as a whole. Rather than the "arrow-like" form of nomad travels set on discovery, conquest, or territorial expansion (as exemplified by Robinson Crusoe or Columbus), Vollmann's travels have the character of a "voyage," like *The Odyssey*: a journey of return and homecoming (Glissant 12). The narrator's voyage is bound to lead him back home again, which detracts from the usual "objective" status of the atlas as a representation of the world.

The itinerary of Vollmann's narrator (or alter ego) is without apparent logic, and its order non-chronological. The journeys reflect a movement of ceaseless meandering without destination. This way of moving through the world resembles the pacing back and fro that one typically tends to do in a prison-cell or waiting room. The novel's text, like the voyage it depicts, is not linear. It is not meant to be read all the way through. Vollmann encourages his reader to "keep [the book] by you as a pillow-book, reading through it in no particular order, skipping the tales you find tedious" (*Atlas* xv). Thus, a digressive way of reading is promoted to match both Vollmann's unsystematic manner of traversing the planet and the skips and breaks of his narration. In the tradition of tabular texts such as Georges Perec's *Life: A User's Manual* (1978) and Vladimir Nabokov's *Pale Fire* (1962), *The Atlas* spatializes information.

The book opens on a title page with an inserted pictorial representation of the globe, while the pivotal chapter depicts maps of the globe as projected from the North and South Poles (*Atlas* 266), showing both ends of the earth's rotation axis. In the front matter are printed reproductions of plates from an old-fashioned atlas depicting Eastern and Western hemispheres and North and South Poles. These images are intentionally distorted in such a way as to resemble the hemispheres of the human brain. In this respect, they reinforce the palindromic form in their mutual attachment, as well as underline the issue of scale. Moreover, these distorted hemispheres form a closed system without a shared "outside," suggesting it is as impossible to move outside one's own brain as it is to step outside the atlas. In the tradition of tabular texts such as Perec's *Life: A User's Manual* and Nabokov's *Pale Fire*, *The Atlas* spatializes information (see Vandendorpe 22–27). Aptly, Vollmann informs the reader that "[w]hat you hold [...] is but a piecemeal atlas of the world I think in" (*Atlas* xv). These words, combined with the distorted, brain-shaped images of hemispheres, are suggestive of the idiosyncratic nature and deformations inherent to Vollmann's and, by extension, to all acts of mapping. Displaying an awareness of these considerations in its paratext, Vollmann's novel, while emulating the atlas (the all-encompassing form par excellence), subverts its claims to "total representation" in its very form. From the beginning it is clear that this textual object is emphatically *Vollmann's* atlas.

During these travels, the narrator visits typically masculine settings like warzones, brothels, bars, boxing rings, and prisons. His travels are motivated by a wish to "capture" all that is different and exotic (a desire that aligns him with American expansionist traditions). His oeuvre is marked by a compulsion to witness and register "everything."③ To this end he collects and archives the stories of those he encounters. In *The Atlas*, he tells of those who suffer under colonialism and globalization: women sold in Kenya, war victims in Cambodia, colonized peoples in Australia and the Americas. He reports bullfights, violence, and his visits to prostitutes. The travels are seemingly endless because of the narrator's continuous departures: "He wanted to see the world, that was all. He wanted to know and love the entire atlas" (224). "Comprehension" of the globe in an all-encompassing representation, however, is impossible. The world manifests itself as excess to representation, escaping "all horizons of calculability (in opposition to the logic of economic and technologic globalization)" (Raffoul and Pettigrew 8). Unable to trace an orb around the globe, Vollmann applies the principle of *addition*, thus creating his own world as a process in expansion. Rather than encompass the globe with his atlas, he traverses it and makes a list of what he encounters that borders on the infinite.

But most of all, he "collects" the female objects of his affection④ and chronicles his experiences with women around the globe. He

---

③ This need to witness all is evidenced by Vollmann's obsession with documentation. He offers extensive appendices of endnotes and sources, underlining the author's idea of the writer as "a recording instrument" (*Rainbow* 3) and his wish to "bear FULL witness" (*Crabbed*) to his subject. As Tom LeClair writes, "[w]ith brutal efficiency we are shown what underwrites [Vollmann's] pathological concern with ocular proof, his need to see everything with his own eyes, however impractical or impracticable it may be for him to do it" (1996). The extraordinary volume of Vollmann's oeuvre is a direct consequence of this self-imposed mission to bear witness.

④ LeClair, in his review of *The Atlas*, causally links this practice of "collecting" women all over the world to Vollmann's youth trauma, "all his 'girls' substituting for his dead sister" (74). And indeed, this connection is at least hinted at in *The Atlas*: "He showed me a binder comprising color glossies of Chinese prostitutes, each woman smiling beside a shiny red car, each glossy professionally mounted onto ivory cardboard. I looked at every page, but my sister was not there [...] I realized that everything I had done was for nothing, that no matter how many young girls I saved I could never undo or appease" (107–08).

repeatedly attempts to "save" these women. This is literally the case in the chapter "No Reason to Cry," where he gives a fictionalized account of his (real-life) experience of rescuing a child prostitute in Thailand. In a larger, more figurative sense, this problematic wish to record the female other is a consistent drive behind Vollmann's writing. He does not compress and amalgamate these women he encounters during his travels. In his Atlas, there's room for all: "could there be any whose recollection he'd ever fail to praise? Their tears and reproaches, silences, farewells, laughter and whispered words were marked on the atlas pages like nations" (*Atlas* 245–46).

The Romantic ideal of capturing otherness manifests itself in *The Atlas* as an ideology of expansion and the nostalgia of open space:

> In pioneer days it must have been that way and more, a man and a woman travelling on together, helping one another, needing each other, not knowing whether they'd make it. These days there seemed no penalty for not being sure. The atlas opened, easy pages lay ahead. (248–49)

The narrator deplores how easy and risk-free it has become to traverse the globe, since it diminishes the sense of adventure in traveling. The center-story that carries the same name as the novel most clearly describes such a fantasy of open space. After having traveled through Pnom Penh and Sarajevo, characterized by conflict and complex, messy human relations, Vollmann's narrator expects to find uncharted territory in the Arctic region, which is described as a space of potentiality: "I seemed to see nothing but solidified space without a predicate. It was a blank space of all possibilities, not excluding loveliness and terror" (237). Vollmann envisions this region as an opportunity to vanish from the face of the earth: "he too would disappear. He was going to travel to the world's edge (which lies in Canada), and he was happy" (207). He arrives at Ellesmere Island in what used to be Canada's Northwest Territories, but is now Nunavut. Significantly, this place is at the farthest Northern point of Canada, close to the magnetic North Pole. The narrator has arrived at the territory depicted on the aforementioned maps printed at the axis of the book. He has finally traversed the globe and reached the limit of the world.

This journey to the limits, however, does not grant the expected transgression, let alone the transcendence that Vollmann seeks. The narrator longs for the landscape as described in Kawabata's *Snow Country*. In this novel, which inspired *The Atlas*, a setting of seemingly infinite snowy plains signals "the end of this world and the beginning of another, the country of pure mountains of sunset crystal which all tunnels are supposed to lead to, the zone of that uncanny whiteness hymned by Poe and Melville, the pole of transcendence" (251). Undifferentiated, lacking contours or markers, Kawabata's blinding white landscape offers a suggestion of the Burkean "artificial infinity" that "impress[es] the imagination with an idea of their progress beyond [its] actual limits" (Burke II, IX, 68). Such an experience, however, has become unattainable in a global world. Even this illusion of the infinite has vanished from Vollmann's globe: "He gazed at Fuji's dull snow far above so many dull white apartments and could not see any beauty" (*Atlas* 251). To his detriment, the once-open plains of Kawabata's sublime snow country are now the site of so many white apartment buildings. Significantly, the sublime experience sought after is not a first-hand memory or knowledge but is mediated by Kawabata's book. One could even wonder whether this mourning of transcendence is indeed typical of late globalization, or if it is not in fact a much older sensibility. It manifests itself as a romantic longing par excellence, which was never meant to be fulfilled.

With this disappointment, Vollmann's alter ego loses faith in the ability to reach new grounds and find unexplored spaces: "Everywhere he went, he'd say to himself: there's nothing for me here anymore. No more nowhere nobody" — having "used up every place now" (202). He realizes that only death would allow him an escape from the all-encompassing Atlas. The poetic wish to exit the grid results in an all-too-real (though blatantly romanticized) near-death experience from freezing.⑤ Leaving this world can only mean no longer being in any world: it is to stop existing.

Vollmann imagines this ultimate alterity, which harbors a last possibility of escape through transcendence for his narrator (a possibility that never materializes), in the form of a woman. Thus in "The Atlas," he configures the icy landscape as the Native American Willow Lady:

---

⑤ While researching *The Rifles*, the sixth volume in the *Seven Dreams* series, which concerns John Franklin's doomed quest to find the Northwest Passage, Vollmann (on assignment from *Esquire*) spent two weeks at an abandoned weather station at the magnetic North Pole and almost froze to death. In the novel he describes the extreme weather and hallucinations he experienced due to lack of sleep and proper food: "Every night now he wondered if he would live until morning" (320).

> The atlas closed. Inside, each page became progressively more
> white and warm. Willow Lady rolled on top of him and took him in
> her arms. She rocked him to sleep. No more nowhere nobody. [...]
> He lay at the center from which the world rotated round and round
> and round. (265)

Such identifications of (open) space as female, with the problematic
ideologies of subjugation and objectification that come with them,
are often seen as typical for U.S. discourse. The idea of geographical
space as "wild, untamed, virgin, needing mastery and manifest
destiny to guide it" is central to popular imaginings of the American
West (Flanagan 77). Here, the Lady is a blank canvas on which the
narrator can project expansionary fantasies. We can understand
Vollmann's female personifications of spaces, landscapes, and
nations throughout his oeuvre as part of both this American tradition
of imperialism and the aforementioned nineteenth-century gender
essentialism.

Vollmann's work becomes informative where his expansionist
quests in these spaces invariably fail. The relations between people in
remote parts of the world remain fragmentary, and the Romantic
unity that Vollmann seeks is unattainable. Otherness, in the final
analysis, cannot be contained. In what follows, we show how the author
employs the spatialized metaphor of the atlas as a commodified
world to bring across the illusory sense of true mastery over the
world and the "objects" he collects. Indeed, he is as much contained
by the world-as-book as these objects are. Vollmann performs the
failure of mastery and control through writing and map making. He
does so by inscribing himself in certain long-standing traditions of
representation that are typically "American."

The Archetypical American Abroad

The conception of the atlas that Vollmann hints at in quotations like
the one reproduced above ("easy pages lay ahead," *Atlas* 294) is a
familiar representation of the world reduced to a portable object. We
can open it on any page we want to, we can hover above and beyond
it. This partial, biased perspective of the atlas is to an important
extent a national perspective. Vollmann's atlas emphatically inscribes
an American outlook on the world and a set of values, a point of
view he cannot escape. This can be deduced from the beginning and
end of the novel. The geographic parameters of the journey are

clearly inscribed within the material space of the book. These are reinforced by one of the major structural features of the codex: finitude. The opening section, "Opening the Book," is set at Grand Central Station, New York City. The closing section, called "Closing the Book," is set at another train station in Sacramento, California (Vollmann's hometown).

As a framing device, these sections indicate a movement from the east to the west coast, which is the traditional route of colonists associated with the American Manifest Destiny. It is the route of expansion, imperialism, and the search for freedom. This pilgrimage embodied the physical and spiritual movement from the limiting culture of the East (of Europe and the "Old World") to the future: the vast, open plains of the frontier — "The east of my youth and the west of my future," as Dean Moriarty says in Kerouac's *On the Road* (15).[6]

Choosing these specific locations to frame his cosmopolitan journeys, Vollmann makes a gesture of implicating himself in this tradition. The myth of the frontier revolves around the desire to escape physical and psychological limitations. Clearly, Vollmann's going "on the road" is likewise motivated by a wish to be free from, and unrestrained by, societal norms.[7] At the same time, this gesture is subverted from the beginning, precisely because his journeys are "bound" between these parameters, emphasizing the unmistakably American character of his quest. This framing foreshadows the incapacity, reflected in his narration, to shake off the U.S.-centered nature of his experiences all over the globe. This local yet mobile point of view already puts the possibility of "mastering" the globe — through travel *or* through writing — into question.

Moreover, *The Atlas* imaginatively conveys the aforementioned insights on the subject of mapping by portraying the subjectivity of

---

[6] The symbolic movement to the West also serves as the background to the journey of the Joad family in Steinbeck's *The Grapes of Wrath* (1939). To mention one more example, Mark Twain's *Roughing It* in 1872 describes the "gold rush" and the wild, lawless society that was founded in its wake.

[7] Vollmann is known for his exasperation with overly restraining social norms. In an interview he exclaims: "Everything that my grandfather used to do for fun is now illegal. People are now discouraged from doing everything my father used to do. We're ruled by safety nazis [*sic*] and safety monkeys. How nice it is to briefly escape them and to have the illusion of a little personal freedom" (Seaman). In his book about hopping freight trains, *Riding Toward Everywhere* (2008), the author repeatedly expresses his longing to live in a less limiting time and place, as denoted by the totalizing "everywhere" of the title.

the traveler-cartographer as emergent *in* this world in relation to actual geographical others, and depicting how this figure is himself "othered." As Michelle Hardesty notes in reference to *An Afghanistan Picture Show* (1992), Vollmann's self-representations (here, by way of his narrator) are "invested in the symbol and myth of the American character, and especially the American character abroad" (101). Parodically modeled after the characters of Mark Twain and Ernest Hemingway, the author-characters in Vollmann's oeuvre take on an allegorical significance, making their achievements and stupidities resonate with those of their nation. Unlike these more iconic representations of American masculinity, however, the stupidities of Vollmann's protagonists by far outnumber their achievements. The emphasis, as Hardesty writes, lies on failure: "Vollmann's narrator is the prototypical American abroad as a well-intentioned failure, a character that resonates with the contemporary imagination of U.S. foreign relations" (104).

This persona enables Vollmann to write about his encounters with geographical others without glossing over or de-emphasizing the ongoing, asymmetrical global power relations that his writing perpetuates and to which it contributes. Instead of "Disneyfying" global relations (Damrosch 10), he foregrounds this problematic aspect of his world-making. Everywhere he goes, he meets numerous actual, concrete others. As Gargi Bhattacharyya writes, the performance of ethnicity is always a kind of ethical display, if we take the ethical to be a statement of intent about our relations to others. She calls this "ethics as part of the lived contract of belonging" (3). In Canada's Northwest Territories, Vollmann's narrator joins native hunters who are hunting after walrus, and is faced with a hostile attitude: "The boy who hated white people sat sullenly with his back turned toward me. [...] I was only allowed along because I had paid three hundred dollars" (*Atlas* 23). At other times, these others look at him and see the possibility of earning money: "Looking up at his giant blinking eye, little girls in red and yellow garbashars stood and tried to sell him packs of cigarettes" (152). Trapped inside the atlas, he is an object of gazes that convey feelings of resentment and hopes of financial benefit.

The narrator meticulously keeps track of the amount of dollars he pays prostitutes for their stories ("'baht': about US $40 in 1993. About what an all-night girl might expect to receive" [393]). In their acknowledgement of the transaction as the story's condition of possibility, these fragments draw attention to the intersection of two meanings of the term "account." As Peter Brooks has pointed out, in "account" the narrative and the financial collide. In the life of a prostitute, especially, "the accounting gives something to recount, money and story flow from the same nights of sexual exchange" (163). Although the narrator of *The Atlas* hungers after a connection with others, all his relations to global others are mediated by money. Sometimes this is literally the case: "As long as he could keep dancing with her (and paying to dance), she'd still be his" (*Atlas* 85). Other times, this inequality is caused by the fact that his money gives him the freedom to leave whenever he wants, whereas the natives do not have this choice: "My guilt about being free to leave has built a silence over time that drowned what she actually said" (11). Paradoxically, the globalized world in its "openness" is a prison for him, causing loneliness, isolation, and exclusion.

The Atlas thus offers a meditation on the type of ethical relationship that Brown calls "horizontal ethics," of border-crossing and encountering the geographic other (53). Unlike Google Street View, which is marked by an "asymmetry of the gaze" (Vaidhyanathan 103),⑧ these others are able to *return* his gaze, and to respond in their own ways to the masculine subjectivity of this well-meaning "ugly American." Gilles Deleuze and Claire Parnet have asked: "In fleeing everything, how can we avoid reconstituting both our country of origin and our formations of power, our intoxicants, our psychoanalyses and our mummies and daddies?" (38). Vollmann's narrator would answer that this is impossible. He cannot shake off his outward "white American-ness" any more than he can transcend his limited, Western perspective on the globe. These aspects of his subjectivity shape his encounters with others in a profound way. This reminds us that cultural phenomena are not static: on the contrary, they revolve around negotiations and exchanges (Aukrust). These stories draw attention to the relational, perceptual, and experiential factors in assigning cultural values. The American subjectivity that emanates from these fragments is not a free, autonomous individual, but only an effect of frictions and asymmetrical (economic) relations with others in different parts of the world. He is "on the move" precisely

---

⑧   This asymmetry, Vaidhyanathan argues in *The Googlization of Everything*, is the main problem with Google Street View: "A person walking down the street peering into residents' yards would be watched right back by offended residents, who would consider calling the police to report such dangerous and antisocial behavior. But with Google Street View, the residents can't see or know who is peeping" (103)

because the political and economic influence of the U.S. is global, thus cannot be escaped.

Ironically, an important part of the American Dream lies in rebirth through traveling, the idea that one can simply hit the road, shake off the past, and become whoever one wants to be (see Fiedler 23–38). Deleuze and Parnet see the corresponding rootlessness of Anglo-American literature as one of its assets (and in fact the source of its superiority over, for instance, French literature):

> One only discovers worlds through a long, broken flight. In [American literature] everything is departure, becoming, passage, leap, daemon, relationship with the outside. [...] American literature operates according to geographical lines: the flight towards the West, the discovery that the true East is in the West, the sense of the frontiers as something to cross, to push back, to go beyond. The becoming is geographical. (36–37)

The Atlas nuances this idea of rootlessness and the related connotations of freedom and autonomy attached to the cultural identity of the American. Whereas Vollmann's wealth and inborn restlessness allow him to expand his geographical horizon, at the same time it is precisely his "Americanness" that prevents him from re-writing himself. The reader soon realizes that the atlas is gaining mastery over its owner, the traveling narrator, instead of the other way around. Far from any position of control, Vollmann's wandering narrator is trapped inside the atlas.

This entrapment inside the atlas is not "just" a metaphor: Vollmann's alter ego at several points reveals an awareness of the material book that contains him and beyond which he cannot move. The narrator's predicament of being caught inside the book is literalized in a chapter called "Inside and Outside," which allegorizes the mechanisms of power and inequality that underlie the production of this monumental collection on a global scope. In a bookstore, a male customer is leafing through the pages of "a thirty-eight color picture book printed on paper as smooth as a virgin's thigh" (*Atlas* 394) when outside a fight breaks out. A male panhandler smashes his female adversary through the bookstore window. Here, boundaries are crossed: it is the violent outside world intruding on the seemingly innocent inner world of books. The customer, trying to help the woman, "opened his book and invited her in [...] Spangles of blood struck the pages like a mystery rain, becoming words which had never existed before" (395). Her blood transgresses the boundaries of the book in yet another collapse of distinctions between outside and inside. The male character, with the best of intentions, tries to save the oppressed female other by "collecting" her in his book, precisely as Vollmann does in his writing. This gesture, of course, has the disastrous side-effect of objectifying her and limiting her freedom.⑨ By literalizing this process of objectification, "Inside and Outside" describes a problematic dimension of *The Atlas*, and indeed of Vollmann's oeuvre as a whole. In archiving the stories of the marginalized, informed by the author's mission of "saving" his sister by witnessing and recording "everything," his oeuvre quite literally objectifies the other. The story makes this ideological underpinning explicit. For all Vollmann's good intentions, he perpetuates existing power imbalances through his writing.

And yet, it is possible to derive from this novel a corrective to the anti-chronotopical control on which Google Earth is fixated. After all, Vollmann's narrator is by no means in a position of control or mastery over his objects of representation — because he himself is just as much part of his atlas. As we have seen, the traveler-character himself does not maintain a position outside of the book. He, too, is encapsulated in the world-as-book, and is aware of this predicament:

> Where is the book you put me in? asked the woman. This is the atlas, he said. This is the book. — And he bent down and touched the pavement. He knew that everything was set upon a single page. Open the book, she said weakly. It's open already. Where am I, then? Am I inside or outside? I don't know, he murmured, suddenly resentful. I don't know where I am anymore, either. I lost my freedom because of you. (399)

This book-space does not allow him the safety of the unobserved gaze. Instead of hovering above the book as a prototypical mapmaker,

---

⑨ In an alternative poststructural interpretation, objectifying the woman character by catching/saving her in a book, limiting her freedom, could perhaps be read differently: if whatever is absorbed in text becomes an element in a potentially endless play of signifiers without beginning or end, the narrativized character would lose the limitations of being a bounded individual, thus being opened to textual contiguity and to a wide semiotic network. That would require an examination of the work's understanding of its textuality, and whether it is consistently maintained. We are at present writing about book materiality, however, with the problematics of objectifying the other through writing, and this allows a fairly comprehensive analysis of the fictional structure.

he is caught in an intermediate space in which both he and the woman are recorded in, and by, the material atlas. Thus Vollmann uses the form of the book as a tabular and "navigable" narrative space and material carrier to unmask as illusory the ideal of a position of overview and of objective representation of the world. Such a conceptualization of narrative space, which refers back to the epic as well as brings to mind adventurous computer games of the present (Manovich, *Language* 244 – 72), is taken further in Danielewski's *Only Revolutions*, to which we now turn.

Around the World in 360 Pages: Danielewski's Revolutions

Like *The Atlas*, Danielewski's *Only Revolutions* covers an exceptionally large territory, while at the same time problematizing notions of "mastery" and resisting the idea of the novel (and the self) as a perfectly self-enclosed form. We argue that the book achieves this in large part through its formal-material aspect, as a textual system that is at once complete in itself and open to the world.

Only Revolutions tells the story of Sam and Hailey through chiasmically juxtaposed stream-of-consciousness monologues. After falling in love at first sight, these perpetual sixteen-year-olds embark upon a road trip through time and space, across the U.S. and its history. The characters flee from their separated and isolated worlds by creating a shared world through endless narration, seeking freedom and transcendence in their romantic unification: the book's subtitle reads "The Democracy of Two, Set Out & Chronologically Arranged." These monologues are narrated from opposite ends of the text.⑩

Through this unusual composition of the page, Danielewski foregrounds the three-dimensionality of the book as meaningful and even indispensable to the narrative. The author has claimed that, with this experimental novel, he wanted to create a book that cannot exist online, to investigate what books do that digital media cannot do: "I think that's the bar that the Internet is driving towards: how to further emphasize what is different and exceptional about books" (qtd. in Cottrell). As a starting point, we describe the complex spatial architecture of this novel.

---

⑩ References to the text will henceforth start with "H" or "S" followed by a page number, to indicate the narrator of the particular citation.

In *Only Revolutions*, everything runs in circles. The signs 8 and II (8 pages, 2 characters), as well as their tilted variants ∞ and = (infinity and equality), recur throughout the book. The first letters of every eighth page together form an infinite loop that goes "... Sam and Hailey and Sam and Hailey...". The book consists of 360 pages, each of which contains 360 words; [1] the page numbers are enclosed in circles that revolve if you flip the pages. This circular structure also comes back in the bodily gestures of reading. In *Only Revolutions*, each half of the story is narrated in portions of eight pages. The reader has to decide on which end to begin, and to turn the book over and around periodically for the narrative to unfold. Alternatively, she can choose to read one narrative in a linear fashion, all the way to the end, and then go on with the beginning of the other one. It is recommended to handle the book like a steering wheel, turning the stories together. In this respect, *Only Revolutions* is an instance of what Espen Aarseth has called "ergodic literature," which requires an effort on the reader's part to traverse the text. In this case, the reader needs to handle the novel to weave a story out of it, to experience the unfolding of the narrative. Aptly, the ancient Greek word *kybernetikos*, which refers to the art of steering, forms the etymological basis for "cybernetics." Thus, Manovich writes, the notion of "navigable space" lies at the origin of the computer era (*Language* 7). As a text that needs to be bodily navigated and traversed, *Only Revolutions* is certainly linked to these developments. As Jessica Pressmann analyzes *Only Revolutions'* unique narrative and navigable space:

---

[1] With its omnipresent circles and the exact number of 360 words on each page, *Only Revolutions* partakes in a tradition of writing under constraint, of which the experiments of the Oulipo movement (*Ouvroir de littérature potentielle*) are famous instances. This was a collective of writers and mathematicians (notably, Georges Perec and Italo Calvino) founded in 1960 by Raymond Queneau and François Le Lionnais, who experimented with the construction of new patterns and structures for literature through severe, self-imposed constraints. The group constructed texts according to lipograms and palindromes, and developed textual methods based on mathematical problems, such as the "knight's tour" of the chessboard. Queneau's *Cent Mille Milliards de Poèmes*, to give just one example, is inspired by picture books for children with each page cut into horizontal strips that the reader can turn around independently, allowing varied combinations of picture. Queneau's book contains ten sonnets, each on a page that is split into 14 strips, one per line. The author estimated it would take a reader approximately 200 million years to read all possible combinations. With its exact number of 360 words per page and 360 pages per protagonist, *Only Revolutions* can be said to build on this tradition.

> The intricate page-design produces a constantly shifting perspective
> that mirrors the movement of Sam and Hailey as they cross the
> terrain of the United States. Moving through the pages of this book is
> like moving through a physical landscape, and the effect draws
> attention to the work's mediality. (*Digital* 160)

Following from its configuration, reading the book necessitates a
material 360° revolution of the object.

Through all these circles on different scales, Danielewski obviously
repudiates the linearity of the conventional novel. The end of Sam's
story implies the beginning of Hailey's story (in 1963), whose end
(in 2063) in turn implies a return to the beginning of Sam's (in
1863). This lends the narrative the form of a Möbius strip, a story
loop with an impossible twist: both versions end with the death of
the other character. The final pages of each half (*Only* 359–60)
prompt us to start over at the other end, so the reading, like the
Möbius strip, has no logical ending. By adopting this form, *Only
Revolutions* enacts the distinctive circular structure of the modern
road narrative, where "[t]ime spent means ground covered" (Ganser
et al. 3), but where, in the end, one often finds oneself back at the
beginning. This circular quality, conventionally working at the story
level of the road novel, here comprises the entire material composition of
the text: the reading is structured by the sensory space in which the
text is inscribed. The circle, like Vollmann's palindrome, forebodes
the *inevitability of return*.⑫ Sam's and Hailey's movements across
the world, like those of Vollmann's narrator, are regressive, always
"running back again." By giving his novel the structure of a Möbius
strip, Danielewski has found another, yet more radical way of
(provisionally) overcoming not only the linearity of prose narrative,
but also the spatial finitude of the codex.⑬

---

⑫ This is already reflected in the characters' opening words: "Samsara!" connotes
    not only drifting or migration, but also reincarnation and transmigration, and
    "Haloes! Haleskarth!" besides transcendence and disembodiment promises
    circularity and recurrence, as Philip Leonard suggests (156).

⑬ As an interminable structure, circularity is even more efficient than digression.
    Hence in "The Garden of Forking Paths," before Jorge Luis Borges' scholar
    discovers the principle of Ts'ui Pen's bifurcating novel he imagines infinite
    textuality as cyclical, a volume whose last pages are the same as the first (97).
    James Joyce's *Finnegans Wake* (1939) is such a text, whose unfinished
    sentence on its last page resumes on its first page, and which therefore
    continues indefinitely. Other variants on this structure include Julio Cortázar's
    Hopscotch (1963/66) and John Barth's minimalist Möbius narrative "Frame-
    Tale" from *Lost in the Funhouse*: "Once upon a time there was a (next page)

This sensory space of the book is foregrounded as a three-dimensional, chiasmic space. Everything that happens is mirrored on the other side, as the narratives gradually and literally get closer to each other until they meet and unite — only to be separated again. The middle pages (*Only* 180–81) function as the axis of symmetry around which all these mirrors revolve. Here, the two monologues become identical, rendering a state of perfect balance between Sam and Hailey, after which they move further apart again. For each page, there are three counterpoints with corresponding lines: for instance Hailey's first page (H1) is counterpointed with the symmetric page in her own narrative (H360), the same page in Sam's narrative (S1), and the symmetric page in Sam's narrative (S360, printed upside down on the same page). This makes the book into a chiasmic space, a space constituted by mirrors and parallels. The chiasm, as Lyotard explains,

> introduces in the course of the text a depth that is not of pure signification, but that conceals and signals a kind of excess of meaning. The figure of the chiasm gives to this meaning — situated on the side of explicit signification, and which exceeds it — the form of the mirror, and therefore inspires a feeling of reflection, the same set of elements repeated, but reversed. (*Discourse* 70–71)

Lyotard writes of the chiasm as a rhetorical figure of the ab-ba variety, and thus of a depth as an excess of meaning. In *Only Revolutions*, however, the chiasmic space is literal, its depth material. The road novel's element of flight and movement begets a whole new dimension. Resulting from the structure of the chiasm, the visual space of *Only Revolutions* is at once a two- and three-dimensional space.

These formal and material elements of the Möbius strip and the chiasm have far-reaching consequences for the relation between the world and the book that contains that world as configured in Danielewski's novel. These consequences start when we pick up the

---

(continued) story that began /once upon a time there was a story that began," etc. This last example also incorporates the materiality of paper in its structure. It is printed along a dotted line and the reader is encouraged to cut the strips of text with paper and glue them together in the form of a Möbius strip. Of course the difference from *Only Revolutions* is that Barth's is a minimalist story, whereas Danielewski's structure encapsulates two centuries of world history. As with Borges and Roberto Bolaño, the difference is quantitative and lies in scale: in this case one sentence versus two times 360 pages.

book to begin reading. Choosing how to read *Only Revolutions* poses an ethical dilemma. This follows from the fact that Sam and Hailey live in different times. Reading one story after another in a linear fashion is an act that produces interlinked, twinned stories of a linear progression from youth to death, with each a duration of four seasons and 100 years. This is a responsible reading that performs a "worlding" of the text and brings historical consciousness into the narration; yet it is also a demythologizing act of reading that splits Sam and Hailey apart. The alternative, cyclical reading, by contrast, is a romantic act that allows them their "being-with" or "being-in-common," sharing a world. This strategy, however, is informed by a selective historical amnesia and also disregards the happenings elsewhere in the world (it is no coincidence that both these faults are often attributed to the U.S.). Either way, the reader is implicated, made complicit.

"Allmighty Sixteen and Freeeeee": The American Dream

Even more than *The Atlas*, *Only Revolutions* inscribes itself specifically in the American cultural imaginary, displaying a number of narrative and mythological tropes that are deemed typical for American literature. Its theme of spatial exploration typifies an American mythology of the individual who discovers his identity by moving outward.[14] At the novel's dual beginnings, the characters find themselves alone ("allone," in Danielewski's spelling) in a vast and unknown space. Fittingly, they begin and end their adventures on foot, traversing a romanticized wilderness evocative of Jean-Jacques Rousseau's State of Nature, not yet compromised by cultural influences. In American mythology, this landscape stands for authenticity and freedom, a place where one can (re)discover one's "true" self. This wilderness in which they find themselves, though seemingly unpopulated, is unmistakably an American landscape. We can conclude this from the species of flora and fauna that they mention, including bald eagles, boreal toads, bighorn sheep, and lubber grasshoppers, Trembling Aspens, Tamarack Pines, and Snowberries. "I'm sooooo

---

[14] Manovich contrasts this external directionality of the American novel to European literature, which is typically more intended toward the psychological, the "inward" (*Language* 27). Similar generalizations are made by Fiedler (xvii–xxxiv) and Deleuze and Parnet (Chapter 2). Because of its outward nature, Manovich likens the prototypical American novel to the computer game (28).

from these uplands, Hailey roars," "From corries and chines. / From the freezeloss and slowwash / slushgushing out of basins / and brooks to miles of / Northern Rock Jasmine growing" (*Only* H35). At this stage, Sam and Hailey are territorialized.

This sense of territorialization diminishes when they build up speed and start traveling the world together. Then, the national setting goes over into transnational movement. Their movements across the globe, seemingly without purpose, could be mistaken for those of a playful user of the Google Earth software with its "smooth zoom effects." One minute they soar above the earth's surface and see the world pass by with an impassionate eye: "agony / of all I skitter by so easily" (S41). The next moment they cross through a city street, locally immersed but still "unassailable." Their narration performs a series of scalar expansions and contractions: an effortless flying or "zapping" from the extremely distant to the intimately close, from national to local, the particular to the general. Sam and Hailey seem to be in full control over their movements across the globe because, as they claim, they know no boundaries. They acknowledge neither laws nor restraints: "I will sacrifice nothing. For there are no conflicts. Except me. And there's only one transgression. Me" (H3). Their global travels are seemingly without borders: "I will sacrifice nothing. For there are no countries. Except me. And there is only one boundary. Me" (S3). Their adventures on the road read like a utopia, a fairytale of unbridled transnationalism. The whole world serves as a geospatial database for their trajectory:

> Amortized. Fueled. Ready to pour it on. / Our new 911 Cabriolet, nelly, natch to lay / a batch from St. Louis. Budapest, Santiago, / Warsaw. Amsterdam, Shanghai, New Delhi. / Lisbon. Every city. Roam. Air sharper. / Promises harder. Driving US from the ages. (H216)

Displaced from the specificity of their original space and location, they come "screaming on from some/transcontinental terrortory" (H227). The transnational here stands for freedom: it promises acts of deterritorialization, disconnection from the nation state.

Yet these transnational wanderings are still inscribed in the national, American framework. Steve Heine's study of cultural variation in various measures of self-enhancement (e.g., self-esteem, self-serving biases, and self-evaluation maintenance) has pointed out that North Americans stand out for trying to live up to their cultural ideal of independence, resulting in identities that prefer to view themselves as independent and distinct from each other. The prototypical American is autonomous, a self-sufficient individual who is complete in herself (110–11). Ironically, the couple's dreams of detachment and autonomy firmly ground these characters in American traditions. Like Vollmann, they are tied to their geographical origins in their dreams of transcending the nation. Sam and Hailey are stereotypically, indeed archetypically American in their repeated insistence on "the Dream": "Everyone betrays the Dream but who cares for it?" (*Only* H360). In their shared story of escape from their particular socio-historical contexts and through perpetual motion,⑮ they are trans-historical personifications of the country that claims to remain "forever young": "Allmighty sixteen and so freeeeee" (S1).⑯ The American framing of their adventure is underwritten by their referring to themselves as U.S. Their Dream is to be continuously reborn through travel. Leslie Fiedler describes the American author in *Love and Death in the American Novel* as "forever beginning," and his country as "a nation sustained by a sentimental and Romantic dream, the dream of an escape from culture and a renewal of youth" (xix, xxxiii).⑰ The circular structure of their navigable Möbius-space allows Sam and Hailey both: a perpetual re-beginning and to be forever sixteen. Their belief in their ability to relocate and begin ever anew ties them to two characteristics of their home country that we have also identified in Vollmann's wanderings: *restlessness* ("Where there's a wheel, there's a way. / And we're always awaying" [*Only* S225]) and *rootlessness* ("allways we will leave US / behind US" [H290]).

---

⑮ The constant motion of their travels is reflected in the repeated inclusion of a symbol of two vertical lines resembling the "pause" icon for instance on a DVD or a computer program. The same symbol is inserted into certain words, such as "Allways" and "Allone". When you see this pause-icon, it means the program is running. Sam and Hailey, the icon seems to suggest, are literally running "non-stop": "We're big engines without brakes" (*Only* H217).

⑯ Pressman notes that this age has symbolic value: sixteen is the age when American youth receive "the quintessential sign of American freedom — a driver's license" (*Digital* 163).

⑰ This perpetual re-beginning comes with an unwillingness to settle that for Fiedler explains why long-term romantic attachment is an uneasy subject for American authors, who avoid the topic of marriage at all cost (xx). This could explain Danielewski's choice of two sixteen-year-olds as central characters. Sam defines marriage poetically as "Where / Love accepting Liberty's end / secures Love's undoing" (*Only* S20). Halfway through, however, these teenagers do get married. As Pressman notes (*Digital* 164), this causes a shift in the novel's tone, conveying a sense of confinement: "The Wheel his no more / We're stuck" (*Only* H312).

Hailey and Sam attempt to reinvent themselves through travel-as-narration. In the juxtaposition of their monologues, identities are presented as fluid: the male goes over into the female, and historically specific details are playfully transformed from one story-half to another. Their automobile, for example, is a different brand and model each time they mention it. As archetypes, Sam and Hailey seem to be above and beyond such material and historical concerns. They are placed at first firmly at the center of their respective idiosyncratic worlds. This sense of control over the world they inhabit includes these characters' own identities. Unlike Vollmann's narrator in *The Atlas*, who remains trapped in his outward appearance and American perspective, the outlaws in *Only Revolutions* are able to rewrite their own identities at will. Such acts of self-invention offer the illusion of total control: of *homo autotelus*, or modern, self-generating man, who is completely self-contained (Eagleton 64).[18] This myth of creative imagination *ex nihilo* is entangled with the idea of freedom in Western history. Thus, Sam and Hailey mythologize themselves and become larger than life as mythical figures. They evade the world beyond their concerns: their respective worlds begin and end with their own bodies and minds. Perfectly self-enclosed, their self-images are of a system without an outside: "I'm unavoidable. No beneath/underneath. No over/above. Just one side" (*Only* SH30);

---

[18]   This idea could be understood as a variation on the well-known *Oration on the Dignity of Man* by Giovanni Pico della Mirandola (1486): "The nature of all other creatures is defined and restricted within laws which We have laid down; you, by contrast, impeded by no such restrictions, may, by your own free will, to whose custody We have assigned you, trace for yourself the lineaments of your own nature. I have placed you at the very center of the world, so that from that vantage point you may with greater ease glance round about you on all that the world contains. We have made you a creature neither of heaven nor of earth, neither mortal nor immortal, in order that you may, as the free and proud shaper of your own being, fashion yourself in the form you may prefer. [...] Oh unsurpassed generosity of God the Father, Oh wondrous and unsurpassable felicity of man, to whom it is granted to have what he chooses, to be what he wills to be!" (7–8). The human being, in this high Renaissance concept, is understood as microcosm or *parvus mundus*, no longer in a middle position within the hierarchically arranged universe but rather capable of choosing and occupying almost any position. Thus humanity is granted an unlimited power of self-transformation. We should not forget, however, that for Pico such self-rewriting is conceivable (even as the purpose of human existence) in a divinely ordered cosmos, not necessarily (as we may infer) in a secular one where freedom *per se* amounts to an illusion. It is not far from there to the fictional perception that the human characters are enwrapped in a prison of guilt.

"I'm the all. The all available / Ever now. Ever here. / Allways unavailable" (S27). They are not *of* the world; they *are* the world.

Yet this by no means makes them "disembodied master subjects" who are able to perceive "everything from nowhere" (Haraway 189). Even if they blow themselves up out of all proportions, Sam and Hailey cannot escape from their idiosyncratic viewpoints. This sense of limited focalization is underwritten by the book's color coding. In Hailey's half of the book, zeroes and the character "o" are synaesthetically printed in gold; in Sam's half they are printed in green, signifying the colors of their eyes, respectively: "gold eyes with flecks of green" (*Only* S7) and "green eyes with flecks of gold" (H7). Their outlook on the world is literally "colored," we see their worlds through their eyes. The effect of this strategy of focalization is one of scale variance. This complex entanglement between what is depicted and the scale of representation also corresponds to a variance in font sizes. The book's typographical composition visually performs the characters' development. Both voices are at first displayed in a large font, with lots of short "sound-bites" and exclamations, creating a "loud" look:

I jump free this wheel.
On fire. Blaze a breeze.
I'll devastate the World.
No big deal. New mutiny all
around. With a twist.
With a smile. A frown.
Allmighty sixteen and so freeeeee. (S1)

When they go on the road, they are able to gradually broaden this narrow viewpoint to include the other. Corresponding to this development, their statements are gradually compressed to a smaller amount of longer, more reflective lines in a tiny font, like a whisper:

And I, your sentry of ice, shall always protect
what your Joy so terrifyingly elects.
I'll destroy no World
so long as it keeps turning with scurry & blush,
fledgling& charms beading with dews,
and allways our rush returning renewed.
Everyone betrays the Dream
but who cares for it? O Sam no,
I could never walk away from you. (H360)

This typographical invention allows for a visual-material presentation of scale variance: the youngster's egos expand and contract as their view of the other changes. By extension, their world changes. The evolving and expanding scales of the text point to a book-world that is always in flux. Contrary to the Googlized view of the globe as a fixed, "fetishized" object, *Only Revolutions*, true to its title, presents us with a world under continuous transformation.

"Chasing US through the [p]ages": History and Worldliness in *Only Revolutions*

We want to be chained in history, but we also want to be unlinked via an escape character (in programming: a backslash, quote sign, comment tag, and so on) that allows us the freedom to be a link unto ourselves or to whom and what we choose.
    Alan Liu, *Local Transcendence* (328)

Danielewski's attention to scale variance, like Vollmann's, already nuances the claim to "mastery" that might be expected from such a masterfully constructed novel. The outlaw couple's romantic dream of escape-through-narration and full control over their worlds is further shattered by the role of time and history in *Only Revolutions*. For Sam's and Hailey's freedom and sense of control are not unconditional. The outside world, culture, and history are at their heels at every turn, questioning their self-proclaimed rootlessness and limitlessness. At times, the emphasis is on active escape ("Driving US *from* the ages," *Only* H216; emphasis ours); at other times they rather seem hunted, passive ("Chasing US *to* our ages," S216; emphasis ours). They have to stay in motion to steer clear of the lasso of time: "Yes, maybe it's time to move on. / Spare some our hurt before / the World retakes what we always / elude when we run" (H209). Their joyride is a flight from a history that forces them to live in two separate worlds. To stand still would mean to be pinned down at different points on the Möbius strip, to be tied to one's historical and geographical contexts. Hence, they do not remain in perpetual motion because they are free: they have to keep moving to *remain* free. This freedom turning into its opposite is another familiar trope in American literature: "The enemy of society on the run toward freedom is also the pariah in flight from his guilt, the guilt of that very flight" (Fiedler xxi). Sam and Hailey are forced to keep moving as they are enclosed in an immanent world. They flee from their guilt of evading the world.

Whether they succeed in retaining their freedom depends on the reader's perspective. Even in dreams of a transnational utopia, as we have seen repeatedly throughout this chapter, the national perspective is not easy to elude. Whereas *Only Revolutions'* characters do, in a superficial sense, transcend the spatial and temporal grid that demarcates their nation-state, that grid does not stop existing simply because they ignore it. One of the ways in which the national impinges on the global, and vice versa, is found in the "chronomosaics." These are columns of historical fragments placed in the inner margins of each page that list events. They are dated from November 22, 1863, to May 29, 2005, with blank entries continuing thereafter until January 19, 2063.⑲ The timelines reduce the events to non-causal, paratactic enumerations:"Yokohama quake & wave, / 3,000 go" (*Only* S118). The dated lists of events resemble a minimalist newspaper, a form that makes comparisons possible across different territorial scales. Like a newspaper, the timeline presents the world to the nation in a way that enforces a global simultaneity and discursive standardization — the local and the foreign are written about in the same way and inscribed in the same daily temporal cycle (see Anderson 2). Thus, in the chronomosaics, the "outside" world is inscribed on the pages of Sam's and Hailey's lives. It is literally marginalized on the page, suggesting the couple's self-absorption and evasion of worldly matters.⑳

---

⑲   These historical events have been collected by the author, who placed a call on his "MZD Forums" (<markzdanielewski.info/onlyrev.htm>) in August 2005 for his fans to submit the historical moments they would want to see mentioned in the book to come. He also asked them for their favorite automobiles, plants, and animals to be included in the manuscript. As the author explains his choice for these elements of reader participation:"It's not just my personal history, but histories that go beyond what I can perceive when I'm looking at thousands of books" (qtd. in Benzon). This example of what Jenkins calls "participatory culture" is yet another way to implicate the reader in the production of the book and make the monumental novel more inclusive.

⑳   The point on the axis formed by pages 80−81, when the lovers momentarily merge on the page, coincides with particularly eventful dates: 1943 for Sam (WWII, Stalingrad) and 1984 for Hailey. These traumatic events precisely coincide with the place where they momentarily dissolve into each other, and are oblivious of the rest of the world. They are aware of this evasion, which is reminiscent of American exceptionalism (Kilgore 188):"Only we can easily escape. Because we're unpunishable" (*Only* S224); "*Circumstantially*, Sam yields. *We're irresponsible. /* — Me: *irresponsible. /* — US: *irresponsible*." (H258).

Yet the historical and the global threaten to catch up with the outlaw couple at every turn. At several points, details from the "gutters" of history find their way into their text. Their clothing, for instance, is always period-appropriate, as Hailey describes Sam as wearing "silk tie, suspenders and loafers" (*Only* H197), while he sees her in "dome hat, bloomers and flats" (S197). When Sam's page bears the dateline "Nov. 19 1945" he sees Hailey receiving five- and ten-dollar bills — "Lincolns and Hamiltons" (S197) — whereas Hailey's page is "March 18 1987" and she sees Sam pocketing fifties and hundreds, "Jacksons and Grants" (H197). This differentialization of contextual details creates a pervasive, ominous sense that the external world is on the verge of impinging upon the lovers' shared world. In spite of their efforts to attain a mythical non-temporality and non-spatiality through interminable autotelic self-narration, Sam and Hailey are thus confronted with the relentless linearity of the chronological archive. The perfection of their closed circle is interrupted by the interference of these temporal and "open-ended" lines, injecting historical consciousness into the world they created.[21] With these hints at historical consciousness, the world seeps in, or rather, exposes itself as always already *their* world; pursued by time, they are worldly, *of* the world.

In *Only Revolutions*, the notion of being chased by time is personified in the figure of the "Creep," a villain that emerges repeatedly at the exact same points in the chiasmic structure. The name of this creep, who pursues Sam and Hailey with a lasso (another loop), is consistently printed in a purple font, as are the

---

[21] The novel's differential handling of temporality may have been nourished by the debate in theoretical physics, which actually has philosophical precursors dating back to antiquity, about the concept and implications of a static block of spacetime as suggested on the basis of the general theory of relativity together with the Standard Model of particle physics. For the time-symmetric laws that apply in these, can it matter at all whether the variable we call time increases or decreases? As is well known, Albert Einstein wrote at the passing away of a friend in 1955, "Now he has departed this strange world a little ahead of me, that signifies nothing. For us physicists in the soul, the distinction between past, present and future is only a stubbornly persistent illusion." Can one say that future events already exist, they just don't exist now? For further discussion, see the volume edited by Duplantier, which includes an analysis of "Time and Relativity"; also the 2016 Time in Cosmology conference at the Perimeter Institute for Theoretical Physics in Waterloo, Ontario < perimeterinstitute. ca/conferences/time-cosmology > and the review by Dan Falk in Quanta Magazine < www.quantamagazine. org/a-debate-over-the-physics-of-time-20160719>.

dates of the chronomosaics. This color coding hints at his character as the embodiment of time and history in the novel: " — Fools. I'm your salvation / Without me you both lose. You'll slip away and never find a role. Time's up. Time to tie you down. Now." (S275). At that point of the narrative, indeed, time would be "running out" were we reading a linear novel, judged by the number of pages left. Luckily for Sam and Hailey, the Creep's lasso is not wide enough to capture them both, and they manage to get away. Still, they are never unpursued, since the Creep just has to wait on the opposite page of the chiasmic structure. The characters always find the creep of time waiting on the other side of the book's chiasmic space: hence, as he announces, "You can never leave me" (S274).

In addition to its combined meanings of "scary" and "stealthily approaching" (as in old age "creeping up on" someone), "creep" is also a term in book design, referring to a situation when the bulk of paper gets particularly large, extending the duration of the act of flipping through a book. Drucker suggests that in book art, this "creep" of the pages can be employed strategically to concretize time, to render it tangible and perceptible "as a literal and spatial feature of the book" (100). This is exactly what Danielewski does. He concretizes (story-) time not so much through the bulk of his carefully crafted work, but rather through his use of small font, his juxtaposition of different blocks of text on one page and the unconventional instructions for handling the book. The Creep is then the structural-fictional embodiment of these manipulations of reading time in *Only Revolutions*.

When we focus on his role of antagonist in the story, this ominous figure of historical time puts Sam's and Hailey's brash assertions of their freedom and transcendence in another light. Inhabiting separate universes that are, moreover, perfectly enclosed in their creator's circular composition, the protagonists are trapped inside the book as a bounded space, like "Vollmann" in his atlas. Sam and Hailey at times seem to be curiously aware of the book's materiality as something that literally stands between them. When their voices become one for a moment, exactly one page before the axis of the chiasmic space, they feel "something wide which feels close. / Open but feels closed. Lying weirdly / across US. Between US. Where we're / closest, where we touch, where we're one. / Somehow continuing on separately" (*Only* 179). The characters could here very well be feeling the book that contains them and comprises their world. What lies between them at this point is one page: a space to be traversed. That this is the closest the two are ever going to get gives a materialist spin to an otherwise classic, idealist story of love and unification.

The motto printed on both ends of the book, "You were there," announces a dream of global relationality. Besides pointing to the way that Sam and Hailey are bound together in each singular opening of the book, this epigraph emphasizes the involvement of the reader who traverses the text, and whose physical work keeps the journey going. *Only Revolutions'* feedback loop absorbs the reader into the narrative system and thus makes her part of this space of globality *within the book*. Danielewski's fans, delivering crowd-sourced content as part of a multim edia participatory culture, are implicated too. Besides referring to the United States and to Sam's and Hailey's romantic "democracy of two," there emerges a third possible meaning of US: a global being-in-common. In the end, this option is not excluded from the textual universe of *Only Revolutions*, but rather lingers as a question that we can project on the timelines for the future that the author has purposefully left open.

Conclusion

The dehumanized and calculated representation of the earth that Google supplies, we noted, produces the mathematical sublime in its users without allowing for comprehension of the earth. Cultural values of waywardness, renewal, and the erasure of history — reminiscent of the American road novel — are encoded in the software. We have contrasted this with the innovative ways in which Vollmann and Danielewski use the materiality of the book, in order to perform experiences of inhabiting the radically immanent world of late globalization. We characterized the late-global situation as one marked by a lack of a "beyond" or an "outside," or with Hardt and Negri a world where the distinction between "inside" and "outside" collapses. Google Earth, we have argued, executes global immanence through ever-more precise algorithmic approximation, in which the tension between partiality and totality remains unresolved. *The Atlas* and *Only Revolutions*, meanwhile, perform the retreat of the outside by playing with the capacity of the book to bind and encapsulate narrative spaces. They use the enclosed space of the book to reflect on this late-global predicament. As we have demonstrated, they exploit the volumetric aspect of the book object, its three-dimensional, spatial affordances, as well as its finite character. They integrate these material characteristics of the book into their narratives, precisely to enact the experience of inhabiting an enclosed world without a beyond, lacking a sense of orientation or external anchoring points.

Both novels imply themselves in an American mythology of the global. In doing this, they partake in a well-established modernist tradition, one to which Gertrude Stein also subscribes when in "The Gradual Making of The Making of Americans" (1935) she writes: "It is something strictly American to conceive a space that is filled with moving, a space of time that is filled always filled with moving" (258). We also find prefigurations of this tradition in the work of Walt Whitman, who romanticizes the state of being always on the move as in "Song of Myself" (1855): "I tramp a perpetual journey" (51).

Yet our case studies also subtend this mythology by problematizing it. Both authors engage in a critical fashion with traditions of American myth-making and their archetypical representations of the American figure abroad. They exploit familiar tropes like the American Dream, dreams of rebirth through traveling, and rootlessness. They subvert these cultural archetypes by revealing how "the American" is framed by traditions and myths that tie it to its own geographical and national context. Rather than propagating freedom or autonomy, these characters fail at "rewriting" the self through travel. Instead, *The Atlas* and *Only Revolutions* insist on the importance of perspectivism and scale as determinate for any world-view. By foregrounding the inescapability of a limited, subjective perspective on the world, Vollmann's and Danielewski's acts of world-forming go against the idea, pervasive in data visualizations, of the globe as an already totalized entity available to the panoptic gaze of a viewer. In both cases, the book has mastery over its owner, the traveling narrator, instead of the other way around. The characters who inhabit their book-spaces are always on the run, wandering around without the promise of transcending their material confinements. Neither free nor in control, they are determined by their itinerary and the spaces they inhabit. These spaces are not only geographical: they also include the book as a space. The material book functions as a container *of* their story-worlds and is contained *by* them. As we have tried to show, the worlds that Vollmann and Danielewski project are highly unstable: the contained and the container, world and book, constantly bleed into one another.

We are reminded of the impossibility of attaining an objective view of a world of which we, as observers, are ourselves a part. The book becomes at once a space to escape *in* and a space from which is impossible to escape. Literature can thus pose a critical corrective to the imaginative norm produced by Google and co., through whose services we engage with the world as a database. At the same time, the material novel teases out the unbridgeable gaps between partiality and totality that are immanent to such technological imaginations of the globe. The novels we studied in this chapter are paradigmatic for the power of literature to offer imaginative alternatives to globalization as a "levelling process of a spreading global consumerism" (Damrosch 11) that leads to "the imposition of the same system of exchange everywhere" (Spivak 72).

Vollmann and Danielewski do not attempt to cover up asymmetrical power relations between the U.S. and the rest of the world. Unlike Google's smooth zoom aesthetics, they do not sanitize their worlds of the problems and messiness of our concrete global situation. This, in our view, is what makes the book-bound novel such a fitting receptacle for imaginative reflections on global relations: it performs this experience of a space that is self-enclosed and simultaneously exceeds all representations. These authors reinvent the book as a space to escape in and a space without escape. Book-bound monumental novels can thus constitute an inclusive sphere of reference in which they implicate their readers in innovative ways, thus rethinking our expanding relations to the world and to others on a variety of scales. In reimagining the world as book, they invite the reader to rethink transnational relationality.

NB. A part of this chapter has been published in Inge van de Ven, "Revisiting the Book-as-World: World-Making and Book Materiality in *The Atlas* and *Only Revolutions*." *Book Presence in a Digital Age*, edited by Kiene Brillenburg Wurth, Kári Driscoll, and Jessica Pressman. Bloomsbury, 2018, pp. 225–46. We greatly acknowledge the author's and editor's permission for the adaptation.

References

Aarseth, Espen. *Cybertext: Perspectives on Ergodic Literature*. Johns Hopkins UP, 1997.

Anderson, Benedict. *The Specter of Comparisons: Nationalism, Southeast Asia, and the World*. Verso, 1998.

Arnar, Anna Sigrídur. *The Book as Instrument: Stéphane Mallarmé, The Artist's Book, and the Transformation of Print Culture*. U of Chicago

P, 2011.

Aukrust, Kjerstin, editor. *Assigning Cultural Values*. Peter Lang, 2013.

Bakhtin, Mikhail M. *The Dialogic Imagination: Four Essays*. Edited by Michael Holquist, translated by Caryl Emerson and Michael Holquist. U of Texas P, 1981.

Barad, Karen. "Posthumanist Performativity: Toward an Understanding of How Matter Comes to Matter." *Signs: Journal of Women in Culture and Society*, vol. 28, no. 3, 2003, pp. 801–31.

Baudrillard, Jean. *Simulacra and Simulation*. Translated by S. F. Glaser. U of Michigan P, 1994.

Benzon, Kiki. "Revolution 2: An Interview with Mark Z. Danielewski." *Electronic Book Review*, 20 Mar. 2007. www.electronicbookreview.com/thread/wuc/regulated.

Bhattacharyya, Gargi, editor. *Ethnicities and Values in a Changing World*. Ashgate, 2009.

Blanchot, Maurice. *The Book to Come*. Translated by Charlotte Mandell. Stanford UP, 2003.

Blumenberg, Hans. *Die Lesbarkeit der Welt*. Suhrkamp, 1986.

Brody, Robert. "Mario Vargas Llosa and the Totalization Impulse." *Texas Studies in Literature and Language*, vol. 19, no. 4, 1977, pp. 14–21.

Brooks, Peter. *Reading for the Plot: Design and Intention in Narrative*. Knopf, 1984.

Brown, Marshall. "Transcendental Ethics, Vertical Ethics, and Horizontal Ethics." *Ethics in Culture: The Dissemination of Values Through Literature and Other Media*, edited by Astrid Erll, Herbert Grabes, and Ansgar Nünning. de Gruyter, 2008, pp. 51–72.

Burke, Edmund. *Philosophical Enquiry into the Origin of Our Ideas of the Sublime and Beautiful*. 1759. Edited by Adam Phillips. Oxford UP, 1990.

Chun, Wendy Hui Kyong. *Programmed Visions: Software and Memory*. MIT P, 2011.

Cottrell, Sophie. "A Conversation with Mark Danielewski." *Boldtype*, vol. 3, no. 12, 2000. www.randomhouse.com/boldtype/0400/danielewski/interview.html.

Damrosch, David. "What Is World Literature?" *World Literature Today*, vol. 77, no. 1, 2003, pp. 9–14.

Danielewski, Mark Z. *Only Revolutions*. Pantheon, 2006.

De Certeau, Michel. *The Practice of Everyday Life*. Translated by Steven Rendall. U of California P, 1984.

Deleuze, Gilles, and Claire Parnet. *Dialogues II*. Translated by Hugh Tomlinson and Barbara Habberjam. Revised ed. Columbia UP, 2007.

Drucker, Johanna. "The Self-Conscious Codex: Artists' Books and Electronic Media." *Substance*, vol. 26, no. 1, issue 82, 1997, pp. 93–112.

Duplantier, Bertrand, editor. *Time: Poincaré Seminar 2010*. Springer, 2013.

Eagleton, Terry. *Ideology of the Aesthetic*. Blackwell, 1990.

Edney, Matthew H. *Mapping an Empire: The Geographical Construction of British India, 1765–1843*. U of Chicago P, 1990.

Eisenstein, Elizabeth L. "An Unacknowledged Revolution Revisited." *American Historical Review*, vol. 107, no. 1, 2002, pp. 87–105.

Ercolino, Stefano. *The Maximalist Novel: From Thomas Pynchon's* Gravity's Rainbow *to Roberto Bolaño's* 2666. Bloomsbury, 2014.

Farman, Jason. "Mapping the Digital Empire: Google Earth and the Process of Modern Cartography." *New Media Society*, vol. 12, no. 6, 2010, pp. 869–88.

Fiedler, Leslie. *Love and Death in the American Novel*. Criterion Books, 1960.

Flanagan, Mary. "Navigating the Narrative in Space: Gender and Spatiality in Virtual Worlds." *Art Journal*, vol. 59, no. 3, 2000, pp. 75–85.

French, Marilyn. *James Joyce's* Ulysses: *The Book as World*. Harvard UP, 1978.

Ganser, Alexandra, Julia Pühringer, and Markus Rheindorf. "Bakhtin's Chronotope on the Road: Space, Time, and Place in Road Movies since the 1970s." *Facta universitatis series: linguistics and literature*, vol. 4, no. 1, 2006, pp. 1–17.

Glissant, Édouard. *Poetics of Relation*. Translated by Betsy Wing. U of Michigan P, 1997.

Haraway, Donna. *Simians, Cyborgs, and Women: The Reinvention of Nature*. Routledge, 1991.

Hardesty, Michele L. "Looking for the Good Fight: William T. Vollmann's 'An Afghanistan Picture Show.'" *Boundary 2*, vol. 36, no. 2, 2009, pp. 99–124.

Hardt, Michael, and Antonio Negri. *Empire*. Harvard UP, 2000.

Hayles, N. Katherine. *How We Think: Digital Media and Contemporary Technogenesis*. U of Chicago P, 2012.

Heine, Steve J. "An Exploration of Cultural Variation in Self-Enhancing and Self-Improving Motivation." *Nebraska Symposium on Motivation* 49: Cross-Cultural Differences in Perspectives on the Self, edited by Virginia Murphy-Berman and John J. Berman, U of Nebraska Press, 2003, pp. 101–28.

Helmreich, Stefan. "From Spaceship Earth to Google Ocean: Planetary Icons, Indexes, and Infrastructures." *Social Research*, vol. 78, no. 4, 2011, pp. 1211–42.

Jameson, Fredric. *The Geopolitical Aesthetic: Cinema and Space in the World-System*. Indiana UP, 1992.

—. *The Political Unconscious: Narrative as a Socially Embodied Act*. Cornell UP, 1981.

Jenkins, Henry. *Convergence Culture: Where Old and New Media Collide*. New York UP, 2006.

Kant, Immanuel. *Critique of Judgment*. Translated by John Henry Bernard. Simon and Schuster, 2008.

Kerouac, Jack. *On the Road*. Penguin, 2000.

Kilgore, Christopher David. *Ambiguous Recognition: Recursion, Cognitive Blending, and the Problem of Interpretation in Twenty-First-Century Fiction*. Dissertation, Univ. of Tennessee, Knoxville, 2010. trace.tennessee.edu/utk_graddiss/891.

King, Adam B. "'Mapping the Unmappable': Visual Representations of the Internet as Social Constructions." CSI Working Paper No. WP 00–05 (2000).

Kwan, Mei-Po. "Feminist Visualization: Re-envisioning GIS as a Method in Feminist Geographic Research." *Annals of the Association of American Geographers*, vol. 92, no. 4, 2002, pp. 645–61.

LeClair, Tom. "His Sister's Ghost in Bosnia." Review of *The Atlas* by William T. Vollmann. *The Nation*, 6 May 1996, pp. 72–75.

Leonard, Philip. *Literature After Globalization: Textuality, Technology and the Nation-State*. Bloomsbury, 2013.

Liu, Alan. *Local Transcendence: Essays on Postmodern Historicism and the Database*. U of Chicago P, 2008.

Lyotard, Jean-François. *Discourse, Figure*. Translated by Antony Hudek and Mary Lydon. U of Minnesota P, 2010.

—. *The Postmodern Explained: Correspondence 1982 – 1985*. Translated and edited by Julian Pefanis and Morgan Thomas. U of Minnesota P, 1993.

MacEachren, Alan M. *How Maps Work: Representation, Visualization, and Design*. Guilford Press, 1995.

Manovich, Lev. "The Anti-Sublime Ideal in Data Art." 1–15 (2002), accessed 1 Nov. 2014. www.manovich.net/DOCS/data_art.doc.

—. *The Language of New Media*. MIT Press, 2001.

McGrath, Charles. "An Author Without Borders." *New York Times*, 28 July 2009. www.nytimes.com/2009/07/29/books/29vollman.html?pagewanted = all.

Moraru, Christian. *Cosmodernism: American Narrative, Late Globalization, and the New Cultural Imaginary*. U of Michigan P, 2011.

Munster, Anna. *An Aesthesia of Networks: Conjunctive Experience in Art and Technology*. MIT Press, 2013.

Pico della Mirandola, Giovanni. *Oration on the Dignity of Man*. Translated by A. Robert Caponigri, introduced by Russell Kirk. Gateway Ed. Henry Regnery,1956.

Pinder, David. "Subverting Cartography: The Situationists and Maps of the City." *Environment and Planning A*, vol. 28, no. 3, 1996, pp. 405–27.

Piper, Andrew. "Rethinking the Print Object: Goethe and the Book of Everything." *PMLA*, vol. 121, no. 1, 2006, pp. 124–38.

Portelli, Alessandro. *The Text and the Voice: Writing, Speaking, and Democracy in American Literature*. Columbia UP, 1994.

Pressman, Jessica. "Big Novels / Big Data." *American Book Review*, special issue: Big Novels, vol. 37, no. 2, 2016.

—. *Digital Modernism: Making It New in New Media*. Oxford UP, 2014.

Raffoul, François, and David Pettigrew. Translators' Introduction. Jean-Luc Nancy, *The Creation of the World or Globalization*, translated by François Raffoul and David Pettigrew, SUNY Press, 2007, pp. 1–28.

Sadokierski, Zoë. "Visual Writing: A Critique of Graphic Devices in Hybrid Novels, From a Visual Communication Design Perspective." Dissertation, Sydney, Univ. of Technology, 2010.

Seaman, Donna. "Boxcars, Shostakovich, and the Poor." *Bookforum*, Feb./ Mar. 2007, p. 52.

Spivak, Gayatri Chakravorty. *Death of a Discipline*. Columbia UP, 2003.

Stein, Gertrude. *Selected Writings*. Edited by Carl Van Vechten. Vintage, 1962.

Vaidhyanathan, Siva. *The Googlization of Everything*. U of California P, 2011.

Vandendorpe, Christian. *From Papyrus to Hypertext: Toward the Universal Digital Library*. Translated by Phyllis Aronoff and Howard Scott. U of Illinois P, 2009.

Vollmann, William T. *The Atlas*. Viking, 1996.

—. "Crabbed Cautions of a Bleeding-Hearted Un-Deleter — and Potential Nobel Prize Winner..." *Expelled from Eden: A William T. Vollmann Reader*, edited by Larry McCaffery and Michael Hemmingson, Thunder's Mouth, 2004, pp. 319–24.

—. *The Rainbow Stories*. Penguin, 1989.

—. *The Rifles. Seven Dreams: A Book of North-American Landscapes* Vol. 6. Penguin Viking, 1994.

—. "Writing." *Why I Write: Thoughts on the Craft of Fiction*, edited by Will Blythe, Little, 1998, pp. 110–15.

Whitman, Walt. *Leaves of Grass*. Facsimile of the 1st ed. Eakins Press, 1966.

Wood, Denis with John Fels. *The Power of Maps*. Guilford Press, 1992.

Woods, Derek. "Scale Critique for the Anthropocene." *The Minnesota Review*, vol. 83, 2014, pp. 133–42.

Appendix

Values and Valuations: Lines of Inquiry

Michael STEPPAT
University of Bayreuth
Mine KRAUSE
(Paris)

> In the semiotic version of cultural psychology,
> values belong to the highest level of semiotic
> regulatory hierarchy. They guide our conduct,
> yet are ephemeral when we try to locate them.
> They are everywhere in human lives, and by
> being there, they are nowhere to be found.
>
> (Angela Uchoa Branco and Jaan Valsiner,
> *Cultural Psychology of Human Values*, 2012)

I. Literature and Values

A Writer's Responsibility

This brief appendix, which does not claim to be complete or exhaustive, offers an introductory overview of some characteristic aspects which can be found in the study of values and valuations. We share the perception that "[t]he subject of values is at the cutting edge in humanitarian studies of recent decades" (Funtova and Sinetskiy 927). The appendix is designed as a basis for considering the potential usefulness of selected approaches to values research in Intercultural Communication (the main focus in Part II) for the purposes of literary study.

In the West, an intimation that literary works are closely associated with value orientations goes back to classical antiquity. As Michael H. Prosser has pointed out in the present book series, the Athenian philosopher Plato "expelled poets from his ideal republic because they did not deal in reality but only in falsehoods"; Socrates would assume that a writer "has responsibility for truth, justice, and goodness," claiming that the continuous search for how to live a virtuous life should be one of a person's major concerns (Prosser 23, 25; see also Nie, *Introduction* Ch. 6.2). For Aristotle, as for Plato in *Phaedrus*, this search is individually distinctive: "the character and value commitments (as opposed to superficial pleasantness or advantageousness) are what each person is *kath' hauto*, in virtue of himself or herself"; an individual is "essentially constituted by values" (Nussbaum, *Love's* 324).[1] From a different perspective, Aristotle in *Poetics* explains that in tragic drama character "reveals moral purpose, showing what kind of things a man chooses or avoids" (6.17, similarly 15.1); articulations in which a speaker fails to choose or avoid anything do not express character.[2] To present an evil man passing from adversity to prosperity does not satisfy "the moral sense" (13.2). Wayne Booth has maintained that the treatment of literary forms in the *Poetics* shows them to be made "of values: values sought, values lost, values mourned, values hailed" (*Essential* 145).

Centuries later in *Ars Poetica*, Horace shifts attention from morality when he pens the oft-quoted lines "Aut prodesse volunt aut delectare poetae / aut simul et iucunda et idonea dicere vitae" (333–34)[3] — aligning a work's aesthetic quality with the usefulness of the represented values for social and material life. Speaking to different social conditions again, and moving literature closer to rhetoric, Sir Philip Sidney in the later 16th century like some other contemporaries (especially Scaliger 7.2, p. 347: qua mores animorum deducantur ad rectam rationem)[4] asserts that the writer's or poet's creation of "delight" has the rather pedagogical purpose "to move men to take that goodness in hand, which without delight they would fly as from

---

[1] Shalom Schwartz's research on basic individual values includes the same emphasis: "People's values form an ordered system of value priorities that characterize them as individuals" ("Basic" 259).

[2] In Book 3 of *The Nicomachean Ethics*, Aristotle further explains the relationship between choice and virtue: "Now if it is in our power to do noble or base acts, and likewise in our power not to do them, and this was what being good or bad meant, then it is in our power to be virtuous or vicious" (3.5, p. 46).

[3] "Poets wish either to profit or to delight; or to deliver at once both the pleasures and the necessaries of life."

[4] See also especially Scaliger 7.2 (p. 347): "Non est poetices finis, imitatio, sed doctrina iucunda, qua mores animorum deducantur ad rectam rationem" ("Imitation is not the end of poetry, but pleasant teaching, by which the habits of the mind may be diverted to proper thinking").

a stranger, and teach, to make them know that goodness whereunto they are moved" (87).

In or just before our time, literary critic Wayne C. Booth has spoken of the ethics of fiction, showing sympathy for deciding "to abandon, at least for a time, the notion that an interest in form precludes an interest in the ethical powers of form" (*Company* 7); for an *ethics of reading* (as Hillis Miller called it), "the virtues of narratives relate to the virtues of selves and societies" (*Company* 11). Booth has averred that "we are at least partially constructed, in our most fundamental moral character, by the stories we have heard, or read, or viewed, or acted out in amateur theatricals"; "*stories* are our major moral teachers" (*Essential* 240, 241). Richard Rorty expresses a similar view, also showing the effect of empathy created by stories that make us understand what it is like to be in a difficult situation: "Such stories, repeated and varied over the centuries, have induced us, the rich, safe, powerful people, to tolerate and even to cherish powerless people — people whose appearance or habits or beliefs at first seemed an insult to our own moral identity [...]" (185).

In a similar thematic context, Christophe André points out that, according to a number of studies, especially a reading of classical literary works (such as novels by Proust) is more likely to promote the capacity of empathy as well as a better understanding of one's social environment ("Plusieurs études ont montré que la lecture d'œuvres de fiction augmente les capacités d'empathie et de compréhension d'autrui, au moins à court terme, et comparée à lecture de non-fiction ou à l'absence de lecture. Les œuvres dites 'classiques' semblent le faire légèrement mieux que les œuvres grand public: sans doute, comme dans le cas de Proust, est-ce lié à la complexité des phénomènes décrits" [14]).

Martha Nussbaum states that "certain works of literature are valuable allies of ethical theorizing, helping us understand issues having to do with moral perception and moral emotion in a way that we could not do well without turning to such texts" ("Literature" 9). She asks whether literature and ethical theory are "allies or adversaries," concluding that "we need good ethical theory as a partner to our reading, so that we will read critically and not passively" ("Literature" 20). Among authors who have advanced a similar preference is Noël Carroll, who declares that "narrative artworks are designed to awaken, to stir up and to engage our moral powers of recognition and judgement," thus encouraging us to think critically and question our value system ("Moderate" 228–29). In another context, he states that it is "natural for us to discuss narrative artworks in terms of ethical considerations," since reading them "engages our moral understanding" (*Beyond* 288).[5] Jean Bessière argues in the same vein, underlining that the ethical tradition of literature as such is reflected by inner conflicts of fictional characters who are in search of guiding values which might provide various answers to the question "How should we live?" Confronted with such ethical reflections, readers are encouraged to rethink their own set of values.[6] Maintaining Aristotle's focus on character depiction, Gregory Currie has maintained that as readers we imagine ourselves in the fictional situation that is represented, in which we have "the same relevant beliefs, desires and values as the character whose situation it is" (257).[7] Yet Carroll

---

[5] Ethics and morality overlap, though they are not exactly identical: "'Ethics' is sometimes taken to refer to a guide to behavior wider in scope than morality, and that an individual adopts as his or her own guide to life, as long as it is a guide that the individual views as a proper guide for others" (Gert; see also Nie *Introduction* pp. 248, 258 on ethical value and moral value and "Conceptual"; Bredella in Baumbach et al. 21, and Müller 20–21). For our purposes, we cannot track the differences with further precision. In his article about music, literature, and ethics, Jean Fisette distinguishes between ethics and morality by stating that the task of ethics is to recognize and establish dominant values in a culture, whereas the task of morality is to make sure that they are collectively respected: "La tâche de l'éthique c'est de connaître et d'établir des valeurs dominantes dans une culture, alors que c'est la tâche de la morale de ce soucier de leur respect dans la collectivité" (39).

Concepts of ethics are only indirectly related to Aristotelian *ethos* as in rhetoric; narrative theory devotes attention to this, and we should not confuse it with the concerns of ethical criticism (see subsection "Ethos and Its Ambiguities" below).

[6] "[...] il y a une tradition éthique qui caractérise la littérature et qui s'est explicitement exprimée d'Aristote à Henry James. Cette tradition est moins celle d'une assertion directe des valeurs que celle de la caractérisation de l'agent humain suivant ce qui est précisément la question éthique: comment devons-nous vivre? Il est tout à fait exact que la plupart des œuvres littéraires portent cette question. Il est encore tout à fait exact, faut-il ajouter, que cette question est un moyen direct pour susciter une réaction du lecteur et ses propres interrogations éthiques. On doit dire que cette perspective définit ce qui peut être tenu pour la manifestation la plus directe du jeu réflexif que porte et qu'engage l'œuvre" (Bessière 7).

[7] Currie also examines the feeling of empathy as an effect of literature, claiming that there is a link between the writer's own value system and the values presented in fictional works which, in his opinion, "record the maker's complex and sustained activity of narrative construction and so are full of clues to the maker's beliefs, values and motives" ("Does" 50). However, this statement is rather questionable since a writer can create characters whose behavior does not correspond to his or her own moral standards.

contends that "[t]he character's emotion does not transmigrate into us. Rather, [...] our preexisting dispositions to certain values and preferences are mobilized by the text's providing an affective cement that fixes our attention on the text and shapes our attention to the evolving story" (231) — which would, if we finish this thought, mean that an already existing empathy is promoted in readers, but that literature cannot overcome a lack of empathy. According to Philippe Sabot, Jacques Bouveresse, and others, writers themselves might not be wholly aware of the ethical dimensions of the narratives they are creating, which also includes their stylistic choices and preferences (see Sabot). Some implicit ethical messages cannot entirely be discovered before the actual reading process of the work in question, during which the reader subconsciously adds his or her own moral vision and judgment. Sabot offers Emile Zola's explanations on *Thérèse Raquin* as an example of a possible discrepancy between the writer's intentions and the reader's interpretation. This proves that values and socio-ethical concepts are (re-)defined while interacting with a literary text in various ways, both on the writer's and the reader's side.

"Literature Would Be Nothing"

From another angle, it has been surmised that the "formation of narrative identities is identical with the development of a set of values that are independent of any given situation and which lend a whole life — or at least certain stages of a life — moral meaning and stability" (Meuter). Narrative ethics will inquire how a use of fictional techniques conveys values "underlying" the narrator's relations to what the narrative depicts and to its recipients; a researcher can then "seek to uncover the ethical values underlying the specific rhetorical exchanges of a particular narrative" (Phelan). This is a research program, extendable to the cultural value items and orientations which social scientists have investigated. After all, as law professor Richard Epstein correctly points out, "the interaction between literature and social science might be seen as synergistic. It is commonplace for literary writers to use fiction and narrative to convey their strong dissatisfaction with the present social, economic, or political order" (988–89). For narrative literature, examining the specific employment of fictional techniques will be the key method to uncover these underlying values.

Of special importance is the brand of ethical criticism developed in China. Nie Zhenzhao calls for a critical theory that approaches literary works on the basis of their ethical essence and educational function from the perspective of ethics (see *Introduction* 13). He argues that "literature is a historically contingent presentation of ethics and morality and that reading literature helps human beings to reap moral enlightenment and thus make better ethical choices [...] literature is essentially a guidebook for the moral teaching of humanity" (Nie, "Conceptual"). The task is, then, "the examination of the ethical values in a given work with reference to a particular historical context. [...] In short, the aim of ethical literary criticism is to offer varied experiences, lessons, instructions and inspirations for our learning, teaching and enlightenment. Without those, I would even say, literature would be nothing; literary critics would be nothing; and ethical literary criticism would be nothing but marks on a page" ("Conceptual"). In this context, we can recall Feng Menglong's Preface to *Stories to Caution the World* (1624) in the Ming Dynasty, in which he affirms that popular historical romances can serve as supplements to historical works for the purpose of fostering virtues in their readers' minds (5–6).

Yet there is a warning: when emotions "draw our attention to the value significance of an object, act, event or opinion," a reader or viewer may identify imaginatively and emotionally with "a particular fictional person in a specific situation" (Wolf 90, 91).[8] This is understandable since a literary work incorporates a certain "ethical spirit" which makes readers think of their personal experiences in life ("Pour Bouveresse, la vérité du roman tient donc en définitive à cet 'esprit éthique' qui l'anime et qui met en contact le lecteur avec sa propre expérience de la vie": Sabot 148). However, the upshot may not be moral learning, but rather a fascination with a text's materiality, its *discours*, so that the experience "need not necessarily lead to an ethically relevant insight and to changes in our behavior" (Wolf 90). This only becomes possible when, drawing on the phenomenology of Bernhard Waldenfels (see the chapter by Steppat and Yang in Volume 9), we accept that it is "not we who approach the text ethically and ask questions, it must be the other way round": a literary representation should be able to "provoke ethical consternation," introducing "rupture, another perspective" (Wolf 98). In contrast, Dominique Rabaté points out that even if a

---

[8] As psychological research shows, considering concrete situations in which people are able to believe that certain values matter can be encouraged by means of narratives such as "[s]hort stories or scenarios" (Jiga-Boy et al. 258).

novel asks certain existential questions, it cannot always answer them because it passes through an ambiguous mirror of the respective representation and plot ("Mais si le roman permet de poser la question, ou plutôt de la mettre à l'épreuve imaginairement et selon un certain rythme temporal, il ne lui revient sans doute pas de pouvoir y répondre, puisqu'il sera forcément passé par le miroir ambigu de la représentation et de la mise en intrigue"; Rabaté 21).

There is a recent pushback, of sorts, as shown in a collection of essays *Against Value*. Its editors loosely define value in a politicized sense: "the neoliberal economy, 'post-ideological' state management, and audit culture," hence "normative, repressive, alienating" — while being "ostensibly virtuous (the good, the beautiful, the happy)" (Ladkin et al. 2). This has echoes of the British development of Cultural Studies (see also the chapter by Tomaselli and Du in Volume 9). Hence the book, which occasionally touches on translation issues but hardly has an intercultural orientation, "resists a defence of the arts or education that is predicated on establishing the value of their contestation of those dominating values, which all too readily provides another market for their expansion"; the arts, that is, may be "expressions of the values they critique" (2). Instead, "the arts and education are fundamentally against value." And when they are, the arts "messily inhabit or haunt the normative, disturbing its order, rather then [sic] seeking new norms" (2); they "resist the predations of instrumentalised thinking" (4).

These assertions partly run parallel to the argumentation of Frédéric Regard (see the subsection "Valid or Alternative Values" further below). They can build on Leo Bersani's and Ulysse Dutoit's claim that art objects as such cannot repair failed social lives; instead, as acts of resistance, art objects "refuse to serve the complacency of a culture that expects art to reinforce its moral and epistemological authority"; they are consequently "at war with culture" (8). To some extent, the observations can be traced back to Alfred North Whitehead's description in 1925 of value as "the intrinsic reality of an event": "the element of value, of being valuable, of having value, of being an end in itself, of being something which is for its own sake" is vital for any account of an event (93; see also Lawrence 147 ff., and the differentiations analyzed by Bode).⑨ Great art then provides "transient" values, "something out of the routine," and thus "transforms

---

⑨ A discussion of the distinction between final and non-final values, in a context of value taxonomy, is offered by Rabinowicz and Rønnow-Rasmussen 30ff.

the soul into the permanent realisation of values extending beyond its former self" (Whitehead 202; see also Pater 249 on "that continual vanishing away"). Likewise relevant is Roman Jakobson's concept of poetic function, which he formulated in 1933: poetic words, their syntactic combinations, and their signification possess their own importance and their own value ("les mots et leur syntaxe, leur signification, leur forme externe et interne ne sont pas des indices indifférents de la réalité, mais possèdent leur propre poids et leur propre valeur": 46). Or one could point to Theodor Adorno's aesthetic theory in which "the function of art in the totally functional world is its functionlessness; [...] The instrumentalization of art sabotages its opposition to instrumentalization [...]" (320).

The volume by Ladkin et al. makes an effort to bring similar insights together with Friedrich Nietzsche's anatomy of nihilism in 1887, according to which we can see "the value of things precisely in the lack of any reality corresponding to these values and in their being merely a symptom of strength on the part of the value-positers. [...] Values and their changes are related to increases in the power of those positing the values" (14).[10] Changes in value are thus at the same time changes in power, so that the strongest can overcome existing values ("die Stärksten überwinden die richtenden Werthe"); value becomes understandable as valuation.

While taking note of this, we suggest that studying the processes of ascertaining and/or attributing value — also known as axiology — can enter into a dialogue at various stages with the processes of determining identity. If we were to adapt the Integrated Identity Matrix model proposed in Volume 2 of this book series, we could then in each context ask whether the values appear at an internalized private level, in small or large social circles, or in larger in-groups; whether they show a degree of self-determination, or interpersonal negotiation, intergroup ascription, or socially imposed roles (Kulich, "Toward" 79−83). There is a correlation with honor, as

---

[10] In the German original, "Werth-Ansetzer" sounds rather like people who are determining certain values: "Daß es *keine Wahrheit* giebt; daß es keine absolute Beschaffenheit der Dinge, kein » Ding an sich «giebt. — *Dies ist selbst nur Nihilismus, und zwar der extremste*. Er legt den *Werth* der Dinge gerade dahinein, daß diesen Werthen *keine* Realität entspricht und entsprach, sondern daß sie nur ein Symptom von Kraft auf Seiten der *Werth-Ansetzer* sind, eine Simplifikation zum *Zweck des Lebens*. [...] Die *Werthe und deren Veränderung* stehen im Verhältniß zu dem *Macht-Wachsthum des Werthsetzenden*" (12: 351). Cf. Cousin's earlier statement: "Une chose n'a pas de valeur par soi; elle n'a que celle que la personne lui confère" (353).

studied by Krause and Sun in Volume 9: "The key to honor processes is that value is assigned by an Other onto the Self"; "Honor is the social process that links identity and value, creating the being-as-identity in individuals and groups. Honor provides an escape from social-nothingness [...]" (Oprisko 46, 57). For social-nothingness, Oprisko cites the paradox of Homer's Thersites in the *Iliad* (Book 2, 211–77), a common soldier who dares to bait his leaders and rails at Agamemnon. Thersites is beaten back by Odysseus into recognizing "the effective non-being of common people," yet since he is named and becomes "the exemplary commoner in the story" he is "honored above all other commoners" with epic fame (Oprisko 95).

Forms of Value

Thus in various ways, an ethical understanding of values, such as the justice and goodness cited above, has recurrently been considered relevant for discussions of literature (see also Grønstad 31–43 and Yang). For some, invoking "la valeur en littérature" means "faire apparaître au choix le spectre du conservatisme réactionnaire" (Vaugeois 28; see also Ladkin et al. 6). Rather, educative programs should beware of using literary works for moral education: "Faire de la littérature un simple instrument d'édification au service de la morale collective" would be to literary works "de simples répliques de l'univers réel" (Laroque and Raulet-Marcel; see also Ştefănescu). It is not the purpose of this appendix to give a comprehensive account of the "ethical turn" and its categories, only to suggest its significance in literary studies.

Ethical values are logically distinct from aesthetical valuations, which are not directly our concern here (see also the classification in Levitin 494, as well as the discussion in Hoffmann and Hornung). Barry Slater provides an overview of the debate on aesthetical values from Kant's *Critique of Judgment* (see also Zangwill) to Janet Wolff's *Aesthetics and the Sociology of Art*, with a focus on the question whether we should assume there is a privileged social class, people with aesthetical interests. As is well known, Barbara Herrnstein Smith has denied that such values are inherent in particular objects:

> All value is radically contingent, being neither a fixed attribute, an inherent quality, or an objective property of things but, rather, an effect of multiple, continuously changing, and continuously interacting variables or, to put this another way, the product of a dynamics of a system, specifically an *economic* system [...] the value of an entity to an individual subject is *also* the product of the

dynamics of an economic system. (30)①

A personal economy is constituted by the subject's needs and resources, while "any particular subject's 'self'" is "also variable, being multiply and differently configurable in terms of different roles, relationships, and, in effect, identities [...]" (Smith 31). Hitlin and Piliavin also speak of this link between identity and values by referring to Gecas, who "suggested that 'value-identities' are important aspects of collectively shared identifications that become internalized at the individual level" (Hitlin and Piliavin 382; see also Hitlin, and Bilsky and Schwartz). Hence valuations and identities are likely to become mutually configured. By analogy, "cultural values shape and are shaped by cultural identity struggles" (Buzzanell 18). This observation is shared by William B. Gudykunst and Tsukasa Nishida, who carried out a study on the impact of culture on individual values in Japan and the United States. In two articles on social identity, Marisa Zavalloni has found that the social and cultural identities of individuals have a direct impact on their personal value system. As for the question of intrinsic as against extrinsic values, extended to intrinsic as against extrinsic properties, it is discussed at length by Zimmerman. In an apparently unpublished 2009 paper "What Is Instrumental Value?" Dale Dorsey, however, does not agree with the definition of extrinsic value provided by Zimmerman, "who claims that one important type of value (which he identifies, mistakenly I shall argue, as 'extrinsic') is the possession of 'potential consequences'" (11).②

In terms of a work's capacity to elicit pleasure or displeasure, since earliest times (as we have indicated) ethical and aesthetic value variants have been closely related: "only by working together with

---

① Arjo Klamer's observation that "[t]he cultural economic perspective compels us to distinguish social and cultural values from economic values" is relevant in this context. See also Klamer's article "Cultural Goods are Good for More Than Their Cultural Value" (http://www.klamer.nl/publication/2011-cultural-goods-are-good-for-more-than-their-cultural-value/). The link between values and economic status has also been highlighted by Hofstede, Inglehart, Sinha, Smith, and others. Inglehart highlights, for example, how economic development leads to a shift in survival strategies which also includes a shift in values. In literary works that deal with intercultural situations, one can observe a clear relationship between economic status and respective value systems. Both the scarcity hypothesis as well as the socialization hypothesis (see Inglehart 221 ff.) can be applied to certain works of fiction (221 ff.).

② https://pdfs.semanticscholar.org/c3f0/09dc9e208fcf0d9e4782c8797f11424c1747.pdf. Accessed Jan. 2018.

morality can the aesthetic value of literature be fully realized" (Nie, "Towards" 88; see also Lamarque). In the Brill and Rodopi book series *Value Inquiry* (since 1992), a volume by Meretoja et al. examines the "Values of Literature"; we will not follow this research pathway (rather than that of values in literature) very far in our context. An important perspective is added in Zhang Longxi's chapter in Volume 9.

A further distinction is possible in that ethical values are not necessarily coextensive with cultural values,[13] though there are overlaps in terms of "the basic values that people in all cultures recognize" such as "restraint of actions, inclinations, and impulses likely to upset or harm others" (Schwartz, "Basic Human" 257, 262). However, the meaning of a cross-culturally recognized value like "honor" (for instance) and its importance might differ very much, depending on whether it is considered an individualistic and gender-neutral or a collectivistic and gender-specific value. These differences are sometimes reflected in the number of expressions available in the respective language, in which one can measure the significance of such a value by the variety of words that exist to describe it (see the chapter by Krause and Sun in Volume 9).

Cultural egalitarianism is defined as seeking "to induce people to recognize one another as moral equals" (Schwartz, "Mapping" 342), while studying cultural values as a union of opposites involves exploring "the foundations of morality" (S. Smith, K. Smith and Christopher 414). Measurable values such as stimulation, hedonism, or achievement, and values of conservation and self-enhancement ("Basic Human") are hard to square with moral categories in any classical sense, while they may suggest how different notions of ethics may apply in specific sociocultural contexts — as one might gather already from Aristotle's *Nicomachean Ethics* 1113a3. The major values identified by Geert Hofstede show next to no overlap with moral categories, while moral aspects may be mentioned in country comparisons especially with regard to the

---

[13] In the early 1990s, Zygmunt Bauman highlighted that "[v]ariety and coexistence have become 'cultural values' [...]" (18). In a related context, Moll et al. point out that moral values as "internalized abstract social norms or rules against which the appropriateness of one's behavior is evaluated" differ from Schwartz's core values as "representations to which one willingly attaches and which comprise an important part of the self"; this is a pitfall in neuroscience research (124).

category "Individualism."⑭ In particular, the categories "Power Distance" and "Masculinity" are indirectly related to certain moral notions, for example to the understanding of a patriarchal, gender-based value like honor in collectivistic cultures. Hofstede's model of cultural dimensions can therefore sometimes be useful for the interpretation of intercultural literature.

In an immediate sense, concepts and research results based on the study of intercultural communication have a certain relevance for interculturally oriented literature, which focuses on cultural encounters and migrations. Thus one can fruitfully study, for instance, disparity in values occurring during communication in television comedies between individuals from an African culture and English/Russian cultures, as Teilanyo does. It is not quite so evident at first sight how concepts from intercultural communication can potentially apply to all kinds of literature. Yet, in a wider sense, a majority of literary works are unthinkable without influences from other cultures, including genre, structure, topics, use of figures of speech, character depiction, or further aspects. Values study as we are tracing it in this appendix rarely seems to consider this aspect of travel, transfer, and transmission of values in connection with the travels of textual discourses. Yet cultural and literary transfers are a core area of intercultural communication research, for the key qualification of intercultural competence. To a certain extent, then, such research may well have potential significance for a majority of literary works and can contribute to intercultural inquiry in this wider sense, having a considerable impact on values.

We should keep in mind that some of the social-science research on values tends to speak to organizational and management culture, so that it cannot be applied without careful scrutiny to the study of literature (what Fludernik and others have called an "economization of culture" is not the aim).⑮ The underlying values which an examination of fictional techniques can reveal may be basic human

---

⑭ Examples: In Malaysia, "Employer/employee relationships are perceived in moral terms (like a family link)" (https://www.hofstede-insights.com/country-comparison/malaysia/). In Turkey, "The relationship has a moral base and this always has priority over task fulfillment" (https://www.hofstede-insights.com/country-comparison/turkey/).

⑮ For the importance of such scrutiny, Steppat in our companion volume 8 (Chapter 5) calls attention to the operation of "praxial critique" as expounded by transversal rationality: an exercise of "discernment in our discursive and institutional engagements."

values, or they may be suitable to "describe, map, and give insight into cultural differences" ("Mapping" 339), whether at a national level or in terms of a variety of subgroups.

In this context, we need to call attention to research which challenges assumptions of a consensus of values within nations, and instead suggests (along with constructivism) an intersubjectivist approach centering on norms (see Leung and Morris). Schwartz already distinguished between values (as "abstract goals") and norms, since the latter "usually refer to specific actions, objects, or situations" ("Basic Human" 259). Recent research originating in the context of management and organization studies, but not exhausted therein, locates the source of cultural influence in a cultural group and the individual's perceptions of it, in order to measure norms rather than individual values — research which becomes relevant in studying honor cultures and face cultures (see Yao et al.). It can, to some extent, become useful in examining fiction which depicts each of these cultures, as described in the chapter by Krause and Sun in Volume 9. Yet we should retain an understanding of cultural norms which explores how these can "serve to reinforce perspectives of powerful groups" and "silence those who would challenge the cultural status quo" (DeTurk 565, 579).

It has been shown that for instance 20th-century Latin American writers have explored national values as reflected in regional customs, examining characters associated with national movements as reflectors of national values (see Ocasio 56–57). In a wider sense, the national and universal have been set as forming "an equation of cultural contact": the latter may be "either the opposite, or a function of the national (specific)," while "universal values are established as a result of complex operations involving specific (mostly national) comparisons" — needing the employment of "interactive, dialogic or multiple-level frames" (Ursa 151). The national is the main level studied by scientists such as Hofstede and Schwartz, while Hofstede extends this to the organizational and occupational levels (206) by additionally mentioning regional cultures and gender cultures. Hofstede furthermore explains that symbols represent "the most superficial, and values the deepest layers of culture, with heroes and rituals in between" ("National" 386). Inglehart and Schwartz group countries into cultural zones and world regions. In this context, the Inglehart-Welzel cultural map of the world, which is derived from the World Values Survey and provides an overview of traditional vs. secular-rational values as well as survival vs. self-expression values, is relevant.

Schwartz is perceptive in reflecting that the nation as such is characterized by its heterogeneous nature: "Is the nation a legitimate unit of cultural analysis? Nations or even their distinct regions are rarely homogeneous societies with a unified culture [...] inferences about national culture may depend on which subgroups are studied" ("Mapping" 355). Knowing that cultural subgroups "espouse conflicting value emphases," he considers survey responses for teachers in different age groups, male vs. female student subgroups, and teacher vs. student samples, concluding that there is a considerable "similarity of cultural value orientations within nations" against "the background of cultural distance between nations" ("Mapping" 340, 357). Heine et al. (2002) suggest that cross-cultural comparisons yield different results depending on the methods used. Minkov and Hofstede find that in-country regions overwhelmingly cluster along national lines on basic cultural values, cross-border intermixtures being relatively rare.

Certainly, culture is difficult to define coherently. Spencer-Oatey, for instance, sums this up as follows: "Culture is a fuzzy set of basic assumptions and values, orientations to life, beliefs, policies, procedures and behavioural conventions that are shared by a group of people, and that influence (but do not determine) each member's behaviour and his/her interpretations of the 'meaning' of other people's behaviour'" (3). In the same vein, Mattos and Branco explain that the "construction of values is an intensely dynamic process, involving internalization and externalization of collective meanings, and is central to what we refer to as personal culture" (11). If one considers culture as comprising "static embedded scripts" which become related to "hybrid contextual integrations" *and* to "dynamic situational responses" (Kulich and Weng 17), cultural groupings will not be exhausted by national, occupational or student and teacher categories (see also Ikeguchi 482). The cultural variables to which, for instance, Branco and Valsiner devote attention go beyond these.

In the present book series, Rosita Albert highlights the dimensions of cultural variability in which Latino immigrants differ from mainstream Americans; Clara Popa discusses the Roma people. While he observes that, "[i]n addition to a dominant culture, subgroups within societies espouse conflicting value emphases," Schwartz surmises a fairly stable dominance order when there are "two or three" competing ethnic groups, yet an "ambiguous and less stable" dominance order when more such groups are in competition

("Mapping" 340, 370).

Intercultural communication pays careful attention to minority groups and their specific values (Kulich, *Applying* 281): "Any study of values needs to consider [...] the regional realities that are becoming increasingly divergent, with unequal levels between coastal and inland regions, urban and rural areas, and other geographical or ethnic situated contexts"; the question is then: "When does one's cultural/ethnic identity/values set prevail (when meeting 'foreigners'), and when does one's geographic or other identity/values set overrule" — as in the form of subgroup values? In showing the inner conflicts of characters who are torn apart between two or more, sometimes rather incompatible cultures, "immigrant literature" highlights precisely this problematic. There are both "theories of cultural integration, suggesting that migrants gradually absorb the values and lifestyles of their countries of destination, and theories of multiculturalism, which suggest that enduring traditions, shared identities, and deep-rooted values persist for many minority groups" (Inglehart and Norris 6; see also Welzel Part A2 "Mapping Differences"; Robinson; then briefly Remland et al. on "Developing a Cultural Identity," and Martin and Nakayama, e.g., 14, 95). Inglehart and Norris also stress that "distinctive social values [are] shaped by collective histories, common languages, and religious traditions, that migrant populations are unlikely to abandon their cultural roots when they settle in another country." Berry, Kim and Boski's theory of intercultural adaptation and adjustment can be significant in this context, underlining that the value systems of assimilators and separators develop in opposite directions (see Chapter 12 by Krause in Volume 8).

At a 2012 conference on "Values in literature and the value of literature" in Helsinki, a focus on the conflict of values in multicultural literature has been provided by Corinna Assmann, concentrating on the topics of religion, tradition, and ritual in Nadeem Aslam's *Maps for Lost Lovers*: "The immigrant situation is [...] often a catalyst for the clash of values, when the conflicting codes and norms of different ethnic or religious groups take on a crucial role in establishing boundaries and furthering powerful mechanisms of inclusion and exclusion."[16]

We should, then, keep in mind that a "'different culture' can exist among different ethnic groups inside one country or region," which often brings with it a different set of values exposed to various

---

[16] See http://blogs.helsinki.fi/values-in-literature/files/2012/05/Abstraktit-blogiin-valiviivalla31.pdf.

interpretations (Jiang and Huang 153).⑰ The chapter by Wen Peihong in the present volume calls attention to minority cultures and their values expressions. In general terms, we should be aware that literature can speak of, generate, or disseminate "unsanctioned, excluded and repressed forms of life as well as their underpinning values and norms" together with "alternative hierarchies of values" (Baumbach et al. 5).

Questions of "The Good Life"

In recent years, sustained attention has been given to "Ethics in Culture" as thematized in a major essay collection (see Erll et al.), including perspectives on transcendental ethics, literary ethics, ethics and aesthetics, and others. This book highlights the key question for those interested in a renewed ethics of moral guidance: "What shall I do to lead a good life?" (1). As mentioned before, many literary works deal with the question "Comment devons-nous vivre?" (Bessière 7). Readers are often subconsciously searching for an adequate answer in the behavior and decision-making of fictional characters. Jacques Bouveresse also focuses on "How should we live?" rather than on "How do we live?" in literary works, or, as Martha C. Nussbaum puts it, on the fact that the reader is invited "to perform ethically significant acts of perception and attention, acts that are themselves part of a well-lived ethical life" ("Literature" 11). Vincent Jouve describes Nussbaum's view of the aim of literature in the same way ("Pour M. Nussbaum, le but de la littérature est de nous apprendre a 'bien vivre'"). Since literature can exceed reality by creating imaginary worlds, readers are confronted with socio-ethical experiences and challenges that broaden their range of existential possibilities and thus widen their horizon.⑱ Among

---

⑰ "Technically speaking, there is no 'American culture' in America that can serve as a common culture [...] America has equipped itself with all the material elements that a modern country is supposed to have, but it is yet to become a nation with its own civilization foundation and culture" (Jiang and Huang 154).

⑱ In a book review, Barbara Carnevali summarizes the role of literature as a moral guide as follows: "La question fondamentale est donc moins 'Comment vivent les hommes?' que 'Comment devons-nous vivre?' Et la littérature y répond justement grâce à sa capacité de dépasser le domaine de la réalité effective et de produire des situations fictives. Elargissant le champ des possibilités existentielles, l'imagination littéraire permet aux lecteurs démultiplier et d'approfondir leur expérience éthique: elle est donc un instrument incontournable de cette activité réflexive que la tradition anglo-saxonne nomme 'perfectionnisme moral'" (482).

others, Nargis Khan stresses the "responsibility of literature in giving us moral education" (6), enabling us to "play our key role as better human being so that we can perform well in our own ecological cycle" (7).

These observations coincide with Steve J. Kulich's report of research in which participants conceive of the highest aim of all values as "happiness and a good life" or "快乐与幸福", with personal, social, and superordinate goals (*Applying* 306). They also match Prosser's highlighting of values which in Aristotle's *Rhetoric* "lead men toward happiness, and thus to a good life" (26). Scrutinizing literature's importance "for the dissemination of ethical values within a culture" is, then, the aim of *Ethics in Culture* (4): not necessarily other kinds of value, and not necessarily across cultures, though some of the chapters are strongly comparative. A few brief spotlights on selected chapters may illuminate this aim. In his own chapter, Herbert Grabes makes the point that works which offer both Horace's *prodesse* and *delectare* (as quoted above) have "best stood the test of time" (42). Ronald Shusterman argues that the reader is challenged to interpret, with freedom of choice, and this "conscious experience" of the nature of judgment and valuing characterizes the "metaethical experience" of the literary work, the form of judgment and value (85). For that matter, in *The Doctor and the Soul* Viktor Frankl emphasizes that aesthetic as well as ethical values "require adequate acts in order to be comprehended," while the acts and the values they allow us to comprehend "afford us a view of only a cross-section of the world" (41). Instead, it becomes necessary "to disclose the full richness of the world of values, and to make clear the extent of its domain" (Frankl 42), which embraces three variants:

> Values which are realized in creative action we should like to call "creative" values. In addition to these, there are values which are realized in experience: "experiential values." These latter are realized in receptivity toward the world — for example, in surrender to the beauty of nature or art. [...] The third group of values lies precisely in a man's attitude toward the limiting factors upon his life. His very response to the restraints upon his potentialities provides him with a new realm of values which surely belong among the highest values. [...] These values we will call attitudinal values. What is significant is the person's attitude toward an unalterable fate. (Frankl 43–44)

For Angela Locatelli, literature transmits values when interpretation serves as an antidote "against the monolithic perspective of any dominant and/or rule-based interpretive community" (27), providing a "memory of time-specific subjectivities" and being an archive of extinct subjects (30). Birgit Neumann focuses more extensively on memory, suggesting that a perpetuation of values is coupled with "a self-conscious reflection of the process of evaluation or 'value-making'" (134−35). She explores the idea that literature offers no unmediated access to values, instead "it actively engages with cultural values," providing new scenarios for "evaluating the imperative to seek/assess value" (132). Tim Gillespie expresses a similar view (not in this book) when he states that "literature does not teach morals in a didactic way; rather it gives us a chance to *experience* moral dilemmas" (18), which may show us how to solve existential problems and lead a better life: "We read ourselves imaginatively into other lives and by this act expand the pages of our own" (17). Even ethically questionable literary works such as Bret Easton Ellis' *American Psycho* or Leila Aboulela's *Minaret* encourage readers to take sides and, by doing so, defend their own moral standpoint, which they can develop while facing such fictional identity crises. In the novel *The Children Act*, where the life of a child is in the hands of a judge's decision and the line between right and wrong seems very thin, Ian McEwan also confronts the reader with a moral dilemma.

Wolfgang Müller in *Ethics in Culture* focuses on narrative fiction in describing three forms of mediating moral values: ⑲ authorial/heterodiegetic narration, which provides rhetorical strategies allowing the reader to discover moral evaluation, varied in restricted omniscience; point-of-view narration with a covert narrator, which "makes it the reader's task to decode the moral qualities of characters and actions" (123−24), varied in ironic and non-ironic uses of free indirect style; and I-narration or character narration, presenting "an individual vision which is not relativized by the superior perspective of an omniscient narrator or the dual voice of point-of-view narration" (127). For novels, this carefully differentiated approach could be adapted to study the value implications of narrative forms and methods, which Müller illustrates by giving examples of novels including Salinger's *The Catcher in the Rye*, Twain's *Huckleberry Finn*, Austen's *Emma*, and others. In a later essay, which includes an example from epic, Müller highlights the depiction of moral

---

⑲ In a comprehensive University of Maryland Ph.D. thesis in 2004, Alessandro Giovannelli analyzes the interconnectedness between artistic/ethical values and narratives: https://drum.lib.umd.edu/bitstream/handle/1903/1474/umi-umd-1595.pdf?sequence = 1&isAllowed = y.

concerns such as kindness and exposure of hypocrisy in Jane Austen's fiction and argues that fiction enables ethics to manifest itself in more comprehensive ways than in non-fictional sources and methods since "narrative techniques can mediate a multitude of attitudes, perspectives, changes of perception, inside views" ("From" 21). This argument can become significant when it is transferred to values, on account of aesthetic mediation and perspective.

We should extend the focus on narrative forms, however, to concentrate on specific textual elements as far as "singular turns of tone, phrase, and figure" in various genres, including the "bafflement" that the lyrical devices are bound to produce, for the purpose of "reading texts closely as texts" (de Man 23). Carroll seems to think similarly to what we have described, when he points out that "in reading a novel, our moral understanding is engaged already. Indeed, reading a novel is itself generally a moral activity insofar as reading narrative literature typically involves us in a continuous process of making moral judgments. Moreover, this continuous exercise of moral judgment itself contributes to the expansion and education of our moral understanding through practice" (*Beyond* 300).

In *Ethics in Culture*, Björn Minx discusses American novels about World War II which communicate particular values, and which thus show a movement in the "value hierarchy between 1948 and 1969" (352). Several chapters highlight authors, *ex negativo*, since the nineteenth century who avoid explicit moral commentary or judgment or express them through polyphony, "dissidence, revocation, negativity, deviance and subversion" (327). By and large, the critical approaches as described tend to concentrate on narrative fiction, and are to this extent generically narrower (or more focused) than the work of Nie Zhenzhao (as in *Introduction*, Chapters 10, 13, 14).[20]

Roland Weidle in 2009, not unlike Müller, observes that "whether a narrator is part of the story world or stands outside it is obviously very relevant for the analysis of value construction and assessment." Similarly, for "the analysis of value construction in narratives the overtness of a narrator or structuring device" is highly significant: is a narrator more overt or more covert? And to what extent does this more overt or more covert attitude influence the reader's moral perception? For "the construction, affirmation and questioning of value positions," variants of focalization as well as of speech representation from indirect speech to free direct discourse

---

[20]   For ethics in lyric poetry, see Lohöfer; in theater studies, see Pewny.

are essential. Anne Leclaire-Halté in 2014 also examines the link between the narrator's voice and the values that are described in a novel, pointing out that a positive evaluation of a character by the narrator can have a considerable impact on the reader's own moral judgment ("Il ne suffit cependant pas que le lecteur s'identifie au personnage principal, il faut encore que celui-ci soit évalué positivement par le narrateur"). Vincent Jouve asks how our values influence our perception of a text, but also how a text can shape our value system ("comment nos valeurs pèsent-elles sur notre rapport au texte? comment le texte agit-il sur nos valeurs?"). However, in this context we should take into account narrative unreliability (see also Phelan or Laurent et al.). As Peter Ackroyd tellingly simulates *The Last Testament of Oscar Wilde*: "I have come to understand why I found myself employing conventional values only to mock at them or turn them into parody [...]" (18 Aug. 1900).

Vera Nünning adds an important point: "At a moment when the legitimization of literary scholarship has become an urgent problem in many countries," gaining competence to analyze "[t]he persuasive power of fiction" in disseminating values is particularly justifying (53). Nünning's analysis of the ethics of fictional form extends to "works that foreground the question of the reliability of narrators or focalizers" (as also studied by James Phelan) and to "multi-perspective works featuring heterogeneous perspectives." If we were to adapt Nünning's (53) catalog of open research questions beyond the purpose of empathy with altruistic behavior, the result could look rather like the following, extendable to film:

- What role do specific cultural valuations play concerning the contents of a particular narrative work or the depiction of the characters?
- In which ways do features such as characters' physical attractiveness, their idealized (or not) personality traits and emotional dispositions relate to the use of fictional conventions in conveying values?
- Which constellations of particular fictional devices regulate the distance between reader/ viewer and character, and invite the reader/ viewer to share the character's values (or not)?
- To what extent are these constellations subject to historical change, what role do cultural values play in any change, and is it possible to relate specific constellations to specific (sub) genres?

In *Ethics in Culture* Birgit Neumann asks, "Can literature contribute at all to the dissemination of cultural values and, if so, where is the ethical dimension that can be attributed to literature to be found?" (131). Martha C. Nussbaum's question is similar: "What, however, is the contribution that literature makes to our understanding of ethical matters?" ("Literature" 5). Concerning cultural values, we can assume what has been argued for modern Russian literature: a "writer intuitively perceives and figuratively reflects timely values. [...] Then, these values reappear in the cultural space" (Funtova and Sinetskiy 932). For intercultural literature, instances of a possible answer can be found in Volume 9, as in the chapter by Sun Yan: this shows how an orientalist and diplomat (Robert Van Gulik) in a series of English fictional works has offered depictions of a famous Tang Dynasty judge as a Confucianist official who attaches supreme importance to accepted moral values. While these are individually applied, at the same time they enable the promotion of Chinese cultural values.

Valid or Alternative Values

Even more relevant to our inquiry is a major essay collection on *Literature and Values* (2009, see Baumbach et al.). As the introduction declares, "the complex and reciprocal relationship between literature and value has not received as much attention as it arguably deserves" (1). The emphasis is not much different from that of *Ethics in Culture*, and frequently speaks of morality: literature and related media can serve the "indirect promotion of values by supplying moral models and presenting practical examples of human behaviour" (3). They "open up possible ways of life, which we can either subscribe to or reject" (3). Yet the editors are aware that "there are not very many approaches that would aptly serve the critic interested in discerning values" — especially suitable highlighted here are those of Wayne Booth and of Wolfgang Müller, as described above (3).

They are supplemented in the volume by discussions of the reader's/recipient's perspective, enabling the reader to experience "a fictitious identification with others, an observation of events and fates from multiple perspectives," and by discussions of the relation between values as disseminated by a literary work and those found "in other discourses and extra-textual conditions" (4) at the time of origin. Drawing on the mimetic structure as mapped by Paul Ricoeur, the volume aims to show how literature can represent "valid, alternative or different norms and values," so that it offers "socially sanctioned or desired, yet more often unsanctioned, excluded and repressed forms of life as well as their underpinning values and norms" together with "idealized or alternative hierarchies of values" (5). With these variables literature contributes to "social conceptions of a good life," which are thematized by Michael Prosser (quoted above).

Volume 197 of the journal *Le Français aujourd'hui* entitled "Littérature et valeurs" in 2017 equally deals with this topic, while providing an overview of different narratives (also including poetry and youth literature) and their impact on the presentation of certain values which shape our identity.[21] A similar focus in the context of education can be found in Laurent et al., where we come across the observation that literature not only offers ideological statements about the exterior world but also builds a universe in itself with its own problems and conflicts of values ("La littérature n'est pas qu'un discours idéologique sur le monde extérieur. Elle constitue elle-même un univers qui connait ses propres problèmes et conflits de valeurs": 5–6). Among other questions, the contributors to this volume ask who decides about the "value of the values" in a literary work, especially in cases where the narrator is not reliable.

How, then, is the literary contribution constructed in each case, "with what literary methods or techniques" are cultural values represented in a text (Baumbach et al. 5)? In the context of education, suitable tasks can include: "underline the sentences which reflect individualism, low-power distance, competitive nature, high-context communication [...]," similarly for cultural determination of characters' specific actions (Natsiuk 185 ff.); analysis of metaphors is a further relevant task (see González Rodríguez and Puyal 122).

Asking about literary methods is significant for the purpose of grasping each of the functions of constructing, representing, and disseminating values. The functions operate within a sociocultural context — the kind of context investigated by intercultural communication studies — so that the literary contribution is "an active constructive process, in which cultural systems of meaning, literary processes of formal configuration and practices of reception are equally involved" (Baumbach et al. 6).[22] Accordingly, norms and values that "actually

---

[21] See https://www.fabula.org/actualites/le-francais-aujourd-hui-n-197-litterature-et-valeurs_80642.php.

[22] See also Luis Fernando Gómez Rodríguez's article, which deals with a similar topic. From a Marxist perspective, Robert Weimann in the early 1970s spoke of a "sociological dimension of value" in that "the social impact and nature" of a literary work, hence the reader's cooperation, can become an index of value. In a similar historical-materialist context, Rita Schober at the same time argued that literature creates a polyfunctional "world of values" in that a valuing subject objectifies itself in the work which readers can then perceive as meaningful and hence compare to their own world. See also Mecklenburg xxvii. In a non-Marxist sense, aspects of Schober's argumentation are adapted by Funtova and Sinetskiy.

exist in the real world" and the possible worlds created in literature "enter into a relationship of mutual influence and change" (6).

This is all the more important when we consider that, as Hubert Zapf has cogently diagnosed, literature not only serves to fulfill normative functions in a society by authorizing and disseminating its valuations. It functions as *"a cultural-critical metadiscourse"* when it represents "typical deficits, blind spots, imbalances, deformations, and contradictions within dominant systems of civilizatory power," revealing these systems to be "structures of severe external or internal constraint" (Zapf 62). Bernhard Waldenfels, studying the boundaries of orders and the conditions of living with alienness, similarly maintains that "[e]ach order has its blind spot in the form of something unordered" ("Boundaries" 77). Cultural criticism compels a discussion of "the ways in which a given piece of literature reflects a changing system of values, and not simply literary values," with attention to interaction between literature and other social domains for a redefinition of our value system: "Literature does not exist in its own discrete space, so to limit our discussion of it to its 'literariness' is to denude it of its crucial links to the other systems that combine to articulate our sense of values" (Hans 15).㉓

As well as metadiscourse, literature tends to offer "a counterdiscursive staging and semiotic empowering of that which is marginalized, neglected or repressed in the dominant cultural reality system," as an *"imaginative counterdiscourse"* (Zapf 63). As Rebecca Kay correctly observes, "marginalized people often use identities, both individually and collectively, as a means of challenging normative assumptions and prescriptive values" (2). Further functions as described by Zapf will not directly concern us here. With some justice, one may query "whether society will grant literature a space free enough to function" in these ways (Grabes, "Literature" 6)? In any case, neither the meta- nor the counter-discourse have often been given full attention in intercultural communication's research on values, though for instance Martin and Nakayama extensively discuss identity development issues (Chapter 5). If we can assume that many characteristics of national cultures were already recognizable at least since the 17th century (Hofstede 210), the literary production of the past centuries is likely to illuminate literature's major functions concerning values in each sociocultural context.

㉓　For the interdependence of "highbrow" and "lowbrow," for instance, as indicators of literary value and the preservation of a literary elite, see Watroba.

In *Literature and Values*, highlighting interactions between text and reader, Lothar Bredella (Baumbach et al. 19 – 42) explains approvingly the positions of authors who assert that "empathy makes us human;" he turns against formalist, psychoanalytical, and deconstructive approaches that ignore or reject empathy (see also González Rodríguez and Puyal, and Djikic et al.). As Martha Nussbaum has explained it, empathy "involves a participatory enactment" without making us feel wholly as the other feels (*Upheavals* 327). She stresses that "cross-cultural understanding" needs "a capacity for sympathetic imagination that will enable us to comprehend the motives and choices of people different from ourselves" (*Cultivating* 83, 85); this means recognizing the value of such imagination for "intercultural communication" (Baumbach et al. 9).

When the fictional organization "makes us realise how the characters feel and think," it "promotes sympathetic understanding" (Baumbach et al. 40). Mar et al. argue similarly: "engaging with narrative fiction and mentally simulating the social experiences represented may improve or maintain [...] skills of empathy and social understanding" (408). Johnson has measured the effect of reading on the development and strengthening of empathy and pro-social behavior. Burwitz-Melzer draws attention to a related issue: fictional texts not only "invite their readers to view subjectively a nation or an ethnic group by portraying specific values, prejudices and stereotypes, but they also offer their audience the chance to exchange their culturally restricted points of view together with a hero or heroine of the narrative, or with the narrator telling the story" (29). In our companion volume 8, Van de Ven and Van Nuenen analyze weaknesses in assumptions of empathy.

In *Literature and Values*, Angela Locatelli stresses the quality of indeterminate literary texts to open multiple perspectives on moral issues, with a space for "experimenting with values, probing alternatives, and challenging current norms" (Baumbach et al. 10). Discussing Hanif Kureishi, Frédéric Regard argues that values like dignity, respect, recognition, and related ones need to be fleshed out in "the body of a story," which should admit a possibility "[t]o become strange to oneself," accommodating "the strangeness of the others' interpretations." In this way, values are produced by "interaction and intersubjectivity"; good and bad are precepts which refuse "to run the risk of interpretation" in a dialogic structure; they "set up barriers and frontiers, which values tend therefore to contest" (Baumbach et al. 209, 212). Together, the writing and the reading bring forth a space characterized by "movement, surprise, newness, 'strangeness'" (213). Discussing the possibility of "intrinsic values in literature," Philipp Wolf in the same volume suggests that a reader develops a view of character traits and the moral quality of actions "through narrative focalization, especially flexible or multiple focalization, temporal progression, description of facial expression and physical detail and the sometimes ambiguous relation of action and speech (particularly in first-person narratives)" (233–34). J. M. Coetzee's fictional works then turn out to be "profound demonstrations of the persistence and relevance of internal values" in the language of humanism (238). Calling attention to the fictional devices is to point in a similar direction to that proposed by Müller, for a procedure able to demonstrate values "fleshed out" in a narrative. Accompanying these chapters in the volume are a range of further case studies of dissemination of ethical values, from classical antiquity to computer games and media scandals.

In the context of a Norwegian research program designed "to generate knowledge about how cultural phenomena are assigned value and how cultural value is changed, displaced, transferred and acquired" (KULVER 2008–12),[24] Kjerstin Aukrust has presented a collection of essays which, while not focusing primarily on literature or film, includes a section on "aestheticization of sexuality and the value of gender roles." The research program points out: "The fact that cultural phenomena are assigned value implies that a hierarchisation occurs within various symbol systems, discourses and practices, which entails passing judgment on quality, taste and values" — with connected issues related to power and control. This actually restates Nietzsche's perception in *The Will to Power* (see above) that "[v]alues and their changes are related to increases in the power of those positing the values" (14).

Studying the depiction of the male hero in American action movies, Anne Gjelsvik in this book shows how the iconography and cultural values expressed in this film genre have been subject to change: "from an extraordinary man to an ordinary man doing something extra, and often his 'mission impossible' is parenthood" (105). Her analysis thus illuminates the relationship between gender and values, which is also the topic of Gry Brandser's essay. Geir Uvsløkk analyzes French writer Michel Houellebecq's creation of

---

[24] For cultural and situational contexts as conditions of value change, also dispositional resistance to change, see Boer and Boehnke 142–44.

works that question traditional assignments of value: liberalism appears as "a regime characterized by the concept of struggle" between individuals, which explains the writer's hostility against masculinist values of "individuality and competition" (78). As for Norway itself, Jørgen Lorentzen and Wenche Mühleisen demonstrate that recent Norwegian fiction links sexuality and intimacy with social aspects, while Julie Holledge and Frode Helland study Norwegian productions of Ibsen's *A Doll's House* for the cultural values that have been invested in the predominant performance tradition.

In their 2014 volume, with a Serbian background, Lopičić and Ilić "examine the construction, dissemination, deconstruction and/ or questioning of personal, familial, national, class, social, institutional, political, cultural, aesthetic and ethical values" in linguistics and literature (1), without explicitly providing a framing or introductory concept. They express a belief that in "our cynical and sceptical times of pervasive relativisms," it seems appropriate to focus on values. Chapter 2 by Danijela Prošić-Santovac examines popular Western fairy tales, finding "gender stereotypes that are detrimental to any egalitarian society," while their Disney film versions "greatly inflate the patriarchal and capitalist system of ideas that dominates the modern world" (3). With a cross-cultural orientation, Tatjana Panova-Ignjatović discusses literary images of Macedonia, focusing on the travel writings of British authors such as G. F. Abbot, H. N. Brailsford, W. Miller, A. Upward, E. P. Stebbing, and I. E. Hutton. Georgiana-Elena Dilă analyzes some plays by Arthur Miller from the viewpoint of character building and value principles, giving these works social and educational impact. Then, three chapters are devoted to the Victorian period in England: Milan Damjanoski shows how A. S. Byatt's *Possession* presents a re-evaluation of the past from the perspective of the end of the 20th century; Sonja Vitanova-Strezova demonstrates how female characters in Dickens' *Great Expectations* undermine the Victorian value system and its stereotypes, and Zornitsa Nikolova investigates how Browning and Tennyson create lyrical personae who, living in their own psychological worlds, provoke readers to question traditional social values. A further chapter is devoted to Umberto Eco's *The Prague Cemetery*. Beyond fiction, Aleksandra Žeželj Kocić looks into Hemingway's *Death in the Afternoon* (1932), where the value of manhood contributes to a value system of bullfighting governed by truth, honor, and honesty.

Ethos and Its Ambiguities

For considering literature, Liesbeth Korthals Altes' work is more substantial than these two essay collections. *Ethos and Narrative Interpretation* differs from all these contributions, though Korthals Altes begins by calling attention to Houellebecq (as Geir Uvsløkk does in the Lopičić and Ilić volume, see above). The focus is now on reception, on the reader's task of interpretation: the author "déplace l'étude de l'*ethos* vers l'espace de la lecture et de l'interprétation"; "on est dans le domaine de l'herméneutique sans laquelle l'analyse littéraire serait amputée d'éléments essentiels" (Brilliant). For Maria Brilliant, the interpretation, construction, and social negotiation of meanings and values becomes essential in this context. Korthals Altes' chief category of analysis is Greek *ethos*, which indicates "a person's or community's character or characterizing spirit, tone, or attitude," for Aristotle one of three major methods of persuasion along with *pathos* and *logos* (Korthals Altes vii). Ethos "pertains to character effects that coincide to create a trustworthy image of the speaker," as being worthy of credence, in any specific communication situation (3).

What counts as an appropriate ethos, and how far do people actually mean their words? A fictional work is uncoupled from its author; writers "have cultivated ethos ambiguities, whether for reasons of censorship, out of provocation, or for sheer delight" (viii). Hence engaging in literary narratives "leads readers into taking perspectives on perspective taking, assessing the value of values" (viii) — or, as Vincent Jouve puts it: "[...] le lecteur est un sujet flottant qui se laisse, en partie, redessiner par le texte." For Jouve this means that, being confronted with a literary text, the reader becomes more likely to question existing value sets while dealing with fiction's affective, emotional, psychological, and ideological aspects.㉕ For readers, ethos ascriptions determine "reading strategies and the value regimes they believe should apply to the work" (Korthals Altes ix). There appear to be faint echoes of the discussion of intrinsic values, and a possible dialogue with the contribution by Frédéric Regard (see above).

㉕ Values as such may not be as significant as the cultural constitution of "evaluative feelings"; social actors do not take values as determinants of action, and it is more commonly "gut feelings and emotions" that appear to inform choices. For this, see von Scheve 186–88.

Korthals Altes sees her main task as reconstructing the "socially encoded pathways along which interpreters [...] assess a discursive ethos" (ix). In a certain analogy with Nietzsche's conviction that facts do not exist but only interpretations, a reader as interpreter[26] engages in a "negotiation of a variety of potential semantic clues, which is itself inscribed in processes through which cultures articulate and negotiate, or fail to negotiate, competing ways of feeling, thinking, meaning making, and value attribution" (x). The questions that occur in this context are "What kinds of assumptions, about literature, about selves, about ethics, do people's reading habits entail?" and "When and how do they consider fiction to involve an author's or their own responsibility?" (xiii). The negotiation process is likely to enable a dialogue with Identity Negotiation (Ting-Toomey, Ying Huang, and others), as a theory explained in the Appendix to our companion volume 8. The meanings and "value positions attributed to narratives, as well as the paths along which we attribute them, are socially fabricated and negotiated";[27] estimations of the author's ethos are involved in the process (x). But why should the author be the chief agent in this? Korthals Altes discusses such aspects as narrative communication and fictionality which require taking theoretical stances, to decide in each case whether to leave out considering real authors and readers (and their ethos):"Under what conditions would readers attach importance to a character's or narrator's ethos, or rather to an author's? [...] And how would such different ethos attributions affect the interpretation and evaluation of a work?" (xi). Such lines of investigation can open a dialogue with Wolfgang Müller's proposed procedures for ethical narratology, as outlined above, just as the general approach might enable a dialogue with Ronald Shusterman's argumentations.

These discussions should "sharpen the interpreter's sensitivity to clues that he or she uses to establish the sincerity, reliability, or authority (or lack thereof) of narrative voices and of authors," an assessment which "affects what stance, what kind of worldviews and

---

[26] Among the different roles of a reader, J. A. Appleyard lists the interpreter, but also the player, hero/heroine, thinker, and pragmatic reader, all of which have an impact on his/her perception of values (pp. 14–15).

[27] Todd May in 2015 defines "narrative values" as ones that enable a life which is meaningful in that it should have a desirable theme such as adventurousness, courage, creativity, integrity, spirituality, or steadfastness; this appears to make narrative especially significant for life, but has little to do with values in literature.

values, one takes a text or its author to convey"; it also enables a reader to reflect "on one's own interpretive and evaluative habits and their underlying values and assumptions" (xiii). In connection with interpretive and evaluative habits, it is worth recalling that "ethos" can also mean "habit." This leads scholars like Reuben Brower and others, with good reason, to underscore the desire to train readers in close reading — *aisthesis* being "Aristotle's most important demand for practical ethics: a full perception of the particular" (Grabes, "What" 49; see also the Introduction to the present volume).

We should not forget, in thinking about the conveying of worldviews, that relative and absolute values can be taken as opposites, but that we nonetheless need to consider them together — in an effort to "accept the radical self-contradiction and unabatable paradox of value" (Connor 2). In a variety of ways, fiction can open the opportunity for readers and viewers to entertain and attempt to understand contradictory orientations. Psychological research in turn studies how "seemingly opposing sets of values may coexist within cultures, and even within individuals" (S. Smith, K. Smith and Christopher 414).

On the whole, research and reflection on values in the literary context have sometimes shown a comparative dimension, but rarely any inter- or transcultural focus as "interaction between cultures" and "communication between non-homogeneous cultures" (Jiang and Huang 153). Such a focus would extend to a dynamic of transformative transfer of the kind that can make potentially *all* literature culturally polyvocal, and hence the object of an interculturally oriented inquiry into values.

To some extent there is a difference from the basic line of questioning in psychological studies of value: human beings tend to affiliate or congregate with others whom they find to be similar or the same, and this is necessary for survival (see Kulich, "Values" 33–34). Because these groupings or congregations form around agreements on shared value priorities, depending on their perceived collective needs, any such grouping differs from other groupings, which is why social science largely focuses on values as distinguishing between them. But by no means exclusively: Schwartz studies personal value priorities ("Basic" 279 – 80), treating "individual values as a psychological property of persons, located in their minds" ("Societal" 42). This is not far from the concerns of literary works, if we follow Martha Nussbaum's Aristotelian emphasis on a "priority of the particular" transferred to fiction, viz., "the salient features of one's particular situation," the "ethical relevance of particular persons," with a "fine responsiveness to the concrete" (*Love's* 37ff.); considering that there can be "a plurality of distinct values," ultimate particulars cannot be subsumed under any epistēmē or system of universals (*Love's* 66ff).⊗ Similarly, "[f]or most readers, characters are one of the most important aspects of a narrative [...] the way the text presents a character is highly influential on the relation between character and reader" (Jannidis). Since the individual is "essentially constituted by values and aspirations" (Nussbaum, *Love's* 324), literature tends to consider distinctions between individuals more than between groups.

But Schwartz, too, stresses that particular values may be "very important" to one person but not to another, so that a system of value priorities characterizes people as individuals ("Basic" 258–59; see also Shearman 158 – 59). Fictional narratives usually consider socio-ethical values at the level of particular characters (their motivation, speech, consistency, and action), with characters' range of interactions and their situations. As a special case of this, we should not forget that characters may represent not only individual personalities, but also a subjacent and parallel dimension of meaning as in allegory. And of course, situations do not exist outside of interpretation. Schwartz reminds us that persons define a situation in light of their own important values ("Robustness" 322); situations, accordingly, whether in society or fiction, are not isolated incidents. It is perhaps for this reason, strengthened by Aristotle's emphasis in *Poetics* 9, that literary analysis in the form of ethical narratology tends to highlight what it sees as depictions of more or less universal moral values. This can lead to a speedy jump from the individual to the universal, all but erasing an awareness of cultural filters. Values in literature have been less often investigated for cultural difference, while even within a given culture patterns of cultural imprint may be traceable. From interculturally oriented values research, literary study may potentially receive or regain impulses for tracing variable forms of imprint.

Richard Epstein warns, not without reason, "that we should beware of the use of literary imagination as a source of social understanding" (1010). Literary studies and social science obviously interrogate their

---

⊗ Achtenberg modifies this understanding a little in her key chapter on "Valuable Particulars": "According to Aristotle, what we must perceive in the particulars in each case is their value," which Nussbaum paraphrases as salience. In this context, "value is a universal that we can know in its universal aspect without knowing much at all about it in its particular instances" (15, 18).

research objects with different methods and aims. Nonetheless, one can try to "identify culture" by studying a society's literature, chiefly seeking to tease out "underlying value emphases" (Schwartz, "Mapping" 341). We are well-advised to recall James S. Hans' assertion that literature "does not exist in its own discrete space, so to limit our discussion of it to its 'literariness' is to denude it of its crucial links to the other systems that combine to articulate our sense of values" (15). In the two *Literature and Interculturality* volumes, values research with an intercultural communication context has already become effective in analyses of (among others) Sino-Canadian and Indian-American literature, American theater, East and West African as well as Turkish fiction, Shakespeare, and comparative studies.

II. Intercultural Communication and Values

Substantive Features

In the following, we will offer a simplified and brief account of major directions in values research as they have become fruitful for intercultural communication. We have already touched on a few of these above. To understand what matters to people and guides them, "[a] central concept" is value, and value priorities have been called the "dominating force in life" (Higgins 43). Hitlin and Piliavin in 2004 have observed the resurgence of the study of values in various disciplines which has undergone several stages, both before and since the classical view of values as conceptions of "the desirable" (Kluckhohn 395). We have already mentioned Shalom Schwartz's conceptualization of "the basic values that people in all cultures recognize." In this context, he considers "the nature and substantive contents of values," which amount to the following six features (see "Basic Human" 258–59, also "Basic Individual"):

(1) "Values are beliefs," and as such they are linked inextricably to emotions and to affect. Whenever they get activated, they become infused with positive or negative feeling. This is important to emphasize because values are not identical with abstract norms or evaluative attitudes which have a stronger cognitive dimension, telling members of a group how they should behave; the affective infusion explains how vital values are for social cohesion.

(2) Values "are a motivational construct" since they refer to "desirable goals" that motivate people's actions. Such goals can be

health, success, justice, or ideas of social order, and many others; their affective roots are decisive for their motivational strength.

(3) Values "transcend specific actions and situations." Obedience and honesty are among such values that may be activated both in the workplace and with friends, or in sports and recreation. Norms and attitudes are different in that they tend to be associated with "specific actions, objects, or situations."

(4) Values "guide the selection or evaluation of actions, policies, people, and events," as "standards or criteria." Usually without being fully conscious of it, people make decisions on what they see as justified or illegitimate, based on what they take to be possible consequences for their attainment of cherished values.

(5) Finally, values are "ordered by importance relative to one another." Thus a person forms an ordered system of "value priorities," such as novelty as against tradition, and it is this system that characterizes people as individuals. ("Many social norms are underdetermined with respect to the collective objectives they may serve"; Bicchieri and Muldoon.) This extends to

(6) The relative importance of values guides specific actions, with a trade-off among competing values.

These features are valid across cultures, while "cultural value emphases shape and justify individual and group beliefs, actions, and goals" (Schwartz, "Mapping" 340).

Feature 1 is strengthened in sociology: "the affective processes that contribute to the emergence and consolidation of socially shared valuations do so through their influence on social action and interaction" (von Scheve 177). Cognitive structures underlying values need to be balanced by a better understanding of the affective domain, and this calls for research investigating "the links between socially structured and culturally shaped emotions and the values that are shared within a group" (von Scheve 190).

Feature 3, however, should not be taken as being unqualified when one studies cultural differences. For instance, "Does individualism mean the same thing in Culture A and Culture B? In what specific domains of the culture are cultural members individualistic in their value orientation?" Cultures are not internally consistent, so that there are "situational constraints" which mediate practices, as a consequence of which a "domain-specific situation-dependent approach" to values research has become necessary (Kulich and Weng 19–20). This equally affects the study of collectivistic cultures. Research on value dimensions since the significant work of Seligman (et al.) has shown that values (and not only attitudes and motivations) are dynamic, blended from various sources. They can thus be situationally determined, and activated by sub- and macro-cultural cues or reordered in response to situational manipulations. Already at an early stage of theorizing, Schwartz was fully aware that research methods embedding values in "concrete and varied everyday situations," while not revealing basic universals, are important "for clarifying the individual and cultural differences that arise when values are expressed in specific judgments and behavior," so that combining abstract measurements with contextually specific methods should "increase our understanding of how values enter into concrete decision-making" ("Universals" 46–47).

Schwartz also records how in different settings people pursue competing values ("Basic Human" 265). For value priorities' impact on actual behavior, he creates a narrative scenario of a particular fictional situation ("Friday, as 5pm approached, Joe was summoned [...]") to illuminate what he describes as the first process through which values influence behavior: it is value-relevant aspects of situations that activate values. At the same time, relevant social groups exert "normative pressure to behave in particular ways in a domain" (Schwartz, "Robustness" 320, 324). Norms embodying a common value system influence behavior as they become part of a person's motives for action (see Bicchieri and Muldoon).[29] Literary discourse, we may observe, operates on the same site. It presents the experience of interplay between values, behavior, and normative group pressures, whenever it depicts conduct in particular situations. In literature and in society, situations are in need of interpretive definition, and they activate values. Psychologically based research can potentially enable a better understanding of such processes.

Cultural values as well as norms have both been employed to explain cultural differences in behavior. Yet Leung and Morris distinguish between a subjective approach, which is centered on values and schemas, and an intersubjective one centered on norms. The latter approach, as Yao (et al.) summarizes it, "locates the

---

[29] In the interplay of "acculturation and deculturation," people who enter a new culture undergo internal transformation "from changes in more superficial areas such as overt role behavior to more profound changes in fundamental values. We are susceptible to conformity pressure from the host environment, often in the form of simple and routine cultural assumptions and expectations extended to us" (Kim, "Long-Term" 340). For this context see also Kim, "Adapting."

source of cultural influence in the cultural group and the individual's perceptions of it," hence "focuses on measuring norms rather than individual values." A norm then "refers to cognitions about the typical beliefs, values, and behaviors of one's group," and focuses on what is "appropriate." When people interact socially, they are "highly sensitive to the social context," which is a limitation of the value approach: cultural patterns across task conditions are not "carried by broad inner values" (Yao et al. 715–16).

Early Concepts and Methods

Important historical lines of inquiry on values research are traced in Kulich, "Values" and *Applying*, and in studies such as those by Oyserman and Spates and partly Boer and Boehnke; our account is based mainly on these materials. In leading up to the more precise study of values, since the beginning of the twentieth century comparative cultural study from psychological perspectives was influential (Wilhelm Wundt), with sociological inquiries into "faiths, notions, codes and standards of well living" (William Graham Sumner in *Folkways* in 1906). William Thomas and Florian Znaniecki in *The Polish Peasant in Europe and America* (1918) pioneered the first sociological concept of value (see Oyserman and also Spates for the early developments).

The influence of values on social action was explored by Max Weber in *Economy and Society*: in his concept, instrumental-rational as well as value-rational types of action are especially important in explaining social order. In this concept, partly adapting Neo-Kantian assumptions, value-rational action is "determined by a conscious belief in the value for its own sake of some ethical, aesthetic, religious, or other form of behavior, independently of its prospects or success" (24–25). It is conscious, involves planning, and does not care about "the cost to the actor," while instrumental rationality is then employed "in deciding upon the means" (Swedberg 287). The value is believed to be "inherent" in a particular way of acting (Swedberg 288). The site of value rationalization is constituted in one of several value spheres: economy, politics, aesthetics, religion, eroticism, and intellectualism. Weber thought value spheres would become increasingly autonomous, each following an immanent logic which can cause tension between them. Guy Oakes has pointed out logical difficulties within Weber's concept of such immanent logic, and has argued that there are cases "in which instrumental rationality qualifies as value rationality": social actors may be "committed to the instrumental assessment of conduct as an intrinsic value" (39).

Yet Hans Henrik Bruun observes that any value sphere's immanent or inherent logic may be either axiological or empirical, and that, while Weber's approach in this regard is "*systematically* less than satisfactory" it nonetheless, and for that very reason, "makes a great deal of sense" (35, 36).

Intercultural communication has discussed the way money and power are "reintegrating the modern global society" by subordinating "hitherto separate value spheres of aesthetic action and institutionalised inquiry" (Young 176, see also 140). Value rationality has been counted among intentional intercultural conflict motives, including ethnic violence, with an ideological quality (see Bergan and Restoueix 85–86). Weber also spoke of "value-idea": there are ideas which give "significance or value" to an object, whether positive or negative; members of a social group or a whole society "are often unaware of the ultimate value-ideas that constitute its culture," while the ideas are dynamic and may change with cultural development (Swedberg 287). The concept was later strengthened by Talcott Parsons. As contributors to Esmer and Pettersson note (100), Weber's hypotheses concerning individualization of values in modern society have been tested with data from the World Values Survey.

At Columbia University in New York, cultural anthropology as practiced with scientific methods by German-American ethnologist Franz Boas enabled a focus on studying "the mind" in primitive cultures. Margaret Mead as his student described Pacific island culture, then the U.S.; Jeffrey Gorer presented "national character" studies. The U.S. Foreign Morale Analysis Division during World War II was significant in advancing the work of pioneering researchers including Clyde Kluckhohn, Florence Rockwell Kluckhohn, Parsons, and others, and then Boas' student Ruth Benedict, who in 1934 had argued that a culture could only be understood by a systematic study "of the motives and emotions and values that are institutionalized in that culture" (Spates 29). After that global war, groups of anthropological researchers at Harvard University around Parsons and Kluckhohn devoted their energies to studying values as cultural ideas, hence developing a concept of values orientations (see Spates). What was to become known as the Harvard Values Study Project began in 1948 under Kluckhohn's guidance. In this context values were seen from a behaviorist perspective as "instigators of behavior 'within' the individual" (Kluckhohn 396), but also more broadly as historically derived ideas with their attached values (Kroeber and Kluckhohn 357). Symbolic interpretations could thus be included. In Boer and

Boehnke's very short and not quite satisfactory description, the Kluckhohn–Rokeach–Schwartz trajectory of research constitutes a psychological approach to personal values, set off from a later political-science approach and a "third family" of theories which explore cultural differences (Hofstede–Triandis–Schwartz). Florence Kluckhohn continued research on a hierarchic structure of values, offering the first theoretically tested multi-level values orientations model (Kluckhohn and Strodtbeck). Here, the target of the orientations could be seen, with hindsight, as a belief system, rather than what was later understood more narrowly as a value orientation (Kulich, "Values" 59). The focus was on rural people; moreover, the approach did not actually enable predictive validity.

From a psychological background, studying values has been especially fruitful. Among the earliest instances of a specific values survey is Gordon Allport's collaborative Study of Values, developed in 1931 to assess the relative importance of six basic personality motives which has been repeatedly updated thereafter. It is a scale of values, without being clearly distinguished from personality theories. A further move to measuring values in various countries was proposed in 1956 by Charles Morris, semiotician and philosopher. He understood values as capable of stimulation by social, psychological, or biological causes, but held that they were not infinitely variable. Instead, they clustered around certain main orientations, so-called Paths or "Ways to Live" such as (for instance) a sympathetic concern for other persons (see Spates 37 – 38). The empirically derived dimensions, their co-relationships and interactions anticipated later research directions, such as Shalom Schwartz's.

From a psychological context again, Leonard V. Gordon developed a Survey of Interpersonal Values in 1960, then a Survey of Personal Values in 1967, the former measuring the relative importance of support, conformity, recognition, independence, benevolence, and leadership in social relations and the latter, ways in which individuals are able to cope with their social environment — while this does not allow a clear demarcation from research on personality traits. Nonetheless, these survey tools have been fairly widely applied. Soon afterwards, in 1969, Robert F. Bales and Arthur S. Couch presented a Value Profile. Incorporating the major concepts already available, their procedure aimed to cover the widest range of value areas, on the basis of a fairly small sample and a hugely complex array of items and variables. They succeeded in generating four important orthogonal factors that were substantiated in later work:

1. Acceptance of authority (which became Geert Hofstede's dimension of Power-distance, or Schwartz's Autonomy at the cultural level),
2. Need-determined expression vs. value-determined restraint (which anticipated Schwartz's Autonomy vs. Embeddedness at the cultural level and also Michael Minkov's Indulgence vs. Restraint),
3. Equalitarianism (partly foreshadowing Schwartz's cultural-level Hierarchy vs. Egalitarianism), and
4. Individualism (to become Individualism—Collectivism as studied by Hofstede and others).

In considering these psychological approaches, we should pay attention also to an adjacent pathway of research by Abraham Maslow (an originator of humanistic psychology) since 1943: the hierarchy of needs. Maslow developed a model in which needs that are located at or near the bottom of a hierarchy have to be satisfied before a person can meaningfully attend to needs that have a higher place. From the lowest position upward, the needs are physiological, safety-oriented, then concerned with love and belonging, then with esteem, and finally self-actualization. For the latter, Maslow hoped to find "figures created by novelists or dramatists," but could not find ones that were suited "in our culture and our time" (150). The "belongingness" need, at any rate, has been "a common theme in novels, autobiographies, poems, and plays" (Maslow 43). The resulting pyramid has been treated as a value structure, with almost interchangeable terminology between needs and values; later research on survival values in the World Values Survey has supported this analogy. Such needs are not automatically ego-centered, as being "healthily selfish" does not empirically contradict a capacity for compassion; any act is as such both selfish and unselfish (for instance Maslow 67–68, 179). Research across cultures has also shown that the safety-oriented needs are opposed to those of self-actualization, while esteem or achievement and mastery needs are opposed to those of belonging. (We can observe that esteem, in another sense, as based on a community's general approval, in some cultures creates or strengthens a sense of communal belonging.) Yet consistent empirical validation of Maslow's suggestive hierarchy as such has not been possible.

Investigating Values Items

A landmark research pathway with a direct focus on values was offered by Milton Rokeach in *Beliefs, Attitudes, and Values* (1968) and then *The Nature of Human Values* (1973). With painstaking groundwork Rokeach offered a distinction between values on the one hand and attitudes, needs, and norms on the other. He emphasized "the central position of the value concept across the several disciplines concerned with the understanding of human behavior" (Introduction 1). With a focus on belief and meaning, Rokeach considered values as "enduring beliefs that a specific mode of conduct is personally or socially preferable to an opposite or converse mode of conduct or end-state of existence" (5). So far as such beliefs are shared and pre- or proscriptive, they include norms about moral principles or standards (see Higgins 45). In a novel move, Rokeach created a distinction between two levels of values: instrumental (operative or practical and largely personal) values as against ones that are terminal (in the sense of ideal or hoped-for); the former include such values as obedience or self-reliance or self-control, the latter such values as social recognition or freedom or self-respect (see Jost et al. 355). Each of these levels is capable of giving meaning to people's actions, and it is not difficult to see how they can contribute to applied studies on political attitudes and behaviors. Schwartz, later, does not find substantive importance in the different functioning of the two levels.

Beyond the instrumental-terminal distinction, then, the "most important" aspect of values may well be that they "operate as *guides for action*" (Jiga-Boy et al. 244). Regarding the enumeration of specific values on each level, Schwartz later commented that values relating to power differences and to tradition are left out (unless we can consider them implied by extension, such as the ideologized dichotomy of freedom vs. equality). In any case, Rokeach did give attention to modification of value systems among migrants and to migrant assimilation; Norman T. Feather adapted the Rokeach Values Survey to study value differences across cultures with samples from Australia, Papua New Guinea, and China.

Rokeach also developed a theory of "belief congruence," later refined as cognitive consistency. The manifold beliefs which a person can hold are normally structured into a form of network having a core, somewhat like an atom. The nucleus consists of the person's primal beliefs, be it about the person as such or external realities. Outside the nucleus are an array of less central beliefs stemming from external sources, and complementing the nucleus. At the perimeter or margin are further beliefs which may have other objects and little consistency with the core and its surroundings. From such a model one can gather that there are openings for inconsistency and contradiction between values. These are especially significant for strategies to counter prejudice based on a person's or group's assumption that members of another group or an outgroup hold values or beliefs which differ from one's own. An ethically oriented learning experience can be effectively triggered by making participants aware of their internal value inconsistency, hence of a cognitive dissonance which undermines the naïve conviction of internal belief congruence. This value analysis can thus become strongly involved in dissecting and potentially overcoming racial and ethnic prejudice against outgroups.

Boer and Boehnke (132) suggest that there is a "first family of value research" (there are three) focusing on human needs as studied by Maslow and gaining concrete shape in political science, especially in the work of Ronald Inglehart. Indeed, in 1971 Inglehart devoted attention to culture shifts in political behavior, and introduced a concept of value change and modernization. The assumption was that in economically advanced societies value priorities would shift from concerns about economic and physical security toward a greater emphasis "postmaterialist" values. A European Community survey measuring such categories in Western Europe had been carried out in 1970. It was expanded to the first version of a World Values Survey (WVS) in 1981–1983 in the later stages of which Inglehart became its global coordinator.[30] As "the largest non-commercial, cross-national, time series investigation of human beliefs and values ever executed," the WVS studies "changing values and their impact on social and political life"; it

> seeks to help scientists and policy makers understand changes in the beliefs, values and motivations of people throughout the world. Thousands of political scientists, sociologists, social psychologists, anthropologists and economists have used these data to analyze such topics as economic development, democratization, religion, gender equality, social capital, and subjective well-being. (Website)

A "live cultural map" over time, beginning in 1981, makes such changes visible. The 1990–1991 survey already covered 70% of the world's population, later growing to 90%. The survey contributes to a modernization concept in suggesting correlations between economic development and intergenerational changes in cultural values such as

---

[30] The survey can be conveniently found at <http://www.worldvaluessurvey.org/wvs.jsp>.

an increase in individual autonomy, gender equality, or sexual freedom. There are indicators that Islamic, African, and South Asian cultural zones are dominated by below-average scores in secular-rational and self-expression values, differing from Confucian and Orthodox, Catholic Europe, Protestant Europe, and English-speaking cultural zones. Esmer and Pettersson offer an overview of comparative value surveys, with contributions by Inglehart and Schwartz.

Values and Cultural Dimensions

The year 1980, as Bulgarian scholar Michael Minkov has pointed out, proved to be "the turning point" in modern values research with the publication of industrial psychologist Geert Hofstede's *Culture's Consequences*. We have already touched on Hofstede's model of cultural dimensions further above; a leading German textbook of Intercultural Communication (by Hans-Jürgen Lüsebrink) actually begins with an extensive introduction to Hofstede's research. A few earlier scholars had explored ways in which dimensions of culture could be analyzed by a factorization process of national character, including Charles Morris and Raymond Cattell. Hofstede's achievement, in the landmark book just mentioned and in later studies, was to greatly expand analyses of this type, with a large IBM-based and multi-national data sample enabling the collection of over 100,000 questionnaires from two human resource department surveys carried out with employees in IBM subsidiaries in 40 countries. Relating the findings to a number of national indices strengthened the case for validity. Hofstede was able to adapt the concepts of Parsons, Kluckhohn and Strodtbeck, of Harry C. Triandis and of others in this enterprise. The initial four key dimensions thus gained were

- Individualism–Collectivism (integration of individuals into primary groups)
- High Power Distance–Low Power Distance (different solutions to the basic problem of human inequality)
- High Uncertainty Avoidance–Low Uncertainty Avoidance (level of stress in a society in the face of an unknown future) and
- Masculinity–Femininity (division of emotional roles between men and women).

Later, with the support of Michael Harris Bond and Michael Minkov there were significant additions:

- Long Term Orientaiion – Short Term Orientation (choice of focus for people's efforts: the future or the present and past; this was

identified by a questionnaire designed by Chinese scholars) and
• Indulgence – Restraint (gratification vs. control of basic human
desires related to enjoying life) .

Hofstede points out that, at an individual level, individualism/
collectivism do not need to be understood as opposites: "they should
rather be considered separate features of personality" ("Dimensionalizing"
202). Hofstede is fully aware of the connection between values and
economic status, as we have already noted above; moreover, he
emphasizes that "national culture scores should not be used for
stereotyping individuals" ("Dimensionalizing" 191 – 92). For our
purposes, it is clear that narrative literature is mostly concerned with
characters, hence with individuals, yet individuals obviously bear the
imprint of culture. As Franz Boas observed, forces that bring about
cultural change are active in the individuals composing social groups.
At the level of societies, the mean national scores gained from 40
countries (later more) served to define and confirm the dimensions.
Each of the countries studied is positioned relatively to other
countries by means of a score on each of the dimensions.③ Hofstede
acknowledges that there are no "real" values dimensions, as these
are created in scholars' minds.

A number of researchers have raised doubt about the feasibility
or validity of Hofstede's neopositivistic approach: there may be no
such thing as a "national culture" based on the nation-state; these
states tend to be dynamic, subject to change and development; they
have multiple ethnicities; the fairly uniform IBM organizational
culture is inadequate to gauge cultural complexity. Ikeguchi gives an
account of studies that, from various disciplines, tend to support or
not to support Hofstede's value framework. The phenomenon of in-
between identities that are trapped between different and often
opposing value systems plays a significant part here. Patchwork
identities are likely to nourish the possibility of patchwork value
orientations. The nation-state was a stable reference that grew less
stable or even broke down with increasing immigration and "nomadic"
existences.

From the important perspective of critical intercultural communication,
Kent Ono maintains that binaristic concepts like Hofstede's and also
Triandis' have "limited analytical or heuristic value today," not

---

③ For "organisational culture and cultural management," the results are conveniently
   inventorized at "Hofstede Insights" < https://www. hofstede-insights. com/
   product/compare-countries/>.

being informed by transformations of thinking about culture in recent decades (89–90). Hofstede has sought to respond to a number of critiques, based on the data at his disposal. In our own book series, Dong and Day have approvingly cited a number of criticisms of Hofstede's work (117–18). Eringa et al. have tested power distance and long-term orientation and found significant differences from Hofstede's original country values, so that these (as Hofstede is aware) are difficult to replicate meaningfully. Conceptually, the values dimensions remain independent, without forming an integrated "system" in Morris' sense. It has been said that Hofstede's dimensions have hardly been influential in the social sciences or the humanities but mainly in terms of international management and training "or wherever a simpler framework is preferred" (Kulich, *Applying* 150). Even so, as the example of Lüsebrink's understanding of intercultural communication shows, Hofstede's work can invite further exploration in a research field which includes attention to language, literature, and the media.

Re-analyzing WVS data in relation to Pew Research Center data, Minkov identified three values dimensions:

- Exclusionism–Universalism (very close to Individualism–Collectivism)
- Indulgence–Restraint (see above)
- Monumentalism – Flexumility ("Flexible Humility") (i.e., self-enhancement which can be related to national pride, as against humility and self-effacement).

These have certain overlaps with some of Hofstede's findings. In monumentalism, the self is "like a monolithic monument: proud, consistent and stable"; the highest scores are obtained in the Arab world and other Muslim countries, the lowest in East Asia (Minkov, "Expanding" 226ff.). Accordingly, migrants from monumentalist societies "prefer to remain distinct," perceiving cultural integration as "a betrayal of their true essence." Minkov has also proposed a further dimension: hypometropia (or cultural myopia) vs. prudence. In societies with short life spans and lack of a lengthy history of intensive agriculture, fairly strongly evident in sub-Saharan Africa and northern Latin America, intra-communal violence is an expression of "mating competition and a fitness contest," as opposed to "a long-term vision and prudent behaviors" which may not be evolutionarily advantageous for such a society ("Expanding" 231). "In communities of intensive agriculturalists, such as those of Africa, and among desert pastoralists where women are jealously protected, as in North Africa and the Middle East, unrestrained mating competition and hypometropia are low" ("Expanding" 231– 32). Further analytical work on the Hofstede-Minkov dimensions could contribute toward an integrated concept that does not leave them unconnected.

Alfons Trompenaars' economics-oriented account of dimensions of culture, which incorporates some work by Hofstede and by Parsons, deserves at least a brief account in our context to show that widely used lists of cultural dimensions do not invariably have a sound empirical or conceptual base. Developed partly with British scholar Charles Hampden-Turner, these seven dimensions (7–D) are structured as follows:

1. Universalism–Particularism
2. Individualism–Communitarianism
3. Specific–Diffuse
4. Neutral–Affective
5. Achievement–Ascription
6. Past–Present–Future
7. Internal–External.

This is designed to enable comparison of a person's range of individual values with those of a specifically national and hence more strongly collective values set. To explain the differences in meaning which individuals give to their interaction with other people, and also with time and with their environment, the team's database contains cross-cultural interview and survey data on the 7–D model and other scales or analysis tools. Critics have observed that the extensive database does not actually prove that seven dimensions are traceable as being independent of each other, and that many appear to belong within the individualism vs. collectivism or the power distance dimensions (cited in Kulich, "Empirical" 76). Even so, Minkov commends the team's presented cases which can be useful to a student of culture (*What* 21).

Cultural Syndromes

The work of Harry C. Triandis is significant in our context, not only because his position has been described as belonging to a "third family of value theories" together with Hofstede and Schwartz (Boer and Boehnke 133). This group of researchers study values as indicating cultural differences, though we should be aware that this does not necessarily set them apart from Inglehart. Triandis became well-known for his urging to consider cross-cultural issues in social psychology and for his ideas of "subjective culture" since the 1970s. Studies of belief and value systems, as well as of affective responses to social situations can be considered up-to-date fruits of a concern with "subjective" culture. This also includes analyses of the well-known binarism of individualism and collectivism, dimensions that have been called cultural syndromes. There is thus a foundation for Schwartz's somewhat similar distinction between Embeddedness as against forms of Autonomy. Triandis explains that the most popular cultural difference to be studied is individualism (independent self-construals, exchange relationships, attitudes, and personal goals) vs. collectivism (interdependent self-construals, communal relationships, norms, and in-group goals). For better differentiation, in the 1990s he mixed this with vertical and horizontal aspects of culture: the horizontal orientation emphasizes equality whereas the vertical emphasizes hierarchy. This results in four cultural patterns:

- Horizontal Individualism (HI): individuals strive to be distinct without desiring special status,
- Horizontal Collectivism (HC): individuals emphasize interdependence without easily submitting to authority,
- Vertical Individualism (VI): individuals strive to be distinct and desire special status, and
- Vertical Collectivism (VC): individuals emphasize interdependence and competition with out-groups.

"Most humans have all four of these cultural patterns in their mind, but use one or another of them, depending on the situation" (Triandis 63). This can break up the binarism which seems initially inherent in such research on cultural difference, and also the cultural patterning which can be less pronounced than variably situative patterning. Further above we called attention to recent research on the "situational constraints" which mediate practices, and these can be seen at work in such contexts. Thus in competitive situations persons in different cultures might use Vertical Individualism (VI), while in situations in which they "share common fate with equal others" they might use or activate Horizontal Collectivism (HC). The frequency of such different kinds of situations can indicate cultural differences.

In value terms, within collectivism "security, obedience, duty to the group, and harmony in interpersonal relationships within the ingroup" are emphasized, whereas within individualism the focus lies on "pleasure, achievement, competition, freedom, autonomy, and fair exchange" (Triandis 70). Further research shows that using a single variable for complex behavior, with individualism and collectivism together, can be misleading. Measuring them separately reveals that "Indians were both more collective and more individualistic than Americans" (Dong and Day 125); what is more, some facets of collectivism have been shown to qualify U.S. Americans as being "more collectivistic than the Japanese" (Shearman 169). Such research also shows that there is no consistently strong correlation between the individualism vs. collectivism variables and the low context vs. high context variables in communication; a collectivist society can have a relatively low-context communication mode.

Psychologist Richard W. Kilby in 1993 described an inventory of at least 29 related types of human value or value domains, without seeking operationalization or rigorous mutual isolation of items in an empirical methodology. This list can be helpful in calling to mind that there are such domains as ideal-self values, subcultural values, aesthetic values, political-economic structuring values, and gender values, among others. Kilby's book offers fuller information on how to understand these.

Integrated Circumplex Model

As we have seen, what engages social scientists' concern is the frequent failure to arrange value patterns into a coherent and thoroughly describable system. Such an undertaking has appeared beyond the means of the majority of analytical tools. Shalom Schwartz, in particular, has addressed this perceived or real shortcoming, by developing an integrated system which addresses both individual and cultural values, studying each at its own level, and thus leaving a precisely conceived space for the idea that value choices at the personal level may differ from those at the level of a whole societal group. Functionalist in its approach, this model "describes an open, not a closed, functional system" (Schwartz, "Societal" 45). The system that emerged is structured by initially 10 individual value types. Beginning in the 1980s, Schwartz explored the idea that there might be a universal psychological structure of human values, which could be revealed by means of a series of large-scale surveys using the Schwartz Values Survey (SVS). He was the first scholar in this research field to employ a multidimensional scaling technique called Smallest Space Analysis. Thus he was able to gain a comprehensive and carefully articulated set of values with systematic internal relations.

The 10 value themes or types are power, achievement, hedonism, stimulation, self-direction, universalism, benevolence, tradition, conformity, and security. Most importantly, as Figure 1 shows, they are placed in the context of a spatial and circular schema with two axes or dimensions: firstly openness to change (stimulation and self-direction) vs. conservation (conformity, security, and tradition), and secondly self-transcendence (universalism and benevolence) vs. self-enhancement (power, achievement, and hedonism). Accordingly, there are both compatible and competing relations among the value types.

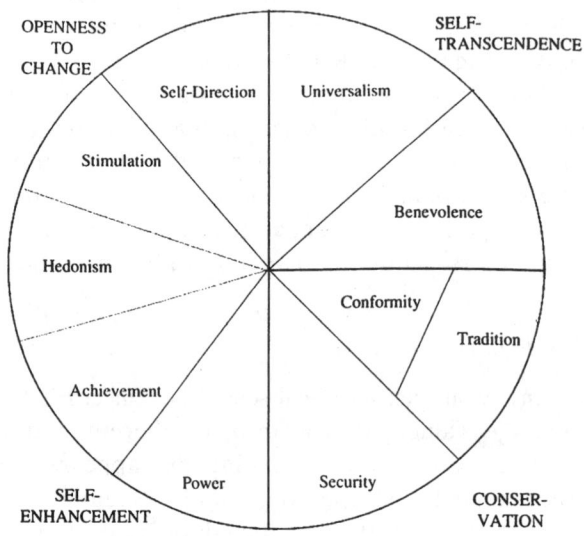

Figure 1: Theoretical structure of relations among values

[from Vol. 4, p. 266]
With the author's permission

Later, Schwartz and colleagues offered a refinement on this, for enhanced heuristic and explanatory power: the revision orders 19 values on the motivational continuum. As Figure 2 shows, it enables distinctions between a focus on personal as against social outcomes, avoiding anxiety or being anxiety-free, and serving self-protection or fostering self-expansion and growth. This reordering was assessed with confirmatory factor analysis and multidimensional scaling. With differentiated subtypes, the potential values are now (see "Refining" for further explanations and the augmented continuum):

Self-Direction—Thought / Self-Direction—Action
Stimulation
Hedonism
Achievement
Power—Dominance / Power—Resources
Face (*maintaining and protecting prestige*)
Security—Personal / Security—Societal
Tradition
Conformity—Rules / Conformity—Interpersonal
Humility (*humble/ modest* , *self-effacing*)
Benevolence—Dependability / Benevolence—Caring
Universalism—Concern / Universalism—Nature / Universalism—Tolerance

Figure 2: **Motivational continuum of**
19 values with sources
[from Vol. 5, p. 210]
With the author's permission

As Schwartz explains (see "Societal"), at the cultural level values are "a hypothetical, latent feature of societies (or groups), a normative system that is independent of individuals and is not located in their minds." Consequently, beyond individuals' own values and norms the cultural level becomes powerful in terms of "the norms, values, and expectations people perceive others to hold as aspects of culture."

The perception is at least as influential as any actual sharing of values. Also, Schwartz highlights the "multiple, proximal cultures (e. g., ethnic, professional, religious, family) that influence individuals." Cultural values mediate many of the effects of institutions on individuals, such as those of economic systems on acceptance of foreign workers. The major value orientations are

- Intellectual and Affective Autonomy vs. Embeddedness
- Egalitarianism vs. Hierarchy
- Harmony vs. Mastery.

As Schwartz explains ("Mapping" 341 ff.), in autonomy cultures people "should cultivate and express their own preferences, feelings, ideas, and abilities," either by pursuing "their own ideas and intellectual directions" or affectively positive experiences." In embeddedness cultures, "[m]eaning in life comes largely through social relationships, through identifying with the group." In egalitarianism, people are induced "to recognize one another as moral equals"; hierarchy by contrast "defines the unequal distribution of power, roles, and resources as legitimate." Harmony places emphasis on "fitting into the world as it is," whereas mastery "encourages active self-assertion in order to master, direct, and change" the environment. Figure 3 shows the structure.

**Figure 3: Cultural dimensions:
prototypical structure**

[from Vol. 4, p. 344]
With the author's permission

On the basis of the results, Schwartz calculated scores for each of the national cultures and distinguishable transnational cultural groups (Western Europe, English Speaking, Confucian, Africa and the Middle East, South Asia, Eastern Europe, and Latin America) on each of these cultural value orientations, generating a map capable of locating 76 national cultures on the cultural orientations. The map resembles some of the findings of Inglehart. Schwartz's research has brought about an integrated system which successfully explains how differences among individuals (with variables such as age, gender, education, and others) can be understood in relation to a broader cultural system of values in which they operate.

In our companion volume 8, we offered a sequence of question cycles which Intercultural Communication research can help us ask meaningfully about literary forms that, in a variety of ways, figure or represent cultural encounter (Chapter 5). The sequence is extendable to film. When we keep in mind that energies of cultural change are active in individuals, we can now derive a basis for fresh exploration of ways in which individual in relation to cultural values become evident in literary works, pertinent to the characters depicted in narratives and their fictional situations — be they cross-cultural or less so. Again, the exploration extends to film. It has been observed that Schwartz's efforts to identify "universal value" domains have been accepted mainly in psychology, communication, mass media, and organizational studies, less so in more situation-focused inquiries like those of cultural studies (Kulich, "Reviews" 53–54). This is borne out in the extensive citations of Schwartz's work in the recent *Handbook of Value* (Brosch and Sander). Yet studying interpretive storylines and narratives constructed by employing images and metaphors can easily benefit from drawing on Schwartz's values circumflex; values as such are frequently cited as research materials in Pickering's *Research Methods for Cultural Studies*. The circumflex has borne fruit in analyzing fictional TV series in connection with political participation (see Besley). If we consider that narrative perspective consists of the way a narrator's values influence the representation, and that narrative communicates values (see Niederhoff), we could ask whether any aspects of fictional interaction constellations are likely to be better understood in light of individual and cultural value structures.

Schwartz is among the few who have expressly studied a gender differentiation: women in many cultures tend to place "greater emphasis on universalism values," which are forms of "self-transcendence" values, and this may be owing to their "status as a disadvantaged group relative to men in most societies. Lower status may make women more sensitive to issues of equality and justice and arouse their sympathy for other disadvantaged groups" (Schwartz and Rubel 1022).

We should not overlook a warning, however, concerning scholars such as Schwartz and Triandis, and evidently extending to Hofstede, that there is a tendency to address values as "stable traits or characteristics" extractable by questionnaires and rating scales, and the ensuing argument that "psychology's best solution to its epistemological crises is to overcome the traditional tendency [...] of studying values as fixed entities" (Branco and Valsiner ix, x). Yet Schwartz has made it clear that "cultural value orientations do change gradually. Societal adaptation to epidemics, technological advances, increasing wealth, contact with other cultures, and other exogenous factors lead to changes in cultural value emphases" ("Mapping" 340–41). While his methodology structures individual and cultural values, Schwartz does point out that "[i]ndividuals, subgroups, and institutions with different interests and traditions are likely to promote behaviors, ideas, and aspirations incompatible with prevailing value emphases" ("Societal" 45), and that endogenous and exogenous forces of change influence each other. Literary works are sensitive to such developments; Schwartz's model for its part indicates sources of change wherever they appear relevant. The prototypical structure should, accordingly, not be taken as immutable. The complementary WVS expressly tracks changes in values. Moreover, while values do not normally change speedily, apart from major ecological challenges, the research shows how they can change in relative importance; such importance ratings vary depending on the contextual reference frame such as cultural minority and majority status or in connection with migration (see Boer and Boehnke 142–43). In relational contexts, "our values may shift in order to appropriate" them, while it can also happen that individuals resist change (Boer and Boehnke 143).

Our book series presents the option of a "dynamic definition" of culture (as an "emerging identity construction system, or growing web of meaningful relatedness": Kulich and Weng 17) in relationship to which values are seen. Communication scholar Sachiyo Shearman agrees that culture is "a dynamically fluid concept," inviting consideration of "[t]he time dimension or the change in certain values" (172–73).

The several influential value frameworks call for comparison.

Schwartz himself has contrasted his model with Hofstede's and Inglehart's, finding correlations as well as conceptual and empirical differences. Yet one can discriminate three combined dimensions in a multidimensional scaling analysis:

(1) "the desirable degree of independence of the person from in-groups vs. embeddedness,"
(2) "the desirability of equal vs. hierarchical allocation of resources, roles, rights, and obligations among persons and groups," and
(3) "the relative desirability of assertively using or changing the social and natural environment" ("Mapping" 373–74).

Having compared the same three cross-cultural value frameworks, Shearman acknowledges that a "universal values framework may entail the risks of simplification and the loss of unique indigenous interpretations of values due to assumptions of equivalence." Yet she finds that the three frameworks do "provide us with a comprehensive, longitudinal, and relative understanding of various values across cultures" (168).

References

Achtenberg, Deborah. *Cognition of Value in Aristotle's Ethics: Promise of Enrichment, Threat of Destruction*. State U of New York P, 2002.

Ackroyd, Peter. *The Last Testament of Oscar Wilde*. Hamish Hamilton, 1983.

Adorno, Theodor W. *Aesthetic Theory*. Edited by Gretel Adorno and Rolf Tiedemann, translated by Robert Hullot-Kentor. Athlone Press, 1997.

Albert, Rosita D. "Beyond Value Differences in Intercultural Research: State-of-the-Art Research on Attributional Differences and Their Implications for Cross-Cultural Interactions." SISU, *Value Frameworks*, pp. 435–63.

André, Christophe. "Mieux se connaître en lisant Proust." *Cerveau & Psycho*, no. 70, 2015, pp. 14–15.

Appleyard, J. A. *Becoming a Reader: The Experience of Fiction from Childhood to Adulthood*. Cambridge UP, 1991.

Aristotle. *The Nicomachean Ethics*. Translated by David Ross, revised by Lesley Brown. Oxford World's Classics. Oxford UP, 2009.

—. *The Poetics*. Translated by S. H. Butcher. 3rd ed. Macmillan, 1902.

Aukrust, Kjerstin, editor. *Assigning Cultural Values*. Peter Lang, 2013.

Bales, Robert F., and Arthur S. Couch. "The Value Profile: A Factor Analytic Study of Value Statements." *Sociological Inquiry*, vol. 39, 1969, pp. 3–17.

Bauman, Zygmunt. *Intimations of Postmodernity*. Routledge, 1992.

Baumbach, Sibylle, Herbert Grabes and Ansgar Nünning, editors. *Literature and Values: Literature as a Medium for Representing, Disseminating and Constructing Norms and Values*. Giessen Contributions to the Study of

Culture 2. WVT, 2009.

Bergan, Sjur, and Jean-Philippe Restoueix, eds. *Intercultural Dialogue on Campus*. Council of Europe Publishing, 2009.

Bersani, Leo, and Ulysse Dutoit. *Arts of Impoverishment: Beckett, Rothko, Resnais*. Harvard UP, 1993.

Besley, John C. "The Role of Entertainment Television and Its Interactions with Individual Values in Explaining Political Participation." *Press/Politics*, vol. 11, no. 2, 2006, pp. 41–63.

Bessière, Jean. "Littérature, éthique et questions contemporaines de théorie littéraire." *Primerjalna književnost* (Ljubljana), vol. 31, no. 1, 2008, pp. 3–13.

Bicchieri, Cristina, and Ryan Muldoon. "Social Norms." *Stanford Encyclopedia of Philosophy*, 1 Mar. 2011.

Bilsky, Wolfgang, and Shalom Schwartz. "Values and Personality." *European Journal of Personality*, vol. 8, 1994, pp. 163–81.

Bode, Christoph. "Literary Value and Evaluation: The Case for Relational Concepts." *Anglistentag 1988 Göttingen Vorträge*, edited by Heinz-Joachim Müllenbrock and Renate Noll-Wiemann, Max Niemeyer, 1989, pp. 310–24.

Boer, Diana, and Klaus Boehnke. "What Are Values? Where Do They Come From? A Developmental Perspective." Brosch and Sander, pp. 129–51.

Booth, Wayne C. *The Company We Keep: An Ethics of Fiction*. U of California P, 1988.

—. *The Essential Wayne Booth*. Edited by Walter Jost. U of Chicago P, 2006.

Branco, Angela Uchoa, and Jaan Valsiner, editors. *Cultural Psychology of Human Values*. Information Age, 2012.

Brilliant, Maria. Review of Liesbeth Korthals Altes, *Ethos and Narrative Interpretation (2014)*. *Argumentation et Analyse du Discours* 9 Apr. 2016, journals.openedition.org/aad/2158.

Brosch, Tobias and David Sander, editors. *Handbook of Value: Perspectives from Economics, Neuroscience, Philosophy, Psychology, and Sociology*. Oxford UP, 2016.

Bruun, Hans Henrik. *Science, Values and Politics in Max Weber's Methodology*. New expanded edition. Routledge, 2007.

Burwitz-Melzer, Eva. "Teaching Intercultural Communicative Competence Through Literature." *Developing Intercultural Competence in Practice*, edited by Michael Byram, Adam Nichols, and David Stevens, Multilingual Matters, 2001, pp. 29–43.

Buzzanell, Patrice M. "Extending and Enriching the Scope and Boundaries of Intercultural Communication." *Identity and Intercultural Communication (II): Conceptual and Contextual Applications*, Intercultural Research Vol. 3, edited by Steve J. Kulich and Xiaodong Dai. Shanghai Foreign Language Education Press, 2012, pp. 12–19.

Carnevali, Barbara. Review of Jacques Bouveresse, *La connaissance de l'écrivain*. *Annales: Histoire, Sciences Sociales*, vol. 65, no. 2, 2010/2, pp. 481–83.

Carroll, Noël. *Beyond Aesthetics: Philosophical Essays*. Cambridge UP, 2001.

—. "Moderate Moralism." *British Journal of Aesthetics*, vol. 36, no. 3, 1996, pp. 223–38.

Connor, Steven. *Theory and Cultural Value*. Blackwell, 1992.

Cousin, Victor. *Du Vrai, du Beau et du Bien*. 2nd ed. Didier, 1854.

Currie, Gregory. "Does Fiction Make Us Less Empathic?" *Teorema*, vol. 35, no. 3, 2016, pp. 47–68.

—. "The Moral Psychology of Fiction." *Australasian Journal of Philosophy*, vol. 73, 1995, pp. 250–59.

De Man, Paul. *The Resistance to Theory*. Foreword by Wlad Godzich. Theory and History of Literature 33. U of Minnesota P, 1986.

DeTurk, Sara. "'Quit Whining and Tell Me About Your Experiences!': (In) tolerance, Pragmatism, and Muting in Intergroup Dialogue." *The Handbook of Critical Intercultural Communication*, edited by Thomas K. Nakayama and Rona Tamiko Halualani, Wiley-Blackwell, 2010, pp. 565–84.

Djikic, Maja, Keith Oatley, and Mihnea C. Moldoveanu. "Reading Other Minds: Effects of Literature on Empathy." *Scientific Study of Literature*, vol. 3, no. 1, 2013, pp. 28–47.

Dong, Qingwen, and Kenneth D. Day. "Revisiting the Relationship Between Individualism/Collectivism and High / Low Context Communication." Kulich et al., *Value Dimensions*, pp. 111–32.

Epstein, Richard A. "Does Literature Work as Social Science? The Case of George Orwell." *University of Colorado Law Review*, vol. 73, 2002, pp. 987–1011.

Eringa, Klaes, Laura N. Caudron, Kathrin Rieck, Fei Xie and Tobias Gerhardt. "How Relevant Are Hofstede's Dimensions for Inter-Cultural Studies? A Replication of Hofstede's Research Among Current International Business Students." *Research in Hospitality Management*, vol. 5, no. 2, 2015, pp. 187–98.

Erll, Astrid, Herbert Grabes and Ansgar Nünning, editors. *Ethics in Culture: The Dissemination of Values Through Literature and Other Media*. De Gruyter, 2008. Introduction by Herbert Grabes.

Esmer, Yilmaz, and Thorleif Pettersson, editors. *Measuring and Mapping Cultures: 25 Years of Comparative Value Surveys*. Brill, 2007.

Feng Menglong. *Stories to Caution the World*. Translated by Yang Shuhui and Yang Yunqin. U of Washington P, 2005.

Fisette, Jean. "Musique, écriture et éthique: L'écriture littéraire comme exploration des relations troubles du sujet à la musique." *Les Cahiers de la société québécoise de recherche en musique*, vol. 11, nos. 1–2, 2010, pp. 39–46.

Fludernik, Monika. "Threatening the University: The Liberal Arts and the Economization of Culture." *New Literary History*, vol. 36, no. 1, 2005, pp. 57–70.

Frankl, Viktor E. *The Doctor and the Soul: From Psychotherapy to Logotherapy*. Translated by Richard and Clara Winston. Alfred A. Knopf, 1972; Vintage, 1986.

Funtova, Daria A., and Sergei B. Sinetskiy. "The Space of Cultural Values in the Modern Russian Literature." *Journal of Siberian Federal University, Humanities & Social Sciences*, vol. 6, 2018, pp. 927–34.

Gert, Bernard. "The Definition of Morality." *Stanford Encyclopedia of Philosophy*, 8 Feb. 2016.

Gillespie, Tim. "Why Literature Matters." *The English Journal*, vol. 83, no. 8, 1994, pp. 16–21.

Gómez Rodríguez, Luis Fernando. "Enhancing Intercultural Competence Through U.S. Multicultural Literature in the EFL Classroom." *Folios* no. 38, July/Dec. 2013, pp. 95–109.

González Rodríguez, Luisa María, and Miriam Borham Puyal. "Promoting Intercultural Competence Through Literature in CLIL Contexts." *ATLANTIS: Journal of the Spanish Association of Anglo-American Studies*, vol. 34, no. 2, 2012, pp. 105–24.

Grabes, Herbert. "Literature in Society/Society and Its Literature." *Literature in Society*, edited by Regina Rudaitytė, Cambridge Scholars, 2012, pp. 1–17.

—. "What Exactly Is the Case? Ethics, Aesthetics, and Aisthesis." Baumbach et al., *Literature*, pp. 43–53.

Grønstad, Asbjorn. *Film and the Ethical Imagination*. Palgrave Macmillan, 2016.

Hans, James S. *The Value(s) of Literature*. State U of New York P, 1990.

Heine, Steven J., Darrin R. Lehman, Kaiping Peng, and Joe Greenholtz. "What's Wrong with Cross-Cultural Comparisons of Subjective Likert Scales?: The Reference-Group Effect." *Journal of Personality and Social Psychology*, vol. 82, No. 6, 2002, pp. 903–18.

Higgins, E. Tory. "What Is Value? Where Does It Come From? A Psychological Perspective." Brosch and Sander, pp. 43–62.

Hitlin, Steven. "Values, Personal Identity, and the Moral Self." *Handbook of Identity Theory and Research*, edited by Seth J. Schwartz, Koen Luyckx, and Vivian L. Vignoles, Springer, 2011, pp. 515–29.

Hitlin, Steven, and Jane Allyn Piliavin. "Values: Reviving a Dormant Concept." *Annual Review of Sociology*, vol. 30, 2004, pp. 359–93.

Hoffmann, Gerhard, and Alfred Hornung, editors. *Ethics and Aesthetics: The Moral Turn of Postmodernism*. Winter, 1996.

Hofstede, Geert. *Culture's Consequences*. 1980. 2nd ed. SAGE, 2001.

—. "Dimensionalizing Cultures: The Hofstede Model in Context." SISU, *Value Frameworks*, pp. 183–215.

—. "National Cultures, Organizational Cultures, and the Role of Management." *BBVA OpenMind*, 2013, pp. 385–402. www.bbvaopenmind.com/wp-content/uploads/2013/02/National-Cultures-Organizational-Cultures-and-the-Role-of-Management_Geert-Hofstede.pdf. Accessed Jan. 2018.

Hofstede, Geert, Hofstede, Gert Jan, and Michael Minkov. *Cultures and Organizations: Software of the Mind*. *Intercultural Cooperation and Its Importance for Survival*. 3rd ed. McGraw-Hill, 2010.

Horace. *The Works*. Edited by Christopher Smart, revised by Theodore Alois Buckley. Harper & Brothers, 1863.

Ikeguchi, Cecilia. "Reflections on the Applications of the Hofstede Value Framework in Contemporary Research and Society." Kulich et al., *Value Dimensions*, pp. 459–503.

Inglehart, Ronald. *Culture Shift in Advanced Industrial Society*. Princeton UP, 1990.

—. "Globalization and Postmodern Values." *The Washington Quarterly*, vol. 23, no. 1, 2000, pp. 215–28 (Copyright 1999).

—. *The Silent Revolution: Changing Values and Political Styles in Advanced Industrial Society*. Princeton UP, 1997.

—. "The Silent Revolution in Europe: Intergenerational Change in Post-Industrial Societies." *American Political Science Review*, vol. 65, no. 4, 1971, pp. 991–1017.

Inglehart, Ronald, and Pippa Norris. "Muslim Integration into Western Cultures: Between Origins and Destinations." Faculty Research Working Papers Series RWP09–007, Harvard Kennedy School, March 2009.

Jakobson, Roman. *Huit questions de poétique*. Editions du Seuil, 1977. (Includes "Qu'est-ce que la poésie?")

Jannidis, Fotis. "Character." *The Living Handbook of Narratology*, 14 Sept. 2013.

Jiang, Fei, and Huang Ko. "An Attempt to Clarify the Differences Between the 'Two Categories and Four Means' of Theoretical Study on Intercultural Communication." *China Intercultural Communication Annual*, vol. 2, 2017, pp. 144–67.

Jiga-Boy, Gabriela M., Gregory R. Maio, Geoffrey Haddock and Katy Tapper. "Values and Behavior." Brosch and Sander, pp. 243–62.

Johnson, D. R. "Transportation into a Story Increases Empathy, Prosocial Behavior, and Perceptual Bias Toward Fearful Expressions." *Personality and Individual Differences*, vol. 52, 2012, pp. 150–55.

Jost, John T., Elvira Basevich, Eric S. Dickson, and Sharareh Noorbaloochi. "The Place of Values in a World of Politics: Personality, Motivation, and Ideology." Brosch and Sander, pp. 351 – 74. Jouve, Vincent. "Valeurs littéraires et valeurs morales: la critique éthique en question." *Les carnets du CRIMEL: Littérature et valeur*, 12 Mar. 2014, crimel.hypotheses.org/730.

Kay, Rebecca. "Introduction to 'Identity and Marginality.'" *eSharp: Identity and Marginality (I)*, vol. 6, no. 1, 2005, pp. 1–6.

Khan, Nargis. "Role of Literature in Moral Development." *International Journal on Studies in English Language and Literature*, vol. 2, no. 3, 2014, pp. 6–9.

Kilby, Richard W. *The Study of Human Values*. UP of America, 1993.

Kim, Young Yun. "Adapting to a New Culture: An Integrative Communication Theory." *Theorizing about Intercultural Communication*, edited by William B. Gudykunst, SAGE, 2005, pp. 375–400.

—. "Long-Term Cross-Cultural Adaptation: Training Implications of an Integrative Theory." *Handbook of Intercultural Training*, edited by Dan Landis, Janet M. Bennett, and Milton J. Bennett, 3rd ed., SAGE, 2004, pp. 337–62.

Klamer, Arjo. "A Pragmatic View on Values in Economics." *Journal of Economic Methodology*, vol. 10, no. 2, 2010, pp. 191–212, doi: 10.1080/1350178032000071075.

Kluckhohn, Clyde K. M. "Values and Value Orientations in the Theory of Action: An Exploration in Definition and Classification." *Toward a General Theory of Action*, edited by Talcott Parsons and Edward A. Shils, Harvard UP, 1951, pp. 388–433.

Kluckhohn, Florence R., and Fred L. Strodtbeck. *Variations in Value Orientations*. Greenwood Press, 1961.

Korthals Altes, Liesbeth. *Ethos and Narrative Interpretation: The Negotiation of Values in Fiction*. U of Nebraska P, 2014.

Kroeber, Alfred L., and Clyde K. M. Kluckhohn. *Culture: A Critical Review of Concepts and Definitions*. Harvard UP, 1952.

Kulich, Steve J. *Applying Cross-Cultural Values Research to "the Chinese": A Critical Integration of Etic and Emic Approaches*. Ph.D. diss., Humboldt U, edoc Publikationsserver, 2011. doi: 10.18452/16426.

—. "The Empirical Foundations of Current Values Research." SISU, *Value Frameworks*, pp. 71–102.

—. "Reviews, Definitions, and Approaches to Values Studies." Kulich et al., *Value Dimensions*, pp. 27–60.

—. "Toward an Integrated Identity Matrix Theory (IIMT) — Proposals for a Dynamic Cultural Identity Framework." *Identity and Intercultural Communication (I): Theoretical and Contextual Construction*, Intercultural Research Vol. 2, edited by Xiaodong Dai and Steve J. Kulich, Shanghai Foreign Language Education Press, 2010, pp. 69–102.

—. "Values Studies: The Origins and Development of Core Cross-Cultural Comparisons." SISU, *Value Frameworks*, pp. 33–70.

Kulich, Steve J., and Weng Liping. "Introduction: Value Dimensions, Dynamic Contexts, and Beyond." Kulich et al., *Value Dimensions*, pp. 1–24.

Kulich, Steve J., Weng Liping and Michael H. Prosser, editors. *Value Dimensions and Their Contextual Dynamics Across Cultures*. Intercultural Research Vol. 5. Shanghai Foreign Language Education Press, 2014.

Ladkin, Sam, Robert McKay, and Emile Bojesen, editors. *Against Value in the Arts and Education*. Rowman & Littlefield, 2016.

Lamarque, Peter. "Aesthetics and Literature: A Problematic Relation?" *Philosophical Studies*, vol. 135, no. 1, 2007, pp. 27–40.

Laroque, Lydie, et Caroline Raulet-Marcel. "Littérature et valeurs." *Le français aujourd'hui*, vol. 197, no. 2, 2017, pp. 5–14.

Laurent, Jean Paul, Karl Canvat, and Georges Legros, editors. *Les valeurs dans/de la littérature: Diptyque*. Presses universitaires de Namur, 2004.

Lawrence, Nathaniel. "Time, Value, and the Self." *The Relevance of Whitehead*, edited by Ivor Leclerc, George Allen & Unwin, 1961, pp. 145–66.

Leclaire-Halté, Anne. "Valeurs et rapport texte/image dans l'album de littérature de jeunesse: étude d'un exemple, *Le Génie du pousse-pousse*." *Pratiques*, vols. 163–64, 2014, doi: 10.4000/pratiques.2259.

Leung, Kwok, and Michael W. Morris. "Values, Schemas, and Norms in the Culture-Behavior Nexus: A Situated Dynamics Framework." *Journal of International Business Studies*, vol. 6, no. 9, 2015, pp. 1028–50.

Levitin, T. "Values." *Measures of Social Psychological Attitudes*, edited by John P. Robinson and Philip R. Shaver, revised ed., U of Michigan Survey Research Center, 1973, pp. 489–585.

Lohöfer, Astrid. *Ethics and Lyric Poetry: Language as World Disclosure in French Symbolism and Canadian Modernism*. Winter, 2014.

Lopičić, Vesna, and Biljana Mišić Ilić, editors. *Values Across Cultures and Times*. Cambridge Scholars, 2014.

Lüsebrink, Hans-Jürgen. *Interkulturelle Kommunikation: Interaktion, Fremdwahrnehmung, Kulturtransfer*. 4te Auflage. Metzler, 2016.

Maio, Gregory R. *The Psychology of Human Values*. Routledge, 2017.

Mar, Raymond A., Keith Oatley, and Jordan B. Peterson. "Exploring the Link Between Reading Fiction and Empathy: Ruling Out Individual Differences and Examining Outcomes." *Communications*, vol. 34, 2009, pp. 407–28.

Martin, Judith N., and Thomas K. Nakayama. *Intercultural Communication in Contexts*. 5th ed. McGraw-Hill, 2010.

Maslow, Abraham H. *Motivation and Personality*. Harper and Row, 1954. 2nd ed., 1970.

—. "A Theory of Human Motivation." *Psychological Review*, vol. 50, no. 4, 1943, pp. 370–96.

Mattos, Elsa de, and Angela Branco. "Exploring the Intersection of Personal and Collective Meanings: 'Responsibility' in the Transition to Adulthood." *Psychology and Society*, vol. 6, no. 1, 2014, pp. 11–27.

May, Todd. *A Significant Life: Human Meaning in a Silent Universe*. U of Chicago P, 2015.

Mecklenburg, Norbert, editor. *Literarische Wertung: Texte zur Entwicklung der Wertungsdiskussion in der Literaturwissenschaft*. Niemeyer, 1977.

Meretoja, Hanna, Saija Isomaa and Pirjo Lyytikäinen, editors. *Values of Literature*. Brill & Rodopi, 2015.

Meuter, Norbert. "Narration in Various Disciplines." *The Living Handbook of Narratology*, 23 Sept. 2013.

Miller, J. Hillis. "The Ethics of Reading." *Style*, vol. 21, no. 2 (1987), pp. 181–91.

Minkov, Michael. "Expanding Hofstede's Model with New Dimensions from the World Values Survey and National Statistics." SISU, *Value Frameworks*, pp. 217–38.

—. *What Makes Us Different and Similar: A New Interpretation of the World Values Survey and Other Cross-Cultural Data*. Klasikai Stil, 2007.

Minkov, Michael, and Geert Hofstede. "Is National Culture a Meaningful Concept? Cultural Values Delineate Homogeneous National Clusters of In-Country Regions." *Cross-Cultural Research*, vol. 46, no. 2, 2012, pp. 133–59.

Moll, Jorge, Roland Zahn and Ricardo de Oliveira-Souza. "The Neural Underpinnings of Moral Values." Brosch and Sander, pp. 119–27.

Morris, Charles W. *Paths of Life*. Braziller, 1956.

—. *Varieties of Human Value*. U of Chicago P, 1956.

Müller, Wolfgang G. "From Homer's *Odyssey* to Joyce's *Ulysses*: Theory and Practice of an Ethical Narratology." *Arcadia*, vol. 50, no. 1, 2015, pp. 9–36.

Natsiuk, Maryana. "Teaching Foreign Culture Values in the Process of Reading Fiction." Studia Anglica Resoviensia, vol. 11, 2014, pp. 178–89.

Nie Zhenzhao. "A Conceptual Map of Ethical Literary Criticism: An Interview with Nie Zhenzhao." By Charles Ross. *Forum for World Literature Studies*, www.fwls.org/plus/view.php?aid = 247. Accessed Dec. 2017.

—. *Introduction to Ethical Literary Criticism*. Peking UP, 2014.

—. "Towards an Ethical Literary Criticism." Arcadia, vol. 50, no. 1, 2015, pp. 83–101.

Niederhoff, Burkhard. "Perspective — Point of View." *The Living Handbook of Narratology*, 24 Sept. 2013.

Nietzsche, Friedrich. *The Will to Power*. Translated by Walter Kaufmann and R. J. Hollingdale. Vintage, 1967. *Sämtliche Werke: Kritische Studienausgabe*, edited by Giorgio Colli and Mazzino Montinari, 1999, Vol. 12.

Nünning, Vera. "The Ethics of (Fictional) Form: Persuasiveness and Perspective Taking from the Point of View of Cognitive Literary Studies." *Arcadia*, vol. 50, no. 1, 2015, pp. 37–56.

Nussbaum, Martha C. *Cultivating Humanity: A Classical Defense of Reform in Liberal Education*. Harvard UP, 1997.

—. "Literature and Ethical Theory: Allies or Adversaries?" *Yale Journal of Ethics*, vol. 9, 2000, pp. 5–16. *Frame*, vol. 17, no. 1, 2003, pp. 6–30.

—. *Love's Knowledge: Essays on Philosophy and Literature*. Oxford UP, 1990.

—. *Upheavals of Thought: The Intelligence of Emotions*. Cambridge UP, 2001.

Oakes, Guy. "Max Weber on Value Rationality and Value Spheres." *Journal of Classical Sociology*, vol. 3, no. 1, 2003, pp. 27–45.

Ocasio, Rafael. *Literature of Latin America*. Greenwood Press, 2004.

Ono, Kent A. "Reflections on 'Problematizing 'Nation'' in Intercultural Communication Research.'" *The Handbook of Critical Intercultural Communication*, edited by Thomas K. Nakayama and Rona Tamiko Halualani, Wiley-Blackwell, 2010, pp. 84–97.

Oprisko, Robert L. *Honor: A Phenomenology*. Routledge, 2012.

Oyserman, Daphna. "Values: Psychological Perspectives." *International Encyclopedia of the Social & Behavioral Sciences*, edited by Neil J. Smelser and Paul B. Baltes, *IESBS*, Pergamon, 2001, pp. 16150–53.

Pater, Walter. *The Renaissance: Studies in Art and Poetry*. 4th ed. Macmillan, 1888.

Pewny, Katharina. "The Ethics of Encounter in Contemporary Theater Performances." *Journal of Literary Theory Online*, 20 Feb. 2012. Accessed Dec. 2017. www.jltonline.de/index.php/articles/article/view/483/1219.

Phelan, James. "Narrative Ethics." *The Living Handbook of Narratology*, 9 Dec. 2014.

Pickering, Michael, editor. *Research Methods for Cultural Studies*. Edinburgh UP, 2008.

Popa, Clara L. "Changing Values in Eastern Europe." Kulich et al., *Value Dimensions*, pp. 441–58.

Prosser, Michael H. "One World, One Dream: Harmonizing Society Through Intercultural Communication: A Prelude to China Intercultural Communication Studies." *Intercultural Perspectives on Chinese Communication*, Intercultural Research Vol. 1, edited by Steve J. Kulich and Michael H. Prosser, Shanghai Foreign Language Education Press, 2007, pp. 22–91.

Rabaté, Dominique. *Le roman et le sens de la vie*. José Corti, coll. «Les essais», 2010.

Rabinowicz, Wlodek, and Toni Rønnow-Rasmussen. "Value Taxonomy." Brosch and Sander, pp. 23–42.

Remland, Martin S., Tricia S. Jones, Anita Foeman, and Dolores Rafter Arévalo. *Intercultural Communication: A Peacebuilding Perspective*. Waveland Press, 2015.

Robinson, Lena. "Beliefs, Values, and Intercultural Communication." *Communication, Relationships and Care*, edited by Martin Robb et al., Routledge, 2004, pp. 110–20.

Rokeach, Milton. Introduction. *Understanding Human Values: Individual and Societal*, edited by Milton Rokeach, The Free Press, 1979, pp. 1–11.

—. *The Nature of Human Values*. The Free Press, 1973.

Rorty, Richard. *Truth and Progress*. Cambridge UP, 1998.

Sabot, Philippe. "Que nous apprend la littérature? Bouveresse, Zola et l'esprit éthique." *Le travail de la littérature: Usages du littéraire en philosophie*, edited by D. Lorenzini and A. Revel, Presses universitaires de Rennes, 2012, pp. 139–50 (Aesthetica). halshs.archives-ouvertes.fr/halshs-00746767.

Scaliger, Julius Caesar. *Poetices libri septem*. Vincentius, 1561.

Schober, Rita. "Zum Problem der literarischen Wertung." *Weimarer Beiträge*, vol. 7, 1973, pp. 10–53.

Schwartz, Shalom H. "Basic Human Values: Their Content and Structure Across Cultures." 2005. SISU, *Value Frameworks*, pp. 257–94.

—. "Basic Individual Values: Sources and Consequences." Brosch and Sander, pp. 63–84.

—. "Mapping and Interpreting Cultural Differences Around the World." 2004. SISU, *Value Frameworks*, pp. 339–79.

—. "Refining the Theory of Basic Individual Values." 2012. Kulich et al., *Value Dimensions*, pp. 191–262.

—. "Robustness and Fruitfulness of a Theory of Universals in Individual Values (The PVQ)." 2005. SISU, *Value Frameworks*, pp. 295–338.

—. "Societal Value Culture." *Journal of Cross-Cultural Psychology*, vol. 45, no. 1, 2014, pp. 42–46.

—. "Universals in the Content and Structure of Values: Theoretical Advances and Empirical Tests in 20 Countries." *Advances in Experimental Social Psychology*, vol. 25, 1992, pp. 1–65.

Schwartz, Shalom H., and Tammy Rubel. "Sex Differences in Value Priorities: Cross-Cultural and Multimethod Studies." *Journal of Personality and Social Psychology*, vol. 89, no. 6, 2005, pp. 1010–28.

Seligman, Clive, James M. Olson and Mark P. Zanna, editors. *The Psychology of Values: The Ontario Symposium*. Vol. 8. Lawrence Erlbaum Associates, 1996.

Shearman, Sachiyo M. "Value Frameworks Across Cultures: Hofstede's, Ingelhart's [*sic*], and Schwartz's Approaches." SISU, *Value Frameworks*, pp. 137–80.

Sidney, Sir Philip. *An Apology for Poetry or The Defence of Poesy*. Edited by Geoffrey Shepherd, 3rd rev. ed. by R. W. Maslen. Manchester UP, 2002.

SISU Intercultural Institute (Steve J. Kulich, Michael H. Prosser, Weng Liping), editors. *Value Frameworks at the Theoretical Crossroads of Culture*. Intercultural Research Vol. 4. Shanghai Foreign Language Education Press, 2012.

Slater, Barry Hartley. "Aesthetics, 3. Aesthetic Value." *Internet Encyclopedia of Philosophy*. Accessed Dec. 2017.

Smith, Barbara Herrnstein. *Contingencies of Value: Alternative Perspectives for Critical Theory*. Harvard UP, 1988.

Smith, Seyda Türk, Kyle D. Smith and John Chambers Christopher. "Respecting the Complexity of Value Systems: Psychological Realism and the Case of Turkish Culture." Kulich et al., *Value Dimensions*, pp. 399–425.

Spates, James L. "The Sociology of Values." *Annual Review of Sociology*, vol. 9, 1983, pp. 27–49.

Spencer-Oatey, Helen, editor. *Culturally Speaking: Culture, Communication and Politeness Theory*. 2nd ed., Continuum, 2008.

Ştefănescu, Maria. "Re-exploring the 'Ethical Turn': Rhetorical Ethical Criticism as a Cross-Disciplinary Project." *Studia universitatis Babeş-Polyai*, Philologia, vol. 54, no. 1, 2009, pp. 275–82.

Swedberg, Richard. *The Max Weber Dictionary: Key Words and Central Concepts*. Stanford UP, 2005.

Teilanyo, Diri I. "Cultural Values and Norms in Intercultural Communication: Insights from *Icheoku* and *Masquerade*." *Intercultural Communication Studies*, 24, no. 1, 2015, pp. 66–81.

Triandis, Harry. "Dynamics of Individualism and Collectivism Across Cultures." Kulich et al., *Value Dimensions*, pp. 61–82.

Ursa, Mihaela. "Universality as Invariability in Comparative Literature: Towards an Integrative Theory of Cultural Contact." *Primerjalna književnost* (Ljubljana), vol. 37, no. 3, 2014, pp. 151–63.

Vaugeois, Dominique. "La Valeur dans les lettres." *L'Art et la Question de la Valeur*, edited by Dominique Rabaté, Presses Universitaires de Bordeaux, 2007, pp. 27–40.

von Scheve, Christian. "Societal Origins of Values and Evaluative Feelings." Brosch and Sander, pp. 175–95.

Waldenfels, Bernhard. "The Boundaries of Orders." *Philosophica*, vol. 73, 2004, pp. 71–86.

Watroba, Karolina. "World Literature and Literary Value: Is 'Global' the New 'Lowbrow?'" *Cambridge Journal of Postcolonial Literary Inquiry*, vol. 5, no. 1, 2018, pp. 53–68.

Weber, Max. *Economy and Society*. Edited by Günther Roth and Claus Wittich. U of California P, 1978.

Weidle, Roland. "Value Constructions in Narratives Across Media: Towards a General Typology." *Amsterdam International Electronic Journal for Cultural Narratology*, vol. 5, 2008–9. cf. hum. uva. nl/narratology/issue/author/authors_cv45.html.

Weimann, Robert. "History and Value in the Comparative Study of Literature." *Neohelicon*, vol. 1, nos. 1–2, 1973, pp. 25–43.

Welzel, Christian. *Freedom Rising: Human Empowerment and the Quest for Emancipation*. Cambridge UP, 2013.

Whitehead, Alfred North. *Science and the Modern World*. Lowell Lectures, 1925. Free Press, 1953.

Wolf, Philipp. "Beyond Virtue and Duty: Literary Ethics as Answerability." Erll et al., *Ethics*, pp. 87–115.

Xie, Ming. *Conditions of Comparison: Reflections on Comparative Intercultural Inquiry*. Continuum, 2011.

Yang, G. "Ethical Turn in Literary Studies and the Revival of American Ethical Criticism." *Foreign Literature Studies*, vol. 35, 2013, pp. 16–25.

Yao, Jingjing, Jimena Ramirez-Marin, Jeanne Brett, Soroush Aslani, and Zhaleh Semnani-Azad. "A Measurement Model for Dignity, Face, and Honor Cultural Norms." *Management and Organization Review*, vol. 13, no. 4 (2017), pp. 713–38.

Young, Robert. *Intercultural Communication: Pragmatics, Geneaology, Deconstruction*. Multilingual Matters, 1996.

Zangwill, Nick. "Aesthetic Judgment." *Stanford Encyclopedia of Philosophy*, 26 Aug. 2014.

Zapf, Hubert. "The State of Ecocriticism and the Function of Literature as Cultural Ecology." *Nature in Literary and Cultural Studies: Transatlantic Conversations on Ecocriticism*, edited by Catrin Gersdorf and Sylvia Mayer, Rodopi, 2006, pp. 49–70.

Zavalloni, Marisa. "Social Identity: Perspectives and Prospects." *Social Sciences Information*, vol. 12, no. 3, 1972, pp. 65–91.

—. "Social Identity and the Recoding of Reality." *International Journal of Psychology*, vol. 10, 1975, pp. 197–217.

Zimmerman, Michael J. "Intrinsic vs. Extrinsic Value." *Stanford Encyclopedia of Philosophy*, 24 Dec. 2014.

About the Authors

Mark Bender is Professor of Chinese Literature and Folklore in the Department of East Asian Languages and Literatures at The Ohio State University in Columbus. He gained his Ph.D. in 1995. He specializes in oral performance and related written traditions of China, including the lore of Han subgroups and ethnic minority cultures. He has published on Suzhou professional storytelling (*pingtan*), oral and written literatures of several Chinese ethnic minority cultures such as the Yi, Miao (Hmong), and Daur, and contemporary minority poets and literature of the environment in the border areas of China. Among his books are *Plum and Bamboo: China's Suzhou Chantefable Tradition* (University of Illinois Press, 2003), *Butterfly Mother: Miao (Hmong) Creation Epics from Guizhou Province, China* (Hackett Publishing, 2006), *Tiger Traces: Selected Nuosu and Chinese Poetry of Aku Wuwu* (Foreign Language Publications, 2006), *The Columbia Anthology of Chinese Folk and Popular Literature* (2011 with Victor Mair), *Hmong Oral Epics* (Guizhou Nationalities Press, 2012), and *The Borderlands of Asia: Culture, Place, Poetry* (Cambria Press, 2017), which features poems by 48 poets in India (Northeast India), Myanmar, China (Southwest China and Inner Mongolia), and Mongolia.

Sandra L. Bermann is Cotsen Professor of the Humanities and Professor of Comparative Literature at Princeton University, and serves as Master of Whitman College. In addition to articles and reviews in scholarly journals, she is author of *The Sonnet over Time: Studies in the Sonnets of Petrarch, Shakespeare, and Baudelaire*; translator of Manzoni's *On the Historical Novel*; editor with Michael Wood of *Nation, Language, and the Ethics of Translation*; and editor with Catherine Porter of *A Companion to Translation Studies*. Her current projects focus on lyric poetry, translation, the intersections between twentieth-century historiography and literary theory, and new directions in the field of comparative literature. A recipient of

Whiting and Fulbright Fellowships, Prof. Bermann has been a visiting scholar at the Institute for Advanced Study in Princeton and the Columbia University Institute for Scholars at Reid Hall in Paris. At Princeton, she chaired the Department of Comparative Literature for many years, served as Master of Stevenson Hall, co-founded the Program in Translation and Intercultural Communication, and led the President's Working Group on the Bridge Year Program. She completed a term as President of the American Comparative Literature Association in 2009.

Du Yiwei is Lecturer at Yuanpei College, Shaoxing University, also doctoral student at Hong Kong Polytechnic University, has been focusing his research interest on translation studies, especially its philosophical side. That is where he found thinkers such as Jacques Derrida, Susan Sontag, and Roman Jakobson relevant to how the West has been "translated" in China. He turned his interests to language and culture after getting a Bachelor's degree in engineering. After gaining the M.A. degree in Applied Linguistics, he published a book *Forms and Meaning: Language, Philosophy, and Life* in 2011, and he is now on the team of a research project sponsored by the China's National Social Science Fund for Young Scholars, titled "Discursive patterns and narrative models of China's image representation in Chinese and British mainstream media."

Mine Krause graduated with a double Ph.D. in Comparative Literature from the Universities of Bayreuth (Germany) and Pau (France) in 2009, after a combined academic focus on literature as well as intercultural German studies and intercultural communication. She worked as an assistant in the Literature and Linguistics Departments of Bayreuth, Ankara, and Granada. Her book publications include *Honor, Face, and Violence: Cross-Cultural Literary Representations of Honor Cultures and Face Cultures* (co-authored with Michael Steppat and Sun Yan, Peter Lang) and *Scandal and Angst in the Works of Albee, Pinter, Ionesco, and Genet* (Peter Lang). Her article on Pinter's *Ashes to Ashes* appeared in Tönnies' *Das englische Drama der Gegenwart*, and her analysis of Elif Şafak's culinary language in *Journal of Turkish Literature*. She was active at the 22nd METU British Novelists Conference in Ankara on Zadie Smith's work. Dr. Krause has contributed to Volume 8 in the present book series, and her article "Screaming Silence of Female Characters in Ayfer Tunç's novel *Dünya Ağrısı*" focusing on feminist issues in contemporary Turkish literature was published in *Monograf Journal* 7 (2017). She is a researcher in the Center for Intercultural Dialogue and also a member of a research cluster on interculturality at universities in Bayreuth and Shanghai.

Steve J. Kulich is Distinguished Professor at Shanghai International Studies University, Director of the SISU International Institute, Editor of *Intercultural Research*, and Academic Coordinator for the SISU MBA program. He received his M.A. from the University of Kansas and his Ph. D. from Humboldt University of Berlin, Germany. In his over 30 years in Asia and 20 years in Shanghai, he has pioneered intercultural training courses, M. A. and Ph. D. programs at SISU, and has helped organize six international Intercultural Communication conferences. With Michael Prosser he has edited the *International Journal of Intercultural Relations* 2012 (4) "Special Issue: Early American Pioneers of Intercultural Communication." He is on the Editorial Board of the *Intercultural Communication Series*, *Intercultural Communication Research*, and the *Journal of Middle East and Islamic Studies* (*in Asia*). Prof. Kulich's work has been published in *Intercultural Communication Studies*, *China Media Research*, *International Management Review*, *China Media Reports Overseas*, *Cross-Cultural Psychology Bulletin*, *The International Scope Review*, and by Edgar Elgar Press (in Xu and Bond's *Handbook of Chinese Organizational Behavior*, 2012), Oxford UP (in Bond's *Handbook of Chinese Psychology*, 2nd ed., 2010), Sage (in Littlejohn's and Foss's *Encyclopedia of Communication Theory*, 2009), Hong Kong UP, Higher Education Press, FLTRP, SFLEP, and Yunnan People's Press, as well as his 2002 columns in English Salon and Shanghai Scene. He has been honored with a "Special Contribution Award" (CAFIC, 2011) and twice with the Magnolia Award (Silver 2007, Gold 2011) from the Shanghai government, as well as a national "Favorite Foreign Teacher" Award (2014). With his team, he has been chiefly responsible for developing and running China's first international partnership Massive Online Open Course with FutureLearn. He is President-Elect of the International Academy for Intercultural Research.

Liu Siyuan is Associate Professor in the School of English Studies at Shanghai International Studies University, where she gained her Ph. D. She has been a visiting scholar at The Graduate School and University Center of the City University of New York (2015–2016) and the Department of English and Culture, McMaster University (2006). Among her major publications are a monograph on *Rake-Hero and Sovereignty: The Representation of Political Conditions in Restoration Comedies* (Shanghai, 2016) and further publications on such topics as Shakespeare's *Hamlet* and Oscar Wilde. Prof. Liu has received several awards, and is currently pursuing a national project on "Seventeenth-Century English Comedies and National Identity."

Mao Sihui received his M.A. in Contemporary Literary and Cultural Studies from the University of Lancaster, U.K., and his Ph.D. in Comparative Literature — Film Culture from the University of Hong Kong. He taught various English subjects and literary/cultural studies courses such as "20th-Century Literary Theories," "Modern British and American Drama," and "Film Culture" at Guangdong University of Foreign Studies from 1982 to 2000, translation and culture courses at the Department of Translation, Hong Kong Lingnan University, from 2001 to 2003, after which he directed the MPI-Bell Centre of English, Macao Polytechnic Institute, from 2003 to 2015. He has been the Executive Director of the English Language Centre and Professor of English and Comparative Cultural Studies, Shantou University (STU), as well as Dean of the College of Liberal Arts of STU since 1 March 2017. He has been Vice-President of the Sino-US Comparative Culture Association of China since 2000, President of the Federation of Translators and Interpreters of Macao since 2007, Executive Director of the International Association for Intercultural Communication Studies (IAICS) since August 2014, and President of the Shantou Association of Foreign Languages and Translation since May 2016. His publications include over ten scholarly books such as *Technologising the Male Body: British Cinema 1957 – 1987*, *Decoding Contemporary Britain*, and *Literature, Culture and Postmodern Transformations: 8 Case Studies from William Shakespeare to James Bond*. He was General Editor of the *New Topics in Contemporary Cultural Studies Series* (6 volumes), and with Doreen Wu co-edited a special issue of the journal *Critical Arts, Media Discourses and Cultural Globalisation: A Chinese Perspective* (Routledge & UNISA). He has also published academic journal articles and book chapters in literary, cultural, and translation studies. He has recently finished a research project on *Representations of Macao in Contemporary Cinema* and is now working on *ELT and Intercultural Communication*. He loves literature, cinema, music, and ice cream.

Agota Revesz has a research position at Freie Universität Berlin. She received her Ph.D. at the University of Theater and Film Arts, Budapest, comparing the work of the actor in Western and traditional Chinese theater. In 2009 she became a cultural attaché for Hungary in Shanghai, and spent six years in active diplomatic service in China. Dr. Revesz is working on a book project exploring the dynamic and domestic context of China's public diplomacy, with special attention to traditional Chinese theater: its sociology, aesthetic crisis, domestic and international reception, and the role it has been assigned by soft power diplomacy.

Olga Sobolev has taught courses in Comparative Literature at the London School of Economics and Political Science since 2001 (European Literature and Philosophy; Comparative Literature and 20th-Century Political History, Contemporary Literature and Global Society). She obtained her Ph.D. from the University of Sussex in 2000 (*Twentieth-Century Poetry of Russian Symbolists: New Aesthetics and Innovatory Qualities of Poetic Language*). Her research interests are in 19th- and 20th-century Russian and European culture, with transitional periods in the development of Russian artistic thought (modernism, Cold War and post-Soviet literature). Recent publications include *From Orientalism to Cultural Capital: The Myth of Russia in British Literature of the 1920s* (with Angus Wrenn, Peter Lang, 2017); "The Symbol of the Symbolists: Alexander Blok in the Changing Russian Literary Canon" in *Reconfiguring the Canon of Twentieth-Century Russian Poetry* (Cambridge Open Books, 2017); "Reception of Alfred Tennyson in Russia" in *Reception of Tennyson in Europe* (Bloomsbury, 2016); *The Only Hope of the World: G. B. Shaw and Russia* (with Angus Wrenn, Peter Lang, 2012); *The Silver Mask: Harlequinade in the Symbolist Poetry of Blok and Belyi* (Peter Lang, 2008), also articles on J. M. Barry and the Ballets Russes, Dostoevsky, Tolstoy, Nabokov, Chekhov, pulp fiction and James Bond, Boris Akunin, and Victor Pelevin. Olga Sobolev and Angus Wrenn have curated four exhibitions on Literature and Philosophy, Censorship in Literature, and the Fabians.

Michael Steppat served as Chair of Literature in English at the University of Bayreuth, Germany, until he achieved Emeritus status in 2015. He also holds a Professorial position of honor in Moscow from the Russian Federation's Ministry of Higher Education and Science. He has been appointed regular visiting professor at Shanghai

International Studies University, extending to advisor functions, as well as visiting professor at Fu Jen Catholic University, Taipei (Chinese Taiwan). After receiving his Ph.D. from the University of Münster (Germany) and later his "Habilitation" both from Münster and from Free University of Berlin, he was a Fulbright scholar at the University of Texas at Austin, then research professor at Arizona State University. He has repeatedly been awarded the Myra and Charlton Hinman Fellowship of Amherst College and Folger Shakespeare Library, Washington D.C.; he has also been granted the position of a Scholar-in-Residence at the John W. Kluge Center of the Library of Congress. He has served in a number of administrative functions, including the Academic Dean's position in his Faculty for many years. To move in a new direction, he developed an internationally cooperative graduate program of Intercultural Anglophone Studies. His book publications include *Americanisms: Discourses of Exception, Exclusion, Exchange*; *Chances of Mischief: Variations of Fortune in Spenser*; *The Critical Reception of Shakespeare's Antony and Cleopatra*; editions of several Renaissance Latin dramas; co-editorship of the New Variorum edition of Shakespeare's *Antony and Cleopatra*; and a monograph on the early work of St. Augustine of Hippo. A collaborative volume on *Writing Identity: The Construction of National Identity in American Literature* (Moscow City University) extends this range. As appointed member of the MLA's editorial team for the New Variorum Shakespeare, he has the honor of continuing to edit assigned plays. Spurred by an invitation from the London School of Economics and Political Science in 2011 to organize a workshop, which turned out to be a first-rate learning experience, Prof. Steppat has increasingly devoted attention to intercultural studies in connection with literature. In 2012 he became Primary Investigator in a Bavarian government-sponsored Sino-German cooperative program on "Identity and Intercultural Communication: Perspectives on America." He has recently co-authored an article on "Considering Intercultural Literature: A Mature Field of Study" (*Intercultural Communication: German and Chinese Perspectives*, ed. Jürgen Henze), and has given papers and conducted workshops on intercultural literary study at various international institutions and conferences in recent years.

Charles Ngiewih Teke is Associate Professor of literature, critical theory, and cultural studies, currently serving as Vice Dean in charge of Programmes and Academic Affairs in the Faculty of Arts at the University of Buea — Cameroon. He holds a Diploma in French Studies, a B.A. in English (1994), an M.A. in English Literature (1996), a Postgraduate Diploma in Sciences of Education (1997), and an M.Phil. in English Romantic Studies (1998) from the University of Yaounde I, Cameroon. With the award of a DAAD grant, he obtained a Ph.D. in English Romantic Philology with a dissertation titled *Towards a Poetics of Becoming: Samuel Taylor Coleridge's and John Keats's Aesthetics Between Idealism and Deconstruction* in 2004 (available as a monograph in 2006) from the University of Regensburg (Germany). During 2003—2004 he served as Advanced Research Counselor at the Institute for English and American Studies, University of Regensburg. He has lectured at the Higher Teacher Training College — Yaounde, the Faculty of Arts, Letters and Social Sciences, University of Yaounde I ; also at the National School of Administration and Magistracy (ENAM) and the Evangelical University of Cameroon. In the period 2012—2015 he was a European Union Marie-Curie (IIF) Experienced Research Fellow at the University of Munich (Germany), where he taught Cameroon Anglophone literature, theoretical criticism, postcolonial and cultural studies in the Institute of English Philology. He has been guest professor at the Bayreuth International Graduate School of African Studies (BIGSAS), Bayreuth Academy of Advanced African Studies (BA), and Institute of African Studies (IAS). He has completed extensive research on eighteen Cameroon Anglophone writers in view of publishing two monographs: *Perpetuating Cameroon Anglophone Literature: A Critical Study of Selected Works* (funded by the European Union Research Executive Agency) and *Encounters with Cameroon Anglophone Writers: Creativity and Critical Perspectives*. He has extensively published scholarly articles in several international journals and reviews around the world.

Keyan Gray Tomaselli is Distinguished Professor in the Faculty of Humanities, University of Johannesburg, as well as Professor Emeritus and Fellow, University of KwaZulu-Natal, where for many years he was director of the Centre for Communication, Media and Society. He completed his doctorate in 1983 at the University of Witwatersrand with a thesis on *Ideology and Cultural Production in South African Cinema*. His recent book publications as author or co-author include *Researching the San* (2015), *Engraved Landscape: Biesje Poort* (2013), *Cultural Tourism and Identity: Rethinking Indigeneity* (2012), *African Cultural Studies and Difference* (2011),

Political Economy of Transformation: The South African Media (2011). He is the editor of *Critical Arts: South-North Cultural and Media Studies* and co-editor of the *Journal of African Cinemas*. Keyan Tomaselli is a member of the Academy of Science for South Africa. He has been hosted by many Chinese universities as a conference keynote speaker and as a lecturer.

Inge van de Ven is Assistant Professor of Online Culture in the Department of Culture Studies at Tilburg School of Humanities (Netherlands). She previously completed research at the Education for Learning Societies Center and taught in the Comparative Literature Department at Utrecht University. She has been a member of the Innovational Research Incentives project "Back to the Book", and Core Fellow at the Institute for Advanced Study, Budapest. Her dissertation is titled *Monumental Novels in a Global and Digital Age* (2015). Her major areas of interest are literary theory, literature and film, literature and new media, digital culture, and narratology.

Tom van Nuenen is Teaching Fellow of Digital Media and Culture in the Department of Digital Humanities, and Research Associate in the Department of Informatics, at King's College London. He has held visiting positions at UC Berkeley, Copenhagen University, Western Sydney University, and Shanghai International Studies University. He specializes in digital methods for the humanities that combine computationally driven corpus linguistics with close reading and hermeneutic analysis. His Ph.D. focused on touristic experiences in algorithmic culture, investigating environments such as travel blogs, review platforms, and video games. His articles have been published in *Tourist Studies*, *The Journal of Popular Culture*, and *Games and Culture*.

Wen Peihong is Associate Professor of English in the School of Foreign Languages and Literatures, Southwest Minzu University, Chengdu, Sichuan Province, P.R. China. She has published essays in Chinese on several ethnic minority American writers. Among her translations are *Winnie-the-Pooh* (2008), *The House at Pooh Corner* (2009) (from English into Chinese), and *Coyote Traces: Aku Wuwu's Poetic Sojourn in America* (2015) (co-trans. from Chinese into English with Mark Bender). Her translations of poems by ethnic minority Chinese poets have appeared in various anthologies and journals in the USA. She was a visiting scholar at Pacific University,

Oregon, USA (2017–2018). Her present research focus is on the comparative study of ethnic minority literatures in China and the USA.

Angus Wrenn has taught at the London School of Economics since 1997, both on the course Literature and Society 1900–present, and the courses Comparative Literature and 20th-Century Political History, European Literature and Philosophy, and Contemporary Literature and Global Society. He has also taught drama on the Text and Performance M.A., taught jointly by King's College London and RADA. He obtained his Ph.D. from King's College, University of London, in 2002, on *The Fiction of Henry James Within the Context of the French Literature of the Second Empire, with Particular Reference to Novelists Published in the Revue de Deux Mondes*. Recent publications include *From Orientalism to Cultural Capital: The Myth of Russia in British Literature of the 1920s* (with Olga Sobolev, Peter Lang, 2017); "Wagner's Ring Cycle and Parade's End" in *Ford Madox Ford's Parade's End: The First World War, Culture, and Modernity* (Rodopi, 2014); "Henry James' Europe" in *The Cambridge Companion to European Novelists* (Cambridge UP, 2012); *The Only Hope of the World: G. B. Shaw and Russia* (with Olga Sobolev, Peter Lang, 2012); *Henry James and the Second Empire* (Legenda, 2009), also articles on the reception of Ford Madox Ford, and of Henry James in Europe.

Ming Xie (Ph.D. Cambridge) is Associate Professor of English at the University of Toronto. He works in modernist and contemporary poetry, literary theory, and comparative hermeneutics. He is the author of *Conditions of Comparison: Reflections on Comparative Intercultural Inquiry* (Continuum/Bloomsbury, 2011) and the editor of *The Agon of Interpretations: Towards a Critical Intercultural Hermeneutics* (University of Toronto Press, 2014).

Yuan Mingqing has obtained a Master of Arts degree from Shanghai International Studies University with a focus on intercultural communication, and a Master degree in Intercultural Anglophone Studies from the University of Bayreuth (Germany), in a cooperative international program. She is currently a member of the Bayreuth International Graduate School of African Studies. Her research interests are in the areas of African and diasporic African literatures, postcolonial studies, as well as transcultural and postcolonial readings of

Shakespeare.

Zhou Min (Ph.D.) is Professor and Associate Dean of the Institute of Literary Studies, Shanghai International Studies University. She is also Chinese director of the Confucius Institute in Waterloo (Canada). Prof. Zhou is deputy editor-in-chief of *The Journal of British and American Literary Studies*. She has worked as a Fulbright research scholar at the Department of English and Comparative Literature at Columbia University, and lecture professor at Klagenfurt University in Austria. Prof. Zhou has been honored as New Century Outstanding Talent by China's Educational Ministry. Among her book publications are *The Transcription of Identities: A Study of V. S. Naipaul's Postcolonial Writings* (2015) and *What Is Postcolonial Literature?*; she is also the translator of *J. Hillis Miller: Selected Works*. Her research areas include contemporary American and British literature, postcolonial studies, cultural theory, and media studies.

About the Series

The *Intercultural Research* book series of the SISU Intercultural Institute (SII) of Shanghai International Studies University (SISU) aims to be a publication in the tradition of an "annual" with each volume (or pair of volumes) focusing on one important topic or theme central to the historical or ongoing development of intercultural communication. With this goal mind, *Intercultural Research* has and continues to seek to publish seminal, cutting edge chapters on the state of the intercultural field in a specific area.

In seeking to cover and help map out the "state of the art" on the designated domain, each volume (or pair of volumes) aims to include diverse theoretical or applied research from indigenous or comparative cultural, intercultural, or cross-cultural approaches, highlight varied paradigms or investigative methodologies on that subject, and provide pertinent "history and status" overviews that track developments, note or critique trends, and suggest important directions for further research developments. The series thus aims to provide a benchmark reference for assessing the current state of the field and an impetus for stimulating future research development on each specified topic.

While seeking to broadly encompass diverse international approaches to any given topic, because of being published in China, the series seeks to especially consider non-Western perspectives. Each volume aims to incorporate contributions that may have greater relevance to studies in other Asian or Chinese societies. For those domains deemed to merit two volumes, the second companion volume generally includes a focus related to Chinese theories and applications (and some chapters or volumes may on occasion be published in Chinese).

In line with international publishing standards for social science and communication studies, *Intercultural Research* has adopted the editorial policies of the *APA Publication Manual* (7th ed.) or *MLA*

Handbook (8th ed.) (these two volumes on literature) along with specific guidelines developed for the integration of Chinese names and Chinese language publications. These "SII APA Integrated Chinese Editing" standards (two documents) can be found on the web site of the Institute (http://sii.shisu.edu.cn) along with model citation, reference, and layout examples. Information on intended future volumes may also be found on the web page. Further inquiries or comments may be addressed to the editors or to the Institute staff at:

icinstitute@shisu.edu.cn

Intercultural Research 跨文化研究

A thematic academic monograph series produced by
the SISU Intercultural Institute（SII） 上外跨文化研究中心

Series Editors: *Steve J. Kulich*，*Michael H. Prosser*

Volumes in the Series

Vol. 1　*Intercultural Perspectives on Chinese Communication*
跨文化视角下的中国人：交际与传播
主编：顾力行（Steve J. Kulich）、普罗斯（Michael H. Prosser）

Vol. 2　*Identity and Intercultural Communication（I）:*
Theoretical and Contextual Construction
跨文化交际与传播中的身份认同（一）：理论视角与情境建构
主编：戴晓东（Xiaodong Dai）、顾力行（Steve J. Kulich）

Vol. 3　*Identity and Intercultural Communication（II）:*
Conceptual and Contextual Applications
跨文化交际与传播中的身份认同（二）：原理的运用与实践
主编：顾力行（Steve J. Kulich）、戴晓东（Xiaodong Dai）

Vol. 4　*Value Frameworks at the Theoretical Crossroads of Culture*
价值观研究的框架：文化与跨文化的理论基础
主编：顾力行（Steve J. Kulich）、普罗斯（Michael H. Prosser）

Vol. 5　*Value Dimensions and Their Contextual Dynamics Across Cultures*
价值观研究的维度：跨文化的动态体现
主编：顾力行（Steve J. Kulich）、普罗斯（Michael H. Prosser）

Vol. 6　*Intercultural Adaptation（I）: Theoretical Explorations and Empirical Studies*
跨文化适应（一）：理论探索和实证研究
主编：戴晓东（Xiaodong Dai）、顾力行（Steve J. Kulich）

Vol. 7　*Intercultural Adaptation（II）: Research Extensions and Applications*
跨文化适应（二）：扩展与应用研究
主编：顾力行（Steve J. Kulich）、戴晓东（Xiaodong Dai）

Vol. 8　*Literature and Interculturality（I）: Concepts, Applications, Interactions*
文学与跨文化研究（一）：概念、应用与交流
主编：Michael Steppat、顾力行（Steve J. Kulich）

Vol. 9　*Literature and Interculturality（II）: Valuations, Identifications, Dialogues*
文学与跨文化研究（二）：价值观、身份认同与对话
主编：Michael Steppat、顾力行（Steve J. Kulich）

Vol. 10　*Literature and Interculturality（III）: From Cultural Junctions to Globalization*
文学与跨文化研究（三）：从文化交汇到全球化
主编：Michael Steppat、顾力行（Steve J. Kulich）